I0562680

POETIC JUSTICE

Thomas Reeder

All of the events, characters, names and places depicted herein are fictional or used fictitiously. No representation is made that any of the statements made in this novel are true or that any incident depicted in this novel actually occurred, nor is any of the same intended or should be inferred by the reader.

POETIC JUSTICE
Copyright © 2015 by Thomas Reeder

Cover images courtesy of the New Jersey Maritime Museum

All rights reserved. No part of this book may be reproduced, transmitted or stored whole, in part or in any manner whatsoever without the written permission, except in the case of brief quotations embodied in critical articles or reviews. For information, please contact Words Take Flight Books (http://www.wtfbooks.net).

Words Take Flight Books printing: 2015

ISBN 13: 978-0692453667
ISBN 10: 0692453660

Printed in the United States of America

For Barb

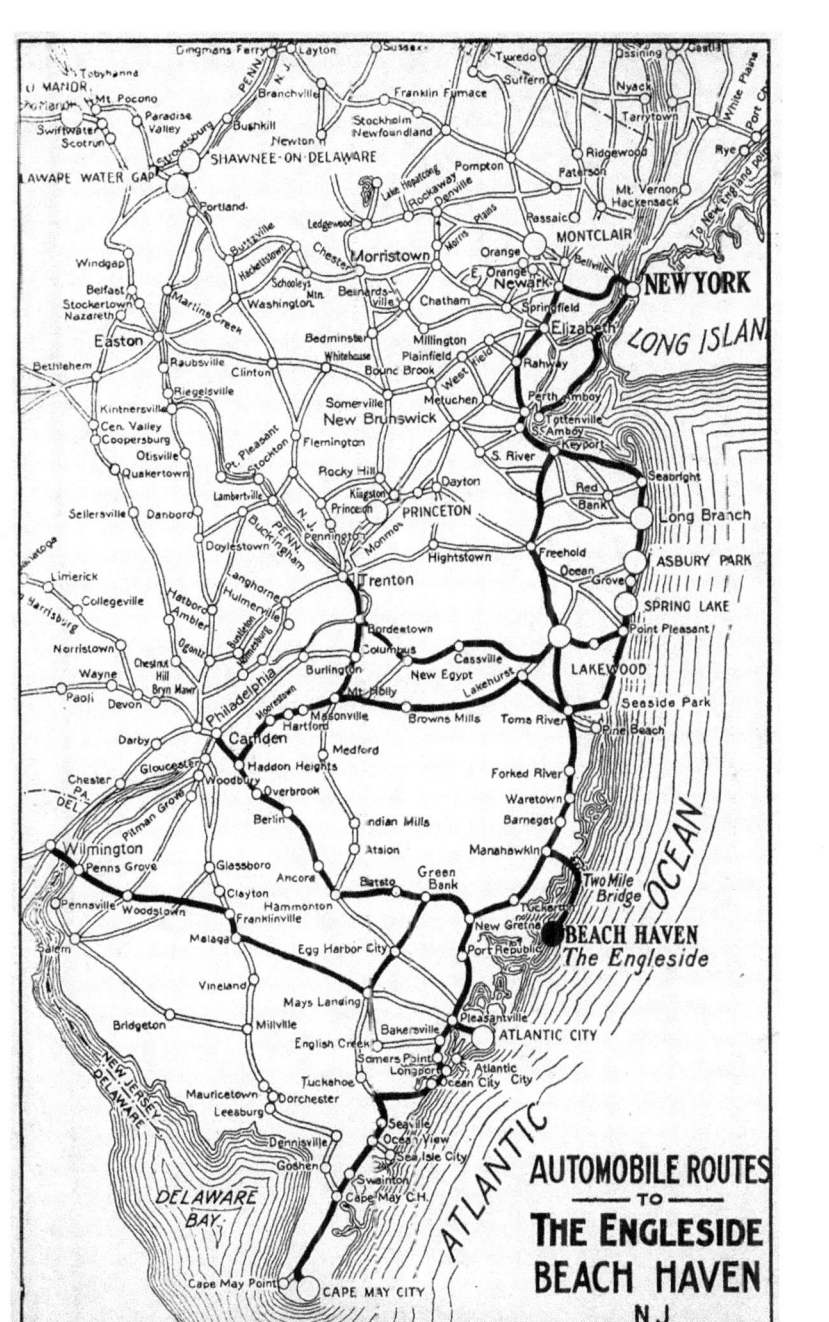

AUTOMOBILE ROUTES
— TO —
THE ENGLESIDE
BEACH HAVEN
N.J.

Saturday, September 15, 1979. 2:38 p.m.

HOW DO I see it?

It would have been October, 1936. Late night, new moon, a stiff, unrelenting autumn wind; as dark as dark can be. Wind rumbling in the ears, water lapping at the shoreline, nine silent figures arrive at the bay's edge in their flotilla of sneakboxes. They silently execute a series of tasks without hesitation or conscious thought, going through motions performed thousands of times before: furl the sails, un-step the masts, secure the tiny crafts at one of the old wooden docks that litter the bay's shoreline. Quickly gathering their rags, rope, wire, knives and God-knows-what-else, placing them in an oversized canvas bag.

Packed, they work their way over to and down the unused narrow-gauge track that wends its way through the marshes toward the lights of town. Moving quickly and quietly from tie to tie, taking evenly measured steps in the all-encompassing blackness. One of the group picks up his pace, steps past another, intentionally bumping the latter as he does so. Giggling, taking turns elbowing each other aside, pokes and shoves, a cap tipped over its owner's eyes. The others smile silently as they move forward, their thoughts on the task ahead. An abrupt "Shush!" and the playful sounds subside, swallowed by the sounds of nature, the hissing marsh grass, the lapping water.

"Like little children – God bless them," thinks the older man to himself. "Just like children." As he walks, he recites a child's poem in a loud whisper, barely audible to the others around him, leaving The Devil's Coffins behind. "*Billy, Billy, one-two-three, Mama's gonna make us a cup of tea.*" An old kerchief tugged from his back pocket, a long, slow, one-handed blow clears his nose, the refolded cloth returned to its nesting place. *"Billy, Billy, two-three-four, Doggy's in a patch of sun down on the floor."*

Several dozen homes grow closer, some as black silhouettes barely discernible against the faint lights beyond them, others marked with dim lights beyond the shaded rectangles of windows, all in a knotted cluster somewhere towards the horizon, endless expanses of black emptiness to both sides.

"Billy, Billy, three-four-five, Sister set the table with forks and knives. Stomach rumbling, mouth dry; should have had something to eat before setting out. *Every man should eat and drink, and enjoy the good of all his labor, it is the gift of God.* Next time: a big meal for all, plenty of cedar water, an hour's nap, then on to the tasks at hand. *Billy, Billy, four-five-six, Baby's got a chunk of ice and takes her licks.* Good boys and girls, all of 'em, makes a father proud. Mama'd be proud, too – is proud – setting up in the clouds looking down, heart bursting with pride at the fine brood that she bore. A fine brood. God-fearing, hard-working, obedient. The salt of the earth. *Billy, Billy, five-six-seven, Family says its daily prayers to God in heaven."*

The wind shifts direction, and for several moments disembodied voices drift through the air. A crowd laughs, some music plays, more laughter and applause: "Must be one of those new-fangled contraptions, open the door, invite Satan into your home, set a place for him at your table. The fools. Not the Lord's work, that's for sure. *Billy, Billy, six-seven-eight, Food's gonna go to waste, so clear your plate.* Special place over here, all right: the ocean breeze and mist, the smell and taste of salt, the gulls overhead crying their anguished cry. A shame what's happening here, a damn shame. *The land is defiled.* Didn't have to be like this; wasn't in my daddy's day, and in his daddy's day and the eternity that preceded them. Had to wait for me."

The tracks cross asphalt now, the group shifting its course to head east towards the roaring sea a half mile from them. *"Billy, Billy, seven-eight-nine, Our daily bread is finished and we feel just fine.* Well, Lord, here we go, doing the good works for you. *Be ye fruitful, and multiply.* My children, my plentiful children, all work with a common goal, and of a common mind: to serve you, O Lord, to serve you."

Pausing momentarily, a dog barks several blocks away. Listening, listening: the groaning of wood as a tree bends in the onslaught of wind, chimes clack feverishly in the inky void to the left. Houses here now, most deserted, but isolated ones with light peeking out from behind closed doors and heavy, drawn drapes. "*Billy, Billy, eight-nine-ten, Clean off the table 'til we eat again.* Mama's rhyme, oh, mama's rhymes. I love that one, makes me think of my toddling years. Innocence. Devotion. Obedience. *When I was a child, I spake as a child, I thought as a child: But when I became a man, I put away childish things.* Daddy brought me up right, Mama and Daddy. God's love and love your God. And we're closer to heaven back home than anywhere else on earth. Home. God's woods, the Pines, filled with an abundance of God's creatures. Eden on earth. Untouched. A refuge from the rest of the miserable world. *I hate them with perfect hatred: I count them mine enemies.* Well, here we are: the Devil's domain."

> *Even maids divinely fair*
> *Must, like flowers, resolve to earth.*

You asked, so that's how I see it. That, or something like that...

Friday, October 16, 1936. 8:15 p.m.

"EVER SEE A dead man?"

"Yeah. A few. More than my share."

Purdy nodded, but his mind was elsewhere. He'd shown up at the taproom minutes earlier, and asked me to come with him. Wouldn't say why, only telling me I'd find out soon enough. The question he had just tossed out suggested a reason, though. And I hate surprises.

We headed west on Dock Road, towards the bay; past my bungalow and the bayberry-choked lot next door. I glanced back: the lights were on, and I knew Holly was in there. The incessant wind was brutal, blowing in off the ocean at our backs, and one hell of a lot colder than I'd expected. Two minutes out in this unforgiving weather and already thinking that anywhere else would be preferable to traipsing about in the dark with our borough's resident "Dick Tracy".

Purdy paused, fumbling with the pack of Camels he'd fished from his coat pocket. Two attempts to light one failed, his trembling hands shaking like dead leaves in a stiff breeze. Whatever was going on, it was apparent he wished he had no part of it. I lit one of my matches, and managed to light the wildly bobbing cigarette clamped in his mouth. Quite a challenge, actually, but it gave me something to do with my numbing hands.

We plodded on while I silently cursed myself for not grabbing a hat. Gravel crunched under foot, its sound carried away in the wind. The frenzied yapping of a dog grew louder. Stands of bayberry rustled loudly. Chimes clacked wildly somewhere off to the south.

"What the hell's going on, Purdy?" I asked, facing straight ahead when I spoke. The wind was deafening, and turning towards Purdy would have exposed my left ear to its full fury, drowning out any anticipated response.

"Soon enough, Porter," he yelled over the roar, staring down at nothing in particular as we walked. He shook his head as if in silent denial of something unspoken.

Purdy paused at the first house beyond the empty lot. I knew it was owned by a guy named Schweickert. It was one of the few that were occupied this time of year, and turned out to be our destination. A small, trim bungalow situated on a nicely manicured property, it was, in the daylight, arguably the most attractive home on an otherwise threadbare street. Given the circumstances, it seemed less attractive at this moment. Parked out front in the street was the town's lone police car, an old, faded black Ford with bald tires; only the word "Police" painted on the door distinguished it as such.

The thin, gawky cop stationed on the front porch stared at us, uncomfortably shifting his weight from foot to foot, hands clasped behind his back. He looked cold. I recognized him as we approached. Earl Schoengarth. He was little more than an excitable grown kid, but he was friendly and well liked in the borough. Knew him from the taproom, as well – the kid could drink. But now he looked ridiculous, decked out in an ill fitting blue uniform several sizes too large and cuffed at all the extremities. Like a kid playing cop. Wouldn't have cut it on a real city force, but I guess he was okay here in the sticks. I nodded to him; he nodded back. Schoengarth looked relieved to have us there, but I might have read more into it than I should. He chewed nervously on a mouthful of something that turned out to be chaw, spewing a brown stream of it onto a porch-side Beach Plum. His aim was impressive. Beech-nut on Beach Plum.

We paused at the door.

"Better take some fresh air while you can," Purdy suggested, inhaling deeply. Didn't sound like this was going to be pleasant.

"Hold on." I pulled a dented chrome flask of Old Overholt from my hip pocket and offered it to him. He looked around – no one of importance was watching – then downed a healthy swig of the stuff. I followed suit. Schoengarth looked on with hungry puppy-dog eyes. I looked to Purdy with a nod towards Schoengarth, but Purdy shook his head an emphatic "No." Rules are rules, I suppose; only a privileged few are allowed to ignore them.

Purdy frowned at Schoengarth. "Why don't you make yourself useful and go look around. The grounds. For anything. You got a flashlight, don't you?" Schoengarth nodded affirmatively and reluctantly headed out to the front yard. Purdy looked after him for a moment, and returned his sad eyes to me.

"Ready?"

"Let's do it," I said.

The front door led directly into a large, well-lit living room. The place was a shambles, and a woman's body lay in a contorted position near the center of the yellow-and-green-speckled linoleum floor. The room was stifling, eighty-five or ninety degrees I'd guess, the air filled with the overpowering stench of death – *death reek*, we used to call it. A gas-fired heating unit, built into the floor, was turned up high – its hot metal clicking in the stillness. Another cop, Rich Hipple, stood across the room, a handkerchief clamped tightly over his nose and mouth in a futile attempt to stanch the smell. He stood at an angle to us, avoiding the horror at our feet. I might not have otherwise recognized someone with his face obscured as such, but how many three-hundred-pound cops were there in Beach Haven? I also knew him from the taproom; we shared nods of greeting. His uniform was as tight as Schoengarth's was loose – maybe they could trade.

I stepped carefully towards the motionless body at center stage. A lone fly buzzed lethargically about the room, annoyed no doubt by our intrusion into her private affair. She was surprisingly loud for her rather sluggish condition. There was blood everywhere, lots of it in wide, arcing smears, some of it pooled, all of it dried and, on the hard surfaces, flaky. Tried to avoid it as I advanced, but it was impossible; it crunched loudly under foot.

The slaughtered body lay in a fetal position on its left side, right arm twisted over and back behind its neck, left arm out straight on the floor. The fingers of both hands looked like blood-covered claws. I saw a riddle of stab marks – the pulpy red mess that had been its head appeared to have been smashed in and was swarming with maggots, all wildly hopping about like a sea of Mexican jumping beans. They made a gentle patter as the dislodged ones dropped to the linoleum below. I'd never seen these things so active before, this particular batch in ecstasy over their current windfall.

A blood-soaked mass of scalp and hair lay on the floor several feet away. She was a blond – or had been. The few areas of her dress that weren't brown with dried blood suggested it had originally been a light floral pattern, but now it was difficult to tell. The body itself was bloated and discolored, the way bodies tend to get when left to their own devices. The bloating, as best I could recall, was a result of the body's natural digestive juices getting carried away and digesting the gastrointestinal tract itself. The discoloration resulted from the blood's bacteria – okay in a live body – having its way with a dead one, releasing gas in the blood vessels and surrounding tissue. *Autolysis* and *putrefaction* were the fifty-cent terms that came to mind, but I couldn't be sure anymore; most people simply called it "rot". Whatever you called it, the results were always the same: and they weren't pretty. And now they contributed to the overpowering smell present in the room. I doubted whether Purdy knew anything of this, and was pretty sure he wouldn't care even if he did. And why should he?

"Can we turn down the heat? Open some windows?" I said, looking to Purdy for approval. Not a particularly novel idea, but nobody else had done anything about it. Made sense to him; he nodded approval to Hipple, who eagerly obeyed. The incessant barking from out back grew louder as the windows were opened.

"Schweickert isn't married. Who is she?" I asked, eyes fixed on the mess at my feet. Looked like a wax dummy, a Madame Tussaud's reject.

Purdy looked to me with a trace of a smile. "Take a closer look," he said quietly.

I fished through my coat pocket for a pack of De Nobilis, the small, dry, twisted cigars I smoke on a regular basis, the ones that no one else seems able to stomach. *Dago stogies* my wife once called them, dredging up a name her father had used years earlier. I offered them around; no takers. Knew there wouldn't be. Lit one and waved its smoking end under my nose, inhaling in a futile attempt to minimize the stench. It just made it worse.

I squatted beside the body for a closer look. Purdy stood off to the side, hands in his pockets, jingling the change in them. Sounded like enough for the week's meals. I stared at the contorted face for a full minute. Something wasn't right.

"She" had a five o'clock shadow.

"I'll be damned. Is…Is this…" I asked slowly as I maneuvered for a closer look.

"If you were going to say 'Schweickert', I think the answer is 'Yes'."

"How the hell can you tell," I asked, squinting at the corpse's misshapen features.

"Well, he – that – has two rings: a high school ring from somewhere in Pennsylvania, and a college ring: he's a Princeton man." He paused to snicker. "Both have his initials. And there's a mole on his cheek, consistent with Hippo's recollections of Schweickert." Purdy, and most of the town, for that matter, referred to Hipple as Hippo. "The rings don't go well with the dress," he sneered.

"My, my, my. What would the neighbors think," I muttered to myself while trying to absorb the incongruity lying before me. There was indeed a mole on his cheek, a half inch to one side of a deep slice in the flesh. I thought back to what Schweickert had looked like when I last saw him: a lone mole the sole blemish on an otherwise unmarked face. I took another look at the "scalp" nearby – it was a blond wig. Hope it wasn't borrowed.

"Who found him?" I asked.

"Woman named Gettinger – Mabel Gettinger. Miss Mabel Gettinger. Lives in the dump next door, only other house nearby 'cept yours," Purdy answered.

"Yeah, I know her. Nosy, old battle-ax. Looks like that actress," I interjected. She was the kind of neighbor who spoke with you twice in eleven years, both times to complain.

"Marie Dressler'd be my choice," continued Purdy. "Claims that Schweickert's dog – the one yapping out back now – yapped all day inside here without stopping. Drove her crazy, so she comes over here to tell him to shut it up. She gets here and knocks, no answer, door's ajar, so being the civic-minded citizen that she is, she looks in. And here we are. Maybe it'll cure her of snooping. Kinda doubt it, though." He paused, looking at the carnage before him, then back to me. "Schweickert's dog – *Daisy* the name – is a pug. Already said that, didn't I? Well, it is. And it's tied up out back, as if you couldn't guess." We could all clearly hear the shrill yapping as if it were in the next room. "Daisy…" mumbled Purdy, momentarily lost in thought. "That's Dagwood's dog, isn't it?"

I shrugged.

"Yeah, Dagwood's dog…"

"Purdy…"

"…and Blondie's."

"*Purdy*…!" I repeated, this time getting his attention. Daisy's interminable barking was an annoying distraction.

"Cute, huh?" continued Purdy, brought back to reality by the persistent yapping. "And that's not the half of it. We get here, not expecting *this* – well, it was quite a surprise. And we find Daisy, this miserable, little, flea-bitten creature – his *pet*, for Christ's sake – running around in circles inside with dried blood all over his snout.

Turns out the little monster's been nibbling away at one of the open wounds. Made an even bigger mess of things." He paused and bent forward slightly at the waist to point at the gnawed neck. "Chewed one of the fingers off. One of the ring fingers, as a matter of fact. That's how we noticed the rings." The pocket change jingling accelerated as he grew more agitated.

"Biting the hand that feeds it, eh?" I murmured.

Purdy's jingling abruptly ceased. Then a trace of a smile crossed his lips; he snorted with what I took to be a suppressed laugh.

"'Biting the hand that feeds it.' Heh, that's a good one." He turned to Hipple. "Good one, huh?" he repeated, a little more loudly. Hipple thoughtfully nodded his head in agreement, the handkerchief still clamped tightly to his face. Evidently Purdy had found my comment more amusing than intended. "I'll have to tell Gibbons that one," he said under his breath, then returned to his account. "I thought Schoengarth was going to lose his dinner right there on the spot. He made it outside just in time, yorked his guts out, then shoves a wad of chaw into his cheek to kill the taste. As if that would make it any better."

"How was he killed?" I asked, hoping he'd given it some thought, while quickly arriving at my own conclusions.

"With a knife: punctures all over him. *Lots* of 'em."

"Got a pencil?" I asked, eyes trained on Schweickert's lifeless shell. Purdy looked mildly surprised at the question, and turned to Hipple with an expression of confusion. Hipple gave the question little thought, and fished through his pockets until he located a yellow wooden pencil stub. Handed it to me; the words "Cranmer Lumber" visible beneath the teeth marks pocking its surface. Holding it by the pointed end, I poked about Schweickert's remains, carefully moving pieces of clothing aside for a better view.

There were numerous knife marks, all right; but judging from the size and shape of the various wounds, at least two different sharp weapons had been used. There were the usual defense wounds on both hands — but *complementing* the knife wounds were a series of pattern wounds no doubt made by a hammer. Still visible on the scalp and forehead were several circular contusions and lacerations all of the same dimensions, and elsewhere on the body were pairs of side-by-side, half-inch wounds consistent with the claw end of a hammer.

"Find any knives? A hammer? Anything else of interest?" I asked.

"Nah, we're still looking for the knife. What's this about a hammer?" questioned Purdy. He sounded skeptical about the possibility of a second weapon.

"Here," I said, pointing out the various wounds obviously not created by a knife. "Find the hammer and you'll have a match — here — here — and here."

"Hmmm. Well, maybe," Purdy quietly responded, more to himself than anyone else. "Maybe not." He tilted his head to one side, squinting at the symmetrical holes.

"You know when it happened? How long he's been dead?" I continued.

"I have no idea," said Purdy. "Blood's all dried, so it's been awhile."

I figured at least a day, but I didn't say so.

"We're still trying to track down Havens," he continued, referring to the town's doctor. "See what he has to say."

The body was room temperature, but that didn't prove much because it was so damn warm in the house. The cornea of the exposed left eye was cloudy, however, and that usually takes half a day after death to happen. As would the settling of the blood in his body, what there was left of it; the regions of Schweickert's corpse closest to the floor had taken on the expected purplish hue, and remained pale where it was in contact with the hard floor's surface — it hadn't been moved. The body was starting to loosen up somewhat from the board-stiff state induced by rigor mortis. Given the room's temperature and Schweickert's body size, his limbs probably would have been locked in position eight to twelve hours after death, and started to relax at eighteen to twenty-four. And the maggots: they tend to hatch about a day after a female housefly deposits her eggs, usually on exposed wounds, the eyes or the mouth – something like that. But none of this is very accurate, and I was just guessing. Like I said: it's been a long time.

I stood up, stretched, and listened for several moments to Daisy's barking. As if I had a choice. I like dogs, but this one wasn't very high on my list. My neck was stiff and ached, and I kneaded it with my left hand as I returned the pencil to Hipple. He reacted as if I had handed him a snake.

"Why did you bring me here?" I asked Purdy. I could make several guesses, but it just seemed easier to ask.

"To help ID the body," he answered, looking somewhat surprised at the question. "Why else?"

"Forget it. Dumb question," I said, reasonably satisfied that he had no inkling of my years with Hack and Hack back in the mid-twenties.

"Can you?" he asked.

"ID him?" I responded.

Purdy nodded.

"Yeah, I'm pretty sure it's him. Kind of looks like him when you get past all the slop, and the top of his right hand has that huge mole on it – noticed it the first time we met and shook hands." I *was* pretty sure it was him. We'd all be sure once they hauled him out of here and cleaned him up. But right now, you had to use some *imagination*.

Purdy seemed distant and preoccupied, and I had a pretty good idea why: He'd been Chief of Police of Beach Haven, sort of, for more years than most people could remember – probably a good thirty years or more. But I'd be willing to bet that in all of that time the most violent situations he'd encountered were the drunken domestic disputes that surfaced like clockwork during the long, lonely winter months. Then there were the ritualistic bar fights at the two rougher drinking establishments in town, but that was just *boys being boys*. And then, of course, the occasional suicide; God knows the island has its share – again, usually during the dead of winter. But of the handful I'd heard of over the years, only one was *really* messy, the rest of them hangings and asphyxiations.

But this. This was different. This was scary for him – and, soon enough, everyone else in town. Scary because it had the potential of having been a random, wanton act of extreme violence, and those are the kind that can happen again, anywhere, and to anyone. Everyone would be up in arms until it was solved, and wouldn't settle for it *not* being solved. It really wouldn't matter much whether the guilty party was found or some poor dupe was railroaded for the crime, just as long as it was off the books and the citizenry could convince themselves that they were, once again, *safe*. Purdy would want this one to go away, and quick. Fat chance he'd *solve* it, though.

I did a long, slow scan of the room. *Gibbons isn't here, and it's just as well*, I thought to myself. Otto Gibbons was the town's other cop, a full-timer in his late forties, and one mean son of a bitch. One never quite knew where they stood with Gibbons; while he was levelheaded most of the time, he was notorious for sudden outbursts of physical violence when provoked. And Gibbons had his own ideas of just what constituted *provocation*. These outbursts were usually directed towards drunks and minor lawbreakers – anyone without the sense to not give him any lip – so the average citizen was usually exempt. Gibbons also had an intense dislike for animals, with cats at the top of his list. He'd lull his neighbors into a false sense of ease by feeding the town's numerous strays from his apartment's back porch…and then, one day while the cats were out there mewing away for old Uncle Otto to make his daily appearance, out he'd come with his rifle, firing away. And he was a good shot, for sure. Fast, too. Cats never seemed to pass the word around, however, and within six months the process would repeat itself.

No, I didn't miss Gibbons, and I'd be surprised if Purdy did.

The living room area of Schweickert's house occupied the front right corner, and a smaller, open kitchen stood beyond, with a small dining table and four chairs visible. Curtains danced wildly in both rooms on the breeze from the now-open windows. To the left of these rooms was a small hall area that led, presumably, to a couple of small bedrooms and a bath. During the brief moments of silence between Daisy's barking and our conversations, I became aware of a low, barely audible moaning or humming. It was coming from Hipple, it turned out; he was still doing his damnedest to avoid looking at Schweickert's remains.

An oval-shaped hooked rug, partially kicked up, lay in the center of the living room off to one side of the body. There were several silver-dollar-sized brown stains on it – a different, lighter color than that of dried blood. Purdy took notice: "Dog shit," he stated, matter of factly. "I think our Daisy must have had the runs." I took his word for it. Daisy, outside, persisted with noisy reminders of his presence. He was growing very annoying.

"Stupid little creature," said Purdy, shaking his head. "Looks like Winston Churchill. Know who he is?"

"Yeah," I said. "The Brit."

"Duke of Windsor loves those things – saw it in a magazine somewhere a couple months ago. Hard to believe…" he said, more to himself than to the rest of us.

The toilet flushed in the small bathroom off the hall and Hipple emerged; I hadn't noticed him leave. He pulled his handkerchief from his pocket and once again plastered it over his face. He walked to a small table midway between the kitchen and living room, picked up a phone and began to dial. I turned to Purdy:

"Maybe it'd be a good idea to leave things undisturbed until the state cops get here?" I asked, conveniently ignoring the disruption caused by the opened windows.

"We don't need the 'staties' here," he responded abruptly. "We know who did it – and Gibbons is out looking for him." That one caught me off guard.

"Really? Who did it?"

"Schweickert's roommate, Miller. Ernest Miller. *Ernie*. Know him?"

I knew him, all right. Not well, but better than I knew Schweickert. Miller was a writer, not a particularly good one, I gathered, but a writer nonetheless. Extremely soft spoken and polite – in the handful of instances I'd spoken with him he seemed to be a genuinely nice guy. Came over and introduced himself when he moved in with Schweickert. I'd seen him a dozen or so times since then drinking at my dump, and at several of the others in town. He didn't seem too particular.

"Miller? What makes you think so?" I inquired.

Purdy looked irritated. "I don't *think* – I *know*. It was Miller. And you'll want to know how I *know* it was Miller, I suppose. Well, I'll tell you. Miller and Schweickert were queers, plain and simple – a couple of fruit flies – and they lived together. They were here every morning and every night. We find Schweickert dead, dressed like this, and he's been this way for some time. Did Miller report it? No. We gotta hear about it from some old, gray-haired biddy up the street, who's probably by now told every other living creature in a fifty-mile radius about it. And in *vivid* detail, I'm sure. These pansies were probably prancing about, doing God-knows-what, when they had a little lovers' spat. Miller grabs a knife and pokes his little lover boy for the last time." Purdy paused and turned to Schweickert's corpse with a look of disgust. "This is an open-and-shut case, Porter. Just another fag slashing. They get 'em all the time in the big cities. But *you* probably know that. Only, unfortunately for us all, this time they decided to do it here in sleepy, old Beach Haven. Thank God, at least, it ain't tourist season." He was fired up now. "Would somebody shut that goddamned dog up? *Please?*" he yelled.

"That's it?" I pursued. "Let me get this straight: Schweickert's found dressed like this, dead as a fence post, and because Miller's not here you've just put one and one together and come up with 'Miller as the killer'. That's *it*?"

"You bet your life 'that's it'!" Purdy sneered. "How many normal people dress like this? And you think if Miller didn't know about… *this*…that he'd dress like this knowing his roommate could come home at a moment's notice? These guys were faggots, plain and simple, and one of 'em killed the other. And *that's* it!" he fumed.

Hipple wasn't paying any attention to the two of us. Instead, he'd just finished his phone call and was now rolling up a nearby section of newspaper; he scanned the vicinity around him for the lone housefly. If Daisy wasn't out back yapping his head off, the fly would quickly move to the top of the "most annoying" list. I silently wished him luck.

"Listen, Purdy," I responded. "I hear what you're saying, but you're making a huge leap here: *Transexuality* doesn't necessarily equate to *homosexuality*. What if all they liked to do was to simply dress up like this in the privacy of their own home?" Purdy snorted. "Yeah, it's a tough one to swallow, but just think about it for a second. What if Miller stumbled across this mess and went nuts? He could be holed up somewhere, staring at the curtains or something. Doesn't help you, I know, but it could explain his not reporting it." I was trying to remain calm, but I hoped to get Purdy's attention. Get him thinking a little more rationally. But it had the opposite effect.

Purdy turned to me, face flushed. "Why don't you keep your nose out of this, leave it to us? This is Beach Haven, not the big city; we have our own way of doing things, thank you very much. At our own pace. We don't need outsiders butting in, trying to change things. You've helped ID the body and I thank you for that," he said with an exaggerated bow. "But if you don't like the way we do things around here, why don't you just go the hell back to Philadelphia, or wherever the hell it is you came from?" His face was beet red now, and he trembled slightly with anger.

I let out a long, slow sigh, stepped toward Purdy and placed my hand squarely on his left shoulder. I towered over him. I bent over slightly and brought my face close to his, until our eyes locked – mine unblinking. I stared at him for several moments before speaking until I knew I had his attention. "Calm...down," I said, slowly and evenly.

He stared at me, muscles working in his clenched jaw. Then, after a pause, the anger seemed to drain from him. His eyes left mine as he let out a deep breath. "Yeah, probably not a bad idea." He slowly moved over to the kitchen, pulled a yellow-painted wooden chair out from the small dining table, and slumped into it. He fumbled for another Camel and jammed it between his lips. Spoke from the side of his mouth while he fired it up: "It's just that this murder has the potential of becoming such a...a...a *big deal*. And it could get kind of messy."

Seemed to me it already was kind of messy.

"Not every day that someone gets slaughtered here," I responded.

"That's for sure," he said. "That's for sure." He exhaled a lung full of smoke, and took another deep pull.

"Mr. Purdy – *Chief*," called Hipple from the other side of the kitchen in a muffled voice through his handkerchief, "did you see – *this*?"

We both looked over, and I stepped into the kitchen to see what he was staring at. After a moment, Purdy dragged himself out of the chair and joined us. We were now all standing in front of a faded white Frigidaire electric refrigerator, maybe ten years old. Scrawled on its front, in what appeared to be dried blood, were the words:

THEY HAVE COMITED AN ABOMINATION AND SHALL
BE PUT TO DEATH.
THERE BLOOD IS UPON THEM.

"Sunday school teacher, perhaps?" I said quietly after reading it several times.

"How the hell did we miss this?" asked Purdy, incredulous that this eye-catching message had, until now, been totally overlooked.

"Mess out in the other room's kind of an attention grabber," I responded, for no particular reason. I moved in for a better look at the hasty scrawl, but a closer inspection suggested that the finger used to write it had been gloved; there'd be no usable prints. "Whoever wrote it…"

"Miller," interjected Purdy.

"Yeah, well, Miller, *whoever*, is a lousy speller. Sounds familiar, though; must have had a Sunday school teacher or someone yell it at me when I was a kid."

"You went to Sunday school?" asked Purdy without much interest.

I looked over to Purdy and a faint smile crossed my lips. "As Ripley would say…" I started, but left the sentence unfinished. Took a quick look around the room to see if there was anything else that Beach Haven's finest had managed to overlook.

Moments later, I became aware of a faint knocking sound from out in the living room. Purdy and Hipple heard it, too; we exchanged puzzled glances. I stepped quickly into that room, the two of them on my heels. After a pause, there was another series of soft knocks: the front door. Purdy let out an exasperated sigh, carefully walked the few paces to the door and threw it open. Outside stood Schoengarth, shivering, gingerly holding a nail hammer that dangled from between his left index finger and thumb. Dried blood covered most of its head, but its claws were cloaked in shadow. "Found this outside. In a bush out by the street," he said almost apologetically, around the wad of chaw stuffed in his cheek. These guys were more at home writing parking tickets.

"Jesus Christ, Schoengarth, what the hell do you think this is, a goddamned social event or something? Don't knock, just come the hell in. You're a *cop*, for Christ's sake, not a door-to-door salesman!" Purdy sputtered. "*Jesus!*"

Schoengarth wiped his feet and entered, pushing the door closed behind him. He'd already seen the corpse in all its colorful glory, but his eyes still went wide when they settled on the decaying mess on the floor. He cupped his right hand over his nose and mouth in a futile attempt to block the smell which, it seemed to me, wasn't half as bad as when we first arrived; either the open windows were helping or, less likely, I was getting used to it. Must've been the windows.

Purdy stared thoughtfully at the proffered hammer for what seemed like several minutes, then took it in his hand and examined it even more closely. He turned slowly to me.

"How'd you know? You done this sort of thing before?" he asked slowly, brows furrowed. "Cop stuff?" It was slowly dawning on him that maybe, just maybe, I had some sort of idea what I was doing. Schoengarth quietly returned to the outside.

"I was never a cop," I responded truthfully, but avoiding the fuller intent of the question. Purdy didn't seem to pick up on the differentiation.

There was a sudden, renewed round of excited barking out back that brought Purdy up short. Teeth clenched, he turned quickly to Hipple: "Your pistol. Give me your pistol."

Hipple looked surprised, but obeyed, pulling the Smith and Wesson six-shot .38 from its holster and handed it to Purdy, stock first. Purdy took it, marched through the kitchen and out the back door. The door slammed. Hipple and I looked at each other questioningly.

"You don't think...?" questioned Hipple.

I shrugged. Purdy's actions were as much a mystery to me as him.

We both flinched as the shot shattered the silence.

"Jesus, did he just...?" he asked, startled by what had just happened.

"Welcome to Beach Haven," I muttered.

Purdy returned through the back door as if nothing had happened. He handed the pistol back to Hipple, who stared at Purdy incredulously.

"You'll want to clean that," Purdy said offhandedly. He resumed pondering the crime scene. Hipple and I just stood there, Hipple staring at him. After a minute or so of awkward silence, Purdy turned to us with a frown.

"What? What are you staring at? I did that dog a favor, you know. It was an orphan, kind of. Nobody'd want a yappy dog like that. And we sure as hell couldn't keep it. Better off this way." The issue was closed as far as he was concerned.

Hipple darted a nervous glance my way, and I gave a slight shrug as response.

And then Daisy started barking all over again.

"Heh, heh, heh," chuckled Purdy, obviously pleased with his little joke. "Had ya going, didn't I? You shoulda seen the little bastard jump when I fired that, *this* far from him" – he held his hands about eighteen inches apart – "Disappeared into his little house like a jackrabbit with his ass on fire." He shook his head. "Kind of hoped it would scare him quiet for a little longer, though." He chuckled again quietly to himself, but it faded as he turned and once again viewed the slaughterhouse around him.

Hipple let out long, slow sigh, and the tension disappeared from the air.

"The dog's *your* problem, Hippo; find a home for it," added Purdy over his shoulder. Hipple's smile faded. Mine grew.

Purdy turned abruptly to me. "You be sure to let me know if you hear anything," he said, "Anything at all. Miller's whereabouts, especially, but anything at all. You hear a lot, I'm sure." I'd been dismissed.

"I'll keep that in mind," I responded, buttoning my jacket. "Done with me?"

"Yup. And thanks," said Purdy.

I wasn't inclined to volunteer any information about Miller – not that I was sure of where he would be, but I had some ideas. Beach Haven's a small town and the island's not a hell of a lot bigger, so it was only a matter of time before they tracked him down. That was, of course, *if* he was still around and not on some westbound train headed for Kansas.

I said goodbye to the two of them and a moment later to Schoengarth outside. This was their problem, not mine, and I was happy to wash my hands of it. Unfortunately, it was Miller's problem, too, and he wouldn't be able to walk away from it quite as easily as I could.

22

Saturday, October 17, 1936. 8:10 p.m.

IT CAME AS no surprise. The taproom's regulars hadn't budged since my abrupt departure. Now they were eager to know what the cops were up to and why I'd been dragged into it. I simply stated that Schweickert had been murdered, that I'd been summoned to ID the body and that I'd fill them in on the details later. There was, of course, a collective groan of disappointment with my inadequate explanation of events, but after a series of ignored queries, the small group immediately launched into wild speculation among themselves regarding the evening's events. I stared for a moment at my cold pork roll sandwich, abandoned a couple of hours earlier, pushed off to one side of the bar. It didn't look particularly appealing anymore – somebody's spent cigarette butt, stubbed out on the edge of the plate, had toppled into it. I swept the mess into the garbage with a muttered curse, grabbed my hat and downed a shot of double-O. Willett, who was working the bar, took notice. I told him that I was heading back out for awhile – as if it wasn't obvious.

I'd left Schweickert's charnel house ten minutes earlier with Purdy muttering to himself and his underlings both wishing they could follow me out of that stinking hell. The fresh autumn air had been a welcome relief.

It was drizzling now. The rain pelted my back with annoying pecks. Once more, I made my way back down Dock Road, guided only by the occasional lighted structures on either side. I passed Schweickert's house again, which sat silently to my left on the south side of the road. Doc Havens' cream-colored '31 Buick sedan had joined the battered Ford out front, its engine clicking as it cooled. He

24

was probably inside checking to make sure the rotting mess was actually dead before phoning the coroner and waking him from a sound sleep. The coroner wouldn't be happy with this one: it's a long ride over from the mainland, but he'd never be able to talk Havens and Purdy into letting him wait until daylight. Scoop it up and move it out – out of sight, out of mind. Well, out of sight at least.

I wandered past Mabel Gettinger's house, caught a glimpse of her peering out around one of the drawn curtains. Boarded-up summer dwellings and undeveloped lots choked with towering bayberry bordered the road the rest of the way. Two minutes later I stood out in front of my destination, one of two remaining lighted structures. Place known as Antlers Grill.

Dock Road doesn't have a whole lot on it. What it *does* have is a trio of year-round bars that are the source of most of its offseason traffic – on-season, too, for that matter. The Acme Hotel Bar was the third, and it was right next door to the Antlers; the Acme would be my next stop if I didn't have any luck finding Miller here. Both sat on the north side of Dock Road, several hundred yards from its termination in a bulk-headed loop at the bay's edge.

This was a wild shot, I knew: Miller could have been most anywhere, and not necessarily here on the island. But I didn't have him pegged for the murderer. I figured he'd probably be sitting somewhere in a state of semi-shock, drinking himself into a stupor. And the Antlers *was* his favorite hangout, with the Acme and my joint distant seconds. Wishful thinking, perhaps, but it was worth a check.

The Antlers wasn't much to look at – just a large, squat four-square that backed up to one of the bay's many inlets, with two stories of partially enclosed porches on all sides. The words "Antlers Grill" were plastered in huge block letters below the upper porch windows, again on all sides, and easily read from a distance from both land and bay. It had been a speakeasy during prohibition – but then so had most of the other former bars on the island – and before that, a hunting and fishing club for some fraternal group from

Philadelphia. But now it was a public bar: Owner Bill Van Kirk had paid his five-hundred bucks at the end of Prohibition back in '33 for a license to sell beer, ale and porter, and that had been upgraded a year later to allow the sale of all alcoholic beverages. The license, that is; the place itself was still in serious need of some upgrading.

I pushed my way in, paused for a few seconds while I scanned the place. It was a large, open room with an oval-shaped bar in the center and wooden tables and chairs scattered throughout. The air was thick with smoke, partially obscuring the forlorn-looking heads of long-dead deer and elk that stared down at me from high up on the walls. One of the sorrier looking of them still suffered the indignity of adornment with some of last year's dusty Christmas decorations. A dozen or so people stood around drinking, throwing darts and making enough noise for a group three times that size. There were empty glasses and half-filled ashtrays everywhere. I wondered if the mess had all been made this evening, or if Van Kirk hadn't gotten around to cleaning up the previous night's rubble. Van Kirk, behind the bar mixing a drink, looked up and nodded a silent greeting, then turned to deliver the results to an anxious customer. I recognized most of the patrons, which wasn't surprising, but only a few of them had noticed my arrival.

Miller was sitting alone at a table in the back by the men's room, or at least it looked like him from a distance. That particular corner was darker than most: a lone, dim overhead bulb dully back-lighting the occupant's head and shoulders. He was hunched over, staring at the tabletop, the glow of a cigarette tip hovering several inches in front of his silhouetted head. After a moment he inhaled, the cigarette's glow briefly illuminating his face. He was drawing designs in a small puddle on the circular table's uneven surface: three rings – purity, body, flavor. Loose change, several faded dollar bills, an open pack of matches and a crumpled empty pack of Pall Malls littered the tabletop. There was a half-full drink of something brown in front of him, several empty glasses sitting off to the side. He looked like he'd been here a month. I went to the bar, got a glass of Camden Ale and a shot of Old Overholt from Van Kirk, then made my way over to Miller's table.

"Hello, Miller." I grabbed a chair with my foot and placed my drinks on the table out of harm's way. "Get you something?"

Miller, in a fog, looked up slowly and, after a moment's searching, recognized me. "Porter – Lew. No. No thanks." His head bobbed slightly as he attempted to focus on me. He was an average-looking fellow: young, perhaps twenty eight to thirty; dark hair parted on the left; a round, squat face with a long, thin mouth that turned down at the corners. He was short – five six perhaps – and his body soft and lumpy, lacking any sort of tone. Short, soft fingers dragged through the liquid before him – bye bye, Ballantine.

I downed my shot then took a long slow pull of the ale. "Tell me what happened," I said as casually as I could.

He looked at me for a moment without expression, uncomprehending. Then it registered, and his head dropped into his right hand, eyes covered. His body shook convulsively, a low moan escaping from slack lips.

"You know?" he sobbed.

"Yeah. Cops found him several hours ago. Called me in to ID him."

Miller shook his head back and forth as if trying to shake the memory of it from his mind.

"What happened?" I asked again, this time more forcefully.

"Oh, God. What happened? Oh, God…let me think. What day is it?"

"Friday."

"Friday. Yesterday – Thursday? Yeah, Thursday. I went home. To Schweickert's, I mean; I have a room there. Went in the front door and, oh, God, there was blood *everywhere*. Fred was…dead. It was horrible. He…he was my…my friend." He sniffed loudly and ran a hand through his unkempt hair. "You – you saw him?"

"Yeah. I saw him."

"I – I sat there for hours, just sat, thinking, not really thinking. I didn't know what to do. I was so…sad. I cried, I slept, sort of, I cried some more. When the sun finally rose, I left. I didn't know what to do, I panicked, I guess. Figured they'd figure I did it, blame it on me. Not that I really care…I…don't really care…anymore." He grabbed his glass, threw his head back, and drained its contents.

My eyes were adjusting to the low light of the bar. I could make out what appeared to be dried blood on his cuff and sleeve. His eyes were bloodshot, there were the tracks of long-dried tears on his cheeks, his hair a mess. Body odor hung in the air about him.

"What'd you do then? I asked.

"I don't know. I walked around for a while, couple of hours, I guess. Outside. I don't remember where, exactly: the ocean, boardwalk, I forget where else. Then I ended up here – and here I am." He sniffed once again. I silently wished to myself that he had a handkerchief.

"You didn't kill him?" I asked.

Miller looked up, stunned. "NO! I told you that. I wouldn't have killed him! He was my friend, my good friend. We had lots of good times together. I didn't…*couldn't* have done that. You've got to believe me," he implored, shaking his head back and forth in a futile effort to make the notion go away. For all the drinks he'd had, he was surprisingly lucid. He slurred a bit, but was lucid nonetheless.

"Not *me* you have to worry about," I reminded him. "Any idea who could have done it? Any enemies? Anyone who hated him? Who would've benefited from his death?"

Miller's gaze became unfocused as he stared out into space. After a moment: "No, not that I can think of. He didn't have too many friends here…but I can't think of any enemies, either."

"What about the way he was dressed? Did that surprise you?" It sure had surprised me.

Miller stared down at the tabletop. "No…not really. Not

anymore…"

Not anymore? I'd get back to that. "How'd you meet him?" I asked. "Originally?"

Miller stared at the empty glass in his hand, turning it slowly, as if he hoped to discover a small pocket of booze hidden in one of its corners. "Fred was a writer…I don't know how well you knew him… but he wrote. Little bit of everything, it seemed: stories that he had published in some of the pulps, mysteries and westerns and some outer-space stuff. And there were some magazine articles that got published. "Hell Comes to Tucson" was one. One of the stories, I mean. It was in *Sagebrush Tales*, if you've ever seen that one." He looked up at me. "Probably not, I guess."

I hadn't, and doubted that few others had. "He got by with the profits from writing?" I asked.

"He had money, family money," he continued, "so it wasn't very important that he earn a living. And he loved it down here, lived here, I guess, for ten years or so. Bought the house."

It was more like five, but I didn't correct him. "And you met him…?" I began.

"Two summers ago. At the Baldwin." The Baldwin was one of the town's two landmark hotels, huge Victorians built back in the late 1800s. "I was down here for the summer, staying with my aunt. She had a room there and got me one. I had just lost my job and was running low on funds. We were both drinking – Fred and me, I mean – and I told him my sad story, how I'd lost my desk job but really didn't like it, didn't like Newark, didn't like the insurance company, didn't like much of anything." He paused for a moment, looked up and around the room, blinking. I don't think he was looking at, or for, anything in particular, but after several seconds of this I looked over my shoulder and checked: nothing, and no one appeared to be any different, just drunker. He finally continued: "What I really wanted to be was a writer." He snorted loudly, as if amused by the thought. "Well, we hit it off. He liked me, told me I could move in with him, he'd help me with my writing."

"Did he?"

"Help? Sure. Well, yeah, as best he could. I wasn't…I'm not very good. But you don't have to be Shakespeare to write westerns." He reached for one of the empty glasses and downed the remains of a melted ice cube. "That's what I'm trying to write: Zane Grey type stuff. It's taking me forever…" His voice choked and he blinked his eyes. It probably occurred to him that he might not *ever* finish it now.

"How'd you manage to pay rent?" I asked.

"Oh, he didn't make me pay rent. I got room and board I guess you call it. For helping out around the house. It was too much house for one person, so I lightened the load, I guess." There were several moments of silence, abruptly ended by the slamming of the men's room door behind him; he jumped as if a gun had gone off by his ear.

"The way he was dressed that night: You said it didn't surprise you?"

He took several moments to compose his response, but it wasn't very composed. "Fred was, well, *different*. Hell of a nice guy, but *different*. He, ah, preferred the company of…of other men, if you know what I mean. It was a seasonal thing with him." Miller fished in his right ear with a crooked index finger as he spoke. "During the summer, there were all sorts of…ah…people vacationing down here that he'd become…*friendly*…with. He was always hanging out around the Baldwin and the Engleside. He preferred the Baldwin, because they had a bar, but he met lots of…uh…*interesting* people at both of them, people of his so-called social standing, I suppose."

I'd heard the random story about homosexuals looking for partners in each of those places, but never gave it much thought. Bill Cobbett, one of the bartenders at the Baldwin, would hang around my joint to drink on his days off, and had – on several occasions – regaled the other patrons with these stories. The stories became more outrageous with each retelling, and one never knew where fact ended and fiction began. Guess it was more fun that way.

"Did these *friends* ever come back to the house?" I asked, pulling a De Nobili from its box and sticking it in my mouth.

"No, never. At least never when I was there. This was only during the summer months, don't forget. The rest of the year he'd spend writing." He thought for a moment. "Well, occasionally he'd take off for a weekend and eventually come back. In good spirits and...uh... relaxed."

"And the clothes?" I asked, firing up my cigar.

"Clothes?" he asked, lost. Then it came back to him. "Oh, yeah, the clothes...I'd lived there I guess for about six months. One night I went out to the movies – *It Happened One Night*, I think it was – or was it *Mr. Deeds Goes to Town*? – one of those. Well, the Colonial's heat was out that night – you know how often that happens – and they were closed, so I turned around and went home. And there he was, all dressed up. Looked like...what's her name? Actress with the legs?" I had no idea who he was referring to. "Joan Crawford, that's it, kind of," he continued. "Well, I was stunned – and he was devastated. He broke down in tears, begged me not to think that he was crazy, anything like that, and went on to explain in a rather disjointed fashion about his lifestyle and preferences." He picked up his glass, remembered it was empty, and replaced it. "Well, I was still stunned; but Fred was such a nice, sweet guy that things six months earlier would have turned me off now took on a human face. It all didn't seem quite so weird anymore. At any rate, I grew to accept, eventually, to become oblivious to, his habits and...uh...needs. During the winter, it grew quite routine to find him dressed that way. Claimed he could write better dressed like that." He shook his head as if it still didn't make any sense to him, then muttered something barely audible – sounded like "cotton whipcord jodhpurs," but I couldn't be sure.

He was silent now. I sat there staring at him. The room had two large, dusty overhead fans, and the one that still worked spun lazily in a futile attempt to keep the smoke from settling. An open window would have been welcome right about now.

"These…friends. Any problems with any of them? Could any of them done this?" I asked, hoping he'd already given this some serious thought.

"I…I don't know. I don't think so. Or, at least, he never mentioned it. Most of them were – believe it or not – *married*, and they'd be down here with their wives and children." He shook his head slowly. "While Mom was talking with other moms and the children building sand castles, Daddy'd be out somewhere entertaining Fred. No. I don't think there were any problems there. Fred didn't talk about it too much and I was always too embarrassed to ask, but I don't think there were any problems." He paused and squinted at the cigar in my mouth, then continued: "What is that thing you're smoking? It smells like hell."

I ignored the question. "Listen, Miller, you're in a bad position. You may not've had anything to do with Schweickert's death, but the cops like to look at things…*simply*."

Miller knew what I meant, let out a low moan and violently rubbed both eyes with his knuckles.

I continued fishing: "So, you're saying Schweickert liked to dress up in women's clothes. He took men as lovers instead of women. That what you're saying?"

Miller, head bowed, nodded affirmative.

"But you: you prefer women, right? You just grew to accept and, I guess, kind of *understand* his peculiarities," I continued, stating what I thought – *hoped* – to be the case. "No cause for jealousy, nothing like that on your part. You just let him go about his business, and pretty much minded your own. Right?"

There was a long, deadly silence, and I knew immediately that I was off base, that Miller was going to have a hard go of it. After half a minute of silence, Miller continued, haltingly, in a voice barely heard above the din.

"That's…not…quite right," he whispered. "It was, at first." He took a deep breath. "He…he was so nice to me. I found myself growing…attracted to him. When he was dressed…*that way*." Tears welled up in his eyes, and he sniffed several times. "It…it's so lonely here in the winters; they're so…*long*."

Miller broke down in tears now, sobbing uncontrollably. Pathetic. No one else seemed to hear him, but anyone looking at him would suspect he had some problems. Me, I *knew* he had problems now: When Purdy finally got hold of him and verified that Miller and Schweickert were lovers, his suspicions would be confirmed and it would be an open-and-shut case with him — and the public. Once the details were revealed, the locals would probably be up for a lynching. At high noon. From the water tower. Bring the children.

"Listen, Miller," I said. "You've gotta turn yourself in and tell them the truth. It's the only chance you have. If you don't, you'll look guiltier than hell. Turn yourself in. *Now*. Tell 'em what you know. All of it. I can take you over there."

Miller, left elbow on table and forehead in hand, fumbled awkwardly in his coat pockets with his right hand. He was, I assumed, looking for either cigarettes or a handkerchief, probably the former, but I hoped the latter. He found and dragged a rumpled linen rag from his left inside coat pocket. As he did so I heard something metallic bounce off the floor. I looked at him momentarily to see if he'd retrieve whatever it was, but a panicked look of realization came over him as he froze in place. I bent over and looked on the floor by our feet. Midway under the table was what appeared to be a long, slender, silver letter opener with an ivory handle. I carefully picked it up by its edges, sat up, and placed in on the table before me. It was smeared with a dried haze, lines of dried dark brown clung to its crevices. Blood. This guy was in deep shit.

"Miller," I said, to get his attention. "What the *hell* is *this*? Why do you have it? Do you know how bad this looks? Are you *nuts* or something, bringing this here with you?"

Even I was beginning to doubt this guy's innocence.

"Oh, my God," he stammered. "I didn't do it. Honest to God, I didn't do it!"

"Why do you…?"

"It was there. On the floor. I just picked it up. I forgot I had it. Oh my God, you gotta believe me: I DIDN'T DO IT!"

He'd risen from his chair now, and it toppled over behind him with a loud thud. He looked like a madman. A few people standing nearby cut short their conversations and were staring at him, waiting to see what happened next.

"Miller!" I barked. "Shut up and sit down! NOW!"

This got his attention; he started to sit.

And then the front door opened with a crash that brought stunned silence to the place. Wind and rain whipped in around the three figures silhouetted in the open doorway. They paused, surveyed the room, and then their gazes locked on us. As they stepped forward into the overhead light, my fears were confirmed: It was Purdy, followed by Schoengarth and – God help Miller – *Gibbons*; Hipple must've been back baby-sitting Schweickert's corpse. Purdy moved slowly towards us. Gibbons, pipe clenched in teeth and smiling, sauntered leisurely behind. Schoengarth closed the door behind them; he remained stationed in front of it.

"Shit," I muttered under my breath, as I looked at the trio over my left shoulder. Miller, who had frozen in place in a half-seated position, now slumped heavily onto his chair.

"Jesus, Porter, what are you doing here?" sighed Purdy as he approached. "I thought I told you to call me…" I stood up and turned to meet him, face to face.

"Oh my God, Lew, help me," whimpered Miller behind me.

"Quiet, Miller!" snapped Purdy. He looked to me: "If you don't mind, Porter," tinged with a hint of sarcasm. I'd never seen him like this before, or at least not before tonight. He looked tired. He looked like he was close to having a stroke.

I let him pass.

He stepped over to Miller, stood – hands on hips – looking down at him. Another sigh.

"Ernest Miller, you're under arrest for the murder of Frederick Schweickert." Miller cowered before him.

"Lew…" Miller moaned. He looked miserable sitting there. "You're pathetic," exclaimed Purdy, shaking his head. "Big, tough guy when you've got a knife, whimpering little Nancy boy when you don't." And then Purdy spotted the letter opener on the tabletop, and brightened immediately. "Well, well, well…what *have* we here?" he said quietly as he picked up the damning piece of evidence. After close inspection: "Well, now, perhaps I was a bit hasty. Look what Mr. Porter's turned up. Looks like the murder weapon to me. Look like the murder weapon to you, Gibbons?"

Gibbons, standing to one side with an unsettling, clenched-toothed grin plastered over his face, removed his pipe and tapped it on a chair-back. Ashes and half-burnt tobacco dropped to its seat. He carefully placed the pipe safely in his pocket.

"Looks like it to me," stated Gibbons flatly, eyes locked on Miller.

"Well, my boy, you're gonna fry for this one, that's for sure," stated Purdy matter-of-factly, turning back to Miller. "Citizens don't like this kind of stuff going on in their backyard." Gibbons started moving in a slow arc around the table, working his way closer to Miller's back. Miller eyed him nervously, turning his head repeatedly, glancing over his right shoulder in an effort to track Gibbons' course behind him.

"Please. I…I didn't do it. I just explained…" stammered Miller to anyone who would listen.

Gibbons took a quick step forward and grabbed Miller's right upper arm in his hand. Gibbons whittled decoys as a hobby – had for years – and had powerful hands, a powerful grip. He squeezed Miller's soft arm tightly. Very tightly.

"Getting into a little mischief, eh, Ernie?" he stated flatly.

Miller became hysterical with fear.

"Lew, oh my God, Lew! Help me! HELP ME!" he screamed.

I stood there, motionless – and emotionless. There wasn't much I could – or would – do.

"They call this the *Queen City*, Miller, always have, always will," stated Gibbons, leaning in close to Miller. "But long as I'm around, the name's not going to be taken literally."

There was some nervous laughter in the room. Schoengarth cracked a smile, but it disappeared quickly when I gave him a long, cold-eyed look.

"Easy, Gibbons," said Purdy, quietly.

"You screwed up, Miller – royally – now you're gonna to pay for it. And it doesn't come cheap," continued Gibbons. "Got a nice, little seat up in Trenton, just your size, still cozy and warm from Mr. Hauptmann. Got it reserved for you. 'Reserved for Ernest Miller'."

"Enough!" Purdy again, more forcefully. He turned abruptly, jammed hands into pants pockets. I could hear the change start to jingle. "Get him outta here. Lock him up. And call Toms River," he barked over his shoulder to Gibbons.

A nickel-plated nipper appeared in Gibbons' hand, which he swiftly slapped on Miller's wrist, yanking the sobbing ruin out of his chair. "Come along, Ernie. Otto's gonna teach you some *decorum*." He started to drag Miller to the front door, and as he passed he looked over at me momentarily, and our eyes locked. I'd swear he winked.

"Lew!" screamed Miller. "Can't you do something? Help me!" He was wide eyed and wild now, but no match for Gibbons' powerful grip.

I paused for a moment before answering.

"Sorry, pal, you're on your own on this one," I stated flatly, then added: "Just tell the truth and cross your fingers." All of them. "And get yourself a lawyer – a *good* one; not one of these local rubes," I added, none too hopefully.

The four of them exited, there were some indecipherable

comments from outside, car doors slammed, and a car pulled away in a spray of kicked-up gravel. The Antlers was dead with silence, cool, fresh air blowing in the still-open front door.

Twenty minutes later, back in the taproom. Almost midnight. I was exhausted. Any other Friday night the place would have emptied out by then, only a straggler or two hanging back. Tonight was different, though – most of the crowd from earlier on remained. And they all wanted a blow-by-blow description of the night's events.

"Gentlemen," I said, wearily, "this is gonna to have to wait 'til tomorrow; I'm just too damned tired to go through it now." There was an immediate roar of disappointment and disapproval. I continued, yelling over the complaints: "Tomorrow, when we open, you'll get the whole story." I hadn't planned it this way, but I immediately realized that tomorrow would be a good day for business – probably a *great* day. The complaints were even louder now. I quickly added: "And the first round will be on the house." The complaints petered out as the thought of a free drink took hold. "Willett," I yelled, "give 'em all a drink on the house tonight, too." I had them in my pocket now, and beat a hasty retreat while their thoughts were temporarily diverted.

Saturday, October 17, 1936. 8:10 p.m.

HOOVER'S LEGS TWITCHED, his nails skittering about the floor's wooden surface, an occasional muffled bark blowing his lip away from his teeth. Sleeping soundly on the floor by the pot-bellied stove, he was immersed in a dream encounter with a squirrel or some other equally vicious creature. Everyone ignored him.

I was stationed behind the bar as usual, surveying the crowd of a dozen or so of our regular customers. The place had been packed at noontime, and I'd told and retold the events of the previous evening to my rapt audience. They had hung on every word and gory detail, and I did my best to not over-embellish in an attempt to tell a *better* story – the truth was good enough. Willett and I'd done our best to keep the drinks flowing. More than once I'd found myself thinking that the occasional brutal murder and attendant scandal would be wonderful for business. By late afternoon, the story had been told to death, and most of the crowd had filtered out.

On the books, the place's official name was the Dock Road Inn, but I don't recall anyone ever calling it that. The regulars all called it "Holly's," in honor, if you want to call it that, of my wife. The sign nestled in the small area of clapboard above the porch roof and below the eaves on the building's north side is more to the point: "Bar." To avoid confusion, I referred to it simply as "the taproom." No one ever called it "Porter's" or "Lew's," or at least I never heard them, but that was okay; Holly had lived in Beach Haven all her life, as had her parents for decades before her. She knew every one of the town's year-round residents by name.

Me? I moved here in the mid-twenties. Became a new Lew Porter, if you will; dressed and acted like a local, and adapted a perfunctory manner of speaking which earned me a reputation as a man of few words while discouraging too many questions about my past. But I was still an outsider, a *mainlander*, a city boy, and with that came an inherent lack of trust. The locals were, for the most part, a tight-knit group. I understood their wariness of anyone from the outside trying to become a part of it. But I'd been around Beach Haven for eleven years now, serving them drinks for just as long, and they'd warmed up to me a lot more quickly than most other newcomers. Bars and alcohol are, of course, the great equalizers.

I'd moved here back in autumn of 1925. The years before were — well, let's just say a *mess* — and I'd made the decision to get the hell out of *that* life and try to start a new one elsewhere. In simpler surroundings. Beach Haven seemed to fill the bill, being a lonely, quiet community of roughly seven-hundred year-round residents. Lonely and quiet, that is, for nine months a year; the summer months of June through August are a whole different story. Then the population swells into the thousands and the endless hordes of vacationers destroy the offseason tranquility. The locals despise these *mainlanders — summer people* as they frequently refer to them. Especially the *uplanders*, who arrive full of arrogance and condescension and turn the usual way of life on end for several long months. But the locals are quick to bemoan any season when the tourists, their pockets full of cash, arrive in less-than-expected numbers. It's a love-hate relationship, to be sure: love their money, love when they leave, and hate everything else about them.

I'd needed a job, any job, and a place to stay, and found both with Holly's old man. Ray Farnham was his name, and he ran a lunchroom-cum-speakeasy known to the locals as "Ray's", with a sign over the door that read "Eats." This same building, of course, is the current Dock Road Inn, and the *Eats* sign was repainted in '33 to the current *Bar*; primarily because it fit. Located near the terminus of the railroad tracks heading south from mid-island, Holly's boasted a clientele consisting primarily of the town's working stiffs – pound fishermen, railroad workers, baymen – anyone else looking for decent, low-cost drinks and a total lack of pretension. Vacationers avoided the place because it looked like a dump from the outside. First-time visitors were always surprised when they entered: it looked even worse inside.

The former lunchroom, needless to say, was a thinly veiled cover for the real moneymaking business, the selling of illegal booze. Ray used to pay the local authorities to look the other way during those *dry* years, so the place wasn't *policed*, because it *didn't exist*. As a result, whenever a fight would erupt – and in those days it seemed to be a weekly occurrence – Ray was on his own. He wasn't averse to wading into an unruly mob with his *friend*, which is what he called the length of lead pipe wrapped in newspaper kept at arm's reach under the bar, and, with a few deft moves, quickly restoring order. By 1925, however, Ray was an older and slower Ray. While he was still game for a donnybrook, the healing of the occasional fractured or broken bone took longer than it used to. That's where I came in. Ray hired me as backup bartender and general all-around help, as much for my size and considerable abilities in handling myself quickly and efficiently – and, some might say, foolishly – during a fight as for my experience decades earlier as a kid working in *my* old man's saloon back in Bordentown. And, as part of the deal, and in lieu of much of a salary, he gave me the large room above the joint as a place to stay.

Ray was an interesting character: friendly as hell, but with moods that could darken as quickly as a summertime storm blowing in over the bay. These were few and far between, however, and no one was ever quite sure what in hell triggered them. He was short and stocky, almost as wide as he was tall, with an Irish brogue undiminished by his years in the states. He was incapable of walking like a normal person, instead swaying back and forth like a clock's pendulum as he slowly moved forward, and rarely ever in a direct, straight line. His snow-white hair crowned a pale, heavily lined face, his white whiskers seemed frozen in time; I can't recall ever seeing him clean shaven, and yet his whiskers never seemed to grow any longer, just a perpetual quarter-inch stubble – kind of an arrested facial hair growth. At the time I first met him, Ray's late wife had been dead for at least a dozen years.

Within a couple of years I'd fallen in love with Ray's daughter, Holly – fallen *hard* in love – and the two of us eventually got married in '28. It was an informal event, as far as events go: just Holly, myself, Ray and anyone else who'd ever spent more than a dollar at Ray's. Justice of the Peace Ellsworth Gwillim presided. Afterwards, everyone headed back to the bar and got sloshed. I knew that Holly liked to drink, but that night she was absolutely amazing: Ray had produced a bottle of Old Grand-Dad that he had hoarded for years, and she went to work on it with a passion. Let's just say that during the course of the night a lot of alcohol was consumed. As a wedding present, Ray had given us the bungalow next door to the lunchroom, and we'd moved in soon after. I liked Ray.

Three years later, in '31, Ray died, leaving his business and a pile of money to Holly. Now, it wasn't any secret that Ray had had a sizable involvement in the so-called *Rum Row* smuggling of illegal liquor from boats anchored off-shore, and had had strong connections throughout the '20s with one of the several crime syndicates operating out of Atlantic City. He'd enlisted and organized a tight assemblage of island smugglers from the pool of local fisherman eager to make a fast buck, and on a regular basis a small *fleet* of old fishing schooners, smacks and leaky scows would wend their way back from outside the twelve-mile territorial limits. They'd be so loaded down with cases of scotch, Canadian whiskey, rum and the like that any one of them would've sunk if an overweight gull had landed on it. Amazingly, the various towns' streetlights always seemed to have problems on those nights, leaving the thoroughfares and cross streets blanketed in darkness and safe for moving the illegal cargo. Ray also controlled the area distribution of the stuff. Needless to say, he had, over the years, amassed a small fortune.

We'd never given the eventuality of his passing any thought, as he always seemed healthy as a horse, full of energy that would've put a teenager to shame. But one night his body simply gave up, and Ray never awoke the next morning. Holly found him in bed, eyes and mouth frozen wide open and staring off into space, as if he had witnessed Death himself enter the room, beckoning.

He had a will, kept it in a large, metal box tucked beneath some loose floorboards. This was in his small office behind the bar, under an old worn sofa. It was locked and Holly had the key. She'd been instructed never to open it – never to even get near it – until his death. She'd honored that request, and had pretty much forgotten about it until the day we found him dead. When she finally *did* open it, however, she was stunned to find stack after stack of tightly tied fifties along with the will which, in simple terms, left *everything* of Ray's to her. And, since the word everything was underlined three times in red pencil, she took that to mean the cash, as well. I didn't argue with her.

We continued running the place as a speakeasy for the next two years, while someone else in the area assumed Ray's role as area procurer of illegal booze. When 1933 rolled around, and Roosevelt committed himself to the one worthwhile goal of his otherwise worthless administration – the repeal of the eighteenth amendment – we promptly applied and paid for a license to sell and serve beer. This was upgraded a year later to cover all the other alcoholic beverages we were already selling. The *lunchroom* charade was dropped, and we became, on paper, the Dock Road Inn. It was business as usual. Except I had to get up on the porch roof and paint over that damn sign.

Sitting at the bar now were Eddie Edwards, Willis Mackey, Joe Carver, and Arvid Dovey. As usual, Edwards and Carver were having another spirited discussion, one that, often as not, would lead to heated words and then a cessation of any further conversation whatsoever while they both went back to drinking. Fifteen minutes later, after they'd both cooled down, the process would usually repeat itself. This time, however, they actually seemed in agreement.

Carver was in his early twenties and worked locally for Stephen Snipes in his plumbing business ("Snipes Does Pipes!"). He was single, not terribly bright, but did a good enough job for Snipes that he'd probably have it for life if he wanted. When he wasn't working, Carver would spend most of his off hours in bars, either alone here at my place or with a group of friends elsewhere. He was a good, fairly reliable source of information regarding the goings on of Beach Haven's more youthful, drinking-age segment: the rookies in their very early twenties. Whenever I saw him, he was usually dressed in his work uniform of drab green cuffed work pants and shirt, with sleeves rolled far up to reveal his considerable muscles, and a pencil that never budged from above his left ear – I think it was embedded there. He had brown hair combed straight back, angular features and was reasonably good-looking. Except for his teeth, which were crooked, arrayed in odd numbers and yellow from constant smoking. Right now, he had a Chesterfield clamped between his lips and was doing just fine speaking around it.

Edwards, known to most everyone as "Deuce," worked as a salesman for a local realtor, Seaside Realty, pushing lots, summer rentals and the occasional house that came on the market ("Your little patch of Heaven by the sea!"). His modest income was supplemented by the sale of various appliances – stoves, refrigerators, radios and the like – which he kept out in his garage. His prices for these items were extremely good, so they moved quickly and he always seemed to have a waiting list. No one ever bothered to ask where he got the things, and he wouldn't have told them if they did: "Don't look a gift horse in the mouth," I once heard him say, as if he were *giving* his stuff away.

Edwards had theories about everything – not particularly well reasoned or logical, but theories nonetheless. Rarely a night would go by when he wouldn't pontificate on some subject or other, usually sexual in nature – or, at the very least, get in an argument with someone. And sex: It permeated his thinking and reasoning, and managed to work its way into most any conversation he had, regardless of whether or not it had anything to do with the topic at hand. Edwards was in his early forties, with a round, youthful face that made him look like the man in the moon. His thinning, sandy hair was short on the sides and back, and non-existent on the top. He wasn't a large man – perhaps only five seven or so – and he looked rather soft and slight. He had the smallest wrists I'd ever seen on a man. But what he lacked in stature he more than compensated for in bluster. His incessant chain smoking of Camels rivaled Carver's. And while many others would make a point of standing at the bar, Edwards always sat.

"Ah, he's a crook," sputtered Edwards, "a bum and a crook." Roosevelt, of course, and no one else within earshot bothered to disagree. "And his wife: She has to be one of the ugliest women I've ever seen. Really, just...*ugly*."

"Well, he's a cripple. Ya think a pretty woman's gonna marry a cripple?" responded Carver, firing down the remainder of his beer as he finished.

"A rich cripple, yeah. He's rich. And love is, as they say, blind. When money's involved, anyway." Edwards paused to have some beer. "Ever notice how all president's wives are ugly?" he continued. "And I don't mean *homely* ugly, I mean *ugly* ugly – *Eleanor Roosevelt ugly*. Why you think that is?" he posited to anyone who would listen. Few were.

Carver thought for a moment. "I dunno."

"Well, I'll tell you why. It's a conscious, psychological ploy on their part, you see? *Think about it*. If they had *pretty* wives, the public would assume they'd want to spend time with their wives. *Ugly* wives are a different story altogether. Subconsciously, people feel their president is devoting all of his waking hours to his duties, 'cause who in their right mind would want to go home and fuck someone who looked like that?"

"A cripple," interjected Carver.

Edwards looked momentarily surprised by the response. "Well, maybe – you have a point there. And that could explain his zeal in putting an end to prohibition."

Carver paused, drink halfway to his lips. "Huh?"

"Well, even if he's a cripple, he'd still probably want to get good and pickled before putting it to someone that ugly. This way, it's legal." Edwards picked a piece of tobacco off his tongue. "God, the thought of face-to-face sex with Eleanor Roosevelt…absolutely terrifying." He quickly looked up at Carver. "And it would be face-to-face. Just 'cause she looks like a dog doesn't mean she'd do it like a dog. She may be ugly, but she's got *breeding*."

"Maybe they've got some Amish in them," responded Carver without much enthusiasm.

"Amish? *Amish*? Like *Pennsylvania Dutch* Amish? *Egg noodle* Amish?" Edwards was baffled by Carver's comment. We all were.

"Yeah, well, aren't they the ones that fuck through holes in sheets so they can't see each other? That would solve his problem. He'd just have to convince her to go along with it."

Edwards stared at Carver for several moments. "I don't think so," he responded, stubbing his cigarette out in the chipped glass ashtray in front of him. "No, I don't think so. Even with a sheet, you'd still know it was her on the other side. Nah, he probably just doesn't do it at all. Maybe a quick wrestle with Popeye behind closed doors, but not sex with the *little* woman," finished Edwards. He motioned to me for another beer, and then seemed lost in thought as his unfocused gaze moved to the large mirror behind me. "Sex with Eleanor Roosevelt…" he muttered to himself, as if contemplating the act. After a moment, he shuddered violently, shaking himself loose from this unpleasant reverie.

Carver squinted at Edwards, and returned to his drink. "Well, that's *his* problem. I've got my own," he said, dismissively.

Mackey and Dovey quietly continued with their drinks. Willis Mackey was owner and proprietor of Beach Haven's Mackey Memorial Funeral Home, and was basically a quiet, low-key sort of fellow. He was always neatly dressed in a dark suit, white shirt, and dark tie, and looked very out-of-place in this dump, but he knew he could come here and drink in peace. Oh, sometimes he'd have to deflect the occasional probing, line-crossing question regarding a customer with a sensible speech about privacy, respect for the dead, the code of honor, and the awesome responsibilities of his position. But everyone knew that if you were patient enough, and kept feeding him drinks, that eventually – when his eyelids suddenly drooped to half mast – you could ask him most any inappropriate question and get an answer. Sometimes rambling and semi-coherent, but an answer nonetheless.

Mackey was tall and thin, probably in his late forties, solemn looking, and balding, with the sole remaining hair on the back and sides still dark brown without a trace of gray. He had sad, sunken eyes, an unsmiling mouth, an aquiline nose and gaunt face that reminded me of a photo I'd once seen in an old *National Geographic* of one of the Egyptian mummies they'd unearthed – Rameses II or III, I think it was. Anyway, Mackey could stand for hours at the bar, quietly playing solitaire with the old deck of cards he carried in his coat pocket, smoking his Kaywoodie pipe stuffed with Granger Rough Cut Pipe Tobacco, the stuff in the heavy foil pocket pouch, ten cents a package. And, for the most part, he kept to himself.

The damnedest thing about Mackey was that he was single, yet he always had women chasing after him. Middle-aged women, admittedly, but women nonetheless, and no one could quite figure out why. Everyone was, however, more than willing to speculate, and the fanciful theories presented in his absence provided the participants with hours of inebriated amusement.

"Saw Holly's poem in the *Times* this week," commented Mackey without looking up, and loud enough to bring me around. "It was pretty good."

The *Beach Haven Times* was the area's weekly newspaper, and it had a little bit of everything in it. Local, national, and international news all summarized for easy consumption, social events, resident comings-and-goings, comics – the whole nine yards; did a pretty good job of it, too. Anyone needing a daily dose of this stuff picks up a copy of the *Philadelphia Evening Bulletin* or *Inquirer*, but *everyone* on the island reads the *Times*. One of its weekly columns was the "Poets' Corner," where anyone who'd ever written a poem could usually get it published. They needed fifty-two of them a year, so lots of the same authors showed up with a fair degree of regularity, and some of their poetry was pretty bad. Awful, for that matter.

"Think so?" I questioned, drying a glass.

"Well, yes. On par with her other efforts." He was being diplomatic: She wasn't very good at all.

"Holly wrote that thing?" asked Edwards.

I smiled a half-smile and nodded.

"Oh. Well then." He seemed at a loss for words, and it was a pleasant change.

Mackey continued: "Of course, she's still an amateur, and there are amateurish aspects to her poetry, but it's a damn sight better than most of the dreck that appears there. At least her poems *rhyme*."

Edwards brightened; he now had something to contribute: "Rhyme, *and* make sense. That Japanese shit that was in there couple of weeks back didn't make any sense at all. And it sure as hell didn't rhyme. Remember?" he asked, looking to each of us for confirmation. There were a few nods. "Must've read it a dozen times and still couldn't figure out what the hell she was talking about."

Carver had grabbed the bar copy of the *Times*, flipped through to the column and methodically folded the paper so that only the column was exposed. "Here it is," he announced. "Yeah, that's her all right." He was looking at the small snapshot of Holly that sat just under the title. Every featured poet got her photo printed – a grainy head-shot – and she was no exception. Only difference was that she was a lot easier to look at than most of them. Carver continued: "'Love Lost,' by Holly Porter." There was a noticeable groan among the patrons who realized that he was about to read it aloud. And probably mangle it in the process.

> As I think of you
> I'm troubled; what did we do
> To our love, for we both know it's through.

Carver paused and looked up. "Phew," he stated, noncommittally. "That's quite an opening."

"I think they get the idea, Joe," I said, trying to get him off the hook.

"Yeah, we get the idea, Joe." said Edwards, reinforcing what I had just said. "But at least it rhymes. *You – do – through*: good solid rhymes None of this *go* and *through* shit." He was riffling through older copies of the *Times* now, muttering to himself: "Where's the one with the Jap shit in it?"

Carver had continued to read silently to himself, and then spoke without looking up. "What's this Poets' Circle they keep talkin' about?"

"Here it is," announced Edwards triumphantly. "Listen to this: It's titled '*Jap Shit.*'

> Fish swimming, nimbly
> Sea of life, cesspool of death
> The ocean, screaming."

He looked up in amazement. "What the fuck does *that* mean?"

"Poets' Circle…it's a club for poets, amateurs," I replied to Carver, ignoring Edwards' question. "Most of 'em live here on the island. Maybe one or two from the mainland; not sure." I didn't bother to add that the club had originally been Holly's idea, that she was its founder.

Gordon Willett had entered the room during this exchange and stood beside me behind the bar. He stared at the upside-down poem that Edwards had just read. "It's called *haiku*," he said matter-of-factly. "It's a Japanese verse form comprised of three non-rhyming lines of…ah…seventeen syllables in total – the first and third lines of five syllables, and the second of seven."

Edwards stared at Willet for a moment, as if he was a visitor from another planet. "Thank you, *Professor*," he stated flatly. *Professor* was the nickname he'd given Willett a while back, and it had, for obvious reasons, caught on. He turned to Carver: "The Poets' Circle is a bunch of old biddies with way too much time on their hands, and the weird idea that they're poets. They write this crap, send it to the paper, and because the *Times* is always looking for filler, it gets published, you see? And we get stuck reading it. No offense, Lew." he quickly added, turning to me. "Holly's the exception."

Her poetry was pretty bad, or at least it seemed so to me. But it was, after all, just a hobby, and it kept her occupied and happy for so much of the time. And off my back.

I looked over at Dovey, who was sitting there silent and uncomprehending. Dovey was an old bayman in his late sixties or early seventies, who rarely uttered a word. He'd sit there all night, just staring with his one good eye at a spot somewhere between the Cutty Sark and White Horse bottles, during his long, slow slide into total inebriation. His face was battered and unshaved, and his lower lip protruded and hung like a pelican's full lower bill. The lip was starting to tremble, my cue to get him off the stool and into an armed chair – quickly. I got Willett's attention, and he gave me a hand pouring Dovey into a chair.

Edwards hadn't let up, continuing his diatribe regarding the Poets' Circle and its members. "They're a bunch of cackling old hens, sitting around drinking tea and murdering the English language. And gabbing, that's mostly what they do — gab away, about anything and nothing, just to hear themselves yak." He finished with a triumphant flourish.

"Isn't that *all* that most women do?" asked Carver.

Mackey scooped up the remains of yet another stalemate. "Speaking of *gabbing*: Does anyone have any idea whatsoever as to what the 'Gab-Fest' I keep reading about is?"

"You mean the posters?" asked Willett.

"I do," responded Mackey.

"There's one out front on the pole," responded Carver, returning an empty glass to the bar. "Another one, Lew. Saw it earlier, but it didn't make sense. I'll show ya," he said over his shoulder as he headed for the door.

"What are you talking about," asked Edwards, puzzled, arms now folded and staring intently at the outcome of Mackey's game.

"I don't see how you could have missed them," responded Willett. "They've been plastered all over the town for a couple of weeks now. Bright red on white."

Hoover jumped up with a start, looked embarrassed, then sheepishly walked over to a cooler spot by the phone booth where he settled in with a thud. Carver reentered, poster in hand.

"Here ya go," he announced, then read:

"GAB-FEST 1936
SATURDAY OCTOBER 24
PATRIOTIC GATHERING - FUN FOR ALL
WALSH FIELD - 10:00 AM
SHARE IN THE GIFT OF GAB"

He looked up, puzzled. "*Gab-Fest. Gift of Gab.* Still can't figure it out, what they're talkin' about," he stated, and then took a long drink of beer.

"A morning of John Philip Sousa with the estimable WPA Orchestra, perhaps?" asked Mackey. "Or a carnival?" He was dealing himself a new hand.

"A bunch of politicians tryin' to win our trust, maybe?" asked Carver.

"Or the Poets' Circle shrews – the really old ones – boring us to tears with personal readings of their wretched stuff. A terrifying thought," mumbled Edwards.

"Why don'cha put this up on the wall along with the other stuff," commented Carver, handing the poster to me over the bartop. I took it, looked it over, and decided it would be right at home with all the other crap cluttering the walls and shelves. Lost, but at home.

The door opened again, and I looked up to see Purdy enter. This time he was alone. He wandered in, gave the place a quick once-over and hung his coat and hat on one of the hooks by the door. He headed for the pot-bellied stove and stood warming his hands for a minute or so. Purdy was in his mid-fifties, balding and what had probably been a sleek frame in his youth was now going to seed, with a rather formidable potbelly straining at his suit's vest. It gave his watch fob something to drape over.

Purdy wasn't really the chief of police of Beach Haven, but he liked to think he was. Actually, he was an elected town councilman, now serving an umpteenth term, whose official duties had always included, among other boring responsibilities, overseeing the borough's tiny police force. He'd found this to be infinitely more interesting – and, dare I say, fun – than overseeing more mundane necessities, such as garbage collection and street lighting. He played it to the hilt: acting like a chief twenty-four hours a day, playing the role for so long now that few people realized otherwise. Most everyone referred to him as Chief and assumed he was on the payroll, but it was just posturing on his part. One thing could be said for Purdy, though, and that was that he was always calm, in good spirits and reasonably friendly with most everyone. Always, that is, except for last night, when he displayed an impressive set of fraying nerves. It was obvious that Schweickert's murder had upset Purdy's routine and the comparative calm of daily life here in town, and he was reacting accordingly – good Purdy, bad Purdy. He had his killer now, or so he was convinced, and Miller'd be shipped north to Toms River soon, if not already, and out of his hair. Then Purdy's life could return to *normal*, and he'd resume being his usual ineffectual self. Miller's life, unfortunately, wouldn't. But that was Miller's problem, and if he had any sense he'd get himself a good lawyer. Soon.

Purdy came over to the far end of the bar and acknowledged the others: "Evening, Mackey. Gentlemen," he called to them. He turned to me as I walked over. "Hello, Porter."

"Purdy," I acknowledged. "Get you something?" In all the years I'd spent in this place, Purdy'd never crossed its threshold as a customer. He preferred Britz's over at Centre and Bay, and I understood why: It was a more *respectable* joint – and a hell of a lot cleaner.

He scanned the shelves behind me. "Rye, thanks. Got any Park and Tilford? Private Stock? Straight up." The man had good taste. I poured him a stiff one. As an afterthought, poured myself one, too. Told him it was on the house and that seemed to make his day – or at least his hour. He took a long pull and closed his eyes for a moment; the tension draining from his body as I watched. He removed his gold-framed glasses and rubbed his closed lids with thumb and forefinger.

"Miller's dead," he stated, matter of factly and in a voice low enough so that the others wouldn't hear.

"*Dead?*" I asked incredulously. I knew Miller was distraught, but I hadn't expected this.

"Yeah. Hung himself. With a knotted sheet. Tied it to the window bars. Stepped off the bed-frame, I guess; another three inches he would've touched ground."

"When?"

"Couple hours ago. Son of a bitch had just confessed, too, like an hour or so before. Said he killed him – Schweickert – out of jealousy, there was another guy involved. A romantic triangle, if you will." He looked mildly disgusted at the thought.

"He confessed? To you?" I asked, stunned by the news.

"Not me. To Gibbons, earlier, in his cell," he responded, fishing a Camel out of its pack, patting his pockets for a match.

"Gibbons? He confessed to *Gibbons*? Did *anyone else* hear this *confession*, or was it just – *Gibbons*?"

"Listen, Porter," he began, patiently. "Gibbons may have his rough spots – and he sure isn't going to win any popularity contests – but when it comes to being a cop, he's a damn good one. Been one for years. Has a natural talent for it. So, if he says to me Miller confessed, then Miller confessed; I'm not going to question it." He fired up his cigarette. "He left a note, too. Said he did it. And signed it."

"What did it say, exactly?"

"Can't reveal that. It's evidence," he said, smoke swirling about his head. You should know better than that." He took another drink.

"Did he say who the third person was?"

"Can't reveal that, either. Mum's the word. Official business," he responded without any emotion, and then looked at me with a slight look of puzzlement on his face. "What is it with you? What's the deal with Miller? Why can't you take things at face value – accept his guilt and stop fighting it?" he asked, and waited for an answer.

Maybe he was right, and maybe not; that was for someone else to determine. But Gibbons: I wouldn't believe a word that lunatic breathed if my life depended on it. Gibbons had only two, tightly related purposes in life: to put as many people in jail as humanly possible and to inflict as much bodily injury on them as he could in the process.

"Nothing I've seen or heard convinces me one way or the other," I responded slowly. "And without seeing the note or knowing exactly what was said to Gibbons, I'll reserve judgment. Keep an open mind. You remember, don't you? *Innocent until proven guilty?*" I immediately felt uncomfortable about the last part; I was rubbing his nose in it.

Purdy sat there silently, staring at the glass he was slowly rotating in his left hand. He wasn't responding to what I had just said. He just sat there. And for the first time in the last twenty-four hours, I had the vague notion that maybe he wasn't convinced of Miller's guilt either. Finally, he spoke: "It really doesn't matter now, does it? We have a written confession. We have a verbal confession – and a body. That's good enough for me. I seriously doubt anyone else is going to pursue this any further. You think otherwise?" he questioned, looking me straight in the eye.

I hesitated for a moment. "You're probably right," I responded. And he was. No one would lose sleep over it, especially if the murderer was tied up in such a neat package, bows and ribbons and everything. "Yeah, you're probably right. It's a dead issue."

I poured another round and we drank silently for several minutes, until the ritual was interrupted by the arrival of my wife. She'd entered through the front and was momentarily occupied with the removal of her coat, scarf and wool cap. All heads turned to silently – and quickly – admire her form, and then turned back just as quickly so she wouldn't notice. She pretended she didn't, and came over to join Purdy and me at the bar's end. I could hear Hoover's tail slapping the floor at a quickening pace. Purdy softened at her arrival and turned to greet her.

"Good evening, Holly. It's been awhile," he said in a pleasant voice.

"Hello, Lucien. How are you?" she responded, taking a seat.

They exchanged pleasantries as I poured her an Old Grand-Dad on the rocks. The next time I looked, it was gone. I refilled it.

Holly, as you may have gathered by now, was an extremely attractive woman. Not a classic beauty by any stretch, but with the kind of looks that got her noticed. She was tall for a woman, about five feet eleven inches, and on the slender side. Her thin, pretty face was framed by long, wavy brown hair that hung to her shoulders and beyond, with high, prominent cheekbones and a long, straight nose. More often than not, her full pouty lips would be set in a half smile that suggested amusement with the world around her. Long, thin legs touched only at the ankles; a nimble child could have ridden a scooter through there. Her posture was wonderful – almost uncomfortable looking at times – and she had, for her frame, nicely shaped breasts. Her eyes were possessed by a distant look, as if lost in thought or daydreaming about some far-away person or place. She was soft spoken but strong willed – always ready to speak her piece with a few, well-chosen words that effectively shut down all but the most argumentative of males. Those words worked less well with females, but those situations arose with little frequency.

"How's Maude doing, Lucien?"

Purdy paused and looked as if he were searching for the right words

"The same, thank you. Pretty much the same. It's…ah…difficult, as you can imagine." He hadn't searched too hard.

"Yes, I think I can. Well our thoughts are with her," placing her hand over his on the bar as a comforting gesture. "And be sure to let me know if there's any way we can help out," she added. This sounded serious. And, unless I was mistaken, she had just dragged me into it.

"Thank you, Holly. Thank you very much. That's very kind of you." He straightened himself out and put away his pack of Camels. "Well, I suppose I'd better be heading home," he announced. "Thanks for the drinks, Lew. I owe you. And try to forget about what's happened the last couple of days. It's over now, and we can all go back to our usual routine. Goodnight," he said, bowing slightly to Holly. And then he left.

Holly looked at the door as it closed, a sad, faraway look in her eyes.

"Maude's his wife?" I quietly asked Holly.

"Yes. They've been married forever. She has cancer of some sort They don't expect her to live much longer, but no one knows for sure." She sighed, and looked at me with brows furrowed. "I've told you all this before," she stated, with mild annoyance.

I shrugged noncommittally. Maybe she had, maybe she hadn't; I seemed to retain only about five percent of what Holly said on a day-to-day basis. So much of it seemed to be so pointless and unnecessary. Like so much of the so-called conversation here in the taproom. In one ear, out the other. Disposable.

"Anyway, their children are all grown and moved away. Jimmy and Julie," she continued. "He has a woman – Mattie's her name, I think – a widow from up in Spray Beach – stays with Maude night and day. Gives him a chance to get out of the house and do his job. It's a shame," she said, sadly.

I had a better idea now why Purdy was functioning so inconsistently these last few days.

"It's the goddamned developers, *that's* what's happening to Beach Haven," Edwards yelled at Carver, loudly enough to get our attention. "Used to be a peaceful, quiet town – think about it – back when we were kids. Nothing like this ever happened. *Ever!*" The subject of Schweickert and Miller must have resurfaced, knowing nods of agreement among the others as Edwards railed on. "Well, maybe some husbands beating up on wives, drunks beating up on other drunks, but that was winter stuff, nothing major. But *this!*" He shook his head in disgust, and returned to his drink. "*This* stinks!" he threw out as an afterthought. "Gives the town a bad name."

"There's no question that the stress of development and ever-increasing numbers of outsiders coming here to vacation and dwell has taken its toll," responded Mackey. "But in a lot of ways it's good for the town."

"Yeah. More bodies for you, McOat," snapped Edwards. Edwards had once learned that Mackey's surname was an

Anglicization of the Gaelic name Mac Aodh, and trotted out his bastardization of its pronunciation whenever he felt like it. "Like now," he continued. "That's the bottom line, isn't it: Fill those boxes!"

Mackey paused, cards in hand and turned to Edwards. "You do me a disservice, my friend," he said sadly, returning to his cards.

Edwards paused, immediately regretting what he had said. "Aw, shoot. I'm...ah...sorry, Willis. I got carried away. I didn't really mean it." He was quiet now.

"What do you make of that?" said Holly, quietly.

"I don't know. They yell a lot, that's nothing new. Don't think I've ever heard anyone raise his voice at Mackey."

Holly nodded in agreement.

"I'm sure he's sorry. Probably worried Mackey won't give him a discount when the wife kicks," I added.

She gave me one of her withering looks. She never found my jokes to be funny, probably because they weren't. She paused for a moment, surveying the room about her, tapping her left index finger nail on the bar's surface as she did so. "When are you going to clean this place up?" she asked – as if spontaneously – quickly changing to a subject I'd just as soon ignore.

"What's the point?" I sighed, knowing full well that this was always a futile stance to take with her. "These guys would reduce it to its former state within a day or so, anyway."

"All this sawdust is, well, *messy*," she continued, looking at the floor with a look of revulsion. Like this was something new. Place hadn't changed since she was in diapers.

"It's there for a reason, *you* know that," I said, looking towards the floor, but not really seeing much of anything in the dim light. It was covered with an uneven layer of filthy sawdust that was replenished periodically with new loads carted over from Cranmer's lumberyard. "Soaks up the spilled beer."

"It's not the beer I'm worried about," she said with a disgusted look on her face.

"Well, when someone retches, it makes it a hell of a lot easier to clean up. Turns into little manageable blobs. Willett'll tell you that." I could see that my line of reasoning wasn't getting through.

"You're impossible," she stated as an immutable fact, draining her glass. "Think about it, though, will you? We could do a lot here."

All I wanted to do here was serve drinks and keep people happy, in peace and quiet. She wanted to enrich their lives or something. "Yeah, I'll keep it in mind," I replied, noncommittally and unenthusiastically. And insincerely.

"Great!" she stated, as if she'd just won some sort of major victory. She tilted her head back one last time and let her glass's dregs drip onto her extended tongue, then licked her lips as she returned it to the counter with a bang. "Bye, hon. See you back at the house," she said as she turned quickly and headed for her coat.

I smiled a feeble smile as she departed. Hoover's eyes followed her as she crossed the room, grabbed her things and left. His tail flopped up and down a couple of times, sending some of that sawdust flying, but he didn't get up from his newly warmed spot.

I knew, deep down, that *he* liked the place just as it was. And he spent a hell of a lot more time here than she did. Case closed. At least for today.

58

Saturday, October 24, 1936. 10:23 a.m.

AUTUMN MORNINGS IN Beach Haven are like no others during the year, and this is arguably the most beautiful time of the year. Today was no exception, with clear, cloudless skies and no breeze. The sun was beating down now and it felt warmer than the low fifties registered on the porch thermometer. Hoover and I were taking our usual morning walk, today more enjoyable than the last several had been, with their stiff winds and occasional drizzle. Octobers were, in general, better than most months here, because it's still warm enough to be up and about during the daytime, yet cold enough to drive people indoors as soon as the sun started to sink – "indoors" meaning preferably my taproom. Best of all, the last of the summer people had by now long departed.

A flock of geese flew overhead in their usual wedge formation, appearing a minute or so after the telltale sounds of their sad honking. Hoover watched them pass, his small brain no doubt weighing the merits of chasing them down versus leaving them be.

Our walk was ritualistic. We'd head a block south from our house on Dock Road over to Centre, then four blocks east to the beach and town's seaside pavilion. Here we'd mount the adjacent boardwalk, head south for four blocks where we'd exit via the Baldwin Hotel's access ramp, then head back west towards the bay again on Baldwin Avenue. Actually, Baldwin was now named Pearl; the street was renamed a month or two earlier, and for no reason apparent to me or any of the people I'd talked to about it. By either name, this street took us past the looming structure of the hotel itself.

The Baldwin Hotel was, by this time, a sad shadow of its former self. Built during the latter part of the town's first building boom, the place was now over fifty years old. In recent years, the porches had all been enclosed and its distinctive little turrets – minarets, someone had called them – torn down. Business had dropped off over the years, too, as the days of the big hotels – with their packed schedules of activities and all meals included – had passed. Through the years, the Baldwin's primary competition was from the Engleside three blocks north, occupying the better part of a block between Amber and South. There really wasn't that much competition, as such, as most visitors had a fairly clear idea of which place appealed more to them.

The Engleside was, from the very beginning, a temperance house staffed by Boston Irish, with a clientele originally consisting primarily of Philadelphia Episcopalians and Quakers. It'd done well for decades, with modern conveniences such as elevators, lighting and plumbing added and upgraded on a regular and timely basis. But now it seemed locked in time, and not a recent one: it was fading fast. Its owner was heavily in debt, the building in desperate need of repair. Few of the rooms had running water – forget about toilets – everyone sharing the bathroom at the end of each hall. And, to add insult to injury, they still wouldn't consider a liquor license.

The Baldwin, on the other hand, was significantly looser and livelier. Always laid claim to a full bar and they served wine with meals. Prohibition didn't stop them, either – didn't even slow them down – as drinks continued to be served to anyone who asked. And most of their customers did; only the drinking vessels changed. Modern conveniences were added here regularly as well; but unlike the Engleside, the tradition continued into the '30s when the outdoor tennis courts were replaced with miniature golf. Still, this and other measures were just bandages on a gaping wound; but while the Engleside was near death – and looked it – the Baldwin was still only bedridden. Late October, however, both were closed for the season and stood as dark, silent, lonely shells.

Our walk would continue two blocks west on Pearl back to Bay Avenue, where we'd traipse the five blocks north back to Dock Road and home. The trip would be interrupted easily a thousand times as Hoover would stop to sniff, then mark, every bush, post and any other object he'd pass and find interesting along the way. An incredible bladder, I'd always think to myself, even though I was convinced that after the first several dozen stops and mandatory leg lifts the old dog was just squirting air. I was fully aware of the importance of this ritual to him, however, policing and securing, as he was, the outermost fringes of his own little world.

Today, I stood patiently while he diligently explored every nook and cranny of a mailbox's right front leg and watched a family late in closing up their home for the winter months ahead. I was vaguely aware of voices off in the distance, which sounded as if from a faraway radio turned up high. My gaze drifted over to a telephone pole, my eyes focusing on the red and white poster tacked to its surface. It was a copy of the one gathering dust on the backbar over at the taproom, reminding me with bold block letters that the so-called GAB-FEST had begun almost a half hour earlier on this very day. Ah, some excitement to break the routine of our daily walk; Hoover could extend the boundaries of his turf. We headed for Walsh Field.

Walsh Field sat on a three-block tract of land bordered on its north, east, and south by Pearl, Bay, and Berkeley Avenues respectively; and its western edge disappeared in the marshes bordering Barnegat Bay. Built a decade earlier, Walsh Field was home of Beach Haven's baseball team and the site of occasional summertime boxing matches. Newly constructed tennis courts sat at the Pearl and Bay Avenue corner, with the Little Egg Harbor Yacht Club occupying the tract's southwestern corner at the end of Berkeley. This club was affectionately known to the locals as the Shit Creek Yacht Club, as it was built in a marshy location previously occupied by a small fleet of houseboats, all with crappers fitted on their ass ends. The crappers functioned as outhouses of sorts, but could actually lay claim to having *running* water: users would wait for the tides to *flush* the area, which quickly became known around town as Shit Creek. And, hence, the yacht club's nickname. One its owners cherished, I'm sure.

The stadium at Walsh Field was an impressive, two-story wooden affair, painted green and backing up to Bay Avenue. A seven-foot fence finished off the playing field's perimeter and was fairly successful at thwarting the freeloading efforts of kids and adults alike, unable – or unwilling – to come up with the entrance fee. The diamond was smooth and well defined, and grass grew in all the appropriate adjacent areas. The place was beginning to show its age, however, with lots of loose and missing boards, and a paint job weathered into memory. No one seemed inclined to do much of anything about it.

Today, however, Walsh Field had been reserved and was now being used for a rally. It wasn't readily apparent just what the *Gab-Fest* was, since it was being held within the walled stadium, shielded from the view of a casual passer-by. This, along with the disembodied voices wafting out from within, served to pique the locals' curiosity. With free admission, turnout was surprisingly high. I headed for the entrance, Hoover following close by with a new degree of enthusiasm, undoubtedly sparked by the promise of thousands of heretofore-unmarked surfaces. Only a handful of people were heading for the entrance at this moment, their perplexed looks and shrugged shoulders suggested that none of them had a clue as to what to expect once inside.

There was a shill out front, but he was surprisingly inoffensive in appearance and demeanor. He promoted the wonders to be found within with a flowery prose that sparked the imagination while saying absolutely nothing of any substance – no one knew what to expect: but whatever was in there, *it had to be good*. We moved forward into the dark shadow cast by the looming front of the stadium, penetrated in innumerable places by knife slits of light streaming between hundreds of weather-shrunken boards. I carried Hoover – didn't want him getting trampled underfoot in the narrow passageways. No one else seemed to notice, or care; dogs were everywhere in this town.

We were admitted into the stadium, but instead of directing us, as usual, up one of the twin flights of wooden stairs into the bleachers on the first and third base sides, we were instead directed out onto the field itself. Once inside, the *Gab-Fest* and the heralded *Gift of Gab* became immediately, and depressingly, clear. GAB stood for the German American Bund, a bunch of high-profile supporters of Germany and, more specifically, that country's *Führer*, Adolph Hitler. I don't think many people took these guys very seriously and didn't consider them to be any sort of a threat, but they'd been getting a surprising amount of publicity as of late and their numbers were growing. The local press had written months earlier of their base, Camp Nordland, located somewhere up in northern New Jersey and a long haul from here. Like a lot of others, I tended to be suspect of groups promoting other countries and other countries' leaders, especially when that country and leader happened to be Germany and its self-important tyrant, Mr. Hitler.

Hitler had, in effect, served notice of his aggressive intentions by withdrawing Germany from the League of Nations three years earlier. A year and a half after that, he'd embarked on a program of rearmament after denouncing clauses in the Treaty of Versailles that prohibited, on paper at least, Germany from doing so. And then, March of this year, spitting in the world's collective face by reoccupying the western German areas demilitarized by that same Treaty sixteen years ago. Once again, the British and French had assumed varying poses of submissive urination and allowed Hitler to do pretty much as he pleased. So much for resolve. No one was quite sure where this would all lead, but there was one thing that everyone seemed to agree on: he was far from through. But Germany was *way over there*, seemingly in another world thousands of miles away, and a lot of people had grown complacent. Surely, they thought, the German populace wouldn't be stupid enough to set themselves up to get their kraut asses kicked a second time. I wasn't so sure, but I always held my tongue when the topic came up at the taproom; it was one of the golden rules of bartending: don't argue with the customers. Or, at least, the ones you think you can sell a few more drinks.

As we filed past first base and into the outfield, I got a better look at the makeshift stage. Parked sideways behind home plate was an old black Dodge flatbed draped and framed with yards of red, white and blue bunting, and a Nazi flag draped over its hood. Lined up shoulder to-shoulder in front of it were half a dozen Bund members, legs spread, arms folded and decked out in a common uniform that gave them the appearance of a bunch of bad-tempered, middle-aged Boy Scouts. They looked more silly than threatening, but clearly *they* took this seriously. Above them, standing on the deck of the flatbed, somewhere mid-speech, stood the *star* of the show. His uniform was the same as the others: khaki shirt, dark pants, black leather boots, black tie and, for a splash of color, a black armband decorated with a swastika in a white circle. His uniform had a different look to it than the others, and it took me a moment to discern the difference: his appeared to be tailored and fit him perfectly. The others were all ill fitting: either too long or short or tight or loose, but too *something*. He was a big man, well over six feet, with short, sandy-colored hair, a prominent beetle-brow shading a pair of small, intense eyes. His features were Teutonic, and he looked as though he'd be more at home in a suit of armor, lopping off heads. Still, he was a good-looking man, or appeared to be from this distance. He had a more relaxed and good-natured demeanor that set him apart from the humorless lackeys at his feet.

There were a surprising number of people here for an event such as this, perhaps fifty or sixty, but there was little doubt that the bulk of them were here solely out of curiosity rather than any sort of support for the cause. The reason for our being herded onto the field instead of into the bleachers soon became apparent: Off to one side sat a dark Ford V8 with the words *Universal News* prominently displayed on both sides. On its reinforced top sat a small platform bordered on its four sides by a tiny, six-inch-high rail. A bored looking individual stood atop this, dressed in shirtsleeves and vest, a battered brown fedora perched far back on his head. He was positioned behind a wooden tripod-mounted movie camera capped by twin film reels – "Mickey Mouse ears" I'd heard them once called. A quick pan of the camera would take in speaker and *rapt* audience alike, and no need to worry about lighting. On the ground to one side was another guy, this one with clipboard in hand, furiously taking notes.

Now, this was a pretty big deal for Beach Haven: having Universal send out a newsreel teams from New York City to cover one of our local events. Unfortunately, it happened to be *this* particular event and one that the town fathers, to a man, would wish hadn't happened here. I wondered how they had learned of this gathering and what it was about it that Universal deemed newsworthy. Granted, they had only sent out their two-man car and silent camera instead of the huge Universal truck loaded down with sound equipment and a small team to operate it; but they must have expected *something* of interest to happen. After all, boredom wasn't their business. These were, you may recall, the guys that had been sued a year earlier for over four million bucks in damages by the mother-to-be who, upon viewing the Universal newsreel footage of "Baby Face" Nelson's bullet-ridden corpse, suffered mental shock that she claimed resulted in the loss of her unborn baby. Journalism at its most sensational meets the legal system at its greediest.

The man on the makeshift stage was in the midst of his buildup now, pacing back and forth slowly with an amused look on his face; I couldn't tell whether he was smiling *with* us or *at* us. A large black megaphone swung loosely by his side and he now raised it to speak, a look of earnestness returning to his face.

"Is this what our forefathers had in mind, I ask you?"

I detected faint traces of a long-suppressed German accent.

"It is not!" he continued. "Deviance, perversion and madness running rampant through our country? It is not!" He paused, lowering the megaphone, still pacing, making eye contact seemingly with every single person in front of him. Rivulets of sweat trickled down the sides of his face, wiped away quickly with the back of his free hand.

"When the *Bible* exhorts us to 'love thy neighbor as thyself,' what does it mean? Does it mean to run out, if you're a woman, and fall in love with another woman? It does not! Or, worse yet, if you're a man — and I use the word *man* loosely — to run out and fall in love with another man? It does not! The mere thought is disgusting! *Repulsive!* It's abhorrent to all people with any sense of decency!"

Uh-oh. Schweickert and Miller were back for a third act. And the unsettling thing was that I noticed several in the audience cautiously nodding agreement.

"*What* is wrong with these people?" he continued. "*What* causes them to go against God's will and perform such unspeakable acts, *unthinkable* acts to anyone with any sort of conscience? What is wrong with these people? What is wrong? I'll tell you what's wrong. They're not God-fearing Christians, that's what is wrong! Why, they're Jews and atheists, people who don't believe in God!" He paused for effect. Or, perhaps, to think of the next thing to say. "And Catholics! People led astray by the pseudo-God Pope! And coloreds, with their animalistic jungle customs. Orientals: chinks and skibbies and what-have-you."

I glanced about the audience during this last volley, and was reasonably certain I could pick out all the Catholics in the group — they were the ones who exited. Twenty feet to my left was one individual who didn't leave, however, seemingly unfazed by this guy's disdain for Orientals. Tak Takarada and his wife, Yumi, both of Japanese descent and probably the only Orientals living within a fifty mile radius of Beach Haven, stood silent and unmoving, staring unflinchingly at the venom-spewing hatemonger pacing back and forth on the stage.

"No, sir! This country's on the path to destruction, a modern-day Gomorrah that's going to be brought to its knees by the insanely liberal policies of its so-called leaders, and the passivity of its lemming-like populace who blindly fall in line behind whatever policies and laws are set forth." He was yelling now. "Lemmings. That's what you are! Lemmings!" He paused and stared them all down with an intensity that was unsettling. He resumed, quietly now. "But it doesn't have to be that way. It's not too late. It's not too late to turn this wonderful country around. To start to rebuild on that remarkable foundation that the great leaders of yore, the great *Aryan* leaders, constructed over a hundred and fifty years ago."

Here comes the pitch.

"In Germany, where the economy was – pardon my French – going to Hell in a handbasket a mere ten years ago, the economy has turned around and in as dramatic a way as imaginable. The National Socialist Party. Adolph Hitler. These are the names that will go down in history as the saviors of a beleaguered nation. For wiping out unemployment. For reining in rampant inflation. And for restoring civil order and pride to a populace led astray, a populace tarnished by the actions of a selfish few obsessed with decadence and perversion. And this same miracle can occur *here* – in the United States." He paused with a knowing smile and there were some hushed words spoken in isolated pockets of the assembled group. "But only if *you* work with *us*," he continued. "*We* have the answer. *We* will show you the way. *We* are the German American Bund. And *we*…"

At this point, I'd grown bored with this fellow's ramblings and fanaticism. My attention drifted to the audience, which was growing uneasy with the direction his speech had taken, then to the newsreel crew who, as far as I'd noticed, had only filmed about thirty seconds of footage. The Bund must have one hell of a publicity department to lure these guys down here from Manhattan and away from a dozen more interesting stories. I turned to a small older man standing to my right, gnawing away at battered stick of fresh-baked bread: "Who is this guy?" I asked, not really expecting him to know.

"Him? Name's Willy Vollbrecht. He's a baker, believe it or not, or so I've heard, somewhere over on the mainland. Don't know where, though." He tore off another chunk with his teeth, paused and studied the half-eaten loaf momentarily as if wondering just where *this* loaf was baked. He resumed chewing, attempting to talk with his full mouth. "These Bund guys have their own camp over there somewhere, where he and his little Nazi friends go to play. Must be loads of fun," he sneered. "I'd rather stay home, listen to the radio."

I nodded agreement, then noticed Purdy off to the side of the newsreel truck. Actually, I noticed Hipple, who's easy to notice; Purdy stood next to him, hands in pockets, Camel dangling from his mouth. I headed over, and Purdy gave a barely perceptible nod of acknowledgment when he saw me approaching.

"Purdy. Hipple," I said as a greeting. "Official duty, or pleasure?" I asked. Hipple cracked a smile but quickly regained an impassive expression, looking to Purdy to answer.

"Just keeping an eye on things, that's all. Make sure things go smoothly." He glanced over at Vollbrecht, who was driving home some other point by pounding his fist on the top off the truck's cab. "No one's getting hurt. And, I hate to admit it, but I will: Some of what this guy says makes some sense. Not all of it, mind you, not even much of it," he added quickly, defensively, "but *some* of it. Stuff about the queers," he added. Why wasn't I surprised?

I looked at the two of them while he spoke. Just what would they do, or *try* to do, if there was trouble? Purdy's an old man and totally ineffectual; Hipple'd have a coronary if he attempted anything more physically taxing than walking into a lunchroom or dunking a sinker.

And Purdy has so little backup manpower: just Schoengarth, Gibbons and a few rookie part timers on call only during the summer. I had visions of Gibbons indiscriminately unloading his revolver into a crowd, then being torn apart by the angered survivors. The Long Beach Township force is nearby on the island, but of comparable size and composition. Given a large enough problem, Purdy would be forced to call in the state police, but their nearest barracks was over on the mainland in Tuckerton, easily an hour away. And that's after the troopers out on the road had all been contacted and gathered. Hopefully, it wouldn't become an issue.

Purdy scanned the audience. "Can't figure it," he said.

"What's that?" I asked.

"Why some of these people are here. There's old man Rosen and his wife. Takarada and his wife. Guy's words must sting. You'd think..." He shook his head slowly, his words trailing off.

Vollbrecht wound up his speech on a thunderous note, something to do with German lineage, Valkyries, Valhalla and God knows what else. After a feeble round of half-hearted applause – more, I suspect out of innate courtesy than agreement – Vollbrecht told the assemblage that he and his fellow members would remain there for several hours more to answer questions, disseminate general Bund information and sign up all those patriotic individuals who wished to join. I couldn't wait to see *that* line, but decided it'd be best for midday Saturday business if I headed back to the taproom and did some work. Some bill-paying work.

I coerced Hoover out of the comfortable bed he'd trampled into a sunny patch of grass. We headed for the exit, cut short as an excited guy I recognized as Bill McKinney trotted into the complex. He paused, gave the crowd a quick once-over, and wiped his sweaty brow with a sigh of relief.

"Morning, McKinney," I greeted him. "What's the rush? You actually interested in hearing this guy?"

"No," he gasped, still trying to get his breath back. "Not at all.

But I got a call from Brunner, said a group of half-drunk Swedes are on their way over here, run these guys out of town." Gerhard Brunner was the owner of the Hudson House and his clientele was comprised of the more spirited elements in town, among them the dozens of pound fisherman who worked for the several local fisheries. These guys were, for the most part, a mix of Scandinavians, with a fair representation of North Carolinians thrown in for good measure – conversations between the two groups must have been headache inducing. They were a hard-working, hard-drinking group, and their bars of choice tended to be the Hudson House on Twelfth and the Hav Inn at the corner of Bay and Taylor. But a handful of them would, on occasion, make the long walk to my place to drink in comparative peace and quiet. They were, by and large, a decent group, and tended to keep to themselves. Evidently, though, not today.

"Any idea how many?" I asked.

"No. A lot, sounded like, but I'm not sure." McKinney wiped the sweat from his lips with the back of his hand, ran fingers through his hair to get it out of his face. "Didn't ask too many questions. Just wanted to get here in time. Haven't seen a good fight in a long while." The guy was still winded.

"Guess this one's worth hanging around. Let's head to the outfield," I said, pointing. "Better view over there."

McKinney nodded agreement as he tucked in his shirt and hiked up his pants. As we walked, my thoughts returned to the Universal News team, who were starting to dismantle their gear. It would be almost as much fun watching them scramble to reassemble their camera.

"These Nazi guys scare me," commented McKinney, giving the small throng of brown-shirts a furtive glance.

"Ah, they're not real Nazis," I responded. "Just a bunch of loud-mouthed, overgrown kids playing army on the weekends."

"Well, maybe they're just playing, but the game's gonna change in a few minutes," he wheezed.

We arrived at what promised to be a good vantage point when Mr. and Mrs. Rosen walked up, clearly dismayed by what they were seeing and hearing.

"Morning, Mrs. Rosen. Irv," I said as politely as I could. Rosen owned a small men's clothing store nestled in among a line of shops on Beach between Centre and South. I didn't know them well at all.

They hadn't noticed me and were startled to hear their names spoken. Once they recognized me, they relaxed somewhat.

"Good morning, young man," said Irv. I guess he didn't remember my name.

Mrs. Rosen smiled a vague smile, but her attention – and concern – remained with the Bund members at the front. "This isn't right," she stated emphatically. "They shouldn't allow this to take place."

"Rabble rousers," I responded. "I wouldn't worry about it. Doubt anyone takes them seriously," I continued, mustering up whatever sounds of reassurance I was capable of. I don't think it was very convincing.

There was hardly a sound as the angry group of a dozen or so fisherman arrived – and if you hadn't been looking you might have missed them altogether. They said nothing, but marched purposefully from the entrance directly towards the sad-looking makeshift stage. The Bund members looked concerned, outnumbered as they were, but nervously held their ground. The fisherman stopped in their tracks perhaps ten feet from the truck and took a moment to survey the situation. An air of excitement and apprehension swept through the remaining audience, who sensed that a real show was about to begin. They weren't disappointed.

The fishermen glanced amongst themselves and, with mutual nods of agreement, raced forward. The guy in the lead swung a massive fist and knocked the closest brown shirt clear off his feet and into the group behind him. Panic broke out as a second fisherman grabbed the Nazi flag from the truck's hood and proceeded to shred it with his bare hands. Some of the remaining brown shirts backed away nervously, while the remainder darted in all directions. One by one, the fishermen caught up with them, driving fists deep into stomachs, smashing jaws, inflicting pain on anyone who resisted. Vollbrecht stood on the truck, seemingly calm and collected, unmoving. Then I noticed why: In his right hand, hanging down by his right thigh, was a large, shiny revolver. The fishermen noticed it, too, and word of it was spread quickly amongst them. Vollbrecht was left alone.

The audience had by now pulled into a tight semi-circle half surrounding the truck. This forced the beleaguered group to run haphazardly around the vehicle – and one-by-one they were caught and pummeled. The smart ones who just fell to the ground and pulled themselves into tight little knots were rewarded with a less-punishing kick or two. A couple of lucky ones managed to break through the crowd to comparative safety beyond. The real beatings were directed towards those who remained and resisted. McKinney had pushed his way towards the front and was cheering the aggressors. I remained at the back, preferring the big picture. The Rosens stood nearby, she hanging nervously on to his right arm, their heads together, whispered comments passing between them. The Takaradas stood quietly off to one side, Tak staring impassively at the melee before him. Yumi avoided it completely, her back turned to it, her face buried in his chest.

The police were nowhere to be seen.

One of the two pseudo-Nazis who had struggled their way through to the back of the crowd now stood at the far side of the Rosens, looking back at the melee he'd managed to escape. His left shirtsleeve was torn at the shoulder, his hair disheveled, his breathing deep. He looked worried, and the Rosens looked at him as if he were a leper. Their stares caught his attention, and his eyes locked on them. Realizing at once they were too old to be any sort of threat, and spotting the yarmulke perched on Irv's head, he directed his anger and frustration at them. Quickly stepping forward, coming face-to-face with Irv: "Kike bastard!" he screamed. "Why don't you go the hell back to wherever you came from and leave America to Americans." Spittle sprayed from his mouth as he yelled.

Irv stood silently as the guy finished his tirade and quickly gave him an ineffectual backhand slap to the face. This accomplished nothing more than knock a few strands of hair down in the guy's face and startle the hell out of him.

"Son of a bitch," the guy hissed through clenched teeth, shaking with mounting rage.

His right hand worked in and out of a fist. This was going to get worse before it got better, so I quickly stepped over, stepped between the two of them. Looking down at him, and as calmly as I could, I said: "Go home."

His eyes moved from Irv to me. He was frustrated and agitated, and words wouldn't form in his mouth. He just stood there shaking with barely suppressed rage.

"Now," I suggested.

He grew redder and shook like an autumn leaf in a stiff wind. His fist tightened, muscles tensed; he hauled off with a roundhouse. He was an amateur, every move telegraphed as if in slow motion. My right hand shot out, engulfed his fist mid-air, terminating his swing with a jolt. Mine was bigger, and I quietly squeezed his fist with enough pressure to bring tears to his eyes. He staggered under the pain, whimpering, clawing at my tightened fist with his left hand, finally dropping to his knees. He was pathetic looking, and I slowly released my grip.

"Now," I calmly repeated.

Sniffing and rubbing his aching right hand, he slowly stumbled to his feet and stood swaying in front of me. He'd lost this one and we both knew it. I thought to myself, and not for the first time, how greater violence had been avoided by a minimal display of carefully applied force.

Force: My dependable ally during my first twenty-five years; call it second nature. That was then, though, and this was now; things had changed. I'd walked away from that world, that life, distancing myself from all that had gone before. Deep down, though, I knew that rotten core of anger remained, and given the wrong set of circumstances could be reawakened like a hibernating bear in the spring. I hoped I was wrong. I hoped that day would never come. But I feared it would.

In the meantime, there was always going to be the occasional asshole like this one, ready at a drunken moment's notice to gum up the works. His kind was relatively easy to deal with, sufficiently intimidated with the *threat* of violence that they'd back down quickly and quietly. This was the approach I'd grown to rely on. Chalk another one up to a thinly veiled threat.

I waited for him to leave. And then he spit on me.

Guys like this... There are times when you can turn a blind eye and deaf ear to guys like this. Times when you can turn and walk away from guys like this, leave them to their hollow rants and raves. Times when you might even hang around, find their antics mildly amusing.

Unfortunately, not this time.

My left hand shot out again and grabbed a fistful of his black tie, dragging him close to my face. Gave him a nasty half-smile. Gave him a moment to reflect on the error he'd just made. Gave him a moment to consider the potential consequences of that error. Gave him a shot to the face with my right fist. Gave him some room to collapse.

I looked at the crumpled heap at my feet, blood spurting from its flattened nose. So much for resolve – old habits die hard, I suppose. Clearly, I'd have to work a little harder at avoiding this sort of situation.

Then there was Purdy, maybe fifteen feet away, standing still, hands in his pockets, just staring at me. He stood motionless for several seconds, then turned and sauntered away, calmly whistling a tune I recognized from an old Busby Berkeley musical. He didn't seem overly concerned about anything that was happening.

Two tattered Bund members spotted their fallen comrade and hauled themselves over to rescue him. I stepped back to give them some maneuvering room while they lifted his limp form by his arms. Blood soaked his shirtfront, and his head flopped from side to side like a rag doll's.

"You'll pay for this, pal," one of them hissed at me. "Watch your ass!" And with that, they departed.

Irv stood motionless to one side, as he had been since the altercation began. A look of consternation clouded his face. Our eyes met.

"I thank you for your intervention on my behalf – *our* behalf," he said. "But there really wasn't a need for violence. So much violence, it's terrible." He shook his head to great effect. He'd just finished smacking the guy across the face and now he's lecturing *me* about violence. "There are, you know, peaceful solutions to problems such as these, and I think it's an absolute necessity to explore all possible avenues of peaceful settlement to disagreements of all sorts." His wife nodded slowly in agreement, clearly pleased with her husband's judicious nature. "But thank you just the same." With that, he glanced at his wife to make sure that she wasn't looking, gave me a big wink and cracked a smile.

The mayhem surrounding us had subsided by now, the battered Bund members limping off to the shelter of their cars. The fisherman stood in a group off to one side, smiling and joking and laughing about their effortless victory, all the while keeping a cautious eye on the small departing group. Vollbrecht, who had remained out of harm's way during the fracas, now climbed off the back of the truck and circled around to the driver's side door. His revolver was nowhere in sight, probably tucked away in the brown leather briefcase he carried. He climbed in, slowly and casually as if nothing had happened, started the engine, and eased the truck towards the exit door – the one intended for vehicles – in the wall beyond first base.

Takarada came to life. He gripped Yumi by her upper arms and moved her aside, then quickly strode over into the path of Vollbrecht's truck. The truck screeched to a halt and stalled. Tak moved around to the driver's side, stepped up on the running board, and let loose a volley of indiscernible words. Vollbrecht could be seen in the dim light of the cab, staring at the incensed Oriental. After twenty seconds or so of this, Vollbrecht restarted the engine, said something to Tak, threw it into gear and started off. He gave Tak a shove, Tak stumbling back off the running board, yelling a few more choice words as the truck lumbered off. Yumi ran over, sobbing, and dragged him off.

As the sated crowds dispersed, I wandered over to the group of fishermen, and they nodded a cordial greeting.

"Drinks on the house at Holly's, boys," I announced, miming a glass in hand and a drink from same, just in case they didn't understand what I'd just said. One of them, who must have known some English, quickly translated to those who didn't, followed by a spontaneous eruption of boisterous approval and slaps to all backs, mine included. Off we went with McKinney in tow. He was more than welcome; I hadn't had this much fun in months.

Forty-five minutes later, the taproom was alive with happy revelers. There were toasts to democracy, to North Carolina and to several other places or people whose names I couldn't grasp through the guttural utterances of those proposing them. Based on the enthusiastic responses, however, each of them must have been worthy of the honor. Sweden, I suppose, and a few other frozen places way the hell over there.

It was a little past noon now, and the place was filled. I worked the bar while Willett manned our tiny kitchen, trying to keep up with the onslaught of drink and food orders. Our menu was bare bones at best, anything requiring cooking available only when Willett was there; I refused to get near the stove in this place. Willett's cooking abilities were uneven at best, the source of many offhanded comments by the patrons. As time went on, however, his cooking hadn't gotten any worse, and he seemed to genuinely enjoy puttering around back there. Our limited offerings included frankfurters on buns, hard-boiled eggs, pickled pigs' feet for the die-hards and something we called the Fisherman's Lunch, a cold platter of thick bread, a chunk of cheddar cheese, an onion and any other arguably appropriate vegetable available locally. This tended to be a tomato during the late summer months, with a large pickle as the fallback. There was no middle ground: the regulars either loved it or hated it.

Gordon's specialty, if you want to call it that, was a Taylor pork roll sandwich on a hard roll with a thick slab of onion and plenty of mustard. This was, surprisingly, the order-of-choice among the regulars. We ordered the stuff on a weekly basis from the smokehouses of the Taylor Provision Co. in Trenton, and they'd ship it in three-pound rolls for two dollars each, postpaid. Pork roll is a regional item that consisted, I think, of unused pork scraps, ground up and mixed with spices and God knows what else, and compressed into dense cylinders of pink meat speckled with white something or other. These rolls of meat were then wrapped in snug cloth jackets, treated in a smokehouse and, as a result, probably had a shelf life of a thousand years or so. When needed for cooking, the user simply sliced off a slab, discarded the fabric wrapper and fried it. Admittedly, it wasn't much to look at, but the taste was sublime and unlike anything else I'd ever consumed, before or since. First-time tasters were invariably put off by its less-than-appealing appearance, but after a first bite they were, to a man, hooked. And, after all, its appearance was less threatening than the large, cloudy jar of pigs' feet.

While I poured drink after drink, Holly's exhortations regarding the interior of the taproom occupied my thoughts. A momentary break in the seemingly endless barrage of orders gave me the chance to step back and take stock of the place while absentmindedly drying glasses with an old bar towel.

The building itself was a two-story structure, the lower level devoted to the taproom and its support. The main entrance was on the east side, from October through March shielded from view outside by a windbreak. When assembled, the three-sided wooden windbreak served as a tiny hall outside the main building. One would enter through its door, and once that door was closed would enter the taproom through the main door. In theory, this would shield the customers from direct blasts of cold air and wind; used properly it did just that. What amazed me, however, and brought on the collective ire of the patrons within, were the people – and there were a lot of them – who would open both doors wide before closing the windbreak's door. Needless to say, that defeated the purpose, and more than once these offenders were pelted with a hailstorm of peanut shells unleashed by the bar's inhabitants. For the remainder of the year, the windbreak was stored disassembled out in the garage behind my house.

The main door into the taproom was a Dutch door, and in the warm summer months the top half was left wide open for much-needed fresh air. The walls of the taproom itself had several large windows covered by wooden shutters, hinged at the top. These were closed and locked during the cooler months, but could be angled open in the summer months to make additional use of breezes and fresh air. The low, overhanging porch roof on the east and north sides of the building thoroughly shaded the door and windows during the heat of summer, and the whole affair was designed in such a fashion as to keep the patrons completely shielded from the view of passersby.

The north two-thirds of the building were occupied by the taproom itself, a long, narrow storage room and single restroom behind it on the south side. The kitchen area and my office were off to its western end; these latter two rooms occupying a narrow addition to the original structure. The third of a trio of closely arranged doors to the right of the bar entered the first three of these rooms; my office was entered either through a door in the kitchen or through a separate entrance from outside.

A long wooden bar ran parallel to the taproom's southern wall, with an enclosed wooden phone booth nestled in the space between the bar's left end and the eastern wall of the room. To the right of the bar were side-by-side doors into the storage room and restroom. Opposite the bar on the north side were a pair of wooden tables with four chairs each, and to the west of them, separated by a three-foot-high half wall, was the building's large coal-burning stove. This time of year Willett would occasionally build a small wood fire in the evenings, but it would be another month before we had a coal fire going twenty-four hours a day. To the west of that lining the western wall were, from right to left, a small storage bin of sorts for storing coal and wood, and two booths with bench seating. Near the corner and the other two doors was the swinging door into the kitchen.

The bar's interior wasn't much to look at – kind of a dump, truth be told – but it wasn't too noticeable due to the fact that we kept the interior lighting so dim. The floor was covered with Cranmer's fine sawdust, whose purity was marred with the indiscriminate addition of peanut shells, cigar and cigarette butts, spent matches, spilled beer and other bits of refuse unidentifiable from the vantage point of one standing. The sawdust served three purposes that come readily to mind. First, it had wonderful powers of absorbency, which made cleanup – or lack thereof – much easier. Second, it served to hide all the other crap deposited on the floor. And third, it afforded a cushion to anyone who happened to fall down – an occurrence that tended to happen more often than one would expect. The place had a perpetual smell of old beer and stale smoke; only the breeziest of days would provide temporary respite from the lingering odor. The interior was kept fairly dark, which is the way the patrons liked it (and the preference of bars in general), and even in the height of summer with the shutters raised the bar's interior retained an acceptable level of darkness.

The counter behind the bar was partially lit by a low, covered light, which afforded only enough illumination for *emergency* uses, such as keeping tabs on just how much each of the customers owed. The bar itself was a plain, dark wooden affair, with the obligatory brass rail running its length and a handful of wooden stools scattered about for use by anyone who'd prefer to sit rather than stand. A huge, old mirror in a faded gilt frame dominated the wall behind the bar. Its visible areas were marred by a number of dark spots where the silvering had peeled off, but most of its surface was obscured by all of the junk sitting in front of it or scotch-taped to its surface. Stuck in the corner of the frame was a twenty-something year old postcard of a sexy French actress named Musidora, stretched out on the beach in a tight, striped bathing suit that accentuated her rather impressive curves, sporting that come-hither look.

The backbar was littered with all sorts of dust-covered odds and ends, most of them brewery-supplied promotional items. My favorite was a painted plaster statue of a smiling Garden State Beer bottle, dancing hand-in-hand with an assortment of New Jersey vegetables, his lecherous eyes fixed on Miss Tomato.

Hanging in various places upon the room's four walls was an assortment of shore-related junk people had donated over the years. These included a couple of name boards from sunken ships (the *Tracy C* and the *Ebb Tide*), old lanterns, fishing and whaling gear, life preservers, the Beach Haven sign recently torn from the deserted Tuckerton Railroad station several blocks away and lots of other crap that escapes me. The most eye-catching item, and frequent topic of conversation, was an old figurehead from yet another sunken ship, fastened to the floor-to-ceiling support post at the end of the low, dividing wall between the coal stove and tables. This was an attractive, busty, redheaded mermaid whose exposed breasts had been worn clean of all traces of paint as a result of years of *fondling* by passing customers. What remained now from the constant handling were two grimy patches resembling shabby looking pasties on a faded burlesque dancer. Mimi, as someone had named her years earlier, had seen better days; I'd swear she wore a sadder look than when I first saw her back in '25. Still well built, though.

I ran the place more as a diversion and for the fun of it than with the goal of making any sort of profit, which I rarely did. We *did* manage to cover all our costs each year: we owned the buildings and had a pile of cash in the bank, so making more money was of little importance to me – and I kept the books. And, as backup, there was a second pile of cash sitting in a safety deposit box in a small bank over on the mainland that Holly didn't know about. It was in her best interest not to know about it, though I doubt she'd see it that way. But that's another story.

At any rate, the taproom's prices had remained unchanged for years and were, almost across the board, cheaper than anywhere else on the island. Holly's afforded the impoverished working stiffs of Beach Haven a place – albeit a threadbare one – where they could get an honest drink for a very reasonable price. Many customers who started coming here a few years earlier out of sheer necessity during the height of the Depression now frequented the place by choice. *The Poor Man's Club*, as it had come to be known to some, still served draught beer for a nickel; admittedly, it was only an eight-ounce glass, but it was still a bargain. Hard stuff was a dime a shot, and those planning ahead could get two shots and two beers for a quarter. I observed the usual bar etiquette of running thirty-day tabs for any customer who wanted me to do so – and many did – and the house would usually pop for a drink every third drink or so. I attempted to be a good, semi-sympathetic listener to anyone needing a compassionate ear, but that was tough sometimes – perhaps the toughest part of the job – and there were days when I felt like leaning over the bar and shaking some sense into some idiot's head. But I didn't, model of restraint that I am.

The division of labor was clear-cut: I worked the bar, kept the books and did all of the ordering; Willett was in charge of the kitchen and the rest room, and kept both of them surprisingly neat and clean. I wouldn't let him do too much cleaning in the taproom itself because I knew the patrons liked it as it was and might rebel if it were to change in any sort of dramatic way. When not otherwise occupied, he worked the bar itself and had gotten pretty good at that, too. He'd committed all the regulars' drinks of choice to memory and had the uncanny ability to recall at a moment's notice exactly what any customer owed – and not just for that particular day, but for the whole month. His other responsibility, and this was a big one, was to keep the coal-burning stove going night and day during the winter months. That wasn't terribly difficult once you got the knack of it, but the thing had a voracious appetite and was unforgiving if its keeper were to slack off. Once it got beyond the point of no return, Willett would have to go through the tiresome ritual of restarting it; he learned early on that it was just easier to remain vigilant. I'd tended the beast for seven years and swore that from then on it'd always be someone else's chore.

Before Willett started working for me back in '32, Holly and I had worked the place together. The taproom seemed a lot smaller back then, but we'd managed to coexist peacefully enough for a number of years. Once Willett was up to speed, Holly phased out her stints behind the bar and now only stopped by for the occasional visit and drink. She was happier that way – and I was *much* happier that way.

"Deuce! King!" Willett yelled from the bar's end. He was holding two platters, each consisting of a pork roll sandwich, a large pickle and a mound of pretzels; he was trying to get Edwards' and Jack Kahn's attention. They came over with half-filled beers in hand, grabbed their plates, settled down on bar-side stools and dug in like ravenous dogs.

Kahn was a reporter for the *Beach Haven Times* and he drove over here from the mainland several times a week to gather information for his regular "Kahn's Column." He was incredibly nosy sometimes, but a storehouse of information of local happenings, particularly local dirt and scandal gleaned from a variety of sources. Most of these sources were of the opposite sex, visited on a regular basis. And, unsubstantiated rumor had it, he'd screw them behind their spouse's backs every chance he got – they liked flirting with *celebrity* and he liked the sex. He was always tired – no surprise there – and repeatedly commented on that fact, much to the annoyance of those around him. In his late thirties, he was, I suppose, what you'd call *dapper*: always immaculately dressed and manicured. His biggest concern in life seemed to be the aging process and the impact it was having on his looks. And, we all assumed, on his ability to score. He was one of those guys the regulars loved to loathe, and he, too, provided them with a ripe subject to speculate about behind his back. His exploits were, by now, legendary; but no one had a clue where fact petered out and fiction took over. Didn't matter, though, because so many of the stories were just so damn entertaining. Like the one about the nymphomaniac Italian twins over in Manahawkin and their love of honey.

"Must've been pretty exciting," mumbled Edwards around a mouthful of sandwich. "All those krautheads getting clobbered like that. Would've loved to have seen it." I thought he was talking to Kahn, but soon realized his comments were directed at me when he paused mid-chew and looked at me waiting for a response.

"Yeah, somethin', all right," I quickly responded, not wanting to look like I was ignoring him. Which, up to that point, I had been. "You shoulda seen the newsreel guys; couldn't believe their good luck."

"Like dogs rolling in shit, huh?" He tore off another mouthful.

"Somethin' like that. Pigs, maybe."

"Here. Let me see that thing," he continued, motioning towards the backbar with a half-eaten sandwich. I turned to see what he was pointing at – it was the rolled poster Carver had brought in a week earlier. I slid it out from between some bottles, held it up questioningly to Edwards. He nodded, dropped the sandwich on his plate, wiped his mouth with the back of his hand, took the poster, unrolled it, and started to read to himself. Out loud, of course: "Gab-Fest 1936. Saturday October 24. Patriotic Gathering - Fun For All. Walsh Field - 10:00 a.m. Share In The Gift Of Gab."

Finishing, he noticed some small print at the bottom of the poster, squinted at it trying to bring it into focus, finally gave up and pulled a pair of reading glasses from his shirt pocket. A look of satisfaction came over his face as the words took form. "'For More Information, Write: W. Vollbrecht, PO Box 28, Manahawkin, NJ.' This Vollbrecht guy lives near here?" he asked, looking up for a response from anyone. Carver wandered in and took a place at the bar.

"He's a baker – over on the mainland. Least that's what I was told," I commented, pouring Carver's beer. "Guess somewhere near Manahawkin." I spun the poster around on the bar to read the small print no one had noticed before.

"I wonder where they practice their goose-steps? Think it's somewhere around there?" asked Edwards, again of anyone. A few others standing around shrugged shoulders and grunted ignorance. "*Goose step* – stupid name," he continued, " – looks like they're all marchin' around with *fixed bayonets*, you get my meaning?" No one did. "You know," he persisted, "*Captain Standish? Pride of the Morning?* The old *Divining Rod?*"

Carver looked up. "You mean a hard-on? Deuce, why don't you just come out and say it, 'stead of beatin' around the bush with all your stupid phrases."

"Jeeze, Joe, you don't have to be crude."

"Same guy said their camp was somewhere around there, too," I said, getting back on subject. "Didn't say where, 'though."

"What guy?"

"I don't know – some *old* guy."

"Did you know that we are actually *south* of the Mason-Dixon Line here," interjected Willett as he passed by.

"What's that have to do with the price of milk?" asked Edwards, but Willett disappeared through the swinging kitchen door as quickly as he'd entered.

"Sometimes I think we're south of the civilized world here," responded Kahn, who'd been quietly eating up to this point, without taking his eyes off the remains of the sandwich in his hand. "But for once, I'm happy to say, our resident genius is wrong."

"What? About the Mason-Dixon Line?"

"Yup. It's the popular designation for the boundary line between Pennsylvania and Maryland, and everyone seems to think it heads due east from there."

"And?"

"It doesn't."

"Where the fuck *does* it?"

"It heads southeast through Delaware."

"Through Delaware?"

Willett reentered the room, tray in hand.

"Kahn says it goes through Delaware," exclaimed Edwards, turning to Willett.

"If we're talking about the boundary surveyed by the British astronomer Charles Mason and surveyor Jeremiah Dixon in the mid 1760s, *that* was drawn up at the behest of the Calverts of Maryland and the Penns of Pennsylvania, to settle an ongoing dispute. Where their east-west border – decided by the British court at fifteen miles south of Philadelphia – ended, so did the line. Or at least in the minds of most people. Therefore, it's not inaccurate to continue that line eastward through our very own Surf City. And it's actually called *Mason and Dixon's Line*."

"What the hell do astronomers have to do with anything?" asked Edwards, exasperated.

"But, technically, you're right," continued Willett. "Mason and Dixon actually continued their survey on a southeast direction through the Delmarva Peninsula, further delineating Calvert's holdings from additional land given to Penn by Charles II. And Beach Haven certainly isn't south of this line."

Edwards stared in disbelief.

"Subsequently, this demarcation was used as the basis for the boundary between what were then known as the *free* and the *slave* states. As such, it was extended westward down the Ohio River to its mouth, continued around Missouri on its east, north, and western sides, then headed due west along the parallel 36° 30'. The eastern boundary followed the old boundaries separating Maryland and Delaware. And south of here."

Kahn nodded his head with a look of satisfaction.

"Christ, who really gives a damn, anyway? What the fuck do Dixon and Mason have to do with *anything?*" mumbled Edwards, slamming his glass onto the bar. "What were we talking about? The krautheads, right? Guess they won't be coming back anytime soon, huh?" He leaned towards Kahn and elbowed him in the side as he spoke. "'cept maybe for some matching lumps, eh?" he chuckled. "A knuckle sandwich?" Kahn tried to ignore him.

The front door slammed and a few heads turned. Tak paused at the entrance with a look of embarrassment over the noise he'd inadvertently made. He shyly wandered up to the bar, nodding politely to everyone nearby. It was difficult to believe that this was the same guy who'd gone after Vollbrecht earlier that day.

Tak and his wife Yumi lived over on Bay Avenue where they operated a Japanese novelties store during the summer with a fair degree of success. They were more practical the remainder of the year, turning over the bulk of their shelf space to such necessities as bread, milk, eggs, canned goods and newspapers – items the year-round locals needed. Tak, a pleasant fellow in his early forties, was a regular at the taproom, stopping by once daily for a glass of sake.

The others looked upon this strange, foreign substance with apprehension, and offers of a taste were always refused. The stuff wasn't locally distributed, but there were a couple of California-based companies that made this alien concoction, reportedly owned and run by Japanese immigrants. Sean Rioux, another customer of ours, kept us stocked with the rare liquid. We never asked where he got it, or whether or not he got it legally; Sean and Holly's father went way back, friends as well as business acquaintances. Sean wasn't actually a *customer*; he drank for free here. Anyway, Tak knew and appreciated just how difficult his beloved drink was to acquire, so he made a point never to have more than one a day. In those instances where his thirst wasn't sated by just one, he'd follow it with a shot of White Horse, sometimes two, on very rare occasion three.

"How are you today, Tak?" I asked.

"I am well, thank you." He was annoyingly polite, always bowing and deferring to others. He offered the glass in a salute, bowed slightly, and fired down a portion of the stuff. Edwards grimaced at the thought of drinking the alien liquid, and returned to his beer.

"New car, isn't it?" asked Kahn, licking his lips, pushing his empty plate away.

"Ah, yes, it is. A fine new car," responded Tak.

"Oh, yeah? What'd you get?" asked Edwards, glancing uneasily at Tak's glass.

"It is a 1936 Hudson Terraplane six-cylinder, two-passenger coupe, dark blue, lots of trunk, ride smooth as silk. A very fine car," said Tak, proudly.

"Hill Busters," commented Kahn, appreciatively.

"Not for a couple of years. Leftover?"

Evidently no one was aware of Tak's confrontation earlier at Walsh Field.

"Yes, yes: leftover. We bought in Atlantic City, in July. Five hundred and fifty dollar, a very good deal. Saturday, July 4, as a matter of fact; Yumi said it was Independence Day for both the country *and* her!" He smiled broadly and took another sip of his drink.

"She gonna to drive it, too?" I asked, prompted by his "Independence Day" comment. Might as well.

"Yumi is only driver," he said. "I do not know how to drive, I never bother to learn."

"What's she need a car for; you can go everywhere on foot?" asked Edwards. Yumi, perched on her old battered bicycle with the oversized straw basket mounted on its handlebars, was a familiar sight in the streets of Beach Haven. Familiar, *and* pleasant. She was much younger than Tak, early thirties, perhaps, and very attractive. Yumi and her bike were the occasional topic of conversation among several of the regulars and Edwards always took part, if not actually initiating the dialog. That is, when there weren't any women around – any women and Tak.

"For her business," he announced proudly. "She make weekly trips to Toms River every Wednesday, takes the better part of the day." Tak had finished his sake and signaled to me for its follow-up.

"That's a lot of car," commented Edwards, with a distant look. Probably jealous, since he was still driving a '26 Superior V, which was what Chevrolet called their four-cylinder touring car that year. There was nothing particularly superior about it now, with its paint all faded, more dents and dings than you could count, and rust that was spreading over it like a disease. Come to think of it, it wasn't too superior in '26, either.

"Toms River? What's there?" asked Kahn, with marginal interest.

"C & C." Tak formed two "C"s with index fingers and thumbs, one of them backwards, naturally. "They are distributors of imported items. She goes once a week, look at their newest... offering," he responded, then paused for a moment. "I do not know what C & C stand for, so do not ask," he added with a laugh, thanking me with a nod and gesture for the White Horse I'd just poured.

I could imagine the kind of offerings that C & C must have. I'd been in Yumi's shop once or twice during the summer, and it was filled with all sorts of dispensable crap geared towards tourists. You know the kind of stuff: incense, tiny little dolls with porcelain heads, wind chimes, firecrackers and sparklers, glazed chinaware with cheesy images of Beach Haven adorning them, lots of bamboo *things*, samurai swords, flags, pennants, some nicer silken items that looked out of place, *that* kind of crap. Or, at least it looked like crap to my untrained eyes.

My thoughts were diverted by an outburst of cheering over by the dartboard. Two tables across from the bar were currently occupied, one by a foursome of Scandinavians – two of whom were playing checkers while the other two looked on intently – and the other by a trio of regulars playing cards. The place was filled, everyone was drinking, all seemed to be having a good time. And Holly wanted me to change the place. What could she be thinking? I guess I had the answer: She wasn't thinking. Just talking. And she was really good at that.

Later that night, around 9:30, the crowd had peaked, the noise was deafening, the atmosphere nearly impenetrable with smoke. We had the north side shutter raised and the glass window lowered in a futile attempt to introduce some fresh air into the place. It wasn't making it to the back, though, and I considered opening the other one. There was a sudden crash of glass, and a hushed silence – starting at the front – quickly spreading over the crowd. I emerged from behind the bar, quickly pushed my way through the group to see what was going on. As I picked my way to the front I saw smashed glass scattered over one of the table's top and the sawdust-covered floor. Billy Ives, who'd been sitting with his back to the window, was standing now and picking pieces of glass out from his collar and sleeves while a friend of his assisted. There were flecks of blood on the left side of his face.

"I'm okay, really. I'm okay." he kept insisting.

One of the Scandinavians whose name, I think, was Olaf, picked up a baseball-sized rock from the floor. It was wrapped in paper, secured with rough, brown twine. He stared at it for a moment, glanced up, saw me taking stock of the situation and handed it to me. If it was a note, he probably wouldn't have been able to read it anyway.

Willett pushed through the group and arrived at my side.

"Get some hot water and soap. And some Mercurochrome or iodine, some gauze," I stated flatly. Willett nodded as he turned and trotted off.

"You sure you're okay, Bill?" I asked.

"Yeah, really; no gaping wounds. Most of it missed me, came through on my left," he said, with a sheepish smile as if embarrassed by the sudden attention.

"Good. Willett's getting some stuff and he'll help you clean up. And you're drinking free for the rest of the night."

"*All right!*" he said enthusiastically; I knew from his reaction he'd be falling-down drunk before the night was done. But he'd forget about his wounds – about everything, for that matter.

I inspected the paper-covered rock in my hand, shaking off the remaining pieces of glass as I turned it. I untied the twine and dropped it to the floor, unwrapped the paper and placed the rock on the table before me. It was a note, a hastily scrawled note, written in large, block letters with a heavy pencil. It read: "YOU PAY FOR THIS. WATCH OUT. WATCH YOUR WIFE. WATCH YOUR KIDS. WATCH YOU FRIENDS. PLESANT DREAMS."

"Spelling and grammar leave something to be desired," I said, offering the note to the curious group around me. One of them, a regular named Tenby, took it and quickly started to read; the others huddled tightly around him for a view.

"Who the hell'd do this," he wondered aloud, not looking up from the document in his hands.

I didn't answer, but I had a pretty good idea: probably my Bund-member *friend* from earlier that day, as he was the only person I'd had any sort of altercation with in recent memory. His threats were probably nothing more than that, intended to give me a few sleepless nights while I worried about possible harm to myself and those around me. But I gave up worrying about small-time stuff like this years ago – save the sweat for the big-ticket items.

And even if the threats *were* real, they could hurt me and they could hurt my wife, but they'd have one hell of a time hurting my son.

That had already happened a long time ago.

Monday, October 26, 1936. 1:35 p.m.

"WOW. THIS IS scary," Carver muttered to himself.

He sat alone at the bar, chin resting in hand, pencil clutched in the other, staring intently at a scrap of paper spread out in front of him. The most recent issue of the *Beach Haven Times* was folded on the bar to his left, open to the *Obituaries* column.

"What's that?" I asked, feigning interest as I continued to dry the glass in my hand.

He looked up at me. "Population's what? Seven hundred or so?" he asked.

"Here? Beach Haven? Yeah, I guess so." I answered, placing the dry glass on a shelf and grabbing another from the sink. "Sounds about right."

"And we average – what? – 'bout two deaths a week?" he continued.

"I don't know; if you say so."

"So roughly a hundred people a year die here in town."

"Sounds high," I said. "Where you going with this?"

He scratched his head and looked at the numbers scrawled on the scrap before him. He looked utterly perplexed. "Well, if I figured this correct – I think I did – by the end of 1943, early '44, won't be anyone left." He looked up at me with a confused, worried look on his face. "We'll all be dead," he stated with an air of certainty.

"It's not that simple," I sighed, asking myself if this was even worth a response. Carver was a moron, but a nice moron, so I decided to elaborate. "Kids are born, people move in, things like that." I left it at that.

"Yeah, but…" he implored, as if he'd factored all of that in. Which he hadn't.

"And two a week sounds high." This wasn't worth arguing.

He returned to the scrap in front of him, lost in thought, chewing on the pencil now held in his teeth. I couldn't figure out why he wasn't working, but it was none of my business.

Aside from a pair of Swedes talking quietly at the booth in the corner, the taproom was otherwise empty. The only sounds were the muffled voices speaking and responding in a foreign tongue, Carver's pencil, which he was now unconsciously – and annoyingly – tapping on the bar's surface, and the occasional clink of the glasses I was drying. A workman from the lumberyard quietly puttied a new sheet of glass in the window from the outside. It was sunny and clear today, and the brightly-lit expanse beyond his silhouette was blinding to eyes acclimated to the darkened interior of the taproom.

The relative quiet was interrupted by the sounds of a vehicle backfiring several times out front. *Must be Fred Buzby*, I thought. Buzby tended to visit here the last Monday of each month, and it was indeed him. He entered with a burlap sack thrown over his shoulder and threw up his free hand in greeting.

"Helloooooo Lewis," he shouted, breaking into his familiar chuckle. He was, consistently, one of the happiest guys I'd ever met.

"Hello there, Fred. The same?" I asked.

"Yesiree," he responded, as I knew he would. He ambled over to the bar, lowered his sack to the floor and pulled from it a pail brimming over with cranberries. He placed it on the bar. This was part of the ritual. Each time he'd visit he'd bring a gift of some sort or other, depending on the season. Things such as huckleberries and blueberries – which he called *hog huckleberries* and *sugar huckleberries* – venison and jars of surprisingly drinkable homemade whiskey. The whiskey was made out of various available local grains or fruits, including corn, peaches, blueberries, apples and who knows what else. In return, I'd treat him to a couple of shots of his favorite,

Watkins Grove Rye, ninety proof. At three quarts for five bucks, it was a rye that no one else was interested in, kept on the bottom shelf solely for him.

"How's the Model T holding up?" I asked.

"Now, don't think funny of this, but she was built in 1914 – *1914 –*" he repeated for emphasis, "and I've driven her ever since, twenty-two years, guess it is, and she still runs just fine!" The Watkins Grove disappeared in one large sip. "She don't look like much no more, but she runs just fine!" he added with a loud laugh.

His Model T had, indeed, seen better days. It was a steel and wood affair, riddled with rust and rot. By design, the cab and large area behind were partially exposed to the elements, protected primarily by the roof overhead and rolled canvas flaps that could be dropped over the open windows in the cold and rain. The years had left the roof as watertight as a sieve, however, and the sole remaining flap was torn and ragged. But the thing just kept on going, and Buzby would bundle up in blankets for cold winter drives.

"What are you selling today?" I asked.

"Cordwood. Need some?"

"No, I'm covered there." I had a shed outside – built as an addition to the main structure – that was filled with coal and wood. Buzby's occasional offerings of wood were fine for the casual fireplace user, but I kept myself stocked by more dependable suppliers.

Buzby lived over on the mainland in the area known as the Pine Barrens, or the pinelands, or, for short, the Pines. It's a huge, undeveloped, sparsely populated area of wilderness comprised primarily of oaks and pines growing in its distinctive sandy soil. I don't know its exact size, but it's huge, as in *Rhode Island*-huge. The handfuls of people that do live there – and there aren't many of them – tend to be clustered in the small forest towns that dot the region, but equal numbers are scattered throughout the forests themselves. These residents were known to outsiders as *Pineys*. Buzby, himself a

Piney, lived in one of these isolated areas.

He was lean, muscular and well-built, not too tall – probably only five seven or eight – with short, bristly, white hair and skin that remained a dark tan the year round. This tan of his was an odd, uneven shade *and* appeared to be the result of long exposure to the sun and small measures of soot and grime. He looked to be about sixty, but I'd been told by others that his age was probably closer to late seventies. His cheeks were hollow, his lips sunken in where numerous teeth were missing, but he still had enough of them to make short work of a bowl of pretzels. Today, as always, he wore an old undershirt years away from seeing white; I envisioned a drawer full of the things back at his house. On top of it he wore a loose, dark canvas jacket, with a grimy cap perched on the back of his head.

He had, for decades, driven his Ford truck over from the mainland on a periodic basis from September through early July, avoiding the island altogether during the summer when, as he once put it, "the summer people are swarming about." He'd visit the various towns that dotted the island, making the rounds on a schedule of his own making, selling whatever seasonal stuff he happened to be loaded up with. These offerings included the aforementioned items, as well as cordwood, charcoal and other stuff of questionable worth. His home-distilled whiskey was a big-seller during Prohibition, and there were some who grew to like it so much during those years that they remained faithful customers ever since.

Buzby was a friendly, good-natured, likable guy and everyone who had lived on the island for any length of time knew who he was. To most of the locals, he was the sole exception to the long-held belief that Pineys were, by-and-large, a crazed, backward, degenerate lot – not to mention a group of deviants, who, for centuries, regularly indulged in the taboo practice of incest, resulting in an insular community of questionable offspring. But Buzby was okay – and I suspect that if anyone had the opportunity to meet and get to know any other Pineys they'd find them to be okay folk and the myths unfounded. Unfortunately, paths rarely crossed; and, as a result, there was a long-standing distrust and fear between the two groups.

"What happened to the window there?" he asked, as I poured him a second Watkins Grove and myself a first. It was pretty bad.

"Rock tossed through it. Some hothead; don't know who."

"That's no good. Glass ain't cheap. No, that's no good," he said, shaking his head in sympathy. "Thought maybe you tossed a customer through it," he added, with a mischievous smile.

"Not me," I responded. "Only get the cream of society here."

"I can see that," he said, chuckling and glancing about the room. "Yup, I can see that."

The Swedes were still in the booth now playing a game with pegs and Carver had wandered over to the open shutter with beer in hand. He watched the workman on the other side put the finishing touches to the new pane of glass. The crystal-clear view it afforded of the outside stood in stark contrast to the filthy pane next to it.

"How's the missus' poetry?" asked Buzby, cracking yet another smile.

"She just keeps getting better," I responded, which was true; she couldn't get much worse.

"Hey, Buzby," yelled Carver from his vantage point by the window. "Who's the guy out in your truck?"

"Him? That's Jonah. Jo-nah," he repeated slowly, as if for emphasis. "What's he doin'?"

"Well, I can't really tell. He's sitting there all hunched over doing something in his lap. Hope he's not playing with his pecker."

"Well, you never know with Jonah," responded Buzby with a chuckle. "Probably whittlin', though. He's always chippin' away at some piece of wood or other, makes all kinds of doo-dads. Some of 'em kind of interesting, some of 'em junk."

"Friend or relative?" I asked.

"Neither – neighbor," answered Buzby, now working on a nearby bowl of pretzels. In his neck of the woods a neighbor could live several miles away, maybe more. "Volunteered to help me out some time back. And the best part is I don't have to pay him. Nosiree. Said he wanted a chance to see the *outside world.*"

"Beach Haven?" asked Carver, incredulously.

"Well, yeah. Beach Haven and the rest of the towns here on the island. And Manahawkin – Waretown – Cedar Run. Few other places like that." Buzby was referring to some of the small towns over on the mainland that stretched in a north-south line near the coast of the bay. "Not too bright, I'll give you that. But he *can* read and write, kind of – I think. And he has a strong back and keeps pretty much to himself. And the price – is right."

"See the outside world?" repeated Carver, in disbelief and amazement.

"That's no bull; that's fact. See the world *and* sell those doo-dads he makes. Now, don't think this is funny, but no matter how worthless some of the things he makes are, he always finds some sucker – 'scuse me – some *customer* over here to buy them. Least that's what I seen since he's comin' with me."

"Well, I *hope* that's not his pecker in his hands, 'cause Mrs. Gilpin's walkin' by and he's just starin' at her, like his eyes are locked on her," commented Carver, stooped over and staring intently out the window.

"Sounds like Jonah," responded Buzby with a chuckle, only this time he kept on chuckling, as if extremely amused by Jonah's antics. "He's got an eye for the women, all right. Maybe that's the reason he wanted to see the world. To see the women!" He kept on laughing to himself while trying to eat another pretzel.

"She's not even pretty," said Carver. "And she's *old.*"

"Don't matter," said Buzby. "They're a novelty to him, like they're from the moon or somethin', so he just likes lookin' at 'em. They seem pretty shaken by him, though. Maybe that's why they buy all that junk from him – just to gets rid of him!" Buzby exploded with laughter, head thrown back, tears welling in his eyes. He laughed so long and hard that, within a matter of seconds, Carver and I were laughing, too. Not that what he said was particularly funny, but it was difficult not to get caught up in his infectious mirth. The Swedes looked on, uncomprehending, but with smiles on their faces nonetheless. After a minute or so the laughter died down, and I felt so good at that moment that I poured Buzby and myself another round.

Lester Simms walked in as I corked the bottle. He tossed his coat on a hook, ambled over to the bar, drew up a stool and sat. Lester was a rail-thin, elderly colored man who worked at a nearby Bay Avenue eatery that served breakfast and lunch. Formerly the cook for a wealthy family with homes both in Philadelphia and Beach Haven, he had, upon their deaths, moved here to live. He'd found a small, unassuming bayside shack that met his needs.

There'd been occasions in the past when Simms would step in to cook here at the taproom. This usually occurred when the regulars rebelled at Willett's mishandling of basic culinary tasks. Fortunately, Willett had improved, over time *and* with a lot of help and guidance from Lester. The regulars were no longer offended by Willett's cooking, and we now saw Lester only when he came in for a drink.

"Lester, how are you?" I greeted him.

"Just fine, Lew. Just fine. The usual, please."

The usual was Guckenheimer Straight Rye, ninety proof, and a slightly cheaper rye than Old Overholt. I always let him have three shots for a quarter and threw in a draught chaser for good measure. I poured the first and followed it with a glass of Camden that hit the bar at about the same time Lester drained the rye.

Lester had short, gray hair that matched the stubble on his face and chin. He was reasonably well educated – more so than some of the locals – and was slow talking, but well spoken. His tired, yellow eyes usually stared at some indeterminate spot on the bar's surface, but he'd meet your gaze when talking with you.

"How's the boy's cooking?" he asked. Some beer foam clinging to his upper lip disappeared under the quick sweep of his tongue.

"Much better, thanks to you. Hasn't poisoned anyone recently. Least not that I'm aware of."

He laughed and motioned for his second shot of rye. He took his time with this one.

He turned to Buzby. "Hello, Fred. Who's the hulk out in the truck?"

Buzby proceeded to re-explain who Jonah was and why he was there. I wandered over to the window to get a look at this guy, but didn't see him, or anyone else, out on the street.

"Where is he?" I asked Carver.

"Ah, he walked off a few minutes ago. Probably had to take a leak — bouncin' around in that thing all day'd make me have to take one, that's for sure."

Behind us, Buzby once again exploded with laughter and Lester joined in; he must have gotten to the part about selling the so-called doo-dads. I turned to see the broad of Lester's back; he was doubled over the bar shaking with laughter and Buzby stood at his side, laughing equally hard, a hand on Lester's shoulder.

No one thought twice about Lester's presence in the taproom, but that wasn't always the case. During the summer months there was a tiny colored population in Beach Haven, the bulk of them employed by whites as help in their oversized vacation homes. Their numbers dwindled to a handful the rest of the year and, by and large, they tended to keep to themselves. I'd first brought Lester in to cook back in '32, shortly after Willett had joined me and made such an initial shambles of the kitchen. I liked Lester a lot, and always insisted that he stick around afterwards for drinks. This raised a couple of eyebrows among the regulars and the few that bothered to say something were promptly told to leave. I'm sure that I lost a couple of other customers during that period, but most of them begrudgingly returned over time when they realized that this was the way things were at Holly's and that it wasn't going to change. By now,

Lester – and Tak, for that matter – were just part of the landscape here, and no one gave them a second thought. No one, that is, except for newcomers.

Lester was a regular, all right, and you could find him here every Monday, Wednesday, Friday, Saturday and Sunday. His budget was fifty cents a day, two-fifty a week, ten bucks a month and I always ran a tab for him. The first of the month he'd wander in with a ten spot in his hand, but during lean months he'd do odds and ends around the place in order to work off some of the debt.

We saw less of him during the summer months and during that period I always figured he was doing his drinking over at the Beach Haven House. That place was unique in town: on the ground floor, there was a single, small room that served as a package store and bar for the town's colored minority. It had its own private entrance off the north-side alley, which kept patrons away from the hotel's main bar, where they *wouldn't* have been welcome. No matter how comfortable he felt at my place, I could understand why he'd feel even more so there among old friends. I never broached the subject with him, however; it wasn't important. And I had to believe that, deep down, he probably never felt completely comfortable here.

"There's the boy. Hard to miss, huh?" said Carver.

I turned and looked in time to see Jonah slowly making his way back to Buzby's truck. He was large and hulking, and dragged his feet as he walked, head down, staring at the gravel directly ahead of him. From what I could see he had dark hair cut short, a round face, large puffy lips and was dressed in dark boots, canvas pants, a dark canvas coat, and under it what appeared to be a discolored two-button cotton undershirt. He looked like a large, overgrown kid, actually, and had the kind of indeterminate youthful looks that could have placed him anywhere from his mid-teens to early twenties. If I had to make a guess, I'd say he was about twenty and would be foolish for making the guess.

"Stupid lookin', ain't he?" added Carver. The pot calling the kettle black.

"Hunh," I grunted, noncommittally, and headed back to my post behind the bar. Carver followed on my heels, returned to his spot at the bar, signaled for another draught and then resumed his study of the obituaries and his hastily scrawled figures.

"Two a week..." he mumbled to himself. "Yup, another nine years we'll all be dead." He took a long drink. "'cept maybe Purdy – we'll n*ever* get rid of him."

"Two *what* a week?" asked Lester.

"Two deaths. Like clockwork," answered Carver. It was a rare week when two people died in Beach Haven, but there were two listed in the current paper and that translated in Carver's mind to two *every* week. "This week we got some old woman over on Berkeley: Iverness Addison, age eighty-three, heart attack. And Lew's buddy, Miller, changing his collar size. That's two."

"Neighbor o' mine found the Addison woman." Lester said quietly.

"Yeah? How'd that happen?" asked Carver.

"Ol' Stump worked for her – 'Stump' Jefferson. Came in early one morning, found her dead, sittin' in a living room chair, eyes and mouth wide open. Face all screwed up like she was scared to death, fingers claw-like, dug in the arms. Spooky as hell, he said. And that's what it was: *Death*. She faced *Death*, eyeball to eyeball, and he won. Always does." He took another drink, followed by a long pull on the cigarette stub pinched between his fingers. There were several moments of quiet in the bar.

"What do ya think *Death* looks like?" asked Carver, more of the group at large than of Lester. But Lester answered.

"White. He's all white," he stated, and downed the remains of his shot.

Tuesday, October 27, 1936. 8:35 a.m.

"'A BANQUET OF fresh raw meat, golden ripe cereals, cod liver oil, charcoal and other beneficial elements. The dog food supreme!'" Hoover sat up on his haunches looking attentive and dog-like as I read from the label of a can of Ken-L-Ration. Charcoal didn't sound like a particularly tasty ingredient, but then rolling in dead animal carcasses didn't hold a lot of appeal to me, either. "Rin-Tin-Tin's food," I continued, spooning the reddish-brown mess into his bowl. Actually, it smelled pretty good – as if that made a difference to Hoover, who'd eat most anything (and probably had one time or another in his short five years). He was at it like a shot and didn't come up for air until he finished inhaling it less than a minute later. Then he just sat there with a dazed look in his eyes, licking his lips, emitting random sounds best left unmentioned.

I wandered into the living room, coffee cup in hand. It was fair out and cold – mid-twenties cold – and I couldn't recall previous October days being like this. A stiff wind didn't help matters; windows rattled and the house creaked while unseen drafts worked at my feet and ankles. Beethoven's *Sixth Symphony* played on the Silvertone eight tube radio I'd picked up for forty-nine ninety-five at the Sears down in Atlantic City a half year earlier. It was tuned to WFPG, every day of the week from 8:00 a.m. until noon, when they broadcast their "Seaside Classics" program of classical music. WFPG was based in Atlantic City, too, and came in crystal clear, unlike some of the more interference- and static-prone stations of Philadelphia and, worse yet, New York.

Our bungalow was situated on the lot immediately to the west of the taproom, on the south side of Dock Road. Facing north, it had a full first floor and partial, unfinished second under its sloping hip roof, with three two-window dormers on the front and sides. Cedar shingles covered both the sides and roof, and an enclosed front porch spanned its width. The porch was bright with four side-to-side windows at either side of the front door and three more at each end. To the west of the bungalow, and twenty feet behind, stood the detached garage reached by a drive of hard-packed sand. The rest of the property was a mix of sand and bayberry, with a few pines scattered about. Native growth overwhelmed the properties to the south and west, the battle with encroaching poison ivy an annual one comparable to the Campaign of Waterloo.

The interior was paneled with pine and was simply, but tastefully, furnished and decorated. Holly's hand was the dominant one here, as she was convinced that she had far better taste than I did, and I was uninterested enough not to argue with her. Tabletops and shelves were adorned with dozens of little statues and knick knacks, which would have lasted about three minutes if I were the one dusting the place. I wasn't, so they'd lasted for years, their numbers swelling on what seemed to be a daily basis, like rabbits unchecked. All this spouse-induced clutter was nothing I could get even remotely excited about; but then, again, she never complained about the mess I'd created – and maintained with loving care – in a small area midway between the kitchen and the living room. So I left well enough alone.

The small area of which I speak was the location of a modest workbench where I'd putter for several hours each morning on an ongoing project. The project was an ambitious one and, to the average person, a fairly stupid-sounding one – a project that occupied huge amounts of time that undoubtedly could have been spent on far more worthwhile and constructive endeavors. But that, after all, was what hobbies were all about. At any rate, my goal was to recreate, in one-one-hundredth scale, a replica of the Cathedrále Notre-Dame at Reims, France.

I'd seen the actual cathedral only once, back in 1918, as we headed for the Argonne forest in northeast France, and a rendezvous with the German army. I was young and green and had no real concept of the hell that awaited us, but deep down in the pit of my stomach I knew it wasn't going to be pleasant. The cathedral dominated the skyline as we marched through Reims, and it was the most incredible, haunting sight I'd ever seen. Which, I suppose, isn't really saying much, when you consider that I was born and raised – if you want to call it that – in the small town of Bordentown, New Jersey, and not a particularly good part of town at that. Under any other circumstance, I suppose, I wouldn't have given the cathedral a second thought. But then, marching into the great unknown, it affected me deeply on some level or other, and I became thoroughly obsessed with the place. It stayed with me through the years, a recurring fixture in my dreams. Finally, settled down here in Beach Haven half a dozen years later, I'd decided to give substance to my memories, and embarked on the long, tedious – and, admittedly, foolhardy – task of reconstructing it in miniature.

The medium of choice – and this adds to the level of absurdity of this undertaking – was wooden matchsticks, cut to three-sixteenth inch lengths and representing the large granite building-blocks of the original. I'd amassed hundreds of pictures and photos of the place, on postcards, in *National Geographic* articles and from numerous other sources. The backbone of the project, however, was a detailed French volume published in 1892, the title of which translated into something like *The Magnificent Cathedrále of Reims*. This was filled with dozens of close-ups and detail shots, as well as architectural drawings complete with measurements and virtually every scrap of information needed to re-scale the structure. Now, ten years after I started the thing, the western façade – which was the front of the cathedral, with its large twin towers – was nearly completed, and work had commenced on both the northern and southern façades and their flying buttresses, back as far as the transepts. I designed it with the western façade independent and detachable from the rest of the structure so that it could be disassembled and reassembled on the off chance that I ever wanted to move the damned thing. Or, more likely, if after my death Holly wanted to toss it into the bay. And at the rate I had been progressing, my sole goal ten years into the project was to finish it before *Death* finished me. It would be a neck and neck race.

Beethoven finished and was followed by the first movement of Edvard Grieg's *Peer Gynt Suite Number 1*, "Morning Mood," when Holly entered the room, wrapped in a white, terry cloth wrap-around robe with its double shawl collar and loosely tied sash. She was vigorously drying her hair with a thick towel and smiled as she passed on her way into the kitchen for a cup of coffee.

"Mornin'," she said. And that's all she said. Talk was scarce at this hour in the Porter household.

It appeared that she'd taken a bath inside today, instead of using the preferred outside shower like I had foolishly done. It was a ritual with us, and one that usually lasted well into November or December. By winter, we'd be forced to shut off the pipes feeding it, due to extended periods of below-freezing temperatures. Nothing was more invigorating or, more simply put, guaranteed to wake you, than a quick, brisk shower in thirty-some degree temperatures. There was an art to making the dash from the enclosed back porch door to the shower stall a mere ten feet away, nestled into the right angle where porch connected to house. A wall of pines afforded further protection from the biting autumn wind. When the temperature dropped to twenty-seven degrees as it did this morning, however, no level of determination and planning could get you in and out fast enough. Forty seconds into the ordeal I asked myself just what the hell had possessed me to do such a foolish thing. Holly, needless to say, had more sense than I did when it came to such things, and while I'd been reduced to chipping ice from my pale, blue torso, she'd merely blotted herself with a nice, soft towel.

"How's the Sisyphean task coming?" she called from the other room. She made an incredible racket shifting items about in the refrigerator; sounded as though she had the damn thing tipped forward, shaking things loose onto the floor. Holly had asked this very same question each and every morning for as long as I could remember, and I gave my usual grunt by way of reply. She carried a pitcher of orange juice to the table, grabbed a couple of glasses, poured us each one, then placed one of them on the table in front of me. Then she dumped a teaspoonful of Cod Liver Oil into hers. Hoover, licking his lips and looking sated, slowly worked his way past her and wandered to his favorite sleeping place under a low corner table in the living room. He let out a belch when he passed, but I'm sure it was coincidental.

"You must be crazy, taking a shower in this cold," she said. It wasn't a question; it was a statement of fact, and one with which I couldn't argue. I looked over at her and smiled, nodding agreement. She downed the vile concoction she'd just put together, her loosely tied robe hung partially open in front of her. She really was an attractive woman and it seemed to me that she was even more so than when I'd first met her. At thirty two, she had the face and body of someone ten years her junior, remarkably free of lines and sags and marks of any kind – unlike her battle-scarred husband.

Holly rinsed her glass, grabbed her cup of coffee and headed to the bedroom for the next stage of her daily ritual. This was the long one – and I'd given up years ago attempting to figure out just what it was she did in there that took so incredibly long. And it's a good thing, too, as the ritual felt to be taking even longer these days.

Soon after, the telephone rang. I made my way to the living room, answered it and – no shock here – it was a female voice asking for Holly. I summoned her and, to my surprise, she was actually dressed at this point. Must have rushed when she heard the phone ring.

I attempted to ignore the half conversation going on behind me, preferring instead to listen to the conclusion of "Solveig's Song" playing softly on the radio. As minutes passed, it became apparent that there was a level of seriousness and concern to Holly's voice usually absent during one of her typical phone conversations. She spoke quietly, her back to me, and when she was finished cradled the receiver. She stood for a minute or two staring out the front window, lost in thought. Finally, she turned and walked over to my side, kneeled on the carpet, placed her hands on my thigh and rested her head on her hands. There was no mistaking it: She was upset about something and it wouldn't be long before I was dragged into it.

"Grace has disappeared," she said.

"Grace? Grace who?" I asked. I couldn't place the name, but that didn't mean a whole lot.

"Grace Peterson. My good friend up in High Point? With the artist husband? Howard?" She kept on going, turning each statement into a question, hoping I'd finally remember something about her. I did.

"The model?" I asked.

"*Former* model. Yes, she's the one," she responded, victorious.

"What do you mean '*disappeared*'?"

"Well, supposedly she deserted Howard. Just packed up and left without a word, without warning."

"It happens. Does that sound like her?"

"I don't know. We're good friends, really comfortable with each other; but who really knows about things like this? Howard's such a shit," she added, with a look of disdain.

"I don't know anything about Grace, except she's a friend of yours and a model of some sort," I said. "Fill me in."

"She *used* to be a model – a fashion model – in New York City. She was *everywhere* in magazines back in the '20s. Very successful, very much in demand."

"Yeah? What happened?"

"What always happens? She got older, she grew tired of the business – and tired of her mother, for that matter. She was her agent –

her mother was, I mean – and controlled her life. I guess it worked out okay when Grace was younger. But Grace is fiercely independent, and she couldn't stand that aspect of it any longer. She cut the string."

"Cord," I interjected.

"'Cord'?"

"As in '*umbilical* cord'."

"'string'," she responded, peeved by my interruption and correction, "as in 'apron string'". Someday I'd learn to keep my mouth shut.

"Oh. Yeah. Continue," I said, feebly.

"Where was I? She was still modeling when she met Howard, I forget where, and, for reasons I'll never understand, was completely taken with him. That's all it took. They fell in love, she retired from the business, said bye-bye to mother and she and Howard got married."

"You don't like Howard?"

"I don't *dislike* Howard, particularly. It's just that he's, he's...such a *moocher*."

"How so?"

"Well, as I said, Grace was very successful, very talented and she'd made a lot of money for both herself and her mother. Howard, on the other hand, is an artist – but in name only. His paintings, if you ever saw them, are pretty bad, very clumsy, very amateurish. And nobody buys them. Or no one with any taste, anyway."

"She must have known that – seen that – before she married the guy?"

"Well, yes. But I guess there's something 'romantic' about an artist, even a mediocre one. And, as they say, love is blind. One thing I'll say for Howard: he *talks* the part very well. If you never saw his stuff and only talked to him about it and art in general, he can be very impressive, very knowledgeable. Even charming...when he's had just the right amount of liquor...and that's a very small window. Did

I mention that? He's a drunk. Or a heavy drinker, at least."

"When did all this happen?" I asked, trying to get a point of reference.

"Friday night, Saturday morning, somewhere during that time. Howard discovered her missing Saturday morning and called the police."

"How long have they lived up in High Point?" I asked. High Point was a tiny little community about twelve miles away towards the northern part of the island.

"Well, let's see. I think she was in the business since she was a teen, in '24 or '25. She met him in '31, I think, and she quit modeling and they got married a year later. That's when they moved to the island."

"They own their house?"

"Yes. She bought it, of course; Howard had no money. Still doesn't. The house has a small gallery out front where they attempt to sell his stuff."

"Who was on the telephone?" I asked.

"That was her neighbor, Betty. I've met her several times, seems pleasant enough. She thought of me and my friendship with Grace; thought I ought to know about her disappearance. Or thought I already knew about it and hoped to learn what I knew. Which, of course, is nothing." She let out a long sigh.

"So, she packed up and moved out. Wouldn't be the first time something like this has happened," I responded.

"Listen, Lew. Grace and I were good friends, very close, as close as two friends can be living in two different towns. She'd talk about their shaky relationship, complain of his unyielding lack of ambition, his drinking, his arrogance, you name it. They were an odd match: He had so little going for him and she had so much going for her. If it wasn't for all the money she'd saved and had socked away in the bank, I doubt they'd have enough to get by. And that was another complaint of hers: she had all the money, did all the budgeting, paid all the bills, tried to keep things under control and he'd always want more. He couldn't understand why she was so tight with her money, couldn't grasp that it wasn't coming from some sort of bottomless money well. He actually had the ball...the nerve to ask her several times why she was so mean to him. Jesus, what a whiner," she said with disgust.

"So, she couldn't stand it anymore," I said. "Maybe she went to her mother's. For a breather."

"The man is spineless, Lew. Arrogant and conceited, but spineless. Maybe she couldn't take it anymore – but if she couldn't, she would have thrown *him* out. It's *her* house, paid for with *her* money, titled in *her* name. She pays the bills. She does *everything*. As for her mother, she loathes her. That's the last place she'd go."

"Another man, maybe? Is she still as good looking as she was a decade ago?"

"Well, she's older, of course. Not old, but older. Maybe in her late twenties. She's a little bit heavier than she was, but she used to be on the thin side. You can see it in her old photos. *You'd* never notice the extra pounds." She was probably right there. "Another man?" she continued. "Maybe. I thought of that. She never mentioned anything about any other men in her life, but I wouldn't really have expected her to. But I suppose it's a possibility." She thought about it for several moments of silence, and then looked up at me. "Still, even if there was another man, wouldn't she tell Howard to get lost? I know I would."

"A lot of people would. But people do stupid things when they fall in love, or whatever you want to call a new infatuation. It clouds the mind, the senses. People don't think things through, don't consider the ramifications." Experience talking, but couched in general terms.

"Hmmm," she said, staring ahead of her. "She's just so...so *sensible*. I can't see her running away, alone or with someone else. At least not without taking everything that's rightfully hers with her," she added. She was stroking my thigh now, and while under general circumstances that would be a good sign – and welcomed – under *these* circumstances it meant something else. I had a feeling I knew what this was building up to. Might as well face it.

"And…?" I asked.

"'And' what?" she responded, looking me in the eye.

"And where are you going with all this?"

"Listen, Lew," she said, as she continued her stroking and cuddled a little closer. "I'm worried about her, worried that something might have happened to her."

"And?"

"Maybe she did run away. Maybe she did go back to her mother's. And maybe she did run off with some guy she met. But maybe, just maybe, Howard had something to do with it." There was a sense of urgency in her voice now. "To get her out of the way – to get to her money. Who knows what he might have done."

"And?"

"Stop saying 'And', would you? You know what I'm leading up to. Are you going to make me beg?"

"Maybe," I said. Why not make her work?

"All right, all right. Please, *pretty* please, would you take a few hours and look into this? For me? You know how to do it. You've got the experience. I wouldn't know where to start, what to do," she implored. She gently stroked both my thighs now, and it felt good. What a manipulator.

"It wouldn't take long," she added, as if she actually knew all that was involved.

This was the first time in the eleven years I'd known her that she ever asked me to dredge up my long-dormant facility for this sort of thing and put it to use. She didn't know all that much about the earlier years of my life, the years before I showed up in Beach Haven. Just a general sort of outline with very few details and a whole lot of gaping holes. What she *did* know, and seemed to appreciate, was my profound unhappiness with those years and that life, and my desire to leave it all behind. She knew that I moved to Beach Haven to put some distance between the two. She knew that I just wanted to mind my own business, keep myself harmlessly occupied, be left alone. And she knew not to ask too many questions. She knew these things. And yet she was now asking me to draw on my former expertise, acquired years earlier and coupled with an innate knack for problem solving, in a former occupation that I steadfastly refused to talk about in anything more than the most general of terms, and only with her.

And that spoke volumes about the importance of this to her. How could I refuse?

"Please, Lew?" she asked, moving in front of me, moving in between my knees. I didn't stop her. "Please?" She was bringing out the big guns now, using her feminine wiles as backup to her powers of verbal persuasion, in an a two-pronged effort to coerce me to agree. These days, for the most part, she kept her wiles tucked away somewhere in a closet for safekeeping, but every so often she'll trot them out, and to good effect. Like now.

"Okay," I agreed, a note of resignation in my voice.

She smiled one of her big, winning smiles and rested her head in my lap. "Thanks," she said, quietly.

"You realize that there's a downside and an upside to this, don't you?" I asked.

"Downside? What, that you don't want to do it?"

"No, not that; that's a given."

"Then what?"

"I was, am and always will be an outsider to the people that live here. Especially those in the other towns on the island, who don't know me from Adam but can *smell* an outsider a mile away."

"Well, yes, I suppose. So what?"

"People don't take too kindly to someone sticking his nose in their business, poking around, asking questions. Especially if he's an outsider."

The smile faded from her face; she knew what I meant. "What's the upside?"

"You've started something, and now we're going to have to finish it," I said, leaning forward and taking her into my arms.

It was late morning and the taproom was empty. Except for Willett. He sat sideways on one of the booth benches, legs stretched out before him, back to the wall, reading. As usual. Willett was a nice, unassuming guy in his early twenties who'd had a tough go of it in life. He'd done a pretty good job of adapting, though. Having lost both parents in an automobile accident when he was only eight or nine, he was turned over to a widowed aunt, who lived a few miles north of here up in Ship Bottom-Beach Arlington. Then she died four years ago when he was eighteen, and he was on his own. He made the rounds of the island looking for work and a place to stay, eventually ending up here in Beach Haven. It was an obvious choice given that it's the island's largest year-round community – but that isn't saying much.

Holly and I had both taken to him immediately, and offered him a job doing whatever was needed here in the taproom. As compensation, we'd given him a small salary and my old room above the taproom to live in. He agreed, and has been with us ever since, growing in the position and, in his shy, detached way, ingratiating himself with the customers. Holly adored him, and he adored her. And me – I soon looked upon him as if a brother. More so, for that matter, than the other two I have – assuming they're still alive.

"Hi, Lew," he said, glancing up at me over the top of the book, then back to its pages. "Coffee's on, if you want some."

"'Morning, Gordon. Yeah, that sounds good," I said, heading for the pot back in the kitchen. Hoover had followed me into the taproom and, after a pause for a quick scratch behind the ears from Willett, had settled in at his favorite spot by the pot-bellied stove.

Willett had the place as straightened as it ever gets, prepped for the day's business. The stove pumped out heat in an effort to keep up with the cold outside and even with the joint closed up securely, cold drafts worked their way in through numerous unseen places. I returned with a full, steaming cup of black coffee.

"Poetic justice, I'd call it," he said from behind the book.

"What's that?" I asked.

"Did you know that Prince Vasili Romanoff, who is the son of Grand Duke Alexander, whose uncle was the late czar of all Russias, is now working as a salesman in a liquor store out in Los Angeles?"

"Why would I know such a thing?"

"And that Nathalie Keschko, who was the Queen of Serbia from 1875 to 1888, was tracked down five years ago and found to be a common beggar in the back streets of Paris?"

"Gordon," I said, patiently. "No, I didn't. What are you reading?" I asked, curious as to what book would carry such obscure and useless information. I cocked my head in a futile attempt to read its spine.

"Oh, just something I picked up at the library," he responded. Willett was one of the most intelligent people I'd ever met, but his formal education had been cut short during his senior year by the death of his aunt. He was a voracious reader of most anything — books, pulp magazines and comic books alike — and had the uncanny ability to retain most everything he read. As a result, he was a storehouse of knowledge on a staggering array of topics of varying degrees of importance and interest. His unprompted willingness to share these obscure tidbits with anyone who would listen resulted in his nickname, conferred by the regulars: "The Professor." When someone innocently asked him once where he went to college, he had responded that he hadn't; he'd graduated from libraries. It was a common sight to see Gordon riding his old bike to or from the town's library, basket loaded with books.

"It's the newest edition of *The Modern Encyclopedia* published by

William Wise and Company in New York. 1934. It's unique in that it's concise: twenty-two thousand articles in a single volume. The staff of the Encyclopedia Americana put it together. They wouldn't let me borrow that – The Encyclopedia Americana, I mean – from the library, but they agreed to this. Fascinating book. But I read about the Queen and Prince somewhere else," he added.

Following Willet's disjointed train of thought provided the occasional epic struggle.

He closed the book and placed it on his lap, and looked up at me, giving me his full attention. Gordon's hair was a perpetual shaggy mess, his chin weak, his body thin and wiry. He was, however, unfailingly pleasant and soft spoken, and always seemed at ease regardless of the temperament of those around him

"Hi," he said with a smile, as if it were the first thing he'd said to me all morning. "Need help with anything? Something for me to do?" It was hard for anyone not to like Gordon, even if his head was in the clouds so much of the time.

"Nothing much, just the usual," I said. "I have to head up-island on some business, don't know when I'll get back. Later afternoon, evening maybe," I added, draining my cup and placing it in the sink behind the bar.

"I can handle it," he said. "It's only Monday."

"Tuesday," I corrected him.

"Tuesday? What about Tuesday?" he asked, confused.

"It's Tuesday, Gordon. *Tuesday*," I repeated. A borderline genius, but trouble with the small things. Like days of the week.

"Oh, yeah. I knew that," he responded. Reassuring.

"I'll leave Hoover here."

"Okay. Bye." He returned to his book. I couldn't wait to hear the tidbits he'd come up with when he was finished with this one.

I dragged open the doors to the detached garage behind my house and climbed into the Ford parked inside. It was a brown '36 V8 five-window coupe, Model 68, slightly restyled from the previous year's Model 48, with redesigned grilles and wheels of pressed steel rather than wire. It'd cost me five hundred and fifty five bucks less than a year earlier, and was one of my few indulgences. And right now it was freezing cold; I hoped it would start. It did, and I headed out to Bay Avenue for my drive north to High Point and the Peterson home.

Long Beach Island is what is called a barrier island, a long thin strip of sand and marsh approximately eighteen miles in length and varying in width from as little as a quarter mile in some places to as much as a mile in others. It sits in the Atlantic several miles off the eastern coast of New Jersey, with the waters of Barnegat Bay at its northern end, Little Egg Harbor at its southern end, and Manahawkin Bay between the two, separating the island from the mainland. Outsiders tended to refer to the body of water in general as Barnegat Bay, however, and some of the locals had started doing the same out of sheer laziness. But they knew better. The island's northern tip was separated from the next strip of barrier land north of it by the narrow Barnegat Inlet, and its southern tip from an outcropping of the mainland and the next barrier island south of it by the Beach Haven and Little Egg Inlets, respectively.

The only bridges spanning these bodies of water were near the island's mid-point, stretching from the town of Ship Bottom-Beach Arlington on the island to the place known as Mud City in the Manahawkin Marshes over on the mainland, touching down on several tiny islands off the island's marshy coastline. There were two wooden causeways: an auto bridge built in 1914, and, eight hundred feet to its north, the train bridge built back in the 1880s for both passenger and freight service. The latter bridge had been used solely for once-a-day freight runs since 1930, and had been totally out of service since November of '35 when a nor'easter had demolished large sections of it. There'd been on-again/off-again proposals for new bridges at either or both of the island's ends, and these had cropped up with a fair degree of regularity during the period I'd lived here, but nothing ever came of them. The market crash of '29 sealed their fate.

Beach Haven Borough was situated toward the island's southern end, and many tourists thought it was the southern-most town. There were, in actuality, several other tiny communities further south, including Holgate and Beach Haven Inlet. Neither of these amounted to much, however, having modest populations during the height of the summer season and were more like ghost towns the rest of the year. St. Albans-by-the-Sea, located on tiny Tucker's Island off our island's southern tip, was little more than a memory now, destroyed for the most part by the ocean's relentless battering and erosion.

I headed north out of town on the island's single south-to-north road – named Bay Avenue here in Beach Haven but Long Beach Boulevard most elsewhere – directions to Peterson's house in High Point beside me on a scribbled scrap of paper. The island was visually unexciting at this end, with long, low stretches of treeless sand hills and dunes as far as the eye could see. The bayside bogs and coves were, for the most part, west of the abandoned tracks that ran parallel to the road, and had, years earlier, been filled in most of the places where they'd cut deep into the island. A few spots still remained, however, where small, wooden trestles spanned some of the wider fingers of water and marsh. Housing thinned significantly at the north end of the borough, with wild growth of bayberry and pine taking over the large, mostly undeveloped, expanses that followed. These areas were interrupted time and again by small pockets of development in the dozen or so tiny communities that had sprung up since the turn of the century. They bore such unimaginative names as North Beach Haven, Spray Beach, Beach Haven Gardens, Beach Haven Terrace, The Dunes, Haven Beach, Beach Haven Park, Brighton Beach, and Beach Haven Crest. Detect a pattern here? The words "Beach" and "Haven" figured into the lion's share of them, with numerous developers of years gone by hoping for a free ride on the coattails of Beach Haven Borough's fame and popularity as a summer resort. If you blinked, however, you'd miss most of them.

North of this series of nondescript communities was the town of Brant Beach, which had some character and charm. This was followed to its north by the more sizable communities of Ship Bottom-Beach Arlington and Surf City, the former the gateway to the island and proud possessor of the most unwieldy moniker of all the island's towns. These two sat at the widest part of the island and were each comprised of a comparatively large number of houses dating back as much as fifty years or so, an eclectic mix of styles both large and small, of grand Victorian homes and tiny two-room bungalows.

My Ford rumbled out of Surf City into the huge, undeveloped Frazier Tract to its north, its tiny heater actually beginning to make some inroads in the frigid air within. My toes were beginning to thaw as I rolled through Harvey Cedars, the island's oldest settlement, located at its narrowest point. It was the only island town with the dubious distinction of not having a single liquor license in effect, a chilling prospect at best. I quickly reviewed Holly's directions to the Peterson house: It was at the corner of Eighty-Fifth Street in High Point, the community immediately following, and would be on the ocean side of the road three blocks past the derelict High Point Inn.

The island was extremely narrow here, with a dozen dead-end streets heading east and west towards the ocean and bay from the single through-road. Eighty-Fifth Street was its topmost cross street, with only a handful of houses in the immediate vicinity. An enormous expanse of pristine wilderness loomed ahead for the couple of miles separating High Point from the island's community farthest to the north, Barnegat City.

There was a lone house off to the right: a gambrel-roofed, two-story, white-painted clapboard affair with a screened-in porch spanning its width, a brick chimney jutting up from its right-hand side. The front yard was actually landscaped – a rarity here on the island – and a white painted wooden signpost, sans sign, leaned towards the road from some low, ground-covering brush off to one side. This had to be the Peterson dwelling – everything was just as Holly had described it, right down to the tarnished brass bell mounted on the post flanking the porch's screen door. The house served the dual purpose of home and artist's showroom, but the absence of the sign suggested that showroom hours and sales were confined to the summer months. I pulled into the hard-packed sand drive, parked, killed the engine, and trotted briskly through the cold, autumn air to the front porch. I knocked several times quickly on the screen door's trim, decided that no one inside could possibly hear it, stepped inside onto the porch, then gave several more raps to the front door itself. No one answered. I repeated the process several more times. There was a small sign screwed to the clapboard to the right of the front door, indicating showroom hours of noon 'til five, Tuesday through Sunday. It was 12:35 p.m. and, in the absence of any sort of posted indication of seasons of operation, I decided that – technically – the place should be open. So I let myself in.

The front room was reasonably large, perhaps twenty-five feet wide by fourteen feet deep, extending the width of the house. A closed door in the middle of the far wall shut the room off from the rest of the house beyond. At the left end of the room was a small flight of stairs, which doubled back on itself at a small landing and terminated at yet another closed door at its top. The room itself was filled with dozens of paintings of various sizes, some perched on easels randomly placed throughout the room, many more sitting on the floor and leaning against the walls, in groups two or three paintings deep.

A quick perusal of his work left me thoroughly unimpressed, striking me as an amateurish attempt at realism, which suffered greatly from a somewhat less than adequate understanding and appreciation of the fundamentals of perspective. But I wasn't here to buy paintings. After calling Howard's name several times and receiving no response, I decided to look into the private living quarters. A closer inspection of the door at the top of the steps revealed a padlock covered with a thick, even coating of dust; no one had been up there for at least half a year. The downstairs door was unlocked. I poked my head in and made several attempts to rouse the fellow, if he was somewhere in the back. These attempts failed as well. After a minute or two looking about and familiarizing myself with the layout of the place, I headed out back. I wanted to see if he had some sort of studio separate from the house, since I hadn't seen any visible signs of a work area within the house itself, or at least not in the parts I'd looked in.

The sand drive led to the back of the house and, as I expected, a second, more modest cedar shingled structure. It was rectangular in shape, perhaps sixteen by twenty feet, with a low, flat-roof and a metal stovepipe poking out of the upper wall at its southern end. Wood smoke poured from beneath its conical cover. Peterson must be in here, I thought to myself as I headed for its door, a rough tongue-in-groove affair with a rusted horseshoe nailed to its center. My approach was cut short by a long, anguished scream from inside the structure, punctuated by a dull thud followed by the smashing of glass. I trotted the last few steps to the door, pulled it open without knocking, and stepped quickly inside.

As I'd expected, the place was indeed an artist's studio. Dozens — perhaps hundreds — of canvases were stacked against the walls in an attempt to keep the central area clear. Before me, in the room's center, stood a man, motionless, arms hanging at his side, head hung low, his back to me. In front of him was a large wooden easel, a three by three foot canvas placed on it, its painted image obscured by the violent splatter of red dripping down its front like some sort of hideous gunshot wound. The remains of a smashed bottle of red paint lay oozing on the floor beneath it. Moments after my noisy entrance, the forlorn looking figure standing before me turned slowly with an awkward shuffle and fixed his eyes on me, head bobbing slightly. He blinked several times and squinted, trying to focus uncooperative eyes.

"Who…who are you?" he slurred. He was drunk, a nearly empty bottle of King of Kentucky Straight Bourbon Whiskey sitting on a nearby chair stood as evidence. Cheap stuff – eighty-nine cents a pint.

"You all right?" I asked. He stared. "I was outside. Heard a scream. Thought you might be in trouble," I added, pointing over my shoulder with my thumb in the general direction I'd just come from.

He looked at me with a sluggish, confused look, as if he didn't recall any of this. Eventually it came back to him.

"Oh. That. My, uh, creative juices aren't flowing today and, uh, I guess I got mad and – guess I took it out on this…this painting." The only thing flowing today was the bourbon. "Who are you?" he asked once again.

"Name's Porter. Lew Porter. My wife Holly's a good friend of your wife. You *are* Peterson, aren't you?"

"Yeah, that's me: Howard Peterson, world-renowned artist, painter of *shit*," he said, almost contemptuously, turning in place to look once again at the aborted mess beyond him. My immediate reaction was that he was a whiner, and I wasn't much in the mood for whining.

"Mind if I ask you a couple of questions about your wife? About her disappearance?" I asked his back.

"No, I guess not," he sighed. "Everybody else has. No privacy, no respect; everybody wants to know what happened." Definitely a whiner.

He wandered over to the chair, grabbed the bottle, uncorked it, took a swig. And then, as an afterthought, unsteadily offered it to me.

"No, thanks. Little too early in the day for me," I lied.

He bobbed his head in acknowledgement, and crashed down onto the small, wooden chair. The bottle was placed on the floor in a position of honor by his feet.

"Tell me about her. Some background. How you met her, that sort of thing," I prodded. We needed to start someplace.

"Grace? She was a model – fashion model, guess you'd call it – in New York. The big city. This is back in the '20s. Her pictures were in all the big magazines, not any magazines I'd read, probably not you either, but, you know, women's magazines."

"I know the kind," I said.

"Well, of course you would. You have a wife, you would have seen them around, lying on tables, bedside tables…"

"Where and when did you meet her?" I interrupted.

"We, uh, met through some mutual friends. 1930, maybe '31, I guess. It was at a party in the city; some friends of mine, the Mortons, were giving it. Friends of *ours*, it turned out." He wiped the sweat off his forehead with the back of his hand. It was surprisingly warm in there, the air thick with the smell of wood smoke. "We hit it off immediately. She was very attractive, beautiful in fact, and was very interested in my work as an artist. And, I should add, in me, also; there was a strong intellectual and physical attraction between us."

Love works in strange ways, I thought. Howard was slight of build, soft-spoken and kind of meek, but like a lot of little guys probably tried to compensate with occasional outbursts of anger and vituperation. He was in his late thirties, curly reddish-brown hair starting to go gray at the temples, a full, bushy mustache. His skin was pale, almost unhealthily so, his eyes red and watery. He looked like he needed a good night's sleep, maybe several. Didn't look like much now, but I could see where he might have been attractive to women a few years earlier, before middle age and alcohol started to take their toll.

"One thing led to another, we dated, fell in love and got married a year later," he continued. A slight smile crept onto his face. "It was a *secret* ceremony; didn't want the *bitch* to know until afterwards."

"'The bitch?'" I asked.

"Yeah. Grace's mother. The bitch. Julia Feeney – *bitch*. She was kind of Grace's agent of sorts – a horrible, domineering woman interested solely in the money her daughter was earning. Didn't give a damn about Grace herself, or how this life of modeling impacted her personal development. Grace was, after all, only sixteen when her mother goaded her into this profession." He pulled a dirty handkerchief from his back pants pocket and blew his nose loudly.

"How did her mother take it?"

"Take what? Us getting married? Oh, she was mad, *very* mad. She couldn't believe that her daughter could do such a thing to her. Took it as a personal affront. And she was worried, I suppose, that we might have babies or something, something that would interfere with Grace's modeling, derail the gravy train. Well, she had good reason to worry: Grace retired from the business as soon as we were married, and severed all ties with her mother. Not that that was any real big deal, though; Grace told me her mother had socked away enough money over the years that she – the *bitch*, I mean – she'd have nothing to worry about in the years to come. That is, unless she squandered her money without an eye to the future. But that would be *her* problem, not ours, wouldn't it?"

"When was this?"

"1932. Spring. We came down here and bought this house. It was the ideal setup for my painting, with this studio here and the house's layout, which accommodates my gallery."

"Why High Point, of all places?" I asked. It was a long way from New York City, and about as different a lifestyle as imaginable. Kind of like moving to Tibet.

"Her father used to bring them to the island when she was a little girl and she had fond memories of the place. He died when she was young." He paused for a moment, considering what he had just said. "I'm not so sure that after we moved here she might have come to realize that her memories were idealized, that the reality of the place was somewhat different – harsher, perhaps – than what she'd remembered." His gaze turned to the oozing red mess spreading on the floor nearby. He reached unsteadily for a large rag hanging off the end of the worktable, and tossed it into the middle of the puddle. It was a futile attempt to stem the flow; he'd have his work cut out for him later on.

"You able to sell 'em year 'round?" I asked, a nod to the paintings, trying to get him back on track.

"No, no; it's hard enough selling them during the summer, when there *are* actually people around. That's Grace's end. From, I guess, maybe May through September, she keeps the gallery open for business. She puts paintings out front on easels to grab people's attention, on those rare occasions when somebody actually passes the place on the way to Barnegat City. The wind's a problem…"

"The wind?" I asked.

"The paintings. On the easels. When it's windy, it's a problem; they keep blowing over," he responded with a hint of exasperation, then continued. "This seemed like a great place to me for painting; quiet, lots of privacy, real estate was reasonable and there was plenty of beautiful scenery and interesting subjects to paint. Especially here at the north end of the island. And the High Point-Harvey Cedars area has a reputation for being a place of inspiration for artists in many fields: Yellin, Blai, Sarah Langley, the Gills, Portinoff and, uh, Beagary. Who else? Oh, yeah, Margaretta Archambault, Fuertes; lots of them." He was still searching for more names.

"I get the idea," I said, having recognized only two names in the list he'd just recited, one as an artist, and the other a guy I'd met in a bar and spoken with at length. Didn't have a clue he was an artist, though.

"Yeah, well. It was fun at first. You know: newlyweds, marital bliss, the sort of stuff that lasts a couple of weeks or so. But then I got to *know* Grace."

"How do you mean?" I was pushing it here, and I had to be careful. I was amazed that he'd answered my questions so willingly up to this point. It was the booze, no question about it. But I knew that the bourbon could, at a moment's notice, work *against* me as well as it was currently working *for* me.

"Did you ever see her? She's beautiful, even now, a few years later and a few pounds heavier. But still beautiful: Any woman would kill to have her looks." It occurred to me that some men might have a similar reaction. "But superficial beauty often hides what's *inside*, what a person's really about." He sat there shaking his head slowly. "Her mother, I guess, had a profound impact on her over the years. It took its toll."

"In what ways?"

"Well, reality kicked in. I thought she had me up on a pedestal, so to speak, but she quickly kicked that out from under me and used it for firewood. I thought it was going to be a relationship of equals, but she quickly took control. She bought this house, which made sense at the time because she had all the money – but it was, and still is, in her name. It's *her* house, not ours. And her money: It's in *her* savings account, not ours. I have to ask her for money every single time I need something, like a little kid begging his mama for pennies for candy. It's embarrassing – humiliating. And she pushed and pushed, telling me that I needed to, as she put it, clean up my act, become self-sufficient and self-supporting. And all I ever wanted to do was paint, just paint. I didn't need this aggravation and hassle; it affected my creativity." He looked very sad now, as if he could cry. His self-pity was growing wearisome.

"And she had this will, too, an old one, that named her mother as the sole inheritor of her estate. She hasn't gotten around to changing it yet, far as I know; said she'd leave it as is until I'd reached some level of self-sufficiency. An arbitrary level, I might add, of her own definition. Impossible!" This was obviously a sore spot with him, and he looked miserable – miserable enough to warrant another swig of bourbon. He paused, wiped his mouth with his knuckle and sniffed, then looked at me again with an expression of confusion.

"*Who* did you say you are? *Why* are you asking me all these questions?" I was afraid he'd come back to this.

"Lew Porter. Remember? Your wife and my wife are good friends. My wife, Holly, was worried about Grace, about her going away." I hoped that this was sinking in, that it was sufficient to appease him.

"Holly. Holly," he repeated several times to himself, staring at the floor. Then it came to him, a slight smile creeping onto his face. "Holly! I remember Holly: the tall, thin, pretty one. The poet, kind of. I remember her. She's nice; I like her," he said. "You're married to her?" he added, a touch of surprise in his voice.

"She's the one. And, yeah, we're married."

He nodded acceptance of what I'd just said. I guess it wasn't impossible to fathom. Difficult, but not impossible.

"Tell me about her disappearance," I continued.

"Well, it happened about a week and a half ago. I was out here painting, like I always am, and she was inside, I guess, like she always is. I worked late that night and fell asleep out here. I woke up in the middle of the night, freezing, and went back to the house to go back to sleep – where it was warm."

"When was this? What day?"

"Well, it was a Friday night. Saturday morning, I suppose, when I came back inside."

"Last Saturday?" I paused, working the date out in my mind. "The twenty fourth?"

"What's today?" he asked.

"The twenty seventh. Tuesday, the twenty seventh. Of October," I added, not quite sure just how out of it he was.

"No, it wasn't just this last Saturday. It would have been the Saturday before that. The…"

"The seventeenth. So, Friday and Saturday, the sixteenth and seventeenth?"

"Yeah, that sounds about right," he said, squinting and scratching his forehead.

"And?"

"Well, I was half asleep when I came in – headed for the sofa and collapsed there. And that's where I slept all night. I, uh, sleep there fairly often. I got up the next morning…"

"What time?" I interrupted.

"Time? I don't know. The usual, I suppose, around eleven, eleven thirty. Something like that. So, I got up, made myself some breakfast, took a bath. You know, the usual."

"And Grace?"

"Well, I didn't realize at first that she wasn't around. I just kind of assumed that she was off doing something. I never really paid much attention to the little things she did to occupy herself; my mind was usually on other things."

"But you finally *did* notice something was different, or that she was missing?" I prodded.

"Well, yeah. Not immediately, but it eventually occurred to me that I hadn't seen her in a while. I took a look for her in the gallery, but she wasn't there. I knew she wasn't in any of the other rooms because I'd just been in all of them over the previous ten or fifteen minutes. There wasn't a note under the sugar bowl on the counter like she usually does when she goes out without telling me. I looked outside, out in the studio, *everywhere*, but she was nowhere to be found." He was staring now through the studio's front window at the rear of his house.

"Then what?" I asked.

"Then? Well, I went back inside, tried to remember if she'd told me anything the day before, about where she was going or something, but I couldn't."

"So the last time you saw her was on Friday?"

"Yeah, early evening, seven, seven thirty maybe; it was after dinner. I had to go back into the house for something and she was in the kitchen making a pie – apple, I think – and we spoke for a couple of minutes."

"What about?"

"Christ, I don't remember. Nothing important, just boring husband-wife stuff. I probably told her the pie looked good. She probably asked me if I'd be working late; she always does. That kind of stuff."

"So, on Saturday, you looked around the house for her, couldn't find her. What did you do then?"

"Well, I looked around some more, then realized that all her clothing was gone, or most of it, and so was the big suitcase usually kept in the closet. She'd run away. Her shoes were gone, too. And her journal, with her writings and poems and addresses and whatever the hell else she put in there. Did I mention her shoes? And the bathroom: Her toiletries were all gone, too, except in her haste she grabbed *my* toothbrush instead of *hers*." He laughed a small laugh to himself. "That's the least of my worries," he added.

"So she ran away? Where to? Her mother's?"

"Her mother's?" he repeated, sarcastically. "That's unlikely – very unlikely. She valued her newfound freedom more than anything else in her life. Anything. She'd gotten out from under the yoke, and I can't imagine her ever going back. That'd be admitting that mother was right and she was wrong. No, Grace wouldn't do that. She didn't need to. She had plenty of her own money socked away and didn't need her mother for anything." He was staring at the floor, pulling on his lower lip. "Anyway, the car's still here," he added, which only muddled things.

"Any relatives nearby that she might have gone to?"

"Relatives? I don't think so. She was an only child. Grandparents are all dead. Never mentioned any aunts or uncles. I don't know of a single relative. Except, of course, the bitch."

"How about friends?"

"Well, she had a couple here on the island and I called them all. All of them except for your wife; I forgot about her. None of them knew anything, not a thing."

"Were these all female friends?"

"Well, yes. Of course they were. If she had any male friends it would have been a long time ago…in New York." He paused for a moment, considering what he'd just said. "But not here. Not on the island."

"Is there any chance that there was another man?" I asked, fingers crossed.

He looked up at me with a strained look on his face. "You sound just like the cops."

"You called the police?"

"Of course I did. I was worried. I *am* worried."

"What'd they do? Or say?" I knew most of the island's cops and had known lots of cops in general over the years. I already *knew* what they would say and do, but I wanted to hear his slant on it.

"Do?" he repeated with a snort. "They didn't *do* anything. They asked a couple of questions – a lot fewer, I might add, than you're asking – then promptly chalked it up to her running away with another man. A case of abandonment, I think they called it." He was shaking his head back and forth now.

"Think there might have been another man?" I prodded.

"I…I don't know. I just don't know," he said quietly. "She's a looker, a real eye catcher, even now. But aside from the summer there aren't too many what I'd call 'hot prospects' among the locals, if you know what I mean. The summer's a different story. There were always plenty of rich swells sniffing around the gallery during the season. All those wealthy, useless young men would come around here, like swarms of mosquitoes, all acting as if they were interested in my paintings but actually jockeying for position to talk to her, impress her with their witty banter and charm. Christ, she was old enough to be their older sister."

"This happen a lot?"

"Well, I might be exaggerating it a little. It happened occasionally. The worst of them was Hawley. Chester Hawley. *The Third*. God, what an arrogant little bastard he is."

"He the rich guy with the estate in Harvey Cedars?" I asked. Everyone on the island knew of the Hawleys and their incredible wealth.

"No, he's the son. The father, *he's* the rich guy – *The King of Cereal,* he's okay. They all live down there in that pretentious bay-to-ocean estate of theirs. What do they call it? *Casa Grande by the Sea,* or some such nonsense."

"What made Hawley the worst?"

"Well, most of the others would take the hint. Grace would be pleasant to each and every person who came in the shop in the off chance they were genuinely interested in the paintings. Whenever she'd determine that their interest was in her and not the paintings, however, pleasantries were dispensed with and they'd get the famous Feeney cold shoulder. That would drive most of them away. Most, of course, except for Hawley; he'd come in at least once a week, smooth talking her, not giving a damn that she was married. An arrogant little prick, that's what he is. She referred to him as 'the Weasel.' Damn thing is, though, he actually bought one of my paintings, one of the more expensive ones. I guess a lot of this was her own fault, brought on by that damned streak of independence of hers."

"How so," I asked.

"Well, she refused to wear a wedding ring and I suppose that confused a lot of these would-be suitors. She said that changing her last name to Peterson was, in her eyes, more than a sufficient matrimonial gesture. She considered wedding rings to be on par with a brand burnt on the hides of cattle, marking them as someone's property. She'd have nothing to do with rings and she was adamant about it. It wasn't worth fighting about. But I guess it didn't help matters, not that she'd ever admit to it."

"Is kidnapping a possibility?" I didn't think so, but I wanted to hear his thoughts on it.

"Kidnapping?" he asked, incredulously. "We're not talking about the Lindbergh baby here. And no one's contacted me since she left. And they would, wouldn't they? If they kidnapped her? But I don't have any money, anyway; she has it all, and I can't get to it. Not now, not *ever*," he added bitterly. Rough times loomed ahead for Howard.

"Might she have gone away by herself?" I asked. We were running out of possibilities.

"Well, I suppose that's a possibility. But wouldn't she have taken the car? We only have the one, and it's still parked out back, untouched. And – well – I hate to admit it, hate to say it, but if I were her and so profoundly unhappy being married to me, I wouldn't run away; I'd throw me out. Think about it: She has all the money, she owns the house, she has it all and I have nothing. She holds all the cards."

"You could have taken her to court."

"I could have, I suppose, but I think she knows I wouldn't. Anyway, even if I did, wouldn't she end up with more than she has running off?" He thought about it for several moments. "Well, maybe not. It's all so confusing. Anyway, the cops think she ran off with another man. She's still reasonably young and good looking, she packed all her things and it would explain leaving the car behind. If the guy had money, it would explain everything." He looked up at me. "And, you know, I think they're probably right: There's no other good explanation." He was feeling sorry for himself now, and his eyes welled with tears. "And me: My future's bleak," he added.

"You have your painting. Maybe move to a more prominent location, to boost sales," I said in a half-hearted attempt to be upbeat and helpful. I wanted to get this over with. My stomach was grumbling, I was tired and hungry, and needed a drink. Especially the drink.

"That'll be the day," he said with a bitter laugh. "I've been doing this for twenty years now, and I have no illusions about my talents as an artist. I'm at best a marginally talented hack doing an unremarkable, workman-like job; I'm not going to get any better. Oh, it's not too hard to sell the occasional piece to wealthy tourists purchasing on a whim. They're in the proper, shore-induced frame of mind, and spontaneous purchases are the norm for them. But my paintings just aren't very good, and they'd be laughed out of any reputable gallery. No, Potter, I have no illusions about my talents. They're fine for here, but that's about all." He barely got the last words out, and took a quick, deep breath in an effort to keep from falling apart.

I let the name slide, wished him luck and got Grace's mother's name and address from him; he didn't know her number. I scribbled my name, number and address on a scrap of paper, told him to get in touch if he needed to talk. I hoped he wouldn't. As an afterthought, I told him to stop by the taproom for a drink if he was ever in the area. I immediately wished I hadn't; I didn't particularly care for the guy, but figured there was only a slim chance he'd ever take me up on it. A slim chance, for that matter, that he'd even remember the offer. I left him slumped in his chair, staring at the floor.

I made a side trip back into his house on my way back to the car. He'd stay in the studio for a while, feeling sorry for himself, polishing off the remains of the bottle. And, should ambition ever strike him, clean up the small pool of red paint congealing on the floor. I headed into the house and made a quick, perfunctory search of the place, with occasional glances out back windows to make sure he stayed put. As he'd reported, her drawers and closets were, for the most part, empty of clothing and shoes. The bathroom was in a similar condition, with only Howard's items, or items of a general nature such as aspirin, scattered about the room. The sole exception was a woman's razor, obviously intended for her legs, which had been left behind on a small, metal basket hung on the side of the tub.

I saved the large mahogany block-front secretary in the living room for last. It had glass upper doors and a closed working surface that locked with a key, hiding the desk's drawers and pigeonholes behind its slanted surface. Fortunately, the key was in the lock. Most of its contents were of a routine nature: old letters, stacks of photos and various other odds and ends of no particular interest.

The exception was a green-covered bankbook. It was the only bankbook to be found, and it was in Grace's name; the bank was the First National Bank of Barnegat: a small, mainland town about eight miles north on Route 9. Entries detailed the history of deposits and withdrawals: The first, and largest, deposit opened the account on April 14, 1932, and there were quarterly withdrawals early in the month every July, October, January and April thereafter of two hundred and fifty dollars each. Deposits were scattered throughout its six and a half year history. Most of these were during the summer months and of modest amounts, assumedly from the occasional sale of Howard's paintings. There were a handful of larger deposits on a much more infrequent and random basis. The source of these larger deposits was an unknown. The account's balance was a staggering $12,432.78, which was only a couple of hundred dollars less than the opening balance. The last entry was dated October 1, 1936, for the standard withdrawal of two-fifty. I quickly copied the account number and her full name on the small pad I always carried with me, and returned the small book to its drawer.

This was troubling: Why would she run away, by herself or with someone else, and leave her bankbook behind? Especially if she went off by herself. An oversight, perhaps? They undoubtedly knew her over there, and I suspect she could have gotten a new copy with a sob story about losing the old one. Something to look into.

"What the hell are you doing," exclaimed Howard from behind. He'd entered the house and room without my hearing, and caught me off-guard standing before the open desk.

"I'm looking for those matches you said would be in here," I quickly bluffed, pulling a cigar from my pocket and jamming it in my mouth before I turned, and hoping he was sufficiently drunk to fall for this.

He stood there with a blank, dazed expression on his face, and finally responded, "Oh. Matches. I said the desk? I meant the drawer. The kitchen drawer. Out here…" he said as he padded off into the kitchen. I hadn't noticed his old, battered slippers before. I followed him into the kitchen and thanked him for the small box of matches he produced from the drawer. Said I could keep them. Thank God for drunks.

I drove the several blocks back to the center of High Point and the sole, year-round luncheonette, a place called Melford's. It faced the boulevard, known as Atlantic Avenue here, on the corner with Seventy-Seventh, diagonally across from the town's fire station. Mrs. Melford didn't complain when I ordered scrambled eggs and ham at a little after two, and the mess she served me tasted a lot better than it looked. Fortified by several swigs of Old Overholt and armed with a fistful of change, I made my way back to the phone booth at the rear of the room. Looked up the number for the First National Bank in Barnegat, fed a nickel into the phone, and gave them a call. The rest was easy: I told the woman at the other end that I was Howard Peterson – I wanted to verify my wife's account balance. I gave her the account number, a last transaction date of October 1, and assumed balance of $12,432.73. After a minute's consultation of the bank's records, she returned and confirmed that that was indeed the current balance, plus interest. No questions asked. Have a nice day.

My second call required the services of several operators, who cheerfully tracked down the number of Julia Feeney's home up in Hoboken, north Jersey. They connected me, and I launched into a second series of lies. Told her that I was with a Manhattan ad agency, that we were looking for a slightly more mature woman for a series of mother-and-child magazine ads we were working on. Would Grace be interested in a return to modeling – or, at the very least, talking to us about it? Told her that just any woman wouldn't do, that it had to be someone whose face had been prominent in magazines five-to-ten years earlier, that the reading audience would subconsciously recognize as someone they once knew or were familiar with. This audience identification was important to us; we were willing and able to pay significantly higher than the going rate to acquire the services of just such a person. Threw in Proctor and Gamble for good measure. Her response – and it was voluminous and bitter – indicated that she'd neither seen nor spoken with Grace in a long, long time. She sounded drunk and mean. I thanked her for her time and cradled the phone as she was midway into a spiel promoting herself for the ads.

I headed back south on Atlantic, satisfied that Grace's accounts were untouched, that she hadn't moved back in with her mother, and that her mother hadn't a clue as to her whereabouts. I wanted to talk with Chester Hawley III about Grace, and crossed my fingers once again that he'd actually be on the island today. Not in Philadelphia or away on some globetrotting vacation, but here. On the island.

The Hawley estate, a sprawling ocean-to-bay piece of property known as White Cedars, sat in the southernmost part of High Point, just north of its border with Harvey Cedars. It had been built a decade earlier by Chester's father, Chester Hawley Jr.

Chester Hawley Jr. was President of Philadelphia-based United States Foods and a self-made millionaire. His company made all kinds of breakfast cereals, items such as Huffin' Puffs and Shaky Flakes, and was the sponsor of several youth-oriented radio shows, including *Brace Manning, T-Man*; *Boots Willis' Old West*; and something called *Beanie Goober and His Friends*. I only know this because there had been a supplement stuffed in the *Beach Haven Times* a couple of months earlier having to do with new construction on the island. And, while not new, Hawley's place was the most photogenic, and graced the lead page in a typically grainy photo accompanied by a brief blurb on his numerous accomplishments. This was followed by two more pages of millionaires' homes on the island, one each devoted to Hawley's neighbor Frederick P. Small of Federal Railway Express and his home *Cobblestones*, and to Frederick Beck's – of the Beck Engraving Co. of Philadelphia – Beach Haven-based home *The Farm* New construction of the more modest homes of the common folk was relegated to the supplement's remaining pages. The Porter home, *Kidneystones*, was nowhere to be found.

The elder Hawley was, for the most part, locally well liked. This was primarily due to the fact that he spent his money freely and indiscriminately, in the immediate area and, to a lesser extent, throughout the island. Autumn was a high-profile time for Hawley. He sponsored an annual regatta each September, which was organized by the Barnegat Light Yacht Club and held out on the bay, followed by an annual Halloween party held in High Point's Milburn Hall. He also supplied everyone in the two adjoining communities with turkeys for their Thanksgiving dinners. They were on their own for Christmas, however.

White Cedars was unusual not only for its size and the immaculate condition of its buildings, but also for the fact that it was one of the few places on the island with a manicured grass lawn, and a big one at that. Everyone was amazed at the amount of time, effort and money thrown at keeping the sprawling grounds green and trim, and considered the undertaking here on this sun-parched, wind-swept island to be sheer folly. Admittedly, though, the results were impressive. The lawn was broken up with a series of impeccably maintained gardens laid out in symmetrical patterns throughout the property. Hell, everything was symmetrical here, which made yet another unstated comment about its owner.

I downshifted as I approached the grounds and took in their layout. As I said, the property stretched from ocean to bay, but the island is fairly narrow here, and the grounds were probably wider north to south. Atlantic Avenue cut through the property and I parked midway through, no doubt spoiling the symmetry. The ocean-side portion of the grounds consisted solely of lawn and gardens easing their way up to the dunes. A walkway had been cut into these and the upper corner of what appeared to be a large pavilion could be seen through the gap. There were no other buildings on this side of the road.

Turning and facing the other half of the property with the bay beyond, there was a bayberry- and pine-lined access road to the left, southern border. This was so boxed in by wild growth that the trucks and cars using it would be shielded from view from the main house and its guest cottages. It was more like a tunnel, but they probably liked it that way since they didn't have to look at delivery trucks and their common, working-stiff drivers. My guess was that it led past the main house and around to its rear, and the servants' entrance. I opted for the open, semi-circular drive out front that provided access to the house's main entrance. This is the one we rich folk use – no servants' entrance for us.

The place was handsome in a huge, overwhelming sort of way, and dwarfed the oversized Victorians built in Beach Haven during that town's formative years. This would have been a cozy home for a family of fifty large people.

I rapped on the front door with its flawlessly polished brass knocker, the sound cutting through the autumn silence, and ejected my spent De Nobili stub into a sandy area with a flick of my middle finger. It looked like a tiny smoking piece of driftwood.

Moments later, the door was answered by one of the Hawley's maids. She was young and petite, with long, wavy, reddish-brown hair – auburn, I guess they call it – and a pale, scrubbed-clean complexion dotted with freckles. She was timid and kind of mousy, not what you'd call attractive, but not unattractive. Just…there. And very young – fifteen or sixteen young. She smelled like starch. I told her who I was, that I wanted to see Chester III if he were available. As luck would have it, he was and hopes of getting this all over with today were immediately bolstered. She ushered me into the living room and shuffled off to retrieve her boss. I disappeared into a large, overstuffed chair.

Unfortunately, it was the maid who returned. Chester was there, but wanted to know why I was there. Told her to tell him I needed to speak with him regarding Grace Peterson, that it was important. She nodded to indicate she'd grasped the message and shuffled off once again. Kind of homely, I thought, but with a cute behind. While I waited, I took in a framed photo perched on a nearby table. It was a portrait of a middle-aged couple; the woman sat while the husband stood behind and to one side. In spite of the positioning it was evident that she was a large woman – a very large woman. The mister and missus, I assumed.

Chester appeared several minutes later. He was, visually, everything I'd anticipated and more: young, early-to-mid twenties, with longish, wavy blond hair combed straight back. He sported a tan all-wool cashmere sports jacket with tucks above its half belt and inverted pleat patch pockets, matching pleated trousers with oversized cuffs, an open-collar shirt with an exposed gold satin ascot and, so help me God, a monocle. Nobody wore monocles – or, at least, no human being I'd ever met. In spite of all I'd ever heard, I still found it difficult to believe that anyone ever had in the past, either. He looked like one of those evil Huns staring down from a wartime propaganda poster. Like Erich von Stroheim – but with hair.

"Lew Porter," I said by way of introduction, while struggling to get up out of the chair. It was like upholstered quicksand. He gave me a quizzical look as we shook hands, and I had the impression that he would have preferred if he could have managed the shake without physical contact. And his hand: It was like shaking an empty glove.

"Mr. Porter. How may I be of service?" He spoke with what sounded vaguely like a British accent. Boston, perhaps – or just an affectation.

"As you may already know, Grace Peterson disappeared a week and a half ago. Grace manages the art gallery up on Eighty-Fifth Street," I added, just in case his memory needed jogging.

"No, I didn't know that. She's disappeared?" he said as he eased himself into a stiff Windsor chair, a look of extreme consternation clouding his features.

"That's how it appears," I said as I sat in the Windsor's companion; I wanted to be able to see him once I was seated. I proceeded to lay out for him the circumstances surrounding her disappearance, omitting a few chosen details from the account. He leaned forward all the while, arms resting on knees, hanging on every word. My story concluded with my visit earlier that day with Howard and a brief, semi-truthful explanation of my involvement.

"Grace is a treasure," he said when I'd finished. "She's stunning, absolutely stunning, and extremely well read. And with a small amount of refinement, she'd be a real trophy for someone from my circle," he added.

I had visions of her head mounted on the wall.

"Unfortunately, she never gave me the time of day. And it wasn't just me: she'd treat all of my friends and acquaintances in a similar fashion, so it had nothing to do with me personally." He spoke as if she weren't married, as if Howard were a pet or a piece of furniture. "Oh, she was unfailingly polite and always friendly, but it was all business with her. Whenever it became evident that we weren't going to make a purchase from her on a particular day, she'd move on to the next customer. Actually, there rarely ever was a 'next customer,' and in those instances she'd return to whatever she'd been doing when I'd entered. With the standing offer, of course, that I shouldn't hesitate to interrupt her if I had any questions whatsoever *about the artwork on display or the artist of same.* It was always abundantly clear that she wished not to be bothered for any other reason." He shook his head, seemingly in disbelief.

"You know, I actually purchased one of Peterson's less-wretched pieces. A boat scene – a fishing boat – surrounded by gulls. Typically amateurish, but a notch or two more accomplished than the bulk of his work, which is uniformly dreadful. Father almost had a fit when he saw it, said it was embarrassing. 'The work of a child,' I think he said. I never hung it. It's up in the attic now, but I'll hang on to it. I paid good money for it, after all. And you never know: Maybe someday Peterson's stuff will be in demand. Doubtful, but you never know; stranger things have happened." He paused for a breath, and I was able to get a word in.

"When did you last see Grace?"

"It's been a while, a couple of months at least," he said, giving it some thought. "Early September. Labor Day weekend, I believe it was. Yes, Labor Day. The McClellan's were with me."

"How often are you here on the island?" I asked.

"Oh, as the spirit moves me. I spend most of my time at our home in Philadelphia, but I visit here fairly regularly. I'm not as taken with the place as father is; it's a bit too rustic for me, not enough excitement, not enough going on. He and mother are of a like mind, however. They love the place, and motor down from the city once a week like clockwork. Unless, of course, there's snow; that's a different story altogether. Otherwise, they arrive here every Friday evening, stay through the weekend and depart early the following Monday morning. And father also takes the train in mid-week, on Wednesdays, and spends the day working out in *The Nook*."

"*The Nook*?" I asked. I figured this question was good for another ten minutes' worth of response.

"Oh, you wouldn't know about that, would you? Father has one of the cottages out back fixed up as an office, or a study, if you will. He frequently locks himself away in there for peace and quiet, no interruptions. His 'Sanity Spells', as he calls them. He'll wander back to the house when he's hungry or wants to talk to someone. *The Nook* is off limits, though; no one goes in there, under threat of disinheritance or disembowelment or having their allowance cut off." He paused for a moment, shaking his head, staring at the floor. "When I was young, ten or so, S.S. pinned me to the wall once when he found me near The Nook. I thought he was going to beat me up or something, but he just pinned me there, my arms held tightly in his fists, feet dangling off the floor, his face an inch or so away from mine. He told me never, ever, to go in there, that father would kill me if he ever caught me near there. Well, it scared the devil out of me, but it got the point across. It's just something that isn't done. Like biting the hand that feeds you." He paused again for a moment or so, and then looked up at me. "Do dogs actually do that, Mr. Porter? Bite the hand that feeds them, I mean? Seems short sighted."

"No dog I've ever owned," I said. The only way Hoover would ever bite me would be by accident, in a frenzied attempt to get to his dog food before the bowl hit the floor. "Who's S.S.? A brother?"

"Yes, my older brother. He moved away years ago. He and father haven't spoken since then."

I wondered why his father chose not to give his first son his name, but didn't ask. I was more interested in the swinging door at the far end of the dining room, some thirty feet beyond Chester. It was ajar several inches, and had been through most of our conversation.

"You have a couple of minutes, haven't you?" asked Chester, rising from his chair. "I'll be back in a jiff," he added, quickly exiting the room. The door in the dining room slowly inched shut. When Chester's footfalls receded into the upstairs, I made my way quietly over to the door, paused, and quickly pushed it open. Or tried to: It only budged several inches before striking something beyond with a loud thud met by a yelp of surprise. I grabbed its edge on the rebound and pulled it open, exposing the maid who'd admitted me minutes earlier. She was rubbing her left forearm, assumedly where the door had struck, and was pink with embarrassment. Her head was down.

"Hear anything interesting?" I asked.

"I...I was just checking to see if Chester needed anything, sir," she responded, hastily. Her response was polite but quiet, almost submissive. Her eyes were planted firmly on the floor at her feet. Maybe the smell was bleach.

"What's your name?"

"Abbey, sir."

"Abbey *what*?"

She paused momentarily, as if contemplating whether or not to trust me with such vital information. "O'...O'Hara," she stammered. I guess she decided I was trustworthy.

"How old are you, Abbey?"

"Sixteen. And three-quarters. Almost seventeen. I'll be seventeen in January."

"How long have you worked for the Hawleys?" I continued. She was more fun than Chester. And not nearly as long winded.

"For a long time now."

"How long is 'long'?"

"They took me in when I was very young, five maybe, and my grandmother could no longer care for me. I've been with them — worked for them — ever since," she responded, quietly.

"Any family?"

"No. At least I don't think so, not that I know of. My parents are both gone: I have no brothers and sisters and there aren't any other relatives that I know of. Not here in the United States, anyway."

"Where were you born?"

"Here. The United States, I mean. In Camden – the Irish section, I think, wherever that is."

"How long did you live there?" I asked. I knew Camden, knew the Irish section – *Potato Hill* they used to call it. Unless she came from Cooper Street. Seemed doubtful, though; it took some money to live on Cooper Street.

"I lived there for a couple of years, or so I'm told, but I don't remember it at all. The Hawleys are my family now. I've been with them since childhood, and they're nice to work for. They're nice to me..."

Her response was cut short with Chester's return. Neither of us had heard his approach, and he looked back and forth between us, undoubtedly trying to figure out *why* we were talking. Abbey shied, almost as if she were afraid of being hit.

"Water," I stated, matter-of-factly, and turned to her. "No ice."

"Yes, sir," she responded quickly. Turning to Chester: "Anything for you, sir?"

"No thank you, Abbey." She disappeared into the kitchen. "How rude of me. I should have offered," he said, but I knew he didn't buy it. Abbey returned, hastily handed me a glass and retreated just as quickly.

"Here, follow me. I have Peterson's painting here." He led me over to a painting that sat on the floor, leaning against the sofa. Surprisingly, it wasn't too bad. Not good, but not *too* bad.

"Better than a lot of 'em," I commented.

"Yes, I thought so. Looks almost like the work of another artist, doesn't it? Everything, of course, is relative, but I figured if I had to be saddled with one of them, this was the least offensive."

The least offensive, perhaps, but still amateurishly executed. It was colorful, I'll give it that. And I suppose it could brighten up the right room. Peterson wasn't destined to be the twentieth century's Winslow Homer, that was for certain.

"No one forced you to buy it. Why'd you bother?"

"Oh, I suppose I felt guilty, visiting the gallery as often as I do with nary an acquisition to show for it. One small painting seemed like a reasonable gesture, and it didn't cost much. I can afford it," he said, as an afterthought. We returned to our chairs.

"You were talking about your brother," I reminded him.

"Oh, yes, S.S. – *Sullivan Stephen* Hawley – but everyone calls him S.S. Or *called* him. As I said before, no one's spoken with him for years. I have an older sister, too. Eunice. She's married, kids and all that, lives up in Albany, of all places. Mother and father, of course. We have the help here: Abbey, whom you've met, evidently, and Milton, our groundskeeper. There are others, of course – all locals – whom we employ at various times during the year as needed, primarily during the spring and summer months. Our primary domicile in Philadelphia – Bala Cynwyd, actually, on the outskirts of Philadelphia – has many more: There's Ellington, Martha, Bonnie...."

"That's really not necessary," I interrupted. "Back to Grace Peterson. Any thoughts on what might have become of her?"

"None whatsoever. Although, I must say, with her looks and intelligence she could write her own ticket. I never could figure out what she sees in that husband of hers. Quite frankly, I felt the fellow to be somewhat of a loser. A lucky one, perhaps, having landed her as a wife, but a loser nonetheless. Her attraction to him was a mystery to me."

"Want to hazard a guess? About her disappearance, I mean."

"Well, I suppose the logical conclusion would be that she woke up one day, realized she couldn't stomach the fellow and took off. And with all of the eligible males expressing interest in her, it would have been reasonably easy for her to connect with one and make a painless exit. But that's solely supposition, you understand," he added quickly.

"You sure that's all it is? You sure you haven't heard anything that might reinforce your supposition? Some gossip, comments made at the club, anything like that?"

"Listen, Porter," he said, somewhat testily. "I've told you what little I know. What the devil's your interest in all this? Jealousy, perhaps? She treat you like she treated the rest of us? *Worse*, perhaps? Is that it?"

I felt like slapping that stupid monocle out of his head, but restrained myself.

"Hardly," I said. "Never met the woman. But she and *my wife* are good friends and my wife is worried sick about her. I'd like to be able to toss her some small morsel of information that would appease her fears, put her mind at ease. My wife, I mean. Calm her down." And get her off my back.

"Oh, I see," he responded, knowingly. "I suppose wives *can* get on your nerves. If you let them. Well, what else do you want to know?"

"I guess that's it. Here's my number," I said as I handed him a scrap of paper with my name and number printed on it. If I did much more of this stuff I'd need business cards printed up. "I'd appreciate it if you'd let me know if you *do* hear of anything that might have a bearing on her disappearance, or a lead to her whereabouts," I added, standing.

"Very well," he responded, following my lead. "I'll walk you to your car. I have a 4:00 engagement. Weekly thing, simply can't miss it," he added, looking at his watch as we walked. "I should have just enough time."

I thanked him for his time, climbed into the Ford and headed out the drive. I slowed a half block south, cut across the north-bound lane onto a side street, made a U-turn, then slid into a spot with a view of the Hawley's drive. I fired up another De Nobili and smoked for maybe ten minutes before Chester drove by in an immaculate brown-and-tan '31 Cadillac V16 Fleetwood Imperial sedan. Milton must have spent as much time washing and waxing this beauty as he did working on the grounds.

Abbey would be alone inside now and I wanted to resume our conversation. She'd listened in on Chester and me, and I could think of several reasons why she'd do so. The probable explanation was that Abbey, simply put, was a compulsive snoop, and listened in on a lot of Hawley conversations. The other possibility, however, was that in telling her I wanted to speak with Chester about Grace Peterson, I had piqued her interest. If so, I wanted to know why. I hoofed it back to the Hawley property and down the curving drive to the front door.

Abbey answered the door a half minute after my knock, and was visibly shaken by my return. She quickly stammered that Chester was gone. I told her I was aware of that, that it was her I wanted to talk to. I moved forward into the house as I spoke; she backed up to make way for me.

"Where were we?" I continued. "Tell me about your position here, your duties. You care for all of them, by yourself?" I had her backed into the main hallway now. It was fun when they cowered.

"Just Mr. and Mrs. Hawley. And Chester, of course."

"The others?"

"Others?"

"Eunice. S.S."

"Oh. Eunice got married and moved away in the summer of 1931…and S.S…I'm not sure where he is. He's not around here, at least. He's been gone since I was a child, eight or nine – the late '20s – before Eunice got married. The Hawleys never speak of him, at least not in front of me."

Abbey's shyness seemed to break somewhat. Due to her comfort with the subjects being discussed? Due to her loneliness and the desire to talk to someone – anyone? Or, just as likely, simply the fact that none of her employers were in the house and she was able to talk. Perhaps a combination of the three. Whatever the reason, she was loosening up somewhat.

"What are your duties?" I asked.

"Oh, a little bit of everything: cleaning, washing, cooking, serving, stocking supplies – most everything."

"Must be some juggling act," I said, considering the scope of her duties.

"Yes, it is. But I've gotten quite good at it and I have plenty of time to keep on top of it, using the days they're not here to catch up. The summer's more difficult: Someone or other's here most all of the time." She was actually smiling a perceptible smile now. Maybe she was warming to me, which would make this easier. Not much to look at, but she did have youth on her side. At my age, that counted for a lot.

"You here all of the time? Year 'round? Ever go to Philadelphia, or wherever their other house is?"

"Bala Cynwyd. No. Here's my home, and here I stay."

"Do you get out much?" I asked. Her existence was beginning to sound like a rather bleak one. Get thee to a nunnery.

"Out? No, never; I'm expected to be here whenever they need me, day or night. And even on the days they aren't here, the missus is always calling to remind me of something or to change her plans. And while she's unfailingly pleasant when things go her way, she's, well, less so on those occasions when I don't answer the telephone on her first attempt. But I have everything I need right here, so it's all right."

"What about food? Don't you go to one of the markets for food and things?"

"No, I just order what we need by telephone – food and any other provisions. The island's shopkeepers are all very obliging and the ones we deal with all deliver – and very promptly."

"You never leave the place?" I asked, incredulously. It sounded more like a prison than a job.

"No, there's no reason to. Well, once in a while I go into the yard, to hang laundry or just to get some fresh air, but I place the pantry telephone in an open window so I'll hear it ring. I always get to it by the second ring," she added, a touch of pride in her voice.

Mrs. Hawley must be *some* bitch. But now: enough of the small talk and on to the good stuff.

"Tell me about Chester," I said, nonchalantly.

Abbey hesitated, the faint smile now fading from her face. She met and avoided my gaze several times. Guess she didn't like me anymore.

"Father or son? Or both?" she asked, a suspicious tone to her voice.

"The son, Chester. The third."

"What about him?"

"Well, is he nice to work for?" It was a lame question, but I needed to ease into this.

"Yes."

"What does he do?"

"Do? Well, he went to college – several of them, actually – for years. He's lived here – here and in Bala Cynwyd – ever since he graduated in the summer of 1934."

"No job?" I knew the answer to this one.

"No, he doesn't have a job." She didn't seem to want to talk about Chester.

"Does he have a girlfriend?"

She quickly looked up at me, but I couldn't read her expression.

"No," she responded, immediately and emphatically.

"How about you? You have a boyfriend?"

"A boyfriend? No. What makes you think that? How could I possibly have…"

"Okay," I interrupted. "I get the point."

She was staring at the floor and looked very uncomfortable.

"Are you finished, sir? May I go now?" she asked, quietly and sheepishly.

"Almost," I said, gently. I felt sorry for her, and for what appeared to be a miserable existence. But I wasn't so sure that she viewed it as such.

"Tell me, Abbey," I continued, calmly, "do you really like it here, cooped up and isolated from the rest of the world?"

She nodded her head "yes," but didn't say a word. I didn't buy it.

"Listen to me, Abbey. It's a free country. You can leave here anytime you want, day or night. No one can force you to continue working here if you don't want to." Sounded like hokum to me, but I pressed on. "You can leave any time. No need to feel any guilt or sense of obligation." My words fell on deaf ears.

"The Hawleys have been really good to me," she said quietly.

"I'm sure they have, but you've been really good to them, too. And for a lot of years. You don't owe them anything at this point. Nothing at all."

"Even if I never get out of the house," she continued, oblivious to my last comments, "even if I'm always expected to be here, the work isn't that hard. And I'm comfortable." She had resumed eye contact.

I knew then that she'd die there.

"Abbey, there's more to life..."

"They've educated me, I have a nice room, a radio. I'm well fed, new clothes, doctor bills paid..." she trailed off momentarily, her eyes leaving mine. She turned a step, busying her hands in her apron. Something she had said. Something she *regretted* having said. She forced herself to continue: "The work here is, uh, fairly easy most of the year, and I...I love the island." She turned back to me and looked at me. "Have you lived here all your life, Mr. Porter? Tell me about it."

Silence fell on the room, with only the cries of some distant gulls and the ticking of the grandfather clock filling the void.

Now, from my experience, there are several types of liars to be found in this world. The first are the natural liars: They lie frequently and effortlessly, the lies imperceptibly woven into the fabric of their conversation. It's impossible to determine where truth leaves off and fiction begins. That is, of course, if you even expect that what you're hearing is something less than the whole truth.

The second type are the common liars, like most of us. We think through the lie and use it cautiously and with a lot of planning – and a good deal of acting and sweating the details. Most of the time we're successful; but it's an effort, and not always a successful one. And, if we trip up, we stumble to regain our course – and that's when we're usually caught, if we're ever going to be caught.

And then there're people like Abbey. It's as if she had a scarlet letter hanging from her neck, this one an "L" for "Liar." She's so obvious in her attempts to lie or, as now, avoid the truth or an unpleasant topic, that a five year old would pick up on it. And I'm a few years older than that.

So, what was it? *Doctor bills?* This didn't sound right and it wasn't *what* she said but *how* she said it, and the clumsy way she carried herself after she said it. Or maybe it was something she said moments earlier that just dawned on her. Either way, it was gonna be fun.

"Who's your doctor? Someone here on the island?"

"No," she said quietly, tensing.

"Havens? Delaney?"

"No."

"Over on the mainland?" I persisted. "Elliott, in Manahawkin? Or Freitag?"

"No."

"Who then?"

Silence.

"Who then?" I repeated, firmly.

"Dr…Dr. Kaye," she finally responded.

"Kaye? Never heard of him. Where's he practice?"

"Some…somewhere over on the mainland, I don't know exactly where," she answered. I could barely hear her.

I looked her over. She'd spent the last ten years of her life on this island, and as a prisoner of sorts. The only time she leaves is to go to a doctor. My curiosity was piqued. "You're young. You appear healthy enough. Why this Dr. Kaye? Why not use one of the locals? Were you sick enough to warrant a specialist?" And, I thought, the sizable doctor bills that would accompany one.

"No," she said, this time emphatically, and loud enough to be heard. Several rooms away.

"Abbey, is something wrong?" I asked, as calmly and reassuringly as I could. "Is there something you want to tell me, but are afraid to – or embarrassed to – about the Hawleys, or living here? Anything at all?" I couldn't imagine why she would confide in me, but I regarded it as somewhat of a challenge.

Timid little Abbey suddenly turned on me like a cat whose tail had just been stepped on, eyes ablaze, teeth clenched, back stiffened, tiny little fists clenched.

"Mr. Porter, I'm going to have to ask you to leave. You shouldn't be here. It isn't right that you're here," she stated, with as much force as she could muster. "You're interfering with my duties and if you don't leave immediately I'll be forced to call the police. I'll call the police *and* inform the Hawleys: *Do you realize just how important they are? Important and – and how* powerful *they are?*"

I had trouble keeping a straight face. Little Abbey, trying to play tough, trying to intimidate me. Pretty feeble attempt, but she's new at it I guessed. Must be listening to too many radio shows. Okay, sister, two can play this game. Lesson number one.

The smile spread slowly across my face and I knew it looked nasty. Words froze in her mouth and her eyes went wide as I stepped in on her.

"*Important*, eh?" I muttered. "*Powerful?*"

She stumbled back on uncertain feet until her back hit the wall, and I was right there. "Sit down!" I snapped as I grabbed her firmly by her upper arms, ready to throw her onto a nearby Chesterfield.

Now, I was forceful, I suppose, but everything's relative: I'd grabbed her more with the force you'd use on a ten year old than an adult. Seemed appropriate at the time, but I never expected the response I elicited: She screamed in pain the instant I tightened my hands on her arms, screamed the slurred words "My arms!" in as agonized a voice as I'd ever heard. I immediately let go, as much out of surprise as concern that I'd actually hurt her. She slumped to the floor, arms crossed in front of her, hands futilely protecting her upper arms, eyes red with tears and face contorted with sobs.

Nice work, tough guy.

I knelt in front of her, gently moved one of her shaking hands aside and carefully pulled up her sleeve. Her arm was a mass of vicious bruises and a quick check of the other arm revealed a mass of similar markings. Then I saw what looked to be the makeup-covered edge of yet another discolored patch peeking out from the high neck of her blouse. I popped the top button, tugged her collars aside, and found her chest to have similar bruises and abrasions. I hadn't seen anything this vicious on a woman since my days back in Camden. Nasty. Well hidden and nasty.

"Who did this to you?" I asked, a steely edge to my voice, fury welling up inside me.

Her eyes were shut tight, tears streaming down her cheeks. She shook her head back and forth, silently refusing to respond.

"Chester? Was it Chester?" I yelled. I knew the answer.

"Please, oh, please," she sobbed. "You don't understand. We're in love. Please don't say anything to him."

"Was it Chester?" I repeated. I wanted confirmation.

She sat there silently for a good half minute, wiping her eyes with the back of a sleeve and sniffing to keep her nose from running. Now she looked more like a twelve year old. Finally, she regained some semblance of composure, took a long, deep breath and looked me in the eye.

"Yes, it's Chester. But it's not what you think!" she quickly added.

"What is it?" I queried.

"Listen, I know you won't believe this, but listen to me. Chester and I are in love. We have been for some while now. It's just that he doesn't want his parents to know, not now, at least, not until the time is right, and then we'll tell them and get married and have a family. But the time has to be right." She blurted this out quickly, hoping to convince me.

"He tells you he loves you and then he does *this* to you?"

"You don't understand. He's very passionate, very physical, very…very…oh! I'm so in love with him and he's so in love with me! It's…it's like we're married already, but we have to keep it secret for a while, just a short while longer, until Chester gets some money thing settled with his father. But *please*, you can't tell anyone!"

It was obvious that she was infatuated with Chester and equally obvious that the guy was taking liberal advantage of her. Of her youth and naiveté, both emotionally and, it appeared, physically.

"Chester says that I'm the only one who understands him, the only one who can help him. He says I'm 'special', and not like any of the other women he's known," she continued. "It's just...just... sometimes, when we're making love, sometimes he...uh...gets carried away and hurts me. He doesn't mean to, and he feels so bad about it afterwards. He cries."

"He's done this to you before?"

She didn't answer my question. She didn't have to.

"It...it's his mother's fault. She's never shown him any love and that hurt him...and sometimes he lashes out. It's his cry for help, for love. I'm helping him. We're working on this together. He doesn't like hurting me, he really doesn't," she continued. "But we're working on it, and he promises me he'll stop. And I believe him."

I wasn't sure whether she was trying to convince me or convince herself. Probably both. Either way, I wasn't buying it.

"He *told* you this, Chester did?" I asked, trying to keep my sarcasm in check.

"Oh, yes. Afterwards, after...everything, he comes back to my bed and comforts me and we talk, for a long time. He's really not like you think he is. But, please, Mr. Porter – you *have* to promise you won't say anything to his parents! Not now, not ever. Chester will have his own money soon, we'll get married. and everything will be... fine. We'll...we'll be happy together – forever – and we'll have babies. Lots of babies."

I was momentarily stunned. Not only had the son of a bitch screwed this poor kid on a regular basis and used her as his own personal punching bag, but he was dangling the old marriage carrot in front of her as bait, as well. And good, old Dr. Kaye probably patched her up each time, with a practice far enough away that word wouldn't get back to the island. Chester may have lost control, but he seemed to retain a certain measure of self-preservation by confining his battering to areas that would be hidden by Abbey's clothing.

"Listen, Abbey, listen carefully: You don't have to put up with this, with any of this. Not with Chester, not with his crazy family. You can leave anytime you want. And if you're too scared to, call me – I'll take you out of here." I pulled out my pad of paper and quickly wrote "Lew Porter. Beach Haven 49" on it, and handed the scrap to her. She looked at it briefly, shook her head and tried to return it. I didn't take it, so she tucked it into her apron pocket.

"But…but I want to stay. I love him. And he loves me. Don't you understand?"

I understood, all right. Chester was using her as his own personal plaything and feeding her an ongoing line of bullshit about love, money, marriage and how nobody understands poor, old Chester. I felt like finding the creep and giving him the beating of his life, one that he wouldn't – *couldn't* – ever forget. I felt like it, but knew I wouldn't: I don't do that stuff anymore. And even if I did, it would only cause Abbey to love the son of a bitch that much more. Seen it happen plenty of times.

There was no convincing her that he was using her, that his intentions were something considerably less than noble, that their relationship was doomed. We talked for a while longer, but I finally gave up trying to get through to her. After some thinly veiled admonitions that she should be *careful*, I wished her the best of luck – she'd need it – and left.

I wasn't going to waste any more time on her. I had enough other things to waste my time on without throwing Abbey and her problems into the mix. I'd given it my best shot, and that was none too good. But I knew I wasn't going to shake her from my thoughts that easily – the whole affair just ticked me off too much.

And me? I wasn't doing so well with my quest, either. I came here to find out about Grace Peterson and ended up with Chester's sordid little affair dumped in my lap. And Chester? Oh, how I disliked this fellow.

I was about to pull out onto the road when I noticed the middle-aged woman in the backyard of the adjacent home. She was going through the motions of hanging laundry, but her eyes were locked on me giving me the once over. I waved to her and she gave a tentative wave back, quickly returning her attention to her wash. Snoopy, old broad – but there were more than a few like her on the island.

Climbing into my car, I spotted Maggie Rowland about a hundred yards north on the boulevard, perched atop her horse Rudolph. Maggie was High Point's mail deliverer and Rudolph was an old gelding named after Valentino – pretty funny, now that I think about it. I knew her father, Stanley – had some drinks with him more than once – and as a result knew more about Maggie than I probably should have. I knew Maggie herself only slightly, but she was always unfailingly pleasant and friendly even when the weather was miserable and her deliveries had become an ordeal.

She was making her late-afternoon rounds, sorting through some letters, as I pulled up and got out. After several minutes of the requisite pleasantries, I worked my way around to the subject of the Petersons. She didn't care for Howard at all, said he was a strange, unlikable fellow. She hadn't seen Grace recently, last time several days before her disappearance.

The disappearance, by the way, was the talk of the town, but no one she knew would fault Grace for leaving the bum. Everyone had their own opinion as to how she should have handled it, of course, and weren't hesitant about voicing it. The abrupt termination of their relationship had been met with almost unanimous approval, with the exception of a handful of local merchants who viewed the loss of a customer – potentially two – on a more practical level.

"He *really* got weird over the last couple of months – weird and *scary*."

"How so?" I asked.

She looked both ways. "You got a taste on you?"

I produced the flask. She downed a hearty swig.

"Well, I guess it was back in August – all the summer people were here – and Grace had the easels out front. You know: the ones with Howard's paintings." She returned the flask.

"Yeah." Rudolph looked impatient.

"So, for a number of weeks running, Howard was out front, sitting on the stoop, waiting for the mail. And I mean every single time I came by."

"That was unusual, I take it?"

"*Very*. Up until that point I might have seen Howard – oh, I don't know – maybe half a dozen times in as many years. And now, all of a sudden, there he is, every single time. He'd jump up, come over to meet me, grunt a 'hello' or whatever – if he grunted anything at all – and quickly sort through the mail."

"Any idea what he was looking for?"

"Not at first. Then, maybe a week or so into this ritual, he shoved a letter back at me, said he refused receipt. Well, I took a look at it and it was addressed to Grace, not him. And he was making such a fuss about it that I just naturally had to look at the return address…"

"And?"

"It didn't have a name, just initials: 'RK' and a return address that included the 'Pallette Building'. Probably wouldn't have remembered that except the building's name reminded me of that actor, you know, the guy with the gravelly voice – Eugene Pallette."

"*My Man Godfrey*. He had the best lines"

"Yeah. *Shanghai Express*, too. What was the one with Paul Muni? Bette Davis was his wife? Pallette's, I mean."

"*Bordertown*, I think."

"Sounds right. Anyway, the return address stuck with me; funny the way that happens sometimes."

"Yeah."

"So, I told Howard in no uncertain terms that *he* couldn't refuse receipt of a letter addressed to Grace, only Grace could do that. And what do you think he did?"

"Tell me."

"He started screaming for Grace, telling her to get out there immediately. Poor Grace probably thought he was dying or something, the way she rushed out. And then he told her what he'd just told me, and told her to back him up, told her to tell me *she* refused receipt."

"Did she?"

"Well, yeah, kind of. Yeah, she did; but my impression was that she did so more to appease her baby of a husband than to refuse genuinely unwanted mail. Christ, what a character. Then Howard chimed in that any future mail bearing that return address should be returned, too, and that he – that *Grace* – would fill out any forms necessary to back up that request. Well, not too surprisingly, many more letters arrived from 'RK' in the weeks that followed. Each one stranger – sadder – than the last."

"Stranger? How so?"

"Well, each new piece bore an increasing number of childish scribbles professing an undying love for Grace. I mean, scribbled all over the envelopes, front and back, up the sides. Really gushy stuff – *embarrassing* stuff. It was awkward as hell for me, but it was pretty clear why Howard got so fired up and acted the way he did regarding the deliveries."

"So, what did you do?"

"Do? Nothing. I mean, I've got a dozen or so of these letters stuffed in here." She patted the outside pocket of her leather mail pouch. "I was going to give them to Grace some day when I ran across her alone, with Howard out of the picture." She shrugged. "That day never came."

"Mind if I take a look at the outsides of some of them?"

Maggie paused, stunned at the question. She quickly glanced about to see if we were unobserved. Satisfied, she unbuckled the flap. "Guess looking at the outsides can't hurt none. But just the outsides." She handed me the wad of letters.

The outsides made for interesting, if somewhat embarrassing, reading – grade school stuff, and not at all threatening. The return addresses were as Maggie had described them, but more so: *Lenox and 132nd, NYC.* I stood there shaking my head.

"See what I mean?" she asked. "Puppy love, huh? Well, someone out there's got it bad for her."

"Yeah, it would seem so. Well, thanks Maggie; I appreciate the info. And keep me posted if you hear anything more about all this," I said, handing the stack of envelopes back to her. She stuffed them back into her pouch without a second look, and didn't notice that I'd pocketed one of them – the one with the most recent postmark of October 10.

Against the law, I suppose, but I didn't think anyone would miss it. No one at all.

That evening I gave a brief accounting of the day's events to Holly, skipping over most of the detail with the promise that I'd fill her in fully in a day or so. I *did* tell her about the letters to Grace, and she immediately came up with the brilliant idea that I should take a trip into Manhattan and track down their source. Now, a trip into Manhattan for the best of reasons wasn't my idea of fun – and to make the trip solely to track down some lovesick idiot made the prospect even less appealing. On the other hand, this was a possible lead to her whereabouts and Holly's unique powers of persuasion battered me into submission. I agreed to go, and on the following day, as much to get it all over with as to act before a lukewarm lead turned frosty.

Manhattan. Camden. Might as well go to Hell.

Wednesday, October 28, 1936. 5:32 a.m.

THE ALARM JOLTED me from a deep sleep at 4:30 and it was still pitch black out. I stumbled out of bed, shaved with only a few bloody nicks, showered outside in what had to be the coldest shower of my life, then gulped down some breakfast and tepid black coffee, reheated from the previous day's pot; it was terrible, but effective.

How to dress for New York was the next issue. I'd been living on the island for so long that I'd lost whatever touch I'd once had with the clothing of choice out there in the real world. Attire that wouldn't warrant a second look in this region would probably get you shipped back to Ellis Island if you had the balls to wear it uptown in the city. Since I had no burning desire to be placed on a slow boat back to Eastern Europe, I dressed in an old suit and tie, and found an equally old pair of dust-covered shoes far back in the closet. *Twelve-years-old* old and far from stylish, but what the hell. At least I'd be better dressed than the vagrants.

There were only two trains into New York City and they departed from the mainland town of Barnegat every Wednesday and Saturday at 6:35 a.m. The first leg of the trip was on the Tuckerton Railroad, with a connection made in Whiting for the remainder of the journey on the Central Railroad of New Jersey.

There had been passenger service between Beach Haven and Barnegat on the Tuckerton Railroad up until 1930, but that was eliminated due to lack of use. Once-a-day freight service continued until November of 1935, when a violent nor'easter wiped out a large section of the bridge between the island and mainland. They never bothered to replace it and fifty years of rail service on the island came to an abrupt end.

I got the Ford started and made the cold, quiet drive to Barnegat; the nearly-full moon providing a surprising amount of illumination. I paid my $1.25 for the round-trip, then climbed aboard the lone passenger car and waited for its departure. The pleasant smell of burning leaves filled the air, which seemed like a strange task for someone to undertake at this early hour of the morning. No more strange, perhaps, than going into Manhattan on a potentially wild goose chase – but strange nonetheless.

The trip itself was uneventful. We rumbled slowly through miles of uninterrupted pines, which were barely discernible in the twilight of early morning. We made our connection in Whiting and continued on. I killed the time reading a copy of S.S. Van Dine's mystery *The Casino Murder Case* – figured it would put me in the mood for Manhattan – if not Manhattanites. I'd been meaning to read it before his next book, *The Kidnap Murder Case*, hit the stores in December of this year. The series' recurring protagonist, Philo Vance, was an incredibly annoying fop, but the mysteries themselves were engaging and Van Dine played fairly.

The sun shone brightly overhead when the Manhattan skyline finally appeared on the horizon, partially obscured by a gray haze. The city's like an aging whore: it looks seductive and beautiful from afar, but up close the filth and decay belies the promise.

We arrived at the Jersey City Depot at the end of Johnson Avenue and I took the ferry across the Hudson to the Liberty Street Depot in Manhattan. I later realized that this was the first – and worst – choice of the two available ferries, the second being the more northerly ferry to the Twenty-Third Street Depot. The one I took, unfortunately, placed me at the ass-end of the city. I hoofed it several blocks east on Liberty, then stopped a guy on the street for directions to the closest subway. He sent me to the Cortland Street entrance of the Broadway-Seventh Avenue local, where I boarded a northbound train. I managed to read a few more pages before we arrived at One

Hundred Thirty-Seventh Street, and from there I again hoofed it east from Broadway. I passed the Hebrew Orphan Asylum, cut through St. Nicholas Park and finally, after several wrong turns, found Lenox. I headed south to One Hundred Thirty-Second Street and arrived at the intersection with spirits low and feet growing sore. Holly had reiterated just how short and walkable the blocks were when heading north or south and, once again, I was glad I hadn't taken her advice, as well intentioned as it might have been. East and west was another story.

The neighborhood was predominately colored, the dwellings predominantly residential. Tired of wandering semi-aimlessly, I approached an older man sitting on a step, drinking from a bottle cloaked in a brown paper bag. It was still fairly early in the morning – I had a fifty-fifty shot that some of his mental faculties were still functioning – and the guy would be coherent. Asked him if he knew where The Pallette Building was located. Must have been lonely for companionship, because he embarked on a concise verbal history of the area, its buildings and its residents. This lasted at least five minutes. Told me how this area had been mostly open plain until the 1880s, when construction of the elevated trains up Eighth Avenue had prompted a wave of development. Row house after row house was erected, similar in design to those flanking Central Park, and sold to upper-class white folk yearning for the wide open spaces. The area's status had diminished somewhat by the end of the war and by the mid-'20s the area had started to integrate. A short ten years later, the street was predominately colored and many of the former residences had been converted to rooming houses. Others, like the one on whose steps he was sitting, had been converted to businesses. And, by the way, *this* building was The Pallette Building. I suppose I should have felt foolish, but how in hell are you supposed to know where a building is if you don't have a building number and there's no sign on the front? My new friend was amused nonetheless.

The Pallette Building was nothing more than a three-story row house, the end portion of a five-unit structure and, as a result of its positioning, the only one with windows on its side as well as its front. It appeared to be constructed of brownstone at the basement and stoop levels, with a lighter stone, maybe limestone, at the higher levels. All of it, however, was now dark and dingy from years of accumulated soot and grime. A slightly lighter rectangle of stone to the right of the front entrance suggested that a sign might at one time have occupied this spot and identified the building. If so, it was just a memory now.

A sign inside the front entrance listed the building's occupants and there were about a dozen of them. That seemed like a lot for this structure until I realized that The Pallette Building actually occupied several adjacent row houses, with doorways knocked through the walls from building to building. I gave the list a quick read in hopes of tracking down the mysterious 'RK' and fourth on the list was "Ralph Kelly Accountants, 3rd Floor." I entered their offices a minute later and faced a bored-looking middle-aged woman perched behind her desk.

"Is Mr. Kelly in?" I asked.

"No, I'm sorry, he isn't," she responded, pleasantly enough. "Can someone else help you? Would you like to speak with Mr. Ralph, perhaps?"

I hesitated for a moment while I absorbed what she had just said.

"What's Mr. Kelly's first name?" I asked, hoping for some clarification of this now-cloudy issue.

"Why, George," she answered, puzzled by my line of questioning.

"Anyone with the initials 'RK' work here?"

She paused as she silently converted a short list of names to a short list of initials, and responded.

"No. No one at all."

I wasn't doing so well. Evidently, the Ralph and Kelly of Ralph Kelly Accountants were two people, not one. I backed out with a quick, vague apology, returned to the lobby, reviewed the list and decided that I'd have to track RK down the old fashioned way: on foot and by mouth.

I visited ten of the remaining eleven businesses, saving the eleventh and largest for last, and grew increasingly frustrated as each gave me a similar response: "No RK here."

The eleventh, Fanfare Films, occupied two of the row houses' first floors, from side-to-side and for their full seventy-foot depth, as well as a handful of rooms on one of the buildings' second floors. As I entered I realized that Fanfare Films differed in another way than just size: It was the only business in the Palette Building which appeared to be staffed solely, or at least predominately, by Negroes. The small, front room was piled high with files, papers, boxes and a lot of other unidentifiable stuff. A woman sat behind a small, battered, similarly cluttered desk, filing her long nails. Light-skinned with freckles, she wore her hair pulled back in the tightest bun I'd ever seen, and did her best to ignore me. I didn't give her much of a chance, though, because I was tired and wanted to finish this up – and get a drink somewhere. I asked her if there was an RK working there. Unlike the others, she consulted a typewritten list in her exercise of converting names to initials. She even put her nail file down to do so.

"No. No RK. Only person here with last initial of K'd be 'Pathé,' 'Pathé' Knauss. And P's no R," she responded. She sounded like she wished she could go back to sleep.

"'Pathé'?" I repeated. "That's not his real first name, is it?" If it was, it was a stupid one.

"No, nobody have a first name like that. Real name's Bobby. Bobby Knauss. But everybody calls him 'Pathé' 'cause he lied to get the job, said he worked for some highfalutin' French moving picture company name of Pathé something or other." She frowned.

"What is it?" I asked.

"What's *falutin'* mean?"

"Beats me."

"Anyway, Pathé something…"

Probably Pathé Frères. I vaguely recalled the name attached to some of the foreign imports I saw as a kid. Maybe on the films of Max Linder, the comedian; but I couldn't recall for sure. Regardless, Knauss' first name must have been Robert, which gave me the sought after RK. Bingo. I asked her where I could find Bobby, and she told me that she wasn't sure where he was — asked if I wanted to speak with the boss, Mr. Goldberg. He might know Bobby's whereabouts and we'd probably have a lot in common. The only guy I'd probably have much in common with would be the owner of the small bar I'd spotted around the corner on Lenox, but that would have to wait. Told her I'd like to speak with Goldberg and she took care of the rest. She couldn't wait to get rid of me.

Sheldon Goldberg was a short, squat man with wide shoulders, a large belly and a five o'clock shadow that looked like smudged soot. Told him I was looking for Bobby Knauss, but Goldberg seemed more interested in talking about himself and his studio.

"We produce films here, 'race' films. Have been for over four years now. We make 'em for colored audiences, *Oscar Micheaux*-type stuff, but more risqué. Know how many theaters there are in the US?" I didn't. "Over *twenty thousand*, that's how many. And of those twenty thousand, only a couple hundred are what we call 'ghetto' theaters. Used to be over seven hundred of 'em, but the Depression and talkies wiped out the lion's share of 'em. And *that*, my friend, is our rather limited market. Oh, there're some special showings in white theaters in a few places, but the coloreds prefer their own theaters, even if they're falling apart, and poorly ventilated and heated. And that's 'cause they feel most comfortable with their own, in their own little rat-traps where they can relax and let loose, where they can interact not only with each other, but also with the film being shown. Ever sneak into a colored theater and watch the group dynamics?" I hadn't. "Well, it's a hell of a show: nothing like us uptight white folk. They know how to have a good time, and we're helping them out by making these movies. We keep the stories simple and fill 'em with the obligatory dance numbers – lots of pretty girls with lots of pretty legs. Those poor guys stuck down south eat this stuff up. We shoot 'em here and wherever we can get a decent location, *cheap*. Single takes and short schedules. Here, follow me, we'll see if we can track down Pathé."

He led me out of his office and gave me what amounted to a mini-tour of the modest complex, talking over his shoulder to me the whole time.

"We're filming *Hell in Harlem* now, a crime film about the protection racket here in Harlem. Next month it'll be *Harlem on the Range* – a western, as if you couldn't guess; we'll film that one over in the woods in New Jersey, make it look like the old west. What we actually do is take your typical Hollywood movie and redo it with a racial slant. Can't be one of the real popular movies – that'd be too obvious. But one of the better second-string films, those are the ones for us."

We paused in front of a tiny stage where a good-looking colored couple was quietly rehearsing their lines. Technicians were nowhere to be seen, so I assumed they must be on a break, lunch perhaps. Which reminded me just how hungry I was.

"That's our big star, Julius Phillips. We bill him as the 'Black Gable.' Micheaux's got Lorenzo Tucker, 'the Colored William Powell'; Bee Freeman, 'the Sepia Mae West'; Slick Chester, 'the Colored Cagney'; and Ethel Moses, 'the Negro Harlow'; so why not? We got a new guy in this film, plays the big mobster, an actor named 'Tiny' Washington. We're gonna bill him as 'the Negro Edward G. Robinson.' Catchy, huh?"

"She looks white," I commented, nodding to the pretty young actress before us.

"Yeah, well, we try to star 'light brights' – light-skinned Negroes; makes the films easier to sell." He looked around the otherwise empty room. "Knauss is our cameraman, only white guy on the crew.

Used to be a still photographer for a fashion photography business, but that folded some years back. Couldn't find a job after that 'cause of his bad reputation, with the drinking and all. So, we got him – and for peanuts. Came in here telling us he worked for Pathé Frères in France – what a load of shit. Taught himself how the movie cameras work, though, and actually does a pretty decent job. Film always in focus and properly framed. Mornings are his best 'cause he's sober then. After lunch he starts to slow down – and after five o'clock, forget it. But we're always done by then, I make sure of that."

I asked if he knew where I could find Bobby and he named a place called "Willie's" just around the corner on Lenox. He said it was a colored place with colored clientele, but Bobby persisted in going there at breaks because it was the closest place to get a drink, and was such a regular there now that nobody gave him a second notice anymore. He inquired about my interest in Knauss, and I instinctively made up a story about our being second cousins; my mother, a cousin of Knauss' father, asked me to look him up while I was in the city. Goldberg looked like he lost track midway through, and like he really didn't care all that much. I scribbled my name, address, and telephone number on a piece of paper for Goldberg to give to Knauss in case I didn't track him down and thanked him for the tour.

Willie's, it turned out, was the saloon I'd spotted earlier on my arrival. It was a rundown little hole-in-the-wall joint and I almost choked on the smoke when I entered. I fired up a De Nobili in self-defense and gave the room a quick once over for Knauss. He was easy enough to locate, being the only white face, the only face not staring at me. Knauss was staring blankly at the tabletop in front of him, two empty shot glasses and a half-full beer in front of him. The fingers of his left hand were wrapped around the beer, and the burning stub of a cigarette jutted out from between them. I got a couple of ryes at the bar and left a dollar, then wandered back to Knauss' table and sat. He gladly accepted the glass I shoved over to him.

Knauss had looked okay from several feet back, but up close was a different story. He had all the telltale signs of an alcohol-ravaged chain smoker, and his nose looked like it would explode if you pinched it. A bad set of snow-white dentures finished off the picture and looked horribly out of place in his pasty face. After verifying that he was indeed Bobby Knauss, I explained that Grace Peterson was a mutual friend of ours, that I lived near her on the island. Told him she asked that I say hello while I was in the city. This last piece of news brought his head up, a look of hope spreading across his features, like the look on a dog's face when you wave a scrap of meat in front of him. He started to talk about Grace – and once he started you couldn't get him to stop.

He explained that he had been Grace's still photographer back in the '20s initially assigned to her sessions on an occasional basis and eventually working his way up to photographer of choice. He was infatuated with her, but she, always pleasant and personable, kept things strictly on a professional basis. And then, one day, he learned that she had quit the business and run off with a guy named Peterson. He eventually tracked down her address in High Point and began sending her letters. At first she responded, letter for letter, but as his frequency of correspondence increased, hers dropped off. He had finally taken the big step, professing his undying love for her and willingness to rescue her from the wilds of New Jersey, but her response to that letter was short and to the point: forget it, and stop bothering her. Undaunted, he began writing to her on a daily basis, but she hadn't responded again since her note of rejection. He was confident that Howard Peterson's allure would eventually evaporate, that she'd grow bored with the isolation and sleepy pace of life on Long Beach Island, and that ultimately she'd return to the city – and to his loving arms. But it had been years since he actually last saw her – probably four or so – and her refusal to acknowledge his letters frustrating.

This guy was a mess. Reading between the lines, I figured he'd started drinking heavily after she got married, and that had cost him his previous job. And, as his drinking worsened, his letters to her had probably gotten sloppier and more overt, degenerating to a point where she wanted nothing more to do with the guy. Who would? He'd returned to staring blankly at the tabletop, head bobbing slightly, lost in a drunken stupor. Goldberg wasn't going to get any more work out of Bobby today. I thanked him and said goodbye, but I doubted he'd remember.

I grabbed a cab back to the Liberty Street Depot and caught the 5:05 p.m. train back to Barnegat.

The clock struck eleven moments before I entered the tiny room Holly used for writing. I settled wearily on a nearby stool, pulled off my shoes and rubbed my aching feet while waiting for her to reach a breaking-off point. Half a minute later, she set down her pen, half turned in her chair and smiled at me.

"Hi. How did it go?" she said, expecting a full report of my findings and knowing that I wanted to put this all behind me.

"Well, here's the way I see it: Grace's disappearance doesn't appear to be the result of any sort of foul play on Howard's part. There's no way that he would stand to gain financially and it looks like he'll actually lose out – both short *and* long term. Here's why: He has little income of his own and all of their savings – hers, primarily – are tied up in a savings account in her name, where he can't get to it. Making matters worse, the house is in her name, too, and, if what he says about her will is true and she eventually turns up dead, which I doubt, or is declared dead, everything she owned – money, house, everything – goes to her mother. Now, maybe he has a life insurance policy on her and stands to gain from her death, but as far as everyone's concerned, she's not dead – she's away on a vacation or something. If she does turn up dead, well, that's another story. And if she never reappears, it'll be years before she's legally declared dead – and Howard'll be in the poorhouse by then. I suppose he could hire a lawyer and contest the will; but, again, that would be years down the road and would cost money he doesn't have.

"Her savings account hasn't been touched in almost a month and her bankbook was left behind. That would suggest that either she didn't go willingly or, if she did go willingly, that it must have been a spur-of-the-moment decision, and probably with someone of sufficient means that her own savings were of no immediate need." Holly looked like she was about to protest, but I cut her short, wanting to get this over with. "Now, the latter explanation may not sound like her, but consider this. All her clothing and toiletries were packed and taken, as well as her oversized journal full of poems and addresses. That sounds like the work of someone who planned to leave and took some time to do so. The former explanation would suggest kidnapping, but that doesn't make a whole lot of sense. There's been no contact in the two weeks she's been gone and kidnappers usually kidnap for money, not for fun. And, if it was for money, Howard doesn't have any; she has it all. Their current lifestyle doesn't really indicate any sort of wealth, so anyone kidnapping her would have had to have some knowledge of her past and her savings. If they knew of her savings account, though, they'd probably also know that it was in her name only, and that Howard wouldn't be able to touch it. No, kidnapping just doesn't make any sense.

"Which brings us back to a voluntary departure. Clearly, Grace wasn't very happy with the current state of her marriage and Howard was growing less tolerable as time went on, so why wouldn't she want out of there? She's still very attractive and always had admirers swarming around her. My guess is that someone finally attracted her – someone with money – and they decided to take off together. Her account's untouched, but I suspect that it won't be for long. She'll show up at the bank someday, reasonably soon, with a story about losing her bankbook, and with the necessary identification to get it replaced. She'll want what's rightfully hers – and also probably come to realize that she has old friends who are worried sick about her and will want to put their minds at ease. You'll hear from her by year's end, I'm sure of it."

Holly sat motionless throughout my little speech, listening carefully to every word and absorbing every detail. What I said sounded logical enough to her but, as she put it: "It just doesn't sound like Grace." I told her to stop worrying, that everything would sort itself out soon enough; in several months we'd all laugh about this incident.

Problem was I didn't quite buy this all myself; inwardly I had some doubts about the whole affair. Nothing I could put my finger on, unfortunately, but the deep-seated feeling that something just wasn't quite right. But I didn't want to worry her with my personal doubts; I hoped to put this all behind me just as soon as possible, and her worrying would make it all the more difficult to do so. After all, I'd come to the island a decade earlier specifically to get away from this sort of "private dick" work and this brief episode had reawakened some former traits and habits that I'd just as soon left dormant. So, I smugly declared Grace's disappearance a non-issue, and hoped that my minimal snoopings would be sufficient to appease my wife's heightened curiosity and concern.

To my surprise – and, I might add, barely concealed delight – she accepted my explanation at face value, and agreed that it was indeed most likely that Grace had taken off with some moneyed, eligible bachelor. She further agreed that Grace's inherent decency would prod her to contact her old friends and put their minds at ease. And, for that matter, to contact Howard and tell him to take a hike.

"That's what I'd do. I mean, if I were in her shoes and was married to a creep like Howard, that's what I'd do," she said, quietly. She looked up at me and a big, sleepy smile came across her face as she cuddled in closer. "Thanks, Lew," she said softly in my ear. "You've earned your fee."

We'd never discussed a fee as such, but she was calling the shots – and I wasn't complaining.

Grace and Howard were left behind.

Friday, October 30, 1936. 8:11 p.m.

"IT'S KIND OF goofy looking. I'd be embarrassed to have a kid of mine wear one, make him look like a sissy or retard or something. What the hell did you call it?" asked Edwards.

"The…ah…*Cranium Cradle*," responded Johnson, stung slightly by Edwards' words.

A small group of us stood at both sides of the bar looking at Johnson's newest invention, a strange-looking helmet of sorts that looked more like a padded cage. The idea was that you strapped this thing onto the little nipper's head and, if misfortune should have its way and the kid fell down the steps or off a swing or something like that, this thing would protect his head from bumps. We were skeptical.

"Looks like the head gear on an electric chair," said Carver.

"Well, it works – and this just might be the big one," said Johnson, optimistically. "Biff's been wearing it for several weeks now," he added. Biff was his two-year-old son, one of four children aged six months to three years. Johnson liked to get out of the house.

The look of pride on his face as he held the contraption in his hands was the same that he displayed every few months when he brought his latest invention in for our review and approval. He was a sign painter by trade, and had a small grocery store he lived above that further helped to pay the bills; but he was doggedly determined to invent something – anything – that would put a pile of cash in his pocket. So far, however, he'd gotten nowhere other than providing barely concealed amusement for the taproom patrons.

"I don't know. I think I liked the leather glove things the best," said Carver. He was referring to Johnson's leather-glove-type apparatus designed to protect winter-dried knuckles from injury. "What'd you call them? *Sava-Knuck*?"

"Long 'A' not short 'A' — as in 'save a'. But I changed its name: *Knuckle-Nickaway*. What do you think?" asked Johnson.

"The suspenders: now *those* were a good idea," said Mackey without looking up. He was referring to Johnson's mini-suspenders, designed to be worn under your shirt and to hold up baggy underpants. I doubted that many people were waiting for that particular accessory.

I heard the front door open and was surprised to see Chester Hawley enter. He was dressed in white: white pants, white shirt, white sweater, white jacket and, yes, white shoes. Skin was kind of flushed, thought — he was drunk. With him were two other rich swells, equally drunk and equally obnoxious. They were making a lot of noise amongst themselves, but nothing I could pick up on. They collapsed into chairs at one of the tables. Chester turned, looked me straight in the eyes and yelled: "Hey! *Bartender*! Three scotches. And make it your good stuff, not the cheap stuff."

The hairs went up on my back. Well, they say the customer is always right. I poured them each a glass of Haig and Haig twelve-year-old blend — the stuff in the pinch bottle — and decided to charge them double for it. Triple, if they ordered another. I had Willett deliver it to them.

"Me, I liked the bald head stuff the best," said Edwards, gently patting the small, but growing, thin spot on the back of his head.

"*Bald-No-More*," said Johnson with growing excitement. He loved the attention his contraptions were getting.

"Yeah, *that's* it. Now that's a product people would buy. Bald people, anyway."

If memory served me, they were referring to a kit Johnson had put together a year earlier, intended to hide bald spots. It contained a jar of some sort of greasepaint mixture, a natural sponge applicator, a comb-like modeling-device for dragging hair-like streaks through the mess, and another jar of cold cream for removing the greasy concoction from your hair and scalp. The kit, he had assured us, would be available in a variety of natural shades. The prototype had been brick red.

Off to the side, Hawley and his companions were growing louder and more obnoxious. Hawley kept making derogatory comments about the taproom, and made it a point to turn in my direction and deliver them at a higher volume to ensure that I heard them. I don't know what his problem was – just showing off, I guess. But I was growing impatient with him. So far, he'd managed to avoid insulting any of the people in the room, which was wise. Especially the Swedes.

"What else ya got in the pipeline, Barry?" asked Carver. Carver always seemed to take these inventions of Johnson's more seriously than some of the others did.

"A good one. Actually, a *great* one. This one's a honey, and it's gonna be *huge*. Everybody's gonna want one," he blurted out with an enthusiasm rare even for him. He had our attention.

"Well, what is it?" asked Edwards, his interest piqued.

"Picture this," said Johnson, hands in front of him, giving shape to the thing he was about to describe. "Custom-contoured toilet seats. Complete with built-in armrests and a plug-in heating element for cold winter mornings. This baby will be the ultimate in comfort and relaxation – take the pressure off your piles, if you got 'em. Make reading the paper a whole new experience." He finished with a confidently satisfied look on his face, awaiting our enthusiastic response.

Hawley was making some more loud comments during this exchange, but we all tried to ignore him.

"Heat, eh?" said Edwards, thinking it over. "That could be nice. That is, if I could ever get into the bathroom." With a wife and five daughters, Edwards probably had a problem there.

"Armrests. Wouldn't they get in the way when you...ah...you know..." asked Carver, trying to find the right words.

"When you go to wipe your ass, is what he's trying to say," interjected Edwards.

"Not in the least," Johnson assured them. "There're little spring-loaded pins at the base of each arm. Just pull the head and arms fold to the sides on hinges, easy as pie."

We all sat there for a moment trying to visualize this, but weren't having a lot of success.

"I don't know, sounds kinda awkward," said Carver. "Wouldn't they bang into the sink and wall?"

"What do ya call this thing?" asked Edwards.

"Well, I'm not quite sure yet. I think I've narrowed it down to two: *Bottom Buddy* or *Bowel-Eze*. What do ya think?" he asked, actually soliciting input from us.

"How about *Pile Driver*?" suggested Edwards. There were a few snickers from the others.

"Or *Unloading Dock*," said another.

"*Potty Pal*," joined in Mackey.

"Wait a minute," said Edwards. "Here ya go: *Crap Shoot*! Am I right, or am I right?"

Everyone was laughing now, Johnson included. After all, these suggestions weren't really too outrageous, considering his original ideas.

"*Bartender*!" yelled Hawley. The laughter drifted off, replaced by dead silence. Everyone looked over at Hawley and his friends. The smiles faded from the friends' faces as they realized they were now the center of attention. Hawley – well, he was a different story.

"What on earth does a person have to do for a drink in this dump? Three more scotches, now! And none of that cheap bar swill!" he added.

There was a moment of silence.

"Move it, *boy*!" yelled Hawley. This guy was unbelievable.

The other patrons slowly shifted their gaze to see what my reaction would be. Calmly, I turned to the group in front of me: "Gentlemen: heads up." They reacted with a bunch of knowing smiles, and casually took their drinks and possessions from the bar.

I circled around the bar's end and headed slowly for Hawley. He stood up as I approached, pleased at first that he'd managed to elicit a response. This quickly shifted to mounting concern as he realized that I didn't have any drinks in my hands, and wasn't smiling. I paused in front of him momentarily, stared in his eyes. Then, slowly, I grabbed his upper arms and spun him around, then grabbed him from the back with fistfuls of collar and belt. If he expected the *bum's rush*, he was disappointed. Instead, I heaved him off the floor and carried him to the bar's end. He protested vehemently all the while, but I tuned him out. I proceeded to wipe down the bar's filthy surface with Chester, his arms and legs thrashing about without effect. I had him pinned, and he offered the resistance of an animated rag doll. When I was finished, I dropped the humiliated kid to his feet and calmly said to him: "Go home."

Chester, near tears and soiled from head to toe with stale beer, ashes, spilled ketchup and other unidentifiable stains, started a half-hearted protest.

"Who...who the hell do you think you are, Porter?" he stammered. "My father..."

I leaned in close and spoke quietly, so only Chester would hear my words.

"Your *father*? Why don't you go and talk to *your father*. Tell him all about you and Abbey, while you're at it. I'm sure he'd be pleased. Now, go home."

Chester stood there for a good half minute, at a loss for words. He looked puzzled, or frustrated, or *something*, but seemed to know full well the meaning of the words I'd just thrown at him. I couldn't read his reaction and didn't really care. I just hoped he had the good sense to get out of there while he could still walk. He backed off slowly, then quickly turned and left in a huff, followed by his two friends. They looked relieved as hell to get out of there. Everyone else looked relieved to get rid of them – and happy that the bar was now cleaner than it had been in hours.

Saturday, October 31, 1936. 12:35 p.m.

THE DATE ON the masthead of the *Philadelphia Inquirer* reminded me that it was, once again, Halloween. Which meant it was my birthday. I sat at a table in the taproom, a smoking De Nobili jammed between my fingers, trying to read the paper. The ash had reached an unmanageable length, so I went to knock it off in the ashtray when I realized that someone – Holly no doubt – had surreptitiously replaced all the heavy glass ashtrays with large surf clam shells. The shell spun wildly whenever I touched its edge. An attempt to place my cigar in the thing ended with the cigar falling out of the wobbly shell, rolling across the tabletop, and falling into the crap on the floor below. Another minute and I would have had a conflagration of wood chips and peanut shells.

"Christ almighty," I mumbled to myself.

Willett entered from outside, open book in hand, and wandered over to my table.

"Hi, Lew."

"Who the hell put these things in here?" I said, picking up the empty shell and holding it up for his inspection.

"Uh, that was Holly, Lew. I told her I didn't think you'd like them too much, but…"

"Throw 'em out and put the glass ones back. And next time she tries something like this, wrestle her to the ground."

"Yeah, right. She'd probably win."

Come to think of it, she probably would; she knows some dirty moves.

"There's some people over at the Schweickert house – an older man and woman," he continued, leaping to another subject.

"Yeah? Who are they?" I asked.

"I don't know. I didn't ask. But they're in and out of the place."

"Think I'll go have a look." I called Hoover, who responded instantly to any gesture that promised to put him outside in the land of targets. We wandered over and found the man carrying a large box of trash out to the curb. I introduced myself while Hoover sniffed the box, and lifted his leg on it. I pretended not to notice.

He introduced himself as Harry Schweickert, Fred Schweickert's father. He pretended not to notice, too. He went on to explain that he and his wife were down for the day from their home in Willow Grove, Pennsylvania. They were attempting to tidy up the house, tossing perishables and boxing up Fred's personal effects to take back home with them. Planning to leave the house furnished, figuring that if the place didn't sell by the following summer they'd rent it out for the season. Said his wife was inside trying to clean up all the blood and dog shit stains on the linoleum floors and refrigerator front, but the soiled carpets weren't worth struggling with at this point. He asked if I could give him a hand rolling up and carrying the several carpets out to the garage for storage, halfheartedly saying that he'd deal with them later on.

Inside, in the kitchen, we found his wife down on the floor. She was on her knees, a pail of soapy water by her side and a large, soapy, blood-tinted puddle in front of her. Her head was down, and she wept quietly. The refrigerator was in a similar half-finished state: Most of the blood had been removed, but a number of partially dried pink smears remained on its surface, and there was a pink puddle at its base. Her husband helped her outside, and I told him I'd finish this chore, which I did. It wasn't, after all, my son's blood.

Back outside, I told them that I'd be happy to keep an eye on the place for them over the winter, and get the name of a couple of local realtors to help with the sale. As they jotted down their name, address, and number on the paper I passed to them, I added that they could give me a call if and when they returned to haul away the furniture; I could dig up some friends to give them a hand. As we said our good-byes, a small group of trick or treaters passed by noisily. The others faded from view as we all focused on the leader of the group, a blood-soaked "monster" wielding a large wooden knife, its blade covered in bright red paint. The Schweickerts seemed visibly shaken by the sight. He stood staring at the spectacle, while she buried her face in his chest. Hoover, on the other hand, followed the small group the length of the road, barking and nipping at their heels.

Later that night I was behind the bar when Holly entered the room. She had a chocolate cake balanced on her right hand, loaded with what looked like a hundred candles. She carried a long, thin, clumsily wrapped package in her left hand. And, to make matters worse, she bellowed the words to the birthday song as she approached. The others quickly noticed and the drunkest of the group joined in singing, if you could call it that. They sounded terrible – like full moon at Bedlam. I wished she wouldn't persist in doing this each year, or at least not in public. I reluctantly completed the ritual of blowing out the candles, and managed to singe my eyebrows. Then Holly encouraged me to open my gift while she divided the cake into enough small pieces to feed everyone in the room.

The gift itself was a good one, as Holly's usually were. It was an old, rusted harpoon that she had purchased from someone up in Barnegat City. He claimed that it was a relic dating back to the late 1700s or early 1800s when whaling was the primary source of livelihood for the island's handful of residents. The pursuit of the so-called Right whale was made by a small number of island dwellers, among them the Inmans, Cranmers and Spragues, names that today are still commonplace on the island and adjacent mainland. After a thorough examination of the harpoon, I gave the room a quick once-over looking for a suitable spot to mount the thing. Holly told me I could use it "to keep the drunks in line." I settled on a thin strip of wall behind the bar, above the mirror. For the time being, however, I propped it up in a corner along with last year's present, which was a similarly rusted clam rake. Someday I'd get around to hanging them both – maybe when I got next year's gift.

There were three guys standing off to one side of the room that I'd never seen before, who'd entered unnoticed some time earlier. They looked humorless and out of place, and seemed to be interested primarily in me. When the regulars finished their cake and drifted back to their drinks, the trio approached. A quick glance around suggested that most everyone else in the room was oblivious to their presence. Holly busied herself with cleaning up the remains of the cake and discarded napkins, and left the room through the kitchen door. Willett alone followed their approach, and he and I exchanged glances. He looked concerned.

"You Porter?" asked the biggest of the three.

"Yeah. And you are…?"

"Smith. Joe Smith," he responded, unconvincingly. "I want to talk to you about renting this place for a night. For a private party."

"I don't rent the place," I said. Not to these guys, at any rate.

He looked quickly about the room, then back to me. "It's noisy in here. Let's go somewhere private and talk about it." Persistent. But then I didn't really think that was the primary purpose of his visit. They weren't locals, and who the hell'd want to rent this dump?

"The storeroom," I said, pointing over my shoulder with my thumb. He nodded approval, and I led, pausing to hold the door while they filed past.

"It's okay," I whispered to Willett as I followed them into the dimly lit room. I closed the door behind me.

"Like I said: I don't rent the place," I repeated to the big guy. His friends were silent and stupid looking. The trio had positioned themselves so that I couldn't see them all at once. And they all kept moving, slowly, and in as nonchalant a fashion as they could muster.

Their hands were out of their pockets now and hanging loosely by their sides.

"Nice place you got here," said the stupider looking one.

"Yeah, that's why I wanna rent it," said the big one.

"Looks like ya do a good business here," said the other stupid looking guy.

I was doing my best to keep my eye on all three, but they seemed pretty good at throwing me off. The smallest of the three picked up his pace and stepped in on me, and the trace of a smile that had graced his face disappeared.

"This all booze?" he asked, turning to the stacked cases behind him. Then, just as suddenly, he spun around with a broad roundhouse. I stepped back to avoid it. The big guy was behind me now. He delivered a solid kidney punch that threw me off completely. Before I knew it he had my arms pinned from behind, and the two others moved in quickly, saps now in hand. I quickly pulled my feet off the floor and kicked out, smashed the first guy in the chest and sent him reeling back into the other. Both of them lost their balance. The big guy's footing was off now. I threw my feet to the floor, flipping him over my shoulders in a single continuous motion. He fell in a tangled heap with one of the others, and my left sleeve went with him. A kick to the face of the first guy down left him out cold, nose broken and bloodied, teeth dislodged. The big guy tried to right himself, but a solid kick to the side of his knee sent him down with a snap and a yelp. I planted my foot firmly on the back of his neck, grabbed his right arm, and yanked it back and up with a twist. It pulled from the shoulder socket with a dull pop. I lifted my foot and gave a forceful stomp eight inches higher, driving his face into the wooden floor with a squish and a moan. The third guy, still on the floor on his butt, was now doing a panicky backwards shuffle on hands and feet, trying to get away from me. I stepped over to him and hauled him up, my left fist filled with his shirtfront. I gave him a face-to-face smile – my nastiest – then buried my right fist in the guy's gut with as much force as I could muster. He went down, retching. A kick to the side of his head left him out cold, face down in a puddle filled with the remains of his dinner.

I surveyed the wreckage before me and satisfied myself that no one was in any shape to offer any further resistance. Aside from some half-hearted moaning and the big guy's clawing at his dislocated shoulder, they were essentially motionless. My kidney ached, but I tried to put it out of my mind as I dragged the three bodies together. The smallest went over my shoulder like a limp, rolled carpet, and I grabbed the other two by their collars. I kicked open the door to the taproom and shuffled into the crowd with my bleeding, moaning baggage.

"Willett!" I croaked. "Get the front door!"

"Oh, Jesus, Lew – are you all right?" he quickly asked, stepping briskly ahead of me to get to the door. "Who were they?" he added before I could answer.

"Yeah, yeah; nothing that won't heal."

Everyone stared at this unsightly procession, mouths open wide. The only sound in the place was that made by the bodies sliding across the floor. A trio of Norwegians, sitting off to the side at a table, were visibly impressed; one of them started clapping. I forced a smile and nodded to him. Willett held the door while I dumped the three out on the porch. Only the big guy screamed in pain as he hit the wood.

"Call the cops," I said to Willett, rubbing my aching kidney. "Drinks on the house," I added, so all could hear.

This, and, I suppose, my victory, resulted in a sudden round of cheers and applause, all the while Willett repeatedly shouting: "Who the hell were they? What did they want?" I worked my way behind the bar and poured myself a stiff pour of Old Overholt, my hands just now starting to shake. Holly reentered the room, oblivious to all that had happened during the minutes preceding, and gave a quizzical look around. All of this ruckus was cut short, however, when the front door was once again thrown open. It slammed against the wall with a resounding crash.

Framed in the doorway stood a man with a Remington twelve-gauge, thirty-two-inch double-barreled shotgun held before him, aimed at no one in particular. His nose was heavily bandaged, both eyes surrounded by large purple-black rings. It took me a moment to realize this was the guy I'd hit at the Bund rally a week earlier. He was livid with rage, probably as much that his three flunkies had failed as miserably as he had with me. He quickly surveyed the crowd, spotted me, and approached. His shotgun now had a target.

The taproom's occupants recoiled at the sight of the gun, fanning out in all directions, backing away, knocking over chairs and crashing into tables in the process. Like the parting of the Red Sea, and there I was at the far side. The sheer number of people in the place became apparent to the intruder, and his rage dissolved into an uneasy mix of uncertainty and nervousness. His eyes darted from side to side as if he expected at any moment to be attacked from both sides. And then Holly stormed forward.

"You stupid son of a bitch," she screamed in a voice loud even for her. "Get the hell out of my – my home!"

With this, the Norwegians kicked over their chairs and grabbed whatever makeshift weapons were available to them – a metal poker, a heavy chunk of wood, a chair. They moved forward to join me; I'd already grabbed two full liquor bottles – cheap stuff, of course – and held them by their necks chest high in front of me. Holly had marched forward, coming to a stop and planting herself directly in his path, hands on hips. The Norwegians and I circled in four different directions, moving towards him all the while. His eyes darted down to the shotgun in his hands, as if counting the barrels and suddenly realizing that two wouldn't be enough.

"Take it easy, buddy, no need for any shooting," I said as calmly as possible, trying to avoid looking at the two yawning holes aimed at my midsection. "Just put your gun at rest and leave, and nobody'll get hurt." I didn't want to panic him, having seen years ago what a shotgun can do at close range.

"Eddie!" yelled a voice from the doorway beyond the intruder. I looked to the source and immediately recognized the man filling the doorway: Willy Vollbrecht. Only now he was dressed in casual street clothes.

"Eddie!" he repeated, this time a little louder. "Calm down. *Calm down.* Take it easy, and leave. We don't need this. Leave. Now." He stated this all in a clear and calm voice, trying to lull Eddie into inaction. Eddie glanced hastily over his shoulder at Vollbrecht, who motioned with a nod of his head to the outdoors. Eddie's gaze returned to us, a look of disgust on his face. He was clearly disappointed in his inability to exact his measure of revenge, but I suspect there was a tinge of relief that he'd stumbled on a way out of an awkward situation of his own making.

"Shit!" he muttered under his breath, as he started to back towards the door. Reaching it, he paused and looked at me. "I don't like you!" he yelled.

My eyes were locked on his. "You're not the first, pal," I responded, unemotionally.

The sound of a siren rose in the distance as Eddie stormed out the door, a wave of relief engulfing the taproom's occupants. I placed my bottles on the bar and stepped over to Holly, engulfing her in my arms. She was shaking like a leaf. The rest of the people in the room slowly returned to their seats and drinks, having had more than enough excitement for one night. The Norwegians kept their eyes on Vollbrecht all the while. Instead of following Eddie, however, Vollbrecht calmly entered the room and approached me, not at all threatening looking.

"Sorry," said Vollbrecht to me, quietly. "Our beef isn't with you. I guess they just got carried away and lost sight of our goals. It won't happen again, I assure you."

"Am I supposed to *thank* you?" I asked.

"Well, believe it or not, I didn't come with them; I got word from someone else shortly after they left as to what their plans were, and hightailed it over here to try to stop them." He shook his head in dismay. "I believe in our cause – strongly believe in it. But for some reason, it seems to attract a lot of…a…" He paused momentarily, searching for the right word. ". . lots of misfits," he concluded. I couldn't argue with him there.

There were several more moments of silence as he looked around at the taproom's interior. "Nice place," he said, quietly. "Reminds me of a joint called 'Heinie's' – on Mickle and Wright, I think it was. Back in Camden – near the tracks. A lot like this. I used to drink there all the time, years back. Camden beer on draught." There was a faint, sad smile on his face now.

"I know the place," I responded. "The blind guy, Fritz, worked the bar. Heinie always playing cards with The Swede. Crummy player piano sounded like hell." Yeah, I remembered the place, all right.

Vollbrecht's smile spread as he lowered his gaze to the sawdust-strewn floor. "I miss the place," he said. "Good times. Neighborhood's gone to hell now, though."

There was an awkward silence of a good half minute before Vollbrecht recovered from his reverie. He looked back at me and flashed another quick smile. "Sind sie Deutsche, mein Freund?" he asked.

I shook my head "no," knowing just enough German to grasp the gist of his question.

"Oh, well, you look it. Well then, goodnight." He turned and started for the door, continuing to speak in a slightly louder voice. "Hope if our paths cross again it'll be under more pleasant circumstances. Heinie's, perhaps? And forget about Eddie," he said, exiting the room.

I stood there for a moment, arm around Holly, her face partially buried in my chest but angled so that one eye could monitor the door. The room had taken on a semblance of normalcy by now.

"I'll be damned," I said, slowly. "Heinie's!"

I ushered her back towards my office. Edwards, his back to us, had a distraught looking Willett off to one side, and was doing all the talking, as usual. I caught a few words as we passed.

"... never heard about the big fight? Well, it was back in '26 – August – and Lew was matched against this big stupid Canuck ..."

Edwards would never give that one a rest.

Saturday, November 7, 1936. 9:58 p.m.

LESTER SIMMS WAS propped up at the bar, a shot of Guckenheimer and a half-finished Camden in front of him, smoke encircling his head from the burning stub stuck to his lips. Sean Rioux was at his left, working on his third bottle of Trent Ale, listening to Simms go on and on about his extensive travels.

"Yeah, lots of pretty places out there – but Monument Valley... whew! That's one of the prettiest."

"Betty says San Simeon's the prettiest," countered Hurley at the bar's end. "You know, Hearst's joint." Hurley had some sort of job at the Ford dealership over on Bay.

"Don't know 'bout no San Simone," said Simms, butchering the name. "Ain't been around long, I guess."

"It's a monument to Hearst's innate bad taste," commented Rioux, quietly. "That and Marion Davies."

Those were more words than Rioux usually spoke in an entire evening. The product of an Irish mother and French father, Rioux was in his mid-fifties, short but solid, and sported a head full of short, white hair. He and Holly's father had been friends and business associates a dozen years earlier, smuggling hooch onto the island throughout Prohibition. Rioux was retired now and sufficiently well off that he never had to worry again about working. Easygoing and hard to rile, the regulars knew never to push too hard as he was rumored to have a violent streak. No one, to my knowledge, had ever seen any evidence of it, though.

Rioux and I had formed an unusual relationship over the years, however. While he wouldn't speak more than a few words to the patrons of the taproom, he and I had been known to sit around for hours, sometimes talking about nothing in particular, sometimes talking about days gone by and sometimes not talking at all – just sitting and quietly drinking. I was, I think, the only one he trusted to keep the stories of his illegal activities and violent past a secret. And not because I have a trustworthy face: I'd told him, too, of my former life, of the things I'd done, of the secrets I'd kept. Things I wasn't proud of, but things that needed doing. And so, each of us armed with information that could have caused the ruination of the other, we had a common, unspoken bond. Each of us knew that there was one other person we could trust, that we could talk to, that we could count on in a pinch. Only one.

He took a long pull of his beer, and turned to me, changing the subject. "What's with the Schweickert place, Lew? They selling it?"

I recounted the details of my visit with the Schweickerts the previous Saturday, finishing with their plans to spend the night on the mainland at the Manahawkin Hotel before heading back home Sunday.

"There're plenty of places here. Why stay in Manahawkin?" asked Hurley.

"Probably don't want nothin' to do with the island, with what happened and all that. The memories," responded Simms. "Bad ones..."

"Where's 'home'?" asked Hurley.

"Willow Grove. In Pennsylvania," I said, drying a glass.

"Ahh," cooed Simms. "Willow Grove Park. Now that's the prettiest. Just beautiful. Ponds with geese, lots of gardens, three rollycoasters – the *Thunderbolt*, the...uh...*Matterhorn*, and a little-bitty one that's scariest than most other parks' coasters." He hesitated, pondering a point. "Make that the *Alps*. With goats on it. And John Phillip Sousa – or he was, at least."

Most everyone knew that while Simms spoke frequently of his extensive travels and knowingly of foreign lands, these "travels" were solely through the pages of books and magazines. Next to Willett, he was the library's most frequent patron. His talk of Willow Grove Park threw us off, however: It sounded as though he might actually have been there once.

A rush of cool, crisp, autumn air stirred the smoke as a slight colored man in chauffeur's garb peered through the open door and entered the room. He paused to take in the place, then strutted over to the bar and Willett. He asked if a "Lew Porter" was around. Willett glanced over at me and I nodded, so Willett pointed me out to him. Instead of walking over, however, the guy turned and left the building without saying a word. He returned a minute later with an older man, gray-haired, later-fifties, distinguished looking in his white suit and shoes – reminded me of the actor in a film I'd seen a year earlier, *China Seas*. Not C. Aubrey Smith, but the other guy. The chauffeur whispered in the older man's ear and nodded in my direction. The old guy straightened, and walked briskly towards me, cane in hand. It was for show only, not out of necessity.

"Mr. Porter," he stated. "Chester Hawley. You can call me Chet; everyone else does." I recognized him as the fellow in the husband-and-wife portrait so prominently displayed back at *White Cedars*.

We shook hands and went through the usual introductory motions. Hawley asked if we could speak in private, so I grabbed a bottle of White Horse, some ice, two glasses and then led him through the kitchen into my private office. After we were seated and drinks poured, he proceeded.

"I believe you've met my son. Several times."

Uh-oh, here we go.

"Well, I want you to understand that I love my son as much as any man loves his son. But I'm not blind. I realize that Chester has grown to be a pompous, spoiled, pain in the ass and I suppose that I'm partially responsible for this. If I had it to do all over again, I'd handle it all differently. Unfortunately, it's a little too late for that and Chester is what he is. And we all, for better or worse, are stuck with it."

I'd been convinced that this guy was going to make a stink about his precious son, but was gratified to see that he had *some* perspective on the situation. I watched him as he silently took a long sip of the scotch, his face harshly lit from one side by the room's sole source of light, the gooseneck lamp on my desk.

"Your treatment of him here in the bar the other night delivered a good dose of humility," he continued. "It didn't sound warranted from the story he told me, but I've come to know Chester and his half truths reasonably well. I asked around and got the full story and, I must say, it must have been rather amusing." He had a curious half-smile.

"But let me get to the point: What's going on? Why were you in my house asking my son a lot of questions – questions I'd expect from the police, but not an ordinary civilian? Is Chester in any sort of trouble? Is he involved in anything – anything at all – that in any way, shape, or form could cause *me* and my family any sort of...ah... *problems?*"

I went on to explain, once again, of Grace's disappearance and the reasons behind my limited involvement, of the loose connection with Chester. I also took the opportunity to mention Chester's disapproval of my speaking with the maid, Abbey. Disapproval, I assumed, due to their *romantic involvement*, for want of a more appropriate term.

Chet looked momentarily startled by the *romantic involvement* part, but quickly regained his composure. He said that he was aware of their ongoing dalliance, but didn't realize that anyone else was. And while he didn't approve of it at all, it *did* seem to be an affair of mutual consent. He'd thought several times in the past of letting her go, but came to realize that the next maid might *not* consent to Chester's attentions and that could cause some real problems.

I had difficulty believing what I was hearing. Unfortunately, she was of legal age in this state and unless Chester had coerced her into having sex with him based upon a false promise of marriage – which he may very well have – there wasn't a crime here. Even if that were the case, the false promise of marriage was immaterial unless she became pregnant, at which time it became a *high misdemeanor*, punishable by a maximum two thousand dollar fine or imprisonment for a maximum of seven years, or both. And Chester could weasel his way out of that by marrying her. But she wasn't pregnant.

"Are you aware of the extent of their involvement?" I asked.

"Well, I…assume that it has progressed beyond the hand-holding stage; I imagine that they may be…*intimate*."

We sat in silence for several moments as I pondered how people of wealth frequently had strange views on various issues, and the Hawley family didn't seem to be an exception to this notion.

"At any rate," I continued, "there doesn't seem to be any sort of crime where Grace Peterson is concerned, let alone that Chester's involved."

Chet seemed relieved to hear this.

"Well then, that *is* good news. I thank you for your frankness, Porter." He paused to drain his glass, and returned it to the desk's top with a clatter. "And I would hope – would fully *expect* – that if things ever turn out otherwise regarding Chester, you'd turn over whatever evidence you had to the proper authorities and let the law take its course. And you'd have my support." He paused, and looked me straight in the eye. "But, if you ever should do anything like that, you'd better be sure – *certain* – of what you've found out, of what you have. Because if you were ever to erroneously implicate my son in any sort of wrong-doing, to bring any sort of unwarranted embarrassment to me and my family – well, that would be a serious mistake."

"Fair enough," I said. And I supposed it was.

Chet grabbed his cane and was half way up when the light went out. Power outages were not an uncommon occurrence in the borough, and a quick look out the window verified that the power was out in the immediate area, although I could see the usual isolated lights elsewhere about a quarter mile away.

"Power's out again. Might as well have a seat for a couple of minutes, see if they get it fixed," I said to Chet as I worked my way across the darkened room. A few missteps later, I'd made it through the small kitchen to the door into the taproom.

"Willett!" I yelled over the voices of the annoyed drinkers inside. "You know the routine!" We had some kerosene lanterns and candles stashed away for these occasions, and he was probably fumbling around for them at that very moment. Fortunately, the power came back on within the minute, much to everyone's relief. It was more than a week past full moon and cloudy as well; maneuvering down blackened streets with a snoot full could be hazardous at best.

I turned to find Chet standing behind me, smiling.

"Well, then: That wasn't too bad, was it?" he said, referring, I assumed, to the brief power outage and not to our conversation. "I thank you for your time, Porter. I'll be going now." And with that, he was gone.

"Who's the stiff?" asked Hurley.

"Chester Hawley. Call him *Chet*," I responded.

Hurley reacted with surprise, quickly looking to the people standing to his sides, then back to me.

"Hawley? Here?"

"In the flesh. But don't count on seeing him again; I don't think this is his kind of place," I said, pulling a telephone directory from under the bar. This one covered Ocean County, and I worked my way through the "Ks" looking for a Dr. Kay or Kaye. There were none to be found. During a brief lull in the chatter I asked if anyone had ever heard of a doctor by that name living on the mainland. The blank stares and feeble headshakes answered my question; I let it ride at that.

An hour or so passed before the next-to-last customer wandered out into the night, leaving Rioux alone at the bar. He drained his drink and wiped his mouth with the back of his hand.

"Dr. Kaye," he said, getting my attention. "This for you, or someone else?"

"Just me," I responded. "It's *personal.*"

He regarded this last comment for several moments.

"There's a doctor of sorts over on the mainland. Lives in Vineland. People call him 'Dr. K', but it's the initial 'K', not the name 'Kaye'. 'K' for Kasabian. Dr. Kasabian." I quickly poured us each another drink while he spoke. "Thing is, though, he's an *animal* doctor – a veterinarian – not a people doctor. But to some, in other circles, he's known as Dr. K. Known as the man to see for more *private* treatment, behind closed doors, no publicity, bring plenty of cash. You know: knife and bullet wounds, abortions, quick-and-dirty plastic surgery, that sort of thing."

I was surprised, but I shouldn't have been. I told Rioux as much.

"But be careful with him. He has a different set of *friends*, people who like having him around, like what he does for them. And you don't want to be on their bad side. And, needless to say, you didn't hear this from me."

It made perfect sense that Chester wouldn't want any regular doctors treating her wounds, particularly local doctors. Word might get out that could tarnish the Hawley image and that could have all sorts of horrible ramifications. Why, Chester might even have his allowance cut, and then how would he pay guys like Kasabian?

I thanked Rioux for the information and decided then and there to visit the good doctor. I wasn't clear as to what such a visit would accomplish, if anything. But, what the hell – if nothing else it would be...fun.

Monday, November 9, 1936. 9:17 a.m.

IT WAS COLD and damp, the sky gray as slate, as I headed over the causeway bridge and into Manahawkin on Bay Avenue. A worn Esso road map was spread out on the seat beside me, folded and flattened to east central New Jersey. Turned south on Route 9 and drove for roughly thirty miles, passing through the tiny communities of Cedar Run, Staffordville, West Creek, Tuckerton, New Gretna, Smithville and Absecon before rolling into Pleasantville. Turned and headed west on Black Horse Pike for another thirty miles and another bunch of nondescript towns – McKee City, Mays Landing, Mizpah, Buena, Landisville and Downstown – before arriving in Malaga. From there I headed south again on 47 to the outskirts of Vineland. A left turn onto Landis Avenue brought me into the heart of the so-called city.

Vineland's pretty easy to get around in, if you know where you're going. Developed by a lawyer named Charles K. Landis in the late 1800s as a fruit farming community, the town is a perfect square, one mile long on each side. The cross streets all head either east-west – most of these have fruit names – or north-south, with intersections all at perfect right angles. These are lined with equidistant frame houses fronted at curbside by evenly spaced trees. Landis sought to attract Italians to his town, thinking them to be the best farmers. He lured them from Philadelphia and New York – some even directly from Italy – by means of hard-selling agents and too-good-to-be-true advertisements. Hopefully, they were all proponents of symmetry.

I stopped at the first diner I saw, the Tip-Top Diner, located on Landis a couple of blocks down from the New Jersey Home for Feebleminded Females. The Tip-Top was a shiny chrome-and-glass

198

affair, and looked to be fairly new. I found a telephone booth inside at its far end by the restroom. A quick perusal of the city directory showed a Dr. Kasabian, Animal Doctor, to have offices on East Quince Street. Within five minutes, I'd located both the street and Kasabian's building a stone's throw from the railroad. His outfit was nothing more than a modest bungalow with another smaller building out back. The smaller one had the sign "Animal Doctor" in large red letters above its door. I drove past, pulled onto the nearest cross street, Sixth, and parked out of view of Kasabian's buildings.

A minute later, I stood inside facing the receptionist – the most brutal looking woman I'd seen in ages. She was short and squat, with a rough, pocked complexion, and teeth that resembled a yellowed picket fence. Her hair, in desperate need of a wash, looked as if it grew in sheets rather than strands. The odor of a general lack of hygiene permeated the air about her. She was working on a crossword puzzle, but hadn't gotten very far. She looked stumped, but she didn't look up, or at least not immediately.

"Kasabian in? I need him," I said, holding my side in the vague hope that she'd mistake me for a prospective patient.

"Nah, he's up to the Overman farm, treatin' a sick horse. Should be back pretty soon. He expectin' you, Mr...?"

"No. Name's Gable. I'll wait."

"Suit yourself," she said with a distinct lack of enthusiasm. She went back to staring at the puzzle and sucking at her teeth. Her breath was beyond description.

The place looked like it was hosed down daily and had the choking smell of some sort of disinfectant. The comingling of odors was making me nauseous.

"Want some coffee?" she asked after several minutes.

"Yeah, I would," I said, not sure that I'd be able to keep it down, but willing to give it a try.

"Well, there's a diner couple a blocks south of here. On the right. Pick me up one, too. Lots of cream and sugar," she said, returning to her puzzle. So much for sympathy for the wounded. I told her I'd changed my mind.

About twenty minutes later I heard someone enter through a rear entrance, and moments after a man poked his head through the door and quietly said something to the receptionist. Kasabian. She muttered an inaudible response and nodded in my direction. He gave me the once over.

He was small and dark, with jet-black hair going to gray on the sides and back, and a distant memory on the top. He had a five o'clock shadow, a large, bulbous nose and glasses that looked tight and uncomfortable. He bore a sour expression and looked tired – already. I told him I needed to see him for a few minutes. He balked, muttering something about an appointment. I repeated my need to see him and *now*. He got the drift and told me to follow him.

We entered a windowless sixteen-by-twenty room filled with the usual stuff you'd expect to find in an animal doctor's office, only lots of it. Once the door was shut, I dropped the "patient" pretense and got to the reason behind my visit.

"I want to talk to you about a patient of yours. Name's Abbey O'Hara. Red hair, young, sixteen, mousy looking. From over on Long Beach Island," I said.

He stopped in his tracks, turned, and gave me a look of bewilderment. Not a very convincing one, at that.

"Abbey O'Hara," I repeated, slowly. "Think about it."

"What sort of animal does she have?" he asked. Cute.

"No animal. *Her*. I want to talk about her."

"You must be confused," he said, quickly. "I'm an animal doctor, not a physician."

"She's a friend of the Hawleys of Long Beach Island. Chester Hawley," I stated, looking over at a tall, wooden, four-drawer filing cabinet jammed in the corner. "Where do you keep your records? Over there?" I said, pointing.

"I'm afraid you're going to have to leave, Mr....ah...whoever you are. I don't have time for riddles, and there's a very sick heifer waiting for me."

"*Gable*," I said. "Let's take a look," I added, moving over to the cabinet. Over Kasabian's objections, I yanked open the top drawer and found files for the letters A through G. I slammed it shut and opened the second, revealing letters H through N, so I slammed that one shut, too, and grabbed the handle of the third.

"Gable!" yelled Kasabian from behind, and I paused at the sound of his voice, which was more of a hiss. "I said *leave*! Now get out of here!"

I turned to find him pointing a small revolver at my belly. It looked to be a Harrington and Richardson target revolver, .22 caliber, seven-shot, double action, rim fire, with its distinctive six-inch octagonal barrel and shiny pearl handles. A sissy pistol – not that a shot from it wouldn't have made a mess of my insides, but it's hard to take a guy seriously when he's pointing a "toy" at you. I smiled my smile; I was more frightened of *Brünhilde* out at the front desk than this weasel. Amateur night. I moved in on him and he instinctively backed away from me, momentarily losing his footing on an open box of small glass vials. My left hand darted out and grabbed the barrel of the pistol, wrenching it out of his limp grip as I quickly slapped him twice with my right, knocking the glasses from his face. I threw the pistol across the room where it disappeared in a pile of periodicals and books. He crashed with a yelp of pain into a white painted steel-and-glass cabinet full of surgical instruments, which tipped back into the wall with an ear-splitting clatter of broken glass and steel. I grabbed his left ear and twisted, hard. He went down on his knees whining, pawing ineffectually at my fist.

"Listen, greaseball: Either you get me what I want – O'Hara's records – or I'm gonna take this office apart looking for 'em." I paused for effect. "But first I'll take you apart, starting with this ear. Which you're gonna be eating."

I gave it another, harder twist, and Kasabian was screaming now;

I hoped I was right about this guy. I also hoped that Brünhilde was used to screams and cries of pain and would assume I was just another *emergency* case having a bullet removed or something, 'cause there was no way she'd miss the racket he was making. Kasabian made some frenzied motions to the cabinet, so I "walked" him over to it. My left fist was growing warm and sticky with his blood. Awkwardly, he pulled at the third drawer, and fingered through the files within. We were interrupted by a loud knock at the door.

"You need some help, doctor?" she asked, matter-of-factly as she opened the door. Florence Nightingale.

I released the sagging doctor and made the door in three quick steps just as she entered. Her eyes went wide in surprise as she spotted the empty table and Kasabian off to one side on the floor, arm draped over the open drawer, blood staining his white smock. But not for long: I hauled off and decked her with a right, and she went down like a bludgeoned steer. Kasabian, observing this with a quick glance over his right shoulder, frantically went back to fingering the files as I returned, emerging with one labeled "H, C." He handed it back to me, then remained motionless and whimpering down on the floor, still on his knees, supported by the drawer.

There were two sheets of paper within the folder, each marked with Hawley's initials. On the first, and in a large, sloppy scrawl that filled a page quickly, were the notations "AOH (w/ CH3) Fem. 6/30/36: bruises, abrasions. 8/5/36: stitches 2 lacerations; bruises. 10/22/36: more b & a." Based on what I read here, Chester had been beating Abbey on an intermittent basis at least since June, and with more serious results in early August when some stitches were required. The final notation indicated that she'd been brought to see Kasabian a mere five days before I met them both at the Hawley residence. I switched sheets and quickly read the second, older sheet: "AO'H (CH) Female: 4/18/36 expulsion, 12-16 wks max. 4/20/36: blood, morph. 4/27/36: ok." I stood there a moment absorbing what I had just read. This added a new dimension to Hawley's abuse of

Abbey in that it indicated that he had impregnated her several months before the random treatments for beatings had begun and that the child had been aborted with some resolved follow-up complications. The guy was an even bigger bastard than previously thought and no wonder that Abbey had tried so hard to avoid my line of questioning.

During this, Kasabian had crawled over to a nearby shelf and grabbed a handful of gauze, which he now had pressed tightly against his right ear. He sat on the floor, back to the wall, legs extended, breathing heavily and whimpering quietly. The gauze grew redder as I watched.

"I'm taking these," I said. "Don't move. Five minutes." I paused and glanced around the room – "or I'll take those dehorning clippers and go to work on your fingers." I gave him my nastiest smile. "And your nose and tongue while I'm at it." I threw in the last part for good measure, and it worked: Kasabian's eyes were squeezed tightly shut, a strange whining moan seeping from his throat. Brünhilde lay motionless, but breathed heavily as I stepped over her otherwise motionless form. It looked like I had broken her nose, but it wouldn't impair her looks much. I made a quick exit, locking the doors behind me.

Tuesday, November 10, 1936. 4:16 p.m.

IT WAS GROWING dark as I pulled up to the front of the Hawley residence. I wanted to see Abbey and hoped that Chester hadn't been lying to me when he had said that he had a weekly appointment on Tuesdays at four o'clock. I knocked, Abbey answered. She was startled to see me again and quickly stammered that Chester – that none of the Hawleys – were home at present. I said that was okay, I wanted to talk to her. She turned away as if dreading the prospect.

"Why do you keep bothering me? Why don't you leave me alone? *Why?*" she asked, exasperated.

"Let's talk about Dr. K," I said. "Or maybe you know him as Kasabian? He's treated you several times for various cuts and bruises – and earlier this year for your…ah…*predicament*. You had an, uh, abortion performed by him."

She stiffened, her fingers searching blindly for something to grab hold of. They found the back of an armless wooden chair, and she dropped heavily onto its seat. She breathed quickly and looked miserable. A minute passed before she spoke.

"You must think I'm terrible," she said, barely audible.

"No. Just young and confused – and much too trusting. He's taken horrible advantage of you," I responded. "Now, Hawley: He's a different story. He's an opportunist of the worst kind. *He's* terrible."

"It…it was back in April," she said quietly, eyes turning red and tearing slightly. "I was, I guess, no more than three months along, so it wasn't like we were killing a baby or anything like that, was it? Just a lump growing inside me?" She paused, and continued. "But it was horrible. I felt wretched for a few days. Absolutely terrible." She shook her head back and forth slowly as she recalled the events. "But that relationship's all over now. All over."

Over? That was news. "How long did it go on for?" I asked.

"Oh, I don't know; a year and a half, maybe. But it's all over now. It seems so strange now, but it didn't at the time." She was staring blankly at the floor.

"But your bruises: You still had them – reasonably fresh ones – a couple of weeks ago. He *still* hits you, right?"

She bowed her head. "Well, that's Chester. He's different. He's changed, or is trying to change. I've told you all about him already. I told you I love him, and he loves me. We're...we're working on it."

Well, I didn't think she was *terrible*, but her mind obviously worked in rather strange ways. Her idea of *all* over was significantly different than mine.

"Listen to me, Abbey. It isn't healthy for you to continue on here. You can leave any time that you want. Pack and I'll take you with me now. Put you up someplace until you can get situated again, start a new life." This was my last shot at convincing her, but I might as well have been shooting at ducks in the dark.

"No!" she stated adamantly. "I couldn't do that to them. They're my friends, my *family*. I couldn't do that to them!" Objectivity was nil here.

"Okay," I said. "I can't force you. You still have my number?" I asked. She nodded affirmatively. "Well, then, hang on to it. Use it if you need to – for *any* reason. I'll come get you. I'm only thirty-five, forty minutes from here." I said this slowly and evenly, hoping it would sink in. "But *be careful*. He ever hits you again, even *threatens* to hit you again, get out of here. Call me – *do something for yourself for a change*."

She looked up and smiled a weak half-smile at me, and gently touched my lower arm. "You're sweet," she said. "You really are. You're so nice to me. It'll be all right – I'll be all right. Honest. But thanks." And with that she leaned forward and gave me a hug, her face pressed into my chest.

There wasn't much else I could do or say, so I said goodbye. As an afterthought I suggested that she do herself a big favor and find another doctor, a local doctor. She nodded in response, but I doubted the decision was hers to make.

I didn't have the heart to tell her that Kasabian was an *animal* doctor.

206

Wednesday, November 18, 1936. 8:19 p.m.

I RESTOCKED THE shelves behind the bar while Willett poured drinks for the regulars. They were well represented tonight – among others, Kahn, Dovey, Edwards, Mackey and, sitting alone at a table, Floyd Tolinson. Tolinson and Holly had dated a decade earlier, right before I'd come to the island, and were still a couple for the first half year or so after I got here. She never said what had happened between them; I never bothered to ask. She and I were married now and had been for a long time, so his frequent visits to the bar didn't bother me. And, from what I could tell, didn't bother Holly either. He kept to himself most of the time when he wasn't playing cards with Ives, and his money was as good as anyone else's. I had no quarrel.

A week had passed since I'd last seen Abbey or had anything at all to do with the Hawleys. I'd managed to put them – her – out of my mind. After all, I'd been sticking my nose in her business, and she hadn't wanted it there. Best to leave things be.

Holly entered through the front entrance and quickly made her way across the room. A worried look clouded her face, and everyone in the immediate area saw it.

"Oh, Lew," she said loud enough so that the others were able to hear. "What's happening? It's Yumi. She's gone. Just like Grace – she's disappeared."

I told her to slow down and start from the beginning, and asked if the cops knew about this.

"Well, she's gone, and under circumstances similar to Grace. All of her personal belongings are gone. I assume that the police know, but I don't know that for a fact. It's obviously becoming public knowledge here in town, so they *must* know. I heard it from Ruth Kinney, who heard it from Betty Hurley, who heard it from...I don't know." Holly was visibly distraught and rubbed her hands together repeatedly as she laid out her disjointed narrative. "I saw her just a week or so ago to discuss poetry. She seemed so happy then, seemed like everything was okay, the same." Holly suddenly stopped talking, lost in thought, brow furrowed with concentration.

I thought back to one of Yumi's poems, the one that appeared in the *Times* a month earlier, the one that Edwards had disliked so intensely. I looked over at Edwards, but his expression was unreadable.

"Lot of this desertion stuff goin' on," slurred Dovey, barely moving. "Must be the weather." His lip wasn't quivering yet.

"Georgie Richards, up in Surf City – his wife Ethel took off, too," chimed in Kahn. "Cleared out all her possessions and took their truck. Georgie's pissed off, reported it to the cops, told them he doesn't care if the bitch – excuse me, Holly – doesn't care if she never comes back."

Holly drifted out of her reverie briefly after her name was mentioned. She smiled a small smile and I glanced over my shoulder at the recipient – Tolinson quickly looked back at his paper. I looked back at Holly, but she had already drifted off again, lost in thought.

"Yeah, Yumi's a real looker, if you like them exotic. And I do," said Kahn. Actually, he liked them *female*; all other considerations were secondary.

"Her poetry stunk, though," said Edwards, coming around once again. Then the bunch of them started arguing about poetry once again.

Holly snapped out of her trance and looked for a moment at the quarreling group, then at me.

"I'll go over and see Tak. See if there's anything we can do," I said, pulling my coat on.

"Thanks, Lew," she said quietly and with a small smile, gently placing her hand on my forearm. It's the small things, I thought to myself. In spite of all our arguments and the disagreements that go on between us – said and unsaid – sometimes there's more conveyed in a momentary touch such as this than could be conveyed in a thousand words.

Now, if she'd only leave the damned ashtrays alone.

I worked my way through cold, dark, windswept streets the four blocks to Tak's home on Bay Avenue. The storefront door, beneath the sign that read "Souvenirs – Groceries," was open. I went in. The lights were on and the place stocked for offseason: the shelves half-filled with bread, cereal, and other assorted staples. Off to the sides was some of the remaining summer stock – useless novelties and knickknacks that always seemed to sell so well to the throngs of tourists wishing to take home a little piece of Beach Haven. I called out to Tak – no response. I pushed open the door at the back of the shop. It led to a small hallway, a locked door beyond and a staircase to the right that led up to their living quarters. I knocked at the door at the top, again to no answer. I pushed the door open and stuck my head in, and was greeted by the overpowering smell of something burning, something reasonably pleasant, perhaps incense. I called out to Tak one more time and identified myself, and this time he responded.

I entered the small room behind the kitchen and found that it had been converted to a small, modest shrine. Tak stood before me, looking quizzically at the small carved, wooden, winged dragon held in his hand. He looked tired and very sad, but a trace of a smile crossed his features as he spotted a friendly face.

"Tak. I heard. I'm sorry," I said.

"Yuyu..." he said, quietly. I'd only heard him refer to Yumi by this affectionate pet name once or twice before.

"Do you know anything about the Shinto religion, Lew?" he

continued, seemingly ignoring my comments.

I told him I didn't.

"We live our lives in subservience to the will of the *kami* and we seek their approval and strive to gain their protection. The *kami* are forces of nature – gods – supernatural powers if you will – and there are hundreds of different *kami* whom we worship. There are *kami* of food, home, healing, purification, thunder, rain, lightening – you name it. In our homes, we worship them daily in these simple shrines, this *kami-dana*. We make simple offerings, and services are brief, but reverent, and attended by all family member." He paused, his voice breaking. After a deep breath, he continued. "Our beliefs – our worship – are centered on the powers of nature. We have a dislike – a *dread* – of contamination, fouling, pollution. Conversely, we have all-consuming need for ritual purification. This dread most evident when someone die. The deceased buried as soon as possible and, after period of mourning, surviving family members go through ritual of cleansing, bathing themselves repeatedly and, in some instances, abandon their home and build new one. The object here is to purge oneself of those impurities that soil individual's nature while in daily contact with the people around him – and world in general." He turned slowly and looked me in the eye. "Yuyu is dead. I *know* it. And yet I cannot…I cannot…I cannot do anything about it."

"Yumi's *dead*?" I asked, startled by what he'd just said. "I was told she'd disappeared."

"That's what everyone else say, what they all think. But I *know*. Yuyu's my wife, and she is a loving, devoted wife. She wouldn't run away, ever. It's not Japanese style. It's not *her* style. No, my friend, Yuyu didn't run off, in spite of what Purdy and his lackeys think. Yuyu is dead. I can *feel* it."

"Why don't you tell me about it, Tak. Maybe I can help," I said. I wasn't clear whether he actually knew what he was talking about – was Yumi indeed dead? – or whether he was just in a state of denial, and couldn't accept the notion that she may have deserted him.

"Nobody can help, now," he said. "But it is kind of you to offer."

"When did it happen?"

"Last Saturday night – the fourteenth. Maybe early the fifteenth," he said. "Yuyu and I sleep in different bedrooms." He paused for a moment and looked up at me. "You would not understand, Lew." He was right; I didn't. "Hers is larger room on ground floor at back of house, behind the staircase, and mine upstairs, on third floor; it just worked out that way. We both went to bed Saturday night, ten o'clock perhaps. Sunday morning, when she did not arise by 9:30, I went in to waken her. She was gone, her clothing was gone. Personal items, everything." He paused for a moment, looked at the simple carving in his hand, then wandered towards the door and steps leading downstairs. I followed closely behind.

"I called police," he continued, descending the staircase, "and Purdy and his men came over and poked around. He declared it *simple* case of desertion, said that is the conclusion the evidence supported. Said I was making mountain out of anthill." He shook his head dismissively. "His counterparts at northern end of island agree with him. But they are blind to truth, all of them. They will not accept possibility that her disappearance is result of some sort of violent act."

We were in the shop now and Tak placed the small figure on a shelf with an array of dissimilar items.

"And the *good* citizens of Beach Haven: it did not take long for news of my misfortune to circulate among them, thanks, no doubt, to Purdy and members of his force. They are a small-minded, gossipy bunch out there. Already I hear the snickers, the hushed whispers, the amused looks when I pass them on street. What is the word? *Cuckold?* That is what they think I am – some impotent old man whose attractive wife has run off with another, more virile, man. Their lack of imagination allows for no other possible explanation."

"Why do you think she's dead? Don't you think there's some other possible explanation?" I asked.

"If you are asking if I have physical evidence of her death, the answer is no. But inside" – he paused and tapped his chest with his forefinger – "I know she is dead. I can *feel* it."

I could just imagine Purdy listening to this, what his reaction must have been.

"How about the region's hospitals – did you check with them?"

"The police did," he responded, wearily.

"And the state police? Were they called?"

"Purdy did all that. He went through all usual motions, I will give him that."

"What else would you have him do, Tak?" I asked, gently. "What would *you* do, if you were in his place?"

He stared at the wall, and there was a slight tremble in his lower jaw. He looked as sad as I've ever seen a person; a lone tear slowly worked its way down his cheek.

"I…I do not know," he whispered.

The room was silent except for the occasional rattle of windows buffeted by the gusting wind outside. He looked up at the shelves of knick knacks.

"What do I do with all these things?" he asked in a louder voice. "This store was *hers* – her *baby*. She loved ordering and arranging and rearranging all these things for summer tourists, loved having them visit the shop, loved talking with them. What do I do with all *this*?"

His voice was growing louder now, and he was acting more erratic as the thoughts rushed in at him, as he grew overwhelmed by grief and the potential of dishonor and humiliation. I realized I was probably doing more harm than good.

And then I noticed his entire frame was trembling violently, his breathing deep and labored. He suddenly lashed out, screamed something unintelligible in Japanese, and smashed the shelf in front of him with his fist. The shelf's contents bounced and shattered on the floor below, Tak grabbed the sides of his head, screamed something else in Japanese and slumped to the floor where he covered his eyes and sobbed. I went over and knelt beside him, placing my hand on his hunched shoulder.

"Easy, Tak," I said, my words falling on deaf ears.

"*Fumeiyo...seppuku...jisatsu...jisatsu...shi...*" he moaned to himself, then "*Yuyu...Yuyu,*" after which he sobbed uncontrollably. I only understood the *Yuyu* part.

"Tak. Listen to me. I'm going to leave now," I said. I felt I was making the situation take a downslide by being there, and wanted to get the hell out before I made it even worse. "You need anything – anything at all – give me a call. Or stop by." I stood up and looked down at the pathetic looking figure slumped at my feet. "Goodbye, Tak. Take care of yourself. I'll keep in touch," I said.

Maybe I should have made an offer to help, to look into her disappearance for him, to see what I could turn up. But I didn't.

"It was sad, Gordon. Really sad." I shelled a peanut, dropped its husk to the floor. "You've known Tak almost as long as I have. I've never seen anything like this before, anything that even *hinted* at this." I popped the two nuts into my mouth.

"Sounds neurasthenic."

"Willet: *English.*"

"Neurasthenic. Suffering from neurasthesia. You know: nervous breakdown. Mental strain will do it. Or exhaustion. Although the distinction between neurasthenia and hysteria is not always clear, they kind of merge into each other. Come to think of it, though, women have a greater tendency to become hysterical than men. The Latin races are more hysterical than Northern Europeans and it's rarely observed among savages. I don't know where Orientals fit in." He pondered this for a moment. "I guess Yumi's departure could have that sort of affect on him. I'll have to look it up when I have a chance."

"He really thinks she's dead, but doesn't have any evidence to back it up with. Least I don't think he does." I attempted to crack another peanut, but this shell gave me a struggle. "He looked like human wreckage, slumped over in a heap on the floor, mumbling incoherent phrases in Japanese. *Jisatsu* is the one I remember, whatever the hell that means; said it a couple of times." Probably the name of a sister. Or a long-lost dog. Or *something*. I went to smash the impenetrable shell with an ashtray when I realized that Willett was staring at me, trying to recall something. "What is it?" I asked.

"Hang on a minute," he said over his shoulder as he stepped briskly out of the room. Hoover was at my feet, sitting up on his haunches, begging. I tossed him a peanut, which he snapped from the air and downed in a single motion. Willett's muffled footfalls padded about the room above. The taproom's three patrons talked quietly amongst themselves at one of the tables. Moments later, Willett reappeared with a large, orange-covered book in his grasp.

"What's that?" I asked.

"*Ripley's Big Book Believe It or Not!* 1934. Some interesting stuff in here," he said, quickly leafing through its pages.

"Does this have anything to do with *anything*?" I asked.

"Here it is," he said, ignoring my question. "Listen: 'Bushido, the way of the warrior, is the ethical code of the Samurai, the Japanese order of knighthood that demands courage, honor, and loyalty to the country...' Let's see... 'Formally abolished with the end of Japanese feudalism, but its ideals still have great influence on today's population of Japan...'"

"Very interesting, Willett, but what's it doing in *Ripley's*?" I interrupted.

"Oh, well, the title is *The Japanese Warrior Who Killed Himself Twice*. Seems he killed himself, was technically dead and then someone revived him and nursed him back to health. Then he killed himself again, and was successful the second time."

"So what?" I asked.

"So, well, it's not the story I want you to listen to, it's the background stuff. Let me finish." He skimmed a little further, and continued. "Here: 'It also requires the duty of hara-kiri, a national form of honorable suicide, or *jisatsu*, by knife and one's own hand.' I *knew* I'd heard that word before," he said, closing the book and looking up with a satisfied expression.

I stared at Willett for a moment. "Jesus Christ – he's gonna kill himself!"

Six minutes later, I arrived back at Tak's, having run the entire distance. I crashed through the front door and ran to the stairwell, yelling Tak's name as I ascended the steps. The kitchen was empty.

"Tak! It's me – Lew," I yelled once more as I made my way over to the small room with the shrine, pausing momentarily as I encountered the unmistakable reek of human fouling.

Tak was in there, all right. His contorted form lay on its side on the floor before me, in the midst of a huge pool of fresh blood. Half-open eyes fixed on nothing, mouth frozen open in a soundless scream, a crimson-stained dagger off to one side. Trails were smeared through the blood as if he'd thrashed about, or tried to move after the act. It looked like hara-kiri to me, all right, or what I thought hara-kiri should look like. His abdominal area was a ruined, blood-soaked mess. I could imagine the traditional L-shaped wound behind the torn and matted fabric. The smell was sickening; I breathed through my mouth in an effort to minimize its impact.

The *kami* weren't going to like this. I called Purdy.

I stood outside on the street, shivering, smoking a cigar, working on my flask. Purdy arrived ten minutes later. It was cold, but the clean autumn air was a damn sight better than the stench upstairs. I offered him a swig, which he took and took again, then showed him the way.

"Doesn't look like it went as planned," said Purdy, surveying the mess before him and breathing through a linen handkerchief. "Just 'cause he's a Jap doesn't mean he knows what he's doing, I guess."

"Maybe," I said, unsure of what exactly a successfully executed act of hara-kiri would look like.

He knelt and looked at the razor-sharp dagger. "This could have caused some of Schweickert's wounds, couldn't it?" he said.

"Are you serious?" I asked, incredulously. "Tak? And Schweickert? Come on, Purdy." I couldn't believe he'd made such a wild, unfounded connection. I hoped it was the strain caused by two horrific deaths in such a short period that led to such a ridiculous comment.

"Yeah, you're probably right," he agreed. "Miller was ready-made for that killing, anyway. And this? This is a suicide. Plain and simple."

I had to agree with his last assertion.

"Any way you cut it, this isn't good – not good at all. Tourist season before you know it. Shop'll be closed. *Christ.*" He shook his head.

He didn't want to stay in the room any longer than necessary, nor did I. I showed him to the telephone in the shop downstairs. He made several calls – one of them for police backup and the other to Doc Havens. While he barked various orders into the phone, I occupied myself by looking at a series of small, inlaid wooden boxes, trying not to think about the remains of my friend upstairs. The little boxes were lined up on one of the shelves next to a half dozen silver necklaces, and closer inspection revealed that each of the boxes had a hidden sliding cover, allowing access to the small compartment inside. Clever, but not a whole lot you could fit inside – maybe a half-dozen wooden matches or something. Nice workmanship, though; enlarge it by a factor of fifty and it'd make a nice coffin.

When Purdy finished, we headed back outside to wait and have a smoke. I made the usual assurances that I'd be available for any further questions and an official statement come morning. Schoengarth, Hipple and Doc Havens all arrived within a minute of each other. They headed inside as a group, leaving me alone outside.

The full impact of my friend's death hit me now and I felt depressed – depressed enough to not feel like heading back home and answering a thousand stupid questions, depressed enough to feel the need to unwind. Flask in hand, I walked the thirteen blocks north to the old Snuggery Dock bayside by the Beach Haven Fishery. I picked up a pint at Gus Potts' liquor store as backup.

May Willis had a houseboat whorehouse that made the rounds of the area's bayside communities. It was a Wednesday night, so the odds were that she'd be here, and she was. May kept the boat stocked with a small group of girls from Atlantic City, any three of whom would be present and working on any given night. Her business was supported almost solely by the pound fishermen here in the borough and elsewhere on the island, but there was always room for interested *outsiders* like myself and I was greeted boisterously by a couple of drunken Norwegians stumbling off the boat and onto the pier.

Inside, I asked May who was available, and she brought out a peroxide blonde named Toby. Nicely padded, a lot of meat on her bones – just my type.

"Hey, big guy! I remember you. *You speak English!*" she said, as if I was a long-lost friend.

Evidently, we'd met before.

Several hours and a pint later, I stumbled home. Inside my darkened house, I crashed onto the living room sofa to sleep. I figured – as I always did in my alcohol-clouded mind – it was the *safest* thing to do. If Holly ever asked why I was out here I could tell her I didn't want to wake her. As if these nights were somehow different than the hundreds of other nights when I stumbled home drunk from the taproom and into the bedroom, making a God-awful racket that could have woken the dead.

There'd be no waking the dead tonight, though – just adding to their numbers.

Thursday, November 19, 1936. 11:36 a.m.

IT TOOK ME close to two hours to write out my statement, and to fill in the various forms Purdy shoved my way. When he was satisfied that the paperwork was in order and there were no loose ends, I said goodbye and left. Not that I was in any particular rush, I was just tired of Purdy. And my head hurt.

I drove north on the boulevard, passing through the various communities that dotted the way to Surf City. They looked like ghost towns, the bulk of their homes and businesses boarded up for the winter, their streets void of people. I passed a single car heading south at one of the numerous undeveloped stretches between towns, stretches of bayberry and pine as far as the eye could see.

The temperature hovered in the low thirties, the sky gray overhead as I arrived in Surf City. I stopped in the first open store I saw, asked to look at their copy of the Ocean County phone directory, and located George Richards' address on North Ninth. I wanted to talk with him, to set my mind at ease that there was no possible connection between the disappearance of his wife and that of Grace Peterson and Yumi Takarada.

The Richards home was on the north side of Ninth, diagonally across from the abandoned Barnegat Railroad freight platform. It was a nondescript little bungalow, similar to a dozen others I'd passed on the blocks to its south: one story and covered with clapboard in dire need of a new coat of paint. The yard was unkempt and overgrown, a narrow drive leading past the left side of the house to its rear, a worn walkway from the road to the front steps. A second path led from this walkway to the drive.

I knocked on the door several times; no one answered. There were some faint sounds of activity coming from the rear of the house, so I wandered around back. Parked at the rear of the house was a nice looking '32 Chevy Roadster two-door convertible, dark green with black fenders – the only thing on the property that looked kept up. Beyond it was a ramshackle wooden garage with sagging, open doors; to its right a larger wooden structure, in much better shape, and this, too, had an open pair of hinged doors. The yard was finished off with an abandoned privy, several old weather-beaten boats in various states of deterioration and other miscellaneous junk partially obscured by the encroaching growth of the neighboring lots, all of them undeveloped.

Inside the larger building was a large, muscular man at work building a new boat; a sneakbox. I said hello. The worker paused, put down his tools, and came over to greet me.

"Lew Porter," I said. "I'm looking for George Richards."

"Well, you found him, friend. What can I do for you?"

"I'm here on behalf of the Beach Haven Police," I lied, "and I'd like to ask you a few quick questions regarding your wife's disappearance."

He asked what in hell they had to do with Surf City, and I mumbled something about inter-departmental cooperation, short staffing, areas of expertise – the usual bullshit. He bought it, told me to follow him into the house where we could grab a beer and talk in comfort. Sounded good to me.

Richards returned with two open bottles of Ortlieb's. He was friendly, easy-going, mid-forties, stocky and solid, full beard and black hair going to gray. He handed me one of the beers, then turned to grab a chair. There was a small, perfectly round bald spot on the back of his head that was still tan.

"Fire away," he said, taking a long pull.

"Why don't we start with a recounting of the events leading up to her disappearance."

"Shit, I've done this a dozen times already; is this really necessary? And the bitch ran off, ain't no 'disappearance'." Mention of his wife seemed to annoy him.

I told him I'd read all the reports, but with his retelling the story some new, previously unmentioned detail might surface, or that a fresh account might put a new slant on things and give us a different view of the proceedings. He bought this, too.

"Well, let me start off by saying that she ran off with another man, I'm certain of it. There were lots of signs leading up to it, signs that I was too bullheaded to recognize. You know the kind: telephone callers hanging up when I'd answer, her telephone conversations cut short as soon as I'd enter the house, that sort of stuff. A husband *knows*. So, now, she's gone, and I don't ever want to lay eyes on the sneaky bitch again. But, you know? I still have trouble believing – accepting – that she's really gone…and for good." A pondering look momentarily clouded his face – one quickly blown away by the breeze of disgust. He polished off the beer in one swig and grunted, "Ahhh, fuck her!" He pulled a cigarette from the pack in his shirt pocket and tapped its end on his thumbnail.

"Tell me about the day of her disappearance," I said.

He sat there for a silent moment, squinting at me, crow's feet looking as though they were carved into his temples. He looked kind of like a suspicious Ulysses S. Grant.

"Well, hell, it was a nothing day, just like most others," he said. "Didn't seem no different. It was a Wednesday. October, uh, 28th, last saw her that evening. I was outside workin' on the boat and out she comes, seven o'clock maybe, and announces that she's going over to her friend Connie's, be back in a couple hours – Connie lives a couple blocks from here on Seventh. So, I finish up around 8:15 or 8:30, and head inside and have a couple o' beers. Get to worryin' about her, so's I call Connie and she tells me she hasn't seen Ethel in several days. Well, I say to myself 'This ain't right,' but what the hell. Ethel wandered in just after 10:30 – I know it was then 'cause I just finished listening to *Gangbusters* on the radio – didn't enjoy it much, though, worryin' about Ethel and all. So, she wanders in, and it don't take no genius to figure out she's been drinkin'. I asked her where the hell she'd been, figuring she's been out doin' God knows what with some other guy, and we got into a big argument. Nothin' new there. She just stomped around and yelled and screamed and made even less sense than usual. Whew, she could be a grade-A bitch when she wanted. Anyway, I wore down after an hour or so of this, told her I was sick and tired of arguing, and was goin' to bed. You see, I had this guy, Amos McNulty, comin' over at 5:30 the next mornin' on his way to work to look at the boat I was buildin'. I must've laid there an hour or so before I fell asleep 'cause she just kept stompin' around, makin' her usual inconsiderate racket, talkin' to herself and drinkin' a few more beers. Next mornin' I was up and out and she ain't in the bed, but I figures she's all pissed off and sleepin' on the day bed back in the sewin' room – nothin' unusual about that, did it all the time after our arguments. Anyways, I show McNulty the boat, but I notice the truck's gone, and I gets to worryin', so I go inside for a look-see. Well, she was gone, all her clothes was gone, all her bathroom crap was gone. Coat, pocketbook, you name it – gone. I was upset, all right, so I went back outside and told McNulty all about it." He paused and chuckled to himself. "Guy musta thought I was crazy, he sure looked uncomfortable. Anyway, I goes inside and call the cops, tell 'em all about her desertion." He stopped for some air, pulled open the drawer in the small, chair-side table to his left, removed a framed photo, and passed it to me. It was a wedding photo, a younger-looking Richards the male half of the duo.

"That's the bitch, back when we got along. Ethel Stoddard Richards. Good days, those; don't know what happened. Anyway, she stole my truck and made a royal fool o' me. God knows what my friends think, so good riddance to her. Hope she drives into the ocean or somethin' – the bay." With that, his tale was finished, and a moment later so was his beer.

I studied the photo and memorized her face. She was an attractive blond, or had been when the picture was taken. Kind of difficult to tell, though; even unattractive women look marginally attractive when they've been reworked for their wedding day. Only lasts a day, though.

Richards took the photo from me and looked at it for a moment, then stood, walked to a nearby wastebasket and dropped it in.

"Ancient history, now. She could come back crawlin' on hands and knees, beggin' my forgiveness, swearin' she made a mistake, it'll never happen again, the whole nine yards. You know what I'd tell her? Get the hell out of *my* house, go back to your precious lover-boy. Just...go the hell away."

We spent another ten minutes going over various aspects of his story; I wrote down McNulty's and Connie's full names and addresses, just for the record. Richards seemed tired and occasionally annoyed, but he went through the paces without too much complaining. When I finally thanked him and left, he was just sitting there, fiddling with a pack of matches, staring at the floor. Probably wondering what went wrong.

Tuesday, November 24, 1936. 12:50 p.m.

TAK'S BODY HAD been hauled off earlier in the week, loaded on a train and shipped back to the small southern California town where his parents still ran a vegetable farm. Edwards and Kahn stood at the bar drinking their lunches, Willett off to my side tinkering with the cash register.

"Thanksgiving day after tomorrow. Holly making a turkey?" asked Edwards.

"Always does," I responded.

Edwards looked around. "Where's Carver?" he asked.

"It's Tuesday," responded Kahn, not looking up from his drink. "The new issue of the *Beach Haven Times* is delivered here on Tuesday. Therefore, Carver must be in the crapper reading the damn thing. As usual. From cover to cover. Maybe twice." Kahn looked up at me. "When are you getting the heat fixed in there, Lew?"

"Hey, Carver! Pinch it off and get out here!" yelled Edwards towards the closed door in the corner. He turned to the rest of us. "Anyone here know why your shits are tapered?" We didn't. "So your ass won't slam shut!"

Carver emerged tucking in his shirt, the *Times* stuffed under his left arm.

"What's new in town?" asked Willett. "Besides Tak, of course."

"Well, there's a picture of the Peterson woman in here and now *I know why* someone would want to run off with her – *what a piece of ass.*"

He opened the paper and spread it out on the bar in front of us. Her photo was next to the weekly "Poets' Corner" column, and it included a lot more of her than the occasional head shot – we could all see why. She was listed as "guest columnist" this week instead of the usual "LBI Poets' Circle member" blurb, and probably warranted the extra attention and full photo because she was so damned good looking. She was dressed in a surprisingly low-cut gown, had the face of a pouty Jeanette MacDonald and the figure of Jean Harlow (pre-Production Code) – reminded me of that film where she sported the negligee, *Iron Man* I think it was. The *Times* always needed any filler it could get and she filled it nicely – she was a looker all right, and a pleasant exception to the norm. Not that Holly wasn't good looking; she was. But a full-length photo would have been wasted on her slim form. Just my opinion; I'm sure others would have disagreed.

And then it dawned on me that this was where Holly knew Grace from: They were both members of The Poets' Circle, and that would account for a friendship that bridged a geographic gap of twelve miles. Had she ever mentioned this before? I decided that if she had, I wasn't paying attention, and that wasn't an unusual occurrence at all.

Willett stood motionless, staring into space, his right forefinger held in the air before him as if about to make a point. Distracted by something,

"What's his problem?" asked Edwards of no one in particular.

"SHHHH!" shushed Willett loudly. He was listening to something – something the rest of us seemed oblivious to. He wandered from behind the bar and over to the cracked window and peered through it for a moment. "Jesus," he murmured excitedly, and ran out the front door.

After a brief pause, the rest of us followed, still baffled by Willett's actions.

There was a young kid, perhaps ten, wandering down the center of Dock Road from the direction of the bay. He appeared to be in a shocked daze as he shuffled along, his pants soaked to the knees, wet sand dripping from his hands and cuffs. Staring straight ahead, he'd yell the words "TRICK OR TREAT!" every five seconds or so, the words breathlessly fading off as he did so.

Others had emerged further down the road. A wool blanket was produced and wrapped around the child. He was quickly carried into Mabel Gettinger's house while Doc Havens and Purdy were called.

Minutes later, the child's hysterical mother arrived, followed soon after by Havens in his distinctive cream-colored Buick. Havens administered a sedative to both the child and his mother, the child mumbling the words "monster" and "bay" over and over. His mother soon revealed that her son had headed out an hour earlier to play bayside down at the end of Dock Road near the Acme Hotel. He did this frequently, and she thought nothing of it. I wondered why he wasn't in school like most other kids his age.

"I'm gonna check it out," I said. "Tell Purdy where I am if he shows up." Havens nodded, and Willett, Edwards, and Kahn all followed on my heels. Kahn hastily jotted notes on a small pad, undoubtedly the basis for a story in next week's *Times*.

We arrived at the road's end several minutes later and instinctively fanned out, looking for something – *anything* – that could have terrified a child so thoroughly. We poked around in the marsh grass that extended north of the road a hundred feet or so. No more than fifteen minutes had passed before Willett stumbled back into view, face gone pale, mumbling "Oh my God" several times over. He fell to his hands and knees and threw up whatever food had been in his stomach, his shaky arm pointing in the direction he'd just come from. "Over there," he managed to say just as a second wave of nausea overtook him. I was over there in an instant.

At my feet were the hideous remains of a dark-haired floater, a corpse in advanced stages of decomposition, so thoroughly repulsive looking that I had trouble keeping my stomach under control. Once I'd composed myself, I pulled a handkerchief from my pocket and held it over my nose and mouth. I knelt beside the remains for a closer look. The only sounds were the hissing of the breeze in the marsh grass and the cries of several gulls far overhead. And Willett's moans.

It must have come in on the tides. Filthy mud-caked clothing was twisted around the thing, a long necklace pulled up in the back, stuck behind its ears and tangled in the long black knotted hair. Its face was beyond description, red in places and white in others, eyes gone and the whole having the appearance of a bust hastily constructed by some demented artist out of globs of wet dough. The hands were crossed at the wrists in front of it, and were swollen into gross caricatures of themselves. Its legs were straight and feet together and, like the rest of it, bloated beyond description. The outer layer of skin was gone from its face, hands, legs and feet and it appeared that some of the bay's residents and, later on, some airborne scavengers had taken the opportunity to feed on some of its exposed areas. Eel grass was tangled up in the mess.

A car screeched to a stop at the road's end fifty feet behind me. The slamming of car doors was followed by Purdy's familiar bark. I stood and waved my arms. Purdy spotted me and quickly made his way through the waist-high grass, a half-dozen people at his heels.

I knelt again and took one last look before the group arrived. It had been a woman, but you couldn't tell that from its bloated features. Her long, black hair, if untangled and straightened, would have been at least one-and-a-half to two-feet long. Her garb, which was now bunched up around her waist and in tatters, left her swollen legs, crotch, and buttocks exposed. It bore a familiar faded red pattern and had at one time been an ankle-length dress. I rubbed a finger along the muddy surface of a length of the necklace, revealing a silver color beneath. It had been a woman, all right, but one you'd never want to lay eyes on in its present state.

Purdy stumbled onto the scene, took one look, and muttered something unintelligible. Gibbons was on Purdy's heels, pipe clenched between teeth and I would have sworn there was the trace of a smile on his face when he spotted the remains. The others arrived a moment later and, with that strange, unshakable fascination reserved for the macabre, all moved forward slowly for a better look. Purdy yelled at them to leave and go home, all of them except Willett. They shuffled and talked in hushed tones amongst themselves, but no one budged. Purdy screamed this time, telling Gibbons to arrest anyone still there in one minute and with that they all took off.

"This isn't turning out to be a good year," muttered Purdy to himself.

Purdy wandered up to the bar and asked for a double of Park and Tilford.

"You guys didn't see this," he said to the others at the bar just before downing the contents of his glass. He filled me in on what had happened in the past three hours since I'd left the body and returned to the taproom. Doc Havens had been called in and rendered the verdict that the body was, indeed, dead. Havens contacted Ocean County Coroner L. Delbert Powell – Del to those who knew him – who had arrived forty-five minutes later. Powell lived over on the mainland in the small town of Tuckerton where he was also the mayor. After a cursory look at the corpse and the comment about it being "pretty well rotted," Powell told Havens to have it shipped over to the E.J. Buchanan Funeral Home in Tuckerton. He said they'd figure out what to do with it later.

I asked Purdy if he knew the corpse's identity. He said he hadn't a clue. I told him I thought it was Yumi Takarada, basing my assumption on the long, jet-black hair, the discernible red Oriental dragon print on her tattered dress and the silver necklace that was similar, if not identical, to some I had seen in her shop. He thought about this and responded wearily that he guessed we should call the state police and get them involved in the off chance that there was some sort of foul play involved. They had ways of figuring out that sort of thing, he said, although it was a mystery to him how anyone could determine *anything* from the mess we'd found near the bay.

Purdy was clearly disturbed by the rash of deaths that had occurred in his sleepy little town over the last six weeks. And so was I – not only for the seemingly coincidental aspect of three violent deaths within such a brief time, but also for the disappearances that had occurred in a similar time frame. These disappearances were also seemingly unrelated, but one of them ended up with the body we'd just found. I hadn't wanted to get involved in this whole mess, but I already was. And on some level or other I was starting – for lack of a better word – to *enjoy* the challenge it presented. I decided to look into these disparate events a little more closely, if only for my own – and, I suppose, my wife's – peace of mind.

Purdy said something that I didn't catch.

"How's that?" I asked.

"I said: When it rains, it pours," he repeated, stubbing out a Camel in the ashtray.

After Purdy left, I grabbed the newest issue of the *Times*, leafed through to the photo of Grace Peterson, and carefully tore it out. When I looked up, Edwards was sitting there watching me, leering. His eyes moved from me to the photo, then back to me.

"Hey, Lew. What's the definition of *jerking off*," he asked.

"I don't know, Deuce. Tell me."

"Having sex with someone you love," he responded. He gave a short burst of laughter, slapped the bar, and went back to his drink.

It took me several moments to figure out what he was getting at.

Wednesday, November 25, 1936. 11:53 a.m.

I DIDN'T FEEL like dealing with the anticipated lunch crowd. I left the taproom in Willett's reluctant hands – he'd have to take a break from the book he was currently reading, a dreadfully thick tome titled *Business Fluctuations and the American Labor Movement* – and headed on foot for Tak and Yumi's neighborhood. Things were going to be comparatively hectic through Thanksgiving, but I figured I could fit in a few hours that afternoon before poking around in earnest come Friday. Yumi and Tak seemed a logical point of departure because of their home's close proximity to my house. That and the fact that I couldn't get the haunting vision of her face – once beautiful, now ghastly – out of my mind and the nagging notion that had I been just a little quicker, and a little smarter, my friend Tak might still be alive today.

I spent the afternoon wandering from house to house, knocking on doors, asking questions. This was somewhat easier than it sounds due to the fact that for every house occupied this time of year there were another fifteen-to-twenty houses closed up for the season, and the houses that were unoccupied, *looked* unoccupied.

My line of questioning was fairly routine because I didn't know what I was looking for, didn't know whether her death had been an accident, suicide, or, perhaps, murder. I asked the usual ones: what were they like, what sort of relationship they had, did you notice any changes over the past few months, any strangers in the area, that sort of thing. I made note of most everything that was said whether or not it seemed of any importance.

It turned out that no one in the area seemed to know the

Takaradas very well. The picture that emerged was very similar to the one I already had as a result of Tak's numerous visits to the taproom, and our frequent, though superficial, conversations. Tak was a loving husband and Yumi a loving wife. No one ever saw or heard of any arguments. Everyone seemed to like them. No one knew of any enemies. They owned their house and car, and no outstanding debts that anyone was aware of. They were frustrated in their attempts to have children, and had considered adoption as recently as eighteen months earlier. They had had a medium-sized black poodle named Smudge who was friendly and slobbery, and frequently tied out in their backyard where he spent most of his time in his doghouse. Smudge had died sometime from three months to a year earlier, depending on the person I spoke with.

Tak rarely left the house, preferring to work or relax in the yard when not occupied with his business. When he did leave, it was for a walk – and almost always to one of four destinations: Frankfurt's pharmacy nearby on Bay, Levinson's Central Provision Market at the corner of Beach and South, the Beach Haven National Bank and Trust Co., or – and this surprised me that it was such common knowledge in the neighborhood – the Dock Road Inn for a drink. Whenever encountered, he was unfailingly pleasant and always willing to help out a neighbor in need.

Yumi was cut from the same cloth. She, too, spent most of her time either inside or out back of their house. The occasional instances when she'd venture out into the neighborhood were always on her battered bicycle with the straw basket. Her weekly trips each Wednesday were common knowledge and she'd close her shop at noon and return around dinnertime. Only a few of the people I spoke with even knew she had a new car, as she kept it garaged at Gifford's a block away on Bay. No one seemed to know the purpose behind – or destination of – these weekly excursions. Her love of poetry was also common knowledge, and while many were pleased to see her pieces end up in the *Times* on a fairly regular basis, few could understand how something called a poem could not rhyme, and most couldn't understand what her poetry meant.

I'd exhausted the neighborhood by a little after six, my last interview in a kitchen where the woman, infant perched on hip and held with one hand, attempted to prepare dinner. My little notebook now held a good thirty pages of notes on the Takaradas. I reviewed them at my office desk, a bottle of Old Overholt within reach. I knew a lot more than when I'd started, but it all seemed so superficial. And none of it seemed to provide any sort of reasonable explanation for the events of the past week-and-a-half.

But then, perhaps the explanation wasn't *reasonable*.

234

Thursday, November 26, 1936. 9:08 a.m.

THE TAPROOM'S BOOKS were spread out before me; I struggled to bring their entries up to date. Sipped my third cup of the strong coffee Willett always had in a pot warming in the kitchen. Maxwell House. "Good to the last drop." Well, good unless you're the only one drinking it and the last drops in the pot have cooked down to a thick, caustic sludge.

The joint was scheduled to be open until noon that day, if anyone cared, and would reopen again that evening. It was empty now, which wasn't particularly surprising. I'd fled my home and the smell of cooking Thanksgiving turkey to try to do some bill-paying work. I figured that with some peace and quiet I might actually get somewhere.

And then Holly entered the room.

She had on her apron and hair pulled back, and placed a ring with two keys on the table before me. She looked sad.

"Yumi's house — I forgot I had them until a couple of minutes ago. She gave them to me a year or so ago. 'In case of emergency,' she'd said. I guess they won't be of any use now. To anyone." She paused briefly. "I'm going to miss her. Both of them, but especially her."

I took the keys in my hand, looked at them a moment, then pocketed them. I wasn't sure whether they'd end up in yet another drawer, or if I might actually have a need for them. The former, most likely.

Holly pulled a chair and sat down across from me.

"Don't mind me, I'll be quiet."

Right.

After a minute or so, she spoke. As I knew she would.

"This place is so dreary," she said quietly, taking in the place with a look of disdain. "It needs some sprucing up. Some redecorating. It's so…cold and inhospitable the way it is now." She stiffened her shoulders in a feigned shiver.

"Stove works fine," I said. "Coal works like a charm, keeps the place warm." This was one of those conversations I didn't want to have, but felt compelled to respond.

"No, it really does need a change," she continued. "Like the Inlet Inn down in Holgate. They do all sorts of marvelous things with natural stuff they collect – *free* stuff. Like now, with their corn stalks, branches of autumn-colored leaves, pumpkins, gourds – stuff like that. And the rest of the year they decorate with shells, driftwood, reeds, branches of bayberry and anything else that isn't tied down and is free."

I grunted and choked down the dregs in my cup.

"Or Britz's. That place is clean and bright and nice looking. Lots of nice woodwork, lots of big mirrors to give it a sense of spaciousness. Or the Acme Hotel, for that matter. Or the New Surf Villa, up in Surf City. God, that place is beautiful – and so exotic looking from the outside."

It looked like Zorro's hacienda to me.

"Or even The Antlers, Lew, with those dreadful deer heads – but at least they're something – *something* – decorative."

"We've got all this nautical stuff decorating the place. And all the beer stuff; that's all free. And the Camden dancing vegetables: I like 'em and I know the patrons do, too – it's a work of art, almost," I responded, knowing full well this would irritate her.

"How can they see it?" she fired back. "The place is so dark you can't even tell if the lights are on when you first come in. And that… *rag!*" She was referring now to the old Indian blanket hanging over the front window. "You always have that *thing* there. No light could ever penetrate that thing." She was getting agitated now, her fingernails drumming a tattoo on the tabletop.

"It might need some patching, but it's functional. Keeps peering eyes and light right where I want 'em."

"And the floor," she resumed, but I cut her off.

"Listen: I like the place just like it is, and so would your father; it's virtually the same place he ran quietly – okay, maybe not so quietly – for all those years. The locals feel *comfortable* here, *like being at home* almost. I don't see any compelling reason to change it. No reason at all." I was annoyed.

"We could attract more people – new people; look at all the extra money it would bring in," she responded, appealing to the mercenary in me.

"We don't *need* any more money."

"It would make it all so much more interesting, less boring."

"Fine. You want a decorator taproom, we'll buy a second place, you can put in palm trees and pink curtains and big windows and whatever the hell else you want to put in. Serve crumpets or something. And you can run the damn place; I'll stick with this joint."

"I don't want to run any bar, that's your job. And we don't need two, one's quite enough, thank you!" she responded testily. "I have friends who have never even been in here, probably scared to death to come in here, with its reputation and all." I could hear her very clearly now.

"Is that what this is all about?" I asked, more than a hint of sarcasm in my voice. "Accommodating a bunch of tea-swilling, poetry-spewing old biddies? Christ, the dough'd be rolling in with regular Tuesday afternoon tea-time poetry readings; really pull in the crowds." I had the vague hope that she'd see some humor in what I was saying, but I knew better than that. Or should have.

"Damn it, Lew, you're so pig-headed sometimes," she yelled, standing up quickly, her chair crashing onto its back. She stomped out of the room, and nobody stomps like Holly. "I have work to do…I've got a turkey to deal with." I wasn't sure whether she was referring to the bird cooking next door or to me.

"A well-reasoned position," I mumbled under my breath. If Holly had her way, we'd drive this business into the ground. Hell, this was the only place in Beach Haven that offered what I offered: unpretentious, cheap, friendly, cozy, accessible drinking and with a minimum of brawls to disrupt things. Well, maybe an occasional visit by pseudo-Nazi goons, but other than that…. My regulars made this their place-of-choice; all the others were last-ditch backups. This was the real thing.

A dump, perhaps, but the *real thing*.

After stewing for a half an hour or so, I fired up the Ford and headed north a couple of miles just past Spray Beach. I knocked on Rhea Scully's door and waited. She lived in a small bayside house by herself, her late-husband, George, a bayman, who drowned accidentally several years earlier. He'd been an occasional customer and a nice guy. I'd stopped here back then to extend my condolences, one thing led to another and I'd ended up consoling her in ways I hadn't expected to – or at least not *consciously*.

I hoped she was home now, and alone.

Rhea answered the door, and a small smile greeted me. She was in her early forties, still in reasonably good shape, and still attractive in a tired sort of way. But she was always happy to see me and I felt that I was performing some sort of good deed by taking her mind off her problems, if only sporadically and for a short while. And, in a pinch, she knew she could turn to me to help with some bills.

Who was I fooling? I suppose I was taking advantage of her situation, but she always seemed genuinely happy to see me. And, come to think of it, I was always – happy, I guess you'd call it – to see her. No harm done, I'd convinced myself.

Not yet, anyway.

I was back home by two p.m., physically relaxed but troubled. An uneasy truce had resulted in a reasonably pleasant Thanksgiving meal, with Willett attending as he so frequently did.

A stomach full of turkey and all the other usual holiday stuff led to a heavy-duty nap. A little after six, some of the regulars gathering spontaneously out in the street woke me with their yelling for me to open the joint. I'd posted a note on the taproom door indicating a six o'clock reopening, so I threw on my shoes and rushed over. I left my coat behind and realized as soon as I hit the outdoors just how cold it had gotten.

Business was surprisingly good for a Thanksgiving night, and a few of the regulars had even brought their wives along, a ritual that occurred only several times during the course of the year. Willett and I were both kept busy, but I spent the occasional slow periods mulling over the occurrences of the recent past.

The power went out town-wide around 9:45, and after a half-hour or so it became evident it wasn't coming back on any time soon. The customers filed out one-by-one as they finished their drinks and we locked up after the last had left. I managed to step on Hoover's tail in the dark; he awoke with a yelp.

Holly was in bed, asleep, when I got home. I managed to pour myself a rye by moonlight in the darkened kitchen and settled back on the sofa to unwind. Something just wasn't sitting well, although admittedly these recent events did appear at face value to be a series of odd, unrelated coincidences. A bloody murder; three wives running off from their husbands, with one of them turning up later a drowning victim; two suicides; and a bunch of north Jerseyans attempting to beat the stuffing out of me – yeah, I'd call those odd coincidences, all right.

Tomorrow I'd head north on the island and talk with the neighbors and acquaintances of both the Richards and the Petersons – if only to verify their stories, and put any doubts about the circumstances behind their wives' disappearances to rest, once and for all. You know – *peace of mind.*

As for Tak and Yumi: Unless something new and significant surfaced having to do with her disappearance and their deaths, there was little more to do. Tak's suicide was obviously just that; but Yumi's drowning was more problematic. An autopsy, if there was one – and I wasn't sure that there would be – might reveal a death from gunshot, knife wound or bludgeoning – wounds that would have been virtually impossible to spot during a superficial examination and in her body's advanced state of decomposition. Similarly, a lack of water in her lungs would indicate that she died before ending up in the bay and water from a different source than the bay would suggest drowning elsewhere, followed by disposal in the bay. But this was now all in the hands of the state police and the coroner, and they might collectively chalk it up to accidental drowning and leave it at that. If it was judged as such, at least it would put the minds of Yumi's friends at ease – Holly's included – and life could go on. On the other hand, while an autopsy could help confirm the theory of accidental drowning, it could instead reveal foul play. And that would open a whole new can of worms, a can of worms that would get me involved.

One thing was for certain: this wasn't going to be a typical Beach Haven winter. More interesting, perhaps. Not as boring. But far from typical.

Friday, November 27, 1936. 8:02 a.m.

THE MORNING WAS cold and gray; the sun having taken a day off. The temperature plummeted into the twenties the night before and had only edged up a degree or so since daybreak. At least the power was back on.

It took me several minutes to coax the Ford from its slumber. Once started, I popped it in gear and eased it onto the road to High Point. I'd put more miles on it in the last six weeks than I had on it and its predecessor over the previous two years. Its heater put up a valiant, but initially ineffectual, struggle against the elements. Condensation freezing on the inside of the windshield demanded repeated swipes with a gloved hand.

Not an ideal day for hoofing it around Peterson's neighborhood, looking for people to talk to. Again, the saving grace was the small number of occupied houses this time of the year. All the year-round residents knew everyone else who was a year-rounder – some better than others, of course – but at least they all knew who I was talking about. A consensus was quickly reached, and it wasn't a favorable one. Peterson was, in one neighbor's unminced words, an "artsy-fartsy phony" who thought "his shit doesn't stink." There was the general notion that he felt superior to the rest of them – the "dirty-necked locals" as a bayman put it – and had somehow managed during his six years in town to have virtually no interaction with any of them. He remained homebound and only surfaced on occasion to head out for another bottle of liquor.

The only locals Peterson *did* have time for were not of the homegrown variety, but from the small group of transplanted artists scattered throughout the community. Problem was they didn't seem to have time for him – or so it seemed to one woman I spoke with, Grace's friend Betty.

It was generally agreed that Peterson adored his wife and she, inexplicably, him. On the rare occasion that one of the locals would comment on Peterson's shiftlessness, Grace would leap to his defense and give the individual a tongue lashing of Biblical proportions, one that he'd soon not forget, one that he'd never again want to endure. The Petersons were city swells, however, and neither of them really fit in. Grace, at least, made an attempt – and that attempt was duly noted and, begrudgingly, appreciated by those I spoke with.

No one, however, had ever seen anything unusual or out of the ordinary. Grace had settled into her new life as a homemaker and homebody, working the small shop in the front of their house when it needed working. She'd spend her evenings alone in the tiny room where she wrote her poetry, continuously reciting lines and phrases to herself. In the summer evenings, when the ocean was calm, the air still and the neighborhood quiet, you could hear her reciting her rhymes, and those who mentioned this agreed to a person that it was very pleasant.

But you never know what goes on behind closed doors. It was apparent that they all seemed to like Grace more than they liked Howard, which wasn't saying much, and the consensus was that she grew tired and fed up with the bum, and took off. They all seemed to agree that, as annoying and stuck up as Howard was, he was incapable of foul play. As one of them put it, "If there was violence to be done, Grace was the one with the balls; *she* would have done it."

It was late morning when I tracked down a telephone booth in Bailey's Groceries on Eighty-First, and searched for the address of Ethel's mother over in Manahawkin. There was only one Stoddard listed; a call verified I had the right person. Said a visit would be all right. Half an hour later, I was seated inside her ramshackle cottage in a tiny living room across from Eleanor Stoddard. Cups of steaming black coffee sat on the table before us, with a bottle of Old Crow off to one side. Eleanor used the bourbon like others would use cream.

Eleanor told me she lived there alone, her husband dead of heart failure some six years back. She never liked George Richards. She hadn't approved of their marriage, but what was she to do when her daughter was starry-eyed in love? They'd been married for only two-and-a-half years, their relationship a volatile one from the git go. Ethel would attempt to pay the bills but George would always fritter the money away. He had an eye for women and, his wife suspected, had several one-night stands during his frequent drinking bouts. Always apologetic when sober, he would try to make amends by buying her gifts that he – that *they* – couldn't afford. The worst of these was the Chevrolet roadster that she loved so much, in spite of its being an albatross around her neck when it came time to scraping together money to pay the bills. There wasn't a one-week period when Ethel wouldn't storm off in the heat of battle and drive over to spend the night with her mother.

When she'd sleep it off, however, it was as if nothing had happened the night before; she'd return home the next morning to her loving husband. Until the next time.

Eleanor hadn't a clue where her daughter was, but she didn't seem worried about her. She'd been known to take off for parts unknown several times in the past when she was really mad, but always returned several days later. She suggested I try her good friend, Connie. When I pointed out that Ethel'd been gone for more than several days now, Eleanor gave it a moment's thought.

"She'll be back," she announced confidently, topping off her coffee with some more of the bourbon.

I got back to the island and Surf City shortly after noon. Polished off a quick ham and cheese on rye at the sole luncheonette that was open and took to the streets in Richards' neck of the woods. If it had warmed up at all since early this morning it wasn't by much, still freezing out.

George and Ethel – "the battling Richards" as one neighbor put it – were known far and wide for their frequent and noisy arguments. They argued endlessly, or so it seemed, and most often about money – or the lack of it. That and George's perpetual late-night drinking jaunts. Ethel'd get to throwing things and making a God-awful racket. This would usually culminate with her stomping out to their new Chevy roadster, screaming at full volume all the way and taking off for her mother's house over in Manahawkin. Like clockwork, however, she'd be back the next day, acting as if nothing had happened the night before, working off a hangover while washing and polishing her car. It was a ritual that was comforting in its consistently happy conclusion, and they would have been concerned only if it ended any other way.

Ethel was younger than George, by as little as five or as much as fifteen years, depending on the source. But she could scream like a banshee and could be heard by their closest neighbors, the Blackthorns; I spoke with the wife, Jessie. She and her husband were one of two other year-'round families on that block and they described with amazement – perhaps with a touch of pride – the fact that she could be heard in the dead of winter with doors and windows tightly closed. Hers was a voice to be reckoned with.

The night she'd taken off was a comparatively mild one, so some of the Blackthorn's windows were cracked – and that night's battle reasonably clear. They'd argued something terrible from roughly 10:30-11 – "after normal people's bedtime." Jessie had managed to fall asleep, but awoke to hear Ethel pull out of their yard and drive away sometime well after midnight, about 2:00 a.m. she supposed. She figured Ethel had waited 'til George was sound asleep to sneak out and leave. In her estimation, they were *both* impossible to live with and their separation could only be a move for the better. At least now she'd had good nights' sleep for the last four weeks.

Tracked down Connie Sneddon, Ethel's frequent drinking companion, or at least according to George. She was of little help, drunk as she was already at 4:30 in the afternoon. Most of what she had to say was superficial and there was little continuity to her rambling narrative. One point she was adamant about, however, was that she had no idea where Ethel took off to.

I found Amos McNulty at his bayside house in Ship Bottom-Beach Arlington, reached by a hundred-foot drive off the end of Thirteenth Street. He'd just arrived home from work minutes before I arrived and offered me a chilled can of Kreuger from his icebox.

"Bad enough," he said, "having to go there at 5:30 in the morning to look at his boat in the cold and dark. But that was topped by getting caught up in the middle of their little domestic drama! One minute he's telling me about the boat – a sneakbox, by the way – and next thing I know he's looking around, mumbling something about his truck. Suddenly he runs off and into the house – left me all by myself. After a few minutes of this nonsense I was fed up and started to leave, when he comes back out, yelling and cursing that his wife had run off on him. All I wanted to do was buy a damned boat, not play Father Confessor."

I headed back to the Richards house when I was finished with McNulty. It was dark now, his house unlit and empty, but the sky was clear and the moon near full; it was easy enough to see. Poked around his yard for a few minutes, trying to visualize the events of that night and the following morning, my breath hanging in clouds before me. Started to leave when I noticed the trash can by the side of the house. I removed my gloves and rummaged through it for several minutes before locating the wedding photo he'd tossed out a week earlier. Pulled it from its frame with hands growing numb, folded it and tucked it into an inside coat pocket, all the while thanking my lucky stars that it was here and not still inside in an un-emptied waste basket.

I wasn't quite sure why I had taken it. But then, I wasn't sure why I'd taken the picture of Grace, either. There wasn't any apparent crime in either instance, so there was no real reason to do so. Old habits die hard, I suppose. Both had been consigned to the trash and I was playing the knight in shining armor by saving them.

Saturday, December 5, 1936. 2:12 p.m.

"YOU EXPECTING BIRDS in here?" Edwards, staring at the rough cedar slab birdhouse sitting on the bar back.

"Gift from Buzby," I said. "For his shot of Watkins Grove," I added, sliding a De Nobili out of its box and clamping it between my teeth.

"Figures," he said, nodding. "Looks like his shit." He went back to reading the paper spread out on the bar in front of him.

Buzby and his assistant Jonah had made their monthly journey to the island the previous Monday, and had inadvertently chosen the coldest day of the year to date. The Christmas season arrived with the passing of Thanksgiving and he'd delivered his usual load of pine trees – soon to be christened "Christmas" trees – to the borough. As recent custom had it, these would be arranged in a line down the center of Bay Avenue for several blocks, adorned with lights. An interesting sight – rather pleasant, actually – except for when one of the town's drunks or elderly citizens would sideswipe some of them, leaving a twisted, blinking shambles out in one of the lanes.

Included in Buzby's annual load was a pile of holly, laurel, cedar and pitch pine boughs, as well as boxes of pinecones. All intended for decorative use and sold to all interested parties. A small, wooden trailer snaked behind Buzby's truck to accommodate this annual load.

Of course, any trip to the island wouldn't be complete without a stop at the taproom, resulting in my "proud" ownership of a cedar slab birdhouse. It was always fun to see and talk with Buzby and this trip was no exception. And, in spite of the freezing temperatures, Jonah had chosen to sit out in the truck, whittling. I even sent Willett out to tell the idiot to come in and warm up, but Jonah had refused. Christ, you'd think the guy was a temperance fanatic or something. Buzby told me the birdhouse was his latest project, over fifty of them back at his house waiting for one of his springtime visits. Maybe Holly could find a use for it then.

The door opened with its usual blast of cold air and in stepped Chet Hawley's colored chauffeur. He went through the familiar routine of verifying my presence before retreating the way he'd arrived. A minute later, Chet entered, deposited his hat, coat and scarf on one of the hooks near the door. He worked his way over to the bar.

"Porter. Good to see you again. Let's have another talk. Private, of course," he said as he pulled a five-spot from his money clip and slid it onto the bar. "Grab a bottle, something good. Have any Dewar's Ne Plus Ultra, twelve years old?"

I said I didn't, motioning to the selection behind me.

"Well, then, the White Label will suffice," he responded, turning and heading for my office. Nervy little bastard. I told Willett I'd be back in a few minutes, and extinguished my cigar.

Once inside and settled, Hawley inquired as to the progress of my so-called case – if there actually was any. I told him in general terms that a series of peculiar, unexplained, seemingly random incidents had occurred in the recent past on the island; I was poking around solely out of curiosity. He paused, slowly rotating the glass of scotch in his fingers, choosing his words.

"As you are undoubtedly aware, I'm a very well known individual on this island – well known *and respected*. As much for my fairness and compassion as for my generosity and good deeds to the various communities and civic groups. I dare say I'm loved by some." He paused and took a sip. "It has come to my attention that some of the locals – my neighbors, my *friends*," he added for emphasis, looking me in the eye, "are growing increasingly upset about an outsider – you – asking so many questions about them and *their* neighbors. Now, I fully understand being an outsider, but my wealth has broken down a lot of barriers, opened a lot of doors. You, my friend, are not in a comparable position. These are simple people. They are used to a style of life and privacy that's remained unchanged for decades. They don't like strangers sticking their noses into their business." He drained his glass and placed it in front of me. I got the hint and refilled it.

"Howard Peterson, his wife Grace, and a number of their neighbors; George and Ethel Richards, and *their* neighbors; the Takaradas, Yutaka and Yuyu, and their neighbors. Not to mention the disruption in my own household." He was looking at his fingernails now, but I knew his mind was elsewhere. "Don't you see? This is a small island with a small population. Everyone minds his own business and expects everyone else to do likewise. But you – you're just stirring up a lot of trouble and distrust between neighbors." He was wearing his best look of moral indignation now. I decided to let him finish, so I said nothing.

"I'm appealing to you, Porter. To your sense of common decency, your sense of fair play: Go back to being a bartender and leave the police work to the police – if, indeed, there is any need for police work. You'll be much happier that way. The residents of Long Beach Island will be happier that way." I waited a moment to make sure he was finished. He seemed to be.

"Chet – I can call you Chet, can't I? First of all, thanks for your concern, both for the residents of this island as well as my own personal wellbeing and peace of mind. What you say all makes sense. When someone starts asking questions, others grow uncomfortable. But when that happens, I always ask myself Why? Is it based solely on principal, or do they have something to hide? Well, I'll tell you what the reason is, what the reason always is: It's a combination of the two; everyone – and I mean *everyone*, from the petty thief cooling his heels in the local jail to the minister preaching to his congregation – *everyone* has something to hide. Not necessarily anything of any significance and, as often as not, nothing illegal – and, in most instances, things that are no one else's business. But everyone has *something* to hide, and that's why they all get jumpy when someone else starts poking around, asking questions.

"Now, in most instances, the reason behind the questioning in the first place is the commission of a crime. If the questioning ultimately leads to Joe Blow down the street getting arrested and sent off to prison, all those others who spent so much time moaning and groaning about invasion of privacy and so forth are the first to applaud a job well done, get the criminals off the street, throw the key away, fry 'em. *Sometimes you have to step on some toes to get the real answers*, follow me? Whatever decisions I make, whatever actions I take, are going to be self-motivated and based on what I think is appropriate, and not dictated by anyone else. Not the good people of the island and certainly not you."

I was finished now, so I refilled my glass; his was still two-thirds full. I sat back with mine in hand, took a long sip, and waited. A week had passed since I last talked with anyone regarding any of the three families he had mentioned, and I'd given the issue little thought myself during that period. But he didn't know that. Chet looked none too happy.

"Is it money? Is that the issue?" He was leaning forward and staring me in the eye now. "I'd be willing to reimburse you – *generously* – for your time spent to date, if you cease now. In the interest of keeping peace and harmony here on the island, of course. As a first step towards smoothing ruffled feathers, if you will."

"I won't," I said flatly.

Chet rose to his feet and stood there glaring at me for a good fifteen seconds.

"Well, then, I guess that settles that," he said. "Good day, Mr. Porter," he finished, turning and taking a step towards the door. He paused, however, and returned, grabbing the bottle of White Label and corking it. He *did* pay for it, after all.

"I hope you know what you're doing, my friend," he added, a touch of threat in his voice. "If any scandals arise out of this that touch upon any of my family or friends…" He stopped mid-sentence, turned, and left.

There was a chill in the air and I wasn't certain it came from the open door.

252

Saturday, December 12, 1936. 4:52 p.m.

"NO, NO, NO! Blondie's the one," yelled Edwards. "I'd fuck her in a heartbeat. I mean, for Christ's sake, *look* at her. She's stacked, tiny little waist, nice ass — a real dish. Wrap those legs around you, you'd be screaming for mercy in no time flat. Wish my wife looked even *remotely* like that."

"If she's such a dish, what's she doin' married to an asshole like Dagwood?" asked Carver.

"Winnie Winkle, now there's a woman," said Kahn, fanning himself with his hand. "Next time you see that one, take a look. I mean, she's not a knockout or anything like that. But beneath the surface, you sense a smoldering sensuality, a savage sexual beast just waiting to be unleashed, waiting for the right guy. Whew! I get hot just thinkin' about it!" I figured if anyone at the bar knew about this Winkle woman's sordid side, he would.

"*Winnie Winkle?* Are you fuckin' serious?" asked Edwards in astonishment.

"Winkle wears too much; she's always bundled up. How about Daisy Mae?" asked Carver.

There were nods around and a general murmur of agreement over this suggestion.

"She's a piece, all right, but kinda obvious. You want somebody a little more subtle," said Kahn. "Like Tillie the Toiler."

"Looks great in a bathing suit," agreed Edwards.

"Ba-ee Boo," mumbled Dovey. It was the first thing I'd heard him say in weeks.

"What the hell did he say?" Edwards asked of the crowd.

"What did you say?" Carver asked Dovey in a voice that could be heard in the next room.

"Bet-y Boop," repeated Dovey, attempting to enunciate.

"Betty Boop?" repeated Edwards. "She's a dog, for Christ's sake!"

"Aw, she ain't so bad," said Carver.

"I didn't mean dog *ugly*; I meant *dog* dog. Like Hoover," he added, looking at the snoring creature sprawled in the sawdust nearby. "The ears; that's the giveaway."

"You have to use your imagination with Boop. But think of that short, skimpy, strapless little black dress she wears. Ya saw something like that in real life, you'd be down on all fours with your tongue draggin', chasin' after her, sniffin' away. Ummm-ummm."

"How about Fritzi Ritz?" asked Mackey. "She's a looker."

"Yeah, but she once looked like that sawed-off little pig-headed dwarf Nancy. I couldn't climb on her – Fritzi, I mean – without thinkin' of Nancy," said Carver with a note of disgust. "I mean, you know what they say about apples."

"Nancy's her niece, not her daughter; might not even be a blood relation," said Mackey.

"Yeah, Fritzi has potential, all right," said Kahn, which immediately moved her a notch higher in everyone else's estimation. "What do you think, Willett?"

"Huh? Me?" he said, looking up from a brief history of the Quadruple Alliance opened on the bar in front of him. "I don't know. Dale Arden's nice. And the way she's drawn, you can kind of squint at her and imagine what she'd look like undressed."

"Maybe Dagwood's hung like a horse," said Carver. "You never know. Maybe it's Blondie who screams for mercy. And maybe it's those weird sandwiches he eats gives him the strength to ride Blondie all night, 'though with those fish you'd think his breath would stink."

"I'll tell you who's the stud of them all," said Edwards. All heads turned his way. "Popeye!" he announced.

"*Popeye?*" asked Carver in disbelief. "*The sailor man?*"

"Yeah, Popeye. Think about it. He may be ugly as a hen's ass, but why the hell do you think that skanky broad Olive Oyl's always chasing after him, trying to get in his pants?"

"'Cause she's even uglier than he is and ugly likes ugly?" asked Carver.

"Well, that, too, I suppose," conceded Edwards. "But it's the spinach!" he announced. "It's the goddamned spinach!"

"Explain," said Kahn.

"The spinach! Think about it. Popeye eats a can of the shit and what happens? All a sudden he goes through all these weird physical contortions and growths, giant muscles zooming up and down his arms and legs, muscles everywhere."

"And then he kicks the shit out of Bluto," added Carver.

"Well, yeah. But we're looking at him with his stupid little sailor suit on, muscles growin' everywhere, but it's what we *can't* see that's the key here."

"And that is…?"

"The hard-on of all hard-ons!" announced Edwards with a look of satisfaction.

There was a moment of silence as everyone stared at Edwards, absorbing what he'd just said.

"How would you know such a thing?" asked Kahn, breaking the silence.

"Well, it just stands to reason. The spinach gets his adrenaline flowing to all his extremities and muscles, and his bone's one of 'em. I just bet you that tucked away in the warmth and comfort of his pants little Popeye's turning into the ol' purple-helmeted warrior of love!"

"And Olive Oyl *knows* this?" asked Carver.

"Well, *of course*. It's one of those *animal instinct* type things. She can sense it, smell it. And by the way she acts, it's pretty obvious she's had a piece of it, too."

"Whew! No wonder she's always makin' all those weird little

cooing noises and gurgles and stuff," said Carver.

"Wish my wife made 'em," said Edwards.

"Okay," said Kahn. "For sake of argument, let's say you're right. Popeye eats spinach, Popeye gets a hard-on, Popeye beats Bluto to a pulp..."

"He wants to get him out of the way so he can jump Olive..." interrupted Edwards.

"Yeah, yeah, yeah. Then Popeye bones Olive Oyl," finished Kahn. "You've explained what Olive Oyl sees in Popeye. Now, explain what Bluto sees in Olive Oyl."

"Yeah, good question," said Carver. "She's about the un-sexiest, skanky little bitch I've ever seen. Why would a big guy like Bluto, who could probably have any broad he wanted down at the wharf, why would he want a dog like her?"

"Ahhh, there's her little secret," responded Edwards. "Her mouth, her throat."

"Her throat? You mean that long, skinny little chicken-neck with the big lump on it?" asked Carver.

"It's an Adam's Apple," said Kahn.

"Women don't have Adam's Apples," said Mackey.

"You sayin' she's not a woman? She's a guy?" asked Carver in astonishment. "Popeye's putting it to another *guy*?"

"No, no, no, she's a woman, all right. She's just got a funny lump. But the lump is part of her secret. She takes on Popeye, all right, but not in the traditional way," said Edwards.

"What...do...you...mean?" asked Carver, leaning in closer.

"She takes him in her mouth. Orally. And in her throat. With the lump."

"Are you sayin'..." began Carver.

"Yup. All of Popeye's manhood, which is considerable, right down here..." Edwards dragged an extended forefinger from his jaw down to his chest. "*All the way*," he added.

"She can do...*that*?" asked Carver.

"Yup. And Bluto knows it. And *that's* what's driving him crazy; he wants a piece of that action."

"Who wouldn't," said Carver.

"Gentlemen, gentlemen," interjected Kahn. "Let's not lose sight of whom we are speaking of. This is Olive Oyl, for God's sake. She's ugly. I mean, *really* ugly. And even if she does…, even if she's good at … at *that*, she's still ugly. A man's got his pride."

"The hell with pride," responded an agitated Edwards. "We're talking a pro gobbler here. Hell, I'd even let *Eleanor Roosevelt* do that to me."

"Wow, *that's* sayin' somethin'," said Carver.

During this spirited exchange, a small Oriental man had entered the taproom unnoticed. He worked his way over to the bar and was directed to me. Said he was Tak's brother, Inoshiro, and had been at Tak and Yumi's house for the last several days packing and clearing out in anticipation of putting the place on the market. The place appeared to have been ransacked some time after Tak's death and before Inoshiro's arrival. He had no idea whether or not anything was missing; nothing obvious was, at least, and if anything was it must have been some smaller, inconsequential item, as lots of valuables were still there, and out in the open.

Inoshiro had assembled a list of items that would be for sale the following Saturday, December 19, and was posting it at various frequented locations about town, which I took to mean the bars, the market, the post office and the bank. Tak had mentioned my name and business to him some time in the past, so he'd decided to stop by and see if he could post the list here as well.

The conversation regarding Olive Oyl and her peers had drifted off as attention turned to the taproom's newest visitor.

"Anything of interest?" inquired Edwards, craning his neck trying to read the list in Inoshiro's hand.

"Mostly furniture. A few appliances. Clothing, the contents of the store. And Yumi's car, which is like new. She kept it under cover down at your local garage," responded Inoshiro.

I told him to go ahead and tack it to the wall somewhere where there was enough light to read it. He thanked me, did so and headed back outside with a wave of his hand.

A swarm of people quickly moved from the bar and crowded around the list, leaving Dovey behind. Edwards had his reading glasses on now, and perused the list, reading aloud.

"Let's see here: an easy chair; a sofa; a nine-year-old RCA Radiola radio, originally two hundred and sixty bucks, now twenty-five bucks; a one-year-old Crossley Shelvador electric refrigerator...." He hummed quietly to himself as he silently read several other items to himself. "Okay, here it is: 1936 Hudson Terraplane, like new, for three hundred and fifty dollars...that's a lot of jack," he said over his shoulder. "A dining room table with six chairs; the contents of the store, et cetera et cetera et cetera." He popped a Choward's Violet in his mouth and sucked on it.

"I'd love to get my hands on that car," said Carver quietly, and to no one in particular.

"I'd love to get my hands on three hundred and fifty bucks," responded Kahn.

Sunday, December 13, 1936. 9:48 a.m.

SUNDAY, DECEMBER 13, 1936. 9:48 a.m.

I flipped back and forth through the Sunday paper's funny pages. Blondie gets my vote, I thought to myself, tossing it aside and grabbing the sports section. I sat at my usual table in the taproom, a second cup of coffee steaming at my side. Sunday morning tranquility; I knew I had at least an hour before they'd start showing up again and hoped to make the most of it.

Then Holly entered the room and silently sat across the table from me.

I folded the paper and gave her my full attention; any other reaction would have been sheer folly.

"Lew," she said quietly. "Are you ready to have another child yet?"

Just like that – no warm up, no lead in. Like a face-full of ice-cold water.

"No," I said. "Not yet." After a brief pause: "I'm not sure I'll ever be ready, with what happened to Eddie and all. I'm just not sure."

Eddie had been my first and only son, born sixteen years earlier. Died five years later, along with his mother, my first wife, Dorothy. I shouldn't say died; they were murdered and they shouldn't have been. The intruders must have thought that the two forms in the bed were of husband and wife, when in actuality they were mother and son. Shotgunned to death, the bed doused in kerosene, the apartment set ablaze. And me: I was out someplace where I shouldn't have been. A day later the cops had asked me to identify the bodies and I tried, I really did, but I couldn't. I was overcome with grief and guilt. Grief and guilt and the overwhelming need for revenge.

The bitter taste and the emotional scars will be with me 'til my dying day; time does little to diminish the memory.

There was a solid minute of silence.

"I think I'm pregnant."

"Are you sure? You *think*?" I asked, caught off guard.

"Well, the signs are all there, but I don't know for sure. I'm going to go see Doc Havens and find out for certain. But, no, I'm not sure."

"Oh," I said, surprised. "Well, then, that's different. That's great." And it was. I don't know that I could have ever made the decision myself, but this one was made for me – kind of.

"You're not excited, are you?" she said, disappointment creeping into her voice.

"Sure I am. Really. I didn't think I would be, but I am. Really."

"No, you're not, are you?" Always turning it into a question.

"I am. I think it's great. It's just that we don't know for sure yet."

"That won't make any difference, will it? You don't want another child, do you?" She obviously wasn't buying it.

"Yeah, I do. The timing's good: we're settled in, things running smoothly and I'm not getting any younger – yeah, it's fine." I was doing my damnedest, but it was like talking to a wall.

"Oh, Lew!" she cried, bursting into tears and stomping out of the room.

Christ, the things I have to do.

I found her back in our house, sprawled over our bed, sobbing. I attempted to console her, reassure her that I did, indeed, look forward to the prospect of another child, but it was difficult to tell whether she was convinced or not.

"I…I know that the loss of your first son was tragic, but…but that was then, this is now," she said through tears.

"Any thoughts on names?" I asked, attempting to be upbeat.

"Oh, stop it – *stop it*, will you? Stop trying to placate me!" she yelled.

"I'm not trying to placate you," I said. "I'm really excited, in my own low-key sort of way, really excited about this. It'll liven up the house. It'll give you something to occupy your time. It'll..."

"*Occupy my time?*" she screamed. "While you're next door getting drunk with your little friends? Occupy my time? You don't want this child, do you?"

She wasn't taking this well and I wasn't doing much to help matters. I gave it one last try: "Holly. I do and I'm sincere about that. Now, please, calm down."

She didn't.

I told her in my calmest fashion to try to get some rest, that in spite of what she thought, I was excited about the prospect of having a child. Let me deal with the Sunday afternoon crowd and we can talk about this more later on.

But I really am happy about this.

Really.

The last straggler left at a few minutes past eleven. I said goodnight to Willett, and heard the snick of the lock behind me. The temperature had dipped back down into the low twenties. I stood in the inky blackness for several minutes, shivering. It was a horrible night out. The stiff wind was unrelenting and of sufficient force to push you around. Aside from it buffeting my ears the only other discernible sounds were the incessant clacking of a faraway set of chimes and the roar of the ocean. Hoover was beside me, leaning into me for warmth. I dreaded the thought of heading back home to yet another unpleasant encounter with Holly. Better to let her fall fast asleep before making my grand entrance; I didn't want to risk waking her. I unlocked the taproom door and Hoover eagerly returned to the warmth inside. I quietly told him I'd be back in a couple of hours, but I don't think he was listening. And if he was, he probably didn't care.

Visiting May Willis and her houseboat seemed like a good idea and, as luck would have it, Sunday nights were one of the two nights a week she docked in Beach Haven. Our year-round population worked in our favor in this particular instance; a few other communities received only a single visit per week and many others only once every two or three weeks.

"Why am I doing this?" I asked myself as I trudged down dark, windswept streets. There was a new moon that night, only the stars overhead offering any sort of illumination, and it was feeble at best. Holly stuck in my mind, my feelings of unease increasing with each step. By this time next year I could be a father once again and then I'd run the risk of hurting not only my wife but my child, as well, should my extracurricular activities ever be discovered. Holly didn't deserve this sort of selfish behavior on my part and no matter how much I told myself that these were meaningless and unimportant flings, deep down I knew otherwise. It was unfair to her and it was just this sort of thing that caused me so much grief years earlier: it got my family murdered. I'd decided to walk the straight and narrow line after that incident and did so for a couple of years. But I'd eventually slipped back into my old ways.

Now it was as if things had never changed.

There never was any harm intended and I suppose I could have taken some measure of comfort in that thought. It's just that I liked women so much, liked their companionship, liked their looks, liked their smell. And my life had always placed me in circumstances where there was nothing but males around: the war, at the railroad, with Hack and Hack, and then, for the last eleven years of my life, at the taproom. And wives, well, they were different. They treated you differently once you were married. Took you more for granted. Replaced the pedestal of the early years with a stubby wooden stool.

Shit, who was I kidding? Okay, one last tumble and that's it. No more. Back to being a one-woman man. That was, of course, assuming that Holly actually was pregnant. Well, even if she wasn't. It was the right thing to do and I didn't want to fuck up this relationship. I loved her far too much to ever want to see her hurt and if she ever found out about these visits – or about Rhea, or about any of the others – she would be hurt. Badly.

I had told myself time and again that the circumstances surrounding the deaths of my first wife and son were a result of my comparative youth and naiveté. But that was just a cheap, shameful excuse and I knew it. I got them killed, damn it, and there were no two ways about it. Me and my love of women.

The lights of May Willis' houseboat twinkled at the end of the street. I should have dressed more warmly for a night like this, and I quickened my pace. Well, one, last goodbye visit, and then it's Maggie and Jiggs time for me.

I wondered if Toby would be there.

Our bungalow was all lit up when I returned a little before 2:00 a.m. A bad sign, I thought to myself; she might be waiting up for me. And if she were, which side would she hit me from: "You don't want this child, do you?" or "Where the hell have you been?" I was too tired for either and hoped for a more benign "Hi. I'm going to bed now." Fat chance of that, though. I retrieved Hoover from the taproom. Had to drag him by his collar to the cold outdoors, legs held stiff, claws scratching a path in the sawdust.

The front porch light glowed brightly, which would have made finding the keyhole a lot easier if I had needed to do so, but I didn't; the door was unlocked. Inside, the lights were on in both the living room and kitchen and it was very cold – the fifties, perhaps. Hoover bounded inside at the prospect of warmth and I'd swear that I could read disappointment on his features when he encountered the comparative coolness of the place.

I was ready to adjust the heat when I realized that the back door was wide open. Closing it, I was overwhelmed by the sickening feeling that something wasn't right. I looked around and it appeared that several pieces of furniture weren't exactly where they were supposed to be. Close, but nudged a little here and there from their original positions. There was a disheveled aspect to the room, but no one item or area was so far out of place as to be obvious.

Except, that is, for my ongoing reconstruction of the Cathedrále Notre-Dame of Reims, smashed into heap of glue-covered pieces of wood, now resembling a tornado-devastated wood-frame home.

A chill ran up my spine as the possibilities took form in my mind.

"Holly," I gasped, making for our bedroom. I opened the door.

The room was torn apart. The bed was unmade and her dresser drawers half out, empty. The two suitcases usually kept in the closet were gone. So were the handwritten books of her poetry, usually kept on the upper shelf of the small bookcase beneath the side window. The adjoining bathroom was a mess, all of her personal items removed. I looked frantically throughout the bedroom, throughout the house, for some sort of a note, or any other clue to her disappearance. There were none.

Holly, all traces of her, gone from the house.

Hoover sat in the middle of the living room, whining quietly in his confusion.

I sat heavily onto the edge of our bed and squeezed my eyes shut. God, not her, too. I may have sat there for several minutes, or several hours. My mind was working none too well at this point, a flood of random thoughts and images pouring in from all sides.

She was gone.

Later, and I have no idea when, I called the operator. Asked for the police station, and left word for Purdy. He called back within a few minutes. I told him she was missing, that it must be an abduction of some sort; she wouldn't have left like this of her own accord. After several moments of silence, he asked if there were any signs of foul play, violence, any sort of a struggle. I described the place as best I could: the furniture's repositioning, the missing clothes, everything that came to mind. After a long pause, he told me he'd be over to give the place a look, but warned me that in the absence of any sort of foul play he would assume that she left of her own free will. What I expected.

Purdy arrived at the house within a half an hour, accompanied by Schoengarth. Cheek swollen with Beechnut or some such, Schoengarth did little other than keep out of his boss' way. Purdy gave the place a reasonably thorough once-over while I sat alone at the kitchen table, thinking things through.

"You know, Lew," he said to me, and I knew I wasn't going to like the rest of it, "you might think you have the perfect marriage, but isn't it just possible that Holly thinks otherwise?" He paused for effect. "Maybe got some ideas from her friends? Think about it."

I already had, and that notion had taken hold. It pushed aside earlier, immediate thoughts of abduction. His bluntness was annoying, however; I gritted my teeth as he finished his words.

"No, that's not possible," I said quietly as I stood and moved into the living room. I think I was trying to convince myself more than anyone else. Purdy looked at me from beneath lowered brows with a look either of pity or contempt, I wasn't certain which. And I didn't care.

There was brown stain towards the edge of the living room carpet and I knelt for a closer look. It was slightly larger than a silver dollar and flecked with pinpoint particles of brown. I dragged my index finger through it, took a hesitant sniff of the residue and realized that it was chewing tobacco juice. Overcome by an unreasonable fury, I stood and spun, took three quick steps over to Schoengarth. He was standing idly by, oblivious to my actions, jaw working on the wad of chaw nestled in his jaw. I grabbed twin fistfuls of his coat front and slammed him against the wall.

"Goddamn pig," I hissed through clenched teeth.

Schoengarth, eyes wide with fear and surprise, stammered "What? What?" while tobacco juice drooled out of the corner of his mouth onto his chin. I pulled him from the wall and gave him a violent shove towards the front door; he almost went down on tangled feet.

"Get the hell out of here," I said in a low, steady voice.

Purdy looked on, concern and confusion clouding his face. He had no idea as to the cause of my petty little outburst. I stood there seething.

"Outside, Earl," he barked.

Schoengarth straightened his coat and dutifully followed orders.

"No call for that," he said slowly, looking my way. "None." It drifted off.

I slumped into the easy chair and fired up a De Nobili. Purdy resumed what little he'd been doing before my interruption. Fifteen minutes and the better part of cigar later, Purdy announced that he was finished. Said I should contact him immediately if there were any new developments. Such as Holly's return or a phone call.

I stood in front of the bedroom mirror, staring at my reflection. I didn't like what I saw at all. Staring back at me was the hardened, feverish look of years gone by, one I thought I'd buried long ago. Unfortunately, circumstances were conspiring to resurrect it from the dead.

You think you know yourself. You think you know how you're going to react in a pressure-filled situation. It'd been eleven, long years since I last confronted the untimely loss of loved ones. I thought I'd built a new foundation for my life. One of stability and strength. One that could withstand any sort of curve ball the fates threw at it. One built of granite and not of spun sugar. Holly was gone now and I could feel eleven years of rebuilding drifting away through my fingers. And the odds were that she was off somewhere, in one piece and healthy – damning me for falling so short at being a husband.

A normal life, I'd thought.

If she left me of her own accord, then it's because I failed her.

And I accept the blame – guess I'm the same old Lew Porter after all. Who was I kidding?

But…if there's some other explanation – if she was taken by force, or there's been any sort of harm done to her – then someone's going to pay – *dearly*. And there will be no doubt: I am the same old Lew Porter. I just won't give a damn anymore.

I'll exact my pound of flesh, whatever the cost.

I spent the night in the dark, lying on the sofa, staring at the ceiling, the play of light and shadow intruding from the outside. "Beach Haven. Christ, this is as bad as Camden," I said to myself and probably more than once. My thoughts were solely of Holly: Was she safe? Was it my fault that she left? Or, was she…not safe?

If I slept at all, my dreams were real enough to make it seem otherwise.

268

Monday, December 14, 1936. 8:02 a.m.

I HAD TO get out of there. As soon as there was a trace of daylight I took a long walk around town. I don't recall where. Hoover followed dutifully, but his heart wasn't in it at this early hour. He collapsed in a heap when we got back to the taproom. I needed a couple of days for the full impact of her departure sink in. To fully resign myself to my plight. For my mind to clear and thoughts to focus. To decide just how I was going to proceed.

And then I'd do it.

I didn't take long for word of Holly's departure to make its way around town and the arrival of each new patron was accompanied by quietly respectful words of consolation – or silence. I was in a foul mood, but attempted to grunt some sort of acknowledgment.

It never failed to amaze me just how quickly some items of news spread throughout the borough. In this instance, it seemed like everyone knew of my predicament, and within a few short hours of its occurrence. As far as I could figure it, there were only three possible sources of this leak of information: Purdy, Schoengarth or the local exchange's operator, Sarah Pruitt. My vote was for Pruitt, since she was notorious for listening in on telephone conversations; any late-night contact with the police would be certain to arouse her interest. One of the job's perks, I suppose.

Everyone seemed supportive and seemed to take the situation at face value: she had run off. But I'd been in this town and this business long enough to have been privy to thousands of unguarded conversations and, as a result, had a reasonably good idea how the local mind-set worked. There would, of course, be an undercurrent of mistrust regarding her departure. There was no question in my mind that the local gossips would let their minds and tongues work overtime. Holly was, after all, one of *them*, and I was still little more than a transplanted *mainlander*. And just what would a guy have to do to cause his wife to run off and leave *everything she had* behind? No doubt, it would be the main topic of conversation for days to come, until everyone grew sick of it. That or a newer, juicier topic entered the rumor mill. The way things were going around here, the latter would be the case; it was just a matter of time.

Anyway, I tried as best I could to keep to myself and Willett did his best to handle the taproom chores and run interference for me. Unfortunately, things didn't always work out as planned; I grew increasingly despondent and surly as the day wore on. The low point, I suppose, occurred a little after dinnertime. There was some guy with a couple of his friends, none of whom I'd ever seen before and didn't even know if they were from elsewhere on the island or not. They'd been drinking heavily for several hours and the most boisterous of the three, a thick, stupid looking individual with the features of a faded boxer, started mouthing off regarding Holly's departure. I'd put up with this all day, but at least from people I knew and liked. This idiot was another case altogether. I don't remember what he said, I only recall being engulfed by a wave of fury and anger. I leapt across the counter, hauled the guy out of his seat and pinned him to the wall with enough force to leave his eyes glazed. Pressing my fist to his jaw, I threatened to knock every goddamned tooth out of the guy's mouth if he didn't shut the fuck up. It wasn't subtle, but I wasn't feeling subtle. This was a level of anger that I'd never displayed before. Everyone in the place sat in stony silence, waiting to see if I was going to kill the guy or not. Willett intervened, God bless him, and told me to calm down. After a few deep breaths I did, and left the stranger on the floor, his back to the wall, legs twisted beneath him. Headed to my office where I sat alone for the next couple of hours, working on a bottle of Old Overholt. Feeling sorry for myself.

Willett knocked at the door a couple of hours later, said Purdy wanted to see me. I told Willett to send him in.

After Purdy was seated with a healthy glass of rye before him, he started asking a bunch of annoyingly suspicious questions – regarding Holly's inheritance of her father's considerable savings, his business and the buildings. He wanted to know if it was still all in her name, or did we now have joint ownership and accounts. I told him it was all hers and in her name, and rightfully so. Anyway, I'd always assumed that she'd outlive me by a lot of years. Asked me if I'd get it all if she turned up dead, and I told him I thought so, but that I'd never actually seen her will. He asked a lot of other questions, some probing, some seemingly innocuous. I did my best to answer them. He was, after all, just doing his job, and as much as I disliked the implications behind some of his queries, I knew what he had to do. And he was doing it.

When he finished, he sat back and took a long pull of his drink. He told me that he already knew the answers to most of the questions – I would have been disappointed in him if he hadn't – and was relieved that I had answered them all honestly. I felt like I was in first grade. He went on to point out the obvious: If Holly didn't turn up, I'd have use of the taproom and house for a good long time.

"All those disappearances give you some ideas, Lew?" he asked. The implication was obvious: I murdered her and made it appear that she'd run off. To have the taproom and house all to myself. It was a stupid idea, but it enraged me – I sat there, teeth clenched, knuckles growing white as I gripped the chair's arm, trying to control myself.

"Calm down, Porter," he said after several moments; "I'm just doing my job. I don't really think you had anything to do with it. From where I sit, it looks to me like she's dumped you. Soon enough, she'll go through the proper channels and grab whatever's hers. Then you won't have a pot to piss in. Until then, I hope business is good," he said, placing his empty glass on my desk. He stood and put his hat back on. "Better stash the profits; you're gonna need 'em," he added, heading for the door. "See you around. And keep me informed." He left the room.

Well, little did Purdy know that I'd always have that pot to piss in. The small fortune I'd tucked away over on the mainland was more than enough to live on for the rest of my days, if need be. I didn't need Holly's money or anyone else's, but nobody knew that – nobody. But it didn't matter; after a day or two of absorbing the full impact of her departure, I wouldn't care what anybody thought. I was just a little touchy now, but I'd get over it. And then I'd figure out what happened to her, if it was the last thing I'd do. If it turned out that she left me – which she probably had, and probably with good enough reason – then I'd accept that fact and move on. On the other hand – well, I'd deal with that if and when it became a reality.

Just a couple of days until my head cleared, I kept telling myself. Then I'd get to the bottom of this.

I wandered back to the bungalow shortly after 10:30 when we'd closed for the night. Willett asked if I'd be all right. I assured him I would be. Christ, he was beginning to sound like someone's mother, but he meant well.

The place was the same as I'd found it the night before, the same as I'd left it earlier that morning. I did some half-hearted straightening in the kitchen, returning everything to as close to normal as I could, struggling to recall just where items had been positioned and stored. It didn't really matter, of course – if I couldn't remember where they went, who the hell else would at this point? *Hoover*, I decided, and continued on.

I stared at the crumpled ruins of the Cathedrále on the floor by the radio. If she did this… But it wasn't like Holly to do something so vindictive, that I knew for sure. And that's what had me so worried about her.

I grabbed a can of ale from the refrigerator, punched a pair of holes in its top, and downed it in three long swallows. I grabbed another.

Things were more disheveled in the bedroom. I renewed my duties as household maid with a sigh – all I needed was an apron and a feather duster. Holly's dresser was moved an inch or so from its usual spot, so I slid it back, its feet reclaiming the depressions in the rug. I knelt and picked up all the items that had toppled from its top: small jars and vials of pleasant-smelling substances important to women. A small red-and-white painted Plaster of Paris replica of the island's historic lighthouse. A glass saucer with earrings spilled out. And a little carved winged creature that sure as hell looked like it was laughing at me, as if it were amused at just how successfully I'd managed to screw things up.

There were a couple of books on the floor. I picked them up and read their spines – the two versions of *The Lure of Long Beach*. The original, I knew, was written back in 1914 by George Somerville to commemorate the opening of the causeway bridge for automotive traffic. The recent re-write, by Charles Edgar Nash, was commissioned by the Beach Haven Business Association to commemorate the fiftieth anniversary of the railroad's arrival here in town. I returned them to the bookcase.

The bathroom off our bedroom also bore signs of disruption. I returned my toothbrush – which had been knocked to the floor – to the holder screwed to the wall; it looked lonely there. Nearby on the floor: an open lipstick tube and a copy of Elizabeth Kite's book of 1913, *The Pineys*. I'd managed to pick my way through this one a year or so earlier, while confined to the house during a particularly violent nor'easter. The lipstick cap was on the floor behind the toilet, and I almost missed it. I placed the lipstick on the small table to the right of the sink, and returned the book to the bookcase in the other room.

I stood silently in the center of the room, surveying the emptiness around me. It was unsettling that things were this messy –

if that's the proper word for the subtle upheaval – and I thought back to the other disappearances on the island. Was there any sort of connection? I didn't see how, but the sheer coincidence seemed that much more difficult to reconcile after each new incident occurred. My feeling of unease – and suspicion of some sort of foul play – grew with each waking moment. But I always came back to the distinct possibility that I was just trying to fool myself, to ignore the obvious: Holly had left me.

Still, and I know there wasn't any one thing that I could put my finger on, but something was rotten in Beach Haven.

Tuesday, December 15, 1936. 11:33 a.m.

"MAN OVER THERE wants to see you," said Willett, nodding at the tall figure slouched over a cup of coffee at the second booth. He had on a long wool Ulster, collar turned up, and from what little I could see of him I didn't – couldn't – recognize him.

"Who is he?" I asked. Willett shrugged. I pulled off my coat and hat, tossed them on a nearby hook, and signaled to Willett for another cup of coffee; he knew enough to bring the pot as well. I went over to the booth and stood at its end.

"What can I do for you, stranger," I asked.

His head was down; smoke swirled around him from the cigarette wedged between the fingers of his right hand. He looked up slowly and spoke.

"Hello, Lew."

I recognized the distinctive voice immediately, but it took me a moment to place it and the face, one I hadn't seen for years.

"I'll be damned," I said. "Quinn! How are you?" I continued, sliding onto the bench across from him.

"Doing well, Lew," he said with a small smile. "And you," he said, glancing around at the taproom's dark interior, "it looks as though you've settled down, made some changes." Returning his gaze to me: "Things going well?"

"Yeah, Bernie, well enough," I responded. I realized that I was smiling for the first time in several days, and it felt good. "It's been a long time," I continued.

"September 1925," he responded. I remembered the date well, and was surprised that he did, too.

"Are you still with…?"

"No," he cut me short. "I'm with the New Jersey State Police now. Criminal Investigations. Have been since fall of '31, back when the Detective Bureau was established. They came to me, recruited me – wanted me to help set it up and take an active part in it. Which I did."

"Goodbye to Hack and Hack, huh?"

"Yeah; no great loss there. But you know that." He looked up at me from beneath his brow. "Don't you?"

No, no great loss, that was for sure.

I'd been approached back in '24 by a guy named Bill Ferguson. He was recruiting people for positions with Hack and Hack Private Investigations, operating out of a Linden Street office in Camden, New Jersey. I hated my then-current job with the Pennsylvania Railroad – working the Camden-South Amboy line – so I jumped at the offer. I moved with my first wife, Dorothy and young son, Eddie, to an apartment closer to the new offices. It never occurred to me at the time just why they'd sought me out, but my new job as clerk paid twenty-five dollars a week – thirteen hundred dollars a year – which was two hundred and sixty dollars a year more than with the railroad.

Hack and Hack, reassuring its customers with the motto "Ever Vigilant," was a well-established detective agency that had been in business for close to forty years. The firm's founder, Douglas Hack, was a Glasgow-born Scottish expatriate. He'd come to the states in the mid-1800s to help out old friend Allan Pinkerton in the latter's newly formed detective agency. Hack was a low-profile sort of guy, but a key player in many of Pinkerton's early, fame-building, exploits. Unfortunately for Hack, Pinkerton was an egotist of the first rank. Pinkerton totally ignored Hack's considerable contributions in his several wildly popular autobiographies, promoting his various achievements as solo rather than group efforts. Adding insult to injury, nepotism ran rampant within the agency, and Pinkerton promoted his sons to key positions while ignoring Hack. After years of being taken for granted, Hack had had enough.

Hack opened his own competing firm in the later 1800s, taking a substantial chunk of Pinkerton's clients and disgruntled employees with him. Hack and Hack Private Investigations was the name, but there was only one Hack, and no one could figure out why a name was chosen that made it sound otherwise. The firm quickly became Pinkerton's leading competitor, and there was no love lost between the two rivals. Hack's firm, however, had a reputation for being somewhat less ethical than Pinkerton's, and frequently took on cases that the latter refused. Nevertheless, there was a lot of overlap, with more than enough strike work in the 1880s for both firms.

Hack paid well, and allowed his employees a lot of freedom to do their jobs. He'd turn a blind eye to the legality – or lack thereof – of any his employee's methods, just so long as the job got done, and the paying client satisfied with the results.

It wasn't long before I was promoted to, and training for, the position of Operative, which was coupled with a hefty salary increase based on hours worked. The days were long, the workweek often seven of them, but I was young and full of moxie, with the potential for over twenty-one hundred dollars a year incentive in itself. It was in this position that I first met Bernie Quinn.

Quinn was at that time a seasoned vet with the firm, having joined Hack and Hack back in the mid-teens. He was assigned to be my mentor and I trained diligently under him, absorbing as much as I could, as quickly as possible. I had a natural affinity for the position and Quinn soon recognized that fact. Somehow or other he'd gotten wind of my less-than-exemplary youth – how much of it I wasn't sure; but he was, after all, a detective. And while he never mentioned it, I always had the feeling that he was concerned about the impact it might have on my doing my job with a clear, objective mind. He was extremely fair and honest, and had taken me under his wing in a vague, fatherly sort of way. I loved the guy.

Quinn had shown me all the various techniques and methodologies of the trade; and while his training was intensive, thorough, and all above-board, I soon acquired other, less ethical approaches from some of the other Operatives. Bluffing, lying, bullying, you name it; it was all a means to an end. It all became part of my arsenal and within a short four months I was a full member of the team, pulling my weight and contributing fully to whatever task I was assigned. Quinn was impressed by my rapid progress, but would repeatedly admonish me with the dictum that one had to exhaust all of the proper approaches to solving a crime before resorting to the less proper approaches. At my young age, however, that seemed like an incredible waste of time. To me, the approach most likely to achieve the desired results in the shortest period of time seemed more appropriate. Come to think of it, I wasn't so sure that I didn't still adhere to that line of thought. Not that Quinn never played dirty; he did. But it was always directed towards the bad guys, the criminals; he drew the line in some murky gray area where the individuals involved were innocent of any true criminal activity – strikers, for instance. The rest of us viewed it more as us vs. them, and the means always justified the ends. At any rate, this conflicting point of view drove a wedge of sorts between the two of us, and we respectfully drifted apart. He kept his hands comparatively clean; I kept my gloves on.

I loved the work and totally immersed myself in it, moving on and, seemingly, up within the firm over the course of a year. Quinn and I had remained friendly and I would occasionally turn to him for advice. Within nine months, however, our contact had diminished to nods of acknowledgment whenever our paths would cross. I had bigger plans in mind. One of the unfortunate by-products of this, of course, was my home life, which rapidly deteriorated. I was rarely at home: The job kept me occupied for inordinate amounts of time and the occasional hours of freedom tossed my way were frequently spent in the sack with some other woman. Secretaries, female clients, wives of clients, the random prostitute, you name it – it didn't seem like such a big deal at the time. After all, I had a loving wife and a five-year-old son at home, for whom I provided financial security, didn't I?

And then things went sour. I left the firm, left Camden, left that world; I started over. And I hadn't seen Quinn again since.

"Lew?" he said softly in that singsong voice of his. I'd drifted off, but my immediate inclination was to act as if I hadn't.

"Where are you stationed?" I asked. "What are you doing around here?"

"Well, usually in Wilburtha, five miles outside of Trenton. But for the last six months I've been stationed over on the mainland – in the Tuckerton barracks, on Route 9. I'll be there for a while, working on some local matters."

The New Jersey State Police had been formed in Jersey back in 1921, its troopers assigned to protect the laws within the state's boundaries, all seventy-five hundred square miles of them. They were stationed in the rural areas first, patrolling on horseback and motorcycle, chasing down fruit and chicken thieves and the like. One of their most newsworthy early projects, if you can believe it, was the tattooing of poultry for future identification. Simpler times, I suppose. But I doubted that was the Detective Bureau's – or Quinn's – reason for coming to Tuckerton.

"Tuckerton? Can't be much of importance going on around here, or at least nothing the average trooper can't handle," I said, hoping for clarification. I didn't get it.

"You keeping out of trouble?" he asked, changing the subject.

"I think so," I responded. "Except for a boxing match a few years back – the locals coerced me into taking part in that, eight or nine years ago. Wish I hadn't." Willett arrived with a steaming metal pot and a second cup of coffee. "So, what have you been up to these past eleven years?" I asked.

He gave me a brief rundown of the highlights of his life during that period: marriage; two new children; a third son from a previous marriage, now a student at the University of Penn; the dog. Lived in an eight-year-old house in Trenton, located someplace known locally as The Island. And, not surprisingly, his involvement in – and frustrations with – the Lindbergh kidnapping investigation four years earlier. He slid a dog-eared photo from his wallet of the wife and kids; they looked pleasant enough, but it was difficult to get a good look from the tiny images.

When he finished, I followed his lead and gave him a brief overview of my unexciting life during that same period. I touched on the highlights, left the low points unmentioned.

"Aren't you omitting a rather important piece?" he asked when I thought I was finished.

"And that is…?" I prompted.

"Christ, Lew; your wife disappears, you don't consider that significant?"

I paused for a moment, fiddling with my cup. "You know about that, eh?"

He gave me a disappointed look. "Lew: I'm a detective. I'm supposed to know these things." He poured himself another cup. "There's no great mystery to it," he continued. "I was reviewing yesterday morning's report on the preceding day's events, and your name jumped out at me. I knew you'd moved down here – I'd grown curious regarding your whereabouts some five years back, and had tracked you down at that point. So, I decided to stop by and see how you were. A few simple questions answered by your young helper over there" – he cocked his head towards Willett – "confirmed that you were *the* Lew Porter. So here I am."

I could only imagine what those questions were.

"Yeah, well, she's gone."

"How does it look to you?" he probed.

"Me? Well, everyone else under the sun, the cops included, think she ran off. With another man, or just to get away from me, who the hell knows; I can just imagine the theories circulating around here. But me? I'm not so sure they aren't right. There's something about it that just doesn't sit well, but I haven't been able to put my finger on it." I paused for several moments, thinking of Holly. "So, what was it brought you down to Tuckerton?" I asked once again, quickly changing the subject.

Quinn looked at me for a moment, and slowly glanced around the room to verify that everyone else was well out of earshot. He leaned in closer to me; his words would be for my ears only. If nothing else, Quinn knew he could trust me to keep a secret.

"Ever hear of the German American Bund?" he asked quietly. The small smile that crept onto my face answered his question for him. "Well, they've been around for a number of years – since the depths of the Depression – operating under the name of Friends of New Germany. They're big supporters of Hitler and all of the so-called miracles that he's worked over there. They think those methods would be equally effective over here. They seem to hate most everyone – Communists, Jews, Roman Catholics, lots of people – anyone who isn't a Protestant Anglo-Saxon or of Teutonic stock. At any rate, their ranks have increased over the last few years, and earlier this year they announced some new plans and restructuring. They changed their name to the German American Bund – "Bund" is German for "League" – and elected a guy named Fritz Kuhn to be their American *Führer*. And – most significant of all in some people's eyes – they tightened their guidelines for membership: being a white Anglo-Saxon Protestant doesn't cut it anymore; now you have to be of German descent as well, and able to prove it.

"Nobody took these guys very seriously for the longest time – and as long as they remained in New York and elsewhere, we didn't much care. However, that all came to an abrupt end a short while back, when they established a two-hundred-and-fifty acre sanctuary here in New Jersey. It's up in place called Andover, in Sussex County; they call it Camp Nordland. You've probably read about it in one of the papers, about their weekend meetings, their pseudo-Nazi garb, the whole nine yards.

"At any rate – and as if one camp in the state wasn't bad enough – they've opened up two more: one near Flemington, up in Hunterdon County, and a second one over on the mainland, in the Pine Barrens. Camp Bismarck is the latter one's name. They started building back in April, had it running full-steam by summer. It's all very secretive and, so far – or so far as we know – legal.

"Why the Pines?" I asked. "Isn't this area rather remote?"

"Yes, but that's a plus in their minds; they can get away with a lot more down here. And there are a lot of Pineys of German descent in the area; I guess they figure they can dig up a lot of new recruits down here. During the Revolutionary War, it seems, Hessian soldiers deserted the British Army en masse after the defeats at Princeton and Trenton, and they fled to the wilds of the Pine Barrens for sanctuary. A lot of Tories did, too, for that matter.

"Anyway, there are three of these camps now, and that's making a lot of people uneasy. The Bund members are a bunch of loud-mouthed rabble-rousers, and we'd just love to have a good reason to shut them down – down and up – and keep them shut. Bismarck: *that's* the one I'm keeping an eye on."

I related my experiences with the local Bund, their ill-fated visit to the taproom and my meeting with Willy Vollbrecht.

"Took on three of them, eh?" he said, a smile coming to his face. "Evidently the years haven't changed you much in *that* regard," he added. "What did you make of Vollbrecht?"

"I don't know. He's slick, that's for sure; a lot more polished than the other gorillas he surrounded himself with. He impressed me as being a reasonably likable guy, if you didn't know what he was up to and just met him sitting at a bar somewhere. But then, I only talked with him for a minute or so."

"That's Vollbrecht, all right; a real charmer. And the charming guys are the worst ones to have in positions like that. Give me a boring, colorless drone, or an obnoxious, loud-mouthed son-of-a-bitch any day – Kuhn, for example. People grow tired of those types very quickly."

"Well, maybe charming one on one, but his speeches show his true colors. Or at least the one he made over here," I added.

Quinn asked a lot more questions about the rally and the ensuing brawl, about their later nighttime visit and about my encounter with Vollbrecht; I told him everything I could remember. I mentioned the newsreel coverage and that got his interest. And I gave him the names of some locals who were there who might be willing to elaborate on events preceding my arrival. He asked that I keep my eyes and ears open, and I assured him I would. I asked him about the camp and the property it was located on.

"No, they don't own the land. It's owned by an old Piney named Stipple – a cranky, old drunk who'd rather jump off a cliff than talk to someone in uniform. A police uniform, that is," he quickly added. "He doesn't ever seem to take part in any of their shenanigans, however, so we guess he's just in it for the money. Smelliest guy I've ever met; I can't imagine he's ever taken a bath. Not in the last couple of months, anyway."

There was a long silence while we drained our cups. I emptied the pot refilling them.

"There's something else that's come to light during my stay down here, Lew. Something totally unrelated. Something that might strike a responsive chord." He paused as he slowly rotated his cup with his forefinger, and I'd swear it was for dramatic effect. Whatever; he had my attention now.

"And that is?" I prodded.

"Well, there have been a surprising number of local *situations* – for want of a better word – that have come to my attention."

"*Situations?*" I asked.

"Disappearances, for starters – a lot of them and all seemingly unrelated. Add to that a surprising number of acts of violence. My experience of the past just doesn't support this level of random occurrence and I've urged the state police to take a more active interest in what's going on around here. They've agreed and the substations of A Troop are all involved on some level or other. We take this a hell of a lot more seriously than the local yokels seem to."

He had my interest now.

"First of all, the autopsy results are in on both of your friends, Yumi Takarada and Yutaka Takarada. Yes, it was, conclusively, Mrs. Takarada's body that was found bayside. What wasn't obvious to the naked eye, or at least I don't think it was – it wasn't in any of the reports – was the fact that both her wrists and ankles were tightly bound with wire; you just couldn't see it due to the excessive bloating of her body. There were signs of a struggle as well. Scraps of flesh and a human hair – not hers – under a couple of her fingernails, and we were lucky there: most of her nails had fallen off in the interim. As you undoubtedly observed, much of her skin was off, too, and the damage to her remains – from both marine and avian life – was considerable. Her lungs were full of bay water, so at least we know she drowned. But it sure as hell wasn't an accident, and it sure as hell wasn't suicide.

"Her husband was a different story. There's no doubt that he killed himself and I don't think there ever was. It was death by knife, or *hara-kiri* as it is occasionally referred to – the Jap name for it. There were the classic hesitation marks, and the reports from the scene indicate a sloppy job on Takarada's part. Death didn't come quickly, and he made one hell of a mess writhing around on the floor while waiting for its arrival. The autopsy backed this up and suggested a logical course of events. First of all, his initial two incisions didn't do the trick and I guess he wasn't aware that they rarely ever did. The traditional Samurai always had an attendant nearby, whose sole duty was to decapitate the Samurai shortly after he had made the ritualistic first move, bringing his incredible agony to a swift end. Takarada should have had such a helper. At any rate, the "L" that he sliced across his gut and up its right side resulted in a horrible spilling of viscera, but not instantaneous death. He must have panicked. At that point he attempted to stab himself in the heart, but there were several false starts when the knife hit his sternum and went no further. Finally, he got it right, but God only knows just how long it took him, or the misery he went through getting to that point. It must have been horrific."

I agreed that it was, and I hoped to never again witness such a scene.

Quinn went on to detail the results of Schweickert's autopsy and most of my conclusions were confirmed. Schweickert had indeed been stabbed repeatedly with two different knives, one a nine-inch butcher knife, the other a shorter six-inch knife. His skull was also crushed in several places from the repeated blows of the hammer found at the scene, and its claw-end had inflicted additional random damage. What I hadn't picked up on were the rope burns on his neck – these were probably the result of a temporary restraint from behind – nor the marks all over his body, hidden by the dress, where he was repeatedly kicked once on the floor. The gnawing damage to his extremities, it turned out, weren't committed by the dog alone; evidently, Schweickert had a problem with mice. Like everyone else in Beach Haven.

I sat there trying to visualize Miller, juggling two knives and a hammer while pulling on a rope clenched between his teeth. It seemed awkward.

"You think Ernie Miller did that?" I asked.

Quinn let out a dismissive snort. "I don't see how the hell he could have, unless he had some help. I only wish we had a shot at the crime scene before your local guy…"

"Purdy" I interjected.

"Yeah, Purdy. Before Purdy declared Miller the culprit and had the place released."

"I heard he left a confession. A written one."

"Yeah. '*I DID IT. I'M SORRY. ERNEST MILLER.*' We have it. It's printed all in uppercase, and every other sample of Miller's writing that we found after-the-fact was in cursive. And it was in pencil, with something soft under it when it was written. He *could* have written it; but, then, again, someone else might have. It's impossible to tell."

"Any thoughts on who *someone* else could be?" I asked. I had my own ideas.

"No comment," he responded flatly. "But not Purdy," he added. "At any rate, no town in its right mind wants that kind of publicity and Miller was delivered as the murderer, all neatly wrapped with a bow on him. As far as they're concerned, it's a closed case. We're keeping an open mind on it."

"And what about Yumi Takarada? That sounds clear-cut – it was murder."

"Yeah, looks that way, huh? Only Beach Haven's officials are of the mind that it happened elsewhere, on the mainland, and that her body just happened to float over here; something ridiculous like that. And the publisher of the local rag, even though it's printed over in Manahawkin, tends to prefer light, upbeat news, and shuns the bad stuff. He couldn't avoid the Schweickert killing, as that was common knowledge. But other than a brief mention of the finding of Yumi's body, he's resisted printing anything further. I suppose that's as much a result of pressure by the town's elected officials – hoping to avoid negative publicity – as it is his own personal reticence on the issue. One way or the other, word will get around – and quickly, I'd guess. I'm surprised you hadn't heard anything yet."

"Okay; that covers the violence. You mentioned a lot of disappearances. Excluding Yumi Takarada, I know of three: Grace Peterson, Ethel Richards and my wife. Am I missing someone?" I asked.

"Your own little world, eh, Lew? Well, Long Beach Island is just an island, and those three you mentioned are just the tip of the iceberg. In the previous fifteen months, there have been many more similar occurrences, but in a more geographically spread out area.

There were two others from elsewhere on this island: one in Brant Beach, the other from Barnegat City. Another one south of here in Brigantine, one from over in Manahawkin, and north of here, one each from Seaside Heights and Seaside Park. And those are just the *reported* disappearances; God only knows how many others went unreported due to embarrassment or shame, or just not giving a damn. A recent check indicates that none of these people have surfaced since they went missing, and you'd think that at least one of them would have. To return to hubby, to sue for divorce, to pick up belongings; for *some* reason.

"Also, there was a murder down in Brigantine; the corpse of a female was found bayside, stabbed to death, nails broken and flesh underneath them, indicating a struggle. Anyway, she didn't stab herself to death; she was murdered, plain and simple."

I fumbled for a cigar while I sat there absorbing all of this new information and its implications. I tried to figure an angle, some sort of explanation, which would tie it in some fashion to my own wife's disappearance. I just didn't make any sense, or at least not at face value. And while what happened to all these others was unfortunate, it was Holly that I cared about. The Takaradas, too, but Holly foremost.

"Listen, Bernie. I don't know what I'm going to do yet. I don't know how I'm going to do it. But one thing I do know: I'm going to get to the bottom of this – assuming there is a bottom – because I now have a personal stake in it. Got that? *Personal.* I don't care how long it takes me, I don't care how many idiots' toes I have to step on in the process. I'm not out to win any friends, I'm just out for some peace of mind and to make right the deaths of two friends." I fired up a cigar. Quinn sat there, staring at me.

"You remember a guy named Ford Sterling? An old-time comedian? The Keystone Kops?" he asked.

I nodded, thinking back to the eccentric slapstick comedian popular in the mid-teens in one- and two-reelers.

"He was extremely popular in the early teens, the most popular film comedian in the U.S. – made a fortune for Mack Sennett. Well, a new guy was hired by Keystone, a little British nobody named Charlie Chaplin, and Sterling quickly grew jealous of his more subtle competition – or so it's been reported. Sterling decided that he was the whole show and decided to go it alone, make all the money for himself. He started his own company and turned out the same kind of shit that Keystone did, but it was an immediate failure. Anyway, twenty years have passed; there were numerous failed comeback attempts; and now, the man who used to be America's most beloved comedian can't get *any* work. And no one knows – or cares for that matter – whether he's dead or alive."

"What's your point?" I asked; I wasn't following this.

"The point is: don't over-extend yourself. Know your limitations. It's far better to be part of an efficiently functioning team than to be a lone wolf. There's security, and frequently wisdom, in numbers. In other words, don't try to go it alone. Work *with* us and not *against* us."

"It's a stupid analogy," I countered. "Chaplin eventually did the same thing – formed his own company – and now, twenty years later, is incredibly popular. Maybe the most popular comedian in the world. Your theory is naïve and self-serving."

Quinn sat there staring at me, formulating a response.

"Listen, Lew, and listen carefully," he began, quietly but forcefully. "Keep out of our way. Keep out of the *law's* way. Don't do anything stupid – like we both *know* you've done in the past. Like we both know you are still eminently capable of doing."

My eyes met Quinn's, and I knew in an instant that, somehow or other, he knew *all* about my past, or at least suspected.

"Kimberly handles things differently than Schwarzkopf did; more *aggressively*, if you will. We still have egg on our faces over various aspects of the Lindbergh matter, and we're determined to never let anything like that happen again." Colonel H. Norman Schwarzkopf had been State Police superintendent since its creation back in '21, and had served three five-year terms before Governor Harold G. Hoffman replaced him with his former deputy, Mark O. Kimberly, earlier in '36. Schwarzkopf's overwhelming ineffectuality and bungling of the Lindbergh kidnapping case and the negative press that it generated, coupled with Hoffman's conviction that Hauptmann was innocent, were the assumed reasons behind the change.

"But whatever you end up doing," warned Quinn, "*stay within the law*. And leave the strong stuff to us." He held an unlit cigarette by its tip, pointing it at me now. "If you get in the way at all, if you do anything whatsoever to jeopardize any potential case we might be trying to build, if we so much as even get a *hint* that you're taking matters in your own hands, *like the old days*... I'll come down on you, and hard. You'll end up spending time rotting in a cell, waiting for some word of your future; you'll *long* for the comparative tranquility of your shitty childhood days...back in Bordentown."

I was jolted by this last comment. Quinn seemed to know so much more about me, about my past – things heretofore unspoken – that it caught me off guard. And if he didn't – if he was only bluffing – he was doing a damned good job of it.

"Quinn, we've known each other a long time now. Were pretty good friends back when and I hope that we can be once again. You always gave me a fair break, probably fairer than I deserved. But let me make this clear: this is *personal* and nothing – *nothing* – is going to get in my way. I just don't give a damn anymore. And if there's paying to be done, someone's going to pay – *plenty* – for whatever's going on here. They crossed the wrong guy."

No one spoke for at least half a minute. Quinn stared at me, I stared back. The muscles in his jaw worked, his unlit cigarette squeezed almost flat. But then he caught me off guard. He broke into a smile.

"I see," said Quinn, looking down and returning the unlit cigarette to its pack. "Well, then; let's just say that we agree to disagree. I don't care if you make a few calls, minor stuff like that. But if you stumble across anything – and I mean *anything* – of any potential significance, I want to know about it. And I don't mean in a day or two, I mean immediately. And keep out of my way."

"Sounds reasonable," I said, because I knew that's what he wanted to hear. I also knew he didn't believe a word of it. *We were playing the game again.*

He fiddled with his cup and stifled an even bigger smile. "Hell, this could be kind of fun," he added.

Things *were* going to get interesting.

Later...

The two-pound, nickel-plated Smith and Wesson .38-caliber revolver was in my right hand, down at my side. I'd stolen it the previous night from a desk drawer in "Boss" Otto Weems' hillside mansion. It felt good, like an old friend, like I'd used it all my life.

I pressed my ear to the closed door. From the other side came a jumble of muffled voices, all indistinct. A single drop of sweat coursed its way down the side of my face. I knelt in the dark, carpeted hallway and squinted through the unobstructed keyhole. Inside, at the far side of the room facing the door, was a large oak desk. Bill Ferguson sat at its other side, large cigar in hand, speaking quietly to the others. Facing the desk were two upholstered chairs. Burl Baggot sat in the one to the right, left leg dangling over its arm, a cigar in his left hand, a drink in his right. He responded to Ferguson; and while his voice was somewhat clearer, I still couldn't make out what they were saying. And I didn't much care. The chair to the left was empty, but it was clear from the voices and the turning of heads that there was at least one more in the room, out of my view, to the left. A moment later he stepped into view, tapped a long ash into the ash stand by the desk and returned to his original spot; I thought I recognized him as one of Baggot's toughs, but I wasn't sure. During this, yet another spoke, a fourth in the room. I hoped there weren't more than that.

Ferguson leaned over and out of view behind the desk. He re-emerged, placing a large carpetbag on the desktop; must have had it stashed in the foot-well beneath the desk. From all appearances it was full. Baggot rose and stepped to the desk, placing his cigar in a large, glass ashtray. He unsnapped the bag and spread apart its two sides. Reached in, and pulled a large stack of bound bills from within. It must have contained a small fortune.

I stood and took one last deep breath.

It was time.

I took hold of the doorknob and turned it quietly until I felt the latch slide free. Took another breath, lifted the revolver and stepped into the room. There were indeed two of Baggot's toughs off to the left, standing close together. I quickly raised the revolver to the level of their heads. Snapped off a single shot at each; both went down in a spray of blood like broken rag dolls. Baggot dropped the bundle of cash and dashed for the coat tree on which his overcoat hung. I closed the gap between us in four steps, steps that seemed to take an eternity, steps that felt as if I was trying to run through water. Baggot moved at a similar pace. I reached him a moment after he reached the clothes tree. Raised the .38 to his temple as he fumbled with the pistol in the outside pocket of his coat. Fired the third of my six shots, blowing the far side of his head onto the spines of the books in the bookcase beyond. I walked over to Ferguson, who had remained motionless throughout all this, riveted to his chair with fear, knuckles white clenching its arms. Only another two steps; as I approached, his mouth moved and he spoke, but if words emerged I didn't hear them. He was trembling and, I suppose, begging for his life.

I didn't care.

I fired a shot into his stomach. He looked down stupidly at the small hole growing red from behind, his white shirt flecked with powder burns. He looked back up at me as if this couldn't be happening.

I fired a shot into his throat. It punched his head back against the chair's leather back. He clawed at the blue hole with his fingers, eyes wide in shock, a steady stream of blood emerging moments later.

I emptied the pistol into his forehead.

The room was quiet, the air reeked of cordite, a smoky haze hung like a cloud. No one moved. No one.

I grabbed the bag full of money, crossed the room, and left the way I came. I pulled the door shut quietly behind me.

I found myself in the walnut-paneled halls of Otto Weems' hillside mansion. I didn't remember walking or riding there, but there was no question where I was; I'd been there dozens of times before, knew the halls, knew the rooms, knew his wife's bedroom. I stood at the door to Weems' study. I knew he was in there, knew he was alone. I opened the door and found him sitting at his desk, pen poised over paper. He looked up in surprise and his jaw dropped as he looked down the barrel of the reloaded Smith and Wesson. His mouth moved, too, but no words emerged. I walked directly to him, pistol aimed at his head all the way. He yanked the middle right-hand drawer open and grabbed for the gun that wasn't there; it was in my hand. Arriving at his chair, I gave it a quick quarter-spin so that its back was to me, and clamped my left hand over his mouth and nose; pinched the latter shut tightly, cutting off all air – Burking they called it. His hands clawed at my arm, but I had his head pinned to the chair. After a minute or so of struggle he went limp with unconsciousness.

Pulled the handkerchief from my pocket and wiped the pistol clean, then placed it in his right hand, carefully wrapping his fingers around it. Picked up his limp arm, bent it at the elbow, and directed the pistol's barrel into his mouth. Placed his forefinger on the trigger, my larger hand wrapped around his, my forefinger on his forefinger.

I waited, patiently.

It may have been five minutes, it may have been five hours; eventually Weems let out a low moan and tried to move his head, but couldn't. His eyes opened a slit, but there was no comprehension behind them. A minute or so more passed before his pupils rolled into view and his eyes flickered to life. And then they focused. On me.

I grinned a twisted smile.

It took him several moments to figure out what was going on, to figure out who I was. To realize that he had a revolver jammed in his mouth. The choked sound that emerged was unearthly, and his eyes went so wide that I thought they'd pop from his head. I applied some pressure to Weems' finger and winced as the back of his head exploded onto the chair and the drapes beyond.

Looks like suicide to me.

I awoke from my dream with a yell, drenched in sweat, lying on top of the covers where I'd fallen asleep. Hoover came to the side of the bed and gave my arm a nudge as I gulped down deep breathes of air. Had this dream dozens of times before, with subtle variations that weren't totally founded in reality. Dozens of times, but they didn't usually get this far.

Holly usually woke me before it did.

It was a day, a September day, eleven years earlier. I'd been with Hack and Hack for a year and a half at that point, thoroughly trained over the first six months and with a staggering number of solved cases under my belt in the year that followed. I was a full-fledged Operative, and a damned good one if I say so myself. Little did I know that there was a singular reason behind all of this, one conceived by Bill Ferguson in conjunction with my former railroad boss, Otto Weems. I was naïve, perhaps, and in retrospect it would certainly seem so, but I fell for it. Which was easy to do; I loved the work, and I rarely gave any thought to the reasons – or the ethics, for that matter – behind my various assignments.

A new, highly sensitive assignment was presented to me: A small group of Pennsylvania Railroad employees were stealing valuable military equipment – and had been for several years. This equipment was shipped throughout the region on their rails and Otto Weems had engaged Hack and Hack to put a stop to it. I'd been chosen, logically enough, because of my former ties and familiarity with the railroad. They wanted me to use any contacts I still had there to see what I could come up with. It was a special project, one with far-reaching implications, and absolute secrecy was imperative.

They had reason to believe that a guy named Jed Scoggins was part of this ring, but wouldn't reveal what those reasons were – which wasn't that unusual. What they were looking for was the ring's meeting place. Once armed with that knowledge they could stake out the place, wait for the group to assemble and then swoop in and make a wholesale arrest. I had to be very careful who I spoke with at the railroad; practically anyone could be part of the ring, and to do so could tip him off. I was never to mention his name. Instead, I was to quietly follow him, note his comings and goings from afar, who he visited, the layouts of the various places he frequented and so forth. Easy enough.

After Scoggins was pointed out to me, I followed him for several weeks without event. Finally, late, one Thursday night, I tracked him to an abandoned blacksmith shop a mile and a half from the railroad yards. Located in the poor Irish section of town, it was an area most people would be wise to avoid at that late hour. Others came and went. I counted seven of them – eight including Scoggins – all very careful to enter and exit without being seen. Little did they realize, of course, that I was positioned a good fifty yards away watching closely, binoculars trained. Later, I cased the place and mapped its layout and exits, knowing full well that this was the joint that Weems and Ferguson were looking for.

It was mid-September when I delivered my full report to Ferguson; I was complimented on a job well done. He told me my part in the case was finished and they'd take it from there. I was disappointed. It seemed that I'd done so little and had so much more to offer; I said as much. But Ferguson was adamant.

They took it from there, all right.

Several nights later, when Scoggins and the seven other individuals were assembled in the small shack, Ferguson, Weems, Hack goon Burl Baggott and two other Hack toughs descended upon the place. Only Scoggins wasn't really named Scoggins; his name was Fred Kinney and he was the brother of an old friend of mine – Phil Kinney – from my days with the railroad. Both Fred and Phil were in there, along with seven others, two of whom I'd also been friendly with. Only they hadn't been stealing anything, valuable or otherwise. They were part of a more militant faction of the railroad brotherhoods and Weems wanted them out of the way. Weems waited outside while the other four stormed the place in a blaze of guns. They killed everyone inside and torched the place. I was unaware of this at the time.

Later, Baggott was assigned to tie up loose ends. Which meant me. I was the only one who could link them to the slaughter at the shack, so that very same night he came over to my apartment with the intention of wiping the slate clean. He entered my dark bedroom and shotgunned the two forms sleeping beneath the blankets. Doused them in gasoline, and set the place on fire. What he didn't realize was that the victims were my wife, Dorothy, and my five-year-old son, Edward, who would frequently climb in bed with his mother when I wasn't home and bad dreams came visiting.

Bad dreams surely came visiting this night.

Me? I was in the room of a Hack and Hack secretary, getting laid. As usual.

I returned home later to the smoldering ruins and found out what had happened. My family had been destroyed when I was in all probability the intended victim. I was plagued with guilt. I should have been there. I might have been able to do something – *anything* – to avoid the slaughter.

I learned of the railroad deaths the next day, and it didn't take long to find out – figure out – just what had happened. I couldn't get over just how stupid and gullible I'd been. I resolved to do something about it.

First, I visited Ferguson and told him I'd gotten the point and would keep my mouth shut, and he bought it. I kept a low profile for the day or two until my wife and child were buried, and watched my back just in case.

And then I went to work.

I stole Weems' Smith and Wesson from his desk drawer and – well, let's just say I carved out my pound of flesh: "*'tis mine, and I will have it.*" Ended up with a bag full of money as well – a bag that was intended as payment for a job well done. A bag whose existence was unknown to anyone outside of the – others. Some trade: a bag full of money for the life of my wife and kid.

I felt empty inside. I quit my job, looked at a map of New Jersey and chose a destination that looked like it would be comparatively remote and desolate, if only for nine months a year. Beach Haven, on the southern end of the long thin barrier island of Long Beach.

Welcome to nowhere.

The clock read four minutes after five. It ticked loudly on the bedside table. It was dark outside now, so I must have dozed on and off for well over an hour. I rolled over and tried to go back to sleep, muffled "woofs" emerging from Hoover's sleeping form beneath the bed; no doubt a dream-in-progress. I stared at the inside of my eyelids for a good half an hour before I gave up.

I eased the Ford down North Ninth and eyeballed Richards' house off to my right. Around 7:30 now – cold, damp and cloudy outside. His house was dark, but the structure out back was lit. I saw Richards moving around inside it, at work on something hidden from view. I parked and killed the engine, headed back to the outbuilding, and knocked loudly on the door. A moment later, Richards pulled it open and squinted in the half-light, trying to identify this unexpected intruder.

"Oh. You again. I don't feel like talkin' no more," he said as he stepped back and started to close the door. It stopped as it hit my foot.

"Listen, Richards – just a couple more questions; it won't take long."

"Get your goddamned foot out of my door," he growled through clenched teeth.

"Listen a second: I'm in the same boat you're in now. My wife – she's disa –"

"I don't give a good-goddamn about your wife, or anyone else's!" he hissed, putting his shoulder to the door and slamming it closed.

My foot slid with it in the sand. I guess he didn't want to talk to me.

I rolled down to the end of the street, turned around and worked my way back to the abandoned freight station. I parked on the west side of the structure in a spot where I could keep an eye on Richards' activities. His change in attitude seemed a little abrupt and I was feeling none too favorably about him now. I sat and watched.

The old, wooden railroad structure helped to block the stiff ocean breeze, but it was cold in spite of that and the wool blanket I'd brought with me. After close to an hour of this, Richards killed the lights in the outbuilding, sinking his property into blackness. Forty seconds later a light went on in his house and then another. Ten minutes passed and I was asking myself just what in hell I hoped to accomplish freezing my ass off like this, when Richards left the house and disappeared once again into the inky darkness. Soon after, lights came on behind the house. His Chevy backed down the drive and onto Ninth and drove past me. I pulled out after him when he was a block away.

It was easy keeping track of him since his were the only moving lights around, with only an occasional lit house punching a hole in the darkness. He headed south on Ocean Boulevard for several blocks, pulling up and parking in front of a small corner store at the corner of North Fifth; I rolled to a stop half a block away and killed my lights. The store had a sign out front that read "Groceries." It was open and well lit, as were the second floor windows above – probably where the owner lived. There weren't any other signs of life for several blocks in either direction. Richards went inside, spent a couple of minutes milling about and occasionally popping into view through the cluttered front window, then reemerged several minutes later. He was munching on a roll and had a fresh package of cigarettes in his other hand. Inside the car, he fired one up, started the engine and pulled off.

Richards turned onto North Fourth, headed west two blocks to Barnegat, turned left and continued south for seven blocks. He parked shortly after crossing South Third in Ship Bottom-Beach Arlington. I passed and pulled onto South Fourth, parking as soon as my car was out of view beyond a vacant house. I headed back towards Barnegat, the wind roaring in my ears, the inky blackness only sporadically broken by the lonely lights in the occasional occupied home. I didn't realize that Richards would be heading in this direction, however, and might have walked right into him if I hadn't seen his silhouette move past the lit windows of the bungalow at the far corner of South Fourth and Barnegat. Once I had him located, however, it was easy enough to keep track of him; and with all of the racket that Mother Nature was making I didn't have to worry about the sound of my footfalls. Cold as it was, it felt good to get out and move. Richards headed several blocks south, then turned west on South Seventh and headed for the causeway; I was half a block behind.

The causeway bridge was actually a series of bridges spanning the bay. Heading east to west, the first small bridge was a drawbridge that led from Ship Bottom-Beach Arlington on Long Beach Island to the tiny island of Cedar Bonnet several hundred feet away. Several more short spans connected Bonnet Island and Solomon's Island before reaching the five thousand-foot causeway that spanned the bay itself. There wasn't much on these other islands except for the occasional fishing shack, but Cedar Bonnet Island boasted two bars that were open year-round, and favorites of the locals. Richards hoofed it across the drawbridge and headed into the bar on the north side of the road, a place called Charlie's Bar and Grill.

I wandered around outside for a short while, peeking in windows and keeping tabs on Richards. He was inside, drinking beer and acting very chummy with a brunette barmaid in her mid-to-late thirties. And he looked warm. She wasn't much to look at, that was for sure, but her figure appeared to be well preserved, and Richards wasn't exactly a stunner himself. It looked like it was going to be a long night; and since my toes had grown numb an hour earlier, I decided to do something about it. I headed across the narrow road to Van's Bar.

Inside, I ordered a Rheingold from the barkeep, a guy in his mid-fifties named Harry Rifkin whom I knew fairly well and hadn't seen in four or five months. There were only a couple of others in the place, and our conversation was interrupted at brief intervals so that Harry could keep them drinking. His wooden leg lent a rocking quality to his walk as he moved up and down the length of the bar – I always grew tired just watching him make his rounds. I sat sideways on my stool so that I could keep an eye on the front door of Charlie's across the street. So far, no one had come or gone.

Harry and I talked about whatever came to mind. He'd heard of Holly's disappearance and I was surprised about that when he first mentioned it, but I guess I shouldn't have been. It was a small island, after all, and most everyone on it had known – or known of – Ray Farnham, and, by extension, his little girl, Holly. We talked about the bar business and, while I was my own boss, Van was his; Harry had sold his tiny bar in Manahawkin a few years back after the onset of Prohibition and had gone to work for Van at its repeal.

We talked about the frequent power outages that plagued the small island communities and how they impacted business. He told me that the drawbridge linking his and Charlie's bar to the island had been stuck in the open position over this past weekend, from the previous Friday afternoon until late Monday morning when it was finally repaired. This, needless to say, had effectively killed their respective businesses for practically three full days, with only a handful of locals making the short trip by boat in their quest for a drink; most others had switched to bars on the island. It wasn't the first time this had happened, and we agreed it wouldn't be the last.

After nearly an hour of catching up, I grabbed another Rheingold and took a seat by the front window, one eye trained on Charlie's front door. I paced myself with the beers, but I was growing fairly weary as midnight arrived and the two bars closed for the night. I was pulling on my coat when I saw Richards step through Charlie's front door, followed a full minute later by the brunette barmaid. They both glanced around as if to check that no one was watching. Richards joined her and both climbed into her car, a beat-up old wreck that looked like it had once been a Ford. Quickly stepping outside, I confirmed that it was indeed a Ford two-door, early '20s, fenders missing and rusted to hell; its paint, which had once been black, was now faded to a dull gray, pocked with huge, cancerous-looking patches of rust. The trunk's lid appeared to have a number of holes punched in it. The car just sat there and I suppose they could have been inside talking, but I seriously doubted it.

After several minutes of nothing she started her car, the cold most likely having gotten to them. The windows were steamed and I could see hands wiping them one at a time from the inside for visibility. I was in a bind now: I was on foot and would have a difficult time following them. She rolled slowly east on Seventh, taking a left onto Barnegat; I ran as fast as I could to try to keep them in view, but the gap widened quickly. Fortunately, there was no one else on the road, her car's lights practically the only lights to be seen. I reached the corner and looked north on Barnegat, but couldn't find them. I slowed my pace to a trot, and arrived a minute later at Richards' car, still parked near the corner of Third. My feet were cold and numb, but I was sweating under my coat. About to give it all up for the night and head back to my car, I noticed the lights of a lone house towards the bayside end of South Third, where it dead-ends. I hung a left and moved on in the darkness, easier now that my eyes had adjusted to the almost total absence of light. The breeze had disappeared and my footfalls were very audible now, but it didn't matter – there was no one to hear them. I found the barmaid's car parked in the yard beside the house – hers, I assumed – which was a small, cedar-shingled bungalow. I could hear their drunken talk and laughter through an open window, drifting out into the now-still winter night air. After several minutes the talk ceased, the window was pulled shut, and the lights went out. I approached the house several minutes later, worked my way around to the back and found a single window that was open four inches. I could hear the familiar grunting and moaning of two adults in the throes of sex, accompanied by what must have been the noisiest bedsprings on the island. I felt dirty, like some perverted Peeping Tom and gave it up for the night. I walked back to my car at a pace more appropriate to a thirty seven year old.

Heading back home down the long stretch of road flanked by soft walls of impenetrable brush, I stared numbly at the overlapping circles of light circumscribed by my headlights on the graveled surface before me. What a waste of a night, I thought to myself. And the barmaid: I couldn't get her out of my mind. Richards was having a hell of a lot more fun than I was right now.

Having a great time – wish I was there.

302

Wednesday, December 16, 1936. 9:48 a.m.

IT WAS MID-morning before the full impact of what Harry had said the previous night hit me: The causeway drawbridge – the only physical link to the mainland – had been stuck in the open position – unusable – the night Holly disappeared. Yet it seemed unlikely that she was still on the island; her disappearance was common knowledge by now, and there just weren't that many places to go, or hide, on this eighteen-mile strip of sand.

I spent the better part of the day and the day following placing calls to the island taprooms that were open year-'round. I knew someone at each place, having lent something to – or borrowed something from – practically every one of them over the past ten years when supplies ran short. Checked that none of them had heard anything – anything at all – regarding Holly's whereabouts, or the circumstances surrounding her disappearance. I called Bill Van Kirk at The Antlers, Gus Tueckmantel at the Acme Hotel, Milton Britz at Britz's and Gerhard Brunner at the Hudson House – that pretty much covered the Beach Haven area. And there was Oswald Riese at his place in the Terrace, "Skinny" Schmidt, who worked for Glenn Coe at the New Surf Villa in Surf City, Charlie Fackler at Charlie's, Harry Rifkin at Van's on Cedar Bonnet Island, and Paul Kaetzel up at his joint up in Barnegat City. I even called "Dutch" Young over at Bonini's at the far end of the causeway over in Mud City. Awkward, sure, but I was satisfied that no one had heard much of anything. What they *had* heard were a handful of theories tossed about as to *why* she ran off, but no one had voiced even the slightest suspicion that she could still be on the island. I received numerous assurances

I'd be contacted immediately if anyone heard – or saw – anything more on the subject, and came away from it reasonably certain that she wasn't anywhere on Long Beach Island. If she was, though, someone was bound to get wind of it fairly soon. After all, taken collectively, these ten guys – eleven if you tossed me into the mix – knew just about everything that happened on the island. Maybe *everything*.

So, if she wasn't on the island, how did she get off? She couldn't have gotten off by car, so the only remaining method was by boat. Which was highly unlikely: I knew for a fact that she didn't know how to swim, probably the only person on the island who didn't. Holly was involved in a boating mishap once as a young kid, had almost drowned. She was, as a result, extremely uncomfortable around water. And while she could, on occasion, be coerced to board a boat, the notion of being on a boat at night, *in the dark*, terrified her. Some are terrified of heights and some are terrified of confined spaces; Holly was terrified of the water at night. There were two specific instances in the previous ten years where we were forced to decline an invitation for a night-time cruise and this was the reason why. Not only that: The weather was crummy the night of her disappearance and the bay would have been extremely rough and choppy. I couldn't imagine her willingly agree to climb aboard a boat – any boat – under those circumstances, even if it were piloted by someone with a lot of experience and self-confidence. She would have waited for better weather and daylight if she could. And that's assuming she even knew that the causeway drawbridge was unusable.

No, it just didn't make sense to me. There had to be more to her disappearance than met the eye.

I tore apart our house in search of any tangible clue that might explain the reason behind her departure. Three solid hours passed, picking through drawers and sorting through closets, to no avail. I sat on the stool in her small workroom, trying to decide what to do next. I stared blankly at the covered wicker basket that held her sewing materials, and it occurred to me that I hadn't looked inside it – ever. Lifted the lid and found two books inside, nestled in amongst the spools of thread, needles and random pieces of material. One of them was her diary for the year 1936, and the other her current volume of poetry and ideas; only a dozen or so pages of the latter were filled. I'd promised Holly years earlier that I would never, ever, look at her diaries unless given specific permission, but there could have been some pertinent information in there. "Hope you don't mind," I mumbled quietly to myself as I thumbed through pages to December 13, 1936. It was filled in.

Sunday, December 13, 1936: started sunny, but clouds arrived early afternoon. Temperature plummeted into the twenties, some sleet and heavy winds in evening. Told Lew the news this morning – hope I'm right. He wasn't very excited, or at least I don't think he was. I was so nervous telling him I acted like an absolute fool, but he can be so pig-headed sometimes. He tried to apologize but I wouldn't hear of it. I should apologize to him. Hope I feel better soon. Need to find out if really pregnant – or just feeling lousy. I'm going soon.

I stared at it for several minutes and reread it several times. I felt numb and light headed. *"I'm going soon."* Where? To see the doctor? Or, perhaps, away? Goddamnit, why couldn't she have been more specific. *"I should apologize to him."* That sounded like she intended to stick around, didn't it? This was maddening: I had no better idea about the circumstances surrounding her departure than before I read it. Should I show this to Purdy? Not a chance. Quinn? Probably not; it didn't really say anything conclusive or even suggestive, one way or the other.

I took the two books out to the living room and settled into my easy chair for a long night of reading. I had the vague hope that there would be something – anything – buried in the diary that might offer a clue as to what the hell was going on.

Some days were covered with only a line or two of comments,

while others were filled with paragraphs of tightly written script. November 18, the day that Holly learned of Yumi's disappearance, was one of the latter. She recounted how she first heard about it, her thoughts on the matter, telling me about it and my initial visit with Tak, and Tak's suicide. She also wrote that both Yumi and Grace Peterson were fellow Poets' Circle members.

Yumi too?

Had she told me this? If so, I didn't remember anything about it, but it made sense. Both Yumi and Grace had had some of their stuff published in the *Times'* "Poets' Corner," and would explain why Holly knew them both so well. Could *this* be a link of some sort between Holly and Grace's disappearances, and Yumi's murder? Seemed unlikely, but in the absence of anything else to go on, I'd go on this. I decided to talk with the remaining Circle members over the next few days.

Assuming any remained.

Thursday, December 17, 1936. 7:38 p.m.

EDDIE NOLAN STOOD at the far end of the bar filling four glasses from the Jacob Ruppert tap, a cigarette stub dangled from his mouth, smoke engulfed his head. The bar was crowded. People milled about the low ceilinged, smoke-filled room, a dozen simultaneous conversations blended into a jumbled roar. I'd stopped in at Charlie's hoping to talk with owner Charlie Fackler about George Richards, but Eddie helmed the bar that night. He used to work at Billy Piggott's little hole-in-the-wall joint on South Thirteenth in Ship Bottom-Beach Arlington, but Billy'd drowned earlier in '36 and the place closed down.

I'd spent the better part of the day working my way through Holly's diary. While there were plenty of interesting entries – and a few surprises – there didn't seem to be anything at all that shed light on her whereabouts. Some of her comments regarding me and the arguments we had in the past were eye-openers. Looking back at some of them with hindsight suggested that perhaps – *just maybe* – she'd been right and I'd been wrong. But that didn't seem of primary importance right now.

I'd also contacted Bernie Douglass, Managing Editor of the *Beach Haven Times*, and asked if he, or one of his reporters, could provide me with a list of all known Poets' Circle members. He said he'd have a woman named Jessica Snook call me back, and she did so a half-hour later. Her voice was raspy and sounded like she had something caught in her throat – a smoker's voice – as she read from her most current list of members, dated January 1936. She said she kept this list so that any given week, when there weren't any voluntary submissions for publication, she'd have some backups to contact and beg for something to fill the tiny column. I jotted down the members' names and towns of residence and, if they had a telephone, their numbers. She rang off. I stared at the list of eight names, amazed that there was actually that many on the island who could – and actually *liked to* – write poetry. Or thought they could. Ethel Richards' name wasn't among them, but since she too had disappeared I added hers to the list. This was in the off chance she'd joined the group some time during the last ten months.

I'd placed a call to Howard Peterson – this was about 1:00 p.m. – and he answered on the sixth or seventh ring. I'd woken him, that was obvious, and he sounded tired, confused, and uninterested in talking. It took him a minute or so to remember me, that I had visited and who Holly was. But, ultimately, he surprised me; it all came back to him. He'd heard nothing from or about Grace, and when asked about the Poets' Circle brusquely dismissed them as "that bunch of chattering hens." When pressed, it turned out that he didn't know any of them at all except for Holly, and he barely remembered her. Or at least he said he didn't; in his current state he would have been hard put to remember his mother. I ended the call when he started whining about his future and what was going to happen to him. I didn't particularly care for the guy.

I wasn't finished with Richards, but knew there was no way in hell he was going to talk to me again. So, I figured I'd try the next best thing: talk to his friends. If he had any, I'd probably find them at his bar-of-choice. And that seemed to be Charlie's.

Eddie wandered down the length of the bar and poured me another Old Overholt.

"So, then, Lew. What can I do for ya?" he asked, pouring himself a glass of water from the tap beneath the counter. There were a lot of coins and bills spread out on the counter before me, and he knew I'd leave it all there as a tip if I left happy. And he was going to see to that.

"How long you been working here?" I asked.

"Since March. Started here soon after that damn fool Piggott wandered out into the ocean. Charlie and the missus take Tuesday and Thursday nights off; I cover for 'em. Some weekend work, too. Mostly, though, I'm up at the New Surf Villa. Gotta pay the bills, ya know. *She* covers for Mrs. Fackler," he added, tilting his head towards the brunette barmaid I'd seen with Richards two nights earlier.

We got to talking about Richards and the barmaid. Her name was Arlene Pretty, although she wasn't particularly, and she worked Tuesday and Thursday nights as well. Richards was there, like clockwork, both of those nights every week, and had been ever since he first laid eyes on her back in June.

Then the lights went out, and the place sank into blackness.

"Shit, not again," I heard Eddie mutter. "Hold on, Lew; let me get a lantern."

He crashed about behind the bar, fumbling around on the shelves beneath in search of his lantern. It was nice to be on the drinking side for a change. A mere ten-to-fifteen seconds passed before the lights flickered-on-and-off several times before deciding to stay on.

"Where was I? Oh, yeah. It wasn't much of a mystery to me – hell, it wasn't much of a mystery to most of these guys – that Richards was nailing her on a regular basis. We're not talking Greta Garbo here, that's for sure, but in the dark – well, she has all the necessary parts…" He paused to look at her admiringly. "Yes, indeed she does," he said, more to himself than to me.

"You know this for a fact, or just guessing?" I asked.

"About her parts?" he asked. "Just kiddin'; I know what you mean. Hell, when two people leave this place a minute apart consistently for five months and climb all over each other out in the parking lot, it doesn't take a genius."

I supposed it didn't.

"And no wonder Richards' wife lost patience with the guy and took off. After five months of this stuff, she had to have gotten wind of it. Ever see her, by the way?"

"Who, Ethel Richards?" I asked.

"Yeah — a real looker. The blond in her hair ain't hers, but who cares? Or at least I think it isn't — sure like to find out for myself, I would. No kids; she sure as hell wouldn't have any trouble finding another guy to take care of her."

The door behind me opened, a blast of cold air hit my back, and the four bills on the counter in front of me started to dance away; I flattened them with my hand.

"Other than Miss Pretty, has he got any friends worth mentioning?" I asked.

"Not really, or none that I'm aware of. Why don't you ask him yourself? He just walked in."

Damn! It was Thursday night; what was I thinking? I put my index finger to my lips, and Eddie nodded agreement, but there was an amused look on his face. Richards pulled up the stool next to me and sat, asked Eddie for the usual. My head was down and my hat pulled low, but I glanced up from under the brim at the mirror behind Eddie and saw that Richards was sitting sideways, his back to me, looking at the far side of the room. I glanced over and saw that he was staring at Arlene, who was joking loudly with four guys sitting at a table. One of them touched her arm briefly, and I could see Richards stiffen on his seat. Eddie placed a beer in front of Richards, who muttered thanks without turning. It seemed like a good time to leave, so I nodded to Eddie, left the change on the bar, and went home.

Friday, December 18, 1936. 10:16 a.m.

I KILLED THE engine and checked my notes: 221 Second Street, Beach Haven – this was the place. Hoover rolled an eye into momentary focus, gave a disinterested yawn and returned to his slumber on the seat beside me. Drizzle steadily pelted the Ford. Mid-thirties and gloomy. I couldn't have picked a more miserable day to conduct interviews. At least Hoover would remain dry.

I trotted up the front steps to the open porch and shook the rain from my hat. Dorothy Frazier lived here and was the first of the surviving Poets' Circle members on my list, three of whom lived in Beach Haven. I hadn't bothered to call in advance; figured she'd be less likely to refuse me if I showed up in person.

Frazier's home was a neat, white-trimmed, two-story cedar shingled house on the north side of Second midway between Bay and Beach. There was a partial third floor tucked up beneath the steep ridge roof with a window at either end, but third floors were generally used for storage since they got hotter than hell during the summer. Any chairs that might have graced the porch during the bulk of the year were now packed away somewhere for the winter months. I knocked several times loudly.

An elderly woman answered and identified herself as Dorothy Frazier; I could call her Dottie. She was short and compact, gray haired, late sixties or early seventies and full of energy. I identified myself as Holly's husband. She led me into her living room to talk. I marveled over her dress, wondering silently just how old it was back when the war ended. I stepped carefully in an attempt to avoid the cats milling about the place, unfazed by my arrival. The place smelled, primarily of cat, but I doubted Dottie was aware of it. A distant teakettle whistled, and Dottie disappeared for a couple of minutes, returning with a tray arranged with two cups of tea, a sugar bowl and creamer.

"So, young man, what can I do for you – as if I didn't know. No, I don't know where your wife went and I don't want to know why she went – that's between the two of you. Have you heard from her at all? She's such a nice girl. Probably visiting a friend or something, but she'll be back. She loves Beach Haven far too much to be away from here for any length of time. I worry about her sometimes: She really should do something about her weight, don't you think? I mean, she's an attractive woman, no doubt about it, but don't you think that she could use a little more meat on her bones? It's none of my business, I know, but I just can't help but feel that she'd be so much more attractive if she filled out a little."

Whew! Insert your penny and listen to the music. This woman could talk; I could take an hour nap and she'd still be going when I woke up.

"Actually," I interrupted, a bit more loudly than usual, "I don't have any idea where she is, nor why she left. I was hoping you might be able to provide some background information, perhaps shed some light, on the other Poets' Circle members, as well as Holly." There: I'd gotten it out. Now I could sit back and listen again.

"Oh, well; all right. I suppose you want to know about Grace Peterson, since she up and took off like Holly did. Well, Grace was a very attractive woman – stunning, in fact – who had the extreme misfortune of having married an idiot. Have you met Howard?"

"Yes, I…"

"Howard Peterson is the laziest, most conceited, arrogant man I've ever met – and I *don't* blame her for even a moment for leaving the fellow. It serves…him…right! Her poetry wasn't bad, though; I would imagine you've read some of it, as it's been in the *Times* on numerous occasions. Some of the others, though – their poetry wasn't for my tastes, let me tell you. I'm a classicist and I like my poetry just so – you know, rhymes? – but some of them have the oddest idea of the proper structure of a poem, the…"

"Dottie," I interrupted, once again; a pattern was being established. "Did Grace give any sort of hint that she might…"

"Oh, heavens, no! Not a peep. She hasn't returned yet, has she?" I shook my head. "Not that I knew her well, mind you. We'd get together four times a year – the first Tuesday in March, June, September and December. We decided to skip our December meeting this year, since several of our members had taken off and several others couldn't be contacted – but we'd get together four times a year and share our poetry. That was the purpose, you see: to share our poetry, not to sit around like a bunch of wives gabbing about the weather and whatnot." She paused for a sip of her tea, and I leapt in.

"And Yumi?" I asked. "Yumi Takarada?"

"Only Yumi I know. Nice girl, that Yumi. Oh, that was such a tragedy, what happened to her, wasn't it? Very nice; pretty, in a funny way; beautiful long, black hair. But I couldn't understand a word she said; couldn't understand her poetry, either, but it sounded so nice rolling off her tongue. It's a shame, that accident; but I guess they don't learn to swim in China. Such a *large* country and so *much* of it so far from the ocean."

I didn't have the heart to tell her that Yumi's death was something other than an accident. Not to mention that she was Japanese.

"How about Ethel Richards? Was she a new member of the Poets' Circle?" I asked.

"Who?"

"Ethel Richards. Lives up in Surf City. Early thirties, blonde, married to a fellow named George?"

"Never heard of her. And believe you me, if I had, I'd remember. I may be seventy two, but I remember names! And if I'd ever met her, I'd most certainly remember. This island isn't that large, and…"

"How about Emily Stackhouse?" I was working from my list now.

"Ah, now. Emily. Do you know her?" I shook my head. "She lives up in Barnegat City. Teaches at the schoolhouse up there, first through sixth graders, before they bus them over to the high school on the mainland. Plain looking, almost drab, but very sweet; a full head of curly, red hair. Oh, how I'd kill for a head of hair like that! Very sweet, as I said, and somewhat shy; she'll probably grow up to be a spinster. Such a shame."

"How old is she?"

"Oh, she's young. Younger than you; early twenties, I suppose. Looks like eighteen, though."

"How's her poetry?" I felt I should ask.

"Ahhh — nice, very nice. She knows how to write a poem. She knows how to structure a poem."

"And Mary McCarthy," I pursued, reading the next name on my list. "Lives down in Holgate?" I added, looking up again.

"Another nice girl and *very* pretty. An artist — paints and sketches, as well as writes poetry. Rather strange, come to think of it, but harmless-strange. She has red hair, too, come to think of it; hers is straight, though. And lots of freckles. And those eyes. She has those strange, pale-looking eyes, rather like a white mouse. She's not an albino, mind you — imagine that: an albino living at the beach! — but she's pale, nonetheless. She really does need to move closer to town, be closer to people; she needs to socialize more, work on her people skills. She lives near Holgate, so I understand, in a small isolated bungalow a quarter mile or so off the road — bayside. I wouldn't want to live in such a desolate area. Why, if something should happen — a fire or something — what would you do? Nobody would know."

"And Agnes Warren? Lives here in Beach Haven, down on Coral."

"Barely know her. She's usually not around; gets together with the Circle once, maybe twice a year. She travels a lot, I think. I can't even recall the last time I saw her — last spring, perhaps?" She scooped up a brindle tabby and placed it on her lap. "Yes, last spring; I'm sure of it."

"And Catharine Copperthwaite, also from Beach Haven?"

Dottie sat erect, an unpleasant expression spreading across her face like ink in water. "Catharine Copperthwaite is one of the crankiest, mean-spirited, joyless, self-centered people I've ever met, and I've met some miserable people over the years, so that's saying something! Her handicap? Well, that's no excuse to make everyone else's life miserable, even if the good Lord did deal you a bad hand early in life."

"What's the nature of her handicap?" I probed.

"Infantile paralysis, I believe; happened decades ago. Left her unable to walk, withered legs, confined to a wheelchair. Fortunately, she's wealthy; she's married to a prominent architect, so ongoing care and attention isn't an issue. He – her husband, that is – spends his workweek working and living in Philadelphia, and comes to town only on the weekends; most, but not all, weekends, and I don't blame him. It's just that she's so – *difficult*. Anyway, there was occasional talk between the other Circle members about just how unpleasant Catharine is and what a damper she put on our meetings."

"Did you do anything about it?" I asked.

"No – and I'll tell you why. She has her own personal demons and they frequently jump out of her mouth at you. But her poetry. It's the only glimpse one gets of the person she *could* have been, given different circumstances. Her poetry is, in a word, *beautiful*; and when you see and read it on the printed page, it's among the best the Circle members have written. Unfortunately, the poetry is usually saddled with Catharine as its presenter – and it suffers accordingly."

Dottie was proving to be a good source for background information about the various Circle members, and I asked a lot of general questions over the next forty-five minutes. Her energy seemed unflagging and my biggest problem was trying to keep her on track. I scribbled notes furiously as she spoke and filled a good twenty pages with my tiny scrawl. As conversation wound down, I thanked her for her time, promising to return some time in the future for another chat. I left with a fair degree of knowledge about the other members, their personalities, and what made them tick – or at least from Dottie's perspective. And, for that matter, whether their poetry was any good or not.

Hoover was all over me when I climbed in the car, sniffing out the scents of cats permeating my clothes. The drizzle had let up momentarily and the fresh December air smelled wonderful after the close confines of Dottie's cat hotel.

Minutes later I pulled up at 102 Coral Street, the house where Agnes Warren lived. Four blocks south of Second, Coral Street was perhaps the nicest street in Beach Haven, lined with a series of majestic structures designed by some of Philadelphia's leading architects back in the late 1870s and 1880s during the borough's infancy. Many of these structures – indeed, many throughout the island – were given names by their owners, names that were prominently displayed on plaques conspicuously mounted on the building's exterior. My personal favorite was number 123, known as "Portia Cottage," a sprawling Victorian with a large wrap-around porch and distinctive twin chimneys joined by an open arch. Its architect, a guy named John Allston Wilson, had designed it back in '83. His family still owned and lived in it.

Warren's house was a huge gambrel-roofed, cedar-shingled affair perched on the southwest corner of Coral and Atlantic and, in spite of its address, its front actually faced Atlantic and the ocean three hundred yards beyond. Hoover again chose to remain in the car, while I walked from where I parked on Coral around the corner to the front of the house. Its first floor was anyone else's second floor, reached by a flight of fifteen steps, at a height where the porch afforded one an unobstructed view of the ocean beyond the dunes.

The place looked sealed for the winter, with shutters pulled closed over most of the windows. I knocked several times loudly and wasn't surprised when no one answered. Then I noticed the note, to the right of the door, fastened at eye level and protected by a small square of glass: "Owner may be reached at 362 Hollander Avenue, St. Petersburg, Florida – October 15 through March," it read. I made note of it.

Catharine Copperthwaite was third on my list and, based on Dottie's glowing reference, I wasn't terribly thrilled with the prospect of this next visit. Her house was six blocks south of Coral at the northeast corner of Belvoir and Beach. It sat alone at the end of the block in this less-developed part of town, nestled in amongst the huge growth of bayberry to its south and west. It, too, was a large structure, newer than those on Coral Street – late teens or early twenties, I'd guess – two stories and sheathed in the ubiquitous cedar shingles. I walked the steps to the front porch, avoiding the long, gently sloped ramp running the length of the house on its north side. Hoover stayed in the car; it wasn't an option this time.

A colored servant answered the door. He made me wait on the porch as he checked to see if Copperthwaite would allow me several minutes. Graciously, she would

He led me down a long, dark hall covered with what appeared to be an easily three-quarters-of-an-inch thick Oriental carpet. Whoever wheeled her about this place got a workout, whether they wanted one or not. He knocked quietly at the thick oak door at the hall's end.

"You know I'm in here; stop that infernal knocking!" barked a raspy woman's voice from beyond. The servant looked at me, raised his eyebrows and opened the door as I smiled in sympathy.

The room was a sunroom, though I doubted that sunshine had ever graced its interior since it was built. The carpets were thinner in here, but still Orientals. Copperthwaite was propped up in an oak wheelchair at the far end of the room, a heavy wool blanket over her lap, an open book face down on top of it. A lone lamp shone over her left shoulder, leaving most of her face in shadow. There was a small circular table to her right with a white lace doily positioned at its center, and set upon it within her reach a clear crystal glass, half-filled with an unidentifiable brown liquid. She reminded me of Alice's Queen of Hearts sitting there, a scowl clouding her face. She was probably in her mid-fifties, but it was difficult to tell – as much due to the lack of light as her physical dissipation. The windows – I *think* there were windows – were smothered behind dark, heavy drapes. Plants were everywhere: on tall floor stands, in pots hanging from the high ceiling, on shelves, everywhere; a mystery how they'd survive and flourish in this dark cave. The air was thick with something unpleasant, but I couldn't determine whether it emanated from the plants, from some concoction that Copperthwaite doused herself with regularly or whether it was the smell of lingering decay. Whatever, it commingled with stale smoke and I resorted to breathing as much through my parted lips as my nose. A small, white Pomeranian with fur stained at both ends barked incessantly, and I knew it was only a matter of minutes before I'd have a splitting headache.

"What do you want?" she asked curtly. There was no mirth in her voice.

I introduced myself, although I knew that her servant had already delivered the particulars. I explained the reason for talking with the various Poets' Circle members.

"Where'd your wife run off to?"

"I don't know. I don't even know that she ran off."

"Did you two get in some sort of argument? You *don't* hit her, do you?"

Who was interviewing whom? I attempted to allay her fears that I habitually brutalized Holly, and I suppose I was somewhat successful as she eventually eased up on me. I managed to ask a few general questions and found her to be, not surprisingly, strong and dominant, condescending, totally void of any trace of warmth or tact, and just downright rude; I could well understand why the other Circle members had some misgivings about her.

She admitted that she liked Holly, in spite of her common upbringing and breeding, but couldn't comprehend how anyone could live with herself while earning a living selling impure spirits to others. Her negativity towards alcoholic drinks of all sorts suggested to me that perhaps the brown liquid in her glass was soda or tea, maybe even prune juice.

She placed a cigarette in a long black enameled holder and lit it. I asked her about Grace Peterson.

"Too good looking for her own good. She was well spoken, but was superficial in her thoughts and conversation. I doubt she has a brain in that pretty little head of hers. I'm not surprised she got fed up with life on the island, especially in that boring little hamlet of Harvey Cedars. She can go back to the city, for all I care. Probably has already."

Yumi Takarada? "I can't figure out why we had an Oriental in the group. She should have been home doing laundry, or whatever it is they do here. And her grasp of the English language was negligible. I couldn't understand a word she said, and her so-called poetry was primitive at best. A shame about her drowning, though; I wouldn't wish that on anyone, even though Orientals value life far less than we Christians do."

I bit my tongue, gripped my notepad tighter and felt my anticipated headache arrive like a roll of thunder.

Ethel Richards? "Never heard of her. Should I have?"

Emily Stackhouse? "A charming, little schoolteacher — or as charming as the natives of this island get. She's the nicest, most decent one of the group and refreshingly intelligent. Her surname, however, is rather unattractive; don't you think? She'll make a wonderful wife someday, if there's a man good enough for her in Barnegat City. Which I doubt."

Mary McCarthy? "She's just out-and-out weird, holed up in her little shack in the dunes with those stupid little parakeets of hers, leading her pseudo-Bohemian existence; she'll get a good dose of reality some day." She shook her head in disbelief. "Goodness gracious, how that girl loves those filthy little birds of hers."

Dorothy Frazier? "Cat woman? She stinks to high heavens, as does her house. The authorities ought to do something about that place; it's a disgrace." This was the pot calling the kettle black. "And she isn't much of a poet; she can't see the beauty in things. She looks at the ocean and sees water, looks at the beach and sees sand. No imagination. None whatsoever."

And Agnes Warren? "Who?" I described her as best I could with the limited information I had. "Oh, her; the mystery woman. She's rarely ever there at the meetings. I don't know why she even bothers to come. She never contributes anything worth mentioning anyway."

I couldn't wait to get out of there. I was used to negativity; I saw it all the time at the taproom. Usually revealed itself in one of two fashions. More often than not an otherwise likable fellow reduced by drink to bad-mouthing anything and everyone who crossed his path, spewing an unrelenting stream of venom in all directions. Or, almost as often, a usually disagreeable fellow relaxed by drink, his defenses down, displaying a far-more likable side to his personality. Jekyll and Hyde vs. Hyde and Jekyll.

Copperthwaite was a different animal altogether. She was wholly unpleasant in person – consistently so, based on others' accounts – and the fact that she didn't drink suggested that this was as good as she got. And I could give a good goddamn about her poetry: I didn't ever sit down and try to hold a conversation with a poem.

It was a little after 1:30 when I fled the depressing confines of her home. Hoover greeted me once again as I reentered the car, thoroughly checking out the new array of smells lingering on my clothing. If I were something lying by the road, he surely would have rolled in me.

An hour later, I rolled into Barnegat City at the northern tip of the island. Fifty years earlier, Barnegat City had been a thriving resort community, linked to the mainland by rail, with two large hotels and a sizable year-'round population. Most of those year-'rounders were the support staff – and their families – for either the town's pound fishery, the island's sole lighthouse or the U.S. Lifesaving Service's local station. In the intervening years, however, the city's complexion had changed and not for the better. While never much of a city in the first place, the appellation now seemed little more than a joke. Severe erosion of the northern tip of the island, coupled with a fervent temperance stance, sent tourists scurrying for Beach Haven at the island's more tolerant southern end. A lack of tourists resulted in a discontinuation of rail service to the north end in 1923, and the two hotels were now gone. The Oceanic had been hit with a typhoid outbreak in 1910 – drowned rats were later found in the water tanks built into the hotel's cupolas – and closed its doors for good in 1914, falling into the advancing sea in 1920. The Sunset lingered on for another decade, but by 1932 only four of its original fifty acres remained – lost to erosion – when it burned to the ground. It wasn't rebuilt.

The lighthouse remained, but its light had been extinguished and its support staff sent packing back in 1930, replaced by a lightship eight miles out at sea in the mid-'20s. The lighthouse had been built in the late 1850s nine hundred feet south of the island's first lighthouse, when that older light proved inadequate and was close to falling into the advancing ocean. Now, some eighty years later, the replacement lighthouse faced a similar fate. The tides had advanced over the years, dooming the lightkeeper's house and forcing the erection of a makeshift bulkhead comprised of derelict automobiles, empty beer kegs filled with sand, and rocks. The threat was renewed with a vengeance back in September when a violent nor'easter pummeled the island and its beaches.

Barnegat City had, for all intents and purposes, reverted back to its roots and was now little more than a transplanted Scandinavian fishing village. Norse names and features prevailed, the children blond haired and blue eyed, the elder males leather skinned, their wives pale and worn. Aside from the fishing industry, there wasn't much else non-residential save a church, a schoolhouse and several taverns.

It was a sleepy, sparsely populated community now and the locals liked it that way.

I took a right at the north end of Central onto First Street and found Emily Stackhouse's tiny bungalow burrowed into a thicket of pine on the south side of the road near where it dead-ended at the dunes. It was a modest, white clapboard affair with dark green trim, but the faded paint was in dire need of another coat. Several hours had passed since the drizzle stopped, and while still overcast things had begun to dry. Hoover roused himself to climb out of the car and explore the area while I mounted the steps to the small open porch. After a minute or so of knocking to no response, I gave up.

I stood by the Ford calling for Hoover when I spotted a young lady sauntering down the unpaved street, an armful of books held to her chest. The head of curly red hair suggested that this might be Emily, so I strolled over to greet her, identified myself and verified that she was, indeed, Emily. She invited me into her home.

The kitchen was larger than I would have expected. I shed my coat and hung it over the back of a chair at the small oak table. Upon her insistence, I took a seat while she quickly built a fire in the small cast-iron stove set in the shallow fireplace. She put a kettle of water on to boil and only then did she remove the long, heavy wool coat she'd been wearing.

My initial reaction had been that Emily was far better looking than Dottie had led me to believe. By no means drab, she had a healthy, fresh-scrubbed plainness that bordered on pretty – not quite there, but darn close. And, of course, she had youth going for her, which might not mean much to another youth, but added points in the mind of an older observer. And her hair: I hadn't a clue as to whether or not the curls were natural, but they were perfect – and combined with a reddish-blond hue, made you want to run your fingers through them. Once the coat came off, I could tell that her figure complimented her face, in spite of the fact that the better part of it was buried under a bulky, wool sweater. I could use my imagination.

She sat at the table's end, elbows planted on it, chin resting on her upturned palms, a pleasant smile spread from cheek to cheek.

"So, you're Lew Porter."

"Yeah," I responded. "One and the same."

"I...I was sorry to hear about Holly. One of the children at school, Timmy Somerville – I teach over at the school on Fifth Street – his mother told me the news, that Holly had left you..." her voice trailed off.

"It looks that way."

"Have you heard from her? Do you know where she is? Is she all right?"

I told her what little I knew, and that I hoped she might be able to offer some scrap of information that might suggest an explanation for the several disappearances and Yumi's death.

She sat there staring at me, and didn't say a word for several seconds.

"I'm sorry; I don't mean to stare," she finally said. "It's just that Holly's told me so much about you that I feel almost as if I know you." She blinked and looked down at the tabletop. "Listen, I'm sympathetic to your plight. I really am. And if you ever need someone to talk to, I'd be happy to. But...I really can't think of anything, anything at all, that Holly said or did, that even remotely suggested that she planned to take off. Maybe it was spontaneous; I don't know." She paused, looked me in the eye. "Do you think...do you think it was a...another man?"

It might have been my imagination, but in the way she phrased the question, I had the uneasy feeling that she hoped the answer was "Yes." I told her I had no idea and switched to Grace Peterson.

"Oh, she's very nice; I like her a lot. And she's a surprisingly good poet; much smarter than her appearance would suggest – so many of the men who see her assume she's the typical – *dumb* I suppose you'd call it – blond. I'm not at all surprised that she left her husband; that guy's an embarrassment. And if I had to make a guess, I'd say that she returned to New York; Harvey Cedars is kind of a shock, I would imagine, after living in a huge cosmopolitan city like Manhattan. But if she ever said anything – gave any sort of a hint – about leaving him or the island, I don't remember it. Her departure was more of a disappointment than a surprise. I hope she gets in touch some time."

The kettle started to whistle, and she got up to make some cups of tea; today's ration of tea would hold me for the next twelve months.

I asked about Yumi, and she paused and turned to me, looking a bit paler than her usual pale coloring.

"That...that was terrible, horrible. She was such a dear, sweet woman. Who could have done such a horrible thing to her?" Evidently, Emily had heard that it was murder and not an accidental drowning. "She was so intelligent. Very soft spoken and difficult to understand sometimes, but her poetry was wonderful – like music."

I asked about the other Circle members, her opinions and comments on each.

"Mary McCarthy is a free spirit. Her poems are nice and well thought out, and I think she could be a real talent someday; but she's kind of a recluse. She's in her late twenties, I'd guess, from a wealthy family in Red Bank. She lives in a small house in the dunes midway between Holgate and Beach Haven – has since 1929, if I recall correctly – and leads an unfettered, non-materialistic existence. She writes reams of poetry. She's somewhat of an eccentric. Have you met her? She's tall and thin, with a head full of long, straight red hair – not copper colored like mine, but red – and a face full of freckles. Her skin's amazingly pale for someone living at the beach year 'round. I think she paints, too, but I'm not sure about that. She makes frequent trips back home to Red Bank whenever she gets lonely or wants a decadent meal. Freedom, but on her terms. She has a bunch of pet birds, too, all living in cages and capable of making an ungodly racket at times. Up all night, sleeps late – one of those types.

"Dorothy Frazier – we call her Dottie – she's, well, kind of strange, but harmless. Her poetry's rather simplistic, but pleasant enough. She loves cats, as you'll discover if you go visit her at her home.

"Agnes Warren – I've met her only once, and can't recall much of anything about her. I seem to recall her just sitting there not saying much of anything. But then she probably didn't know the rest of us like we already knew each other, so maybe she was just shy, or intimidated, or whatever. I don't even recall her poetry, or if she read any.

"Catharine Copperthwaite? Now, there's one of God's creations gone wrong. Mrs. Copperthwaite – I can't bring myself to call her by her first name – is one of the most miserable, unromantic people I've ever met; truly dreadful. She's a living, breathing example of how wealth can poison the soul and I hope that she grows bored – or fed up – with the group and leaves; I don't think there's a single one of us who can stand seeing her and listen to her miserable grumblings and complaints." She fingered her teacup, staring at it for a moment. "It's going to be…difficult, going to the next meeting, whenever it is…everyone I really like…" Her voice trailed off.

I gave her a moment, then asked about Ethel Richards. That brought her around, but she'd never heard of the woman until a few weeks back, when the mother of another student had mentioned her disappearance in passing.

We both sat there for a minute in silence. She continued to finger her teacup, and would occasionally look up at me and give a small, shy smile, then return her gaze to the chipped cup. I looked out the window behind her at the streak of bright orange where the setting sun was tearing its way through the heavy mass of gray clouds. It lasted for only a half-minute and then the outdoors returned to grayness even darker than before.

I felt comfortable talking with Emily, comfortable sitting in her kitchen, comfortable being with her and not speaking a word; I felt as if I'd known her for years. There was a hollowness in my stomach as my thoughts moved to Holly: God, how I missed her, missed the sound of her voice, the warmth of her body.

"Would you like to…ah…stay for dinner? Nothing fancy, mind you, but cooking for two's no harder than one, and I'd love the company."

I was tempted, but for all the wrong reasons.

"No, but thanks; maybe some other time, if that's all right. I have some other stops I need to make and I have to get back to the taproom. Friday nights are always busy," I said, grabbing my coat and thinking to myself how I'd love to stay. Willpower, that's what it was; good thing I hadn't had anything to drink. She walked me to the front door.

"Thanks for everything," I said, pausing one last time to quickly examine her face. She stood facing me, looking up into my eyes with a charming little half-smile gracing her face.

"The pleasure was all mine, Lew Porter. Be sure to stop by again soon. Anytime." She paused. "I'd love to see you again." Her hand briefly touched my arm and something happened inside of me, something I knew shouldn't have.

Hoover was lying in the yard staring attentively at some birds when I emerged, and he joined me at the car. It was 3:15 when we headed back south.

We rolled into Surf City twenty-five minutes later. I took a detour to check out Richards' house and, once again, he was out back in the lit-up outbuilding, his house dark. He was annoyed at something, stomping around and cursing, the crash of the occasional thrown item audible over the Ford's idling engine. I kept on going. Emily kept creeping into my thoughts and I didn't struggle too hard to eject her; there was something very appealing about her.

Hell, there was a lot that was appealing about her.

When I arrived in Beach Haven I made the momentous decision to squeeze in one last interview, so I continued on in the direction of Holgate and Mary McCarthy's house. If I could take care of this one, I figured, I'd have spoken to all of the surviving members – or all excepting Warren, who was a thousand miles away in Florida. I could ease into the weekend with that chore behind me.

After a couple of false starts, I finally located the sand road that led back through the low tangle of brush to McCarthy's house. It had been marked with a small horizontal strip of wood, nailed to a stake driven into the sand, with the letters "MMC" painted in white. Just like Emily had indicated.

Daylight was almost a memory as I slowly made my way down the narrow road. I emerged several hundred feet beyond in a parking area large enough to turn around in, a small, modest structure off to one side. My headlights were on now and straight ahead of me laundry hung on a line, dancing in the breeze. Several pieces hung at odd angles by a single pin and others had pulled loose altogether, lying about in the sand nearby or tangled in the leaves of an adjacent bayberry bush.

I killed the lights and engine and sat for a few moments, the silence interrupted only by the ping of my cooling engine, the sound of leaves doing battle with the breeze, and the flat clack of a wind chime somewhere distant, bayside.

The kitchen lights were on inside her house, and as I approached the low sounds of a radio became audible. As I stepped onto the small covered porch, the boards groaned loudly under foot. No one answered after several knocks. I let myself in and yelled loudly to announce my presence. A half-eaten bowl of cereal sat on the kitchen table, the milk long ago evaporated. By its side was a mug of coffee, half gone from evaporation and skimmed over.

I called out one last time as I looked at the two dead parakeets lying on the bottom of their cages; no one answered, no one was home. A faceless voice droned on in the background about the preparation of clam fritters. I turned off the radio. Silence descended upon the building, broken repeatedly by boards creaking and windows rattling in the on-again, off-again gusts of wind.

It didn't take long to search the tiny place. Her clothing and toiletries were all gone, leaving the bedroom and bath comparatively void of signs of occupancy. It was evident that she had lived alone, however. A family photo – two parents and their tall, thin daughter, I guessed – sat on a chair-side table. On its back was written "Mum and Dad, Summer 1934," and I memorized the girl's face. I hoped that I would see it again some time in the future – smiling.

I stood there for a long time, overwhelmed by a feeling of helplessness. Another one gone, and this time it looked as if it were against her will. Unless, of course, it was spontaneous – but no one is that spontaneous. No one except, perhaps, a madman. Was she kidnapped? And the others: were they kidnapped, too? What would be the sense in that, the motive? Kidnappers do it for money, and no one – at least to my knowledge – had asked for any, from anyone.

Holly...

I felt like screaming. Like punching a hole through the nearest wall. Like my world was going up in flames around me. I stormed through the door towards my car.

Hoover trotted out from the brush and up to my side, nuzzling my hand with his snout and giving a few tentative licks. Amazing how that dog could calm me down. I sat in the sand and scratched him behind his ears, and he joyfully fell onto his side, legs kicking at the air. I stared into the darkness, the breeze hitting me square in the face. It brought tears to my eyes.

Or, at least I think it was the breeze.

My mood blackened as the night wore on. I'd placed an

anonymous call to the police regarding McCarthy – anonymous because I just wasn't in the mood for any more of Purdy's insinuations just now – and figured they could traipse out there, survey the scene and draw their own stupid conclusions. I hadn't budged from my seat at the taproom table, smoking one cigar after another, drinking quickly and heavily. Willett knew I was best left alone and managed the bar on his own. Come to think of it, he did a pretty good job, all alone back there, fielding orders on a Friday night.

Holly's disappearance was dragging me down; and now, with McCarthy's vacant home discovery tossed into the mix, my concerns for Holly's safety and well-being intensified – and my appreciation of the role she'd assumed in my life grew with each waking moment. I was miserable – and tonight it was obvious to everyone around me. Sitting there, grumbling under my breath, the regulars instinctively knew to avoid me.

And then, as luck would have it, George Richards slammed through the door.

I recognized him just about the same moment he spotted me sitting there. I wasn't in the mood for games.

"Here for that drink?" I yelled, an edge to my voice. The place went silent. Richards glared at me, and I realized I had never extended that offer to him, only to Peterson.

"Why in hell are you askin' so goddamned many questions 'bout me?" he yelled. "You want to know something, talk to me!" he continued, approaching. "I'm gettin' goddamned sick and tired of your snoopin' around, askin' neighbors questions, stickin' your nose in my business!" He pushed his way through chairs and people, his fists tightening into solid balls. "Keep it up and I'm gonna teach you a fuckin' lesson!"

I stood to meet him, a nasty smile plastered across my face. If that fazed him, he didn't let on. Hoover, lying under the table at my feet, lifted his head towards the approaching hulk and let loose with a long, slow, bare-toothed growl.

I yelled to the dog to shut up, but he just lowered his growl a notch or two. I turned back to Richards, who stood facing me, eighteen inches separating our faces.

"Just try it, Richards – but you better make the first one count... I'm not Ethel."

Richards went red with rage, and shook like a dead leaf in a stiff ocean wind. But he saw something in my face, my steely gaze. Something that made him think twice. Something that made him think better of forcing the issue. Richards made a quick scan of the staring faces around him, and turned back to me, the veins fighting at his neck.

"You son of a bitch," he muttered, saliva foaming at the corners of his mouth. "Just stay out of my life," he added, turning quickly and stomping back towards the entrance. "Just stay the hell out of my life!" The door slammed behind him.

"Bye," I said quietly after-the-fact, then spit a loose piece of tobacco from the tip of my tongue. Everyone around me started talking at once, asking each other who he was, what was going on and what they'd just witnessed was all about. The booze was getting to me, and I slumped back into my chair as someone – I don't know who – asked if what he said was true – that I was poking around asking questions about him, prying into his private life.

"I wouldn't be asking if there wasn't a reason to," I snapped, louder and shorter than I needed to. The place fell silent again, and stayed that way for a bit until Willett's familiar voice broke it.

"You know, Lew, I'd be kind of pissed off, too, if someone was asking a bunch of questions about me, behind my back," he said. There were some low murmurs at that, and I had to assume they were comments of agreement. But I didn't give a damn at that moment; it was an occupational hazard, one that I'd formed a tough skin towards years earlier.

"Shut up, Willett," I snapped without thinking. Like I was yelling at my dog. "And who the hell do you think you are, anyway, the goddamned owner of this place? *Shut up* – and do your goddamned job," I snarled as I grabbed my bottle of Old Overholt, took a last, long pull, then stomped out of the place. Right now I was about as popular as the eel grass blight.

I walked the streets for hours, aimlessly, and have little recollection of where I went, or what I did. Later on, as the cold night air and my continuous movement helped to clear some of the alcohol from my brain, I found myself on the boardwalk staring out at its sole fishing pier. Its southern end had been whittled away over the years by the encroaching waves, and I laughed a mirthless laugh as I thought of the parallel to the gradual destruction my life was undergoing. I took maintenance pulls from my flask now, but my drunken state had reached a point of equilibrium: I was tired – very tired – but that was about all.

I was feeling sorry for myself.

I was making bad decisions.

I found myself driving through the night. Towards Barnegat City. Towards Emily's.

But why? Oh, who was I fooling? Of *course* I knew why – I just didn't seem, at that moment, to know any better. Or care.

Hauling myself up to the door, I knocked – loudly. And followed it with words.

I remember her answering after what seemed an eternity. I remember her look of surprise…confusion…pleasure…excitement. Or at least I think I do.

The pieces in between are a blur, but there's no mistaking what we did. I remember her bed, the passionate tangle of limbs, time collapsed. I wavered from consciousness to sleep and back again, seemingly dozens of times, and each time she was there, touching, probing, kissing – rousing me from my slumber time and again. I'm not sure whether my heart was actually in it, but my body was.

And, truth be told, so was hers.

332

Saturday, December 19, 1936. 5:06 a.m.

EMILY WOKE ME early the next morning a little after five and this time it wasn't for pleasure: She thought it best that I leave well before daylight, before there was any chance that one of the locals might see a stranger emerge from the young teacher's home.

We stood at the door for several awkward moments of silence. I looked at the situation more clearly now and it was obvious I'd made another Porter-sized blunder, one that I'd probably feel guilty about. I mumbled some rambling inanities, but she appeared happy and, it seemed to me and for want of a better word, aglow in her new relationship. She brushed my cheek with her fingers, and stood on her toes to give me a goodbye kiss. I responded somewhat hesitatingly with a quick, noncommittal peck on her cheek. The corners of her mouth sagged imperceptibly.

"Can I see you again?" she asked. The house went silent for several seconds, the ticking of a far-off clock the only intrusion.

"I don't know," I finally answered with a sad lack of decisiveness. "It's probably not a good idea. I mean…Holly; I'm a married man…" I cut it short as I realized just how lame my comments sounded. I needed to get out of there.

I glanced back at her house as I drove back to Central, in time to see the lone bedroom light wink off and the house disappear in the darkness.

An hour later I stood in my bathroom, staring in the mirror at my unshaven face. I didn't like what I saw, didn't like it at all. As hard as I tried, I couldn't come up with any sort of justification for what I'd done, not a scrap of it, and I was usually pretty good at justifying the unjustifiable. Anger welled up inside me, anger at myself, anger at those primal urges festering inside of me, anger at the unseen forces wreaking havoc on my life and the lives of so many around me. Only after I'd punched a six-inch dent in the plaster and lathe wall did the uncontrollable shaking of my body subside. I fell across my bed – fully dressed – and sleep descended upon me as quickly as the light had switched off back in Emily's bedroom.

Hoover roused me from the dead sometime early that afternoon. I stumbled to the back door to let him out. My head was pounding, my stomach on edge, and several fingers of my left hand – the one I seemed to recall punching the wall with – hurt like a son of a bitch. Swollen, they looked like three links of knockwurst.

I put on coffee and shaved, then took a long shower outside, alternating hot and cold water in a futile attempt to goad my body and mind back into a state roughly approximating normalcy. After dressing, I scrambled some eggs, toasted some bread, then attempted to shovel the mess into my throat; but it seemed that neither my hand, the fork, nor my mouth were working as efficiently as they usually did. Hoover got the leftovers.

I sat on the edge of my bed, staring into the mirror hanging over Holly's bureau, silently chastising myself for being so selfish. Why the hell did I always feel this ongoing compulsion to jump into bed with any woman willing to join me? Simply because it felt good? That seemed a pretty lousy reason to keep doing it, to keep betraying the trust of the woman who loved me.

You'd think I would have learned a painful and enduring lesson a long time ago, when my philandering placed me elsewhere while my wife and son were slaughtered. I'd kidded myself for years that Weems and his hired thugs from Hack and Hack were the sole culprits, but they had help – my help. If I'd been home as I should have been – as most husbands would have been – Dorothy and

Eddie would still be alive. I might not have survived, but it was me, after all, and not them, that was the intended target. And, for all I know – and I've conveniently ignored this fact since then – Weems may very well have chosen me as the patsy for reasons other than my naïveté and relationship to the intended victims. He may very well have known that I was fucking his wife, too. And frequently.

Christ, that's it – no more. I had to stop. I couldn't go on ruining others' lives in my ongoing pursuit of momentary pleasure, while convincing myself that I wasn't doing any harm. I was – and it was incalculable. I'd been something far less than a model husband during all of this. Something less than a *man*, when you really got down to it

I'd really made a mess of things.

My mind was made up. I couldn't undo what I'd already done at this point, but I sure as hell could make myself useful – by keeping a clear mind, avoiding distractions and immersing myself in the task of unraveling the tangled web of seemingly unrelated problems plaguing so many on the island. If there was any wrongdoing involved – and I emphasized *if* – I'd see to it that the perpetrators paid their pound of flesh. There'd be justice, all right. *My* justice. And I didn't care how long it took me, or how much it cost me. I'd solve this, or die trying.

And that probably wouldn't be much of a loss.

The small, winged, wooden creature looked down at me from atop Holly's bureau, silently mocking me. "You're getting on my nerves, friend," I said, scooping him up and shoving him in my pocket. "We're going for a walk."

I paused inside the taproom's door and looked at the assembled group, much the same group I'd treated so shabbily the night before. My friends. One by one they noticed my arrival and the raucous din quickly fell to a low murmur as they speculated amongst themselves just what to expect from me now. I felt like a fool.

"Gentlemen," I said, and the weakness of my voice surprised everyone, "I…I want to apologize for last night. For the last few days. For my lousy attitude and behavior. I know you guys don't have very high expectations of me – or for anyone else – when we're behind these doors, but I…I've sunken far below that modest level. I've had a rough few days, but that's no excuse. I guarantee you it won't happen again, or at least I'll try my damnedest to see that it doesn't. And if it does…well, it won't."

My little speech was well received, I suppose in part because they now knew they could drink in peace without keeping one eye on me or worrying about my next outburst. My announcement that drinks were on the house was received even more enthusiastically.

I gave Willett a hand with the sudden rush and, when things calmed down a notch, I dug out the wooden creature from my pocket and placed him in a prominent spot on the backbar, among all the other dusty crap accumulated over the years.

"He looks kind of at home with the dancing vegetables," I said to Willett, then pulled him aside and made a private, sincere apology and swore that I'd keep my drinking under control in the future. He seemed happy with the overture – both to him and the group at large – and its timing, as the patrons were starting to grumble about the city boy and his unpredictability. I'd compromised several years of hard work and camaraderie, and it would take some time before I fully re-earned their trust and good will.

I quietly nursed my hangover while Willett took a few minutes to wrap my swollen fingers. I told him I'd slammed them in a car door, which seemed like an easier explanation than the truth.

By five o'clock my stomach had come to an uneasy truce with the rest of my body, and my headache had receded from my eyeballs to a less-obtrusive overall dull throb. Willett cooked up some pork roll and potatoes for me, which I wolfed down. Behind me, at the bar, I could hear Edwards talking to Carver and Kahn.

"So the Mother Superior tells these two nuns – one of 'em gorgeous and stacked, for a nun anyway – to paint this empty room at the back of the convent, but warns them not to get a drop – not even a *hint* – of paint on their habits. They discuss it between themselves, and decide that the safest way to do it is to lock the door, strip off their habits, and paint the place in the buff. No one's gonna see 'em, right?" said Edwards. "Well, they get the room half done when there's a knock on the door.

"'Who is it?' asks nun number one.

"'The blind man,' replies a voice from outside the door.

"Well, they look at each other for a moment and shrug; what can be the harm?

"So, they unlock the door and let the blind man in.

"'Nice tits, sisters,' he says. 'Where do you want these blinds?'"

The trio broke into gales of laughter and I found myself smiling broadly.

Mackey and Ives entered, shed their coats and worked their way over to the bar to a flurry of greetings.

"Sale over?" asked Kahn.

"Yeah," said Ives, "most of the stuff moved and most of it for less than the asking price."

"Even the Oriental junk?" asked Edwards. Ives nodded, and I realized that they were talking about the sale at Tak and Yumi's home.

"Who got the Hudson?" asked Carver.

"What a beaut: like new, alright. Only seven-hundred-and-thirty-four miles on it, and a full tank of gas, to boot!" responded Ives, taking a long drink from the glass of Garden State Ale Willett had placed in front of him. "And believe it or not, there was some guy there just to buy that car; pushed his way to the front and insisted – well, kind of – that he be dealt with immediately, no haggling over price, just cash for title and then out of there."

"Whadaya mean, 'Kind of'?" Asked Edwards.

"Well, the guy was dumb," responded Ives.

"What did he do, ask dumb questions or somethin'?" asked Edwards.

"Not stupid dumb, *dumb* dumb. You know: *mute*."

"Who was he?" asked Carver.

Ives shrugged and looked over to Mackey, who was working on his bourbon and a game of solitaire laid out in front of him. Mackey paused, looked up at Ives momentarily, shrugged ignorance, and returned to his game.

"Nobody I'd ever seen before," he continued. "I was near him – close as I am to you – when all this was goin' on. He paid full price – three hundred and fifty smackaroos – no questions asked, no test drive, no nothin'. Name was Milton something-or-other. That's all I got, saw that much and nothin' more when he printed it out. Milton. Milt the Mute. Paid cash, mind you, grabbed the title and keys, and left before we knew it." Ives paused and finished his beer.

"What do you call a guy who can't read?" asked Kahn.

"Dumb," chuckled Ives. "Stupid, maybe. Who you thinkin' about?"

"Louie," replied Kahn. "And he's not dumb or stupid; he's a genius in the darkroom." Louie was an old guy who acted as photographer and all-around darkroom wizard for the *Times*. And, evidently, couldn't read a lick.

"Jeez, what the hell's Louie got to do with this? From the island? Was the dumb guy from the island?" pursued Carver.

"I'm not sure," said Ives, wiping the foam from his mouth with the back of his hand. "Somebody there – Wally Snipes, I think it was – said he was sure he'd seen him at some point or other, long ago at the north end of the island. Wasn't sure where or when, and had no idea who this guy was. Who cares?"

The conversation segued into sports and sex, and I sat there staring at my mug of tepid coffee. My mind, already fragile from the previous night's onslaught of alcohol, felt like it was going to explode. What the hell was going on around here? What was the connection, if, indeed, there was one, between the missing Circle members and Yumi, the dead one? Did the others plan their disappearances – the abandonment of their husbands – due to mutual dissatisfaction and unhappiness? Holly, Grace Peterson and

Mary McCarthy seemed an unlikely trio, but stranger things had happened. McCarthy's departure looked very suspicious, that was for sure, but it *could* have been a spontaneous, hasty exit. But why? She had no husband to beat a hasty retreat from and her beloved parakeets didn't fare too well in the maneuver. And Holly. It wasn't likely that she'd leave her current book of poems and diary behind and yet take the other, older ones. That is, unless it was an oversight in haste. And Yumi was definitely a case of foul play of some sort: the wire on her wrists and ankles bore mute testimony to that fact. But was it murder, or perhaps something kinky gone terribly wrong? And if it were the latter, who with? Tak? Or someone else? And poor old Tak clearly killed himself, but it could have been guilt instead of remorse. Who'd ever know?

If there was some connecting thread between some or all of these occurrences, some guilty third party, what was the purpose or goal? There'd been no ransom notes, so kidnapping seemed a highly unlikely explanation for the disappearances. And Schweickert. There was seemingly no connection whatsoever between his slaughter and the rest of it; it was viewed as just another weird coincidence, but was it? Richards. His wife supposedly took off, too; but did she know any of these others? The people I spoke with said no, but that really proved nothing. There wasn't a Poets' Circle connection here; and, aside from Schweickert, that's a potential common thread tying the rest of them together.

I finished the coffee and stubbed out my cigar. The sheet of paper in front of me was, by now, covered with an intricate maze of interconnecting doodles that I'd absentmindedly created over the last hour or so. Richards stuck in my mind, and I turned him, and the circumstances surrounding his wife's disappearance, around and around, viewing them from every angle.

If Richards' wife didn't leave of her own choice, if there was instead some sort of crime here – murder, for instance – could he have been behind all of the other disappearances, setting them up as a smokescreen for the faked disappearance he planned for his wife? Seemed like a stretch, but who knows? His neighbor said that Ethel left at 2:00 a.m., but that could have been anyone leaving. And Richards claimed that she left in the truck; that didn't make sense, because the new Chevrolet was hers — was her pride and joy — and if she took off of her own volition she sure as hell would have taken it instead of his battered old truck. If Richards committed a crime, on the other hand, he might have wanted to keep the newer, nicer, more valuable vehicle and lose the old wreck. Something was off here, and warranted further examination.

The dull ache in my skull intensified with thought, and I resolved to make my mind a blank slate for the remainder of the day, take it easy to facilitate my body's recuperation.

Tomorrow would be a healthier day. Tomorrow I'd resume in earnest.

Tomorrow would be the beginning of the end.

Sunday, December 20, 1936. 10:47 a.m.

I WAS JUST north of Surf City and someone was following me. The car was too far back to identify by make and model, but its shape was distinctive, its color dark green and there hadn't been any other cars around to take its place. I'd thought nothing of it for the first leg of my journey, but a stop for coffee at a corner store in Ship Bottom-Beach Arlington gave it ample time to catch up and pass. A minute after, when I was back on the road, there it was again, like a pesky green-head fly.

Emily was a nice kid, so I wanted to see her once again, briefly, to set things straight and tie up loose ends. She deserved as much and I felt uneasy about my night with her.

Long Beach Boulevard was a twisty unpaved road north of Surf City, although each year the paving seemed to extend another mile or so, working its way from the town center towards Harvey Cedars and that town's brief length of paving. The bayberry, pine and occasional oak were much thicker as you headed north, the view of the road beyond frequently blocked by the dunes and foliage. I rounded such a bend with my new friend several hundred feet behind, spotted a small sand road off to the right, slammed on my breaks and quickly backed in. Nestled between some rolling dunes about fifty feet in from the road, I saw my friend drive by moments later: George Richards' Chevy. I pulled out after him with feelings a mix of annoyance and amusement, and followed at a comparable distance as he headed into Harvey Cedars.

He pulled into Gailey's at Eighty-First, eased up to the Standard pump out front and got out of his car to wait for the attendant.

That's when I drove by and his eyes locked on mine as I passed. He just stared.

It was almost noon when I arrived at Emily's, but she wasn't home. I stood by the edge of the road trying to decide what to do next, when the bells of the nearby Presbyterian Church over at Seventh and Central began to chime. Maybe she was at church. I decided to give her a few minutes, and wandered down to the end of First where I had an unobstructed view of Central for a good half-mile.

Another gray, depressing day. Looking up at the low jumble of stratocumulus clouds, I heard her walking up the graveled road. She had a small black book in her hand – a bible, as it turned out – and a handful of fellow churchgoers could be seen in the distance peeling off at their respective streets.

She seemed glad to see me and, after a few words of greeting, we walked quietly down the road to her house. Inside and coats off, I launched into my little speech, and while I tried for sincerity, it came off as self-serving and lacking spontaneity. Or at least it sounded – felt – that way to me.

I told her I'd taken unfair advantage of her and her trust. She was a nice kid, I was fond of her, and perhaps, under other circumstances, this could have gone somewhere. But now it was impossible. I was a married man, and loved my wife very much. Granted, I hadn't a clue where she was, but I had to remain optimistic and work on the assumption that she would return sometime soon. And I didn't want to mess up what I had at that point. I'd done that too many times in the past. Another screw up, another failure, would probably kill me – one way or the other.

When I'd finished she let out a little laugh, then turned her back to me and remained that way – and silent – for several minutes. Eventually, and after a few deep breaths, she turned back to me and gave a little smile. She told me she liked me – a lot – but she understood. And she was jealous of Holly. She said something quietly in French, but it might as well have been in Chinese for all I understood of it.

After a few more awkward minutes, I left, and she spoke some parting words as I approached my car.

"If things don't work out, Lew…" and then her voice trailed off.

I didn't look back.

I drove in a daze. I felt relieved on one level, like a worthless pig on another. *Nice work, Lew. Not content to fuck up just your own life, you've gotta go and fuck up someone else's as well…*

Enough of Emily. Start thinking about Holly.

As I rolled through Harvey Cedars, Richards' Chevy fell in line a distance back and resumed its leisurely pursuit. This guy was getting to be a pain in the ass; just what was he trying to prove?

I returned to the taproom with a five-foot pine I'd picked up at a stand on Centre off Bay. Willett gave me a hand setting it up near the front where one of the tables had been; we'd pushed the tables together, and while it was cramped it afforded us sufficient room.

Throughout the afternoon and early evening, the tree slowly evolved into a full-fledged Christmas tree, with patrons helping out with the decorations. These were informal and makeshift: corks and string for balls, pieces of sawdust for snow, some decorative fishing lures and so on. A plug-in advertising piece from the good people at Schmidt's of Philadelphia, placed behind the tree against the wall, changed colors once it warmed up and the effect, viewed through the branches of the tree, looked surprisingly good.

It was a nice tree and it helped in a small way to fill some of the emptiness of the room, perceived if not actual.

Holly would have approved.

344

Monday, December 21, 1936. 10:16 a.m.

MCNULTY HAD A telephone and it was listed in the Ocean County directory. I got through to his wife, who gave me the office number of the small plumbing business he ran in Ship Bottom-Beach Arlington with another guy named Welch. McNulty was there – they both were – and I asked him a few follow-up questions about Richards. He told me that his 5:30 a.m. appointment with Richards was Richards' choice, not his; he would have preferred some time after 4:30 p.m. when he closed up shop, but Richards was adamant that 5:30 was the only time it could be done. Reluctantly, McNulty agreed, even though he usually didn't crawl out of bed until 6:15.

Mary McCarthy would have collected her mail at the small Beach Haven post office, so I stopped in and paid a visit to Faye Entwistle, the town's postmistress of sorts. Faye frequented Britz's in her off hours, and I knew gin to be her drink of choice; a quart of Booth's House of Lords Dry Gin broke the ice and put her in a responsive, talkative mood. After a quick check, she told me that McCarthy's mail hadn't been picked up since Saturday, November 14. The oldest letter in there was local, a bill from the Central Provision Market. It was postmarked the 14th, and should have been picked up on the 16th, but the two weekly magazines usually placed in her box early Saturday mornings were gone for that week. And, weather permitting, Mary McCarthy always rode her bike into town daily to retrieve her mail, some time between 8:00 and 9:00 a.m. like clockwork.

Later that afternoon during a lull in business, I left Willett reading a book on the Kafir Wars, and headed for my office. My notes on the local events were growing daily and they were arranged in a rough, chronological order on the desktop. I transferred the basics to a new sheet of paper and stared at it, trying to find a common thread.

Fred Schweickert – Oct 15, 1936
Thursday: murder (unrelated?)
Grace Peterson – Oct 16, 1936
Friday: disappearance
Ethel Richards – Oct 28, 1936
Wednesday: disappearance (unrelated?)
Yumi Takarada – Nov 14, 1936
Saturday: murder? accident?
Mary McCarthy – Nov 14 or 15, 1936
Saturday or Sunday: disappearance
Holly Porter – Dec 13, 1936
Sunday: disappearance

Three in October, two in November and – so far – one in December. Varying days of the week. All on Long Beach Island. And two probable murders.

Were Schweickert's and Ethel Richards' disappearances unrelated to the rest? Neither had anything to do with the Poets' Circle, and the former was the only male on the list. If you dropped those two from the list, that left one mid-October, two mid-November, and one mid-December, all females, all Circle members. So what? What's the pattern? Or is the pattern the fact that there is no pattern? It could, after all, be sheer coincidence; but that seemed about as likely as my being nominated for sainthood.

I puzzled over my notes for several hours, took a break around 6:30. Stepping outside for a smoke, I noticed a lone car parked at the far edge of the road, its engine idling. It was Richards' car.

I left him sitting in the cold.

Tuesday, December 22, 1936. 6:38 p.m.

I COULDN'T GET Richards out of my mind. He was up to something – his on-again, off-again tailing made that obvious – but just what I didn't know. His wife's disappearance was fishy, no question about it. She took off with the crummy truck and George Richards had orchestrated having a third party witness at the house when he supposedly discovered her disappearance. It stunk, alright, like a bluefish rotting in the midday sun.

Richards reportedly chased after his brunette barmaid girlfriend Arline Pretty every Tuesday and Thursday night. It was Tuesday night, and working on the premise that Richards would rather get laid than sit in a freezing car – and who wouldn't? – I decided to check out things a little more closely during his absence.

I bundled myself in some warm clothing, loaded a few items into my trunk and drove north. Checked for Richards' car on Barnegat between South Third and Fourth, and it was parked right where it had been a week earlier. Richards was at Charlie's, and it was a safe bet he'd be at Arline Pretty's later on. I had some time.

Arriving in Surf City, I parked several lots away from Richards' house and killed the lights and engine. The street was semi-dark, illuminated somewhat by the glow of a quarter moon. The only house with any lights sat far down at the end of the street. I grabbed the leather bag from my trunk and worked my way back to his house. It was incredibly cold out – mid-twenties cold – and my frozen breath hung in the air before me like the exhaust from a car.

I went to work. The doors were locked but easily picked and within a minute I was searching the inside, flashlight in hand. I took my time, going through drawers and closets, sifting through papers, the whole nine yards. An hour and a half later I was done and nothing had jumped out at me, nothing appeared out of order.

Back outside, I searched the garage first. Aside from a selection of rakes, shovels and the usual stuff hung on its three walls, there wasn't room for much else aside from the absent car. The other outbuilding was padlocked and this took a little longer to pick; I was getting rusty in my old age. This search took considerably longer than the garage, taking in the boat-in-progress, dozens of boxes, cans, workbench drawers, a few derelict pieces of furniture and so forth. This too revealed nothing of significance, although I did stumble across a stack of pornographic photos stuffed in an old paint can – professional stuff, looked French or German.

I went through the old boats dumped in the yard, and sifted through the other pieces of junk, one of which was an old rotted icebox. I saved the abandoned privy for last. It was empty except for an old, yellowed Sears-Roebuck catalog tossed off to one side; a look down the hole revealed that it had either been filled in or its sides had collapsed over time.

I stood in the faint moonlight, trying to decide whether I'd missed anything – and got the sinking felling I hadn't. Flashlight in hand, I poked around aimlessly one last time in the futile hope that I'd overlooked something in the yard.

About to give up, I spotted the bush growing behind the privy. I pulled it aside to see if anything was between it and the small building's back wall. It was dead and moved aside without any resistance. I got down on my knees and examined the sand beneath the loose bush and brush. It was looser and lower than the surrounding sand, and had been dug up some time not too distant.

I started digging with a trowel retrieved from the garage. Within five minutes, I'd scraped out a hole eighteen inches deep when the tool met with resistance. Working with my hands, I dug out the perimeter of a large flat object, loosened it, and pulled it from the hole. It was a pocketbook.

I went through it thoroughly, and quickly identified it as Ethel's. It was filled with a lot of superfluous junk, but also items of importance, things you'd never leave behind if you were going away – for a day or forever – things like her automobile operator's license.

"Son of a bitch," I muttered to myself. No wonder he didn't want me snooping around.

I went to rebury the bag and return the area to its previous state, but hesitated; I removed the license and pocketed it, then buried the rest. The license, I figured, would serve as some sort of evidence later on, if needed; there was still plenty of other identification left in the bag.

Fifteen minutes later I had the area restored to its previous state, the trowel returned to its resting place. I double checked the grounds and things looked reasonably untouched.

I got the hell out of there.

Wednesday, December 23, 1936. 12:10 p.m.

BY NOON THE temperature had only climbed to about forty degrees, but the sky was bright and clear, and the sun surprisingly warm; it felt a good fifteen degrees warmer.

Christmas was only two days away, so I walked over to the Central Provision Market at South and Beach and purchased a chicken, potatoes, onions, green beans and some rolls, then stopped in at Gus Pott's liquor store on Bay and picked up three bottles of white French wine. I dumped them off at my house.

I filled the Ford's tank with Sunoco at Gifford's, made a quick stop at the Beach Haven National Bank and Trust Co. for some spending money, then headed north for the mainland. I reached Route 9 around one o'clock and headed south a mile or so to the tiny community of Cedar Run. A small airport named Pollypod Airfield was supposed to be somewhere in the vicinity, but I had to stop and ask directions before I could find it.

Pollypod Airfield sat in an open field of packed sand out in the Pine Barrens, and consisted of a single, relatively smooth, landing strip and a boxy wooden building large enough to house two airplanes. A pair of large sliding doors sat wide open. The words "Pollypod Airfield" were painted in tall block letters high up on the wall, the words "Wesley Shinn, Prop." beneath. There was a small walk-in door on the building's left side, and a tin Red Man Chewing Tobacco thermometer screwed to the wall to its right.

There were two planes, one parked inside the structure, the other outside in the sun. I recognized the one inside as a mid-twenties Stearman biplane, but didn't know planes well enough to be able to identify the other, which was a monoplane. A man whom I took to be Shinn was kneeling on the ground, seemingly oblivious to my arrival.

I pulled up next to an old Ford truck parked off to the side, and wandered over to the lone figure. He was hard at work doing something, seemingly oblivious to my arrival.

"You Shinn?" I called out.

He raised his head and flashed a big smile. "Yup," he said. "Give me a second and I'll be right with ya."

Shinn was in the process of rolling up a long series of five-foot tall cotton letters. Each of these was stretched between a pair of vertical parallel bamboo poles, the tops and bottoms of which were tied to long lengths of rope. Guess it spelled something, but I couldn't tell what.

"What's that?" I asked in total ignorance.

"Letters," he answered. "New idea I had last year. Hoped it'd generate a little extra income, which I could use."

"What do you do with 'em?"

"Well, I had this idea: billboards in the sky. Ya see 'em by the roads year-'round, but all them people cookin' out on the beaches in the summer, what do they have to look at? Nothin', 'cept maybe the water and each other. So I thought, why not make a big sign o' sorts, drag it behind my plane, and fly back and forth up and down the coast, shovin' the advertisin' in people's faces. 'Course it only works one direction; the letters are backwards when you turn around, so I heads back over the bay. Show 'em headin' north, hide 'em headin' south."

"Burma Shave? That kind of stuff?"

"Nah, just local stuff. Only did a couple last year. Gonna be a big business someday, mark my words." He finished tying three lengths of rope around the bundle, dragged it the few feet to the truck and maneuvered it into the back.

"Pull your car over there," he said, motioning to a spot by the hanger. He climbed into the cab, fired up the engine and pulled off.

"So, what brings you here? What can I do for ya?" he asked after we were parked.

I introduced myself, verified that he hired out by the hour and said I wanted him to take me on an exploratory flight low over the pines in the nearby vicinity. We agreed on a price.

"We'll take the Robin," he said, pointing to the monoplane. "Give me a couple o' minutes to clean up," he added, then disappeared into the side door.

We were up in the air within fifteen minutes. I sat in one of the two wicker seats bolted to the floor behind Shinn's lone seat and he explained that this was the newer of the two planes. It was a 1928 Curtiss-Wright Robin, with a twenty-four foot length, forty-one foot wingspan and a six-foot constant chord – that was an enormous wing for a plane this size, he enthusiastically pointed out. Had a cruising speed of eighty-five miles per hour, big wheels on the main gear, squared-off trailing edge to the tail fin, and a whole bunch of other specs that meant nothing to me. Sounded like it wouldn't crash, though.

When he let up for air I gave him my general parameters for exploration: I wanted him to start at the bay by the causeway and head west low over S40. As sand roads were spotted heading north or south from S40, I'd want him to check out their course and destination. When we were finished with S40, we'd head back to its intersection with Route 9 and repeat the procedure with the southern, then northern, legs of Route 9.

Then, while I looked, he piloted and talked. I had a large pad on my lap and sketched rough maps of roads, trails and landmarks as we spotted them. The terrain below us was, for the most part, an endless rolling tangle of dull green and brown, interrupted only by the occasional cluster of a small community's buildings, or the roof of a piney shack; the latter would crop up in the middle, seemingly, of nowhere. There was a gentle roll to the land not evident from the ground below. Buzby had once told me that the Pineys had names for practically every topographic upheaval – the low spots as well as the high – but that I should never waste my time trying to find a map that listed them: it didn't exist.

Every so often Wes would yell to me, pointing out various items of interest below while he dipped and circled for a clearer view. He gave me a crash course on the topography, pointing out cranberry bogs, dwarf pines, tall oaks, Atlantic white cedars and hundreds of small- to mid-size streams. The dwarf pines looked as big as the other trees from that vantage point, but in actuality were only shoulder height. The white cedars always appeared bunched together in long, twisty lines, and Wes explained that they grew along the banks of streams.

The streams, he told me, all flow east out of the Pine Barrens to the ocean; farther west some of them flow to the Delaware. But in either case, the Pine Barrens is always the source, not the destination. And the streams' water, he explained, is brown like scotch, sometimes like bourbon. Known as cedar water, it's colored by the cedar trees crowding the streams' banks and by the plentiful iron deposits in the ground. Sea captains used to stock up on the stuff for long voyages because it remained drinkable – *potable* was the word he used – for far longer than regular water.

Seven or eight miles inland, and several miles northwest of the hamlet of Brookville, we flew over a series of small clearings in the midst of the pine forest below, dotted with a series of newer-looking buildings. Traces of a long, winding drive snaked its way eastward through the growth.

"What's that?" I yelled over the roar of the engine, pointing to the compound below.

"That? *That* is Camp Bismarck," he responded. "Never heard of it?" I said I had. "It's pretty quiet during the week," he continued, "but the weekends are a different story. The so-called German American Bund – American Nazis, actually – that's where they meet and do whatever adults dressed up like Nazis do. Lots of marchin' and formations, from what little I've seen. They were the guys over your way a few months back, ones held the rally. Got beat up pretty bad, I heard."

He circled around for another look, I supposed, because he wasn't finished talking about them.

"It's a little quieter down there now that the weather's turned cold, but there's always a couple o' hardcases that are there all the time. Makes me nervous, sometimes, when I fly over and they're out there shootin' their guns; figure they might get tired of shootin' at stationary targets someday."

We headed back east. I concentrated on the twisted mazes of two-track sand roads below, forking out in seemingly random directions, making sharp turns in every direction, frequently rejoining with the roads they'd split off from. Wes told me that some of them were two hundred years old, a mixture of old stage routes, lumber roads, access roads to the region's once-prevalent charcoal pits or connecting roads for towns that disappeared decades ago. He pointed to an odd geometric pattern below surrounded and filled with green. Said it was the remaining foundations of one such town, place once known as Beetle Back.

My interest in the roads was something less than historical: I was looking for Richards' truck. Based on the assumption that Ethel didn't leave of her own accord – which seemed fairly obvious to me – and that Richards dumped it somewhere, this would be the logical general area. The neighbors said they heard the truck leave at 2:00 a.m. and McNulty was at Richards' talking with him at 5:30, so that gave Richards only three-and-a-half hours to drive it somewhere, dump it and get back home. I figured an hour, an hour fifteen at most each direction, assuming he had a ride back somehow. That put me over here. He'd want to get as far – and quickly – away as possible, so that suggested either S40 or Route 9. The maze of roads to nowhere throughout the Pine Barrens would offer an easy route into the midst of the forests, and it would be easy enough – especially with some advance preparation – to get the truck off to the side and hidden.

I know. It was a long shot.

Three hours later the sun hung low in the sky and the fuel hung low in Wes' tank. He told me we had only fifteen minutes more before we'd have to head back. I sensed the futility of our efforts.

That is, until I spotted the small square of metal in the brush below. The sun glistened off its partially dulled surface when viewed from our present angle.

I told Wes to circle around and around again even lower, and several more times before I was sure of it. Below, about forty feet in from yet-another, windy two-track, was the exposed roof of the cab of a small truck, its hood and the bed behind covered for the most part by dead brush. I wasn't sure, obviously, but it looked promising. And while it wasn't bright and new, it looked to be in far better shape than the handful of other tarnished, rusted hulks we'd spotted.

We were approximately six miles west of the bay – three miles west of Manahawkin – and roughly a mile and a half south of S40. A sizable stream – Wes told me it was named Cedar Run Creek – snaked its way southeast a quarter mile south of the truck's resting place, and the two-track headed north to S40. I told Wes we could stop looking once we'd followed the sand road back to S40. That was fine by him.

He circled around, passing over some more Piney shacks below, when there was a dull thud off to our left.

"She-it," he yelled as he banked quickly. "Moonshiners," he added, pointing over his shoulder with his thumb at the left wing. "See it?" he yelled. "He put a shot through my left wing, the bastard…"

I spotted the hole, and craned my neck to look at the clearing below, now actually at a weird angle out my left window. There were several ramshackle structures, abandoned rusted vehicles, wagons, and boats. A tied dog jumped about, no doubt barking at us. Nearby was a lone man standing in a clearing in the midst of the structures, aiming a rifle up at us. Fortunately, another man rushed into the clearing and knocked the first's rifle aside, grabbed him and dragged him towards one of the buildings.

"They're all over down there, runnin' their illegal stills – been doin' it for centuries. Some of them are more touchy than others and take potshots. First time it's ever happened to me – guess all the circlin' around drew their attention. Happens all the time to them slow, low-flyin' blimps out of Lakehurst Naval Air Station; guys down there think the sailors are on the lookout for stills and'll report 'em. Crazy, ain't it, tryin' to take out a blimp with a rifle?" He chuckled and shook his head, but got out of there quickly.

He followed the two-track towards S40, which was difficult to do as its course switched directions several times, several stretches hidden from view. I scribbled notes regarding various points of reference, optimistically hoping I could retrace our steps from the ground.

We touched down back at Pollypod as the sun dipped below the horizon, the sky went orange, and the mercury in the Red Man plummeted.

358

Thursday, December 24, 1936. 10:34 a.m.

CHRISTMAS EVE, I thought to myself as I rolled up to the causeway a few minutes after 10:30. The drawbridge was down, so I slowed to fifteen miles per hour and eased my way onto the first of the bridges. The boards rumbled loudly as I rolled on. The remains of innumerable smashed clamshells – dropped from high above by gulls in order to get to the unlucky tenants inside – crunched under my tires. A dozen years earlier, when the bridge was practically the only hard surface around and automobile tires were structurally less tolerant of sharp objects, flats were the norm on a trip across the bay. Travelers who knew better scheduled their crossings to coincide with the daily sweeping of the bridge surfaces, thereby minimizing the risk.

Yesterday's sunny warmth was by now only a memory. The temperature hung in the mid-thirties, a stiff ocean wind buffeting anything in its path. The bay was at low tide and yet the water was surprisingly high and extremely rough. It lapped at the bridge from beneath, creating a strange thudding sound.

Once again, Richards had followed me north from Beach Haven, but pulled over and ended his pursuit at the causeway's entrance. Which made things easier for me: I'd worked out a rough plan to lose him once we hit the mainland, but now it appeared I could concentrate on more important things. The guy was annoying. And, I feared, dangerous.

Two hours later and more K-turns than I could count, I gave up trying to locate the entranceway to the elusive road I'd spotted the day before from high up above. I pulled into a spot outside the

National Hotel in Manahawkin, went in, ordered a beer. Found a booth and called Willett back at the taproom. Told him I needed a guide familiar with the Pine Barrens, and wanted him to dig up Buzby's address. Gave him the booth's number and settled in at the bar. I had a liverwurst sandwich while waiting for his call back.

By 1:15 I was armed with some half-assed directions Willett had gathered from several sources. I crept westward on S40 looking for a small road off its southern side, marked by a rock – shaped like the continent of Africa, I was told – to its left, a dead pine to its right. An hour – and innumerable curses – later, I knew I needed some more help. I spotted a shack off through the trees, pulled in its drive and chugged my way through to a clearing. A Piney of indeterminate age – forty, I'd guess, but he could have been sixty – sat in the yard staring at me; I'd interrupted his basket weaving.

Told him I was looking for Fred Buzby. This guy was shy – the staring had stopped just as soon as I'd emerged from the Ford – and he looked everywhere but at me. He hiked up his pants, sniffed and pointed towards the southwest.

I looked at trees. Lots of them. "How do I get there?" I asked, hoping for something a little more specific.

He spit, took a deep breath, wiped his nose with his sleeve – the condition of his sleeve indicated this was a habit with him – and proceeded to give me directions of sorts, using his hands more than his mouth. He motioned down the drive, a finger slice to the right, a cocked thumb to the left "...road" he muttered, more gestures, "...a point" a thumb cocked to the right, and so forth. I strained to follow him, putting words to his gesticulations, and hoped he'd correct me if I was off base.

"Yup," he concluded, so I thanked him and left. Within a short fifteen minutes, and as things failed to fall into place, I realized once again I needed help. Coherent help. The question was, where?

My patience had just about evaporated when I spotted a thick column of smoke rising from the dense brush on the north side of the road, several hundred feet in. It took me another five minutes to locate the drive leading back. I chugged through to a clearing and pulled to a stop. There was an old wooden shack with a chimney belching smoke, its windows covered on the inside with newspaper – Piney insulation, I supposed. There were two vehicles parked outside: one, an old rusted sedan that appeared inoperable, the other a surprisingly new – for the area, at least – '34 Pontiac touring sedan that actually appeared to have been washed sometime within the last month. It looked about as out of place as makeup on the Mona Lisa. I knocked at the door and hoped for better luck.

"Who's that?" called a raspy voice from the shack. I took it as an invitation and opened the door. Inside were three people: a younger couple and a wizened, old Piney, who squinted at me with bad eyes. The younger woman was seated at a small, wooden table, a baby in her arms. A younger man, whom I took to be her husband – I'm not sure why; the way he touched her upper arm, I suppose – stood by her side. Both were dressed in garb that would have gone unnoticed on any small town's streets, but that looked vaguely out of place here. The older man, presumably the owner of the shack, was more typically dressed for the area. The couple looked as startled to see me as I was by their attire in these environs. I guess they didn't get too many outsiders paying personal visits – just the occasional lost clod like me.

"Sorry to barge in on you like this…" I began.

"Who are ya? What do ya want?" the old man repeated before I could finish, wanting to get to the point.

I explained as quickly and in as few words as I could. An old mangy hound wandered over and sniffed at my pant leg. The woman stared at me as if I was a wanted criminal, the infant clutched to her chest. Friendly place.

When I finally mentioned Buzby's name, the old man dropped his brusque manner and chuckled. He led me over to a window, peeled the newspaper aside and, in a much friendlier tone, proceeded to launch into a detailed set of directions. Within a minute I knew I would find the place, and after sincere thanks, left quickly. The hound escorted me to the door. I think he wanted my leg.

I arrived at Buzby's at three. Buzby was bundled up warmly, working at the back of his truck; Jonah sat on the ground playing with a goat. The goat looked smarter.

"Well, well, well. If it ain't Lewis Porter," he exclaimed, walking over to greet me. "Merry Christmas!"

We shook hands. I returned the holiday greeting and nodded the same, silently, to Jonah when our eyes met. I explained what I was looking for, in as much detail as I could muster. He listened intently, working the gray stubble on his chin between thumb and forefinger. When I got to the part about the trigger-happy Piney, he started to chuckle.

"Yeah, it all fits," he said, nodding. "Probably Jonah's kin, the Leeks. They're all ornery and crazy; he's just stupid," he added quietly. He chuckled again. "They're moonshiners: always have been, probably always will be. Not that there's anything unusual 'bout that, mind ya; they're just more...*cautious*...'bout it. Very protective of their turf. Not at all friendly to outsiders. Nope, not at all." His voice had returned to its original volume, and I hoped that Jonah couldn't hear what he was saying – especially the "stupid" part.

He proceeded to explain how to get to the sand road. I pulled my pad from the car and he laid it out in pencil, emphatic that I walk the mile and a half in from S40, as the sound of my car would alert the Leeks that I was there and they might decide to make it uncomfortable for me. I glanced over at Jonah, but he was down on his back tickling the goat's belly. Buzby wished me luck, said he'd keep Jonah occupied for awhile. I promised a full explanation when I saw him again in a few days.

The sky was an ugly dark gray as I walked down the sand two-track, lug wrench in hand, collar turned up for warmth. I'd left the Ford parked back on S40 fifty feet east of the entrance. The wind was significantly worse now, the trees and brush bent under its onslaught. The racket was sufficient that I probably could have driven, but sound can travel unpredictably in the wind and had decided to heed Buzby's advice. I had to hurry now, with perhaps only forty-five minutes or so before the gray twilight was chased off by the night. And when it gets dark in the Pine Barrens, it gets *black*.

Twenty-five minutes later – and dumb luck this time around – I stood by the small truck deserted in the brush. It sat thirty-to-forty feet off the sand road, but the brush between was still sufficiently matted down to catch the eye. I uncovered it as best I could. The locals must have stumbled upon it – its wheels and tires were gone. The license plate had been removed, and the serial numbers had been partially chipped off. I lit a match and got down close, and could piece together what appeared to be A372637, or something close to that. Richards had unsuccessfully attempted to render it unidentifiable.

Inside, the front seat had been removed; again, I assumed, by locals for use on some broken-down porch somewhere. The height of Piney luxury, no doubt.

Now, Richards may have thought he was clever, but he was just as stupid as so many other impulsive criminals, drawing up intricate plans while overlooking the obvious. In the small glove box, folded neatly under a dirty rag, was a handwritten receipt from Cranmer's Lumber Yard, dated September 12, 1936, made out to "G. Richards, Surf City." What a fool. I stuffed the receipt in my pocket, finished my search, and quickly headed back to S40 and my car.

Twenty minutes later, I was back in the Ford returning to the causeway. It was dark now, a freezing drizzle pinged off the car's surfaces. My lights and wipers were on, but visibility was limited to the reach of the lights, which dissolved into blackness about thirty feet ahead.

Richards occupied my thoughts. He claimed that Ethel ran off on him, but so far the evidence indicated otherwise. Her pocketbook and all her identification were buried out in his yard behind the privy, and the truck she was supposed to have run off in sat out in the Pine Barrens, abandoned and unsuccessfully rendered unidentifiable. And George: He was dogging my every move on the island, keeping an eye on me for reasons that now seemed apparent. The guy had to be involved and I decided then and there to contact Quinn and give him everything I had. Just when I could contact Quinn was another issue. Tonight was Christmas Eve and tomorrow the holiday itself; so even if I left word for him when I got back, it might be several days before we actually spoke. Richards meant nothing to me, and I had no personal stake in the disappearance – murder? – of his wife. It would earn me points with Quinn, points that could be cashed in later on when I needed them.

I steered the Ford slowly onto the now-slick surface of the causeway bridge, proceeding at a crawl, boards rumbling beneath my tires. The relentless wind buffeted my car all over the place, the bridge's slick, icy rain-coated surface not helping matters. My wipers struggled to rearrange the mounting slush, the fading light coming from headlights growing dim with accumulated ice. Salt water lapped up and over the bridge's surface at uneven intervals. It could be worse, I supposed; it was only a mile between the bridge's start in the Manahawkin meadows to its first terminus at Bonnet Island and I had the roadway all to myself. Little comfort in that thought, but the only comfort I could summon up as I fought with the steering.

I squinted at the black horizon ahead and could, with the shift of rain and sleet, occasionally spot a line of twinkling lights dotting the island from Surf City to Ship Bottom-Beach Arlington – the *string of pearls* I'd heard them called. They'd disappear as quickly as they'd appeared, and reappear fitfully as the elements permitted.

I wasn't enjoying the ride at all. The cab was filled with the groan of the engine, the unsettling rumble of boards and the staccato clicking of icy rain on the Ford's exterior. Waves pounded the bridge from beneath, with the occasional crest breaking high and momentarily hiding the surface from view. My knuckles white from my grip of the wheel, it was all I could do to keep the car creeping in a semi-straight line.

And then, when it seemed as though things couldn't get any worse, there were several loud pops and a discernible thud, followed by the familiar flopping of a flat tire. I rolled to a stop and sat for a bit, cursing quietly to myself as visions of a warming glass of Old Overholt drifted away. A flat tire in the middle of a storm in the middle of nowhere, lashed by wind, icy rain now turned to sleet, and occasional waves: could it possibly get any worse? And on Christmas Eve.

Shit.

Grabbed the lug wrench from the passenger seat and climbed out into the inhospitable elements. I felt both driver side tires in the dark, and they were okay. The passenger's side tires were a different story: *both* were flat, and I only had one spare. An annoying situation turned horrible. Now I'd have to walk the rest of the way to Bonnet Island, and from there to Cedar Bonnet Island where I could go to either of the bars and call for assistance. That is, if at least one of them was open for business on Christmas Eve. And I hadn't yet decided on the lucky recipient of that phone call.

Leaned in the open door, killed the Ford's lights and engine, and crossed my fingers that no one would plow into its rear if crossing the bay in this mess. Then I started the long, slow walk east, fumbling my way along in the total blackness of night. Pulled my collar up and my hat down low, and hoped that my eyes would soon adjust sufficiently that I could make out shapes, anything. I slid one foot after the other to try to avoid tripping over any unseen obstacles, and kept my free arm moving in front of me to ward off God knows what; the other still held the lug wrench I'd forgotten to leave behind. The sleet drummed on the top and brim of my fedora, while the wind buffeted my body. At this rate it would be New Years before I reached land, or at least it felt that way. My thoughts returned to a warming glass of Old Overholt, something concrete to keep me going.

I hadn't stumbled along for more than thirty seconds when I was overwhelmed by the chilling feeling that I wasn't alone. The same feeling that everyone has at least once in his life. The same feeling that served me so well several times during the war. Can't describe it – it just happens and it's unmistakable. I paused and listened, and for a moment thought I could hear a whispered word or two carried on the wind. I froze: I still couldn't see a thing – like a blind man – and yet I knew I wasn't alone. I now knew the blowout was planned and knew that if others were out there – and they were – they could see a hell of a lot better than I could.

I took several slow, deep breaths. Switched the lug wrench from my left hand to right behind me, held it down close to my side where I hoped it would go unnoticed. Resumed my forward movement as if nothing were the matter, but knew full well that if someone were going to attack me it would be soon. Before my eyes had a chance to adjust to the dark and the odds evened out.

Staring at the horizon I found that I could discern, through the sleet, the twinkling string of lights from the town beyond. And in the midst of the string was a gray break and it was getting larger, obliterating lights to the right and left as it grew.

A silhouette, and it was advancing.

I dove to the ground and scrambled furiously to one side a moment before the roar of a shotgun blast ripped through the night. Wood splintered beside me, pellets tore at my left side. I sprung forward on hands and knees, ending in a mad roll as a second explosion illuminated the world around me. A blizzard of wood chips and splinters tore at my face and clothing. The air filled with choking smoke and the stench of creosote. I knew the shooter would be momentarily blinded by the muzzle's flash, and quickly scrambled to my feet, lunging towards the clicking sounds of the weapon being reloaded. Swung the lug wrench low and with all my might. There was a shriek of pain as a leg was smashed. The screamer crashed to the bridge surface, the shotgun landing with a metallic thud nearby. I didn't give him a chance to react. Brought the wrench down as quickly and as forcefully as I could. Ribs were smashed, followed by horrific, panicked screams. A second swing and the unearthly sounds were cut short as a skull crumpled under the blow, replaced by a low, short gurgle that trailed off within seconds.

There were footsteps behind me. I turned as he leapt, and his aim was bad. I pivoted, and he crashed to the boards, taking me with him. I dropped the wrench. We scrambled in the darkness, and I felt a knife slice through the air, tearing at the dangling fabrics of my coat and shirt destroyed by one of the shotgun blasts. A second slice cut through my burning, wounded flesh. I grabbed the knife-wielding arm, and with a violent downward yank snapped it apart at the elbow over my rising knee. A scream of pain, and I took a quick, pounding punch at its source. I felt the snap of a jaw and the smashing of teeth under my torn, bloodied fist. He crumpled with a moan.

I heard a third one – how many of these guys were there? – fumbling behind me, patting the wooden surface, looking for the shotgun. I scrambled as fast as I could for the side of the bridge, over the timbers that edged it and below the lowest rail of the pipe railing. Legs swung madly in the dark in hope of a foothold instead of the freezing water below. I made contact with a piling and the bolted end of a large cross-member. Holding on with one hand, I quickly and quietly swung under the bridge. Another deafening blast lit up the night, sucking the air from above me, splintering wood, pocking the metal, pellets and debris everywhere, my hand torn loose from its hold. I was wedged securely atop the beam now, heart pounding, lungs gasping for air.

I listened to the racket above, the garbled screams of the one with the punched-in face eliciting a response from the shooter: "Where are ya? Where the hell are ya?" Scrambling sounds as they connected, muffled yells: "Shut up! SHUT UP!" and "Oh my good

God almighty…" Sounds of dragging – probably the body of the first attacker – and shuffling as my attackers made their way west down the bridge.

I waited for minutes, for a cessation of all sounds of activity, hoping to get back up to the bridge's surface before the dull throbbing in my side turned to real pain. The sound of an automobile's approach from the west brought me up to peer over the edge. They weren't on the bridge – I would have seen them in the headlights – and they hadn't enough time to get beyond the approaching vehicle, which was at least a hundred feet on the mainland side of my parked Ford. I strained to think – where were they? Hiding on the far side of the parked Ford? Down in a boat? I hurt too much now to think, and my clothes – what was left of them – were soaked through. I stumbled up onto the bridge and flagged down the approaching auto. The driver, a guy named Gil Conard whom I recognized as the owner of a service station in Surf City, reluctantly picked me up. Seeing the woeful condition I was in, he agreed to drive me to Doc Havens'. I mumbled a promise of free drinks for a night, and there was little question in my mind that he'd take me up on it.

Doc Havens had office hours on Tuesday and Thursday nights, and played bridge most of the others. I held no illusions he'd be open on Christmas Eve, and he wasn't, but he was home and saw me immediately. He spent an hour and a half removing pellets and splinters that were, thankfully, all close to the surface in what turned out to be superficial wounds. The knife slash was similarly superficial and easily stitched and he cleaned up the rest of the abrasions on my knuckles, palms, knees and elbows. I told him I'd accidentally dropped my shotgun and it had discharged, but I don't think he bought it for a moment. I assured him I wasn't in any sort of trouble. I borrowed his phone to place a call to the state police barracks in Tuckerton, leaving a message for Quinn to contact me at his earliest opportunity. This call seemed to set Havens' mind at ease.

"It's Christmas Eve, Lew," he said as he used the better part of a bottle of iodine on me. "You should be home wi…" He paused. "You should be home," he resumed.

While Havens applied bandages, I thought back to the attack. Surely it was Richards – who else was so pissed at me, or felt threatened by my actions? But where would Richards find a couple of goons willing to kill a stranger? And who was it I killed in the struggle, assuming the first attacker was, indeed, dead when I was finished with him and they'd dragged him off. Richards himself, perhaps?

When Havens was finished I paid his bill in cash – fortunately I hadn't lost my wallet in all the scuffling – and asked to use his phone one last time. I gave Oskar Freund a call at his house in North Beach Haven; his wife Undine answered. After a heartfelt greeting and wishes for a Merry Christmas, she trundled off to get Oskar.

Oskar, born in Austria, had come to the United States in his early twenties sometime around the turn of the century. He worked as a mechanic at Gifford's Garage on Bay Avenue between South and Amber, and frequently spent lunch at the taproom reading the previous day's Evening Bulletin and drinking bottled Ortlieb's, a lager he swore was closer to the beers of his homeland than any others he'd had here. I told him that, yes, I knew it was Christmas Eve, but that it was very important that I get some replacement wheels and tires for my Ford, and I needed a loaner auto for a short while, as well. He agreed, promising that the loaner would be parked in the alley south of the garage in one hour, keys and mounted tires inside.

I popped some Bayer aspirins and walked the mile back to my house, shoes and clothing soaked through. I didn't give a damn; the cold damp air made me feel surprisingly alive, and the pain subsided – if only temporarily – as I worked my way down Bay Avenue.

An hour and a half later I was home, cleaned up, warm and dry, draining a glass of Old Overholt. Hoover sat at my side staring, looking hungry, so I grabbed a can of Red Heart Dog Food and stared at its label: beef, fish, cheese, "no cheap fillers," "puppies cry for it...dogs demand it."

"Is that true?" I asked Hoover. He didn't answer.

I tuned in WFPG. They were playing Christmas carols. Hoover finished with his meal and wandered over to the sofa, licking his lips, a satisfied look on his snout.

"Might as well come on up, pal," I said, patting the cushion beside me. "Nobody's gonna yell at you now."

Hoover obliged, and moments later we were both snoring loudly.

Friday, December 25, 1936. 5:30 a.m.

I WOKE CHRISTMAS Day with a start, my heart pounding, when the alarm clock on the bedside table sounded at 5:30 a.m. Sometime during the night – I didn't remember when – I'd wandered from the living room sofa to my bed. Hoover had elected to remain behind, and didn't even lift a lid when I stumbled through the room to the kitchen.

My body was stiff and ached all over; I popped some more aspirin. I was dressed and knocking at Willett's door by six. Twenty minutes later we'd hoofed it the four blocks over to Gifford's and retrieved the loaner. Forty minutes after that were out on the causeway parked in front of my ice-encrusted Ford. Willett went to work on the wheels while I poked around, eating aspirin and looking for traces of the previous night's encounter.

About fifty feet west of the Ford, teetering on the edge of the bridge, was a three-foot long strip of wood studded with nails. The source of my punctured tires, no doubt, chipped and splintered where it had flipped up behind one of the tires and struck the Ford's chassis. It had ended up there, out of the way of any future vehicles making the crossing.

The damage from the three shotgun blasts was obvious, and I found traces of one of the attackers' blood, diluted by and frozen into the now-thawing icy mess.

There was nothing else to find, or I didn't find it if there was.

We drove the two autos back to Beach Haven. I found myself checking the rear view mirror for signs of Richards and, for once, he wasn't there: dead, perhaps? We returned the loaner and headed back to the taproom where Willett put on a pot of coffee. I bolted down several cups of the steaming hot liquid along with a couple of day-old rolls retrieved from the kitchen.

I knew what I had to do. I wasn't thrilled with the prospect, but it needed to be done. I was taking this personally now.

I grabbed a roll of dimes from the cash register and pocketed it, and sat at a table for the better part of an hour making detailed notes on a sheet of paper. I added name and phone number at the top and summoned Willett to join me at the table.

"One more thing, Gordon. Call Bernie Quinn at the state police over in Tuckerton," I said, placing the paper in front of him and pointing at the number, "Tell him I told you to tell him about each of these items listed here."

The list enumerated and detailed all of the things I'd discovered about Richards: his girlfriend, the buried pocketbook, his persistence in following me, the abandoned truck in the Pine Barrens and the attack on the causeway. I downplayed certain aspects of that attack.

"Make sure you get through to him. It's important. Tell him I'm going to pay George a visit. If he wants, he can join me; if he doesn't – well, I'll handle it my own way." I paused, then added, "I know it's Christmas, but you've got to get through to him, one way or other, and pass this stuff on. Even if he's at home." I added what I knew of Quinn's Trenton address at the top of the sheet.

Was Richards even at home? Hell, was Richards even alive? I'd find out soon enough.

Willett headed off to place the calls. It was a little after 9:30 now. I stretched and took stock of my physical condition; everything still worked, but not without effort and accompanying discomfort. I popped some more aspirin and pulled on a pair of loose brown leather gloves. It was a tight fit: The three left-hand fingers were still swollen from their encounter with the bathroom wall. And my right hand – its palm and knuckles scraped raw from the night before and now bandaged in gauze – balked at being sheathed. I stripped off a few layers of gauze and finally managed to shove it in. After several minutes of discomfort the pain subsided.

I drove slowly north toward Surf City. It was snowing now, and there was a half-inch accumulation. The occasional occupied house that I passed, in Beach Haven and in the handful of communities north, all seemed to have fires burning in their fireplaces, lit trees in their windows, and decorations outside. I felt hollow.

That's where I should be, and what I should be doing. Where normal people are and what normal people are doing. Instead, I have no one left. I'm spending Christmas — Christ's birthday — confronting a murderer, playing the avenging angel. Things haven't changed that much, after all. Time to grow up, pal, and get a real life. But I guess that isn't in the cards, is it? Fate's dealt me a shitty hand, dictating where my place in life is. Maybe next time around.

Maybe…if there is a next time.

I pulled onto North Ninth and into Richards' driveway, blocking the Chevy parked at the side of the house. It was snowing heavily now. As I got out I saw a small group of carolers at the far end of the street, arranged in front of a small house with smoke streaming from its chimney. Their collective voices could be heard through the falling snow. "Silent Night." It sounded beautiful. I wanted to follow them around.

Maybe next time.

I wrapped my fist around the roll of dimes in my right side pocket. My hand was sore, but not nearly as much as my left side, which was sore *and* stiff. I made my way to the small porch and front door, snow crunching and squeaking underfoot. I knocked, then knocked again and waited.

Richards answered, dressed in an old plaid flannel bathrobe and heavy, unlaced shoes. His hair was disheveled, his eyes red, and while he looked like he'd just climbed out of bed after a bad night's sleep, his skull was in one piece and his jaw functional. I know this for a fact: his jaw dropped when he saw me standing before him.

"Merry Christmas, Richards," I said calmly.

"What the hell do you want," he said, wearily. "Don't you have anything better to do than bother me?"

"Decide to take a holiday break from your island journeys?" I asked.

"What's that supposed to mean?" he asked, confused.

"Wife turn up yet?" I asked. "I thought she might've come back for her pocketbook."

Richards' look of weary annoyance shifted to one of alarm.

"She took it with her," he said quickly.

"In the truck, George? Why didn't she take the Chevy? I sure as hell would. And why take the truck," I continued, as Richards' eyes darted from side to side, "only to dump it out in the Pine Barrens?"

Richards went pale.

"We found it, Richards. A few miles west on S40, about a mile south on that little sand road. Where you dumped it. And, make no mistake about it, we *know* it's yours," I added.

Richards' shoulders sagged as he let out a low sigh. He looked defeated.

"OK," he said, as if a burden had been lifted. "Come in, let's talk."

"No, why don't you come out here," I responded.

"Alright. Let me get a coat." I could barely hear him.

He turned and as he took a couple of steps into the house I immediately questioned the wisdom of letting him retreat inside. I could still see him through the doorway, however, as he fumbled with a coat on a hook. He turned to return within seconds.

The snow was falling heavily, and the sounds of the carolers had grown more distinct as they worked their way up the street. How pretty they sounded.

Richards appeared at the open doorway, walking. He'd taken on a crazed look and held a revolver at waist level. It was pointed at me. In the moment before he fired I leapt to my left, the explosion ripping the air almost simultaneously. My bandages pulled loose and pain shot through my side. I wasn't sure if I'd been hit. There was a second shot as I hit the snow-covered ground, and this one tore through my hair and scalp. A crab-like scramble took me to the back of my parked car as blood flowed down onto my face and eyes. A third shot kicked up the sand and snow by my leg. Richards continued forward, picking up the pace. I scrambled around the rear of the car and glanced under the car: Richards was approaching quickly now. I got on my feet and ran the length of the car in a crouch, pulling open the driver's door as I passed. Richards fired another shot as he cleared the back, punching a hole in the open door. My side on fire, I ran madly towards the rear of the house, feet slipping in the snow, hugging the brush in a desperate attempt to obscure Richards' view. Another shot tore through the bayberry by my shoulder. The garage appeared locked. I ran to the larger outbuilding, pulled its one open door shut behind me. Another shot splintered wood near its center. I worked my way to the rear in the dim light, past the sneakbox sitting up on wooden horses. Grabbed a shovel off the wall. Cleared blood and snow from my eyes, if only temporarily, with a backhand swipe. My side was red with fresh-flowing blood. From reopened wounds, I hoped and not from a fresh bullet hole whose presence had yet to make itself felt.

I heard Richards' crunching footsteps arrive outside the building's door. *Fucking cowboy, crummy shot; let's hope my luck holds.*

The door moved slightly then held. I envisioned Richards grabbing the handle then hesitating.

There was a moment of dead silence, with only the muffled voices of the carolers off in the distance. My heart pounded in my chest. Lousy shot or not, he couldn't miss at this distance. Or could he? I took a deep breath.

The door yanked open and the room was filled with gray daylight, Richards silhouetted in the doorway, a large revolver in his hand. I kicked out at the back of the boat which lunged forward at Richards as the horses toppled. Richards stepped back quickly and awkwardly from the crashing boat. I drew back and threw the shovel with all my might as Richards lifted the pistol and pulled the trigger. There was a loud click and nothing more; it was empty. The shovel missed his torso but instead hit his upraised left arm, blade first, at the shoulder joint. There was an audible snap and Richards yelped in pain as he stumbled back into the snow, panicking over the empty revolver. I rushed forward, scooping up a full can of varnish by its handle. I tossed it overhand, causing Richards to jump to one side. It caught his useless arm. Richards kept pulling the trigger, as if attempting to will bullets into the empty chamber. I grabbed and threw a length of lead pipe, javelin-style, catching Richards squarely in the middle of the chest. He shrieked in pain as his feet went out from under him. Landed flat on his back with a thud, the air knocked out of his lungs. I leapt onto the prone figure and straddled him. Richards smashed the empty revolver against the left side of my head. Things went double before me, my skull felt as if it would explode. Blinking heavily, I laboriously grabbed the arm and pinned it to the ground with my left knee on the upper arm. Likewise with his left, even though that arm appeared to be useless. I grabbed his throat as tightly as I could and watched Richards' face go red in silence, his mouth open, nothing going in or coming out. His pinned right arm twitched under my weight, his legs danced wildly. He made several feeble attempts to strike with the revolver, but there was little force behind the blows.

Methodically, I removed the roll of dimes from my right pocket and clenched them firmly in my big fist. I gave Richards a smile that caused his eyes to bug in the sheer horror of what he anticipated was coming.

I paused for a moment, blood streaming down my face, my scalp a sodden mess. The world spun around me, and I felt as if in a dream. The carolers were a house or two away, singing "God Rest Ye, Merry Gentlemen."

How appropriate. I'm gonna enjoy this.

I drew back my fist and smashed it into Richards' face. His nose crushed with a spurt of blood, several teeth loosened,and there was a disembodied gurgling shriek. I delivered two more smashing blows to his face, leaving it a bloody, gasping, groaning mess. I stumbled to my feet, got my balance as best I could, and delivered a well-aimed kick to his side. I thought I heard a rib crack, maybe two, before I staggered and fell onto the snow-covered ground.

Blood seeped into the snow at my side and around my head, turning the pristine white powder a vivid crimson. I listened to the pretty singing for seconds or minutes, drifting off into darkness as the snow began to collect on my body.

Christmas trees…Santa Claus…Snowfalls…Laughing children. I became a snowflake, spiraling down from the heavens towards the vast white emptiness below. Billions of flakes surrounded me, dancing in rhythmic and spontaneous patterns. The flakes all had pitchforks, and they all poked at my side as we tumbled. Busby Berkeley. Cold. Cold…

"Lew! Lew! You all right, Lew?"

The voice cut into my dream, my sleep. I wanted it to go away.

"Lew! Goddamn it, wake up."

I drifted back to consciousness, the snowflakes melting away before my unfocused eyes. The sky above was blocked by a large dark shape. I blinked. I blinked again. Slowly, Quinn's face came into focus, a burly state trooper visible over his shoulder.

My side and pants were soaked with blood, and my gloved fist was starting to turn a dark brown from the wetness inside. I turned my head and verified that Richards was still there, another trooper kneeling over him.

"I got him for you," I mumbled.

"Christ, you're a mess, Lew. Hang in there," said Quinn.

"So's this guy," I heard the kneeling trooper say. "A really big mess."

I blinked my blood-filled eyes again and wiped them with the back of my hand, and smiled at Quinn.

"The cavalry – nick of time," I said, a laugh cut short by a stab of pain. "Pocketbook – behind the outhouse – under it," I added, motioning vaguely with a lifted hand.

Quinn turned and nodded to one of the troopers, who promptly disappeared, taking the nearby shovel with him.

The carolers arrived and pressed forward for a better look at the carnage. My head cleared somewhat, and I proceeded with a lengthy, if somewhat rambling, explanation of the events of the past two days. A bloodied Richards was hauled off and taken into the house to await an ambulance. My story was just about finished when we were interrupted by the return of the trooper. He looked a bit pale.

"The pocketbook's there, all right, but that's not all: I think we may have found Mrs. Richards, too," he said, nervously.

Quinn stared at him a moment, then looked back to me with an arched eyebrow.

"Looks like you may be on to something," he commented calmly with a trace of a smile.

I ended up back at Doc Havens', with another round of patching and cleaning, and more serious reprimands about taking it easy and giving my battered body a chance to recuperate. The only bullet that had touched me was the one that grazed my scalp, and other than losing some hair to the seeping furrow on the upper left side of my head, the damage was minor. I had a splitting headache, though – undoubtedly from the blow to the side of my head – and any scabs that had formed on the previous day's wounds had pulled loose.

By early afternoon I was stretched out on my sofa listening to Christmas carols on the radio. My side sent out warning signals every time I moved the wrong way, and my right hand was re-bandaged and sore. The left side of my face was swollen and bruised purple. I felt like a prune wrapped in a napkin.

After a couple of hours staring at the wall, I couldn't stand it any longer. I hobbled over to the taproom – it was closed for Christmas –

and invited Willett back to my place for an impromptu, don't-get-your-hopes-up, Christmas dinner. That sounded fine by him, and he said he'd be over in an hour after finishing up whatever it was he was doing.

The cooking kept my mind off my various aches and pains for several hours, and the meal turned out surprisingly well. Thank God for Holly's *Joy of Cooking*, which I vowed to return to more often in the future.

Actually eating it, though, was a bitch.

After our meal was finished and Willett had cleaned up – he'd insisted, God bless him – we sat in the living room drinking wine before a roaring fire. Two lost souls.

We talked for hours. Willett told me about his childhood; I followed suit. We both tried to keep it upbeat, but our respective tales were unavoidably peppered with depressing elements. Willett had a Christmas present for me: three hand-rolled Cuban cigars wrapped in a red ribbon – he sure as hell didn't purchase them in Beach Haven, though he never did say where he got them. I had a present for him, too – actually had it for over a month now – but it was out in the garage, and I didn't have the energy to go and get it. He wandered out with a flashlight for a look – it was a new set of Encyclopedia Britannica – and returned excited and appreciative, the Index volume in hand.

"Do you have any idea where she is?" he asked quietly at a break in the conversation.

"Holly?" He nodded. "No, Gordon, I don't. I wish I did."

There was an extended silence. I realized that his eyes were growing red, and he casually swiped at each with a knuckle.

"I guess you miss her, don't you. Maybe almost as much as I do," I said.

He nodded slowly. "I…" He paused as his voice cracked, cleared his throat, then continued. "I love her. Like a mother. Like a sister. I don't know; it's hard to explain. But she's been – you both have been – so good to me over the last four years."

We spent the next five minutes silently staring at the fire, lost in our own thoughts. The mood brightened considerably with Eddie Cantor on the radio cracking jokes. By the time his segment was finished we were both laughing heartily. We switched over to beer.

"What's the story behind this?" asked Willett later on, staring into one of the three large crates holding the ruins of my Reims Cathedral model. I'd dumped it there in a moment of pique a week and a half earlier.

I told him. Uncle Sam had needed bodies to fight the war back in 1917, so I'd joined up, Europe looking more attractive than the U.S. at that particular time. After several months of basic at Camp Dix in the Pine Barrens, I was transferred to Camp Merritt up in Cresskill for processing, then shipped over to Europe out of Hoboken. Later, in 1918 – probably August or September – we marched through the French town of Reims on our way to the Argonne. The cathedral in Reims took my breath away. It was unlike anything I'd ever seen before, and its delicate beauty entranced me. Hundreds of statues adorned it: fifty six were of French kings and were arranged on its front, and there were angels everywhere. One in particular had stuck in my mind over the intervening years, situated above the front's left portal: a female angel, wings unfurled, smiling a smile unlike any I'd ever seen before or since – sort of a bemused Mona Lisa smile – looking at something held in her right hand. I'd never figured out just what it was she was holding, but that smile spoke a thousand words, different words, I suppose, to everyone who viewed it. She haunted my dreams for the days that followed, just as the horror awaiting us haunted my dreams for the next eighteen years. I'd appropriated some postcards and a booklet on the Cathedral, and took them with me – and have them to this day. The Cathedral was already war-damaged at that time, and restoration work had been ongoing ever since, with estimates of completion sometime around the turn of the next century.

Willett urged me to return to my hobby – my passion, he called it.

"You've got to rebuild it, Lew. Learn from your mistakes and build it better," he said. "You can't give up on it. I mean, the French haven't," he added, somewhat sheepishly.

His little speech sounded corny to me and I sure wasn't a Frenchman. But he was sincere and spoke from the heart – and he was, after all, right: about the model that was destroyed and, it occurred to me, *my life in general*. Yeah, he was right.

"By the way, Gordon," I added during a pause in the conversation. "Did I tell you that we have to go get my car again?"

Thursday, December 31, 1936. 11:07 a.m.

I FELT LIKE absolute hell when I woke up the day after Christmas. I decided then and there to take it easy for several days, give my wounds a chance to heal and my head an opportunity to stop pounding. I say "decided," but I doubt that my body would have allowed otherwise. I spent a lot of time sleeping. When I wasn't sleeping I took a lot of long slow walks for the exercise and to keep my body from seizing up. It warmed considerably during this stretch – with lows of only thirty-five degrees and highs of an unseasonable sixty-two degrees – so the weather was conducive to these frequent jaunts. Additional hours were occupied with reading, which helped keep my mind off other things. I wandered over to the taproom at least once daily, but did nothing that required any significant level of exertion. I left the real work to Willett.

By Tuesday, though, my thoughts had returned to Yumi and her murder, and the nagging – if potentially unimportant – question of just who it was that had purchased her car and why – and if the "why" was of any importance. I placed a call to the Department of Motor Vehicles in Trenton and weaseled my way through to a helpful individual willing to indulge my questions and bend the rules a bit. After some checking, he responded that they had no record of the purchaser of a '36 Hudson Terraplane previously owned by a Yutaka Takarada of Beach Haven; their records still showed Takarada as the owner. He suggested that I call back in three-to-four weeks; maybe they'd have something then.

Late Wednesday morning I was sitting alone in the taproom reading the paper when Purdy entered. He looked tired and distracted, and moved more slowly than usual. In a surprisingly quiet and conciliatory tone, he begrudgingly complimented me on the breaking of the Richards affair; but quickly reasserted his firmly held belief that there weren't any connections whatsoever, that the other disappearances and deaths were just what they appeared to be. Maybe he was right.

"And Holly?" I had asked.

"I don't know," he'd said, and paused. "I just don't know. I knew her pretty well – and her father before her – and I just can't picture her running off like that. For *any* reason." He looked up at me. "After all, you're the outsider here, if you know what I mean." I nodded; I knew. "If she wanted you out of her life for some reason or other and you refused to leave – well, she could have easily achieved that without leaving the island herself. She could, for instance, have hired some of our fun-loving Swedes and Norwegians – or some of those Goddamned North Carolinians, for that matter – to convince you that other parts of New Jersey would be more conducive to your physical and psychological well being. If you know what I mean."

I knew.

"And you," he'd continued, "from what I hear from Quinn, you'd pack up and disappear if there were a conflict, not chop her up and feed her to the gulls or whatever." He paused again, staring into the distance with a contemplative look on his face, his eyes reddening and growing moist. "I need to get back and check on my wife," he added suddenly, pulling himself together to leave.

"It's Maude – that's her name, isn't it? Is she okay?" I'd asked.

"*Okay?*" he'd repeated. "Heh, well, I guess you wouldn't have any reason to know. No, she's not *okay*. She's got cancer, and she's rotting away before my eyes, loaded up on morphine and babbling like a baby. No, she isn't *okay*. She's not...*okay*." His voice had been a mix of bitterness and resignation. He looked back at me. "Thanks for asking, though. People just don't appreciate what they have 'til it's yanked from them. Then, it makes a difference. A big one."

I knew.

He turned to leave, and I called after him.

"For the record – and for what it's worth – I *don't* know where Holly is. But I sure as hell wish I did. For better *or* for worse," I'd said.

He paused and turned.

"I never really suspected you of anything, Lew. Just getting your goat. Part of the job – getting people's goats…" His voice trailed off.

"Well, thanks, I guess, for the vote of confidence."

That was Wednesday.

Buzby stopped by on Monday, per his informal schedule, while I was on my couch dozing. He left a jar of his newest batch of distilled whiskey for me as a belated Christmas present and it sat on the backbar awaiting my return. Its *drinkability* was the source of much speculation and I was immediately goaded into sampling it as soon as my coat was off.

"Well, it's just as cloudy as usual," I'd said, holding the jar up to a light and viewing the contents. It looked like dirty dishwater. "Maybe even more so." I unscrewed the heavy lid and held the open jar under my nose. I winced. "Smells like the usual stuff. Maybe stronger; hard to tell." My nostrils were burning.

"Come on, quit teasing us," said Edwards, speaking for the crowd. "Taste the damned stuff!"

I nodded agreement, but my heart – hell, my stomach – wasn't really ready for this. I took a tentative sip, and it felt like lit lighter fluid coursing down my throat. It brought tears to my eyes and a rasping cough to my throat; it was a good thirty seconds before I could get words out. "Whew! That could be his best yet."

The group broke into applause, and I poured shots of the nasty stuff for all who wanted. And, not too surprisingly, they all did.

I felt reasonably well by Thursday, and the bruises on my face had turned to a sickly looking yellowish-brown, which at least was less obvious in low light. I looked jaundiced.

Quinn arrived unannounced and I was glad to see him; I knew he'd now be able to tie up some loose ends regarding Richards. I grabbed a fresh pot of coffee and we settled in at a booth.

"You get a confession?" I asked, lighting a De Nobili.

"Oh, yeah," he said, lighting a cigarette, smiling slightly. "And thanks for only wrecking his left arm. He was still able to sign legibly with his right." He tossed the spent match in the ashtray. "Yeah, once he was all cleaned up and tended to, and his mind had cleared, he sang like a parakeet – do parakeets sing? – and filled in all the gaps. You probably know half of this already, but here it is. Richards had met and fallen hard for the barmaid at Charlie's Bar and Grill up on Bonnet Island off Ship Bottom – Ship Bottom-Beach Arlington, I guess it's called – a round-heeled floozy named Arline Pretty. By the way, what the hell kind of a name is that for a town? Sounds like two towns."

"It was. Go on."

"Anyway, he had it bad for her, and she had what he wanted. He also wanted to dump his wife Ethel – they'd been at each other's throat for years – but she viewed things differently. So, he decided to take matters into his own hands.

The Peterson desertion up in High Point gave him the idea: make it appear that Ethel had done the same. So he strangled her to death – he used a length of clothesline, by the way – and buried her corpse in the hole beneath the old outhouse along with a bag of lime. He picked the lime up at Cranmer's here in Beach Haven. Then he gathered up all of her personal effects and put them in the truck. Followed by Pretty, they headed over to the mainland, pausing midway over the bridge to dump Ethel's clothing and stuff into the bay. Then they headed into the Pines and onto the old road off S40 where you later found his truck. It was a full moon out, or close to it, so he had plenty of light to work by. He stripped off the plates and got rid of anything he thought could possibly tie the truck back to him. Or at least he thought he did; the receipt you found was a glaring oversight. Richards wasn't too sharp, as you may have noticed.

"Anyway, he was covering the truck up with brush when he was interrupted by the arrival of some not-too-friendly Pineys. Richards, for some reason, is scared to death of Pineys. He hopped into Pretty's car and they drove off, but the Pineys unloaded a couple of barrels of buckshot into the rear of her car, probably to scare them off rather than with intentions of harming them. The pellet marks and holes are still there in the rear of her car; we checked.

"Later, he stumbled across Ethel's pocketbook – a big loose end – so he hastily added it to the hole out back with the intention of digging it back up and discarding it elsewhere later on when things died down. As you probably noticed, the pocketbook was rather shallowly buried; that was due to the rush he was in.

"Word of the two subsequent disappearances made Richards feel even more secure that his crime would be viewed as just one more in a series of desertions. And as far as his friends and neighbors were concerned, it was. But your snooping, Lew, was worrisome. He started to unravel and began dogging your steps whenever he could."

"And the bridge?" I asked.

"The guys who attacked you? He had nothing to do with that and there's a bar full of people that swear he was there all that night, as usual, trying to climb into Miss Pretty's pants – as usual. We arrested her, of course, and she independently verified most of what he said. With her own slant on it, of course. She claims Richards forced her to accompany him out into the Pines to dump the truck, and she swears she had no prior knowledge of his plans to kill Ethel. You know, the usual sob story."

I sat there listening to Quinn's summary of Richards' deeds, and felt a certain level of satisfaction in having had a hand in bringing the cold-blooded murderer to justice. But a question begged to be answered: If Richards wasn't involved in the attack on the bridge, who was? And why?

"So," Quinn continued, "it looks like you've solved a crime and we're appreciative of that. But aside from using the other disappearances as a smoke screen, that's where the connection ends. It was an isolated crime."

And I was back where I started – nowhere. But Quinn had something I felt I could use, that might possibly help to connect the dots.

"Quinn," I said, "you mentioned several weeks back that there were a number of other disappearances that occurred in this general area a year or so ago. Can you get me a list of the names, dates, and addresses of those involved? The usual stuff?" He looked at me for several moments without expression. "Please?" I added. I hoped he didn't want me to beg.

A faint smile came over his face as he withdrew a small notebook from his inside coat pocket, and from that pulled a folded, typewritten sheet. He handed it to me.

"What's this?" I asked as I spread it out on the table in front of me. He didn't answer, but it was self-explanatory. It was the list that I'd just asked for. Quinn had already prepared it in anticipation of my request – but I knew he wouldn't admit to it and I didn't waste my breath asking.

"Ah. Thanks," I said, scanning the names, and there were a fair number of them. One victim, Virginia Leonard, disappeared from Brant Beach on Long Beach Island on January 24, 1936; another, Eileen Hunt, from Barnegat City – also on the island – on October 28, 1935; and a third, Dorothy Silsby, from Brigantine on September 27, 1935. A fourth, Julie Massey, had vanished from Manahawkin on May 19, 1936; a fifth, Annie Ryan, from Seaside Heights on March 22, 1936; and a sixth, Elizabeth Perry, from Seaside Park on February 22, 1936. Lillian Van Pelt, the stabbing victim he'd mentioned from Brigantine, was found bayside on November 2, 1935, and had been dead for roughly a week at that point. I reread the list several times, but it was just names, dates and locations – nothing more.

"Lew," Quinn interjected, and I knew what was coming, "I've

said it before and I'll say it again: play by the rules and feed us anything you find that has anything to do with this – any of this. And don't think for a moment that you didn't get lucky with the Richards mess," he added, returning the notebook to his pocket and scooping up his pack of cigarettes. "You did, but things could very easily have turned out differently and you could be cooling your heels in a cell up in Toms River right now. Or worse."

"Don't worry," I assured him as he stood up to leave. "I'll be a good boy."

I was lying, and we both knew it.

We had a good crowd that night to celebrate New Year's Eve, a lot of them with their wives in tow. Everyone got drunk, which in and of itself was nothing new, only tonight they got a little more drunk than usual. I'd hired Lester Simms to put on a fancy spread for the group and Edwards hauled in an old record player and a stack of 78s. Everyone seemed to enjoy themselves and while I did my best to get caught up in the spirit of things, my mind was elsewhere. There were a lot of missing people – too many of them – and they were all women. And a lot of them from close to home.

Real close.

Monday, January 4, 1937.

I USED THE weekend to gather as much preliminary information as I could regarding the various disappearances. This was, for the most part, from local sources and much of it by simply putting Beach Haven's phone system to work. I figured another couple of days of taking it easy would put me back in fighting trim – or at least hobbling trim. Come Monday, the real legwork would commence. I would look into each of the disappearances in chronological order, for no good reason other than it appealed to my sense of order. Assuming I had one.

I called Jack Kahn at home and picked his brain, and was surprised at how much info he was able to dredge up. I could have waited most any twenty-four hour period and found him at the taproom: but one-on-one, without interruptions and distractions, was what I needed. We spoke several more times over the weekend, after Kahn had gathered even more information from old notes, the newspaper's files and from conversations with acquaintances at other papers.

"Shorty" Hewitt, the backup bartender at Paul Kaetzel's joint up in Barnegat City, was an old acquaintance and proved to be a good source of local scuttlebutt regarding the Hunt disappearance. There wasn't much that happened in that sleepy little town that Hewitt didn't get wind of somehow or other. Fortunately, Emily Stackhouse's name never came up in our conversation and that was fine by me.

I spent a couple of hours Sunday afternoon talking to several year-round neighbors of Mary McCarthy's. I use the term "neighbor" loosely, as they all lived a quarter to a half mile away. They helped to flesh out my image of Mary as a person, but offered little that seemed of any real importance. I returned to McCarthy's property for another look around. The cops had been there – and while I knew it had probably only been two or three of them, the area looked like a small army had held maneuvers on the grounds. There were several sets of tire tracks farther in than where McCarthy or I'd previously parked, and the ground was littered with cigarette butts, a candy bar wrapper and an empty Bugle Boy chewing tobacco wrapper. Looked like they'd made an afternoon of it.

The laundry had all been removed from the line and the adjacent bushes. The lights were off inside and the door locked now, and I could see the laundry stacked on a kitchen chair, neatly folded. I couldn't imagine the cops doing that, so I chalked it up to a thoughtful friend or concerned relative. It didn't seem to matter much either way.

I poked around some more outside, but it seemed an exercise in futility. Aside from the drive out to the road, the only other access to the house was a narrow winding path that worked its way back to the bay. Dense thickets of brush fenced in the rest of the property's perimeter and if there were any additional paths through the tangle I never found them.

I spotted something of contrasting color several feet under a bayberry bush and found a long piece of driftwood back by the house to fish it out with. It was a dark blue bandanna, tied to be worn as a headband. It was stained with sweat and fitted for a head larger than mine, so it wasn't a piece of Mary's scattered laundry and it was doubtful it even belonged to her. Who did it belong to? Who the hell knew? It could have been there for four months as easily as two weeks. Probably a fisherman or hiker or bather; it could have been most anyone. I pocketed it anyway and headed back to my car.

On Saturday morning I visited Agnes Wormley at her house. Agnes was the librarian at Beach Haven's Free Public Library, which was closed for the holiday weekend. For that matter, it seemed to be closed most of the time, with access to the institution's books a catch-as-catch-can affair. I asked her if she would loan me a set of keys to the place so I could peruse the past year's newspapers uninterrupted and at will. Being the sweet woman she was, she agreed. The bottle of sherry didn't hurt.

Early Monday morning, I took the drive down to Atlantic City. I figured my inquiries were going to take me several days, and I sure as hell didn't feel like making the round trip more than once, so I searched out a hotel – a cheap one.

The Surfside Hotel was anything but, located a good six blocks back from the beach, at the corner of Drexel and Tennessee. It had seen better days – probably back in the previous century – but it was cheap and open for business. Parking was a different issue altogether and even offseason I was forced to park nearly a block away on a side street. I paid for two nights in advance and, just for laughs, signed in as Alfred Landon. The guy behind the desk didn't bat an eye.

I headed the three miles north to the small ocean-side town of Brigantine. As the crow flies, Brigantine was only about fifteen miles from Beach Haven. But the crow drove a Ford, so it was closer to fifty. I figured I'd devote the rest of Monday looking into Dorothy Silsby's disappearance and Tuesday into Lillian Van Pelt's murder; Wednesday could be spent wrapping up loose ends, if needed. I didn't hold any illusions that I'd actually come up with any answers or solutions, but I did want to get a sense of just what it was that happened, how it happened and why. Call me ambitious.

Dorothy Silsby had disappeared from Brigantine back on September 27, 1935. Kahn had called a friend of his at the *Atlantic City Beacon* and gotten Silsby's address, and picked his friend's brain for the story's details. It was juicy stuff, for Brigantine at any rate and a mild scandal at the time it had occurred.

"Who was it," Kahn had asked me, "that said, 'As the French say, there are three sexes – men, women, and clergymen'?" I hadn't a clue, but the guy was probably a Brit.

Dorothy Silsby, a minister's wife in her mid-thirties, just picked up and left one night while her husband was attending to some church business. Only it turned out that the "business" was a one on one in his office with a grieving widow; he was comforting her in his own, unique fashion – and himself in the process. Or at least that's what the town's busybodies conjured up. It very well may have been an innocent meeting, but with Dorothy's desertion it evolved into an unseemly affair, with Dorothy fleeing her husband and the area in shame and despair. Church attendance soon dropped off due to the parishioners' growing conviction that their minister was a lecher. The humiliated widow eventually packed up and left town, her house selling soon after. The breaking point for Reverend Silsby – this according to one of the parishioners I interviewed – was finally reached one Sunday when the sum total of his congregation consisted of the town idiot and a senile old woman named Rose. After conducting an abbreviated service, Silsby went home and packed, taking off in the dead of night with whatever personal belongings he could stuff into his old model T.

"And the funny thing is," Kahn had added, "everyone seemed relieved that he was gone, like this was the expedient solution to their moral problem. And the poor S.O.B. was probably a complete innocent."

Maybe. Maybe not.

I spoke with a number of Silsby's neighbors and parishioners, and to a person they were convinced that there had been an illicit relationship of some sort. The problem was that their theories ran the gamut. Some thought his wife had an affair with another parishioner or an outsider. Others insisted the Reverend had an affair with the widow (or, according to some, an endless string of affairs with an endless string of women). Still others were convinced the two of them – husband and wife – engaged in something unfathomable, like threesomes. You get the picture. But no one had any tangible evidence of any of this; it was just what they'd heard.

And if Dorothy Silsby was a writer of poetry or anything even remotely creative, it was news to each and every one of them.

Tuesday was spent looking into the stabbing of Lillian Van Pelt, whose partially decomposed corpse was found in the marsh grass bayside on November 2, 1935. I'd found her address and a summary of the discovery in a newspaper – the *Atlantic City Beacon* – published shortly afterwards and on file at the Beach Haven Library. I located her neighborhood and interviewed the handful of year-'rounders I was able to track down. They all seemed eager to talk about it, but I sensed that they would have been just as eager to talk about the weather. Probably more so.

Van Pelt was in her early twenties, single and ran a small grocery store out of the front of a house she'd inherited from her late parents. Her neighbors grew concerned when her shop remained closed for the better part of a week and there'd been no signs of anyone at her home. Her immediate neighbor, a trusted friend since childhood, had a spare key to the house, so she'd let herself in to see if everything was okay. It appeared that Van Pelt had gone on an unannounced trip, since most of her personal belongings were gone. The neighbor'd thought it unusual, but not worrisome. The last time she'd seen Lillian alive was in church the Sunday before her body was found; that would have been October 27.

Poetry? Not Van Pelt. All she ever did was listen to the radio from dawn until bedtime, both in her house and in the small shop. When she wasn't working, I was told, she was sleeping; but she worked a lot. Store hours were from 8:00 a.m. to 8:00 p.m. every day, with extra time spent restocking shelves, bookkeeping, placing orders – that sort of stuff. So, when you threw a couple of meals and household chores into the mix, it left very little time for sleep. Who had the time to sit down and write rhymes?

And more than one of those I spoke with mentioned the inconvenience of having to walk several blocks to the next closest outlet carrying the *Philadelphia Evening Bulletin*. The woman had nerve, was the implication.

Van Pelt's body had been found out by the bay by a trio of local kids – twelve year olds – and it wasn't a pretty sight, having been picked at by an assortment of wildlife. She had been repeatedly stabbed in the chest and neck, and her throat had been slit through to the spine. Like a teakettle lid, someone said.

I checked with the local police – Brigantine's department consisted of two full timers – and verified that nothing more was ever discovered regarding the murder. It was still considered an open case, but a case that no one had given any thought to lately. Conventional wisdom, if you want to call it that, was that the murderer was a transient – a hobo, perhaps – and that the locals had nothing further to worry about. A transient with a very big knife, it would seem.

"It's just not gonna get solved," said Chief of Police Lemuel Petrie, "unless some feller wanders in off the street and tells us he did it." That didn't seem likely.

And, of course, since this all occurred after Dorothy Silsby's disappearance, but before the Reverend had departed, there were even some who went through some mental gyrations to tie him to the murder in some fashion or other. It seemed to me that the people of Brigantine had even more time on their hands than the people of Beach Haven. We were a close second, though.

I finished Tuesday afternoon in a dump of a local bar called Crowley's, where I had a bunch of Garden States and a ham and cheese sandwich that was light on the ham and cheese and heavy on the bread and mustard. It was filling, though.

Crowley's sat on a dingy alley situated between Sewell and Caspian. As luck would have it, Seeley's Alley turned out to be one of the city's low-rent scuffer hangouts. It didn't take long to find a serviceable-looking brunette named Florence, nor long after that to get my money's worth. Not that the money was considerable.

I know – so much for avoiding distractions. But this, I told myself, was a minor distraction.

I wandered back to The Seaside a little after 9:00 p.m. The place looked deserted – even the guy who should have been manning the front desk was elsewhere. I crashed into bed, and after a good thirty seconds or so of trying to organize my thoughts, fell into a deep, sound sleep.

398

Wednesday, January 6, 1937. 7:38 p.m.

THE SEASIDE'S BED didn't feel very comfortable when I woke up a little after 5:30 Wednesday morning. It seemed futile to try to go back to sleep, so I grabbed my things and left. I stopped in Tuckerton at a small greasy spoon, had eggs and bacon, and was back at my house by 9:30. Willett had Hoover with him, so the place felt empty when I got there, as deserted as The Seaside the night before. The place seemed like a tomb with Holly gone.

I tended bar that night and it was a refreshing change of pace. Mackey, Edwards and Kahn were among the eleven customers – and Mackey seemed preoccupied, Edwards seemed annoyed and Kahn seemed bored. All as usual.

"Have any luck down south?" asked Kahn without looking at me, stubbing out his cigarette.

"Some, I guess – nothing worth mentioning," I said, wrestling a full keg into place and realized as I did so that today was the first day that I actually felt reasonably ache-free. "Thanks again for the background stuff, by the way. I'll fill you in when I actually have something." I really didn't want to get into this with everyone else around. Kahn was a good source, though, and at some point I'd be sure to feed him something – assuming there ever would be a "something" – as tangible thanks for the work he'd done.

"How's business?" I asked Mackey, quickly changing the subject.

Mackey looked up from beneath heavy lids and I noticed that the right sleeve of his dark blue suit was peppered with cigarette ash. He noticed me notice and blew it off.

"Got a full house," he answered quietly.

"What's a full house, McOat?" asked Edwards.

"Two."

"Two? The Kilmer woman and who else?"

Mackey hesitated, drink halfway to lips and turned to Edwards.

"I guess you haven't heard – I assumed everyone had heard." He took his drink.

"Heard what?" exclaimed an exasperated Edwards.

"Maude Purdy," replied Mackey matter-of-factly.

"Purdy's wife?" repeated Edwards. "She wasn't that old, was she? Like fifty-ish?"

"Cancer," I said.

Mackey said nothing more.

"No, no, no; it wasn't the cancer," said Kahn quickly. "She... ah..." He paused to look around and make sure that only the four of us were in this conversation. We were. "She shot herself. One shot. In the head," he finished in a loud whisper, bending his right hand into the shape of a pistol and sticking his index finger in his mouth pointed at the roof. His thumb "hammer" closed. "Boom," he added for effect.

Mackey shot a glance at Kahn and returned to his drink. It was okay if someone else let the cat out of the bag; at least *he* hadn't betrayed any professional confidences.

"She blew her brains out?" yelled Edwards. A hushed silence fell over the place at his sudden outburst. Edwards turned red as he glanced around the room and he waited for conversation to resume. Mackey shook his head in disgust; Kahn looked amused. Edwards leaned in to us and repeated his question, this time in a loud whisper.

"Yeah," said Kahn. "Last night. With one of Purdy's revolvers."

"Whew!" exclaimed Edwards. He looked genuinely surprised. "What the hell's going on around here? Everybody's killin' themselves."

"Miller, Tak and Maude Purdy: that's three in as many months. When was the last time before that someone killed himself on the island?" thought Kahn out loud.

"Well, there was that Postmaster up in Surf City – hung himself back in October. And the Cadwalder sisters a few years back with the poison," said Edwards.

"Oh, yeah; I'd forgotten about them."

"'cept maybe Miller's suicide wasn't a suicide, if you get my drift?" added Edwards.

Mackey and Kahn both looked up and about nervously, seeing who might have overheard Edwards' comment.

"You better keep that kind of thought to yourself, friend," cautioned Kahn. Mackey nodded agreement.

I knew what Kahn was getting at – Gibbons had been on duty that night and had an interest in the case. And while I didn't think that Gibbons would ever resort to cold-blooded murder, he was the sort to goad and taunt a guy on the edge into doing it, then stand by and watch the death dance. Saturday night at the movies. Maybe grab a bag of popcorn.

If you lived in Beach Haven, you sure as hell wanted to stay on Gibbons' good side. At least most of them did. Personally? I couldn't have cared less.

Especially now.

Thursday, January 7, 1937. 11:09 a.m.

VIRGINIA LEONARD HAD disappeared from her parents' home here on the island in Brant Beach a year earlier – January 24. Kahn had remembered the incident, but said the circumstances were never clear and that no one was even sure that she'd actually been on the island just before that date. And the Long Beach Township police, of course, chalked it up as parents overreacting to a runaway daughter. I spent the day filling in the gaps.

Ginny, as everyone called her, was in her early twenties and the single daughter of a wealthy Philadelphia couple. She was using their summer home offseason to write, claiming she needed the solitude to concentrate. There were no year-round residents living near the house, no one to observe her coming and going. There was a local shopkeeper who remembered her occasional visits, for newspapers and odds-and-ends foodstuffs, but the days tended to blend together in his mind. He wouldn't even attempt to recall when he'd last seen her.

Her parents had grown concerned when repeated daily telephone calls went unanswered and they eventually made the trip to Brant Beach to check up on her. The house was open as if recently occupied, but she wasn't there – and all her personal belongings were gone. They neither saw nor heard from her again. Curiously, her typewriter was still there on the kitchen table, a blank sheet of paper by its side.

They estimated the disappearance date based on a couple of items: the dates of old newspapers stacked up in the house, the postmark on an opened envelope found in a wastebasket and the postmarks of uncollected mail at the post office. So, while it wasn't definite, January 24 was a reasonable estimate, give or take a day or so.

There were no signs of foul play, so the cops all but ignored her parents' entreaties. It sounded familiar.

I let myself into the Leonard's place — the lock was cheap and easily jimmied — and took a look around; but aside from confirming the layout, I found nothing of interest. After all, a year had passed and the house had been used in the interim.

I spoke with her parents by telephone and they remained convinced that harm had come to her, that her disappearance was not one of choice. But they had nothing to back that up with other than a gut feeling. Gut feelings counted for a lot in my book, though. They asked me a lot of questions — probably as many as I asked them — then ended up begging for my help in finding her. I told them I'd do what I could and would let them know what I found out.

And her writing? According to her parents she was intent on writing "the great American novel," although they had never read a single word she had written and none were ever found. One thing they were sure of: She hated poetry and felt it to be a lazy person's writing.

I stopped in at the post office on my way back home and Faye Entwistle passed my mail over the battered wooden countertop. There were close to a dozen envelopes neatly stacked atop a small box wrapped in brown paper. Back in my car I took a closer look at the package. Its return address read, "Fanfare Films, The Pallette Bldg., Lenox & 132nd, NYC," its postmark December 31, 1936. Inside, on top of wadded up newspaper, sat a letter.

Dear Mr. Porter:

Knowing of your relationship to Robert Knauss, I regret to inform you of his passing. He fell asleep in his room while smoking and died in the ensuing fire. Fortunately, no one else was hurt. This happened on December 23. There was a brief article in the *New York Post* regarding the incident, which I've enclosed.

His personal belongings were few, but his landlady is holding several boxes of his clothing. She told me that she'll hold on to them until spring, at which point they'll become a casualty of her annual housecleaning. She gave me a few other odds and ends, which are enclosed in this package. These were found on, and in, his bedside table and miraculously survived the fire.

The only two people that I know of (aside from locals and fellow employees) who knew Mr. Knauss were you and his friend Grace Peterson. I have sent her a similar note regarding his death. I spoke with some of the regulars and the owner down at Willie's (Bobby's favorite hangout), but none of them know anything much of his past and nothing of any friends or kin. As second cousin, you're the closest relative that anyone knows of.

Please have any interested party contact his landlady regarding collection of his clothing. Her address is:

Daisy Smith
88 West 134th Street
New York, New York

Please feel free to contact me with any further questions.

Regards,
Sheldon Goldberg

Another one bites the dust, but at least this one was unintentional. Or at least it seemed to be. And it was a rather sorry state of affairs when I was considered one of Knauss' closest friends. I turned to the article stapled to the letter.

Burned Body ID'd

HARLEM - A dead body found severely burned on a bed in a 134th Street rooming house has been positively identified as that of Robert M. Knauss, 34, of Harlem, authorities said yesterday.

Knauss's bed caught fire shortly after 10:00 p.m. on Wednesday.

Evidence recovered at the scene indicates that a cigarette caused the blaze.

Building owner Daisy Smith called the fire department, while roomer Malcolm Jeffreys attempted to confine the blaze with an extinguisher. Firemen arrived in time to save the building and its occupants, but Knauss was burnt beyond recognition.

Coroner F. Aubrey Daniels had the body removed to the 96th Street Morgue where tentative identification was made Thursday morning by Knauss's dentist, Dr. Frederick Mathews, of 110th Street.

Foul play has been ruled out.

I fished through the wadded up paper until I reached the package's contents. There was an inexpensive pocket watch and old high school ring that were badly discolored from the fire, his set of white false teeth, a pair of reading glasses, some spare change and a wallet. The wallet was thin, holding only a Social Security card, an ID card, a scrap of paper with Grace Peterson's address scribbled on it, and a tiny black and white photo – a long shot – of a youngish couple I assumed to be his parents way back when. There were no paper bills to be found.

Not much to show for thirty-four years on this planet.

I went over to the Mackey Funeral Home shortly after 7:00 p.m., to attend Maude Purdy's viewing. It seemed that most of the town wandered through the small room over the course of the hour, though I suspect that some were there more out of curiosity than out of respect. Mackey had made a valiant effort to piece her back together, but she looked terrible: thin, haggard and her face misshapen, she looked as if she'd been carved out of a large chunk of discolored soap. Death isn't kind. I stared at the woman I hadn't known while a pair of elderly women behind me commented on how natural she looked.

They must have been looking at someone else.

Friday, January 8, 1937. 11:36 a.m.

I THANKED THE postmaster and wandered out to the street with the Hunts' address scribbled on a scrap of paper. Eileen Hunt had disappeared from her parents' home in Barnegat City back on October 28, 1935. Kahn had remembered the story and the family's name: Eileen Hunt, a teenage girl of sixteen, had stayed at home that night while her parents and younger sister went to the movies at the south end of the island. When they returned later that night, she was gone. She was assumed to be a runaway by both the local cops and by a private detective later hired by the grieving parents. Joe Grimes, the Toms River-based detective, had proved ineffectual.

"But you know private dicks," Kahn had said. "He may have taken the easy way out, parroting the police line and pocketing the cash without ever having lifted a finger." It happened.

I spoke with the parents and it was evident that they still didn't buy the runaway theory. They clung to it, however, as an optimistic alternative to their worst, unstated fears.

When I finished with the Hunts and several neighbors, I walked the two blocks over to Paul Kaetzel's bar. While it seemed unlikely, my fingers were crossed in the hope that I wouldn't run into Emily. I kept my eyes open, anyway, ready to peel off down a side street if anyone resembling her stepped into view.

"Shorty" Hewitt was propped up behind the bar. After a few minutes of small talk and a couple of draughts, I got around to asking him if he had any idea who this Milt the Mute was. He didn't, but he threw the question out to the half-dozen patrons scattered around the smoke-filled room. None of them did, either. For that matter, none of them knew any mutes at all – some dumb people, but no mutes. Nobody knew of a '36 Hudson Terraplane, either, but I doubted that any of them would recognize one as such if it crashed into the bar.

I downshifted the Ford to a crawl as I drove through High Point, looking down each of the side streets for Maggie and Rudolph. I spotted them on West Seventy-Sixth, braked, backed up and pulled down the road to meet them.

Did she know Milt the Mute? No, there weren't any Milts or Miltons on her route, or at least none that ever received any mail. There was one guy who could be a mute – either that or the shyest person on the island – but she didn't know his name. He worked as a caretaker south of there. Down at *White Cedars*. The Hawleys' place.

Damn it! That's why the name sounded so familiar; Chester had mentioned it – his groundskeeper – during our first conversation. And now it made some sense. That's where someone would come up with three hundred and fifty bucks cash to pay for a car and with no haggling: Milt had purchased the car under instructions from one of the Hawleys. But why? It warranted a closer look, though – at some point.

Well, it was a good theory, at least.

Monday, January 11, 1937. 10:23 a.m.

I'D SPENT THE weekend working the bar, with a mind towards keeping the business afloat. Not that Willett wasn't doing just fine on his own, mind you, it's just that I felt it needed that personal touch every so often. That and I was tired of driving all over the place.

I wanted to wrap up my brief look into the previous year's disappearances, however, so that I could resume with the ones that really concerned me – and that took me to Seaside Heights. But first, since I was in his neck of the woods, I decided to pay a visit to the so-called "private dick" Joe Grimes in Toms River.

Grimes wasn't at all what I expected. He was a small, balding man with thick glasses, pasty skin and bad teeth. He was parked in a cramped office above a barbershop and sat sideways at his desk facing me in my armless oak chair. Our knees almost touched in the close confines and his breath reeked of tobacco and coffee.

It turned out that he actually did do some work for his fee. He related the facts of the Hunt disappearance as he remembered them, his memory jogged by the pile of notes in the dog-eared folder lying on the desk next to him. There was a lot of superfluous detail that no one else had relayed to me – and while it must have taken some time and effort to collect, it amounted to nothing. When he was finished with his story, he added that it was his gut feeling that something bad had come of Eileen. But it was a only gut feeling, with nothing tangible to back it up, so he had kept his thoughts to himself and relayed just the facts. And the facts all pointed to Eileen having run away.

Annie Ryan had disappeared from her home in Seaside Heights

the year before on March 22. I had vaguely recalled that "Shorty" Hewitt at Kaetzel's had mentioned something of this back when it happened, so I gave him a call and he provided the details as best he could remember them. She was in her early thirties, reportedly attractive, and the wife of one of our group, a bartender named Mickey Ryan. He worked long hours at a place called Kelley's Taproom, and was there as usual the night she vanished. As far as Shorty knew she'd never turned up, but he doubted he would have heard if she had. Only bad news seems to get passed on and circulated.

Kelley's wasn't difficult to find – the first guy I stopped on the street knew exactly where it was, and in spite of the cold drizzle was willing to give me directions. Mickey was right where I expected him to be, wiping down the bar. I ordered a draught, struck up a conversation, and eased it over to the topic of his wife. He was resistant to talk about it until I told him of my similar plight, which seemed to genuinely upset him.

Not surprisingly, everyone jumped to the conclusion that Annie had run off, some going as far as to intimate that Mickey must have done something reprehensible to cause her to do so. With conventional wisdom all of a like mind, it had been real easy for him to fall in line and come around to the same conclusion. But it'd always nagged at the back of his mind – "What if...?" She'd never been seen or heard from again, and it *could* have been as they said, but he just didn't *know*. And that was the hard part.

The details were familiar. He came home a little before midnight on a Sunday night – it was a cloudy Sunday night and as dark as they come due to a new moon – and found her gone. The signs were an orderly departure: nothing was out of place, and her bags and personal possessions were gone. The police indulged him but did little else, and repeated calls to her friends and relatives turned up nothing. It was as if she'd vanished off the face of the earth. Mickey felt their marriage to be a pretty good one, as far as marriages go.

Not that there wasn't the occasional rough edge, but they loved each other and he just couldn't see her running off with some other guy or, for that matter, just running off.

He reached beneath the bar and produced a dog-eared photograph of an attractive young woman with long, curly, light-colored hair. It was taken from the shoulders up, and she smiled for the camera. Not at it, but for it.

"She's pretty," I said.

"Yeah," he said wistfully. "And you'd never know."

"Know what?" I asked.

"Oh. Yeah — how would you know? It's what never made any sense to me. Everybody was so quick to jump on the 'she ran away from home' bandwagon, but it just didn't make any sense."

"Why was that?"

"Why, she's blind. Blind as a bat."

Mickey was pouring himself drinks at this point, so I switched the conversation from his wife to another disappearance, that of Elizabeth Perry. Perry had vanished from the next town south — Seaside Park — a month before Annie on February 22, 1936. I hadn't been able to get much of a lead on this one, but Mickey remembered it vividly as an uncomfortable coincidence. He was aware of Perry's disappearance at the time it happened, but hadn't attached any particular significance to it. Annie's subsequent disappearance, however, cast it in a whole new light.

Elizabeth Perry, a plain-looking nineteen year old, had disappeared along with her seven month old baby girl. This was on a Saturday night, while her husband was out bowling with his league over in Toms River. All of her things were gone, as were the baby's, leading everyone to the immediate conclusion that she had left of her own accord. Where she had gone, however, was anyone's guess, and as far as Mickey knew it was still a mystery. It was Mickey's opinion that her husband Paul must have been having some difficulties dealing with the responsibilities of marriage and fatherhood. Why?

Because he never seemed overly upset about it, taking the stance of "Let her go if she wants to" and "The kid will be better off with his mother." Not what you'd call a concerned individual, although Mickey admitted that he might be putting on a gruff exterior for any one of a variety of reasons, male vanity the most probable. At any rate, within several weeks of her disappearance, Paul was jumping a barmaid at the bowling lanes he frequented. According to Mickey, it was Paul's turn, as most every other guy who frequented the lanes had had a shot at her at one time or another. Only Paul was stupid enough to be serious about it.

By late Monday afternoon – and a hell of a lot of drinks later – I wasn't in very good shape for the drive back to Beach Haven, so I decided to spend the night and poke around a little more on Tuesday. I lined up a room in a private home with a sign out front – "Rooms for Rent." It wasn't much, and the place smelled of cats, but the bathroom was right across the hall; it would do. I wasn't ready to turn in just yet – it was only a little before six – so I hoofed it back to Kelley's to finish off the night. I liked the place and I liked Mickey; it was one of those taprooms that immediately feels comfortable, like an old pair of pants. They served food of sorts, and I filled myself with corned beef and cabbage. Mickey and I talked into the night about nothing in particular, and at some point when the words weren't flowing too well I decided to call it a night. Somehow, I made it back to my room.

Tuesday, January 12, 1937. 11:17 a.m.

PERRY'S NEIGHBORS DOWN in Seaside Park reiterated much of what I already knew, but they did manage to flesh out the story a bit. All seemed to agree that Paul was fairly immature – even more so than his wife – and that they had been too young to get married and have a child.

I tracked down Paul at his job in a small food store on the main road through town. It wasn't much of a job, but I got the feeling that he wasn't much of an employee. I spent five minutes asking him questions during a morning break where he smoked two cigarettes in rapid succession. He seemed indifferent to the whole situation, and acknowledged that they were all probably better off this way – it had been a stormy marriage. And she was welcome to the child; he'd never wanted one so early on, anyway. Like it was her fault.

I finished up the day back in Seaside Heights, gathering some independent, third-party information regarding Annie Ryan's disappearance. Then, in what seemed like a good idea at the time, I returned to Kelley's for a quick draught before the ride home. One turned to many, and I spent yet another night bullshitting with Ryan. By night's end – and after switching over to rye – I was in a state similar to the night before. I ended up sleeping on an old sofa in the back, at Ryan's insistence. He didn't have to insist too hard.

Later...

Gibbons, pipe clenched in his teeth, glared at Miller through the bars of the small cell, wordlessly urging him to put an end to it. He produced a length of rope. Tossed it through the bars to Miller. Miller sobbed uncontrollably. Tears flowed from bloodshot eyes, coursing down his cheeks, dampening the front of his torn white shirt.

"Do it," urged Gibbons, though I couldn't hear his words. "Do it."

Miller dragged himself over to the high barred window, tossed the end of the rope over one of the horizontal bars, and tied it securely. He fashioned a rough noose out of the other end while swirls of thick tobacco smoke clouded the air in the tiny cell. Gibbons watched, eyes squinted and motionless, a half-smile frozen over clenched teeth. Miller stepped up onto the bed's iron headrail and tightened the noose around his neck. He turned slowly to look one last time at Gibbons.

"Do it."

He did it.

Gibbons puffed contentedly on his pipe as Miller jerked convulsively in his long, agonizing, death throes. After what seemed like an eternity, Miller was motionless. Gibbons tapped the spent dregs from his pipe, pocketed it, and left quietly.

Miller's eyes slowly opened.

I awoke with a start, drenched in sweat, breathing heavily. It was a good half minute before I remembered where I was, and why I was there. I stumbled over to the tiny sink mounted on the wall nearby and drenched my face in cold water. This stuff was getting to me, and I didn't like it. I just wanted my life to return to the way it was, to the simpler existence of a year earlier.

But I knew it never would.

I knew it never could.

Wednesday, January 13, 1937. 10:38 a.m.

I'D FELT BETTER.

A mess of fried eggs, bacon, toast and greasy potatoes coated in something red sat uneasily in a swamp of coffee down in my stomach – and threatened to resurface if I gave it good reason to. The Tip-Top Diner of Toms River was added to that list of places to avoid.

I drove slowly south on Route 9, silently thanking Mother Nature for putting an end to the drizzle of the last two days. It was still gray and overcast, but every now and then the sun managed to claw its way through, if only for a few, fleeting moments.

Julie Massey had lived in Manahawkin with her husband, Greg, up until she disappeared one Tuesday back in May of 1936. He was a carpenter by trade, though reportedly not a very good one; he was out of work more often than in. Nor, for that matter, a particularly reliable one; he was drunk more often than sober. Eddie O'Reilly, a business acquaintance of Jack Kahn's, and a reporter for Manahawkin's weekly paper *The Beacon*, had filled me in on the Masseys as a couple, and Julie's eventual disappearance.

As far as he knew, Greg still lived in a small cabin on a nameless road off Stafford that dead-ended at Turtle Cove. According to O'Reilly, Greg had arrived home late the night of the nineteenth in his usual drunken stupor and had fallen asleep on the living room couch. He came to the next morning dressed, with a pounding headache, and stumbled off to God knows where – it certainly wasn't a job, as he was in the midst of one of his frequent unemployed stints. But it wasn't until he returned home later that day and found the place empty that he came to the realization that he hadn't seen her at all that day, hadn't seen her since dinner the night before. She was, by all reports, a terrible cook and dinner was the only meal he'd force himself to have with her – after a hard day's work, he once said, most anything looks reasonably good. Greg had taken the same "To Hell with her if she doesn't want to stick around" attitude, thinking, like many of the others before and since, that she'd willfully abandoned him. And that's the way it had looked, because all of her clothing and personal possessions were as gone as she was. The police had made a half-hearted inquiry of her family, all of whom lived within a mile of her home. None of them had a clue as to her whereabouts. Her disappearance was not, to O'Reilly's knowledge, pursued beyond the few brief questions put to immediate family members and was regarded by most in the area as the not-too-surprising departure of a woman thoroughly fed up with living with a drunken, habitually unemployed, abusive husband.

Their cabin was only a mile or so off Route 9, and it was the last stop I was going to make on the way back to the island. It was easy enough to find – it was one of only three small dwellings on the road, and the only one with a rotted wooden dresser and remains of an ancient easy chair adorning the front lawn, and an old sneakbox propped up by the side. The place was in desperate need of repair, with a roof patched so many times over the years that little remained of its original materials. It stood out like a sore thumb here so near to town, but wouldn't have looked out of place a mile or so into the pines.

I knocked at the front door in the off chance that Greg was actually home. With his track record, I figured the odds were even: He was probably out of work and sleeping off the previous night's fog. There were cats everywhere, wandering about in packs too large to count. A few of them looked far less healthy than the rest, and one the others all avoided appeared to be dead. One of the cuter ones – a kitten, of course – did circle-eights in and out between my ankles as I knocked again and again, each time a little louder.

Much to my surprise, a pale, haggard-looking young woman answered the door, a grayed dishtowel crumpled in her hand. She stood there for a moment, motionless, wrapped in a threadbare pink bathrobe and who knows what else, looking me up and down; probably Greg's newest female friend and par for the course. I identified myself, and told her I was looking for Greg.

"Well, you might find it kinda difficult to believe, but he's actually working today," she said with a sniff, slowly wiping chapped, already-dry hands on the towel. Her nostrils looked as dry and raw as her hands.

"Oh," I said, and from all I had heard, I was surprised. "I wanted to talk to him about his wife Julie and if…"

"You're talkin' to her," she responded, cutting me off.

That caught me off guard, and I guess it showed.

"Oh, I see; you're another one of them who still thinks I'm missing. Well, I'm not. I'm back here – for better or for worse. I'm back here, all right." She didn't sound too thrilled.

"Do you mind my asking where…"

"Here we go," she said, cutting me off once again and sounding as though she'd been asked this question a hundred times before. "Greg's a … handful. Reached a point where I had to get away from him, so I went and stayed with my cousin Jeanne for a while. Down in West Creek." A cat fight broke out nearby in a fury of hissing and meows, and she instinctively threw the balled-up towel at them, punctuated with a yell.

"I was worried what he might do," she continued, "if he found me – he has an awful temper, you know, and the drinking don't help, 'specially now that it's legal and all – so I told her – told the rest of my family – to play dumb. They're good at that. They supported me; don't none of them care much for Greg." She was hugging herself to keep warm, and looked up at the gray sky. "Let's go inside. You want to go inside?"

I said I did, and followed her in. The cabin's interior was

surprisingly better than its exterior; while still shabby, it was neat, clean and significantly more inviting than one would imagine from the dreary exterior.

"Want some tea? I can fix it up pretty quick," she said.

"Tea'd be fine," I responded, though I yearned for something stronger. The hair of the dog that bit you, I thought to myself.

She wandered into the kitchen area, which was a scant dozen feet away. She continued to talk as she lit the fire beneath a kettle of water. "Who'd you say you were?" she queried as I sat on a sprung sofa.

I explained who I was, what I was trying to do and why I was trying to do it. She looked visibly saddened when I got to the part about Holly.

"Oh, that's so sad," she said, and sounded as though she meant it. "But that's not the case here," she quickly continued. "I just got fed up with Greg – his laziness, his drinking, his temper and, um, impulsiveness; you know. But running away didn't seem to change much. I got lonely pretty quick and Jeanne turned out to be even worse than Greg. Well, kind of, in her own way. So, I came back." She poured the boiling water into a cup, added a tea bag, and brought it over to me. She sat in a similarly sprung easy chair.

"Greg was actually kind of like a changed man, as much as he could change. He seemed happy to have me back, and has actually cleaned up his act somewhat. His newest job – he's working for Len Tatum here in town – he's actually managed to hold on to it for four weeks and two days now, today being his third. And he hasn't, um, hasn't hit me in almost as long," she added, looking to one side as she said it. Ah, love, I thought.

We talked for another ten minutes or so, and conversation drifted from Greg and her flight from him to more mundane topics. Actually, she did most of the talking; I was content just to listen and sip my tea. She seemed grateful just to have some company, and non-combative company, at that. Finally, during a momentary lull, I returned to the original topic.

"You think you made the right move?" I asked. "I mean, are you happy – or happier – now," I added when she gave me a puzzled look, "or do you feel like, maybe, you've chosen the lesser of two evils?"

She looked at me silently for several moments – looked me straight in the eye – and I realized that, up to this point, she'd looked most everywhere else but at me directly. "You offering to take me away from all this?" she asked slowly, tilting her head slightly at the shabby surroundings. "If you are, I'll be packed in a minute," she added, resigned to her situation. She knew I wasn't, and her comments seemed a combination of loneliness and desperation. I told her I was flattered, but, in a word, no.

The cats needed her.

It was early afternoon when I rumbled off the causeway bridge back onto the island. I felt better now, having thrown an egg salad sandwich and a couple of draughts into my stomach back in Manahawkin. North into Surf City, parked at the ocean end of Eleventh Street and wandered up through the dunes and onto the wind-swept beach. The seaside pavilion, built nearly forty years earlier by real estate developers hoping to lure prospective buyers to the area, sat vacant and lonely looking. I walked up to the second, open level, and took a seat on one of the anchored wooden benches facing the ocean. It was pleasant enough out now – the sun had broken through and the temperature had risen to the unseasonably high fifties – and there wasn't a soul to be seen. Sat there for close to an hour, sifting through the information I'd gathered over the last ten days.

There was a depressing similarity among the majority of the disappearances, a similarity that kept pulling me back to the events of the last three months here on the island. Too many women were packing up and taking off, or it sure seemed that way. Maybe this sort

420

of thing happened on a regular basis and people like me were just oblivious to it. Maybe only when a similar occurrence touched a family's lives did they actually become aware of the dozens of others in the same boat. Maybe, but I didn't think so. At least Julie Massey had turned up after the fact – alive, well and miserable.

I drove by the Beach Haven Free Public Library at Third and Beach later that afternoon and was surprised to find it open. I located November 1935 copies of *National Geographic* and *Saturday Evening Post*, and settled in a reproduction Windsor chair to leaf through them. When I found what I was looking for, I surreptitiously tore a few pages from each, quietly folded them and stuffed them into my coat pocket. It was okay to do so, I convinced myself – there weren't any articles on the backs of those pages. Or at least none of any interest.

Thursday, January 14, 1937. 1:13 p.m.

ABBEY O'HARA LOOKED stunned when she opened the door at *White Cedars*.

"Hi, Abbey. How are you?" I asked, and really meant it.

"Oh, goodness; come inside," she said, quickly grabbing my sleeve and ushering me through the front door. I looked back over my shoulder at the small adjacent home, to see if the middle-aged porch-sweeper was still watching me. She was and she had that "Who the hell is that?" look on her face. I waved to her from the doorway. She gave a tentative wave back.

I wanted to find out what was going on with Yumi's car – assuming that Hawley did indeed have it – and this was the obvious place to go to find out. Abbey was a bundle of nerves over the fact that I had returned, and told me so. The Hawleys, after all, didn't seem to care for me and would be furious to find that I'd been there during their absence. And they were absent, back in Philadelphia, but due to return early this evening; she and the groundskeeper were the only ones there at present. She was reluctant to talk, afraid she'd be caught and perhaps – God forbid – lose her job. She answered my questions with short one-and-two word answers – usually evasive answers – standing all the while with her back to me, staring out the window at the misting rain.

No, she hadn't heard anything about any of the disappearances on the island.

No, Mr. Hawley had not purchased the '36 Hudson Terraplane; I must be mistaken. Why would he possibly want an old, used car? He'd buy new, if he were going to buy. *I should know that.*

No, she'd never met an Oriental woman or man. Not recently, not *ever*. Never heard of Yumi Takarada, never heard of Yutaka Takarada, never heard of the nickname "Tak." They owned the car? So what?

She implored me to leave. The Hawleys could, after all, show up earlier than expected; it's happened before.

I asked her about the groundskeeper, told her I thought his name was Milton. She confirmed that and where I could find him. She motioned me to the window, pulled aside the curtain, and pointed to a small, white clapboard-covered cottage. It was neat and trim like all the other buildings on the property, surrounded by dormant rose bushes; smoke poured from its chimney. That was where he lived and if he had any sense when it rained, that's where he'd be. She seemed eager for me to move out and on, so that I'd become Milton's problem if the Hawleys returned earlier than expected.

"If you need to, call me," I reminded her, scribbling yet another note with my name and number. She looked at it a moment, pocketed it in her apron and thanked me; they were the softest words she'd spoken since I'd gotten there. And, I suppose, deep down she meant it.

Milton's cottage was a ten-second dash through the light falling rain. Reaching the overhang that afforded some shelter from the elements, I announced my presence using the polished brass knocker shaped like a three-masted schooner. Several moments passed, and it occurred to me that he might be deaf as well. The door opened as I was getting ready to head for the nearest window, having intended to wave my arms about like a madman in a last-ditch attempt to get his attention.

"Are you Milton?" I asked, speaking slowly and letting him see my lips. He looked me up and down, paused and nodded slowly as he stood aside to allow me entrance. He pointed to the small table with three chairs off to one side of the main room. I shed my wet coat, hung it over the back of a chair, and had a seat. He sat across from me and lit a cigarette. The place was warm and cozy; a big, inviting fire crackled in the small fireplace. The main room – and it was small – spanned the width of the building and had a tiny kitchen area at its right end. Beyond, offset at the rear of the cottage, was a small hallway with three doors; the left door would lead to a bedroom, the right door to a tiny bathroom, and the center door to a closet or, perhaps, the yard beyond.

Milton seemed aloof and disinterested in my presence. He was short, perhaps five and a half feet tall, stocky, appeared to be in his late fifties or early sixties. His head hung forward most of the time, chin almost touching chest and without much of a neck worth mentioning. He'd look at you from beneath his bushy eyebrows, his head maintaining this strange, broken-looking position. His gray hair was cut short, there were puffy bags under his eyes, his stomach strained at his work shirt, and his hands had the coloration of someone used to working in the dirt and sand. He reminded me of a mole dressed in work clothes.

I told him who I was and asked if he could understand me. After a pause that seemed like an eternity and convinced me that he couldn't, he surprised me by nodding the affirmative. It looked like an effort for him, though, and I could see that he was about as happy to have me there as he would have been to have a clogged toilet.

Well, it'd worked a lot of times before, so I dug into my inside coat pocket and pulled out a virgin bottle of Old Overholt. Milton's eyes brightened considerably as it hit the table and he was halfway to the cupboard when I suggested that he grab two glasses. He poured us each a healthy measure and a smile actually crossed his face when I told him he could keep the rest. The ice was broken.

I produced a pad and pencil and slid them over to him after verifying that he could write, and launched into my questioning. He nodded "No" when I asked if he had heard of any of the island's disappearances. When I ran through the list of names of those individuals for both this and the preceding year, he responded to the name "Ethel Richards" by writing on the pad: "Her husband killed her." Eileen Hunt's name also elicited a response: "Didn't she run away?" I filled him in on what little I knew, both the facts and the speculation, with emphasis on the former. At least Milton was more animated now, nodding to each of my statements, sometimes "Yes," sometimes "No," sometimes just a vague, non-committal nod and a shrug; but at least he was paying attention. He poured us both a second drink, his noticeably fuller than mine.

I abruptly switched the "conversation" to the Hudson Terraplane and the Takaradas. He looked at me suspiciously from behind his bushy white brows, and shook his head to indicate that he had no knowledge of either. Now, I wasn't at all convinced that I was getting the truth – from either Milton or Abbey – but there wasn't a whole lot I could do to get them to admit otherwise. Which was understandable: They'd known and worked for the Hawley's for years – perhaps decades. Abbey barely knew me, and Milton, well, he knew my rye better than me.

I spent another fifteen minutes asking all sorts of general questions about the Hawleys and Abbey without learning anything new. Milton reached for the pad during a lull and I watched a lethargic looking mouse amble across the room while Milton scribbled a note. He pushed it back to me. "I have to prepare for the Hawleys," it read. Milton rose from the table, walked purposefully to the front door, put on his coat and hat, then stood there staring at me – time to go. I took a moment to jot my name and number on a piece of paper, hesitated a moment, then added my full address; it's difficult to call someone when you're a mute.

I trudged back to my car. Curtains in both the Hawley's residence and Milton's cottage were pulled aside slightly, and I could feel the two pairs of eyes burning holes in my back as I climbed in. Yeah, I'm going. Pulling out of the long drive, I glanced over at the adjacent property and that same middle-aged woman was watching me again from her doorway; nothing seemed to get by her. I made a hard turn, pulled into the barren parking area beside her house, and trotted up to the front porch.

"Name's Lew Porter. You may have seen me visiting the Hawleys in the past," I said in as charming a manner as I could muster after dealing with Abbey and Milton, who had been about as responsive as tree stumps. "Nice house you have here," I added, giving the place the once-over; not a sure-fire comment, but it usually helps break down barriers.

"Well, yes I have, young man. And thank you; I try hard to keep it as presentable as possible," she responded, and continued to talk and talk, about anything and everything and nothing of consequence. At least she invited me in; I figured it would be a week before my coat would dry out. And anyone who calls me "young man" is okay in my book.

Again I promoted that I was working with the police – *which* police I was careful not to specify – and that seemed to grab her interest. Her name was Edna Williver, and she was pleasant enough, perhaps fifty, and a widow.

"As you well know," she said, reminding me of a spinster teacher I'd had back in Bordentown, "there aren't too many people – people or cars – this time of year. I try to keep an eye on *White Cedars* – that's what the Hawleys call that place – because I never know if someone's there or not. There was a break-in several years back that you may or may not have been aware of – winter of 1933 or '34, I believe it was. Nothing important was stolen, just some pillows and blankets and the like, of all things, but it dispelled the notion that there's *never* any crime here on the island. There is, and I could tell you stories that'd make your hair curl." Maybe not make my hair curl but probably put me to sleep. I nodded and smiled knowingly.

"There was a similar crime down in Beach Haven," she continued with a concerned look clouding her features, "a year or so ago. A former police officer – maybe you knew him? – and a drunk to boot, and he stole the same type of necessities from one of the big hotels down there when it was closed down offseason. The Baldwin, I think it was." I remembered, and it was. "I would imagine that the next time it happens there might be a reward, not that I'm interested in a reward, mind you. It's my civic duty and the Hawleys are good neighbors. They're rarely there, and with *White Cedars* across from me I never have to worry about some ugly little shack being built within view of my front porch." She had it all worked out.

I fired some questions at her regarding the disappearances and while I didn't learn anything new, at least she responded. She had heard of the Petersons, of course, and based on everything she'd heard about Howard – before and since – didn't blame Grace for taking off, not a whit. As for the Richards, she found the whole affair to be a frightful business and hoped they'd give George his comeuppance – I took that to mean *the chair*. And Schweickert's murder down in Beach Haven, followed closed by Miller's suicide, was beyond comment.

"What's happening to this island?" she queried. "We've had more death and misery here in the last year than I can remember during any similar period of time over the last forty-three years." I guess I'd aged her prematurely. "Actually, there were two suicides down there, weren't there?" she continued. "Three, if you count that Postmaster in Surf City. And the drowning, too – that was in Beach Haven, wasn't it? Though it's anybody's guess where that body came from; maybe a mainlander – a Piney, no doubt – with too much to drink in his boat. Why, just a year ago there was that poor fellow who got stuck in the mud off the banks of Sink Hole Creek and drowned – that's just a little south of the causeway, if you didn't know." She'd worked herself into a fit of despair by now, and sat staring at the floor, wringing her hands. Time to change the subject.

I produced the three pages torn from the *Saturday Evening Post* and *National Geographic*, flattened them out, and slid them over to her; they were all ads for the 1936 Hudson Terraplane. "Ever see this car? In dark blue?" I asked. She took the pages and picked through them, one by one.

"Oh, sure; every Wednesday. Pulls into *White Cedars* over there, around noon. The delivery drive." This caught me off guard.

"*White Cedars*? This car?" I repeated.

"Sure. Stays all afternoon, then leaves at the end of the day."

"Around what time?"

"Just before five. I'm always trying to tune in WOR about then, on the radio – they play music at five. Great show; I always listen to it while I make dinner, have a glass of sherry. Course if I can't get a signal I'll listen to Larry Cotton on WJZ."

"Did you ever see the driver?" I asked.

"Well, yes; it would be hard not to. A Chinese woman, I believe. A maid I suppose, or some sort of house help. Probably laundry." She shook her head in disbelief. "I can't imagine why anyone needs so much help running a house. Why, you should see just how many people they have working over there in the summertime. It's obscene, I tell you; like a small army."

"You said Chinese. Are you sure she's Oriental?"

"Well, I guess so; Chinese or Japanese or one of those places over there. Or, at least that's what she looked like to me, but I never really gave it any thought otherwise. It is far enough away that it's hard to tell. She has long, straight, black hair and all; that much I could tell. What is she? Mexican? Hawaiian? Something like that?" She was straining to visualize the driver.

"I think your gut reaction was pretty close," I said. "Did you ever see her do anything other than drive in and out again?"

"No, never. She just always drove the car down that drive – it's like a tunnel, it's so overgrown – and to the back of the house. And that's out of sight from here, hidden from view by the house and brush and what-have-you. I figured she had a job to do, and went right to it. Why? What's she done?" she asked with growing curiosity.

I told her that she hadn't done anything, that I was more interested in the car. She told me she hadn't seen the car in at least a couple of months, and had forgotten about it until I brought it up. We spent a few more minutes talking about the Hawleys and then I left in a flurry of thanks and promises that I'd stop back again some time.

This was an unexpected turn of events. The Hawleys evidently knew Yumi, either socially or on an employer-employee basis. But Yumi had told her husband she went to Toms River every Wednesday, to C & C Distributors. And one of the Hawleys may have bought her Hudson after her death, although everyone I'd spoken to over there had disavowed any knowledge of such a purchase.

I pulled into a dingy eatery – the Harbor View Diner – just south of Toms River on Route 9. There was an empty phone booth in the back by the restroom. It had been slow going in the rain, but it was just a few minutes after four, and I hoped like hell to catch someone at C & C before they closed. It was listed under the "C"s all right, but not quite where I expected to find it. I jotted down the number and address, and after getting some straight-forward directions from an overweight, gum-chewing waitress, headed back outside to my Ford; it was impossible to reach without stepping in at least two puddles.

"C & C International Importers and Distributors" read the small sign by the door. The building was an old three-story structure made of brick, and sat alone in a treeless area by some tracks in a seedier part of town. The door was open, so I went in. Just inside sat a dumpy old woman with smudged reading glasses. She was wedged uncomfortably in an armed chair behind an oak desk, working on what appeared to be the business's books. I told her I wanted to speak with the owner. She yanked herself free from the chair and waddled into the back, pulling her skirt into place as she passed from view. A minute later she returned to escort me down the same hall, which was tough going, more so for her than me. It was lined with dozens of opened and unopened crates, which reduced the walkable area to roughly two feet. This was lit by a single, dim light bulb, exposed and hanging overhead from a wire. She pointed to the half-open door near its end, and I could see and smell the smoke-filled office beyond. It, too, was crammed full of crates brimming over with excelsior and various unidentifiable odds and ends.

Charlie Corcoran was a short, trim, middle-aged man with thinning hair and the look of someone with more worries than you'd care to hear about. After some quick introductions, he went on to explain that he and his brother Eddie were the C & C, and they'd been in charge of the business since 1914. That was when they taken it over from their father and uncle, but the uncle had to come out of retirement and run it for the short period during the war when Charlie and Eddie worked for Uncle Sam.

I asked Charlie about Yumi and her weekly visits.

"Takarada? Yumi Takarada? Sure, I remember the name; who the hell could forget a moniker like that. But it was always catalogs sent – to Beach Haven, right? – and orders taken, by mail. Maybe a phone call or two, but never in-person visits. Who the hell'd want to visit a dump like this?" He let out a derisive snort. "There are some, of course," he added quickly. "Guy from Camden, another from Trenton; local guy from Toms River, but he doesn't count. And once a year two guys – not so 'sure' about them, if you get my meaning – from Philly. But never any women."

"Are you positive? Could someone else have dealt with her without your knowing?" I asked.

"We're talking women, right? Females? Opposite sex, with boobs and all that? Here? Yes, I'm sure. And I know my brother: any female ever sets foot in this place and I sure as hell would hear about it. Bullshit stories: them hot for him, getting into their pants, that kind of nonsense. Wouldn't matter if they were old or fat or crippled or whatever; he'd have a story. Nah; if there was a jane in here I sure as hell woulda heard about it. What is she? A chink? *That* woulda made a great story." He smiled to himself, no doubt fantasizing a *great* story at that very moment.

I left a few minutes later and made yet another dash to my car, hat pulled low over my eyes. So, now I knew where Yumi went every Wednesday afternoon for close to five months. Now that I knew where, the question was why?

The Surf Villa, located in Surf City at Fifteenth and the boulevard, was an unusual-looking place for the island. It looked more like a Spanish hacienda than a place to get dinner, have some drinks and, if the spirit moved you, do some dancing. A guy named Perry, formerly with the National Hotel in Manahawkin, took over the place a month earlier, and was in the midst of renovations. If you didn't mind the mess and the possibility of sawdust in your beer, you could still buy a drink and marvel at just how slowly some workmen work. It seemed as good a place as any to kill some time while deciding my next move.

Abbey either lied about the Hudson or was ignorant of its existence. The latter was entirely possible due to the fact that she rarely stepped out of the house and, when she did, didn't venture far. The car could be stored in any one of several outbuildings – and if she hadn't seen it brought in would be none the wiser. That is, of course, if the car was even on the Hawley property and not somewhere over on the mainland.

Milt was another story. Billy Ives had told us that the purchaser of Yumi's Hudson was a mute named Milton who'd paid three-fifty in cash for it. That pretty much singled out Milton the groundskeeper, 'cause he fit the description to a T, and would have access to that kind of cash if Chet Hawley – or, I suppose, one of the other Hawleys – gave it to him. Why would he lie about such a thing, though, unless there was a good reason to? Well, I guess he could have lied because he didn't know me from Adam – why the hell should he concern himself with the truth when dealing with a perfect stranger, and a nosy one at that? Because I gave him a fifth of booze, that's why. I wasn't convincing myself on this issue, but wasn't going to let a small matter like that get in my way. I wanted to verify for sure whether or not the car was there and, if it was there, what was so special about it.

Both Abbey and Milton had mentioned the Hawleys' scheduled arrival later today, but thinking back to my previous conversation with Chester, he'd told me that they always came down on *Friday* night. Why would they come down a night early? Especially in the dead of winter? Was it a smoke screen? Maybe it was just a convenient way to get rid of anyone they wanted out of the house and off the property. Well, I guess I'd find out.

It was pitch black out. The rain had settled down to a light drizzle now, but even if it were clear out it would have been just as dark, being only two nights past a new moon. I left the Ford in the drive of a vacant house a quarter mile south of *White Cedars*, and made my way up the road with the aid of my flashlight. The batteries were past their prime, so I made a mental note to replace them before I did anything else important requiring its use. Might as well be lighting matches.

I worked my way down the Hawleys' access road, shielded from view by the thick tangle of brush on either side. There was a turnoff to the right several hundred feet back, which emerged from the thicket and led to the back of the main house where there was a turnaround. I took stock of the property, flashlight now stuffed in my inside coat pocket. I was careful to stay far enough away from the two inhabited buildings so that the dim pools of light spilling from their windows wouldn't illuminate me.

In addition to the main house and Milton's small cottage just beyond, there were three additional cottages set off to one side – assumedly for guests – and a fourth, larger cottage towards the property's rear, bayside. This fourth cottage was, for the most part, obscured by wild growth. Only its roof, and a bright light mounted under its eaves, were visible; *The Nook*, if my hunch was right. Several other structures were scattered about the property as well. There was a sizable privy – dormant now – which was larger and, I dare say, in better shape than half the summer dwellings on the island. A rambling, barn-like structure sat off to one side towards the back, with several vehicle-sized sliding doors, as well as three or four randomly placed doors for entrance. And there were several other smaller buildings whose purpose was anyone's guess. I looked carefully at the main house's windows for any signs of life aside from Abbey, and if the Hawleys were there, I didn't see any signs of them. Inside or out.

I started with the tiny buildings.

The first was locked with a simple padlock. I slid the folded leather carrier from my outside pocket, chose the right pick, and had it open in under a half minute; I wasn't losing my touch, just slowing down. The inside was filled with wooden lawn furniture, carefully wrapped and stacked on the floor as well as hung from numerous hooks higher up on the four walls. Some nice stuff, but a bitch to paint.

The barn-like structure had locks on every one of its doors. I chose a smaller door located midway in the front, and hoped that it would afford access to the entire structure. Once inside, I pulled the flashlight. The four parking slots were empty except for the farthest one, which was occupied by a small, older truck, probably used by Milton or some of the other help they had during the summer season. It was clear now that the Hawleys weren't here – unless, of course, they arrived on foot, which was about as likely as my swimming to Atlantic City. There were several workbenches, a wide assortment of automotive tools mounted on hooks hanging above, and shelves stocked with cans of oil, antifreeze, auto wax; that sort of stuff.

The two adjacent rooms were not locked on the inside. The first was dedicated to the upkeep of the Hawleys' property, with a wide assortment of mowers, spreaders, trimmers, hand tools, fertilizer and the usual things rarely found on the island. The second, larger room was a wood-working shop, with heavy workbenches on two sides, piles of used and unused wood, a large wood-burning stove, and enough tools – both manual and power – to stock a Sears and Roebuck showroom. I spent a good half hour poking around this building, but nothing of any significance caught my attention. Nothing, that is, except a half-consumed bottle of Early Times that I found stashed in a drawer under some rags.

The privy, which stood off by itself a good seventy-five feet away, was unlocked. It had six separate entrances and compartments, each of which was empty and clean as a whistle. Its obsolescence was confirmed by the fact that the individual seat lids were all screwed shut. Pity the person in desperate need.

Each of the three cottages was similarly padlocked and just as easy to break into. They were roughly fifteen feet in width by twenty in depth, their insides identical. A small sheltered front porch led into a cozy living room the width of the place, with a fireplace to the left and a Murphy bed built into the opposing wall. Beyond this room was a modest bedroom with double bed and dresser, and a bathroom with the expected amenities. Outside, attached to the rear of each of the three, was a simple stall with a shower and small dressing area.

I returned to the access road and followed it back. The thick hedgerow on either side fell off as the road neared the bay, and the drive terminated in a large turnaround skirted by several more small buildings I hadn't spotted from my previous vantage point.

The first, which was unlocked, was a small, single room stacked high with several decades' worth of old newspapers and magazines. I could only guess as to the reason for keeping this stuff, but hoped that some young neighborhood kids never chose this place to experiment with smoking.

The second was yet another garage, this one more modest in size, with a single sliding door at its front, a walk-in door on its left side, and not a window to be found. Both of these doors were locked as well, so I went to work on the side door's lock and had it open in twenty seconds; I was getting better at this. Once inside, I flicked on the flashlight and was greeted with the most welcome sight I'd seen in ages: Yumi's Hudson Terraplane. It'd seen better days, though: The wheels had been removed and it was up on blocks, and the rest of the vehicle had the appearance of being partially dismantled. Its front seat had been removed and stood on end in a corner, leaning against the wall. The floor mats were stacked on an old, paint-splattered kitchen table shoved up against the side wall. A small shelf, above and off to one side, held a dusty lantern, which was half full of kerosene. I lit it to give the room some overall illumination, but continued to use the flashlight for the more shadowy, out-of-the-way places. Returning to the Hudson, I found both its doors, trunk, and hood to be open. The spare tire cover and the tire itself had been removed and rolled off to the side where it sat with the rest of the car's wheels and whitewall tires. I went through the large trunk fairly quickly – access was easy, and it had already been emptied of everything. Jack, lug wrench, flares, rags – all of these sat in a pile on one of the benches. I spent a fair amount of time in both the front seat area and behind it, peering and probing into every space I could think of with flashlight and fingers, but to no avail. The rocker panels had been removed, and the glove box was open and empty. Several wires hung limply from behind the dash, pulled loose from and never returned to their original resting places. The engine compartment was, for the most part, unmolested, but it appeared to my novice eyes as if some of the wires had been pulled aside. The dust on the two fenders had been wiped clean at their peaks as if someone's torso had rubbed on each, while jockeying for a better reach into the areas under the hood.

After a good forty minutes of this exercise in futility, I sat uncomfortably on the driver's-side running board with my back against the rear fender. Whoever was looking and whatever it was they were looking for, must have met with success, because this sorry sight had been thoroughly picked over.

What the hell was going on? Were Yumi and Chet having an affair? Or was she having an affair with Chester, the son? Chester was much younger than her, and, according to the nosy neighbor, Yumi's visits were always on Wednesday afternoons, the same day that Chester had said that his father returned to *White Cedars* to work in *The Nook*. Interesting work, it would seem, if you can find it.

Yumi was a weekly visitor for close to five months. She lied to her husband about the destination and purpose of her trips, and then she died a horrible death. Chet or Chester has Milton snap up the car at the sale, then bring it back to *White Cedars* and tear it apart. Looking for something? Evidence of some sort? Something that could implicate him in her murder? Or just to cover up their illicit relationship? But if he were looking for something, what was it and why would he think it was in her car? Tak's brother Inoshiro had mentioned that the Takarada house had been tossed soon after Tak's suicide, so perhaps this was the last place the intruder knew to look for whatever it was he was looking for. Well, whatever it was, if it *was* here in this car, it was found a long, long time ago. What the hell was going on?

And then I saw it, just as I was stood to leave. Sticking in the ignition was the car's key, and dangling from it at the end of a short piece of wire were two additional keys and a small inlaid wooden piece just like the one I'd seen back in Yumi's shop. I pulled them from the ignition and took them over to the lamp for closer inspection. Yumi's original set of keys. The three of them were crudely labeled "CAR," "F" and "B" in red nail polish; the latter two may have been for her home's front and back door locks. Remembering the key that Holly had given me back on Thanksgiving, I fished out my key chain and compared the key with the one labeled "F" – it was a match. I fiddled with the wooden slab for several seconds until I located the sliding panel. I opened it, revealing a brass key wedged inside. Was this it? Was this what all the searching had been for? It appeared to be a door key rather than an automobile or padlock key, but that didn't narrow it down too much. I turned it over in my fingers, and the initials "CH" were written on the reverse in a similar red polish.

I pocketed it, took one last look around the room before extinguishing the lantern and exited through the side door. I took a moment to relock the padlock, but was cut short by the unmistakable pressure of a gun shoved in the middle of my back. I put my hands up slowly – I didn't want to rile my captor – then turned even more slowly to face the consequences. A flashlight clicked on and shone directly in my face, momentarily blinding me. But then its beam was redirected first to the door behind me, then slowly down and up the length of my torso, ending up on the key held between my fingers. This guy was silhouetted by the house lights beyond, and I could tell that he was staring at the key. As my eyes adjusted, I recognized him as Milton. He stood there, unmoving, his double-barreled shotgun aimed at the middle of my chest. After several moments passed, he lit a wooden match with his free left hand and lit the cigarette wedged between his tight unsmiling lips. He looked again at the key in my hand, then to the garage beyond where he undoubtedly knew the Hudson was stored. He glanced to both sides and over his shoulder as if verifying that no one else was about, then back to me. With a long slow sigh of resignation, Milton indicated the cottage beyond – *The Nook* – with a slow tilt of his head. He lowered the shotgun and placed it under a crooked arm, pulled out his pocket watch and angled it so that he could read its time, then held it out before him. He tapped at its face with the nail of his forefinger, and held up five extended fingers for a few seconds until I got the message, loud and clear: I had five minutes only and they'd be best spent in *The Nook*. He turned and left as quietly as he had arrived. I stood there for a brief moment staring dumbly at his receding form. Christ, that was close. But why was Milt cutting me a break? I didn't have time to ponder it now, however. Having regained my composure, I turned and trotted briskly to the off-limits cottage lit solely by the outside light under the eaves.

I was going to pick this lock, too, but decided to try the new-found key; it was a match, and I was inside within seconds. I didn't have time to waste. I turned on the interior lights and began a quick search of the place. No one would be able to see *The Nook*'s lights from the main house even if the windows were uncovered – which they weren't – and Milton already knew I was there, so what the hell. I spent four quick minutes taking in the layout of the place, absorbing the furnishings adorning the room, and the assorted objects scattered about. According to Chester, no one entered this place except for his father. It was unremarkable, and looked not unlike so many other private offices or dens. The one potential difference, however, was the room beyond which was dominated by a large double bed, with a small bath off to one side. I quickly searched through the drawers of a small dresser. It seemed to be filled with various articles of Chet's clothing but, deep in the bottom drawer buried under a stack of folded shirts were several items of women's clothing – some undergarments and a flimsy nightgown. They could have been Mrs. Hawley's, but I doubted it; these never would have fit on the large woman whose photo I'd seen back in the main house months earlier. On Yumi, yeah, but not Mrs. Hawley.

I had to get out of there. Milton could change his mind at any time, and if he blew my head off here in the sanctity of *The Nook*, it would look to the entire world as if I'd broken into the place with burglary as a goal.

Which, I suppose, wasn't that far from the truth.

I killed the lights and locked the front door behind me, trotting silently over to and down the access road. I kept my eye on the main road ahead for any signs of the police, in case they'd been called. Finally made it back to my Ford and got the hell out of there.

I sat in a booth near the corner of the taproom, nursing a beer and trying to ignore Edwards. He was railing on to anyone who'd listen that King Edward VIII's recent abdication of the crown *proved* his theory that the King, now reduced to the lowly status of Duke of Windsor, had knocked up Bessie Wallis Simpson, and the two *had* to get married. During all this, I mulled over the evening's discoveries while staring at the key in my fingers. Chet Hawley, it appeared, had Milton purchase Yumi's Hudson and had torn it apart looking for – and unsuccessfully so – her key to *The Nook*. It seemed obvious that they had been having an illicit affair, and after Yumi's murder Chet had wanted to retrieve any possible links between her and him. It's anyone's guess just what was obtained – if anything – when her house had been ransacked, but the key to *The Nook* was still out there somewhere and Chet wanted it back. Her key ring was the obvious place and it was worth three hundred and fifty bucks to get it. The key wasn't where he expected to find it, however, even though it was right there under his nose. He tore apart the Hudson looking for it, but to no avail. It was, in his mind, the one loose end and one that he seemingly could do no more to eliminate.

"Got a minute?"

The voice jarred me from my reverie, and I looked up to find Purdy standing before me, rainwater dripping from the brim of his fedora. I told him to have a seat, but didn't bother to signal Willett for a round of drinks; I knew this wasn't a social call.

"Knowing what an active interest you have in all these unrelated disappearances and unfortunate *accidents*," he began slowly, stripping off his wet raincoat and draping it over the edge of a nearby chair, "I figured I'd bring you another piece of news. Hot off the press." He settled into the seat across from me.

"Yeah? What's that?" I asked. I wasn't sure I wanted to know.

"Well, there's another one, another runaway. This time up in Barnegat City. A young schoolteacher. Name's Emily Stackhouse. Funny thing is, she didn't have anyone to run away from." He jammed a Camel between his lips and put a match to it, then added,

"But maybe that's not news to you, eh Lew? Rumor has it you knew the woman. But what I don't know is just how well." His eyes met mine. "Well, did you?"

"Did I what?"

"Know her?"

"Yeah. Not well, but I knew her. Talked to her a couple of times."

"What about?"

"Things."

"What sort of things."

"You know; stuff."

"Stuff."

"Yeah; stuff."

"What kind of stuff?"

"You know, this and that." I was in no mood to talk to Purdy, and wasn't giving much thought to what I was saying. Emily. Now she was gone, too. I wasn't bringing anyone around me any luck.

Purdy stood there, staring at me and simmering, muscles working in his jaw.

"Mr. hot-shot detective," he said finally with a bitterness I'd never heard before. "You stupid son-of-a-bitch. Who the hell do you think you are? Come to our island, act like you know it all. You mighta been somethin' in Camden – yeah, I've heard all about that – but this isn't Camden."

"Give it a rest, Purdy," I said wearily, slowly rotating my glass between my fingers.

"Know it all, huh? Show us dumb backwater hicks how it's done, eh? You're so goddamned smart. Well, you don't know shit."

"You gonna make some sort of a point?"

"You think you're so clever, so sneaky, whoring around with half the woman on the island. You think I don't know that? You think that everyone who knows you doesn't know that? Did you really, truly think that *Holly* didn't know that? Well, I did, they did and whether you buy it or not, *Holly* did."

I didn't have a smart answer.

"And I'll tell you somethin' else, Mr. Conspiracy: If you weren't so wrapped up in yourself, your sneaking around, your jumping into bed with any willing snatch, maybe you would've paid a little more attention to your wife, to her needs. Maybe you would've noticed that what's good for the gander was also good for the goose!" He stopped abruptly.

"Tolinson," I muttered.

"I...I didn't say that, Lew," he stammered.

"Tolinson," I repeated. How could I have been so stupid, so oblivious to all the signs? Holly'd been having an affair, and with her former boyfriend of years gone by. Purdy was right for once: I was a stupid son of a bitch. And my own worst enemy. I let out a long sigh. "Maybe someday I'll learn," I muttered, more to myself than to Purdy.

Purdy just stared at me for a long while, not sure what to do or say next. I think he would have quietly backed out the door, given the chance.

"Well, at any rate, the Stackhouse woman is gone," he finally said quietly. "Let's just hope you'll be part of the *cure* and not turn out to be part of the *cause*," he continued, picking a piece of tobacco from his tongue. I wasn't too sure *which* I was at this point. "But that's not my jurisdiction. It's someone else's problem; got enough of my own, don't need to add in someone else's," he muttered.

He stared off into the distance, smoke circling about his head. "Used to be a quiet place," he continued. "A family place – take the kids to the beach, take a quick swim in the ocean."

I heard only half of what he said. *Tolinson.* God, what a fool I'd been.

"A family place," he continued. "Months and years'd go by, not much change from the previous. But now..." He stubbed his cigarette out in the ashtray. "Now the place's going straight to hell." He stood and grabbed his coat.

"Purdy," I said, and he paused and turned back to me. "I'm sorry – about Maude. You doing okay there?" I didn't know what else to say.

"Okay?" he repeated. "No; I'm not doing *okay* there. It isn't over yet. Oh, sure, she's dead and gone and buried in the ground, but it isn't over yet. *That's* the problem. Coroner declared it a suicide, but there's been some talk of murder – don't ask me by who; I don't know – and that guy Quinn from the State Police spent a good hour or so asking me some supposedly informal questions. Wasted the better part of an afternoon."

"What kind of questions?"

"Like, where was I when she shot herself? Told him I was downstairs, reading; the nurse – Mattie – had the night off, and I heard the shot. What could I do? I mean: What could I do?" He shook his head in sad acceptance of the way things were changing, on all levels. He waved a weary hand to me and turned to leave. "Keep out of trouble," he added over his shoulder, then vanished through the crowd.

Could Purdy have done it, I asked myself? Was he capable of doing it? He was, and could have, I decided. And, faced with a similar situation, so were a lot of other people. It's tough watching someone you love slowly deteriorate before your eyes, to suffer through months of prolonged misery and agony. Lots of people are capable of taking that irrevocable step, regardless of the potential consequences. But, given the laws, they'd be foolish not to try to cover it up, to make it look like death by natural causes or suicide, because to do otherwise was as good as killing yourself, or at least had the potential to be. Well, at least that's what I'd do.

And Emily. Poor, sweet Emily. The news of her disappearance was a shock all right, and I hoped that she *had* only gone away rather than whatever the alternative to that was. And *that* I didn't want to contemplate.

And then there was Tolinson.

Quinn phoned a little later to deliver the same news about Emily. He asked what I'd been up to, whether or not I had anything to tell him. I told him I didn't, but when I did he'd be the first to know. He verified that there'd been no other regional disappearances this season worth mentioning, and seemed surprised – perhaps annoyed – to hear that Julie Massey was alive, well enough, and accounted for; I had the distinct impression that some heads would soon roll at the Tuckerton Barracks for the sloppiness of the local investigation.

I reviewed my notes, and scratched Ethel Richards' and Julie Massey's names from the list.

Dorothy Silsby, minister's wife. Brigantine
September 27, 1935. Friday. (disappearance)
Lillian Van Pelt, single shopkeeper. Brigantine
October 26-ish, 1935. Saturday-ish. (murder)
Eileen Hunt, teenage girl. Barnegat City, LBI
October 28, 1935. Monday. (disappearance)
Virginia Leonard, single daughter. Brant Beach, LBI
January 24, 1936. Friday. (disappearance)
Elizabeth Perry, young mother. Seaside Park
February 22, 1936. Saturday. (disappearance)
Annie Ryan, bartender's wife. Seaside Heights
March 22, 1936. Sunday. (disappearance)
Fred Schweickert. Beach Haven, LBI
October 15, 1936. Thursday. (murder)
Grace Peterson. High Point, LBI
October 16, 1936. Friday. (disappearance)
Yumi Takarada. Beach Haven, LBI
November 14, 1936. Saturday. (murder)
Mary McCarthy. Holgate, LBI
November 14 or 15, 1936.
Saturday or Sunday. (disappearance)
Holly Porter. Beach Haven, LBI

December 13, 1936. Sunday. (disappearance)
Emily Stackhouse. Barnegat City, LBI
January 12, 1936. Tuesday. (disappearance)

Except for Schweickert, all of the people on the list were women. Of the twelve events, nine of them occurred on a weekend sometime between Friday and Sunday; nine out of eleven if you excluded Schweickert. This season, all were from the island and, with the exception of Schweickert, all were members of the Poets' Circle. Schweickert was the odd man out, so to speak. Last season, only two were from the island and none of them were known to be poets. Geographically, most of last season's events followed a south-to-north progression, with only the two island-based incidents a reversal: The first occurred in the more northerly town of Barnegat City, followed by the second in the more southerly Brant Beach. And November and December of 1935 were without incident – or, at least, without a reported or discovered incident.

And Yumi? What was she up to besides an affair with the elder Hawley and why was she killed? Was there any sort of connection between these dozen seemingly random incidents? And, if so, what was it? It might be a wild goose chase, I though, trying to make that connection, but deep down I felt there was a large, unique-shaped piece of the puzzle missing: the keystone, so to speak. And when I found it, everything would fall into place.

If I found it.

Friday, January 15, 1937. 9:52 a.m.

THERE WERE ONLY four families that lived year-'round anywhere near Emily's house in Barnegat City and I was lucky enough to find the lady of the house at each residence. One of them was doing the wash, two others were hanging their wash and the fourth was baking bread in her kitchen. Each of them was more than willing to talk, but none of them had anything remotely useful to say. And the baker actually seemed happy to see me, having spotted me before, she said, at Emily's.

Two of them were of the mind that Emily had simply grown bored with Barnegat City and decided to head elsewhere. By the far-off looks in their eyes as they spoke, I had the distinct feeling that they'd almost be tempted to do something similar, if not tied down with the responsibilities of family and household. The third had no opinion whatsoever, said she'd never given it a moment's thought – and who cared anyhow? The fourth, an older woman, who appeared to have the weight of the world resting on her stooped shoulders, commented that something was rotten with the whole affair. Emily was thoroughly devoted to the school and her students and the notion that she'd just picked up and taken off was unthinkable. So much for consensus.

The sky was clear and crisp, and the sun felt good in spite of the constant breeze. A gull drifted lazily overhead, hoping I'd be the source of a scrap of food. Huddled over, I managed to fire up a cigar and leaned against a pine tree to contemplate what little I'd just learned. Minutes passed as I stared at the exterior of Emily's home. Carried on the wind was the intermittent clacking of a nearby set of wind chimes, and their mournful sounds reminded me of the dancing bones from an old Disney cartoon I'd seen years earlier at the Colonial Theater. Or was it Mickey playing a skinny cow's ribs like a xylophone? Maybe it was the cow's teats? My mind was wandering.

"What can I do for you, stranger?" intruded the voice off to one side.

I looked over to see a stocky man, perhaps early to mid-thirties, dressed in dungarees, flannel shirt and heavy canvas jacket. He stood on the side steps, a wrench held in his left hand. I wandered over, hand extended, introduced myself and told him where I lived. He was Emily's brother, name of Joe Stackhouse. Lived over on the mainland in Waretown, a small little crossroads roughly eight miles north of Manahawkin, midway between Barnegat and Forked River. I went on to explain that while Emily and I were casual acquaintances, she and my wife Holly were pretty good friends, fellow poets. That brought a slight smile and chuckle, and I gathered that he thought no more of poetry than I did. I expressed my concern over reports of her disappearance and asked if he knew where – or how – she was. He didn't and he said it with a far-away look that revealed nothing.

"Figured I better close the place up until she returns," he added, then paused as he stared out at the treetops. "Don't want the pipes freezin' or nothin' like that."

"Where did the two of you grow up?" I asked.

"Waretown," he responded, lighting a cigarette. "Still live in the same place. Was just the two of us – and mommy and daddy, of course. Well, there were two others, but we never knew 'em; died soon after birth. A little boy and a little girl. Often wondered what it woulda been like had they made it, a brother for me and a sister for Emily. Oh, well; it worked out okay. Emily and me get along just fine." He puffed for several moments with a contemplative look engulfing his face.

"How'd she end up over here?" I asked.

"Oh, that. Daddy was a bayman and we both grew up close to

the water. Probably spent near as much time on it and in it as we did on dry land," he said with a small laugh. "Anyways, we'd come over here every so often, and somethin' about the place – Barnegat City, I mean – appealed to Emily; couldn't get the place out of her mind. Well, when she became a teacher, this was the place she wanted to be." He frowned for a moment. "Never could figure out just how she managed to get the job. It's not like they have a bunch of teacher jobs over here; she's the only one. Guess she was in the right place at the right time. Heh, that's somethin'. Never happens to me. Ever happen to you, Porter? In the right place at the right time?"

"Rarely," I said. "Very rarely. More often the wrong place at the wrong time."

Stackhouse let out an amused snort mixed with smoke, tossed the spent butt to the ground, and started to walk to the rear of the house. "Come on," he said with a beckoning gesture.

"Emily ever indicate any sort of unhappiness with life here on the island? Any disappointments? Anything else you can think of that might explain where she went?" I asked as I followed.

"Can't think of any. Pretty much of a homebody, Emily was. Waretown, then here; never showed no interest in anyplace else, least not that I can think of. And she loved them kids," he added as he removed the wooden cover to the crawl space and placed it to one side. He lowered himself to the ground, and scooted underneath like a crab with a mission. "Be back in a minute; stick around." His feet disappeared into the darkness. A minute or two of silence followed, interrupted only by the wind and the incessant clacking of the chimes. This came to an abrupt end with the sound of metal on metal. "Open the spigot, will ya?" came the voice from beneath. I did, and the pipe drained to a trickle then a drip. Stackhouse emerged soon after, and brushed the damp sand from his knees and lower arms. "Hate that job," he said, dismissively, and paused to consider the tasks remaining. "Guess that should do it, 'ceptin' the fridge." I tossed my cigar and followed him inside.

"Does she have any friends – childhood or otherwise – over there in Waretown that might know something?" I asked as he pulled various foodstuffs from the small refrigerator.

"Not too many. Betty Jamison's the best. They were inseparable all through school – joined at the hip, I used to tell 'em, like them Hilton twins I saw in that movie a few years back. You know, the circus one? Anyways, Betty's married to a worthless S.O.B. now, but likes him for some reason none of us'll ever figure out. Last name's *Skaren* now – Betty *Skaren*. Talked to her just yesterday; it was news to her, but she's got other things to worry about now."

"Any others?"

"Only 'Red' Ridgway. Real name's…hell, I don't know what her real name is; always called her Red, 'cause of her bright red hair. She and Emily, together, looked like sisters 'cause of their hair. Anyways, Red's married, too, with more kids than I can keep track of – must be a hundred of 'em. Talked to her too yesterday and she hasn't seen or talked to Emily in a couple o' years. Three or four letters, but nothin' in 'em worth mentionin'. Or so she said."

He placed the last of the refrigerator's contents into the box, shut the door and pulled the plug. "S'pose I should wash the damn thing out," he said, more to himself. "Aw, hell with it; she can do it when she comes back. Serve her right." He carried the box outside to the metal garbage can, and I followed.

"Just those two friends? No others?"

"Man, you sure ask a bunch of questions," shaking his head. "That's pretty much it, friend. There was one other – Clara Shlau – but she's dead. Died two years back, maybe three. And that's it. 'course she *knew* some other people, but we're talkin' friends here, right?" he said, wiping his hands on the blue handkerchief pulled from his back pants pocket. "I mean, Waretown's not big, not like some places."

"So where do you think she is? Emily, I mean," I asked, as delicately as I could.

Stackhouse paused and looked at the ground, pushing a small pile of sand around with the toe of his left shoe. "I don't know," he finally answered. "I...just don't know. But I hope to God that she's all right." He looked up and added, "She's my only living kin. Can't tell you just how much she means to me. I...I couldn't bear it if something happened to her." He quickly blew his nose, and returned the wadded rag to his back pocket. "But she's all right, I'm sure of it. Probably just up and took some time off, and forgot to mention it to anyone. You know women." Then he screwed up his face and looked at me. "What's your name again, Porter? Your first name?"

"Lew. Short for Lewis."

"But you're married, right? Hmmm. Must be another. Last time I talked to her – back in December, I think it was – she mentioned a fellow named Lew, or somethin' like *Lew*. Quite taken with him, so I recall. Didn't mention his last name, though. You might try findin' out who he is, 'cause he might know somethin'. Just a thought." He paused and looked out at her yard, while I stood there silently feeling like a heel. Stackhouse grumbled, "Goddamned chimes. Loud enough to wake up the dead...." He paused again, perhaps reflecting on his choice of words. "Well, got to lock up and head back home. Nice meetin' you," he said, offering his hand.

The chimes. Where had I heard the chimes before? Just here, or someplace else? There they were, a mere fifteen feet away, hanging unobstructed from a low branch on a red cedar tree. I wandered over for a better look. The chimes were attached to the branch with a four-inch loop of rough twine. Its top consisted of a triangular frame of five-inch twigs, each piece tied to the next with the same twine From the three corners hung three rows of oyster shells strung on twine roughly a foot-and-a-half in length. The breeze moved these lines of shells easily, bumping them into one another, producing the distinctive flat clacking sound I'd heard before. Somewhere. But where?

And then it came to me. I'd heard it before while wandering

around Mary McCarthy's property. The sound had come from far behind the house, out towards the bay – or at least that's the way I remembered it. And it wasn't the sound of metal chimes; rather the distinctive flat clacking of these strings of oyster shells dancing wildly before me, or something very similar. Was it my imagination? Maybe, but I didn't think so.

Forty-five minutes later, I stood in the center of McCarthy's back yard, listening intently for sounds emanating from any direction. A half hour later, when I'd just about convinced myself that I was mistaken, I heard it. Far off, bayside, and barely audible over the wind, but it was there; I was sure of it. I headed down the beaten path through brush and sand, pausing every so often to listen. The sound grew louder as I neared the bay.

I emerged from the tangle of brush to an area of eel grass roughly fifty feet wide bordering the bay. Another breeze produced another round of clacking sounds, and I quickly located the source. It was a set of oyster chimes, similar to the ones at Emily's, hanging a good six feet off the ground from the branch of a huge bayberry bush. Closer inspection revealed a design that differed only with a rusty can lid replacing the triangular frame of twigs; three holes punch in a triangular pattern secured the knotted ends of the twine holding the rows of shells.

Coincidence? Maybe. But maybe something more than that. Were there others? I didn't know, but I sure as hell intended to find out.

Peterson's house looked much as I remembered it, although someone had actually raked it since I was last there; very few twigs and dead leaves remained scattered about. The shades were still drawn on the bedroom windows, and I had visions of Howard, with his unconventional hours and heavy drinking, sound asleep inside. My gut told me he wasn't selling a lot of his artwork these days.

I saw Grace's friend Betty on her front porch, shaking out a dust mop, and she paused to wave. I waved back and continued my search. Which, ultimately, yielded nothing even remotely resembling a wind chime – a birdhouse and two bird feeders, but no wind chime. Discouraging.

There was no reason to check out Ethel Richards' house, so I headed back south to Beach Haven. I pulled up to the curb in front of the Takarada's Bay Avenue house and shop. This fronted the avenue, with only the concrete walk separating the two. There was a sign out front, fastened to the wall, which read "FOR SALE: HOME AND STOREFRONT" and had a local phone number listed below. I headed to the back down the narrow alley that separated their house from the adjacent building, and gave the tiny back yard and surrounding areas a thorough search. The place had been cleaned up, probably to make it more presentable to prospective buyers; Tak's brother Inoshiro would be my guess. There was nothing left here, assuming anything had ever been here.

I parked on Dock Road out in front of my house. I was going about the day's work in a rather half-assed fashion, winging it, but it couldn't be helped. Or so I told myself. I had nothing better to do anyway, except maybe run my business. That's what I had Willett for, however, and I felt confident that he could run it all by himself. Into the ground, perhaps, but he could run it.

Hoover crawled out from under the porch to greet me, sitting in the sand to watch and see what I was going to do next. I positioned myself midway between my house and the taproom, and then just stood there, listening. Five minutes and a handful of stiff breezes later, I decided there was nothing to hear worth mentioning. And Hoover's slow, methodical licking of himself was growing annoying.

I took a long, thorough look through the branches of the area's trees and bushes, behind the garage, under the eaves – any place I could think of where something could be hung, but to no avail. And anything that had been here should still be here: I knew I hadn't done anything outside that even remotely resembled yard work since October. I always leave that sort of stuff until spring – and even then sometimes conveniently forget about it. Holly never forgot, though.

As I walked the property and explored the reachable areas of the vacant lot next door, I had the depressing feeling that I was getting all worked up about nothing. Mary McCarthy and Emily had been acquaintances, after all, and perhaps they had both acquired a set of wind chimes of similar styles. But if they had, why would Mary have hung hers so far away, at bayside, almost out of earshot? Hoover ambled behind me all the while, marking each bush in his usual fashion, as if in an attempt to make my search more methodical. What would I do without him?

Schweickert's house sat vacant, the doors all locked, windows shuttered, pieces of plywood covering those without shutters; it appeared cold and lifeless. The porch furniture, garden hose, lawn chairs, clothespins – everything that had once been out and exposed – was gone. A large padlock secured the garage door. I peeked through a separation in the roughly boarded sides; the garage was stacked full and high with a wide assortment of items – many more than when I'd helped Schweickert's father with the carpets. Then I noticed that the lock was sitting loosely in place: Someone had pried the metal hasp and base loose from the wood, and then slid the loose screws back into the stripped holes when they were finished. From a few feet back it looked as secure as the day it was installed. I carefully removed the assembly, pulled the door open wide enough to permit entry, then squeezed in for a look around.

All the stuff that had once adorned the lawn had been hastily shoved into the interior, along with an assortment of boxes filled with pots, pans and other household items wrapped in newspaper. The carpets were rolled, tied with heavy twine, and stacked like logs off to one side, just where we had left them months earlier. Except one. It was untied and partially unrolled on the floor, and I recognized it as the oval-shaped hook rug that had witnessed Schweickert's murder. Surrounding it were dozens of spent cigarettes – dinchers, half of them – as well as a couple of pulp magazines, some funny papers, a couple of Tijuana Bibles and six empty Kreuger beer cans. *Keglined*, I thought, and impenetrable without one of those handy new metal gadgets to punch holes in the top to get to the good stuff inside. Evidently, some of Beach Haven's more industrious youths had appropriated the place as a clubhouse; I'd have to keep an eye out for them.

The carpet was a sad looking sight lying there trampled into the garage's dirt and sand floor, and precious little Daisy's stains were still quite prominent, if you looked for them. There were also several smaller dark brown stains that I hadn't noticed earlier near one of its edges, and I took them to be dried blood – Schweickert's blood. And all that was left of the poor guy.

I located the three lengths of discarded twine, rolled the carpet as best I could, retied it and maneuvered it atop the pile of boxes and various other odds and ends. If the little squirts returned and wanted a carpet back down on the floor, I hoped they'd reach for one of the more accessible ones. Working the unwieldy affair into a low spot between two lawn chairs, a shaft of low, late-afternoon sunlight cut across its surface and, as fate would have it, some of the larger stains on its surface. Something struck me immediately as not being quite right, and then it came to me: The stains we'd foolishly written off as left by Daisy did not, in fact, look even remotely like runny dog feces. There were little dried flakes of something in each of them, and I moved in for a closer inspection and – hesitatingly – a sniff: they were tobacco juice stains, with tiny little remnants of chewing tobacco clinging to them. Schoengarth's a bigger slob than I had realized, I thought to myself; as bad as Hoover, leaving his mark everywhere he went. I'd have to keep an eye on the boy next time he was in the taproom.

I left as I had entered, re-seating the worthless lock in its original position, assuring myself I'd return and replace the unit and lock when time permitted. I would have assigned the task to Willett, but I doubted he knew which end of a screwdriver to hold.

I walked the property listening for any sounds of a chime, but there were none. Some of the property's bushes had been yanked out or severely cut back, either by the cops looking for some additional evidence, or by a laborer trying to move his ladder closer to the house to board up the windows – maybe both. Daisy's empty doghouse sat off in a corner of the back yard, a bowl off to one side brimming over with dirty rainwater. Hoover sniffed the latter but refused to drink; toilet bowl water was more to his taste.

Discouraged after another fifteen minutes of wasted effort, I was ready to leave. Hoover was half hidden under a nearby bush, tail and back end exposed, snarling, tugging at something. I gave him a call, and he attempted to back out, but something clenched in his teeth was caught up on a branch. I reached over and held the bush aside, and a moment later he emerged, triumphant, a broken stick-and-twine tangle clamped firmly in his jowl, oyster shell-strung twine trailing from it. It was the remnants of a wind chime, a close match to the other two. This was definitely a three-biscuit night!

This renewed my interest in the lot between our homes, figuring that a similar chime could have been tossed in its midst and left to slowly disintegrate in the elements to its various component pieces. I waded into the thick of it, and did my best to poke around at the ground below the brush. My best was none too good, however; it was like a needle in a haystack. This didn't last too long, and eventually I straightened, stretching my aching back and still tender side. The sun was now low in the sky, and I knew that I had no more than another twenty minutes or so of usable daylight.

And then I saw it, or at least I thought I did. Lying on top of a smaller bayberry were several shells – and it suddenly dawned on me that anything tossed in this tangle would, more likely than not, get caught up on the upper surface and not work its way down to the ground. The shells turned out to be some random ones accidentally dropped by gulls, but there were other clusters that warranted checking. For naught, it seemed; one after another proved to be the discards of gulls. I worked my way from cluster to cluster towards the back of my property, the odds that I'd actually find something rapidly diminishing as I did so.

I finally found it a mere eight-to-ten feet in from my property line, several shells and twine caught up on the surface, the bulk of it hanging down out of view. This, too, was a close match, and gave me four of the damned things: one each at McCarthy's, Emily's, Schweickert's and, assumedly, my house – *Holly's* house. A chill went through me as I struggled to figure out just what it all meant and why they were there.

Willett sat behind the bar, absorbed in a copy of *American Detective Magazine*. I dropped one of the units – the one from Emily's – on the counter in front of him. He looked up at me, then down at the chime. Putting the magazine aside, he picked up the chime, considered it for a moment and blew lightly on it to hear the sound it made; some others at the far end of the bar glanced up briefly then returned to their muffled conversation.

"So?" he asked.

"Any idea what it is? Tell me about it. Anything. Consider this a test," I challenged him.

"It's a chime. A wind chime."

"Hoover could've told me that. What else? Ever see one like it before?"

"No, or at least not that I noticed. Or remember." He fingered the shells. "They're oyster shells, of course."

"Of course."

He looked up at me, annoyed. "Hey. What the hell do you expect from me? '*A bivalve mollusk of the edible species of the genus Ostrea*?'"

"Sorry," I said, but I wasn't; I only wanted him to return to English.

He returned to the chime. "The twine – it's rough. Doesn't look store bought; it looks manmade – crudely manmade – from some plant or something. I'm not sure."

Hearing that, the fellow at the far end of the bar looked up, and sauntered over for a closer look. "Mind?" he said, looking from me to Willett.

"Be my guest," I responded. Willett handed the chime to him. The front door slammed as the others left the building. I recognized him as a bayman named Jim something-or-other, but didn't really know him at all.

He took the chime in his left hand, felt the twine between finger and thumb of the right, and returned it to Willett.

"That there's handmade, all right. Or at least it sure looks handmade. My vote'd be the Pines, someone over there made it," he said, wandering back to his seat.

"Thanks," I said to his back, then returned to Willett. "Anything else, Sherlock?"

"Aw, come on, Lew. What else is there?" he asked. "Except the wood. White cedar, I think. This white cedar?" he called down to Jim, holding the chime aloft.

"Yup, think so" said Jim, draining his beer.

I told Willett to give him a beer on the house, which he did. When he returned, he continued. "White cedar. Or, if you'd prefer, *Chamaecparis Thyoides*," he added with a hint of sarcasm. "You don't find much of it here on the island anymore, if there even is any left. Used to be a lot of them here a hundred years ago. The Great Swamp – ever heard of it?" I nodded, but knew it only by name.

"See ya," said Jim as he headed out. Willett and I were alone now, which was unusual for this time of day.

"Used to be up where Surf City is now," he continued, "a big forest of white cedars, thousands of them, but a big nor'easter wiped them all out. There were a few stragglers, here and there, but I think they're all long gone now." He looked again at the chime. "At least that's what I think it is. Our friend concurs."

The door opened once again and in walked Tolinson. He hesitated when he saw that no one else was in the place, but it was too late to retreat. He asked for a beer and headed for his usual table. I followed.

"You know where she is?" I asked, settling in a chair across from him.

He froze mid-drink, returning the glass to the table and nervously licking the foam from his lips. "Who? Where who is?" he finally said.

"Cut the crap, Tolinson. You know who and I know who. *Holly*."

The color drained from his face and he began to fidget. "I...I don't...Why would I..."

"Christ," I muttered, shaking my head. "Relax, Tolinson; I know about it – about you and Holly. I'm not gonna do anything. I'm not happy about it, that's for sure, but I'm not gonna do anything." My fingertips drummed on the tabletop.

Tolinson wanted to be anywhere but there. "I ...I'm sorry, Lew. Really. I'm sorry. It just... it just kind of..."

"Yeah, yeah. Listen, I don't want to hear about it. Understand? I don't want to hear about it – not a damned thing. All I want to know is if you know where she is. Is she all right? That's all that matters. That's all that's important to me."

Some of the tension eased from his body as he realized I wasn't going to kill him on the spot. "No. I don't know where she is. I don't know what's happened to her." He wiped the condensation from the sides of his glass with the tip of his index finger; did the same to a trickle of sweat on his brow. "I wish I did. Wish I had the peace of mind."

We both did.

An hour later and settled in alone at my booth, I sipped a beer, sucked on an unlit cigar and pondered one of the chimes. What possible connection could these have with *anything*? Unfortunately, it was a year now since the earlier disappearances. If any of these things had been left at those locations, I doubted they'd still exist in any tangible form. Returned it to my side coat pocket, tipped my head back, closed my eyes, thought of Holly. Oh, how I missed her.

Hoover sauntered over and laid down at my feet with a thud. Within a minute he was snoring loudly.

Saturday, January 16, 1937. 11:15 a.m.

IN THE GRAY winter light, the Hawley residence looked more like a mausoleum. It was much colder today – the mid-thirties – the sun having decided to take a day off. The Ford's tank was near empty as I pulled up out front and I made a mental note to refill it when I was finished here.

Abbey answered the door, as usual, and looked startled to see me there again so soon, and this time on a weekend. Before I could get a word out, she'd given a hasty look over her shoulder then squeezed out the half-open door, pulling it mostly shut behind her.

"Go away," she exclaimed in a loud whisper. "They're all here today! *All* of them!"

"I hoped they would be," I said. "I'm here to see Chet – the old man," I added, just in case there was any confusion.

She stared at me for a moment as if I was crazy, then her shoulders sagged and she let out a deep sigh of resignation. "All right," she responded, reopening the door and leading me into the foyer. "Wait here a minute." She walked off, shaking her head in disbelief.

Four minutes later Chet entered the room, Abbey on his heels. He paused for a moment when he saw my unsmiling face, then turned to Abbey.

"That will be all, Abbey; I'll call if I need you," he said to her. She gave a perfunctory nod and quickly disappeared from sight. "What's this all about, Porter?" he asked, returning to me. He looked none too pleased to see me.

I told him we needed to talk, in private. He suggested that we take a walk on the grounds outside while we do so. He dug a coat out of a nearby closet, and led the way.

"You know, don't you?" he asked quietly once outside. I nodded yes. "I figured it was only a matter of time. I've taken a look at your background – had an acquaintance of mine in the detection business make some inquiries about you. Interesting story. We talked to an old timer at Hack and Hack – remember them? – and that fellow's comments about your innate abilities and dogged determination made me realize that my goose was cooked, that it was only a matter of time before you put the pieces together and figured things out."

"Sutton?"

"No. Byerly – Theo Byerly. I suppose I should have come to you first and opened up, but you weren't working in any sort of official capacity, and I wasn't sure – in fact, I'm not sure – just what your motives are."

"Why don't you tell me all about it," I said as we crossed the road heading towards the ocean. "About Yumi."

Chet took a deep breath, and exhaled slowly. "I'll give you basics, Porter. The more intimate parts are none of your business." Having dictated the parameters, he continued. "I'd accompanied my wife on one of her many shopping expeditions, this time down to Beach Haven; this was back in May of '36. We stopped in Yumi's store and while my wife was trying to decide just how best to spend my money, I met Yumi. I was immediately enchanted with her. Well, I went back again later – this time alone – and the two of us talked for hours. This was May, remember, and business was very slow. At any rate, there was something that clicked between the two of us almost immediately, and she was as interested in me as I was in her." He paused as we crested a dune. The vast, churning ocean lay before us, and there wasn't a soul to be seen. He looked up at the dozen or so gulls circling slowly above the beach, all looking for something to eat.

"Herring gulls," he said, looking at the large gray-backed birds with the black-tipped wings. "Except for that one," he said, pointing to the single larger gull. "That's a black-backed gull." He watched them for a minute or so, and continued without averting his eyes from their flight. "Gulls are fascinating creatures: powerful, independent, resourceful and highly adaptive; they're both killers *and* scavengers, and wait for the right – and safe – moment to secure their food. They eat whatever's available: fish – although they are incapable of diving – shellfish, worms – they'll follow plows to get at them more easily in the up-turned earth – insects, garbage, and carrion. They even prey on eggs and other gull chicks, if need be. But it's the carrion that's the easiest to get." He watched as two screeching gulls performed *threat* displays over a dead crab. "They make up the sub-family Larinae which, along with terns, who make up the sub-family Sterinae, comprise the family Laridae, order Charadriiformes. It's possible that some of those out there will outlive us, Porter, but there's no question that their species will outlive ours: they've been around for sixty million years." He smiled with admiration. "It's survival of the fittest; I could watch them for hours. In fact, I do just that sometimes."

I felt like I was back in elementary school, but at least this was one less thing to learn from Willett. "You were saying? About Yumi?"

"Oh, yes," he responded, brought back to earth. "She was lovely, not in a youthful way, but in a mature, middle-aged way, and she was as taken with me and the attention I was lavishing on her as I was with her beauty, charm and wit. One thing led to another, and after several more visits, evolved into a relationship – an affair, in the vernacular – sometime in June."

The posing ceased as the larger of the two gulls charged then flew off with the crab's remains dangling from his yellow bill; the loser looked disappointed.

"How'd you manage these assignations?" If he was going to use big words, I'd throw in a few of my own.

"At first, in Beach Haven. She'd come up with some excuse or another to leave the house and business for several hours, then I'd pick her up at a pre-determined location and we'd go off – at first to deserted stretches in the dunes, but that was too risky; later, back to *White Cedars*. This was a cumbersome process, to be sure, and in July Yumi convinced her husband that she needed an automobile for her business. She arranged it so that she'd be away, on business, every Wednesday afternoon; but, in actuality, came here. To me. We'd meet in my private cottage, which has a private road of sorts that's sheltered from the view of the main house and its occupants; I suppose you know that road well by now," he added, casting a glance my way. "Anyway, she could come and go without being seen by those I was most concerned about. I figured if anyone else saw her pull in the drive, they'd assume her to be one of the many help or delivery people that come and go from *White Cedars* on a regular basis."

"Weren't you concerned that one of the family members might stumble across her, coming or going, or *there*?" I asked. I would have been.

"Not really; *The Nook*'s off limits to everyone, but I had a story all made up, just in case: an interior decorator, Oriental motif, you know; I've developed a wonderful poker face over the years."

"How long did this go on?"

"Through the summer and into autumn. Her last visit here was on November 11, just three days before her disappearance." He paused and turned to me. "You have to believe me, Porter: I loved the woman. She brought joy and happiness and a feeling of youthfulness into my life. I worshipped her. And I had nothing whatsoever to do with her disappearance and subsequent death, nothing at all. I lived for each week's visit, and, had it continued, had she lived, I'm not certain what it would have evolved into. She was, after all, still very fond of her husband. Perhaps devoted would be a better choice of words. That seemed very clear, but remained unstated, as she would never speak about him to me – never once – about him or much of anything else regarding her private life. She was a poet and spoke mostly in generalities, of life and of the beauty in the world around us. She was an incredible woman, unlike any I've ever met before, or could ever imagine meeting in the future. You have to believe me: I had nothing to do with her death."

He paused for a moment, staring out at the sea. His eyes looked moist, but it could have been the wind.

"Any thoughts on who might have killed her? Or wanted her dead?" I asked.

"No. None at all." He turned his back to the sea. "Let's go back," he said. "It's cold up here." We headed back through the dunes in the direction of *White Cedars*.

"I feel a lot of remorse over her husband's suicide," he continued. "From everything I've heard, he killed himself in a fit of despondency over the disappearance of his wife, out of profound grief. And I understand that grief: I feel it myself over Yumi's death. It's funny, though; even though Yutaka killed himself, I feel, in a strange way, almost guilty. If he had discovered what was going on between Yumi and myself, what she was up to and just how she was exploiting his trust, he may very well have taken the same self-destructive steps that he did over her disappearance. And for that I feel ashamed. Can you understand that, Porter?"

Boy, could I.

"How did you connect me to her?" he asked, changing the subject back to me.

"There were only seven-hundred-and-thirty-four miles on her Terraplane's odometer when she disappeared and some quick math indicated she would have put on at least twice that amount making weekly trips up to Toms River. I figured her trips must have been more local, to either the northern part of the island or just over the causeway to Manahawkin or that general area. A visit to C & C, the distributor she supposedly visited, confirmed that she'd never ever been there in person – or if she had it was only once or twice and no one remembered."

"That's not much," he said.

"In one of our earlier conversations," I continued, "you referred to Yumi's husband Tak with the unfamiliar 'Yutaka', which I would have expected. But you referred to Yumi with the familiar 'Yuyu', which I *wouldn't* have expected; to my knowledge, Tak was the only other person who used that term of endearment."

"I remember that. I realized my mistake as soon as I made it, but there was no turning back at that point; I hoped it would go unnoticed." He shook his head, no doubt thinking to himself what a stupid slip-up that had been.

"And the tone of your second visit to my place a month ago was so different than the first that it sent up warning signals. You went from support to threats and that evolution seemed unlikely. And, I might add, and just for the record, I don't respond very well to threats. You expressed concern for your son, your family and your neighbors, but it seemed to me that you might really have a more personal stake in this than you were letting on to. That second visit, you'll recall, was only a week or so after Yumi's body was discovered, and that added a new layer to my informal investigations: disappearances are one thing, and may be totally innocent, but this was murder, plain and simple.

"Also, I have a witness – not anyone that works for you, by the way – who placed an Oriental woman here on a weekly basis at just those hours when Yumi should have been at C & C. Now, as you well know, there aren't too many Orientals in Ocean County, let alone Long Beach Island."

Chet crossed the road silently, staring at the dormant lawn ahead of him.

"The Takarada residence was professionally tossed after their deaths and clearly something specific was being searched for, since nothing of worth to the average burglar was taken. The quick, haggle-free purchase of Yumi's car got me to thinking – it had been stored offsite, and could have been overlooked in a thorough search of the house and grounds. A check on the purchaser of her car led me back here to your place, and in her car was the key to your cottage, which assumedly you gave her to let herself in, quickly and discreetly. Obviously, you looked but didn't find it."

Chet had stopped and was staring at me. "It was in there? You found it? In *there?*" I nodded yes, and he shook his head with disgust. Someone had screwed up.

"That would explain all that happened previously. The key was potential evidence to link her to you, and you wanted it back," I continued.

"Yes, you're right," he admitted, resuming his aimless walk. "I hired a couple of people, who shall remain nameless, to search the place – thoroughly. They came up empty handed, of course, after spending two solid nights there. Our relationship probably could have gone on forever without being discovered – at least by anyone who mattered – but who would have ever guessed that what happened would actually happen? Be that as it may, however, I swear to you that I'm guilty of nothing more than an illicit relationship…"

"And breaking and entering…" I interjected.

He waved that off as of no concern, and continued, "…and my concern has never been with any sort of implication with her murder. My concern has been solely with the impact that my ill-considered extra-marital activities would have on my marriage and my family. And nothing more."

"You didn't kill her?" I asked, bluntly.

"No. And you can check that, if you want. The night of her disappearance – Saturday, November 14 – I was with fifty or so others from early evening on. At a surprise testimonial dinner, given for me, over at the Mason's Lodge in Toms River. They presented me with a mantelpiece: a wooden ship with a barometer and clock set in its starboard side. We all went bowling – and drinking – afterwards. I ended up inebriated, not surprisingly, so I spent the night – along with my son, Chester, who was also an attendee – with a lawyer friend at his home in Toms River. Didn't return to the island until Sunday morning after breakfast. Ten o'clock, maybe. Edgar Shore's his name. The lawyer, that is; I can give you his number if you want to check up on it."

You didn't have her murdered?"

"No. I told you that. And why would I? What possible purpose could it serve?" he asked.

I couldn't think of a good reason, but that didn't mean anything; history is filled with murders committed for the most tenuous of reasons. Even so, I didn't really think Hawley was guilty of anything more than being an unfaithful husband and crummy father. And maybe being an S.O.B. in the business world, but that was a different issue altogether.

"Any thoughts? On who might have done it?" I asked.

"No, none. As I said, I knew very little of her life beyond our little get togethers." He thought for a moment. "Her husband, perhaps? Maybe he got wind of what was going on and murdered her in a fit of rage – then couldn't live with the guilt?"

It sounded vaguely plausible, but I thought back to Yumi's corpse: wrists and ankles bound in wire. She had drowned and I doubted very much whether Tak could have pulled off that sort of murder. It seemed more like the work of several people, not a lone individual. "Maybe, but I doubt it," was all I said in response.

"It's the only thought I had," he said quietly.

"Well, I'm going to do some further checking, but if what you say is true – and I have no reason to doubt that it is – you have nothing to worry about from me."

"What about my wife?" he asked.

"What about her?"

"If she were to find out about…"

"Listen, Hawley. I couldn't care less about your private life. What you do is your own business. My only interest is with the disappearances around here, my wife's included and foremost, and the handful of murders that have taken place. And I don't know whether there's a connection or not, but I aim to find out," I added, flatly.

"Then our concerns are the same. Look, Porter. I'd be interested in bankrolling your investigation – quietly, of course – to help you find and bring Yumi's murderer to justice – or, well, whatever. What do you think?" he asked. Suddenly, we were close to being on the same team, and I wasn't sure I liked that. But I liked money, and I'd rather spend his than mine; I'd been buying a lot of gasoline lately.

"Okay," I agreed, "but with the understanding that if I should find that you are involved... well, we'll deal with that issue if and when it arises."

I left with a check.

468

Sunday, January 17, 1937. 11:48 a.m.

"CHET HAWLEY?" THERE was a long hesitation. Quinn continued, slowly and evenly. "What's he have to do with anything?"

"It was a simple enough question, Bernie. Do you know who the guy is?" I asked once again.

"I know *of* him, like a lot of other people, but I don't know the man personally; we travel in different circles, if you hadn't noticed. Now, I asked you a simple enough question: What does he have to do with anything?"

Quinn was being evasive, and I had the feeling that he knew a lot more about Hawley than he was admitting. Maybe feeding him something would put him in a more generous frame of mind, so I spent the next few minutes telling him everything I'd learned about Chet's affair with Yumi. And Chet was, after all, paying for this phone call.

"I'm not terribly surprised," said Quinn when I had finished. "Hawley has an okay reputation with the press and his peers, but like anyone else with similar money, power and influence, he's been involved in some things that might raise some eyebrows and, as a result, sell a few less bowls of cereal."

"You could help me verify Hawley's innocence by having someone check up on his story about the testimonial dinner at the Mason's Lodge. And, while you're at it, have someone check up on Hawley's whereabouts on the nights of the other incidents, the various disappearances."

"That's a lot of checking, Lew. Why would I possibly want to put some of our resources at work just to help you out?"

"Well, look at it this way: You'd be helping Hawley out. And, if he truly is innocent of anything more than simply jumping in the sack with Yumi, wouldn't you just as soon establish that now and be armed with that information? Rather than after some enterprising reporter, or some over-eager investigative type stumbles across some information that ties him into this the way I did? And makes a public stink? As you said, Hawley's an influential guy…"

"And why make waves if there isn't a good reason to," he finished.

"Something like that."

"Protect his good name."

"Yeah, something like that. What do you know about the son, Chester?" I asked.

"I hear he's a spoiled brat – an arrogant, conceited little brat. But that's what money does to some people. Or so I've heard. Why?"

I filled him in on Chester's affair with the young maid Abbey and her subsequent abortion back in April of 1936.

"I knew I didn't like the little prick. Who performed the procedure?" he asked with a note of bitterness. Quinn's a Catholic and he took his religion seriously. Or, at least the parts he wanted to take seriously.

"Who knows?" I evaded. I didn't want him going after Kasabian just now, but planned to feed the quack to him later on. "But I thought you might want to hear this stuff up front instead of accidentally stumbling across it later on, at a potentially more embarrassing time for the Hawleys."

"And I appreciate it," he said, somewhat skeptically. "Why are you being so thoughtful, all of a sudden?"

"Because you asked me to, remember?"

"That and you want some favors," he pointed out.

"That's incidental," I said, unconvincingly. "And they are, in effect, favors to Hawley. If he's innocent, and there's no reason to drag him into this, let's establish it and move on."

There was a good half-minute's silent consideration before Quinn responded. "I'll get back to you," he finally said, then hung up the phone. I had the distinct impression that Quinn knew more about Hawley than his initial responses had suggested.

I wondered if he knew about Holly and Tolinson?

Wednesday, January 20, 1937. 3:26 p.m.

WILLETT WAS IN bed – yorking into a basin, if the last two days were any indication – trying to recuperate from whatever it was that hit him in the night early Monday morning. Which landed me back in the taproom, effectively covering for the guy hired to cover for me. If it lasted into the weekend I'd probably go up and shoot the kid, put him out of his misery.

Purdy entered, hung his heavy wool overcoat on an open hook, then wandered over and took a seat at the bar. He placed his hat on the seat next to him. The place was otherwise empty, the last of the lunch crowd long gone, and the first of the after-work crowd at least an hour away.

"Rye, Lew. Park and Tilford – if you still have it…"

"I do," I said, reaching for the bottle.

"Make it a double. Straight up." Purdy looked weary. He watched silently as I poured his drink, gave a hint of a smile, and took a long slow pull. A wave of warmth seemed to course through his body as he fingered the glass. Finally, after a second pull, he looked up from under half-closed lids. "You still snooping around?" he asked. "You have some sort of theory, or something? Just what the hell is going on? I mean, do you *really* and *truly* think there's anything to it?" He sounded exasperated.

I gave him a reasonably honest answer – one that skirted the details, of course – and reminded him that I had an active interest in it all, owing to Holly's disappearance. I just couldn't buy that it was all coincidental but, in truth, I'd like nothing more than establish that it was, that Holly was, indeed, down in Miami Beach, soaking up the sun, congratulating herself for finally making the split.

Purdy nodded. "Maybe you're right," he said. "Maybe there is something to it. I don't know. I just don't know. It's all just too *big* and confusing for a small town bull like me. I never had any training for this sort of thing. Never thought anything like this would ever happen. *If* something's even happened. It's just all too confusing." He paused long enough to take another drink. "Well, if you're right, if it is something more than just a cruel coincidence, good luck. Just let me know if you stumble onto something in my jurisdiction; don't make me look like a complete fool."

"Agreed," I said. It seemed like a reasonable request, but I hadn't agreed to just *when* I'd let him know.

I poured him another round, and he didn't resist it.

"How are you doing, Purdy?" I asked, switching gears. "The state cops still bothering you about Maude?"

"Oh, that guy Quinn," he said, shaking his head and holding his forehead as if holding back a massive migraine. "Yeah. On and off. They seem very skeptical. They want me over there – Tuckerton – tomorrow morning. Have some more questions they want to ask me." He massaged his temples as he spoke.

"They shouldn't be," I said, having made a quick decision I hoped I wouldn't regret. "After all, I was with you when it happened. Remember?"

Purdy looked up, confused, his brows furrowed. "What?"

"Think about it, Purdy," I cut him off. "I was there, that night, asking you all sorts of questions about the disappearances, about Miller, about all that stuff that we'd spoken about before. *Remember?* Then there was the shot, upstairs and we both ran up. Except I stayed in the hall, just like you told me to. You went in, then returned and sent me home. Told me you'd take care of it, and you'd let me know if you needed me as a witness. *Remember?* Then you called the authorities or doctor or whoever the hell it was you called. *Remember?* Well, here I am: your witness." I stared him in the eyes, and he stared back, studying me for a moment.

"What's your game, Porter?" he asked slowly.

"What are you talking about? There's no game. It's my story, and I'll stick with it if anybody asks me about it. It's the truth. *Remember?* And no one's around that can prove otherwise. *No one.*"

Purdy just stared at me.

"And if you don't – or didn't – remember any of this, well, I can only guess that the shock of the event put it out of your mind. Temporarily, of course. And you *were* in shock. *Remember?*" I reached to pour him another drink, but he covered his glass with a flattened hand. I withdrew the bottle.

Purdy stared for several minutes at the bar's surface, and finally broke the silence when he let out a long, deep sigh. He put his hat back on, drained the last drops of rye from his glass, got up, and slowly headed for the door. He didn't say a word.

Well, Porter, you're in it now.

476

Friday, January 22, 1937. 4:09 p.m.

THE TUCKERTON BARRACKS of the New Jersey State Police sat in a clearing off Route 9, roughly a mile north of the town of Tuckerton. It was comprised of two clapboard-sided buildings, the first a smaller structure facing the road, fronted by a covered porch running its width, the by-now-familiar logo of the New Jersey State Police emblazoned on a sign hanging from its eaves. The second was a larger, more utilitarian structure beyond, which I took to be the living quarters. Smoke poured from chimneys in both of the buildings and a heavy rain pelted the ground. The numerous puddles that had formed on the uneven packed sand lot were pocked with raindrop strikes. I parked as close as I could to the smaller building and managed to dash to the front porch without getting thoroughly soaked.

A trooper led me down a short hall to the second door on the right, knocked twice briskly on the closed door and yelled out my name in response to the muffled grunt from the other side. Another indecipherable grunt was the response, and the trooper told me to go on in.

"Thanks for coming, Lew," said Quinn from behind his desk, standing and extending his hand. The room was tiny and as cheerless as a storeroom, with a battered oak desk that dominated the room, a pair of armed oak chairs, a bookcase, a tall, four-drawer wooden filing cabinet, coat rack and air thick with cigarette smoke. I tried to pull out a chair but there was no place to pull it; I slid into it, knees brushing the desk front.

"Place is tiny," I said, looking around. Yellowed shades sealed us in.

"Yeah, well, there's rarely ever anyone in this building. Couple of troopers out on the road most of the day, and several more back in the barracks," he motioned over his shoulder with his thumb towards the large building beyond. "There's a guy up front during the daytime, but at night the place is empty – the telephone rings out in the barracks and the lightest sleeper answers it. This isn't Atlantic City or Toms River," he added, shoving his pack of Lucky Strikes over to me. "This is just a small stop in between." I returned the cigarettes to him and we both lit up. The cigarette burns along the desk's edges were too numerous to count.

"Guess you're looking forward to heading back home," I finally said. The place was dismal.

"I'm counting the days. Problem is it's kind of difficult to count the days when you don't have a date of completion. So, instead of counting down, I'm counting up," he explained. Made sense to me.

"So? What's up? Why am I here?" I asked. There were places I'd rather be.

"You asked me to look into the Hawleys. That's why," he answered, exhaling. My reaction signaled my interest, and he continued. "As we both suspected, both Chet and Chester's alibi for the night of Yumi's disappearance and murder – working on the assumption that she was murdered that same night – is air tight; everything checks as Chet had reported to you. And, to tie up any potential loose ends and resolve any lingering suspicions, we looked into Chet's whereabouts for each of the other dates." He paused as he opened a folder and referred to the typewritten sheets inside. "Schweickert was murdered on a Thursday night, October 1, while Chet was attending a board of directors meeting for United States Foods in Philadelphia, then back home afterwards. Grace Peterson disappeared the following night, Friday October 16, and Chet wasn't down here that weekend, either; he and his wife attended a wedding in Bryn Mawr – that's a few miles west of Philadelphia – on Saturday, but spent both Friday and Saturday nights in a local hotel. I've got the name in here somewhere," he mumbled as he fished through loose scraps of paper. "The William Penn Inn," he said triumphantly. "Imaginative, huh? Christ, everything around there's the William Penn *this* or the William Penn *that*. Anyway, we know about Ethel Richards. Yumi, too. Mary McCarthy? She disappeared, we think, on either the November 14 or 15, the day after Yumi's murder. We know where Chet was on the fourteenth, and he headed back to Philadelphia with his wife mid-afternoon on Sunday the fifteenth. By the way: have you ever seen his wife? *Whew*, not what you'd expect." He shook his head in disbelief. "And your wife, Holly; she disappeared late on Sunday December 13, and, once again, Chet had headed back to Philadelphia earlier that day. I keep saying Philadelphia, but they actually live in Bala Cynwyd, which is just a couple of miles west of the city – near Bryn Mawr."

"What about Chester," I asked, flicking an ash into a glass ashtray with "The Stacy Trent Hotel" printed on its bottom in red.

"What about him?" he responded. "I don't see how he could – or should – be tied to any of this other than the fact that he was sniffing around Grace Peterson – as if he were the only one. Chester took off for Florida – Key West, of all places – with a friend – *no*, not Grace Peterson – a male, guy name of *Caswell Kimberly*," he hesitated for a moment as a smile crossed his face. "Yes, Caswell Kimberly. They left the day after Thanksgiving, and he plans to stay down there until it starts to warm up back here. Has the place down there from November 15 to May 15. That's his usual routine, by the way: mid-November to mid-May. Been doing it every year since his late teens. Last year, he spent it in Spain and Portugal. Tell me, Lew, what the hell would you do in Spain and Portugal for six months? Watch bullfights? Well, it must be tough, living a life like that."

"*Caswell Kimberly*?" I repeated.

"So, at any rate, yes, he was here for Schweickert, Peterson and McCarthy, but so were a thousand other people on the island.

Thousand sound high to you, Lew? It does to me, but it's almost impossible to get an accurate count of the year-'rounders as opposed to the absentee homeowners. And the transients, for that matter, at the fisheries. Anyway, forget about him; he's just a spoiled, obnoxious rich kid, but that's all." He killed his cigarette, leaving its remains with those of its brethren.

"Okay, so we're at a dead-end with the Hawleys," I said. It's what I had fully expected, but it left us with nothing. Quinn was staring at me with an amused look. "What's with the look?" I asked. "Is there something else?"

"Doesn't this raise any questions in your mind, Lew?" He was playing games with me now, and I knew that I was missing something. Knew it, but not too proud to admit it.

"Okay, Quinn; spill. I'm not in the mood for guessing games."

He nodded his head slowly. "You're slipping in your old age, Lew; you've drawn a wrong conclusion."

Silence hung in the air between us as I furiously thought through everything he'd just told me, searching for any possible conflicts with that which I already knew. I didn't get very far. "Yeah?" I said, trying to act casual.

"A couple of pieces didn't fit together quite right, so I took a couple of troopers with me out to the Hawley residence. This was yesterday, when I knew that Abbey would be there and no one else of importance would. She panicked when she saw the uniforms and it was easy to intimidate some additional information out of her."

"What pieces didn't fit?" I asked.

"*Think about it, Lew.* The Hawley kid was in Europe November 1935 through May 1936, and she had an abortion when only a few months pregnant in April of 1936. He *couldn't* have been the father." He grabbed a tied brown paper file folder from the corner of the desk, opened it in front of him, and removed some typewritten documents. "One of the troopers knows shorthand," he added, touching the typewritten stack. "It turns out that the old man – Chet – is a bigger creep than either of us figured." He tossed the typewritten report over to me, and its lead sheet bore the title "Interview with Abbey O'Hara, Thursday, January 21, 1937, 11:06 a.m. to 12:34 p.m. Conducted at the residence of Chester Hawley, Jr., High Point, New Jersey." I scanned it as he continued. "*He* was the one who was screwing her on a regular basis, Lew, not his son. Every Wednesday, just like his latter routine with Yumi."

"Chet? The father?" I asked, failing to mask the surprise in my voice.

"One and the same. Abbey, in her youthful naïveté, was flattered by the attention and regarded the son of a bitch as the father figure she so missed. God only knows what *her* father was like, but I didn't get into that. This went on since she was fourteen. *Fourteen*. Can you believe that? And it lasted until soon after he got her pregnant and procured the illegal abortion for her." He paused as he fingered the framed photo of his kids sitting on his desk, and continued. "Soon after, his interest waning and his ardor dampened, he met Yumi and she soon replaced Abbey as the object of his attention and affection."

I sat there, speechless, a rotten taste in my mouth. Abbey had as much as told me herself, but I was too thick to pick up on it. "...*that relationship's all over now. All over.*"

"Well, like father, like son," he continued. "Chester saw her despondency and quickly jumped in, and she welcomed the new, youthful attention with open, lonely arms. Only Chester wasn't Chet, and while both of them are opportunists of the worse kind, at least Chet was gentle with her, and, at some level or other, there was an almost-caring relationship between them. Chester's another story altogether. He's rough with her and uses her solely for his sexual gratification, and I don't think he's ever said a kind word to her outside of the bedroom." Quinn tossed a pile of letters to me, and paused while I opened and skimmed through several of them. They were all passionate notes from Abbey to Chester, and were almost embarrassing to read both for their innocence and raw sexuality. "*Inside* the bedroom's a different story," Quinn continued. "That's where he flatters her and makes empty promises and so on, and she eats this stuff up. She's convinced that the guy's really all right, that she's going to bring him around some day and she'll become fairy princess to his dashing prince. Christ, how do these people convince themselves of such things? Anyway, she's counting the days until his return, like the bride to be on the morning of her wedding. I plan to have a talk with that boy when he returns, one that he'll remember. And respect." Bitterness crept into his voice. I handed the letters back to Quinn.

"The old man, eh?" I repeated, dumbly. "Christ, she's young enough to be his granddaughter." I sat there in silence thinking this all through. Quinn held me in his unwavering gaze.

"Disgusted, Lew? he asked.

I let out a snort and nodded.

"Well, it gets *worse*."

"Worse?"

"Yeah. Worse. We did some checking into Hawley's background, and came up with some stuff that isn't covered in his bios, all those *son-of-a-prominent-Boston-shipbuilder* stories. Do I have your attention? There're a lot of names and dates here."

"Fire away," I said.

"Okay. Chet's father, Chester Hawley Sr., was, indeed, born in Boston in 1855, and married a woman, eight years his junior, by the name of Abigail. This was in – let's see – 1879. Chet – our Chet – was born a year later, in 1880, and a daughter and second son born soon after both died in infancy. Chester Sr. died in 1890 when Chet was ten and off in a private school, and soon after Abigail met an older, well-to-do Austrian immigrant named Wilhelm Vollbrecht; they were married in late 1891. They moved shortly thereafter, for business reasons, to Camden, but she insisted that Chet continue his private education, and she had a lot of Hawley money to see that he did.

"Wilhelm and Abigail had a son together a year later named Wilhelm Jr., but everyone called him Willy – Willy Vollbrecht."

I sat forward in my chair. "Willy Vollbrecht? Brown-shirt Vollbrecht? Of Camp Bismarck?"

"One and the same," he responded, jamming another Lucky Strike between his lips.

"And he and Chet are *brothers*?" I wanted to make sure I heard him correctly.

"Half brothers. But except for briefly during the holidays, however, the two boys – twelve years apart in age – rarely saw each other. One can assume, I suppose, that there was some jealousy on the younger brother's part: Abigail continued to spend Hawley money on Chet's upbringing and education, but Wilhelm insisted on a more austere and disciplined upbringing for Willy."

"Twelve years is a big gap," I interjected. "You think Willy ever really looked at it as older and younger brother, at least back then when he was a kid?"

"I really don't know. What I *do* know is that Willy was a handful of trouble and when his father Wilhelm died in 1909, seventeen-year-old Willy took off, and mama didn't try to stop him. *That* kind of trouble."

"Where'd you dig all this stuff up?" I asked.

Quinn laughed as he lit his cigarette. "Believe it or not, old Abigail's still alive, living in an old, run-down Victorian in Camden, on Cooper Street between Second and Front, across from Johnson Park. Used to be a nice neighborhood – Camden's *Society Hill* – but that didn't last. House sits in the shadow of the RCA Victor plant now, but there are still a fair number of Irish in the neighborhood. It's just her, a maid and a cook, and she's living out her years on a stockpile of Hawley cash. She felt more at home surrounded by others of Irish descent and moved there during the war. She switched back to her maiden name when she did so, I assume due not only to anti-German sentiment, but to more readily fit in; she was, after all, Irish by birth."

"And you talked to her?"

"Yeah. And she sure does like to talk about the old days and the impressive success of her oldest child. Willy's departure must have been under rather unpleasant circumstances, but she wouldn't elaborate, and refused to speak any further of her younger son. 'He's no son of mine,' she kept saying. Anyway, Willy got into the bakery business as a teenager, while older half-brother Chet finished his education at Harvard and got into the cereal business. Now, Willy married some local woman named Elizabeth Krauss – not a *blue blood*, to be sure – and they have a daughter. The wife dies giving birth, but the baby is healthy enough. Willy struggles along for a few years, but he was rarely ever at home, spending most of his waking hours toiling alone in his little bakery. His landlady was largely responsible for the young girl's upbringing, perhaps even her survival. Her name – the landlady, that is – is Millie Packard, and she's alive and not so well, and almost as talkative as old Abigail is. Millie was the source of most of this latter information regarding Willy.

"Half brother Chet, by now worth a rapidly growing fortune and living in Philadelphia – make that Bala Cynwyd – helped Willy out time and again with cash gifts and who knows how else. Willy eventually remarried, this time to a reportedly brutal woman named Thea something or other. She's totally unaffectionate towards the young girl, and, in desperation, Willy searches out mother Abigail and turns care of the daughter over to her. With me so far?"

I nodded, staring at the unlit cigar in my fingers. I had the sickening feeling I knew where this was heading, but I wanted to hear it from Quinn, and in his words.

"Abigail gives the child her own last name, keeps her for a year or so, then ships her over to her other son Chet, who she felt could more adequately provide for the youth's needs and upbringing. Thea disappeared several years ago – some people think she returned to

Germany, while others think she ran off with a storekeeper named Kaplan who disappeared around the same time. No one's sure, and no one seems to care." Quinn got up and cracked one of the windows, filling the room with a rush of cool fresh air. "And Willy," he resumed, returning to his seat, "now alone and with far too much time on his hands, finds a growing fascination with the successes of Germany's National Socialist Party and Chancellor Hitler. When the English translation of *Mein Kampf* was released here in '33, it became Willy's bible. He got involved with The Friends of New Germany, which is now – as you know – the German American Bund, and was instrumental in building it up to the annoying mess that it is today."

"What did Chet make of this?" I asked.

"Chet, it seems, is always willing to help out with a gift of cash; he helped foot the bill for Camp Bismarck."

"How the hell did you find *that* out?"

"From my new friend, Ozias Stipple. He owns the land and we threw him in the slammer for a few days when he refused to answer our questions. He might be stubborn, but it seems the old boy has a weakness for drink – a couple of days of abstinence were more than he could bear. He admitted that he was leasing the land to Vollbrecht, who mentioned to Stipple at some point or other that he had a brother who was bankrolling the affair, and that money wasn't an issue. Vollbrecht, of course, only has one brother."

He paused again while this all sank in, the room filled with only the sound of heavy rain drumming on the roof.

"By the way," resumed Quinn after the pause, "did I mention that Vollbrecht's daughter's name was Abbey – short for Abigail – and that when she assumed her grandmother's maiden name became *Abbey O'Hara?*"

"Jesus Christ," I muttered as a chill ran up my spine. My fears were confirmed.

"That's right, Lew. Respectable old Chet Hawley is Abbey's *uncle*, and his shit-of-a-son Chester is her *cousin*."

"She knew this?" I asked, incredulously. "*Knows* this?"

"I haven't spoken with her since I pieced the lineage together – and I'm not sure that I want to. I don't know, to answer your question. But I believe she does."

"What are you going to do about it?" I asked. There was an edge to my voice. "Do you intend to do something about it?"

"No," replied Quinn. "Or at least I don't plan to at this point."

"And just why the hell not?"

"Calm down, Lew; sounds to me like you're a little closer to this – more involved, should we say – than I thought you were. We spoke with Kasabian at length – when were you planning to tell me about him? – and he, of course, denies everything. Tore his office apart and found absolutely nothing tying him to the Hawleys." Kasabian must have destroyed his records after my visit. "We can prove Abbey's relationship to the Hawleys, but as for the sex angle it would be her word against the two Hawley's – and that's if we could even get her to testify. She swore up and down that she'd deny everything if we ever tried to do anything about it. She was adamant about that. And, try to keep this in mind: She's not unhappy with their rather twisted relationship. But even if she changed her mind and push came to shove, who do you think people are going to believe: a common maid or the King of Cereal? The man has deep pockets, Lew, and the stuff in them buys a lot of legal power, if need be – not to mention leeway. By the way, you really did a number on Kasabian's ear, or at least I assume it was you; I haven't seen that maneuver since Hack and Hack, and it looked like your handiwork. He claimed a horse bit his ear."

Quinn's words were rolling off deaf ears; all I could think of was the Hawleys and a kid robbed of her youth. "Something needs to be done," I muttered to myself. "Somebody needs to do something."

"Well, that *someone* isn't going to be *you*, Lew. I don't want you steamrolling into the Hawley household and using your typical ham-fisted tactics to try to put an end to this. I'll talk to Chester when he returns from Florida and try to put the fear of the police into him, but I suspect that even if that works for the short term, it probably won't have much effect for the long."

"That's bullshit and you know it."

"Maybe so. But Chester's not thinking this through too clearly, not thinking of the possible ramifications; he's just acting on his primal urges. Maybe a strongly worded warning will have the desired effect and steer him in another direction."

"I don't buy it," I said flatly.

"She's a willing partner, Lew. Don't forget that. And *that* makes the task that much harder."

The wind shifted and the rain beating against the window was blowing in through the crack. Quinn slammed it shut. I shook my head again, looked up at Quinn, and repeated my mantra: "Somebody needs to do something. *Somebody.*"

Quinn, still standing, returned my look and shook his head. "Let it ride, Lew. Let us handle it."

Quinn's idea of handling it was worlds apart from mine. I let out a derisive snort.

"For the record, Lew, Where were you the night of January 5? This year? A Tuesday night? he asked offhandedly, switching gears. I had expected this at some point, but not now. I played dumb.

"I don't know; that was three weeks ago. Is it important?"

"Yes, Lew, it's important. Give it some thought."

"Got a calendar?" I asked. He pulled one from a nail on a nearby wall and laid it flat on the desk in front of me. I went through the motions of thinking back, day to day. "Oh, right; I was at Purdy's house," I said. "With Purdy," I added, looking back at Quinn and returning the calendar to him. "He must have told you that."

"He did. Recently."

"We were talking about Schweickert, Miller and the rest of them when we heard a shot. Sounded like a car backfiring, except it came from upstairs." Quinn remained motionless, staring at my eyes as I spoke, while I did my damnedest to keep from blinking. "We both ran upstairs – he went first, and I just instinctively followed – but when we got to the hall outside his bedroom door, he told me to wait there. Which I did. He went inside and I heard him let out a cry of anguish."

"What'd he say?" asked Quinn. His voice was as flat and cold as ice.

"I don't know. 'Oh, my God,' or 'Oh, my God, Maude,' or something like that. I wasn't taking notes."

"And?"

"I yelled in to him, asking if everything was all right, even though I had the sickening feeling it wasn't. He didn't answer immediately, but finally reemerged, as gray as a dirty sheet."

"What'd he say?" repeated Quinn. I didn't like sitting while he stood, so I got up, stretched, and lit my cigar. *Then* I answered.

"He stated what had happened: Maude had killed herself, with *his* pistol. He asked me to leave – nicely – said he could handle it from there, would contact the authorities, which I took to mean the coroner and the cops."

"Local or state?"

"Beats me. What's protocol?" I asked, feigning ignorance. "Anyway, he said he – they – would get in touch with me if they needed a statement or witness or whatever. I assume that wasn't necessary, 'cause no one's asked me about it since then. Until now."

"Do you have any witnesses, anyone who could place you there?" he asked.

"Purdy."

"You know what the hell I mean."

"That was three weeks ago. How the hell should I remember that? I see a jumble of people most every night at the taproom and one night tends to blur into the next. Ask me about last night and I might be able to tell you. Ask me about three weeks ago and it's not so easy."

Quinn asked a lot more questions and I responded as best that I could. I put the emphasis on my perspective, on things that only I would know and that Purdy couldn't contradict. After another ten minutes of this, Quinn finally settled back into his chair. He seemed skeptical of the story I'd just laid out for him, but was finished pursuing it. Or at least I thought he was. The question in my mind was had he bought it? There was no real reason for him not to, aside from the fact that Purdy had not initially mentioned my *presence*; although, evidently, he did finally take the ball and run with it. Purdy and I weren't good friends by any stretch of the imagination, so there's no single good reason why I'd lie for him. That is, of course, unless Quinn thought that Purdy had something on me, and was blackmailing me into lying for him. I'm not really the blackmailing type and Quinn knew that, but Quinn could possibly conjure up some sort of scenario where I was involved in Holly's disappearance, Purdy found out about it and was holding *that* over me. Unlikely, but stranger things have happened. I wasn't worried about it.

"Well, taken at face value," he finally said, scratching his cheek, "this closes the book on Maude Purdy's death. Not that the book was ever really open," he added. "You'd testify to this, if need be?"

"I'm a law-abiding citizen, aren't I?" I responded, not really answering his question. This time he let out the derisive snort and looked at his watch.

"Tea time," he said, reaching into a drawer and pulling out a bottle of Watkins Grove Rye. We were finished with business – for the day, at least.

Sunday, January 24, 1937. 2:12 a.m.

BOTH OF THE buildings were dark and quiet as death. I silently made my way to the porch of the smaller one and checked the door – to my surprise, it was unlocked. The door to Quinn's office was a different matter altogether and I spent a half minute playing with the lock, flashlight tucked under my left armpit, before it opened.

The shades were drawn, but it didn't matter much. The windows were out of view of the barracks behind us, and Quinn and his men would all be asleep at this late hour. I locked the door behind me, dropped the large canvas bag to the floor, angled the gooseneck desk lamp low to the desk, turned it on and stowed the flashlight. I found the file folder and documents I was looking for – he'd forgotten to lock his drawer – and spent some time leafing through them, setting the important ones aside and marking their locations in the stack that remained. Another ten minutes was spent setting up the tripod, the camera, and the lights. I measured the distance from the empty stretch of wall to the Graflex's focusing plane and took a reading with the Weston exposure meter; I'd been given very specific instructions to follow and had paid well for them. Now, it was in my hands not to screw up things. This was a little more exacting than pouring drinks; I took my time. When everything was ready and I'd checked and double checked my notes, I carefully tacked the first sheet to the wall without making any holes in it, held my breath, and released the shutter.

It was a few minutes before four a.m. when I left the building and silently made my way back to the road and my car that I'd left parked a quarter mile away. If Quinn could see me now.

Later on, around 6:30 – after an early breakfast at Spivey's on Bay Avenue consisting of a mess of corned beef hash, fried eggs, potatoes and coffee – I headed over to Louie's. Louie lived in an immaculate little cottage on Eighth facing the north side of the elementary school. As promised, he was up, and I returned everything to him along with instructions – and two twenties and a ten. Maybe he couldn't read, but he sure could identify numbers. He was the happiest I've seen him in years and told me to come back in twenty-four hours.

Monday, January 25, 1937. 1:26 p.m.

"HELLOOOOOO LEWIS," HE shouted, and broke into his familiar chuckle. Buzby ambled across the room and settled in at the bar.

"Hello there, Fred. The same?" I asked. I was behind the stick this afternoon.

"Yesiree," he responded, "like always." He looked over at Willett, who was propped up in a booth reading. "Gordon," he said, nodding. Gordon glanced up, smiled and gave a small wave with his free left hand. Buzby's attention returned to the glass in front of him. He licked his whiskered lips as he watched me pour the Watkins Grove and approached the brimming full glass with all the reverence usually afforded to a chalice of consecrated wine. While he was performing his ritual of consumption, I placed one of the wind chimes in front of him.

"Ever see one of these?" I asked.

He paused for a look. "No, can't say I has. From over my way, though."

"The Pines? How can you tell?"

"Well, just look at it. That there's white cedar, and this here – " he fingered the rough twine, "'tain't store bought, no sir. It's *devil's breath*, if I'm not mistaken; grows in the salt marshes. Has long, tough fibers inside that can be twisted into a twine like this. The Lenni Lenape used to use it years ago and ya still finds some people over there usin' it. Easier to go out and buy a ball o' twine, though," he added. He took another sip and after a long, satisfied sigh, Buzby dug into the canvas sack he'd dropped on the bar. "Almost fergot! Got somethin' for ya," he said with a chuckle. I expected no less.

He placed the small wooden carving on the bar, twisted it so that it faced me, and looked up with a smile. "Whadya think, Lewis? Whadaya think?"

I picked it up and surveyed it closely, then compared it to the carving I'd placed on the backbar a month earlier, the one I'd retrieved from Holly's bureau.

They matched.

"Where'd you get this?" I asked, examining it more closely.

"That? That's a *Leeds-Peeper*," exclaimed Buzby, scratching behind his ear.

"Explain," I said.

"Well, ya ever heard of the Leeds Devil? Ya must've."

"Tell me about it," I said. I'd heard stories of the Leeds Devil – the Jersey Devil to some – but I wanted to hear it from him.

"Well, there was a woman – long time ago, mind ya – lived in Leeds Point. That's down south a here, near Smithville – Higbeetown. Ya know where I'm talkin' about?" I nodded. I knew the area. Not much to know.

"Well, story has it she scorned a preacher man who was trying to convert her, save her soul. He didn't like that – you know how theys can be, all self-important like. Anyways, he tells her her thirteenth child's gonna be the child of Satan, and sure enough the kid comes along and's ugly as sin. Looks like a kangaroo with cloven hoofs, a big old goat head, a long tail like a snake and big wings made of leather – ugly little bastard. And ornery, too; he'd chew and tear at his mama's skin whiles nursing and finally went and killed his mama – his daddy, too; though it wasn't really his daddy – and ate them. And at four years old!" He paused and took another drink, then resumed. "Little monster sets out wanderin' through the Pines, tearin' out the throats o' pigs and horses and sheep and deer – you name it. Drank their blood, he did. And babies. He *loves* babies; eats 'em whole."

"*Loves*? Not *loved*?" I asked as I poured him a refill. I wanted him to keep talking.

"Well, now, don' think this is funny...but, people think he's still out there. Only comes at night, though, so's people hang up lanterns around their houses to scare him away; he don't like light. Been doin' it for years. Let me show ya," he said, extending a hand for the small wooden figurine. I handed it to him.

Buzby proceeded to demonstrate the carved wooden Leeds-Peeper to me. It was roughly five inches tall and a carved variation of the mythical creature he'd just described. "This one's fancier than most," he said, flicking the tip of one of its leather wings with his fingertip, then flicking the long, thin leather strip that represented its tail. He pinched its head between two fingers and twisted it around on an invisible joint. It unfastened from the torso and the torso separated into two halves, which came loose from a base consisting of the legs, buttocks and tail. Inside the hollowed-out halves of the torso was a trio of tiny carved wooden babies nestled in its stomach, and closer inspection showed them to have anguished looks of pain and misery. "People give 'em to their kids," he continued, "as playthings. Only they hold off showin' them the insides until the kids misbehave, then tell 'em this is what happens to bad little boys and girls!" Buzby let loose with a loud whoop of merriment, then polished off his glass.

"But where'd you get this one?" I asked. *Where did the one on the backbar come from?*

"Why, Jonah carves 'em. Sells 'em, too. I told you that, didn' I? Sells some of 'em here on the island, when he's got 'em. But they takes a while to make, so that's only sometimes." He dragged his sleeve across his mouth and took a long, slow look around the place. "When you gonna hang them?" he said, nodding at the clam rake and harpoon gathering dust in the corner by the kitchen and bathroom doors.

"Soon," I responded without much thought as I emerged from behind the bar. "It's on my list." I worked my way slowly across the room, empty glass and dishtowel in hand, and squeezed between the two empty tables for a look out the window. The shutter was half raised, so I had to stoop to see Jonah. He was out in the street leaning against the right front fender of Buzby's Model T, whittling.

"What other kinds of trinkets – doo-dads, I think you called them – does he make?" I asked, staring at the strange young man beyond.

"Jonah?" He responded, mouth half full of pretzels. "All sorts o' things. The Leeds Peepers, o' course, little carved wooden puzzles…"

"What sort?"

"Oh, you knows, balls in cages, linked chains, that sort o' thing. Noisemakers, too – he calls 'em 'music makers' – thems kind o' things." He shoved another pretzel in his mouth.

Jonah whittled, unaware that he was being observed. It was windy and extremely cold – the mid- to upper-twenties – but he seemed oblivious to the chill, hunched over in his canvas coat. Then, without warning, he leaned forward a few inches and let loose with a stream of brown chewing tobacco juice. It splattered on the road's graveled surface, and steam arose from the new little puddle.

"I'll be damned," I muttered to myself as it sunk into my thick skull. "I'll be goddamned!" My head swam and I steadied myself as visions of carved creatures and tobacco stains filled my head – little winged creatures in my wife's and Yumi's possession, and tobacco stains on both my carpet and Schweickert's.

"I'll be back in a minute," I said to Buzby, dropping the glass and towel on the nearest table. Buzby held up a pretzel by way of salute, and jammed it in his half-full mouth.

I stepped out front and walked over to Jonah, who was still working on the scrap of wood in his hands. My hands worked themselves into fists, but I paused, took a slow, deep breath and forced myself to calm down. I stepped in front of him and stood there for a moment, but if he noticed me he didn't let on.

"How are you?" I finally asked, forcing out civil words.

Jonah just shrugged without looking up.

"My name's Porter. Lew Porter." I wanted to pound his face. *To a pulp.*

"I know," he said around the lump of tobacco wedged in his cheek, and still not looking up. Even in the breeze I could still pick up traces of body odor.

"What's that?" nodding to the carving. "A Leeds-Peeper?" I took another deep breath and exhaled.

"Umm hmm," he uttered. It was worse than talking to a little kid.

"Sell many here on the island?"

"Some," he mumbled.

"What have you done with the women?" I asked, point blank.

Jonah's knife froze mid-whittle, but he didn't look up.

"The women. The ones that have disappeared. Where are they?" I pressed, this time with an edge to my voice.

Jonah stood there motionless for a spell, and slowly looked up at me. Our eyes met. He was silent and unmoving, but I could tell there was a lot of frantic activity going on behind the dull staring eyes.

"You're going..." I began.

Jonah lunged forward with a shriek and threw the weight of his body into mine. I tried to step back but my heel caught on the edge of the step, and I landed on my back half on the porch. My head hit with sufficient force to momentarily scramble my thoughts. I heard Jonah bellow, but by the time I'd pulled myself up he was a good fifty feet away, running wildly due east down Dock Road.

"Willett!" I yelled, but I'm not sure why. I set off after Jonah, passing the dropped carving that lay towards the side of the road.

He ran like a panicked crab, but it was all I could do to keep pace with him. Once past the abandoned railroad tracks, Jonah cut off to the right, heading southeast through the lumberyard, dodging between the tall stacks of wood randomly placed throughout the premises. He disappeared from view part way into the wooden maze, so I had to anticipate his course. Emerging from the yard onto

Centre Street a block south of Dock, I spotting him a quarter block away, still heading east, running towards the intersection with Bay Avenue and the town's only stoplight. The island's, for that matter.

"Goddamn it! Stop! I want to talk to you!" I shouted, running as fast as I could. I was out of shape and a cramp grew on my right side just below my ribcage. I took deep breaths and applied direct pressure with a knuckle in hopes of keeping it from growing worse.

Jonah ran through the shadow of the south side of the Colonial Theater, angling out of view in front of the looming structure. I reached Bay and looked northward. Jonah, a quarter block north, had paused – bent over, hands on thighs, gasping in deep breathes of air, his exhalations vaporized in a cloud before him. He was in as bad of shape as I was. He froze as he spotted me, and quickly darted between two parked autos and into the street.

That was a mistake.

The south-bound LaSalle took his legs out from under him and I saw his limp torso fly into the air, hit the sedan's roof and tumble off behind. The coal truck just behind bounced perceptibly as it rolled over his body, and the Dodge and the Hudson just behind the truck finished the job; but all I saw of it was a lone boot which spun through the air and landed on the sidewalk. There was a mounting screech of brakes and the truck rear-ended the LaSalle with a roar that sent the careening vehicle over the curb and into a street light pole. The Dodge and Hudson took turns rear-ending the vehicle before them, followed by a comparative silence punctuated only by the hiss of steam from several damaged radiators, and the wailing of the Dodge's stuck horn.

I made my way past the wreckage and found the remains of Jonah. The shapeless, raw, twisted mass was barely identifiable as a human form, a cloud of vapor forming above in the chill winter air. Blood oozed from everywhere. I approached the lifeless thing, its clothing torn and twisted throughout the raw flesh and meat. I was stunned, took a deep breath and choked back the taste of bile.

Within moments people began to emerge from several nearby buildings. The truck's driver emerged, took one look at his handiwork, then covered his eyes with his hands and leaned against a nearby vehicle for support. There was a lone scream, soon followed by a chorus of others as more and more people arrived to witness the carnage. I couldn't see the LaSalle, but several people were attending to the driver of the Dodge, and the driver of the Hudson sat sideways on the edge of his seat, feet planted on the pavement, sobbing into a bloodied handkerchief. A barber, comb and scissors still clutched in his hands, stood to one side mumbling something indecipherable in Italian. He crossed himself.

I sent one of the more composed arrivals back into his shop to call the cops and knelt by the mess in the road. I'd never know, now – at least not from Jonah.

I lost track of time, but found Buzby standing beside me after a while. He moaned softly to himself as he looked down at the sodden mass.

"Well, I'll be… What happened to him? It is a him, isn't it?" he finally said.

"Jonah," I said. "It's Jonah. Or at least what's left of him."

"Well, I'll be," he repeated. "What spooked him? What's he doin' here?"

"I…don't know," I lied.

"Well, seems to me you should. You chased him here, didn' ya?"

A dog wandered in through the crowd, sniffed the puddle of Jonah's blood, and began to lap it up. Buzby kicked him in the flank, and the insulted creature took off with a whimper.

"He ran. I just followed," I said, standing.

"Oh," he said simply, as if that explained everything, but the look he gave me suggested he suspected otherwise. Given the horrific nature of Jonah's death, though, Buzby seemed surprisingly calm.

Doc Havens pushed his way through the crowd. He paled when he saw the heap on the road, and yelled out to anyone who'd listen to call an ambulance. Several gulls circled impatiently in the sky above us.

"His kin – the Leeks, was it? The cops will need to inform them. Who should they contact?" I asked as I led him back to the sidewalk.

"They been called?"

"The cops?" I asked. He nodded. "Yeah. Few minutes ago."

Buzby scratched his chin. "Well, there's his daddy, Leviticus; he's an ornery old so and so, a real hermit – a re-cluse. Then there's his simple-minded older brother – oldest, I guess – June. For Junior, I think. Then a pair of twins, I think; don' know their names. Seems to me a couple more died over the years. Don' know if there's any others, 'cause they ain't sociable like most folk out there."

The siren of the town's ambulance grew from off in the distance as the crowd swelled. It seemed that most everyone in Beach Haven was here, people I'd never seen before.

"I guess Leviticus is the one to contact," I said as I mentally filed Buzby's information.

"Then there's the girls – ha! – real ugly girls; look like ugly guys." A look of distaste crossed his face. "You know kinda where they lives, right? Up beyond that old sand road you was askin' about?" I nodded this time. "But ya better tell the po-lice to be careful. Tell 'em to announce loudly that they're there – and why – and who they are. Can't be too careful with the Leeks." He looked around and rubbed his upper arms. "Cold out here," he added, changing the subject, and warily eyeing the circling gulls above.

"Yeah. I'll pass the stuff about the Leeks on to Purdy – to the cops," I said, "so they'll know who to notify, and what to do – with the remains. Thanks."

It *was* cold out, and the sweat I'd worked up minutes before sent a chill through me. The town's faded black police car slid to a noisy stop on bald tires. Purdy and Hipple got out from opposite sides. Purdy's eyes locked on mine, and he walked straight through the crowd to me.

"What's going on, Porter? What do you know about it?" he asked, and then he spotted Jonah's remains. "Jesus in heaven," he muttered. "What the hell happened to – to – *that?*" Purdy yanked a handkerchief from his rear pants pocket and wiped the sweat that had suddenly appeared from his face. "That's worse than – than Schweickert. Maybe even the Takarada woman." He quickly glanced around to make sure no one heard his utterances, and looked back at me. "Well?"

I gave him an abridged recounting of what had transpired, omitting the chase and beginning with Jonah stepping out into traffic. I introduced him to Buzby, who said nothing that contradicted with my story. Or, for that matter, added to it. Purdy just stood and stared at the mess, shaking his head and I noticed that the large pool of blood was already starting to skim over in the freezing cold. Someone had inadvertently stepped in it, dark crimson shoe prints dotting the area to one side. I'd had my fill, and I announced to both Buzby and Purdy that I'd be back in the taproom if anyone needed me for anything. Purdy said he was going to wait around for the basket.

I headed back down Centre, leaving Buzby behind staring at his former helper. I silently cursed myself for spooking Jonah into running. Now, the one person who had the answer to at least some of what had been going on was dead, and the answers died with him. Or, at least I thought he had the answers.

What did I actually have? Both Yumi and Holly had copies of Jonah's so-called Leeds-Peepers and there was dried tobacco juice spittle on both Schweickert's and my own living room carpet. Oyster shell wind chimes were found at both Schweickert's and my property, as well as at McCarthy's and Emily's. But what did that prove, if anything? Jonah *could* have just sold the damned little carvings to the two of them, and the tobacco stains *could* have originated with Schoengarth, as I had previously assumed. And the wind chimes? They could have been a coincidence. Three of the four individuals were fairly good friends – knew each other from the Poets' Circle –

and might have seen and liked the original purchaser's chimes so much that each ran out and bought one for themselves. It could have happened that way, but I didn't think so: Jonah was just too threatened by my questions to not be involved somehow or other. Or so it seemed.

And if he was involved, odds were he hadn't acted alone. Whomever murdered Schweickert had to have had an accomplice; there were just too many wounds of varying sorts for one person to have inflicted, or at least that was a reasonable assumption. And Yumi? It would have been a real struggle to have dealt with her alone, but it was possible.

I just couldn't put it all together, no matter how hard I tried. Yumi's body was found bayside, as was the Van Pelt woman's corpse a year earlier down in Brigantine. Holly's disappearance occurred at a time when the bridge to the mainland was unusable and the only way off the island was by boat. If Jonah was involved, had he come over to the island by boat? If he had, it was consistent with at least some of what I knew.

How many of the crimes and disappearances were related? I still had no real proof that the rash of disappearances was anything more than what they appeared to be: willful abandonment and desertion. I had no real proof; but somehow I knew it to be. And if they were abductions, what became of the victims? Where were they? Were they even still alive? And was there any connection whatsoever to the trio of violent murders I knew of? The elusive puzzle piece was still missing, but I knew I'd find it sooner or later.

I just hoped that Jonah's accidental death wouldn't put any of the missing women at further risk. Or, for that matter, my involvement in his death, should details of the events become common knowledge.

I stared at my pile of notes, my hand wrapped around a half-empty glass of Garden State Ale. I was tired – bone weary – and wanted nothing more than to fall into bed and sleep for a couple of days. I'd only gotten a few hours sleep Saturday night, and none at all

Sunday night, which I'd spent sneaking around in the dark over at the Tuckerton barracks. And the beer wasn't helping now. I only needed to hold out a couple of more hours, at which point I could collapse into bed with a reasonably clear conscience. A handful of patrons were clustered by the bar, talking and laughing about the usual inanities, but they were just a distant buzz in the background.

I tried to focus on the summarized list of incidences. Last season (and I was loosely defining "season" as the offseason from September through the following March): one incident in September; two in October (one of them a murder); none in November or December; and one each in January, February, and March. This season: two in October (one of them a murder), two in November (again, one a murder), one in December and one in January. All were females with the exception of Schweickert, who was found dressed as a female; could he have been mistaken for a woman, then killed when the deception was discovered? I refilled my glass at the bar and lit up a De Nobili. I knuckled my burning eyes, but it didn't help. Stood, stretched, wandered aimlessly around the room.

Those damned wind chimes were found at four of the six incident sites from this season, twice hanging and functional, and the other times somewhere on the premises or adjacent property. In each month with two incidents, one of them was a murder – and it was always the first of the two, followed a day or two after by the second. Was this significant, or just an unhappy coincidence?

"Lewis," yelled Buzby from the doorway. "Outside. Wanna talk to ya."

I stubbed my cigar and followed him out. The fresh air would be welcome, if only briefly.

"What's up, Buzby?" I asked. Buzby stopped and turned, facing me.

"What's goin' on, Lewis? Somethin's up, I can smell it. Was Jonah involved in somethin'?"

I shoved my hands in my pockets and looked over at the sun

disappearing behind a dark bank of clouds.

"If he was," he continued, "ya gotta tell me, 'cause where I come from, we like to take care of any problems ourselves. Yes, sir; we take care of any problems ourselves. No *po*-lice. No outsiders buttin' in. We keep our own house clean. Yes, sir; we keep our house clean, all right."

Silence hung in the air between us. Finally, I answered, "I don't know." It was evasive, but true.

"This have anythin' t' do with all them women? Ones disappeared?" His question caught me off guard, but I tried not to show it.

"I don't know."

"Hmmph. Like hell ya don't!" he snorted as he climbed into the cab of his truck. "Like hell."

I stepped to the open passenger door to close it and Buzby looked at me sadly, shaking his head. "S'pose ya got a good reason, fer not talkin' an' all. S'pose ya do," he repeated.

I pulled my handkerchief and wiped my nose, and at that moment spotted the small canvas bag, sealed with rough twine, on the floor tucked beside the passenger's side of the seat – Jonah's side. And out of Buzby's view. Buzby fished a small bag of tobacco out from under his seat and proceeded to roll a cigarette. I hooked a crooked finger through a loop in the twine, slid the canvas bag out of the truck and lowered it to the ground. Its heaviness surprised me, but I managed the task without Buzby noticing. There was the faint clink of glass on glass as it settled on the ground.

"Think I'll do some pokin' 'round," he said around a smoking cigarette. "Ya got anythin' else to tell me, ya knows where I live. See ya 'round," he concluded as he put the truck in gear. I shoved the passenger door shut as the truck moved forward, and stood there until it rounded the corner and disappeared on Bay. Then I reached over and grabbed the bag. It was heavy and filthy.

Inside the storeroom, with the door closed behind me, I dumped the bag's contents on top of a stack of crates. I separated the various items and took stock. Some wooden matches in a small jar with a screw-on lid; an onion; a small, clear glass pint liquor bottle half filled with some cloudy brown contents; a folded piece of paper; a hand-sharpened pencil with "W.F. Quincy, Insurance, Barnegat, New Jersey" printed in red on its white surface; a chunk of wood roughly five inches square; a thin, ragged piece of old brown leather; another small jar with a pile of tiny tacks in it; a completed Leeds-Peeper; a small chunk of bog iron the size of a candy bar; a half-whittled piece of wood in the rough form of two balls in a cage; and a rusty one-and-a-half-inch nail. Last of all, there was a stick, twine and oyster shell wind chime, just like the ones found at the several sites.

So, Jonah was the source of the chimes, as well. I unfolded the piece of paper. On it were written the words: "BAKING SODA." It meant nothing to me. As I tossed it back on the crate, I noticed some printing on its reverse side. Picked it up again and read the back: "CATHRINE COPPERWAITE-138 CORAL STREET." Catharine Copperthwaite. I thought back to the bitter, wheelchair-bound woman I'd spoken with weeks before. Another one of the Poets' Circle members, and one of the few still around, along with elderly Dorothy Frazier and her house full of kittens, of course, and Agnes Warren down in Florida for the season. Here was Copperthwaite's name and address, in Jonah's possession. Why?

I returned the contents to the bag and carried it, along with my notes, back into the taproom and to the end of the bar. Willett stared at me, I think with an air of concern; the others were oblivious to my return.

"I need to think," I said, blinking burning eyes. "I'm going back to my place, get some sleep. Watch things, will you?"

I stared at the ceiling, shoes off but clothes still on, lying on top of the covers. Think, Lew. It's got to be there. Think. *What sort of lunacy is going on here? What sort of lunacy...*

I fell into a deep sleep for several hours, and drifted into a parade of twisted, interconnected thoughts and details. *Running...Trucks crashing...Gulls...Murder...Lunacy...Visions of dead people...Piles of dead people...And lunacy...Lunacy.*

Lunacy.

I awoke with a start.

"Oh Christ," I muttered. "Can it be?" I glanced at the loud ticking clock. It was 8:32. Dark outside. Still night. Went into the bathroom and splashed cold water on my face and hair. Repeated the process several times until I was sure I was awake. Stood in the middle of the bathroom staring at the mirror, eyes blinking stupidly.

"Can it possibly be?" I muttered once again.

I flipped through books in the bookcase until I found the three books retrieved from the floors of the bedroom and bathroom after Holly's disappearance. I flipped through the first two and found nothing. Grabbing the third – Elizabeth Kite's *The Pineys* – I opened it to the page marked by the dust jacket's front flap. It was the title page, and hastily circled in lipstick were the words – the title – *The Pineys*. She told me, right here, and I had been too hasty – too stupid – to notice.

I slipped on shoes and ran back to the taproom. I pulled Jonah's canvas bag from the bottom desk drawer where I'd stuffed it, and once again dumped its contents. *It's lunacy, all right – lunacy.* I twisted the head off the Leeds-Peeper – the one place I'd failed to look – and pulled the two sides from the base. Inside was a tightly folded piece of paper, soiled and limp from extensive use and repeated folding. I carefully flattened it on the desk in the circle of light from the gooseneck lamp. It was an itemized list of names and addresses, names that were all too familiar to me: Yumi Takarada, Holly Porter, Agnes Warren, Catharine Copperthwaite, Dorothy Frazier, Emily Stackhouse, and Mary McCarthy. Lines were drawn through all of the names – Holly's included – except for Warren's and Frazier's, which had X's through them, and Copperthwaite's, which had not yet been touched. A sudden chill worked its way through the length of my body.

"Gordon!" I said, stepping back into the taproom. "I need some old calendars. Now! Where can I find them?" I breathed heavily and was impatient for a response.

"Aw, c'mon, Lew; *think!*" he said, exasperated, but my mind was a blank. "*The storeroom,*" he added, finally.

"Oh, yeah," I muttered as I moved quickly into that room.

Plastered all over the walls were large color calendars dating back to the mid-1920s, courtesy of the local ice company, emblazoned with life-like paintings of scantily clad young women. Each of these, with the exception of the current year, had only the page for December remaining, but behind the last page of each, printed on the cardboard itself, was a tiny calendar of the twelve months for that year. *What sort of lunacy...*I thought to myself as I pulled out my notes, grabbed the calendars for '35, '36 and '37, and circled some dates. I stepped back into the taproom.

"What do you know about lunar phases, Gordon?" I asked.

"Well, it's a little less than a calendar month – about twenty-nine-and-a-half days, a tiny bit more – between new moons. And there's the Metonic cycle, named after the Greek astronomer named Meton, of course, where after nineteen years the cycle repeats itself, with the new moon falling on the same day as it did at the beginning of the cycle. There's also..."

I returned to the storeroom while he was still answering. I stared at the calendars, checking dates, counting silently to myself as I moved the pencil backward from incident to incident.

"All of them," I finally muttered to myself. "Every single one..." I returned to the taproom, numb.

"What's going on, Lew?" asked Willett, a trace of concern in his voice.

"Paper. Get me a piece of paper, will you?" I asked quietly. He returned from the backbar and placed it on the counter in front of me. I wrote out several addresses and some notes, double-checked what I'd written, and handed it to Gordon.

"Gordon, this is very important. You need to follow my instructions very carefully. Okay?"

He nodded. "Yeah, sure; what is it?"

"Here's what I want you to do. Call Bernie Quinn at the state police barracks in Tuckerton. This number here..." I paused and pointed at the paper, "...and tell him if I haven't called the barracks and left word by..." I looked at my watch, "...by 10:30 tonight, that he should grab some troopers and come looking for me. I'll be at this address. Tell him he should be very careful when he comes in." Gordon scribbled notes to himself as I spoke. "And tell him he should send some good men to this other address here. They should look around the place – tear it apart – *as if a life depended on it*. Use those words; he'll know what I mean. Got it? Okay, wait an hour and then place the call. Not before then." As I finished, I realized my voice was a dull monotone, and sounded like death. My eyes were fixed on some vague point in the distance.

"What is it, Lew?" he asked. "What's going on?"

I turned slowly to him and answered.

"I'm going to get my wife."

I knelt in front of my open bedroom closet door and cleared its floor. The loose board pried up easily with the edge of a shoehorn and then I removed the two boards beyond it. Lifted the tightly wrapped musette bag that had been tucked off to one side and out of sight, blew the dust from its surface, and carefully unwrapped it. Inside was my old Colt .45 caliber automatic, model 1911. I wrapped my fist around its hard rubber grip and re-familiarized myself with its heft and feel. It felt good – just like the old days. The bluing of its metal surfaces glistened while disrupted dust motes danced crazily in the strong shaft of light from the bedside table lamp. It was an old friend, and this particular night we'd renew acquaintances. The Colt model 1911: adopted in March of that year by the U.S. Ordnance Dept. as the standard service weapon for the U.S. Army, Navy, and Marine Corp. And the army's gift to me when The Great War was over and my tour of duty ended – only they didn't know it.

Removed several ammo clips and two boxes of shells from the bag, loaded my weapon and stuffed the remainder in my coat pockets. Kicked off my shoes and replaced them with a pair of heavy boots, tied tightly. *Just like old times.* Grabbed my hat, a powerful Eveready flashlight, the large Manila envelope – already addressed and stamped – and the piece of raw meat tied up in heavy brown paper.

Ready as I'd ever be. Tonight, at least.

Pulled the warmed-up Ford to the curb in front of the post office, got out, stuffed the envelope into the mail slot, and continued on. Thirty-five minutes later, I rumbled across the wooden causeway bridge towards the blackness beyond, the vastness of the Pines silhouetted against a sky bright with the light of a near-full moon. Was I doing the right thing?

Who cared?

510

Monday, January 25, 1937. 11:26 p.m.

THE FIRST SIGN of life was the smell of pine smoke. A southerly wind delivered it from ahead, and soon after the glow of several windows hung in the blackness below the gray sky.

Quinn hadn't shown at 10:30. Another twenty minutes passed before I gave up on him and left my car parked a mile and a half behind on S40's hard sand shoulder; this couldn't wait. A near full moon dominated the sky, and while it helped in traveling the dark two-track, the strong headwind slowed things down. At least that would cover my sounds and, I hoped, my scent, knowing full well there was a big unsociable dog tied up ahead; I didn't need him barking for the last five minutes of my approach.

He didn't and he didn't even hear me. The chunk of meat landed on the sand inches in front of him. After a start and several obligatory barks at the darkness around him, curiosity – and hunger – overtook him. He wolfed down the raw, poison-laced chunk of beef.

Four minutes later he was dead.

The Leeks' property sat in a clearing in the pines at the end of the two-track. The doghouse and its late inhabitant were at the entrance to the clearing off to the right. The house – it was the only structure with dim lights in the windows – sat at the far end. To the right beyond the doghouse, and set down in a haphazard fashion, were three small shacks. To the left of the clearing were two larger buildings, the first an open-front structure housing what appeared from a distance to be a horse-drawn wagon and several sneakboxes, and the one beyond a similar-sized, barn-like structure that I took to house some sort of livestock. Behind these buildings was the rusted, scavenged remains of a small truck, and leaning against the closest side of the open structure were several sneakboxes in various states of disrepair. Above these hung a dozen or so muskrat pelts that had been left to prime up in the cold January weather, accompanied by a handful of small traps. Nearby sat a splint-shaving horse surrounded by piles of white oak splints, and a half-made basket constructed from them. In the center of the clearing, swaying in the stiff wind, stood a lone, tall pole with a small, square, gable-roofed purple martin house at its top. There was stuff strewn everywhere, heaped in piles and scattered randomly, with care taken to keep a large circular trail open, I assumed, for the use of their wagon.

To the right of the house led a sand path which forked, its left trail leading to a barely-discernible privy back in the trees, and its right trail vanishing into the darkness of the looming pines; a well sat between the two legs of the fork. All of the structures were made of clapboard and all of them looked like a stiff wind could reduce them to rubble.

After establishing to my satisfaction that there weren't any more dogs, I worked my way over to the two structures to the left. The moonlight was sufficiently bright that I was able to find my way around and get the lay of the place with relative ease; what the Leeks had so assiduously avoided was now my ally. The wind was a godsend, drowning out the sounds of dried leaves crunching and twigs snapping under foot, and I was able to move quickly. I paused to pull the Colt from my waistband, jacked a cartridge up into the barrel, slid the safety off and kept it at the ready.

The first structure, its front open to the elements, took all of thirty seconds to search. Aside from the wagon and sneakboxes were a long, crude bench, a variety of old tools, piles of split wood, and a jumble of other miscellaneous items. It was otherwise unoccupied.

The second, barn-like structure took somewhat longer to check out, but it too was uninhabited by anything other than two old mules, a cow, and a bunch of roosters and hens. I entered through a door at its north end and slowly made my way from room to room, ignored for the most part by my furry and feathered companions. There weren't any windows in most of the rooms, so I was able to use the flashlight without worry. In the final room were piles of dried salt hay and black grass, stored I suppose as feed for the four-legged residents. I exited the way I'd come in.

I angled around the fenced-in area behind the building, working my way through the darkness towards the house. A number of the windows were lit, but were covered from the inside by newspaper. Muffled voices could be heard as blurred silhouettes moved about occasionally beyond the yellowed paper. The third window gave me a view: The newspaper on its inside was old and torn, a small flap on its mid-right side providing a small triangular-shaped gap three quarters of an inch high at the outside and with a width of a couple of inches. It afforded a decent view of the large room's interior without risk of my being seen by its occupants.

There was a large fireplace on the opposing side, faced with stone and capped by a rough-hewn mantle. A fire blazed and crackled – the source, no doubt, of the pine smoke – and the mantle itself was lined with candles and several earthenware jugs. Above it hung a faded reproduction of "The Last Supper" framed by a set of deer antlers. The walls of the room, or at least the two I could see, were otherwise bare except for a framed embroidery that read "Home, Sweet Home" and a trio of snapping turtle shells with something unidentifiable painted on the backs of each. The two windows to either side of the fireplace and the single window at the far end of the room were all covered with newsprint, and one of them had the additional adornment of a pair of faded burlap curtains. A double-barreled shotgun hung on the wall, another stood in the corner and a third, sawed-off shotgun sat on a nearby table; the first two looked like old Remingtons, but I couldn't be sure. Several boxes of shells sat on the table.

The room's center was dominated by a long, rectangular wood

table with eleven chairs: four on the left side, five on the right, and one at each of its ends; eight of these were occupied. Standing at the far end was the man I took to be the patriarch Leviticus, as he was the senior of the group, although probably only in his late forties or early fifties. He was a large man, thin and wiry, but clearly muscular, with close-cropped hair all gone to white. There was a discernible growth of white stubble on his face, one that was heavily lined and tanned with the look of leather left in the sun too long. He spoke solemnly in muffled tones to the group assembled before him and only when he raised his voice could I understand what he was saying. The seven seated before him – five males and two of the most brutal-looking females I'd ever seen – stared blankly at the table top, palms flat against its surface. The chair at the end opposite Leviticus was empty, as were the two chairs to its right. Placed in front of the first side chair was a large earthenware bowl filled to the brim with what appeared to be the brownish cedar water of one the area's streams. Submerged in it was, I think, a dead bluefish, its tail fin hanging over the bowl's edge.

"If thine enemy be hungry, give him bread to eat; and if he be thirsty, give him water to drink. For thou shall heap coals of fire upon his head," he thundered suddenly, and there was a jumble of low voices in response. Leviticus paused to pour some brown liquid from an earthenware jug into a mug. He held it up in front of him – it looked almost as if he was saluting the iron fixture that hung from overhead and illuminated the table with a dozen candles – and mumbled a few words, then quickly drained its contents. He refilled the mug and held it chest high in front of him.

I exhaled on my hands to keep them warm, and angled closer to the window in an attempt to better hear what was said inside. The house protected me from the wind, but windows rattled on the far side with each new gust, the stronger ones eliciting some groans from the creaky wooden structure. Trees on all sides swayed and twisted in the inexorable onslaught.

"June!" barked Leviticus. The male to his immediate left blinked several times and slowly stood. His jaw was misshapen, its coloring a sickly yellow-brown, and looked as if it had been broken and poorly reset some time in the recent past. He awkwardly spit a stream of tobacco juice off to one side, took the mug, mumbled something and drank its contents; some of the liquid ran down his chin and stained his shirtfront. He was rail thin, roughly thirty years old, with a face deeply lined and scarred from years of acne. He was partially bald, with long wisps of unkempt yellowish-gray hair hanging limply from the sides. His beard, which was completely gray, was stained a reddish-brown below his mouth, no doubt from his use of chaw.

"Ezekial!" said Leviticus loudly, pouring another mug while June settled back into his seat. The person to his immediate right, facing away from my vantage point, rose and now took the mug, turning into view as he did so. Perhaps in his late twenties, he was round and pudgy, and almost babyish in his looks. He wore bib overalls and a large discolored hat with its earflaps hanging loose, and had a long unkempt beard that hung in matted clumps down to his chest. His similarly unkempt black hair hung in greasy strands from beneath his hat. By the way he handled himself I could tell that he possessed great strength, in spite of his soft-looking outer appearance. He drained the mug without saying a word.

"Titus!" The male to Ezekial's right rose slowly. He was similar in build to Ezekial and from the back they looked much alike – but this one was comparatively clean-shaven. Ezekial stroked Titus's back as he stood, and I took these two to be the twins that Buzby had mentioned. Titus stared blankly as he took the mug and never once met anyone else's gaze; he looked like a sleepwalker. When he sat back down, Ezekial again began stroking his back, leaning towards him in a barely perceptible fashion. They looked affectionate.

"Etta!" The large woman at June's left rose slowly, a smirk on her round face. She was overweight, with short, reddish-brown hair. At a quick glance she looked as much like a man as a woman both facially and in build, but closer inspection revealed the slightly softer contours and proportions of her gender. Male or female, she was one of the ugliest specimens of humanity I'd ever seen. She said something unintelligible, but with bluster, then turned to the others with a toothy smile, the few teeth that remained thick and yellow with scum.

"Emma!" Etta's sister sat to her left and may also have been a twin – or just similarly unattractive. Her hair was comparably short and she sat staring with a quiet intensity, her clasped hands stuffed between her thighs. She didn't respond at first to Leviticus' call, appearing to be lost in a daze. Etta elbowed her and got her attention, made a comment, after which Emma rose quickly to take the mug. Only then could I see her face and she had surprisingly clear and clean looking skin. This was marred primarily by the snaggletooth that protruded between tightly closed lips. She never said a word, either.

"Micah!" The overweight male at Titus' right stood slowly, his tight bib overalls and long sleeved undershirt straining at the seams. He placed something small on the table in front of him. He was filthy with grime and sweat, his clothes stained with ages of inattention. He scratched his groin unselfconsciously as he ambled to the end of the table, paused to take his drink, wiped his mouth with the back of his hand and returned to his seat. Only then did I see his face. He appeared to be in his early-to-mid-twenties, and there were the dried traces of a runny nose on his upper lip. His fingernails were unusually long and yellow and, not surprisingly, caked with dirt. He sat and picked up the object on the table – it was a length of string – and he resumed playing with it, wrapping it around an index finger.

"Noah!" The last of the seven, to Micah's right and with his back to me as well, rose quickly. He strode to the head of the table and took the required drink, then turned into view. He looked to be the youngest of the lot, with eyes set too far apart and a long, sparse beard growing from his neck and jaw; his face was otherwise void of hair. He uttered a few indecipherable words, struggling to speak; a cleft palette was my guess. His head bobbed slowly and continuously, as if nodding agreement with anything and everything that was said by others. He had a vague, dreamy look about him as he returned to his chair. His aim was bad and he got hung up on its arm as he sat.

It was an unattractive group at best, and I had no idea what this ritual – the drinking from the mug and the fish in the bowl of water – was all about. And, just as frustrating, it seemed that the only words and sentences I was able to discern were the inconsequential ones. Leviticus poured himself another and asked something of the group. They looked from one to another. Finally, Micah stood. Leviticus stood facing Micah without any show of emotion, but I'd swear that I sensed something like paternal pride in the way he held himself and puffed out his chest. He took Micah's soft shoulders in his large tanned hands, leaned forward and spoke closely into the young man's ear. Micah nodded and stepped out of sight, while Leviticus opened the large book before him, flipped to a marked page, and began to read in a booming voice that was clear and distinct.

"Behold, the Lord will lay waste the earth and make it desolate..."

Micah returned to view wearing a coat and hat. He retrieved his piece of string and listened for a moment.

"... and He will twist its surface and scatter its inhabitants..."

Micah left.

I pressed myself deep in the shadow of a rain barrel. Inside, planks squeaked under foot and the door opened.

"... as with the maid, so with her mistress..." boomed Leviticus' voice through the opening.

Micah waddled straight towards the middle of the three shacks to my right, his hands jammed in his coat pockets. He unlocked the windowless door and disappeared inside. I stayed put for a moment, trying to decide what to do next. Micah emerged a minute later, preceded by a woman. It was difficult to see her in the shadow cast by the small structure, but when they stepped into the moonlight I could see her back as he guided her towards the sandy trail. Her hair was long and curly, and appeared to be light brown or blonde. My immediate impression was that she was younger, twenties to mid-thirties at the oldest. Her clothing was ragged, and the kerchief that capped her head, coupled with her hesitant, stumbling gait and outstretched arms, suggested that she was blindfolded. Micah had a handful of the back of her blouse, and steered her up the path.

I followed from fifty feet behind, knowing full well that the blast of the wind would hide any sounds that I made. The moonlight cut through the canopy of pine overhead, the awkward couple disappearing and reappearing in the alternating shafts of gray light and darkness. I wanted to know where he was taking her, to see if there were any additional structures on the Leek property. Once satisfied, I could return to the main compound and make a thorough search of the other structures.

There were several occasions when I thought I'd lost track of them, but I kept to what felt like the trail and would, eventually, see their silhouettes flicker ahead of me. The ground gave way to a slight incline, and I struggled up the side of a small hill in darkness. Several minutes later I saw a clearing beyond, and slowly worked my way towards the edge of the woods I'd just traipsed through.

The clearing ahead was small but comparatively well lit by the moonlight. Micah jerked the woman to a stop, stepped around her and took a handful of the front of her blouse. They resumed their walk, with Micah now leading instead of pushing. They stumbled up to the top of a sand ridge and again he had her stop. He paused and looked around, but didn't spot me in the shadows a mere twenty feet away. He turned to the woman, took her shoulders and slowly turned her around.

Then I realized the ridge wasn't just a ridge; it was the edge of an open pit. I saw her face. Her eyes weren't covered by the kerchief. She was pretty. And she was blind.

She was Mickey's wife, Annie Ryan.

Micah produced a vicious looking hunting knife. He quickly took a fistful of her hair and, in one sweeping motion, pulled her head back and sliced through her throat. Deep.

Instinctively, I rushed him.

There was a geyser of blood, an audible gurgle carried on the wind, and Annie dropped in place, half falling into the pit, her twitching legs still visible over its side.

Micah didn't hear me, didn't see me. He jabbed the knife into the sand and reached for the exposed legs.

I scrambled up the rise. He turned and saw me, shock registering in his eyes. I sank my fist into his gut. He doubled over, retching. I grabbed his knife, yanked his head up and back by a fistful of hair. I jabbed it as hard as I could through the side of his neck, its tip exiting the opposite side. His eyes bulged in horror. Words froze in his throat. Fat hands clawed at the air. I jerked the knife forward and his nearly severed head fell backwards like the lid on a coffeepot. I shouldered him in a spray of blood and his fat, limp carcass fell to one side. I leapt into the pit and took Annie's lifeless form in my arms. Dead.

The bastards.

I clawed my way back towards the Leek's compound, my Colt clutched tightly in my right hand, Micah's knife slid in my boot. They'd done it, all right; they'd kidnapped the missing women – every last one of them, I was sure – and, by God, they were going to pay for it. Annie had disappeared – been kidnapped – back in March, and three more since then: Peterson, McCarthy and Holly.

Oh, God: Holly. My mind reeled, my body ached for revenge. These bastards would pay, every last one of them – with blood, with the last faint wisps of life that seep out of the husk. They'd pay all right.

They'd pay – *me*.

But before I dealt with them, I had to find out who remained, who was alive, and get them the hell out of there, to safety. I just hoped to God that someone – anyone – was still alive. And if it had to be just one… I rubbed my eyes with the back of my right wrist as I fended off branches with my left hand. The lights of the Leek house appeared through the trees ahead.

The first shack's sole window, at its rear, was boarded over. I expected the door to be locked, but it wasn't. The hasp was open wide, and an unlocked padlock dangled uselessly in the dark shadow that masked the building's front. I grabbed my flashlight, took a deep breath, and held my .45 waist high. I threw the door open as I clicked on the light, did a scan of the inside, and quickly determined that none of the Leeks were in the small building. My brief perusal registered a pair of beds at either side of the room, an armless wooden chair, a simple wood table with a pitcher and basin on it and a chamber pot beneath, and a small wood-burning stove. I killed the light, stepped inside and pulled the door shut behind me. It was much warmer inside, in the fifties. When I turned the flashlight back on, its beam glistened off a pair of panic-stricken eyes staring at me. It was a woman, and she was lying on the bed to the left, covers half pulled in a jumble to her chest. She was gagged, and both raw wrists were tied tightly to the bedposts with cord turned brown from ages of dried blood. Her long hair hung in filthy lifeless strands, framing a face smudged and streaked with grime. And yet there was something almost pretty about the face. She blinked in the beam of the light. She looked terrified. She looked – like Grace Peterson.

"Grace," I said as I approached.

She couldn't see who I was with the light trained in her eyes, and looked terrified. I placed the flashlight on the nearby table and went to work on the knotted gag.

"My name's Porter," I said quickly. "Lew Porter."

She stared dumbly. The name meant nothing to her.

"Holly Porter's husband," I added quickly.

She understood, and a look of hope came into her eyes.

"I'm going to get you out of here," I said as the gag came loose.

She sucked in lungs full of fresh air. "Oh, my God! Oh, my God!" was all she could say at first, then quickly added, "My wrists. Please, my wrists."

"Are you okay?" I asked, working on the cord.

"I – I'm okay. Oh thank God you're here!"

"Are there others?" I asked, glancing over at the other bed. It was empty, stripped down to its lumpy stained mattress. "Is there anyone else – like you? Here?"

"I think so – I'm not sure," she said, wincing as I struggled with the cord that bit into her raw wrists. "There were. I've heard voices – female voices – screams – from outside somewhere." She blinked heavily. "There was one in that bed," she nodded towards the other bed, "a long time ago, I don't remember how long. Her name was Lizzie – one of them called her that – but we never talked. The gags…"

Lizzie. That would be Elizabeth Perry.

"What did they want you for?" I asked. I gave up on the knots, and pulled the small penknife from my pants pocket. It quickly severed her bonds.

"Oh, God," she moaned, grabbing her right wrist with her left hand and clutching them to her chest. "I – I – oh, God." She shook her head back and forth.

"Shhhhh," I said. "Calm down. It's all right now." I hoped.

She took a deep breath and fixed her gaze on the far wall. "Babies," she blurted out. "Babies. They sell them, I think. I guess."

"Babies?" I repeated, incredulously.

"Oh, God; it was terrible. Those filthy animals would come in – every day, every night. They'd force themselves on us. We were tied, couldn't fight back. They – they want babies…." She fought back a sob.

"They won't. Anymore," I said.

"I – I'm actually safe now. Sort of," she said.

"What do you mean?"

"I – I'm *pregnant.*" She took another deep breath. "They were successful. One of them." Tears welled in her reddened eyes. "They leave me alone now. The old man is crazy, but he won't let them near me now. Except – except for the women. Etta and Emma. Etta – " She squeezed her eyes closed tight. " – that pig! *That goddamned pig!* She – she – Oh, God; it's horrible. She – "

"Easy," I said, stroking her hair and trying to calm her. I didn't need her yelling. I hadn't noticed that she was pregnant, and probably wouldn't have if she hadn't said so; there was a slight bulge under the covers, but it could have just as well been the result of a lousy diet.

"I'm sorry. Oh, God, I'm so sorry," she blurted.

"That's crazy," I said. "Why should you be sorry? It's not your fault."

"It is my fault! The poems – "

I froze when I heard the word. "Poems?" I repeated. "What about the poems?"

"It was horrible. They forced themselves on us. The old man. Grunting – hot, stinking breath in my face – my ear. Like a rutting dog. I – I couldn't stand it. I started reciting my poems to myself. To keep my mind off what was happening. To keep from going crazy. To myself. Out loud." She took another deep breath, and exhaled slowly. "The old man – he loved the poetry. Told me I was his favorite. *His favorite!* Like some goddamned teenage boy! Made me recite poems every time from then on. Said it made it more – more *exciting* for him. Oh, God," she said again, shaking her head.

"How long have you been – pregnant? How long – "

"Listen to me!" she said quickly. "He loved the poems, the way they sounded. He loved having me recite them while he – he – "

"I understand," I said quietly.

"No! No you don't! He – he had my journal. He found the names – the names and addresses – of the Poets' Circle members. *'More like you,'* he said. *'I'm going to get more – like you.'* Oh, God. Mary. Emily.

Yumi. *Holly*. Are they safe? Did he get them? Did he?"

A wave of nausea passed over me as my worst fears were confirmed. The bastards.

"He did, didn't he?" she finally said, quietly. "I sealed their fate. Oh, God, please forgive me."

"You'll have your revenge," I said flatly. "We both will."

Silence hung in the air between us. I took several deep breaths and collected my thoughts. There wasn't time to waste.

"Listen. I need to get you out of here – you and the others – before I deal with – with *them*. Can you walk?"

I helped her to a sitting position, helped her swing her stiff legs over the side of the bed. Holding on to my arm, she tentatively placed some weight on her feet, and attempted to stand. Her legs buckled, and I grabbed her.

"Like a baby," she muttered. "Let me try again."

She did, with my assistance, and managed to stand. "I – I'm weak. But I can manage, I think." She took several tentative steps as her confidence grew.

It would be slow going, and I didn't need her slowing me down while I looked for the others. "Listen," I said. "The Leeks: Do any of them come here this late at night?"

"No – not usually. The – the one with the eyes: He brought wood for the fire an hour or so ago. That will be it for the night. Etta, sometimes..." Her voice trailed off as she stared at the wall.

"I'm going to check the other buildings, see who else is here. You stay here. You'll be safe; I'll keep an eye on the door, on the Leek's house. Take this," I said, pulling the .45 from my belt. "Lie under the covers, like you're still tied up. If anyone gets in here – and they won't – but if they should, wait 'til they get close to you, as close as I am now, and point this right here – " I patted the center of my chest " – and pull the trigger. Both hands. It'll have a big kick, so hang on tight. It's ready to fire – the safety's off – so don't touch the trigger unless you need to. Understand? Can you do it?"

"Oh, I can do it, all right. It'll be my pleasure," she said, staring at the huge automatic weighing down her right hand. "It will be a pleasure."

"Okay. I'm gonna get the others, then I'll be back for you. We'll get the hell out of this place." I grabbed the flashlight from the table. "I need to take this with me. You okay?" I asked.

She sat on the edge of the bed, staring at the glow in the cracks around the wood stove's door. She didn't answer, instead muttering the name "Deborah."

"Deborah?" I asked. "Who's Deborah?"

She looked up at me, sadly. "I am. That's what the old man calls me: Deborah. *If a woman have long hair, it is a glory to her,*' he says. That's the other reason I was his favorite: my hair. Every night that he came here he'd stand outside and say, *'Awake, awake, Deborah: awake, awake, utter a song. Make sweet melody, sing many songs, that thou mayest be remembered.'* And then he'd come in and – " She paused a moment, looking in my eyes. "I hope he comes back tonight." She looked at the Colt. "Oh, I'd love to see him now. Up close. It would be a pleasure – this time."

Leviticus and his bible quoting. I felt like shoving a bible down his throat and watching as he slowly choked to death on scripture.

"I'll be right back," I repeated. "Get under the covers now." She nodded and did so. I took a quick look outside and verified that no one was about, then pulled the door shut behind me. I thought of Micah and Annie; the Leeks had plans for these women tonight, and wouldn't leave them alone for too long.

Micah had left the door to the second shack unlocked. Inside, I gave the place a quick search. It only had a single bed in it, and it was empty. Annie Ryan had been this building's sole occupant. *Had* been.

The door to the third shack was locked. I quickly rummaged through one of the nearby piles of refuse and came up with a flat, rusty length of iron roughly the size of a ruler. There was enough play between the padlock and hasp to wedge the strip of iron in between the two, hinged pieces. I yanked back as hard as I could and pried the assembly free from the building with a squeak of metal on wood. I glanced over my shoulder at the Leeks' house: all was still.

I entered quickly, pulled the door shut behind me, and clicked on the light. "Holly," I called as I scanned the room. There were two beds, both occupied. The figure on the left was twisted to one side, face and hair obscured by a blanket tugged high. The covered figure breathed loudly in sleep. The woman on the second bed, partially covered by a blanket half on the floor, was gagged, her wrists tied to the bedposts. She was awake, eyes wide in horror.

"Lew Porter," I said quickly, as I went to the side of her bed. "Holly Porter's husband." I sliced the gag from her mouth. "You are – ?"

"Mary," she gasped, taking in a mouthful of fresh air. "Mary McCarthy. Please help me. Please!"

"I will," I said. "Hold still." I cut her restraints.

"Do you know what – what they've done to us?" she asked.

"I know. And they won't do it anymore." I looked to the other bed. "Is that Holly?" I asked. I was afraid of the answer.

"No," she said, sadly. "No, it isn't Holly."

"Do you know where Holly is? What happened to her?"

"No. I'm sorry, I don't."

I stepped to the other bed while Mary sat up, rubbing her wrists. "We have to get out of here – quick," she said.

"We will," I said over my shoulder as I sat on the other bed's edge. I pulled the cover down and shone the light on the sleeping woman.

It wasn't Holly. I don't know why I thought there was a chance it would be, in spite of what Mary had just said. Wishful thinking, I suppose.

The woman moaned and slowly twisted onto her back.

It was Emily.

"Emily," I said. "Emily. It's Lew. Lew Porter." Her eyes opened as I cut the gag from her mouth. She lay there, staring at me, not saying a word. I brushed the matted red hair out of her eyes and stroked her cheek. "Lew Porter," I repeated. "Remember me?"

She stared. Her eyes slowly widened in horror. She sucked in air. And then she yelled at the top of her lungs: *"YOU BASTARD! YOU MOTHERFUCKING BASTARD! GO AHEAD: KILL ME! KILL ME!"*

"Emily!" I yelled, shaken. "It's me!" I reached to cover her mouth, to stifle her yelling. It didn't work. Twisting violently like a fish dying out of water, she let out a sustaining, blood-curdling scream that tore through the night. No one could miss it – *no one.* I made a fist and slugged her. She went out cold, her screams cut off as abruptly as it had started.

"She's crazy," Mary stated matter-of-factly. "They drove her crazy. Weeks ago. Poor kid."

"Christ. We've got to get out of here. Fast!" I said. "Wrap yourself in a blanket. Grab one for her; I'll carry her." I ran to the door and looked out. The Leeks' house looked still, no outward sign of life. Maybe they hadn't heard her scream. I *hoped.* "I'm going out to get Grace. I'll be right back."

"Who?" asked Mary wearily.

"Stay put!" I responded, ignoring the question.

I trotted back to Grace's shack and opened the door. "It's me: Lew. Don't shoot!" I said before entering the place; I didn't fully trust an edgy rape victim with a loaded weapon. I pulled the door shut and flicked on the light.

"I'm ready," she said sliding out from under the covers. "I think I can walk okay," she added.

"Take this." I threw a blanket to her. "It's cold out, and we have a long walk. Let me have that," I said, pointing to the Colt.

We both froze as we heard the door latch click from the outside. I snapped off the light. The latch rattled and the door opened, moonlight spilling onto the floor just inside, the large silhouetted figure casting a thick shadow in its midst. The person held a lantern turned low, stepped into the room, and pulled the door shut.

"Hey, there, babycakes," said the voice. "It's momma." It was a female. Etta. Grace grasped my sleeve from behind as Etta placed the dim lantern on the floor. She bent over and turned up the light, illuminating the shack's interior. She turned and froze as she saw the two of us. And then she smiled.

"Well, well, well," she said. "We have company." She sucked loudly on her teeth.

Grace slipped the Colt into my hand, and I raised it towards Etta.

"Sit down and shut up," I said

She looked at the .45, then back at me. "Big gun. Big man. But I need my lovin' from babycakes over there, and nothin's gonna stop me." She slid the razor-sharp hunting knife from her belt. "And you: You better get the hell outta here before my brothers get here – my brothers and *daddy*."

I didn't move.

She stepped slowly towards me. "You wouldn't shoot a woman, now would –"

The .45 punched a hole in her chest and tore the words from her throat. Her lifeless form dropped in place and hung up on the bed's post. Her knife clattered to the floor.

"Let's go," I said.

"Let me see that," said Grace without emotion. She held her hand out for the Colt.

"No. Let's go."

"My friend – my savior. Let me see." Her hand hung in the air, palm up.

"No! We don't have time."

"I'm not going 'til I see it," she said.

"Christ," I muttered to myself. "Here." I handed it to her. "The deliverer of death to your tormentor. Satisfied?"

She eyed it for a moment, turning it in her hand. A smile crept across her features.

"Now let's get the hell out of here. No way they could have missed that."

Then Grace held the Colt in both hands and aimed it at Etta's head.

"Jesus," I said grabbing for it. Too late.

The place shook with the roar of the second shot, and the right half of Etta's head disappeared, opened up like a smashed melon. Bits of Etta were splattered everywhere. I wrenched the Colt from Grace's hands, grabbed her sleeve, and dragged her towards the door. "Let's go!" I yelled.

The door opened, and in stepped Emma. She looked at us in shock, then down at the crumpled heap hanging limply from the bedpost. Her mouth hung open as she slowly looked back at us, then at the Colt in my hand.

"*Now*," I said to Grace.

With a loud hiss, Emma charged. I lifted the Colt and fired as I slipped awkwardly in the mess on the floor. Emma's left arm twisted back and around as the slug tore through it.

"KILL THE BITCH!" yelled Grace from behind.

Emma spun around and careened to the floor, smashing the kerosene lantern with her fall. In an instant, the entire corner went up in flames, Emma shrieking in its midst.

I yanked Grace behind me and leapt for the door, avoiding the licking flames. Emma stumbled to her feet, her clothing on fire, and ran out into the darkness shrieking like a stuck pig, her smashed left arm flopping uselessly.

Grace stumbled as we ran, but managed not to fall. We passed the second building and reached the third, the grounds now glowing from the fire behind us. I glanced back to see the bone-dry wooden building go up in flames, the wind blowing tongues of fire and clouds of sparks towards the nearest empty building. Doors opened and slammed back at the Leek house, and voices shouted.

"Get out here! Now!" I yelled to Mary, who raced to the door.

"You two – go! That way," I pointed towards the sand road. "Stick to the shadows. It's over a mile to the road. My car's there. You hear anybody on the way, head into the brush and hide. I'll bring Emily. And take this," I added, pulling the hunting knife from my boot and handing it to Grace. "Just in case."

They both nodded hurried agreement and took off. I looked back: no one was in sight. That was bad. They knew I was there and knew where I was. There were five of them, and they were armed, or at least some of them were.

I went inside to get Emily. She had regained consciousness, and resumed screaming when she saw me. The side of her face had swollen where I'd hit her. I grabbed the discarded gag from the floor and tied it hastily, reducing her frenzied screams to a series of loud moans and grunts. She twisted violently as I cut her restraints, scooped her up, and threw her over my shoulder. She twisted and turned, kicking and pounding at my back with her fists. I tried to steady her with my right hand, the one clutching the Colt.

I stumbled back outside, looked around quickly for signs of life, and started for the sand road. The second shack had caught fire now, and the compound glowed a pulsing yellow-orange. The air was filled with the sound of gusting wind and the crackle of flames. Emily twisted and turned like a gyroscope, and it was slow-going on the sandy ground. I felt like slugging her again.

I'd covered a mere fifty feet when I sensed someone behind me. I slowed and turned. Titus stood there behind me trembling, an old Iver Johnson .38 held in both hands and pointed in my general direction. My immediate impression was that he'd never used it before.

"Stop!" he said softly as he pulled the trigger. Or tried to: the trigger lock was still on. A look of panic overtook him and tears rolled down his cheeks as he looked at the ineffectual thing in his hands.

"Amateur," I hissed as I lowered the Colt and fired once. Titus dropped in a heap on the sand as the last traces of life spilled from his body.

I could make out voices yelling off in the distance, but couldn't tell from where. Emily twisted and bucked like a crazed dog. She was jeopardizing both our lives and I couldn't take it any longer. I smacked her on the side of the head. She went limp, and traveling became easier.

I glanced around once again and spotted a shadowy figure dart between the barn and the wagon house seventy-five feet away. I didn't see anyone else. The road was only twenty-five feet away, and I could feel the warmth of the blaze on my back. The dog's house was straight ahead, the dog's lifeless form right where I'd left it.

And then the tall figure stepped from behind a nearby pine and lifted one of the Remingtons.

I leapt to my right and threw Emily's limp form as far as I could, which wasn't far at all. There was a simultaneous flash and roar, and I felt my left leg yanked back at the knee. I hit the sand and raised the Colt, squeezing off two quick shots before there was a second roar. His aim was off. Sand kicked up and stung my face and eyes. I blindly squeezed off a third, and clawed at my face in a desperate attempt to clear my vision. There was blood everywhere. More than sand had hit my face, and my thoughts raced like the water in a flushed toilet. I lay on my back blinking and squinting, the hazy images before me all cast in crimson. I heard agonized shrieking to one side, and knew I'd hit my target – hadn't killed it, but sure as hell put it out of commission. My left leg burned and felt like an anvil. I struggled to sit, but couldn't. I took deep breaths as the glowing crimson treetops spun overhead and smeared into a yellow-green stain.

A towering form stepped into view. I blinked and focused. It was Leviticus – with Grace, kneeling on the ground in front of him. He held a fistful of her hair, her head yanked back, the barrels of the sawed-off shotgun shoved in her mouth. She gagged and grimaced from the pain, blood trickling from her scalp and the corner of her mouth. He stood there a moment, staring at me.

"Drop it," he said.

I did. It was empty, anyway.

"You," he said after a moment. "You're the barman, aren't ya?"

Not for long.

He slowly slid the barrel from her mouth, kicked her to the ground, and aimed it at my head. "Well, then," he said slowly, "goodbye."

There was a deafening roar as his head disappeared in a red mist, a rain of wet bits of matter showering the immediate area. What remained of Leviticus dropped from view. A series of blasts followed immediately from a number of different directions and distances, punctuated by shrieks and screams. Then, as suddenly as it had all started, all was silent.

I heard a low moan and a sob, and a warm hand clenched mine.

"Lew," I heard Grace say.

Another looming figure, silhouetted in the glow of the flames beyond, stepped into view, a smoking shotgun held in the crook of his arm.

"Who —" I struggled. "Who are you?"

"Ya shoulda said somethin' Lewis. Ya shoulda said somethin'."

"Buzby…"

"Like I said, Lewis, we take care of our own. Won't be no more trouble now, no sir. We take care of our own."

Another lone shot roared in the distance, and several voices yelled and responded. Buzby looked over his shoulder, gave a thumbs up, then returned to me.

"I didn't see you," I said quietly. "Neither did she."

"Damn right ya didn't," he said, wiping his nose with the back of his fist. "Ya didn't. Damn right."

Buzby — the world — faded away.

Tuesday, January 26, 1937. 11:03 a.m.

"MR. PORTER?"

THE voice came to me in a dream. It was a talking fish. A bluefish. A big one.

"Mr. Porter?" it said, once again. Must be feeding time. "How are we this morning, Mr. Porter?"

I felt a hand on my shoulder. I opened my eyes slowly. A nurse in white hovered over me, or at least I hoped it was a nurse – and not an angel.

"You're in the hospital, Mr. Porter. Paul Kimball Hospital – in Lakewood. I'm nurse White," she said. How appropriate.

"What time is it?" I asked. As if I cared.

"11:00," she answered. There's a call for you, a Detective Quinn with the state police. Are you up to it?"

"Quinn," I repeated, trying to place the name. Things weren't working so well today. They had me pumped full of something – something soothing. Or at least I hoped they did.

"Yeah," I said, struggling to sit. She had a telephone in her hand, and stepped over to the jack in a nearby wall. I fumbled for the bottle of water by my bed, slopped some into a cupped hand and splashed it on my burning, crusted eyes. There was a bandage on the left side of my face. I splashed a few more palms full, and felt around my head for damage. Aside from the bandage, some of the hair was shaved from my scalp, and a thick, greasy substance was smeared all over it and into the hairline. Nurse White returned with the telephone.

"Quinn?" I said.

"You sure know how to step in it, Lew."

"Yeah. Up to my ankle. Is – uh – Grace okay? And the other two? Mary and – uh – Emily?" I ran my hand up and down the length of both legs; they were still there, although the left one was tightly wrapped at the ankle.

"Grace is fine. She's tough, that one. McCarthy, too. Emily – well – they're keeping an eye on her…I don't think she fared as well."

"Yeah," I sighed. "I think you're right."

"I didn't get Willett's message 'til well after 10:30, Lew. We got there as soon as we could, but by the time we got there it was over – whatever it was that happened there. What the hell did I tell you about going it alone?"

"Let's cut the bullshit, Quinn. You know damn well what you were doing, feeding me information all along, knowing full well I'd do your dirty work for you – the stuff you guys didn't want to dirty your fingernails with. Well, you got your wish. And I'd do it again, given the chance." I barely got it all out, and I was exhausted.

There were several moments of silence before Quinn resumed, with a chuckle. "Calm down, Lew; you're in the clear here. Anyway, when we got there, the entire place was on fire."

"Everything?"

"Everything. Even the goddamn doghouse. Empty kerosene cans strewn about. Half dozen bodies stacked up in one of the buildings – dead, of course. Dead and burnt beyond recognition. Looked like a bunch of boxers, all tightened up in that so-called *pugilistic stance*. Coroner's got them all now; shipped them up to Swayze in Trenton, see what he can come up with."

"There's a…" I struggled to count heads in my mind, but kept losing track. "There's a couple – I think – more. And women: There's at least one in a pit southwest of the compound. Annie Ryan. One of the Leeks should be there, too."

"We found them – Christ, did you do that to him?"

I didn't answer.

"We did some digging around the pit, found a couple of shallow graves. *Women* is all we know so far..."

My heart sank. "Holly?" I asked, reluctantly.

"No, not Holly. These were too far-gone – advanced stages of decomposition – been there too long. Definitely not Holly."

There was a long silence.

"Holly," I said slowly.

"No sign of her. I'll keep you posted on that. And we're still looking around, still digging; we're not finished yet, not by a long shot. The Leeks, though: I want to know what happened up there, *everything* that happened."

"I'll tell you what I know."

"That's what I want. What I expect."

"Okay, Bernie. Just do me a favor."

"Yeah? What is it?" he asked skeptically.

"Give me twenty-four hours. To let my brain clear. Let me piece this all together – fill in the gaps."

"You'll stay put?"

"I will."

"Okay, then. It's a deal. I'll see you there, noon tomorrow."

"What – what day is that?" As if it really mattered.

"Wednesday."

"Okay," I sighed as my eyes rolled back into my head and the telephone slid to the floor.

The fish was waiting for me.

Wednesday, January 27, 1937. 11:59 a.m.

"HERE'S WHAT WE'VE found," said Quinn. "Then I want to hear what you have to say."

"Fair enough," I said, sipping water through a glass straw.

"Like I said yesterday, there wasn't much left of the Leeks' house and outbuildings. They were all ablaze when we got there and nothing more than smoking heaps of cinders by the time they'd burnt themselves out. We found you out cold on the ground. You were a mess: buckshot had torn up your leg and taken part of your scalp off. The Peterson woman was there on the ground next to you, unconscious too. Stackhouse was nearby, semi-conscious and making a lot of noise. The McCarthy woman was out on S40 when we got there, flagged us down; might have taken us longer to find the entrance if we hadn't seen her. Not that your directions weren't clear, mind you. And then there was the pile of corpses, of course, a half dozen of them. We're fairly sure that these were the remains of the Leeks, and that someone had dragged them all into the wagon house, piled them up and covered them with dried salt hay, then set them on fire. The building collapsed and burnt on top of them, but we eventually managed to fish them out."

"Was one of them missing a head?"

"As a matter of fact, yes."

"That's the old man – Leviticus. Someone shot him – blew his head off – as he was getting ready to kill me."

"*Who* shot him?"

"I have no idea. But I'd sure like to thank him."

"I guess you would. Anyway, all that remained besides the bodies were the fire resistant items: metal wood stoves, bedsprings, dishes, that kind of stuff. That's in the compound itself; we did some further digging in the area near the pit, and found three more shallow graves with women's corpses in them, in similar states of decomposition. And if that wasn't bad enough, we also found the bodies of two babies. Not much left of them, either."

"How old?"

"Coroner figured only a few months, but there wasn't a lot to them; he'll have a better idea later on. By the way, did I mention that two other babies – these two alive and well – were left here on the hospital's doorstep late last night? Both healthy, both six months to a year old and no note; a phone call to the front desk alerted the staff, so they weren't out front for too long. Both of them were asleep in baskets, just like in the old Bible stories. You know, baby Moses."

"He wasn't left on a doorstep."

"No, but they put him in a basket, didn't they? Same difference. Anyway, we went to the other address you gave us – Sam Bozarth was the fellow's name – and tore the place apart. Your hunch was right: He was involved with the Leeks. Acted as their middleman, between them and the outside, the so-called civilized world. *They were selling babies*, Lew, and making a surprising amount of money in the process. The Leeks provided them and Bozarth lined up purchasers. Bozarth kept detailed records of the transactions, dates and amounts, but – unfortunately – no names or addresses. Just a brief description of each customer, enough for him to keep track, but not enough for us to go on."

"Did you get Bozarth to talk?"

"We're, ah, *questioning* him now. He'll talk, all right, given enough time. We figure there's someone else – in the city – who actually lines up the purchasers, then puts them in touch with Bozarth."

"Philly?"

"That's our guess, but we'll find out for certain. Philly or Camden."

"What do you make of them?" I asked. "The two babies?" I had a pretty good idea, but wanted Quinn's slant on it.

"Well, obviously someone stepped in and saved your butt, so we figure they either found them there in the compound or tracked them down to whomever they'd been sold to. Either way, they're safe now. They'll put them up for adoption once they've checked them out and nursed them back to health."

"I guess two out of God-knows how many is better than none."

"I'd say so. We do the best we can and all else is history."

"I suppose so. What about Grace? And Emily and Mary? How are they?" I asked.

"So-so," he responded. "The Peterson woman was pregnant – I don't know if you were aware of that – but she miscarried yesterday. She's all right otherwise and took her loss surprisingly well. But I guess that's understandable, given the circumstances.

"Mary McCarthy was released to her parents in Red Bank and they have a private doctor keeping an eye on her. She's a mess – thoroughly traumatized by the events of the last couple of months – but she'll do all right, or as well as can be expected. Says she never wants to go back to the island, though. Know anyone in the market for a house?"

"Not off hand. I'll keep it in mind."

"Well, let her know if you do. Emily Stackhouse is another story altogether. She's stark, raving mad and thinks that everyone – myself included – is one of her tormentors. When she isn't staring at the wall in one of her periodic catatonic states, she's screaming bloody murder at the top of her lungs. We couldn't get anything out of her and had her shipped up to the Psychiatric Hospital in Trenton. They'll know what to do with her. We didn't."

Yeah, they'd know what to do with her, all right: add her to their assemblage of nut cases and maybe – just maybe – if by some remote chance her condition improves on its own, might get around to releasing her. Otherwise, she was lost and among the lost.

"And, by the way," he continued, "you were right. The woman in the pit was Annie Ryan. Her husband ID'd her yesterday. Nice guy; took it hard, though."

They usually do.

"Now tell me everything you know, everything you've figured out. And make sure it all ends up with your visit to the Leeks' the other night. I have Peterson and McCarthy's stories, so I know the basics, but I'm sure there're some big gaps you can plug up. Based on what the two of them told us, the Leeks would probably all be dead now even if we'd found them all alive – strung up in neat rows from some convenient tree. I want to know what you found, how you put it all together, how you ended up there. Way I see it, you could've gone in there, cut off their balls, fed them to the chickens and the people around here would *still* regard you as a hero." Quinn sat back in his chair, crossed his legs and fired up a Lucky. "So, Lew…"

I looked over at him as I repositioned myself in the bed.

"*Everything*. No convenient omissions."

I nodded agreement as I fluffed the pillow. *Fat chance.*

"The Leeks decided to go into the baby-selling business," I began.

"Why?" asked Quinn. "Who would want one of these black-market babies?"

"I don't have an answer for that. Why would someone – some couple – want to illegally acquire a baby? Why not have their own children or adopt some through proper channels? I can think of several reasons, a couple of them reasons I'd rather not think of. And I know you can, too. But, the bottom line is that there were people out there who wanted them and were willing to pay money for them."

Quinn shrugged. "Like I said, we'll get Bozarth to talk. This is important to us, and to a lot of people around here. He'll spill, eventually."

"Will there be much left of him when he does?" I had visions of a medieval torture chamber.

"You should see it up in Toms River. There's a mob of locals camped outside beneath his window, screaming for blood, screaming for Bozarth. They have him spooked, all right, and in another day or so we'll threaten to release him. He'll know what that means and he'll talk."

"And if he doesn't?" Bozarth looked pretty tough to me.

"Well, then, I guess we'd resort to some other tactics, time-proven methods that are – shall we say – not *officially* sanctioned."

Ah. Medieval torture chambers make a twentieth-century comeback – in New Jersey.

"So," I continued, "who knows why, but you'll find out. Eventually. At any rate, at some point the Leeks determined it was a lucrative business to be in and they needed a constant supply. Now, they had two options: steal them or produce them. Stealing babies wouldn't have worked because the very first incident would have outraged parents and locals alike, and brought in the authorities almost immediately. There are, after all, a lot of people with the Lindbergh baby still fresh in their minds, just itching to string up the next person with the gall to try something similar.

The second option, producing babies – or, if you will, *harvesting* babies – required one essential component: mothers. As far as I know, Etta and Emma Leek were the only women in the Leek family, and at best could have produced two children a year. They probably wouldn't have been too thrilled with the idea and matters would have been further complicated by trying to find some participants – other than their brothers and father, of course – willing to impregnate them. Two babies a year, at best, are not the kind of numbers required to make a lot of money. So, they needed prospective mothers and came up with a scheme to get them. Enter Sam Bozarth and his connections."

"He's Leek's brother-in-law, by the way; Leviticus' dead wife's brother. Her name was Deborah Bozarth, way back when. Bozarth has a record as long as my arm, and that's just the stuff he got caught on. This is the Pines, after all, and a lot of things go on here that the authorities never find out about."

"I figured there was probably a connection there. A lot of these families have been in the area for centuries and everyone seems to be related to everyone else on some level or other."

"Continue," said Quinn, exhaling a cloud of smoke.

"So, while a baby's disappearance would have gotten a lot of attention and caused an immediate uproar, a woman's disappearance would be a different story altogether. It could be due to a criminal act, of course, but could just as well be totally innocent, the woman having chosen to leave for her own personal reasons. The Leeks counted on this and went to a fair amount of effort to leave behind sufficient evidence that pointed to the latter assumption. Given that, here's how I think it happened..."

"You *think*?" interrupted Quinn.

"Yeah, I *think*. Punch holes in it if you can. It's my theory, backed up with facts. You got a better one, then go with it. But this is how it happened, I'm sure of it. Or as sure as I can be. Now, are you going to keep interrupting me every time I take a breath?"

Quinn puffed on his cigarette. "Go ahead."

"The kidnappings all occurred in the fall and winter months of September through March, when the shore communities were all but deserted. The few people that are there have the good sense to stay inside. If you check the dates of the kidnappings against a calendar, you'll find that they always – with a few exceptions that I'll get to in a moment – took place on a new moon. Now, this could be due to some mystical mumbo jumbo, but my guess is that it was a result of a more practical consideration: The new moon is the darkest night of the month and they could move about the area without worrying about being seen. In the absence of an artificial light source, you can't see anything around here in the blackness of a new moon."

"It's not like Trenton," he nodded. "There's always a glow there, no matter how dark the night."

I took another sip of water. "The Pines are crisscrossed with hundreds of creeks navigable by sneakboxes – the *Devil's Coffins* as they're known to the locals – which have a draw of only a few inches, and can get around quite easily in shallow water. As Buzby once said to me, 'They can follow a mule as it sweats up a dusty road.'"

Quinn cracked a smile.

"One of these," I continued, "a branch of the Westecunk Creek the locals call the Six Mile Branch – flows right past the Leek's property and eventually works its way on out to the bay near the town of West Creek. The Leeks, of course, had a bunch of sneakboxes, probably one for each of the family members."

"There were some pretty cold months during these periods," said Quinn. "How would they have managed when the creeks froze over?"

"I don't know. Maybe they carried them – they're light enough for a man to carry – or drove them out to the bay, which freezes over less often than the freshwater creeks that feed it. Sneakboxes are usually outfitted with runners and can function as sleds on ice – and with the aid of an ice pole, you can manually propel them most anywhere. At any rate, a bunch of them would set out, use the creeks and bay to get around, do their dirty work and return as silently as they came."

"We found a couple of boats up front that escaped the blaze. Odd looking things – low and flat, kind of spoon shaped, maybe twelve feet long by four feet wide, and covered, with a cockpit?"

"That's a sneakbox, all right. Somebody in the Pines designed them about fifty, sixty years ago, and they're uniquely adapted to the needs of the baymen. And that, I'm sure, is how they got back and forth to the island and the other communities where the missing persons were reported. Keep in mind that the causeway bridge was unusable the night that Holly was kidnapped; the night after, too. A boat was the only way they could have gotten her out."

"Working on the assumption that Holly *was* kidnapped," said

Quinn.

"You talked to Grace. She told you about old man Leek and his love of poetry, and his discovery of the names and addresses of all the other poets? She was kidnapped, all right. Just like the others, just like her friends Grace, Mary and Emily. And think about all the others: Silsby, Hunt, Leonard and Perry are all unaccounted for; but we found Annie Ryan over there, and both Van Pelt's and Yumi's corpses were found bayside. Yumi's had clearly been in it — the bay, that is — for a long while. The Leeks came by bay, no question about it."

"Okay, we'll go with that," he said. "Continue."

"So, with each new abduction, the Leeks were clever enough — perhaps *crafty* is a better word — crafty enough to gather and remove all of the victim's personal belongings: clothes, shoes, toiletries, jewelry and, as we've seen, other personal items such as diaries and journals. They packed this stuff into suitcases, if they could find them, and took the suitcases with them. That way, when the women were discovered missing, it appeared to be nothing more than a planned departure. And keep in mind that this was always during the long fall and winter months, with many of the abductions occurring during the dead of winter, when tradition has it that the locals all tend to go a little stir crazy. Heavy drinking, domestic upheaval and spousal abuse tend to peak during this period each year, and the notion of a woman abandoning her husband certainly isn't unheard of. It usually works the other way — the husbands taking off — but it isn't unheard of. As for the single women, it appeared that they'd gone on a trip without mentioning it to anyone — to visit friends or relatives, to go to Florida, who the hell knows where? And, the amazing thing is, virtually no one seemed to care — or was concerned enough to care.

"The Leeks didn't always get it right, though; sometimes they took too little or too much. Grace Peterson's leg razor was left behind and that's something one wouldn't expect a former model to overlook. And Holly's current, unfinished book of poetry was left behind, too, and she always took that with her wherever she went. Poke around a little more closely at the other homes and I'll bet you'll find other odds and ends that they should have taken with them, but didn't."

"Could be an oversight, forgotten in the rush to get away quickly by a woman racked with guilt over abandoning her husband…" he interjected.

"Do you really think so, Quinn? Given what you've seen and been told so far?"

"No. Not really."

"Okay, then; let me finish. They – the Leeks – also took pains to straighten up any signs of a struggle. For whatever reason, they were less thorough when they grabbed Holly and there were some visual clues that she'd been taken by force. Unfortunately, the clues were subtle enough to not be too obvious, and I was stupid enough not to pick up on them.

"The first year, assuming that last season was their first – and you might want to check back two seasons and see if there were any missing reports back then…"

"We did. There weren't."

"Okay. So, last year – fall of '35 to spring '36 – the Leeks were more ambitious, heading as far south as Brigantine and as far north as the Seasides, moving northward each month. This was probably to avoid any appearance of a pattern, and to render a point of origin less obvious to anyone who might have had suspicions of wrongdoing. The coldest month of last year – when I say year I'm referring to the Leek's active season – was January, with near-zero temperatures and plenty of ice. The Leeks decided to stay closer to home, venturing no further than our little island directly across the bay, and the town of Brant Beach. This year – this season – they started to get a little cocky since no one had caught on to their routine and there hadn't been a single word of suspicion raised in the local press or among the local authorities."

"How would they know that? They actually *read* a local paper?"

"This isn't Siberia, Quinn; they could very easily have picked up a paper in Manahawkin, and Jonah had lots of opportunities during his travels with Buzby. And Jonah, at least, could read, so some of the others must have been able to, too. But word gets around fast in the Pines and everyone seems to know everything about everyone – or at least everything that people don't take the pains to hide – sometimes faster than it appeared in the weekly papers. Buzby has mentioned the informal network of information dissemination several times in past conversations. Claimed he heard things about people before they even happened to them. An impossibility, of course, but it conveys a point."

"Well, they did a pretty good job of covering their tracks; you have to give them that."

"I suppose. Anyway, Fred Buzby told me he took on Jonah Leek as an unpaid helper this past September – and at Jonah's suggestion. It made sense for Buzby: Jonah wouldn't cost him anything and he was strong, and Buzby isn't, after all, a kid anymore. Jonah had ulterior motives, however, and guidance from his father. His purpose was to check out the various neighborhoods that Buzby visited on his monthly rounds and to look for a likely subject – a single, young female of childbearing age. How he'd figure out that they were single is anyone's guess. I suppose one could determine that if they had the run of someone's house, but it's unlikely that Jonah had that luxury; more likely his determination was made based on the presence or absence of a wedding ring. That's what got Grace Peterson in trouble: She refused to wear a wedding ring; and the casual observer might have thought that she was alone in the house as her husband was rarely to be seen. He always slept until early afternoon, spent his waking hours in the building out back that he used as a studio, came and went by the back door, and virtually never left the premises.

"The first season the Leeks were probably a little less organized in their approach. Once they'd arrive in a town after dark, they'd creep around from house to house, peeking through windows until they found a likely subject. Then it was a relatively simple matter of gaining entrance – nobody locks their doors anyway – and overpowering the woman. Then off they'd go, leaving as silently and unobtrusively as they'd arrived. You'll recall that during the first season each of the victims was, in actuality, either single – Lillian Van Pelt, the shopkeeper from Brigantine, and Virginia Leonard, the young writer from Brant Beach – or all alone at an hour when spouse or family should have been around – Eileen Hunt's family was at the movies, Dorothy Silsby's clergyman husband was off giving solace to the needy…"

"Yeah, I heard about his method of giving solace," said Quinn.

"Rumors, but I heard them, too. Anyway, Annie Ryan's husband Mickey was off tending bar and Elizabeth Perry's husband was out bowling. They were all alone and that was the biggest requirement.

"This method worked, but it was risky. So, this year they put Jonah to work, pre-selecting their subjects so that each subsequent abduction was quicker and more efficient. Jonah would carry one of his homemade oyster shell wind chimes with him, which looked innocent enough to anyone who saw it, and he'd hang it at the subject's property. This served as an audible marker when they returned several days later in the dead of night. They'd stash their boats, listen for the clacking of the chimes and make their way in that direction. Probably didn't work all of the time, but it sure didn't hurt. Buzby, by the way, usually visited the island the last Monday of the month, unless he had something really good that he needed to unload. This was frequently – and coincidentally – just days before the new moon. In two instances, it was actually the same day. The rest of the time a couple of weeks might elapse before their return, but as long as no one noticed and chose to remove the chimes, they'd still be there, in place, serving as a marker. They were, after all, not very conspicuous, and my guess is that people heard them but didn't give them any thought. I heard one at Mary McCarthy's, off in the distance, and it didn't register. The one at Emily Stackhouse's *did* catch my attention, as it was hanging right there in the yard and was particularly active one of the days I was there. But, again, it wasn't the sort of thing that stood out; it seemed to belong there. I found similar discarded chimes at Schweickert's and in a bush in the lot by my house; and, if I remember correctly, I seem to recall hearing one the night Purdy dragged me over to identify Schweickert's corpse."

"What does Schweickert have to do with all this? How's he fit in with the Leeks' plans?"

"Be patient – I'm getting there. My guess is that, when they remembered, the Leeks would pull down the chimes when they were finished. They'd discard them, often nearby, so that they wouldn't run the risk of attracting attention. But sometimes, in the heat of it, they forgot."

"Then how do you explain the chimes at McCarthy's? She was abducted the day *after* Yumi's abduction. Shouldn't the chimes have been at Yumi's instead?"

"There may very well have been chimes at Yumi's, which we never found. Maybe Jonah staked out several homes in advance? Or maybe, when Yumi's abduction failed, he might have sailed over the next day, checked out the next nearest name on the list and marked it. Her chimes were bayside, where he would have landed and hung them without being seen. They were a more hastily made affair, substituting a can top for the usual, more elaborate twig and twine creation. We'll never know for sure."

Quinn stubbed out his cigarette and immediately jammed another into his mouth. As an afterthought, he offered me one. I wasn't in the mood.

"Grace Peterson told me – and may have told you, too – that, to take her mind off the horror that was happening to her during her first night in captivity, she tried to put her mind elsewhere by reciting one of her poems to herself. A good idea, I guess, if you can call it that, but unfortunately she did it out loud, and the old man was taken with it. He loved the poetry, and forced her to recite poems every time thereafter. And when he found her journal in with her stolen belongings, he found the names and addresses of her fellow Poets' Circle members, all of them living on the island. Now he had a list to work from, a list of first choices, all of whom could continue the tradition of poetry recital while he worked on making babies."

"That's sick," said Quinn, shaking his head. "That's really sick."

"Yeah, it is; but I doubt he looked at it that way. And who knows what his sons thought. They probably didn't care, just as long as they were in on the fun. Anyway, Jonah now had a list to work from and all of the addresses were in towns that Buzby made stops in. All, that is, except for Mary McCarthy's house down towards Holgate, which might be another reason Jonah would have sailed over and searched out her house when they needed a quick backup, knowing full well that Buzby'd never go near the place."

"So, let me make sure I'm with you," said Quinn. "The Leeks wanted babies to sell and they needed young women to serve as mothers. So, they sailed back and forth to nearby communities and kidnapped them. They did this first at random and all over the map. Then, this year, they stayed closer to home, restricting themselves to Long Beach Island. Jonah was sent over to search out likely subjects and marked their homes with his wind chimes. Later on, Peterson's journal provided a list of names and addresses that served as their, um, menu. And, all the while, they disguised their abductions to make it look like the victim had taken a trip or something. This is a tough one to swallow; sounds like something churned out by Carroll John Daly."

"No argument there, but you've got the gist of it," I said. "On second thought, I'll take one of those," I added, nodding to Quinn's pack of Luckies. He tossed me one, along with a pack of matches.

"You said that McCarthy was a backup," he resumed.

"Well, think about it," I said as I lit the cigarette. "Think about the new moons and when the abductions took place. Last season, Van Pelt was murdered in late October – probably the 27th, a new moon, which was the last day she was seen by anyone. Her murder, unfortunately, was probably the result of a kidnapping gone wrong – she was, after all, only of use to them alive. The very next night – almost as dark as the night before – Eileen Hunt disappeared from Barnegat City. If you don't get it right the first time, try again. Only this time, the Leeks were tired from their long trip the night before, so they picked a destination closer to home. Not that Barnegat City is close, but by comparison to Brigantine it sure as hell is. They may have also figured Van Pelt's body might have been found quickly and that the area would – potentially – be swarming with cops.

"This season you have Schweickert," I continued.

"I was wondering if you were ever going to get around to him," said Quinn.

"Yeah, he's unwittingly part of this whole mess, too. He was, as you well know by now, one taken with wearing women's clothes. Unfortunately, his timing was bad and he was in full garb when first spotted by Jonah – through a window, I would imagine. Jonah misidentified him as one of the fairer sex and chalked him up as the next abductee. When the Leeks arrived to make the snatch, imagine their surprise when they found that the fertile young lass intended to be the mother of one of their children was actually a man. I can hear the old man now, railing on, spouting scripture regarding perversion while his children tore the poor guy apart. You saw his refrigerator, didn't you?"

"I saw the photos."

"Well, it was from the *Bible*: 'If a man lies with a male as with a woman, both of them have committed an abomination; they shall be put to death, their blood is upon them.' Leek paraphrased it and mangled the spelling, but that's where it came from. Anyway, they dealt with Schweickert on the spot, stabbing him with at least two different knives, and beating him to a pulp with the hammer that was found on the premises. He was found on Friday, October 16, and had been murdered probably the day before; October 15 was a new moon. Undaunted, they snatched Grace Peterson the next night, the 16th, and their pattern of poets began.

"Yumi Takarada's abduction went horribly wrong, too, as we've seen. Her husband last saw her on November 14, which was, once again, a new moon – although her body wasn't found until a week and a half later. McCarthy was alive on the 14th, but wasn't seen after that, so she may very well have been abducted the following day.

"So, as you can see, each failed abduction was followed up by a successful one – and most likely on the following day."

"Not a very impressive track record," said Quinn. "A failure for every couple of successes."

"They made an effort to improve their odds, actually."

"How do you figure?"

"Well, after two thoroughly bungled attempts – Van Pelt's and Schweickert's – they put an additional safeguard into effect. And, by the way, there may have been a third bungled attempt. There was an elderly Beach Haven resident named Addison who supposedly died of heart failure on October 16, but a witness claimed she looked like she was scared to death. It wouldn't be too much of a stretch to imagine the Leeks somehow following the Schweickert failure with this second failure – she was, at eighty three, a few years past prime child-rearing age – before getting it right with Peterson, and that would have been *real* incentive to implement some additional safeguards.

"So, instead of having Jonah simply mark a house with his chimes, they also had him go to the door and confront the potential subject, to verify that she was suitable for their purposes. His ruse was the attempt to sell some of his handcrafted items. The most interesting things he made were the so-called Leeds-Peepers – and both Yumi and my wife actually purchased one from him. Yumi's husband was handling one when I spoke with him several days after her disappearance, but at the time I mistook it for an Oriental carving; at a quick look, it appeared to be a small wooden dragon. Evidently, he didn't give it a second thought, either, returning it to the shelf of items for sale in her store. Holly must have purchased one, too, and when I found it I took it to be one of the many useless little knick knacks she always had lying all over the place. That one's sitting on the backbar in the taproom. You might take another look at McCarthy's and Stackhouse's and see if a Leeds-Peeper, or some other Piney craft, is lying around. Needless to say, their additional safeguard wasn't of much use. While it would have prevented another fiasco along the lines of the Schweickert screw up – and what were the odds of that ever happening again? – and, perhaps, the Addison screw up, they still managed to bungle Yumi's abduction. All brawn and no brains, I guess. Yumi was found dead, as you well know, her wrists and ankles tightly bound, but with her mouth free. My guess is that she struggled violently on the way back to the mainland, freed herself of her gag, started screaming bloody murder and was killed and dumped on the spot. Or, perhaps her boat capsized and she drowned. Either way, the result was the same: one more aborted abduction, with Yumi very dead.

"I hadn't heard about the Addison woman," said Quinn as he jotted her name down on a small pad. "You have any others I should know about?"

"I don't think so. Ethel Richards figures into all of this only because her husband George took advantage of the situation to murder her. The remaining Poets' Circle members are Dorothy Frazier, who is also an elderly woman, Catharine Copperthwaite, who is a cripple in her mid-fifties and Agnes Warren, who has the good timing to spend the offseason down in Florida. When Jonah was killed by the truck, I found Copperthwaite's name and address in his possession, so he may have been on his way to check her out. As for the other two, both their names were crossed off a complete list of Poets' Circle members he carried with him, so that would suggest he'd already checked them out and deemed them unsuitable for further consideration.

"I'll want any pieces of physical evidence that you have."

"Yeah, I'll get them to you." I looked around for a place to deposit the cigarette butt, and Quinn took it from me. "And, to further compound my stupidity in this whole affair," I continued, "Jonah, who was totally void of any sort of social graces, left his calling card-of-sorts at two of the crime scenes, maybe more."

"What was that?"

"The physical evidence of his rather nasty habit of chewing tobacco. At Schweickert's, we observed brown stains on the living room rug, but assumed them to have been excrement left by his miserable little dog. Or at least Purdy did, and I foolishly took his word for it and gave it no further thought. A later check showed the stains to be tobacco juice, thoughtlessly spit out at some point during their visit. And, adding insult to injury, I pigheadedly assumed that the puddle of tobacco juice on the floor of my kitchen after Holly's abduction was caused by the one of Purdy's cops – a young guy named Schoengarth – and gave him hell for it. I only wish that he'd spoken up and told me otherwise, but he just stood there with a stupid look on his face and took my verbal abuse."

"You can be rather intimidating sometimes, Lew."

"Yeah, I guess maybe I can. Anyway, who knows if there were tobacco stains anywhere else? At this point, we'll probably never know; they would have all been cleaned up or trampled over long ago."

"Couldn't Schoengarth have left the stains, as you originally suspected?"

"I don't think so, now that I've thought about it. Purdy told me that Schoengarth started a mouthful after seeing Schweickert's corpse and going outside to throw up – to kill the taste, I suppose – and didn't go back inside after that. And, at my house, Schoengarth was genuinely stunned when I pinned him to the wall. In retrospect, I don't think he had a clue why I was angry. And with good reason, it turns out."

"Okay, I guess it all fits." Quinn stared at his pad, shaking his head. "You have to admit, though, it all seems pretty farfetched. I mean, without Peterson's and McCarthy's testimony – and the other physical evidence at the Leek's place, of course – I'd have a lot of trouble swallowing it."

"I can see that. You have to remember, though…"

"Remember what?"

"I had a personal stake in this."

"Sure, I understand. But we still don't know for certain that they abducted Holly. It's possible that she wasn't one of their victims."

"She was," I said. "I'm sure of it now." I was. And while I'd avoided thinking about it previous to this conversation, it was clear to me now that she was dead. Thanks to the Leeks – may their souls rot in Hell.

"Well, let's wait and see what the coroner comes up with and see what else we find, if anything. Tell me about the Leeks' place, what you found there."

"Well, once they got their victims back to their place in the Pines, they'd imprison them and force themselves on them on a regular basis until their unwilling participants became pregnant. Then they'd leave them alone. Thoughtful of them, huh? Once the child was born, I'd guess, the mother was kept around as a nursemaid until the sale was set up, and then she was killed, to be replaced by a new victim."

"Why not keep her around? Have her bear more than one child?"

"I don't have an answer for that. Damaged goods, perhaps? Who knows just what went through the mind of that Bible-misquoting maniac. And maybe one of the victims managed to kill herself, the sad, but expedient, alternative to a future of ongoing misery and horror. All I know is that the only ones that were there – alive – when I got there were the four most recent kidnap victims."

"Holly wasn't one of them, Lew, and her disappearance occurred during that timeframe. That *could* mean that they didn't kidnap her."

"Yeah. Or it *could* mean that she's already dead. They killed Annie Ryan soon after my arrival and the rest were soon to follow. My guess is that they knew I was on to them and were in the process of eliminating any incriminating evidence."

"How'd they know you were on to them?"

"As a result of my pursuit of Jonah, and his subsequent death. And, don't forget, they knew I'd been poking around their property a month ago, although what they didn't realize is that it was by sheer coincidence; I was looking for Richards' truck. They were the ones who attacked me on the causeway bridge. Junior Leek was one of the survivors and he still bore the scars of our encounter the night I got there. The way I originally spotted the truck was by plane and someone – I'm sure now it was one of the Leeks – took a shot at us. I don't know whether they ever connected me with the plane – but even if they didn't, it was one more incident to fuel their paranoia."

"Later on, before I located Richards' truck on the ground, was when I stumbled upon Bozarth's house in the Pines. And it was strictly by accident when I unwittingly stopped there to get some directions. The incongruity of the new Pontiac parked out front failed to connect and I should have realized that something was very wrong when I went in. The well-dressed couple inside, holding a baby, regarded me with terror when I entered. Bozarth was smooth, however, and diverted my attention and put me at ease. I should have sensed something wasn't right. But I didn't and didn't make the connection 'til much later."

"I guess Bozarth would have mentioned the incident to the Leeks afterwards. There couldn't have been too many strangers looking for their house over the years, especially *outsiders* like you."

"Yeah, seems likely. Anyway, the graves your people have found are undoubtedly the graves of last season's victims. And the infants' graves were probably of babies who died at birth or soon after. Their delivery and care was, after all, primitive and unsanitary at best."

"Okay, Lew; hold on. You're jumping all over the place and I'm losing track of just what you did, when you did it and why you did it. So, why don't you start at the very beginning, when you first became aware or involved in this mess and tell me the whole story, in sequence."

I did, and in detail, starting with Purdy's request to accompany him to Schweickert's house. I went into as much detail as I could, but omitted the parts that had little or nothing to do with the Leeks. And that included Chet Hawley's affair with Yumi; even though she was a victim, her relationship with Hawley had nothing to do with her kidnapping and death. I wanted to put a lot of distance between myself and Hawley, anyway.

Just in case.

It was a little after 3:30 when Quinn finally drew the inquisition to a close – and I was exhausted. Going through the last three months' events in detail, while Quinn questioned and probed, had been a useful exercise, however, clarifying in my mind a number of details and connections I hadn't previously pieced together. It was – fortunately – his problem now; all I wanted to do was go back to Beach Haven, tend bar and piece my life back together.

Without Holly.

Thursday, January 28, 1937 – Wednesday, February 10, 1937.

THEY RELEASED ME from Paul Kimball ten days later. Willett was waiting outside for me in the Ford and beeped the horn to get my attention. I hopped down the steps, steadying myself with the railing while holding my crutches in my left hand, eager to get the hell away from the place after a stay that seemed far too long. I gave silent thanks that he hadn't demolished the car during the ride over – Willett was a notoriously inexperienced and inept driver – and crossed my fingers for the ride home.

I made a number of calls and visits over the days that followed, as much for my own peace of mind as to tie up the remaining loose ends of the whole affair. They helped, but not as much as I'd hoped.

I caught Grace Peterson in the midst of packing. She looked tired, but was in surprisingly good spirits for someone who'd gone through the hellish events that she had. She told me that when she'd finally been released from the hospital and returned to her home by a state trooper, Howard had refused to talk to her, refused to have anything to do with her. He hadn't visited her in the hospital and now sealed her out as if she didn't exist. So *she* threw *him* out of the house, put it on the market and was moving out. She wasn't sure just where she'd end up, but she was sure of two things: it wouldn't be on the island or anywhere even remotely close to it, nor would it be with her mother. I wished her well and we vowed to keep in touch. Unfortunately, vows of that sort have a way of being broken.

Mary McCarthy had decided to stay with her parents in Red Bank and it was probably a good choice, even if only for the short term. She'd emerged from her ordeal in one physical piece, but in a rather fragile emotional state. Her parents had the wherewithal to provide the appropriate ongoing medical attention, but it was anyone's guess as to whether it was doing more good than harm. She'd sort it out eventually and at this point seemed to be enjoying all the attention and coddling, attention that would have driven her up a wall a mere six months earlier. Her future plans were nonexistent, except for one item: as with Grace Peterson, the island, which had once been a haven of natural, unspoiled beauty and splendid isolation, was now for her Hell on earth; nothing could ever lure her back. Her house in the dunes sat empty, a "For Sale" sign planted in the sand out by the road.

Emily Stackhouse seemed to be beyond hope. Locked up and under ongoing observation at Trenton Psychiatric Hospital, she'd throw violent fits every time a male would approach her, be he an orderly, a doctor or one of the establishment's administration. And that was, at first, fairly often. They tried to arrange it so that only women would deal with her – and while that seemed to work initially, it was often difficult to schedule. Within a week or so, however, her reactions to the women became as violent as they had been to the men. So, Emily had a cozy little padded room with a single window high enough in the wall to allow light, but no view. Meals were delivered through a tiny hinged opening at the base of the door, with dinner always laced with sufficient drugs to allow a later daily cleaning of the cell and her unconscious body. And, I suppose, it afforded her a good night's sleep. I didn't try to visit.

Holly? There were no signs of her anywhere near the compound. Quinn's men had unearthed eleven graves in total, eight of which contained the remains of adults. Annie Ryan, of course, was found in the open grave, and had been identified by her husband. Dorothy Silsby's remains were found in a second, and had been positively identified by her dental records. A third showed signs of having recently given birth – the telltale parturition scars were found etched in the surface of the pelvis – and was the right, short height – five feet – to be new-mother Elizabeth Perry. Of the remaining five, one was of a teenage girl and the right height to have been Eileen Hunt's remains; and another was a female between the age of twenty and thirty, and the right height to have been Virginia Leonard's remains. The final three females' remains were chalked up as Jane Doe I II, and III, and were probably of other unfortunate victims abducted at various times in the past. None of them, however, were Holly's remains, as she was considerably taller – by several inches – than the tallest of these.

Then there were the three other graves. One, it turned out, was that of a newborn, either born dead or who died shortly after. The other was no more than several months old when he or she died. The third was of a youngster, perhaps twelve or so, perhaps a boy; they couldn't determine much more than those vague parameters. Who were they? The next person's guess would be as good as mine and I tried to give the issue no further thought.

Willett told me I should be proud of what I'd accomplished. I had, after all, brought a reasonably speedy end to the reign of terror hanging over the island – a reign that no one seemed willing to acknowledge back while it was occurring – and saved the lives of three women who most certainly would have died otherwise. Add to that the fact that I'd brought George Richards to justice, a singular act that otherwise may very well have never taken place.

All true, but they were hollow victories. What had been the tradeoff? My wife was gone, a woman I'd grown fond of was in a madhouse, a pair of friends – husband and wife – were both dead and several others I'd never known were dead as well. And one of them, Annie Ryan, should by all rights still be alive – and would be if I'd been a little more on the ball.

Add to that the fact that a lot of old wounds had been reopened. I'd been forced to revisit the slaughter grounds of a previous marriage that had ended in death for both mother and child, and my wholesale act of vengeance on those responsible. I'd swept those years and acts aside, and thought – naïvely so – that I could start a new life, in a new place, with new friends, as if the previous twenty-five years had never taken place. A new Lew Porter. I should have known better, however; you can't escape the past. The best you can ever hope for is to come to terms with it – and, if you're lucky, make peace with it. I hadn't, though, and found myself forced to confront what I had once been. And, I suppose, what I still was.

The thing is – and this puts my stomach in knots – that in spite of all the loss, death and destruction that had befallen the inhabitants of this little world known as Long Beach Island, in spite of the havoc that had been wreaked on my family and friends, in spite of *all* that had happened over the last few months, aspects of it had been kind of – for want of a better word – *fun*.

And the Hawleys? A Piney named Flemyng stumbled across father and son while taking a walk with his hound, Snip. It was early February, and Flemyng and Snip were working their way north on Slocum's Log Swamp Road, which parallels Slocum's Branch, a small offshoot of Westecunk Creek. Flemyng spotted something out of place among the white cedars lining the creek and found Chet's bullet-ridden body hanging by the neck from one of them. The gulls that he'd so much admired in life had pecked out his eyes. Chester III's body was found nearby, tied to another tall cedar. His tongue was cut out and a bullet had been fired through his left temple at point-blank range. Both of them had been emasculated, but the missing appendages were long since gone. Chester's shirtfront was torn open and a swastika carved by knife point on his chest.

True to form, it was backwards.

A day later, two dozen heavily armed state cops raided Camp Bismarck and everyone was arrested. Everyone, that is, except Vollbrecht, who jammed his .45 into his mouth, threw his left arm up stiffly in a Nazi salute and blew off the top of his head as a trio of troopers approached. Vollbrecht's relationship to Hawley soon became public knowledge, and a couple of his more hot-headed Bund members – guys named Reinhold Arnheim and Karl Seitz – were eventually convicted of helping Vollbrecht murder his half brother and nephew. They spilled under intensive grilling: Vollbrecht planned the abduction and murder, and Arnheim provided the muscle; Seitz was the one with the knife. They found out who did it and how they did it, all right, but no one ever knew *why* they did it.

No one except me.

And, I suspect, Quinn.

Later, I watched from the front window as they carted off the boxed remains of the Cathedral. When they were gone from view, my focus shifted to my reflection in the window's pane. My thoughts drifted to the words Purdy had spoken three months earlier, the words that served as an introduction to this whole mess. I muttered them silently to myself.

"Ever see a dead man?"

I was looking at one.

Thursday, February 11, 1937. 7:52 p.m.

I SLID A Garden State across the bar to Dovey and pulled one for myself. Kahn sat a couple of stools to his right, working the day's crossword in a copy of *The Evening Bulletin*. It was slow tonight. Slow and cold. Willett had the stove loaded with coal, but it was difficult to forget that it was in the low twenties out.

Mackey and Carver sat at the table nearest the stove, hunched over a game of dominos. Carver made his move, finished off his beer and wandered over to the bar.

"Hey, Kahn, how can you tell if your wife is dead?"

The place went silent, Kahn looked up in shock and Carver went pale as he realized just how inappropriate his joke was.

"Oh, I'm, uh, sorry, Lew. It's just a dumb joke…" he stammered.

"It's okay, Carver. Really," I said. "Go ahead and tell your joke."

"You sure?"

"Yeah. But you better start over again – recapture your rhythm."

"Oh, yeah; right." He turned back to Kahn, though by now everyone was listening. Except maybe Dovey, who was beyond listening. "How, uh, how can you tell if your wife is dead?"

Kahn shook his head in disbelief. "I don't know, Carver. How?"

"Well, the sex is the same, but the dishes pile up."

I think I was the first to laugh and soon the rest joined in. Except Dovey.

A half hour passed. Mackey and Carver abandoned the dominoes for the radio plugged in by the phone booth. "Kate Smith's Bandwagon" had come on at eight and they weren't about to miss a moment of it – or at least the comedians.

The door to the windbreak closed with a resounding thud, followed by a pause that seemed to last an eternity. Fred Buzby finally entered the room, pulling a heavy battered wool coat from his wiry frame. He tossed it onto a nearby hook.

"Helloooooo Lewis," he shouted and once again broke into a familiar chuckle. It sounded forced, if only to me.

"Hello there, Fred. The same?"

"Yesiree," he responded. As he always responded.

"This one's on me," I said quietly, pouring him a stiff one and doing the same for myself. I offered a silent toast that he acknowledged and the two of us drank without another word. There was an unspoken knowledge we both shared and we chose to leave it that way. Business as usual. For the time being, anyway. I poured two more.

Finally I said, "Didn't expect you for another couple of weeks, if then."

"Yeah, well, man's gotta do what his spirit tells 'im to do."

"Don't think I ever saw you over here this late at night. Long ride home, this kind of cold."

"Like I said..." He finished his drink. "Well, thanks, Lew. Hit the spot."

"Thank you, Fred," I said. And meant it. Mackey and Carver were huddled by the radio, laughing at Henny Youngman's jokes.

Buzby paused, tunneled into his pants pocket and withdrew a fist that he held out in front of him. Something in it. Something for me, I gathered. I held out an open hand beneath it, palm open. His fingers relaxed and a gold chain slithered out of it into a heap, my fingers closing around it.

Holly's necklace – the one with the small shells.

I blinked several times through wet eyes, staring at a small loop of chain peeking out from within my trembling fist. He might as well have dumped her corpse at my feet.

"Found it, Lew, but can't tell ya any more than that. Sorry," he said, in the saddest voice I'd ever heard him use. "Sorry," he repeated, then slowly walked across the room and gathered his belongings. Carver and Mackey joined in with the radio's tinny laughter.

"Where?" I shouted after him. "*Where?*"

There was a muffled thud and the place went dark.

"Jesus H. Christ," yelled Carver from the blackness. "Not again — not during the punchline!"

"Goddamnit," I cursed. "Willett! Get some light in here, will you? Wait up, Fred."

"In a minute," responded Willett's muffled voice, either from the kitchen or bathroom.

Someone lit a match – Carver. Someone else opened the door to the coal stove, bathing nearby objects in a pale orange glow – Kahn. I grabbed a kerosene lantern from under the bar and fumbled with its shade.

"Where, Buzby?" I said once more, striking a match. "Where?"

Buzby paused, door part way open. "The Pines," he responded over his shoulder. "In the Pines." With that, he left.

Mackey opened one of the shutters and looked outside. I was numb, staring at the necklace clenched in my left hand, glimmering in the lantern's glow.

"That's funny," said Mackey. "We're the only ones in the area *without* power."

The silence was shattered by an unearthly shriek from outside, followed up by a sickening, wet crack that shook the building.

"What the hell?" muttered Carver as his match faded to black.

The door exploded open, slamming against the wall, hinges groaning with the strain. All eyes were riveted on the open doorway as the figure stepped in out of the darkness into a shaft of dim light. It was huge, ax held in its right hand and the other arm dangling useless by its side. Filthy, charred and torn clothing hung in shreds from its frame, exposed body parts a festering horror of fire-ravaged flesh.

Emma Leek.

She stepped forward, ax swinging in a constant arc over her head, scanning the room like a crazed, rabid animal. Crashing to my right as Mackey and Carver jumped from their seats and stumbled backwards out of her path, tripping over chairs, tables and anything else in their way.

"Where?" she screamed in a blood-curdling bark. "WHERE?"

Someone – Kahn, it turned out, and of all people – went after her with a chair, but a violent swing of the ax knocked both him and his ineffectual weapon through the air, slamming into the darkness. Another swing was slowed by the stove's pipe, which collapsed from the impact. Orange sparks filled the air and scattered across the floor.

"*WHERE?*" she repeated. And then her eyes met mine. "*You killed me!*" she hissed, raising the ax high in the air.

"Get out! Get out!" I yelled to the others.

Dovey, 'til now oblivious to it all, gave a violent shudder, clumsily slid off his stool, then stumbled towards the front door. Right in front of Emma. Her attention shifted to him, her hand tightened on the handle, her muscles tensed. Dovey was as good as dead. Someone shouted his name from the darkness, another yelled for him to get the hell out of there. They might as well have shouted at the moon. I jumped up onto the bar and dived for Dovey, tackling him as the ax cut through the air behind me. We slid through sawdust, crashing into one of the booths. The ax tore into the bar, wood splintering in all directions. Wood shavings and dust clouded my eyes. I tried to pull loose from Dovey, but he clung to me like a drowning man. The ax was wrenched from the wood behind me. I slugged Dovey in the jaw. He let go. I rolled onto my back. Emma turned and roared, charging, ax held high.

"No!" screamed the voice to my right. It happened so quickly. Willett grabbed the old harpoon and dived. Emma charged. Willett slid across the floor. The harpoon raised as Emma leapt.

It was like time stopped. Emma froze in the air, eyes gone wide, mouth screaming a soundless scream. The butt of the harpoon wedged under my arm, against the table's leg, Emma skewered on its end, teetering momentarily in the air above me before her feet returned to the ground. Eyes glassed over as her body slid forward on the shaft, the rusty spike emerging from her back, her dying weight dragging her down slowly, inexorably. With a deep guttural gurgle, her eyes went dead, her legs slack, landing in a blood-soaked heap on the two of us.

Muffled voices as her lifeless corpse was dragged off. I scrambled to my feet, drenched in her fetid blood. Willett looked shell shocked, similarly soaked in her blood, lying motionless on the floor, head up against the wall, staring off at nothing.

She was dead, all right. I knelt by Willett, wiping the blood from his eyes and face.

"Gordon. You okay?"

"Yeah," he said in a barely audible whisper. "I think so."

He didn't look it.

"You saved my life, Gordon. Jesus Christ, *you saved my life!*" I blurted, running fingers through the sodden mess of blood, sawdust and hair clinging to my head. "Thank you."

What else could I say?

Lanterns were brought over. Mackey reluctantly checked to make sure she was dead. Kahn, blood trickling from a gash in his hairline, helped Willett to a chair. Carver tried to move Dovey, but he was out cold. Probably wouldn't remember any of this come morning.

"Christ almighty," muttered Kahn. "What in God's name – *who* – is it?"

Carver stumbled into the light, visibly shaken. "Holy shit! What the hell is that?" And then he paused, looked around, and back to us. "Buzby?" he whispered.

"Oh, Christ," I moaned. "Buzby. I think she might have…"

The front door swung open, hinges groaning. A figure stumbled in from the darkness, weaving from side to side. Buzby. Right hand

568

pressed tightly over the stump where his left hand had been, blood gushing from his fingers.

"Someone call Doc Havens. *Quick!*" I yelled, jumping to my feet. "Get some rags – *something!*"

Buzby walked right past us. To the coal stove. The open door. He paused for a fleeting moment and then plunged his bleeding stump into the hot coals. A hiss of burnt-flesh smoke filled the air. His eyes rolled back and he collapsed to the floor in shock. So did Carver, white as a sheet.

Willett was on his feet by now, headed behind the bar and quickly filled a pail with ice. Handed it to me. I jammed Buzby's cauterized stump into the center of it.

Kahn let out a deep sigh. "Nobody's gonna believe this one. No one."

I nodded agreement.

An hour and a half later, Buzby'd been hauled away in an ambulance, Emma'd been hauled away in a basket and Purdy'd released the site. Willett mopped up the floor, furniture was returned to its place and the stovepipe had cooled sufficiently to be propped back in place. Aside from the front door hanging cockeyed on its hinges and a noticeable gash in the bar's edge, the place looked relatively normal.

Except it was empty. Oh, Willett and I were both still there, but Kahn, Carver and Mackey had all left after a few quick, stiff drinks. And, of course, Dovey was still there, slouched over in a chair and out to the world; might as well not been there.

"Call it a night?" I asked wearily.

"Sounds like a good idea. What about him?" Willett nodded to Dovey.

"Let him sleep it off. He won't remember a thing, anyway, so it'll be like any other night to him."

"Yeah, I guess so." Willett paused, looked at me. "I was scared,

Lew. *Really* scared."

"We all were, Gordon. *Shitless.*"

He smiled a faint smile and nodded. "Tomorrow?"

"Another day," I said.

And with those few words came a revelation. With all that had come to pass, with all the upheaval and loss, I still had family. Not in the traditional sense, but family nonetheless.

As Willet reached for the door, it opened. Edwards.

"Gentlemen. I'm not too late, am I? How about a quick one, Lew?" he said around the Camel bobbing in his mouth. Somehow, he hadn't heard.

"Deuce. Not tonight, okay? We've…"

"Whoa! What's that?" he asked, sniffing the air. "Ribs? Barbecued ribs? Any left?"

Author's Note

THE PRECEDING WAS relayed by Lewis Porter, eighty, during a series of interviews conducted during the months of September and October, 1979, in his home in Waretown, New Jersey. Gaps in the narrative were addressed through a series of correspondences by mail that followed over the next seven months.

Porter's recall was prodigious, aided by frequent referrals to several in a stack of journals kept by his side, cross referenced with two yellowed calendars for the years 1936 and 1937. Most of what you have read was taken directly from transcripts of the recordings made during those interviews, and the hand-written correspondences that followed. Contemporary news dailies were also referenced for purposes of clarification and confirmation.

Porter died by his own hand in July 1980.